The BLACK UNICORN

The BLACK UNICORN

George the Good

GEORGE THE GOOD

iUniverse, Inc.
Bloomington

The Black Unicorn

This is a work of fiction. All of the characters, names, incidents, organizations, and dialogue in this novel are either the products of the author's imagination or are used fictitiously.

iUniverse books may be ordered through booksellers or by contacting:

iUniverse
1663 Liberty Drive
Bloomington, IN 47403
www.iuniverse.com
1-800-Authors (1-800-288-4677)

ISBN: 978-1-4759-4133-3 (sc)
ISBN: 978-1-4759-4134-0 (ebk)

Printed in the United States of America

iUniverse rev. date: 10/09/2012

Contents

CHAPTER ONE

Rules of the Trail

Birds caroled in the branches one gray spring morning when Unicorn caught his long-legged son scrambling out of the Nest in the heart of the forest. Unicorn moved across the roots of the great tree to block Blackie.

"Hold up there, son!"

"What's up, Papa?" squealed Blackie, dancing over the damp ground. He tossed his head at the great white beast looming above.

"Stand still! Come over here in the light. I want a look at you before you bounce away to play with those fawns."

"Sure, Papa, you can look at me."

Swishing his tail, Blackie took skittish steps around his father.

"Stop jumping." Unicorn poked Blackie with his great horn. "Let me get a look at you."

Blackie stood stiffly on skinny legs as Unicorn sniffed him over. Except for his shining eyes and pink horn, Blackie was dark as midnight.

Unicorn shook his head. "I can barely see you against the tree trunks! That color doesn't come from my side of the family. My grandsires were all silvery white like me."

Blackie twitched and squirmed.

"Stop jumping!" Unicorn yelled. He circled Blackie, studying his coat. "No cuts, no scars, that's good, but your ankles—You've been running through briers."

"I just run, Papa!" cried Blackie, tossing his little horn. "Briers are where I run."

"Slow down, then. Keep your eyes open when you run. No need to get youself cut up like an old boar."

Unicorn stepped back, sighing. "You look fine now, but I fear the future. Look to your coat, look to your coat. You'll want to keep it clean and perfect like mine."

Blackie hopped to face him. "Can I go? Can I go?"

Unicorn stepped forward again

"You can go when I say you can go. This is an inspection. Mama says I have to look you over before we go on a journey."

"A journey!" Blackie jumped in the air. "A journey, you and me? Where we going, where we going, where we going?"

"Settle down!" Unicorn rapped him with his horn. "Silence! I'm not taking you anywhere till you settle down!"

Blackie ran in a circle, tossing his head. "Where, where, where we going?"

Unicorn yawned. He lifted a hoof, knocked it against a root to shake off mud. "To think I had to get up early for this. Who gets up this early?"

"Me!" squealed Blackie. "Me, me, me! Every morning, Papa, I get up early!"

"Wet behind the ears," mumbled Unicorn. "Too young to go anywhere, but she insists. 'Take him on a road trip,' she says. 'Show him the world. You can protect him out there and teach him the way of the roads. He'll learn about humans.'"

Swishing his tail, Blackie grinned up at Unicorn. "I want to learn, Papa! I want to learn everything, everything! Can we go?"

Unicorn slammed a great hoof into the earth.

"We'll go when I say we can go! Listen to me, son. There are rules for travel, rules of the trail. Here in the forest, you know, we're safe, safe as anywhere, but it's different in the human world. You can't run around like a mad thing out there. You've got to follow the rules."

Blackie whispered the words, "The human world—"

"Dangerous!" Unicorn exclaimed. "It's always been dangerous, Blackie, but now for some reason, it's worse. Down at the village, they tell me that bandits are out, raiders running all over the place. Some say they've even heard Hellhounds howling at night."

"I'm not afraid!" cried Blackie, jumping up and down. "I've got my horn!"

"That's why we're having this talk, Blackie. I want you to keep your horn. Listen, Blackie, the dragon has been seen. Twice!"

Blackie gasped. "The dragon!"

He shivered, the image of the monster flooding his mind—the great worm with her broad wings, her jaws, her fiery breath!

"Yes, the dragon."

Unicorn pulled his ears back and turned to the ferns under the tree. "Just like your Mama to choose this moment to send us on a journey. Worse time she could have picked. Run to her, Blackie. Tell her goodbye. We'll leave as soon as you get back."

He chomped at the ferns and mumbled with his mouth full. "'Spend time with him,' she says. 'Togetherness, father and son.'"

Blackie whirled, snatched a bite of fern, and dashed up the path, kicking off mud. He sniffed the dewy air, hearing squirrels scratching up trees before him. He jumped a stream, stopped for a drink, paused to sniff a broken eggshell in the trail, and dashed on.

Mama was eating grass on a hillside where lightening had blasted a tree, opening a hole to the sky. Blackie ran up to her and rubbed her with his nose, sniffing her warm, milky scent. She turned her head to caress him.

"Papa's taking me on a journey, Mama! I'm gonna see the world! I'm gonna see humans! I'm gonna see the dragon!"

Mama kissed him with a sigh. "Of course, you'll see the dragon, dear, you're a unicorn. But not yet, I hope. Promise me, sweetheart, that you'll listen to Papa. Don't drive him crazy with questions. Be as quiet as you can. Look after him and bring him back safely to me."

Blackie fell back, startled. "Me, Mama, me? You want me to look after Papa?"

Mama nodded. "Go easy on the poor beast, Blackie. Don't run him too hard. Papa's not as young as he used to be, you know. Keep away from humans if you can, but if you do get with them, don't drink their wine. And don't let Papa drink it. He can't stand that stuff."

Blackie hopped around happily. "I won't drink wine, Mama! I'll look after Papa, I promise!"

"That's the spirit, love." Mama kissed his nose. "Go now, have fun. The Lord be with you."

"Goodbye, goodbye!"

Blackie galloped down the trail, tossing his mane. The forest was damp and alive with clouds of scents—the earth, the trees, roots, bark, leaves. At a fork in the trail, Blackie reared from sheer joy. He gulped in the breeze, pawed the air, dropped to his hooves, and ran on.

Unicorn was eating mushrooms on a hill. He jerked around when Blackie galloped up, shouting, "I saw Mama! She says we can go, Papa, but we can't drink wine!"

"Stop right there!" yelled Unicorn. "Pull yourself together!"

Blackie stopped, panting. Unicorn glared down at him, shaking his head.

"What'd I tell you about rules of the trail? The first rule of travel among humans is to stay silent. You move like a shadow, eyes open, mouth shut. You see everything, say nothing. Humans are always gabbling like geese, but not us. We're creatures of the forest, quiet as the wind. We come and go before anyone sees us."

Blackie swished his tail and looked away. Unicorn pointed down with his horn.

"Here, eat something before we leave. Mushrooms here, Blackie, sprouts over there. Good food. That's another rule in the world of humans—you eat when you can, but always watch what you eat. No oak leaves or yew. Even with ferns, you have to be careful. If you don't know what you're eating, ask me, especially if it smells bitter or spoiled."

"I will, Papa."

Blackie gobbled a mouthful of mushrooms and leaped up, swallowing.

"Blackie!" shouted Unicorn. "Don't guzzle those mushrooms! Slowly, slowly, eat slowly. Savor the taste, please. Mushrooms is prime eating."

"But Papa, Mama says that you gobble mushrooms. She says you can clear out a patch in half a minute."

"What does she know?" grumbled Unicorn. "I know what I'm doing. I pace my eating."

"So, let's go, Papa! I'm ready to go!"

Unicorn sighed. He shook a hoof at Blackie.

"Another lesson, Blackie! Quiet down, now. This is serious! Do you remember those rascals from the village, Bunly, and that bunch of humans that caught you with ropes a month ago?"

"Sure, Papa, I'll never forget them!" Blackie nodded vigorously, grinning at Unicorn. "You saved my life! You galloped up like a hero and kicked them around. You had them squealing like field mice."

"Yeah, well, what if I hadn't run up?"

Unicorn bit up the last mushroom.

"You were lucky that I got there on time. I won't always be around, you know. You've got to learn to take care of yourself. Humans out there—they'll shoot you for your hide, for your horn, or just for fun. They'll make you fight goats if they'll catch you, or make you carry a princess around."

"What's a princess, Papa?"

"Something to stay away from!" Unicorn snapped, stamping a hoof. "Point is, the world of humans is dangerous. You've got to follow the rules. So whatever happens out there, you stay behind me. Another rule, most important of all—no fighting! Don't attack anything—no bears, no badgers, no polecats! If you get stunk up or torn, your Mama's going to blame me, so you stay behind me. You run when I run, hide when I hide."

Blackie nodded. "Sure, Papa, I'll run, I'll hide. Can we go?"

"I'll go tell Mama we're going, then we'll take off. You wait for me. Stay here. I won't be a moment."

Unicorn moved up the path. Blackie sighed and looked around. He sniffed the air, tasted a leaf from a vine, stepped over to the sprouts. He bit off a mouthful and chewed, flicking bugs from his ears, but he couldn't stand still. He lowered his ears and charged a tree trunk to shake out his horn.

SMASH!

He bounced back, dry leaves and twigs falling on his back.

"Stop that!" shouted Unicorn, running back up the path. "You settle down, now!"

Blackie grinned. "I'm settled, Papa. Can we go now?"

"All right, all right, we'll go in a minute. Here come the foxes. I want to ask them what's going on."

"Oh, no," sighed Blackie, "not foxes!"

5

"Always keep an eye out for foxes!" insisted Unicorn. "Foxes are smart. They know how to survive."

Blackie heard a soft scratching. A pair of foxes drifted out of the trees, looking sharply around. They glanced up at Unicorn, then sat back and stared at Blackie, their ears up, pink tongues hanging out of their mouths.

"I asked them to drop by so you could study them," said Unicorn. "Now, foxes are animals that live by the rules. They're quick, alert, quiet. They don't crash through trees like deer. If you can't smell a fox, you don't know that it's watching you."

"Well, yeah, Papa," said Blackie, "but foxes eat frogs and bugs. I don't want to eat such stuff."

"Foxes eat what they eat. That's the way the Lord made them. Come on, let's go, but watch how they move. You can learn a lot from foxes."

At that, Unicorn took off with the foxes running ahead of him, trotting lightly down the path, heads high, ears perked. Coming last, Blackie watched them for a few paces, then turned his head to catch the smells of lichens and wildflowers. He looked at a molehill in the path and watched Unicorn's tail brush off a deerfly.

The foxes ran with them for a mile or so. Twice, they barked a warning and slipped off the path, but it was only a rattling limb and a pheasant bursting into the air. At the end of their range, the foxes skittered back, chattered farewell, and vanished silently. Unicorn stopped under a hazelnut tree to sniff the ground for old nuts. Blackie tasted a leaf on a bush.

"I wouldn't hang around those old foxes, Papa," Blackie said, looking up. "Foxes are boring."

Unicorn moved to sniff a bush beside him. "Boring? Foxes? Let me tell you about foxes." Unicorn chomped a mouthful of leaves. He swallowed.

"Foxes, now, foxes know how to live. First of all, they eat everything—squirrels, mice, mushrooms, berries. We're stuck with vegetable food. The rule about food is that the more things you eat, the more food's available to you. That's important in hard country or winter."

"Winter, what's winter like, Papa?"

Unicorn shivered.

"Winter's the hungry season. In winter, the wind stabs like a thorn. Everything's frozen, all black and white, nothing green to eat. You'll see winter soon enough. These old seasons roll around before you know it."

He sighed.

"Foxes, now, they're sneaky and smart. A fox can catch a crow. Make you laugh to see a fox play dead till some old rook flies down to peck him up for lunch. Brains, Blackie, that's what they've got. Brains and patience, that's how you survive out in the world."

Unicorn moved to some small white flowers with triangular leaves. He sniffed, gobbled. Blackie tried the blossoms, tart but tasty. Unicorn lifted his big head, shook it back and forth.

"You don't know how lucky you are, Blackie. You think Grandpa ever took me on a journey? Not Grandpa, he was always too busy for me."

"But Grandpa was a hero!" squealed Blackie, jerking around. "Mama's told me tales about Grandpa. He fought dragons! He fought lions! I want to be just like Grandpa."

"No, no!"

Unicorn jumped in horror. His shout rang through the forest. Unicorn shrank away, swinging his long horn back and forth, ears high, listening.

Birds sang. Bugs whined. Leaves rustled above their heads.

"See what you did?" hissed Unicorn. "You made me shout! Hunters could have been near with their bows, bandits with their spears. What you said there—that's what I fear most. Never, never want to be like Grandpa. Grandpa was a mess!"

"But he's famous, Papa! Mama says that humans sing songs about him."

Unicorn shook his horn. He snorted.

"Songs, stories—all nonsense! Who cares about songs? The way Grandpa chased after knights and horses, he was a fool! You think he ever took me on a journey? He had no time for me. He was always off when I was young, traveling here, traveling there. He never stayed at home. Only time I saw him was when he got torn up in a fight. He'd show up at the Nest then, but I wasn't allowed to bother him. He had to recuperate."

Unicorn repeated the word with disgust, "Recuperate!" He spat in the bushes.

"So I'd wait for him while he healed, but he was off again. Grandpa was no fun at all. I wish you could have seen his coat!"

Unicorn rolled his eyes. "Bear-scratched, arrow-shot, ratty as a badger! Cuts, burns, scars—Grandpa was ripped and slashed from ears to tail. What do you expect if you fight dragons? His horn, you should have seen his horn, Blackie! A good foot of it broken off, just a jagged stump."

Unicorn stretched out his neck. Unicorn's horn was pearly white, straight and strong.

"Now, this is a horn! It's perfect, not a scratch! And my coat, the only scratches you'll find on me are down at the ankles where you can't see them. Even if you try, you can't avoid all the briers and thorns in the forest."

He swung his long neck to look up and down his flanks with an approving eye, then snapped his attention back to Blackie.

"So ask yourself, Blackie, why is my coat so fine? Living foxy, that's what. Living foxy! While Grandpa ran off to fight dragons, I hung around the foxes and learned the rules. I eat good food and get my sleep. I run enough to stay in shape and always, always stay out of fights. Who wants to get burnt by dragons when there's berries to eat in the forest?"

"But, Papa—"

Blackie swung his little horn under Unicorn's, reached up to touch his nose.

"I know you don't like to fight, but the way you saved me last month, chasing off those villagers, I'll never forget that! I think you're brave underneath. I think you're a hero, too."

"A hero!" snorted Unicorn. "You can dunk me in the Fountain the day I'm a hero! You think I just charged up on Bunly and that gang? Not me. Mama told me to follow you that day. She sensed there'd be trouble, so I watched from the bushes till their backs were turned. I ran them down before they knew it. Heroes are fools! Those old unicorns chasing after lions and Hellhounds, they all died young. Not me, I don't fight anything. No one's ever heard of a unicorn living as long as me! Never! I set the record 'cause I live foxy. I live by the rules. I'm alive and happy and plan to stay that way."

"I hope so, Papa."

"You can bet on it," snorted Unicorn, stretching. "Why seek out trouble? With the forest around and the village down the road, we've got sprouts and mushrooms in springtime, berries in summer, and plums, peaches, apples. Oh, so much to eat! Cherries, you've never tasted cherries or strawberries. Let the dragon fly in peace, I say. You stick with me, and we'll live forever."

Unicorn sighed. He shook his coat and looked regretfully at the blossoms and bushes about them.

"Well, Blackie, since you want to see the world, we have to go on this journey. If I could trust you to keep quiet, I'd find us a nice clover field. We'd relax there a week or so, live on blossoms, skip all the hassle of travel. But I know you. You'd go running to your Mama as soon as we got home. You'd tell her everything, then she'd scold like a bluejay. I'd never hear the last of it."

"So let's go, Papa!"

"All right, all right, we'll go."

Unicorn sniffed his familiar hills once more, then turned to the path. Blackie leaped for joy following Unicorn's tail. He panted and sniffed and looked at everything.

CHAPTER TWO

Running Papa

Following Unicorn turned out to be maddening. Blackie found himself trotting through new territory, plunged into a world of fresh sights and smells. He quivered to take it all in at once. He itched to romp and roll and explore everything, but Unicorn poked along. He tasted bushes, sniffed cross-trails, perked his ears at every twig-fall. They ambled up and down hills and across streams where Blackie couldn't hold back. He jumped in the water to splash about while Unicorn hissed at him.

"Stop that! Stop splashing! Come along!"

Paths ran into trails that widened and fed into a lane where Blackie saw his first wagon tracks. He ran ahead to sniff around a campground, a place where humans had stopped for years. It smelled of cloth and wood chips and burnt meat, an especially nasty odor. Near the ashes of an old fire, he found a broken pot with ants running over it. Blackie poked the pot with a hoof. He turned it over.

"What's this?"

Unicorn glanced back. "That's a pot, something the humans threw away."

Blackie examined bones scattered beyond the ashes. He wrinkled his nose at the stink and ran after Unicorn.

"That pot, what's it for?"

"Quiet," whispered Unicorn, "we've come to the road. We have to be careful from here on."

Sunlight blazed down where the road was chopped back to the width of a wagon. The light turned shadows dark and mysterious in the forest beyond the stumps where lizards sprawled, blinking sleepily. Unicorn stopped at a patch of bright yellow blossoms around a stump. He sniffed a blossom and grinned.

"Dandelions. Here's a treat, Blackie, dandelions. Delicious, their leaves, too. I've told you about dandelions."

Blackie bit off a dandelion. "Tasty, Papa, but shouldn't we keep on? We haven't gone very far."

Unicorn swung his head down to crop the blossoms. He swallowed. "Who's in a hurry?"

"But Mama—"

Blackie paused for a big bite of dandelions.

"Down by the village—" Unicorn began. He swatted a bee with his tail. "Down by the village, where the land's cleared of trees, they've got fields of dandelions. Sunflowers, too, heavy with seeds in late summer, and gardens with green peas and strawberries, luscious red strawberries. Wait'll you taste strawberries! We've always got the village for a midnight raid, but we'll skip it today since Mama wants me to show you the wide world. You'll see dandelions all over the place out there, too."

Unicorn trotted off with Blackie dancing behind. Around the next swing in the road, they found a large patch with matted green leaves and tilting stems of purple blossoms.

"Clover!" Unicorn shouted in delight. He ran to the clover and plopped down in it. More bees flew up.

"You can gobble clover, Blackie, roll in it, take a snooze. Come to think about it, I'm a little frazzled this morning. Your mama poked me up early to catch you at dawn. Napping in sweet clover—that's the way we live."

He stretched out his legs and sniffed the air, then lowered his head into the leaves and yawned.

"We'll get off to the world in awhile. I'll just rest . . . my . . . my . . ."

His eyelids closed and he snored.

Blackie tasted the clover around the edges of the patch. Delicious! He chewed happily until he got bored. He poked Unicorn with his horn.

Unicorn snorted, rolled over.

11

"Come on, Papa," urged Blackie. "Let's go. I haven't seen the world."

Unicorn's mouth dropped open. He started snoring.

Blackie poked him again. "I'm thirsty, Papa. Come on."

Unicorn twitched, babbled something, snored on.

Blackie looked around. He wasn't sleepy, not a bit. He was thirsty. He walked down the road, turned, looked back at Unicorn gleaming white in the sunlight, a leg thrown over his head.

"I'll just look a little farther."

Blackie trotted around a bend and stopped. Something stank, horrible. Blackie wrinkled his nose, but he was curious. He left the road to squeeze between fringy young trees until he saw it. A deer, dead, legs sticking out stiffly, bugs running over its head. Its blackened side was torn open to show white bones.

"Oh, no!"

Blackie gagged in his throat. Sick to his stomach, he ran panting down the road till the air smelled sweet again. A trail turned off the road, twisted between trees, and angled down to a stream where sparkling water gurgled over shiny rocks into dark clumps of leaves.

Shuddering at the picture of the deer in his mind, Blackie stepped into the stream. He sniffed the water bubbling and frothing around his hooves. He stretched down his neck and drank, shook his muzzle, drank again. He wandered down the stream, splashing out of the sunlight as hills swelled to both sides to shadow him.

The channel narrowed, deepened above his ankles. He came to a sandy pool with trees reflected on the surface. Bubble-footed bugs skated on top of the water, tadpoles darted below. Blackie drank again and listened to birds singing in the trees.

Blackie stood in the middle of the pool, water to his knees, watching ripples wash the banks. He looked down at his reflection—black nose, pink horn, bright eyes. He struck the reflection with a hoof. His face splintered.

He backed out of the pool to the mossy bank, swung sharply to run up the hill, and smashed his head into the rock wall beside the stream.

WHAM!

"Ow!"

The blow threw him back on his haunches. Pain stabbed Blackie's forehead. He yelped again, tears running down his nose.

"Ooh, ooh, ooh!"

He shook his head. Pain throbbed over his eyes with each movement.

"Papa!"

Blackie jumped back up the stream bed. He scrambled through the trees, forehead aching with each step. Once on the road, he eased along to avoid jolting his head. He held his breath when rounding the turn into the deer stink and hurried to Unicorn, sleeping on his back now, legs spread to all corners.

Blackie rubbed his nose against Unicorn. "Papa, Papa, I hurt my head!"

Unicorn snorted and rolled away, legs flopping over. Blackie poked his shoulder with a hoof.

"Papa, wake up! My head hurts."

"Wha—What?"

Unicorn lurched awake, blinking. He stumbled to his hooves, jerking his horn back and forth, looking for danger in the forest. Blackie saw green stains on his hide.

"Papa, my head—" wailed Blackie. He ran around to Unicorn's nose. "I hurt my head."

Unicorn's eyes focused on Blackie. He jumped back with a cry. "Oh, no, your horn! It's crooked, bent like a pig's tail! What'd you do to yourself?"

Blackie tried to rub his nose against Unicorn. "It hurts, Papa."

Mouth open in horror, Unicorn pulled away. "What will your mother say?"

He grew furious, started yelling, waving his horn back and forth.

"Two hours! We've not been gone two hours before you go and ruin yourself! You look ridiculous! Your mama—she's going to blame me! She's going to say it's my fault!"

Blackie felt tiny under the tall trees. He dropped his head, crying, "I didn't mean to, Papa. A wall, I hit a waaa . . . a wall by the stream. I didn't s-s-see it."

"Why me, why me?" moaned Unicorn, holding a hoof to his head. "Why do these things happen to me? A wall! Middle of the forest, and he hits a wall! Where would anybody find a wall in the forest?"

13

He kicked the clover with a hoof.

"What do I do now? Go home? Face the music? No, no, not yet. I better stay away for a while. That horn might straighten itself out. Anything's possible. At least, I can tell her that he saw the world!"

He took another look at Blackie. "Didn't I tell you to be careful? Now, you look like a freak!"

Blackie lowered his head to touch his horn with a hoof. It was bent, definitely twisted. It hurt.

Blackie cried as Unicorn stepped out of the clover into the road, headed away from home. Blackie yearned to run the opposite way, back to Mama. She'd kiss him and make it better, but no, Unicorn went stomping off through the trees, mumbling to himself.

"Now, we've got to keep going till the stupid horn straightens out. Maybe it'll fall off. He'll shed that baby horn sooner or later. With my luck, it'll stick on till the very moment she sees it! Why me, why me?"

"Papa, Papa!"

Blackie tried to squeeze by, but Unicorn shoved him with a hip. "Don't push! Stay back!"

"Papa!" cried Blackie. "Why don't you heal me? Use your magic horn!"

Unicorn didn't hear. He muttered to himself.

"Why do I let her talk me into these things? I knew something'd happen, something bad. I told her he's too young. We should have waited until next fall when he's got some sense. I knew he wouldn't listen to me. He runs out first thing, mutilates himself, and I get blamed for it! A wall!"

"Papa, your horn!" yelled Blackie. "Touch me with your horn!"

"My horn?" repeated Unicorn, looking over his shoulder. "What about my horn?"

"Hold up, Papa, stop!" Blackie begged. "You can heal me with your horn!"

Unicorn stopped under low branches. He turned to Blackie with a sigh.

"No use, Blackie, my horn can't heal you. It's lost its power."

"Mama says you can heal anybody!" Blackie protested. "You just touch them with your horn and they're healed."

"I can't." Unicorn shook his head. "Not anymore. I gave up healing years ago. Let's keep going. Sooner we find somewhere to rest—"

He turned back to the path.

"Please, Papa, please," begged Blackie, limping behind. "I know you can heal me! Why won't you try?"

"Healing doesn't work for me," Unicorn insisted, trotting along. "I'm out of practice, haven't healed anyone in ages!"

He jumped a tree branch lying across the path, its leaves brown and dead. Blackie stepped over gently not to jar his aching forehead.

"The humans," Unicorn explained, slowing down, "they got to be too much for me."

Stopping in a sunny spot in the road, he sniffed the bushes.

"It was your Grandpa, you see. He insisted on healing every human that begged him to. It got to the point that hordes of humans followed him into the forest, creeping along on canes and crutches. What a sight that was—all those cripples climbing over him, pawing at him, bloody and nasty. Lots of them died in the trails, trying to get to him. I'd find corpses all over the place, horrible things!

"When I was a couple years old and went roaming myself, they came after me, too, begging me to heal their aches and pains. I went along with it for a while, healing this one and that, but more kept showing up. It got disgusting! They wore me down until I turned around and came home. I retired from travel, and that ended it. When I refused to heal anyone, they stopped coming around. After awhile then, my power died away, and I could live in peace."

"Please, Papa," screeched Blackie, "give it a try, won't you? My head hurts!"

"Okay, okay!" Unicorn swung his glowing horn through the sun. "But I warn you. My horn doesn't work anymore. You want touched, I'll touch you. Then you'll see."

He tapped Blackie's tender horn with a click.

Blackie felt a spark of something in his forehead. The pain slackened. The throbbing stopped.

"Papa, it's better!" squealed Blackie. "You can heal!"

"Nah." Unicorn inspected Blackie's horn. "Still looks the same, bent."

"But the pain! You took away the pain."

"I did?" Unicorn looked surprised. "Well, if it helps, I'll try again."

15

Unicorn touched his horn to Blackie's head. The pain vanished. Blackie blinked. He grinned at Unicorn.

"See, Papa, you did it! You can heal."

Unicorn looked ruefully at Blackie's bent horn.

"I wouldn't call that healing, but if you feel better, that's good. I didn't think I could do anything. But keep it to yourself, okay? Don't tell anyone. I don't want them pestering me, not beasts, not humans. We better travel on while we can. Let's try to get some distance before nightfall."

They trotted on again. Blackie shook his horn. It felt weird, but it didn't hurt. He had to duck under hanging branches, though. The twist in his horn tended to hook onto twigs.

The trail slid down a muddy bank to a stream where Unicorn pointed to sharp-toed tracks. Blackie sniffed the prints while Unicorn explained.

"That's dogs, a bunch of dogs. You've got to watch out for dog packs, Blackie. They'll give you a hard time if they can. The trick is to never let them get you running. If a dog snaps at you, just kick it in the nose. That'll keep it off."

"I will, Papa."

A mile or so farther, Unicorn found a cracked piece of leather harness beside the road. Blackie sniffed it as Unicorn explained about humans and horses—their wagons, saddles, straps, whips. He shook his head.

"Those poor horses, you'll see how humans treat them. They beat them with sticks. They whip them and work them to death with their plowing and pulling, hauling heavy loads from one place to the other. When the beasts grow old, they skin 'em for their hides. It's mostly the human males that do it, but you stay away from the females, too, Blackie."

Blackie looked up when Unicorn raised his voice.

"Three summers ago, I spent a month up at Darr with a couple of girls. You wouldn't believe how they treated me, that Princess and Dorinda. They hitched me to a chariot and drove me around like a jackass. They made me carry them everywhere, then wait around like a fool for their pleasure. They had a rooster used to sit on my head. Oh, I got tired of that quickly enough. I kicked off the harness and ran away!"

16

"What's a princess?" asked Blackie. "Mama told me that someday I'd find a princess for myself, Papa. What is it?"

"Oh, I hope not," shuddered Unicorn. "Sorriest thing in the world, a princess is our weakness. Seems like, sooner or later, we all run into one. We just can't resist them."

They walked up the road, side by side.

"Just pray you never meet yours, Blackie," said Unicorn in a serious voice. "You see, a princess is the ruling maiden among humans. She's got a perfume on her like . . . like—Well, I can't describe it. Better than peaches, better than strawberries! It pulls you in, draws you to her. If you meet one, you'll see. You just can't hold back."

He sighed. "Lucky thing about smells is that you get used to them in time. Then, you can break away, but at first—"

"So you've traveled through the world of humans," said Blackie brightly. "Like Grandpa!"

"Oh, no," Unicorn snorted, "not like Grandpa. Grandpa went looking for trouble. He sought out adventures, heroic deeds like the ancestors. Bunch of nonsense, if you ask me. Oh, I was curious when I was young, but I was mainly after food. Got plenty of fine dinners from humans, too, the only thing they're good for. Picnics in summer, feasts in winter. I got to know the buttery crunch of pastry, I can tell you. Cookies, oh, ho, ho! Cookies!"

Unicorn stopped to smell a tuft of dark hair caught in a tree beside the road. Blackie sniffed the hair. It smelled strong, strange.

"What's that?" whispered Blackie.

"That's bear!" Unicorn looked around, sniffing. "Must be a big one with fur that long. Those creatures will be roaming all over the forest by summer's end, but you stay away from them, Blackie. Even if a bear seems in good temper, you never know when it'll turn vicious."

Blackie snorted scornfully. "I'm not afraid of a bear! I'll charge a bear! We unicorns can whip any beast, can't we, Papa?"

Unicorn stopped in the road. Angrily, he whacked Blackie with his horn.

"Don't you ever listen to me? What do I keep telling you? Sure, you can whip a bear—you're a unicorn! When you grow to your full strength in a year or so, you can whip a lion or a tiger, but they'll scratch you to pieces while you do it. It's not worth it! Stay out of fights, that's the topmost rule."

Unicorn stamped down a hoof with a thump.

"Do . . . not . . . get . . . into fights! If you're in trouble, use your legs, run away. Even better—"

He tapped Blackie's forehead. A jolt of pain shot through Blackie's head.

"Keep alert! Think! Use your brain. Stay out of trouble in the first place. And please, please, stay silent in the forest! You've been chattering like a sparrow. Quiet, now. Come on."

He trotted off, shaking his head, grumbling to himself. They followed the road through an area of high hills that had Unicorn breathing hard by the top. Just beyond the summit of the highest hill, the forest fell away to a plain of rippling grass dotted here and there with tree groves. Unicorn looked to both sides. He took a long sniff, pricked up his ears, and listened.

Blackie looked up and blinked. He'd never seen such a sky. Spreading as far as he could see, the heavens were a bright blue like a bird's egg with puffy clouds rolling along. Chirping birds flew up from the grass.

"High country, open," said Unicorn, nodding with satisfaction. "You've never seen open country, Blackie. In open country, you use your eyes. It's safe enough if you keep watch to all sides. No one can sneak up on you here. Just smell that grass! Good place for a run."

Unicorn took a deep breath. Tossing his horn, he lifted off his front hooves and thumped down.

"So what do you say, Blackie, want to shake out your hooves? Think you can outrun your old dad?"

With a cheer, Blackie bounded into the knee-high grass. Unicorn threw up his horn, leaped off rear hooves, and galloped past Blackie. Blackie pulled back his ears, stretched his neck, and dug into the sod with all four hooves. Wind fanned his face. His mane fluttered as he swished through the grass with full heart, but Unicorn kept ahead, driving forward, his horn low, tail stretched behind.

Filled with joy, Blackie ran and ran. Far ahead, he saw a deep gully cutting across the field. Unicorn pulled up at the edge and reared high, kicking front legs. He trumpeted. Blackie thrilled at the call. He ran up beside Unicorn and threw himself down in the grass. He rolled in the softness till the sky swayed when he looked up.

Blackie pushed to his hooves, laughing and panting. He shook grass seeds and stubble from his coat and gazed at his father. Unicorn's head was down. He sobbed for air, sweat raining down his shoulders.

"Hey . . . Papa!" panted Blackie, running over. "What's wrong?"

Unicorn choked and coughed, gasping for breath. His eyes were glassy. Foam slobbered down his chin.

"Never!" he wheezed, shaking his horn. "Never . . . let me . . . do that again!"

"Papa, Papa, you're great!" yelled Blackie. "You run like a hero!"

Unicorn fell into the grass, shuddering. Blackie backed away a step. He stared down with concern.

"You all right, Papa?"

Chest heaving for air, Unicorn lifted his head and glared at Blackie. "Blackie, Blackie, you'll be . . . death of me."

Blackie stepped close and rubbed Unicorn's wet neck with his nose. "Don't talk, Papa, just rest. Rest a little."

Unicorn dropped his head. He closed his eyes, scraped in a broken breath. He puffed it out again, breathed in, breathed out. He softened into uneasy sleep.

Bugs buzzed down and walked over Unicorn's sweaty body. Blackie stood a moment brushing off the bugs with his tail. Blackie felt alive, muscles stretched from his run. He shook himself, aware that he was thirsty again.

He left Unicorn and walked along the gully, looking down the muddy sides into scraggly brush and trees below. He bit the long strands of grass leaning over the edge.

He came to an old log thrown across the gully to the other side. He lifted his front feet to the log and looked down again. The bushes below had yellow and blue flowers. He listened, but didn't hear water trickling down there, only bugs and birds.

"Must be water somewhere," he thought. "It'd be easy to jump down there to see, but how'd I get out? The sides are too high to jump, and the gully goes on and on in both directions."

Thirstier than ever, he ran back to Unicorn. Unicorn was snoring, his sides rising regularly.

"I'll stand guard, let him sleep a little longer."

The breeze blowing across the field cooled Blackie's damp face. He chewed seedy grass stems till they tasted too dry to swallow. He yawned, shook his mane, and looked up. Clouds rolled gracefully in the wind, moving steadily across the sky.

"Clouds, clouds, I wonder where they come from?"

Birds flew back and forth. Bugs whined about his head. Something bit him on the ear. He swung his neck around and swept his head with his tail. He looked across the field, remembering Unicorn streaming along at full gallop. What a sight that'd been!

"Oh, Papa."

Blackie's head drooped. He locked his knees and closed his eyes for a nap.

It seemed he'd slept only a moment before he woke to Unicorn's groan. Unicorn was struggling to his feet, looking wildly about.

"Where am I? Where am I?"

"You're here, Papa, with me." Blackie stepped over to nuzzle his father. "We're traveling to see the world."

"Oh . . . oh, yes," Unicorn panted. He dragged in a breath. "I almost . . . almost went into my charge back then. Haven't run like that for ages! I can't do that, never again."

"You were great, Papa!" cried Blackie. "Let's run again!"

"Run again?" screeched Unicorn. "What did I just say about running? Look at me!"

Unicorn tossed his head. He shook his coat, trying to steady his breath.

"I'll be sore for a week after that run. I'm still sweating. Gotta cool off, catch my breath. Mad, I must be mad, racing around like a colt. What in the world was I thinking?"

Unicorn looked well enough, so Blackie shook out his coat and turned to the gully, feeling dryer than ever. Unicorn limped over beside him and sniffed disgustedly at the ditch.

"No use jumping down there. We'd never get out again."

"There's a log over here, Papa!" cried Blackie, running to the tree trunk across the gulf.

Unicorn followed slowly. He sniffed the log and frowned. Blackie prodded it with his horn. "Do we cross on this, Papa?"

Unicorn looked along the gully to both sides. He sighed.

"I guess we have to. Either cross here or circle around to the flats, a couple miles down. There used to be four or five logs here, a real bridge. Horses could cross it. Humans must have carried them off. We can cross on this log, though. Watch me, I'll show you."

Unicorn placed his front hooves on the log. One at a time, he reached up his rear legs and stepped slowly out on the log, staring straight ahead.

"Like this, Blackie. One step at a time. Don't look down. Hey! What are you doing?"

Blackie hopped onto the log. It rolled slightly under his weight. Unicorn screeched as his left rear hoof slipped off the trunk, swinging him off balance. He tried to pull back, but his right hoof slipped the other way. He fell with a squeal, thumping down upon the log, clinging with legs and shoulders like a squirrel astraddle a tree limb.

Blackie ran out on the log. "I'll help you, Papa!"

"Get off! Get off!" shrieked Unicorn. "What are you trying to do, kill me?"

Blackie backed down the log and jumped off. Unicorn hung tight, sweating and panting, as Blackie danced around the end of the log.

"Hold on, Papa, hold on! Reach up with your hoof! Pull yourself up! You can do it! You can do it! It's easy!"

Groaning, Unicorn stretched up a rear leg. He had to shoulder his body forward to shift enough weight to scrape a knee up the trunk. Gasping, he tried to rock his weight forward.

"I can't do it!"

"You can, Papa, you can!" squealed Blackie. "You're almost there! Another push! Another push, Papa!"

Unicorn shuddered. He gave up and the haunch slipped down again. He shuddered, wheezed a moment, tried pulling up a shoulder. Clinging with rear legs, he dragged up his right front leg, stretching out his neck for balance. He got a hoof on the trunk to hold himself, wobbling and trembling, while he pulled up the other front leg. Finally, he had both hooves planted.

"I'll never get up! I can't do it!" he moaned.

Jumping up and down, Blackie cheered him on. "You're halfway there, Papa! Pull up your back legs now! You can do it!"

It was impossible. Unicorn couldn't pull up a hind hoof without rolling himself off the log. Finally, he let go with his front hooves. He plopped down and dragged himself forward by inches, throwing enough weight on his front shoulders to scoot his rear forward a worm's length, then settling down and reaching again with front shoulders.

Slowly, painfully, inch by inch, he scraped himself over the log. He shuddered in deep breaths, terrified he'd fall off any moment. When he reached the far side, he let himself roll off the log. He flopped down in the grass, foamy and sweaty, choking for breath.

Blackie ran across the log and jumped down beside his father. "See, Papa! You did it, you did it! I told you, you could!"

"Get away!" gasped Unicorn, eyes squeezed tight. "Get away from me!"

Blackie backed off and cropped a mouthful of grass, staring anxiously at Unicorn. Unicorn lay still a long time without moving. Only his heaving chest showed he was alive. Blackie ate more grass, looked at the sky, watched grasshoppers jump around.

"Papa!" he called. "Papa, are you all right?"

Unicorn rolled over. Without looking at Blackie, he crawled painfully to his knees. He pushed up on trembling hooves. Panting, he inspected his legs, scraped and torn by the log. Blood trickled from the scratches.

He shook his head, sighed deeply, and limped across the field. Blackie trailed behind, silently watching his father.

CHAPTER THREE

Gardens

Unicorn limped over the field, head low, horn down. Blackie followed silently, glum and depressed. He was thirsty, stone dry. He wanted to speak, to say something to cheer Papa, but this seemed a good time to stay silent, so he plodded along, looking at the clouds. He thought of the sparkling streams at home.

Back at the Nest, he could run down the hill whenever he wanted a drink. Out here in the world, he had to wait until water came along.

The broad track they followed narrowed into a distinct road on the far side of the field. It descended into a tree-shadowed ravine where flies swarmed about their ears. At the bottom of the ravine, they found a small clearing scattered with dry leaves and a fire site next to a stream bubbling through rocks.

Blackie smelled the water twenty yards away. He couldn't stop himself. He ran through the brush to throw himself into the stream, splashing and rolling on the stony bottom, then jumped up, shivering. He shook his coat and drank deeply. He drank again and again. He lifted his head to look at Unicorn. Unicorn was lying downstream in a pool, half-covered with water that reflected the clouds above. Eyes closed, head resting on the mossy bank, Unicorn breathed heavily, letting the flowing water wash the sweat and blood from his body.

Blackie shuddered with pity as Unicorn rolled over, exposing cuts and scratches up and down his legs. Poor Papa, how that run had worn him down! He needed refreshing, restoring. Papa needed healing.

Blackie thought of his horn. It was bent. It was damaged. Could his horn heal the way Papa had described? Blackie had never tried to heal anyone, but he crept toward Papa as Unicorn pushed painfully onto his fore hooves, then to his rear. Panting, Unicorn looked sadly at his reflection in the pool—legs scratched, smudged black from the log.

"Papa," Blackie whispered, "my horn—"

Unicorn glared at him. "Back off! Stay away! Keep your distance! Pushing, pushing, always pushing at me! You knocked me off that log!"

"It wasn't my fault, Papa! I didn't touch you!"

"Oh!" Unicorn waved his horn. "I can see how it's going! Before you came along, I was happy. I had my life under control! Now, it's 'Blackie this,' and 'Blackie that'! You'll squeeze me and squash me till I won't have room to breathe!"

"I'm sorry, Papa. I won't do it again."

Unicorn thrust out a scabby leg.

"Look at that leg! My beautiful coat, scraped, scratched, scarred! That's never going to heal! I'm injured! Wounded! I'm torn and tired and miles from home—ruined! And it's all your fault!"

Blackie lowered his head. "I'm sorry, Papa. I won't push you again."

"Gotta rest," muttered Unicorn. He limped down the rocks beside the stream to a leafy shelf under bending branches. He shook himself, set his hooves for a nap.

Blackie was tired, but he didn't feel like sleeping. He sniffed along the stream, smelling deer and foxes and a host of strange smells, one especially sharp and strong. He found tracks in wet sand, broad pads of something big that had squatted to drink.

He turned back to Unicorn's resting place. By lifting front hooves onto a fallen tree trunk, he could reach his muzzle into a cluster of green branches. He tore off twigs and chewed, stopping now and then for a drink.

Shadows darkened the reflections in the stream. The air grew heavier, smells stronger as bugs swarmed and stung. Blackie shook his mane, swept his tail about.

He heard a yelp, not a fox's "yip," but a gruff warning. He turned his head to see a scrawny yellow animal watching from upstream with intelligent brown eyes. Its mouth was open, its tongue hanging out.

"Has to be a dog," thought Blackie, swinging to face the creature. "Hi, there!" he said aloud.

The dog didn't answer. It stared at him with lifted head and yelped again.

Frowning at the dog, Blackie moved closer to Unicorn.

"Dog packs," Papa had said, "watch out for dog packs." Was this dog in a pack? Would he have to kick it in the nose?

"What do you want?" Blackie asked. "Where do you come from?"

The dog said nothing. It sniffed at him and panted, then turned and pattered up the stream.

"So that's a dog," thought Blackie, smelling its track. "Didn't look fierce to me. Wonder where it came from."

He stayed beside Unicorn, who snored as the sun sank. Darkness fell, dense and perfumed. Bird songs died away to hoots and murmurs. Blackie ate the shoots and leaves he could find about the stream. In the dusk, he stepped next to Unicorn and locked his knees to sleep.

He sighed and thought about the dead deer and the dog. He relived the thrilling run, pounding through grass with the wind in his ears. Oh, yes, and poor Papa stuck on the log. That had been scary. What if Papa had tumbled into the gully? How could Blackie get him out?

"Mama says I should look after Papa. How can I look after him if he won't listen to me?"

Blackie had a strange, dreamy night. He was so tired that he slept deeply, but kept waking to the ripple of the stream and the rustle of branches about him.

Unicorn was up and moving at dawn. Blackie heard him splashing in the pool, washing his ankles, mourning the scratches.

"My coat, slashed to pieces! A lifetime of care thrown away!"

Blackie stretched out his shoulders. He took a long drink in the stream, then followed Unicorn upstream to the clearing where dogs ran from under shadowy wagons to bark at them. Unicorn ignored the dogs, but Blackie stared at them and at a pair of dark creatures tied to a branch beside the stream. He took a deep sniff of humans and animals, fire, and pungent cooking smells as Unicorn limped into the road under the brightening sky.

With a groan, Unicorn stepped up to a heavy jog. "Ooh, I ache, I ache—every muscle aches! We're not going much farther today. We'll take a look at a couple villages, then head back to the forest where we belong!"

They trotted silently around a bend before Unicorn spoke up again.

"This is the world I warned you about, Blackie, the world of humans. Men, with their dogs, their bows, their spears. You have to keep your eyes open around here. You'll see castles, churches, villages—humans everywhere, and humans will give us trouble."

"Why, Papa?"

Unicorn pulled up at a patch of straggly grass. He took a bite before answering.

"That's just the way they are. They worship you one moment and shoot you the next. Worse than wolves. Wolves, now, you find wolves in the hills. They run in packs like dogs, but you know what you're up to with wolves. With humans, you never know."

Blackie sniffed the grass, looked up. "Will wolves attack us? Do we fight them?"

Unicorn choked on a mouthful of grass. He spat out his words.

"We don't . . . fight . . . anything! Wolves, we don't worry about, not this time of year anyway. In winter, the starving season, wolves might give us a chase. I had a pack after me in the mountains one winter. I drove out a lamb for them and they left me alone."

Blackie's mouth dropped open. "Papa, you didn't! Not a baby sheep!"

Unicorn nodded his head, grass spears hanging from his mouth.

"Sure, I did. Saved me from a fight. That lamb was small. Nobody missed it. It was the foxy thing to do, but don't fret now. Wolves won't bother us in summertime, and we can outsmart the humans. Come on."

A mile or so farther, a broad path joined their trail from the right. The trees had been cut away on both sides, widening the route into a serious road with deep wheel tracks in low spots. The smell of humans was heavy here, particularly at clearings every few miles where they found briers, mounds of ashes, and patches of grass.

They were grazing on fresh leaves where a tree had been cut down when they heard something rattle down the road. Blackie looked up to see a horse plodding slowly toward them, a hornless creature, reddish-brown, that came up to Unicorn's shoulder. Bound to a cart by leather straps, it shambled along, head down, eyes half-shut. A man with a stick dozed on the front of the cart, rocking back and forth with the movement.

"Leave it alone," warned Unicorn, but Blackie was too curious to hold back. He trotted toward the horse, sniffing. It tilted its head to look at him.

"Hey, cousin," it neighed, "kill this man for me. If you pull off the harness and turn me loose, I'll follow you around the world."

Blackie ran up to the beast, touched his nose to it. It smelled tired, dirty.

"Hello," said Blackie. "Are you my cousin? Why are you tied up? Do those straps hurt? Does that man beat you?"

The man on the cart woke when the motion stopped. He stared at Blackie, lifting his stick.

"Get away! Leave my horse alone!"

"Come on, Blackie!" ordered Unicorn, trotting past the cart. "Don't bother that nag."

Blackie stayed back a moment, asking questions, then ran to catch up with Unicorn. The horse pulled around to follow, but the man yelled at it and struck it with his stick.

Blackie looked over his shoulder. "So that was a horse, Papa! Why don't we set it free? Why can't it go where it wants?"

"That horse doesn't want to be free," said Unicorn, slowing to a limp. "It wouldn't know what to do if we turned it loose. It'd tag after us for a while, slow us down, get us into trouble. Horses are born to pull wagons."

Blackie caught up with his father.

"Well, I'm glad I'm not a horse. I wouldn't let anybody hit me with a stick."

It wasn't far before the forest ran out, chopped away into a sunny wasteland of stumps and thistles. This area smelled of wet wood chips and shavings. Soon, they walked between small fields surrounded by thorn fences. Humans stood in the fields, shielding their eyes to watch them. Dogs came running from all sides to surround them, barking wildly.

"Is this a dog pack?" asked Blackie, nervously drawing close to Unicorn.

"No," said Unicorn, eyeing a big-headed mutt that ran close, snapping yellow teeth, "just village dogs, but they need a reminder of who's who."

Down smashed a hoof, and the dog scampered away, howling. The other dogs backed off, barking even louder.

"That's the way you handle dogs. Come on."

Blackie followed quietly. They trotted steadily a mile or so before Unicorn stopped to graze at a clover patch just outside the log fence of a small village. Blackie bit up dandelions along the edges of the clover and gazed at the flowering thatches on the hut roofs across the fence. He smelled smoke and sewage and humans. He heard thumping and banging, chattering and yelling.

"Unicorns!" cried light voices. "Lucky unicorns!"

A pair of girls in brown and yellow dresses ran barefoot around the fence. They dropped their bundles and began hopping up and down. They clapped hands and sang. To Blackie's surprise, he understood their words.

Unicorn, Unicorn, grant my wishes.
Fill my bottles, fill my dishes.
Keep me safe from wolves and bears.
Answer all my prayers.
Answer all my prayers.

Unicorn gave them a look of disgust.

"No princess there. Already begging. That's what you get around humans. Come on, Blackie. Let's get out of here."

He turned into the path around the village fence. Blackie followed, the girls running beside him, patting his flanks.

They called in their high voices, "Stay with us, Unicorn, stay! Aunt Josie's sick with the fever. Stop with us. Heal her! Heal her!"

Unicorn trotted faster, and the girls fell behind.

"It never stops," grumbled Unicorn. "They always want something."

"I can understand their speech," said Blackie, looking back at the waving humans.

"Of course you can." Unicorn slowed again. "You're smart, you're a unicorn. We understand humans, but they're dumber than donkeys.

They have no idea what we say. Best to pretend you don't understand them."

Catching up with the road on the far side of the village, they passed a stone castle with its tower and banner. Blackie got a whiff of the stagnant moat running around the castle. The drawbridge was down for the day.

"Castle Shrems," said Unicorn, pointing his horn. "I used to stop by here for dinners. The castle was in good shape in those days, and they put on regular feasts when I dropped by. Then old Shrems spent himself poor on a wedding and tried to catch me for the reward."

"What reward's that, Papa?" asked Blackie.

"Aw, there's always a reward for a unicorn," grumbled Unicorn. He grew silent.

After another mile of lanes and fields, the road returned to forest though they kept running into humans—woodchoppers with carts, peddlers with packs, boys with baskets of birds' eggs. A baldheaded man in a brown robe knelt to them as they passed by.

"Oh, oh!" said Unicorn, suddenly. "Those men in green, hunters! Watch that pair, Blackie. Watch the bows. Run into the trees if they shoot at us."

The men in green stopped to squint at them. Blackie heard the young one say to the older, "But we can't shoot a unicorn. The Bishop'd hang us!"

"Let's take a chance," said the other, pulling an arrow from his belt. He spat on the ground. "That big horn's worth a score o' silver."

"Run!" cried Unicorn.

He crashed through the brush with Blackie at his heels. They plunged into the dark forest, circled quietly around the men, and returned to the road a half-mile beyond, Unicorn panting again.

"Oh, how I'd hoped . . . no more running. I just wanted to . . . to take it easy, today."

"You should've charged those men!" cried Blackie, fiercely. "You'd have run them down before they could lift their bows!"

Unicorn shook leaves from his shoulders, muttering to himself. "He never listens, never learns."

The road was empty for the next few miles. They came to more fields and another castle with its village. Here, they turned into a quiet lane that passed around the outskirts of the settlement and back into the road on the other side without bothering the humans. Trotting along, Unicorn recalled his years of adventure.

"Oh, yes," he mused, "castles. Worst thing about castles is all the humans squeezed inside, noisy, stinky, quarreling. The fights I've seen—They'll fight at a look, a word, or just because they're bored. Taverns are bad as castles, but it's knives there instead of swords. Castles have the best food. Oh, the dinners at Furland and Darr, royal feasts with veggies and fruits, cakes and cookies!"

Unicorn smacked his lips at the memory.

"Peaches, salads, cobblers, cookies! Best food in the land! The Princess and Dorinda—horrible girls, but at least, they fed me well. I'll say that for them, they fed me. If I were you, though, I'd keep away from humans. That's the safest."

Unicorn talked about Darr, his adventure of three years before.

"That time wasn't my fault. I was eating watercress in the forest when this Prince showed up and captured me. How he did it, I don't know. I've thought and thought about it. Somehow, he had a power over me even stronger than the princess who enthralled me when I was young. He could make me do anything he wanted, so he rode me up to Darr and turned me over to the females. They made me race horses and fight goats. So undignified, but the dinners—"

Describing the feasts made Unicorn hungry again. He looked around carefully when they came to the next village, then pushed through a hedge into a garden. Blackie followed into paradise—rows of lettuce leaves and pea pods more delicious than all the scattered greens of the forest. He chomped happily beside Papa until a human saw them and began yelling.

More humans ran up with sticks and hoes. Dogs chased them down the garden path until Unicorn broke through the hedge into the next garden where they found young cabbage plants. They moved around the village from garden to garden, gobbling as they went with dogs and humans chasing after.

That morning was an education for Blackie. He learned how quickly dogs can run and how slowly humans dragged along. The real lesson came from Unicorn's introduction to the vegetables in the gardens, their tastes and textures. Crunchy yellow carrots, sharp red radishes, pungent white onions, chewy green spinach—Blackie tried them all, and found them delicious.

"Papa, this is wonderful!"

"Oh, you have no idea!" cried Unicorn, chomping down on the spinach.

Choking on a mighty mouthful, he gulped and gasped, "Wait . . . wait a couple weeks until it's berry time. A month later, the orchards burst out with fruit! Hay, grain, nuts—you've got a whole world of food ahead of you!"

He was just reaching down for the spinach when a sharp arrow smacked down into the green plants between them.

"Time to move on."

Unicorn jerked up the spinach plant in his jaws and trotted off, shaking dirt off the roots. Blackie looked at the humans running down the garden path, the females waving hoes while the males pulled their curved bows to shoot arrows that thumped down five or six feet away.

Unicorn ran through the spinach to the next hedge and jumped it with ease. Blackie fell a little short. He cleared the hedge and crashed into a prickly gooseberry bush.

"Watch the thorns!" yelled Unicorn, darting around the spiny bushes.

"Oh, oh, oh!"

Blackie tore himself from the scratchy sprays and followed Unicorn down the path to the outer hedge where they broke out into the lane circling the gardens.

"This was how I lived when I was young," said Unicorn, trotting along the road with dogs barking after. "I traveled from garden to garden, eating the freshest and sweetest veggies in the land. I loved that life until the humans caught me one time."

"You got caught, Papa?"

Blackie glanced back. The dogs had dropped away.

"Back in those days, Blackie, I used to go running with the Hunt in autumn. I'd be nosing about a harvest festival and hear the long horns echo across the land, so I'd head for the campgrounds. After the run was over each evening, the hunting parties had feasts, spectacular feasts! All the nuts and pears you could eat! Why, the bread they served was slathered with summer's jams and jellies, and they gave me relishes and olives and pickles."

Unicorn paused, a faraway look on his face. "Pickles, I haven't tasted a pickle for years. Tangy little things."

He smacked his lips, then caught himself.

"It's not worth it, Blackie—that's what I'm trying to tell you. One morning, we were chasing a stag through the forest."

"A stag?" questioned Blackie. "You were chasing a deer?"

"Sure, different days they hunted bear, foxes, boars. That day they were chasing this big buck. And me, I was running ahead of everyone. I was sniffing the air and feeling like I could run forever. Suddenly, the path swung sharply and I missed the turn. I skidded into this dead tree. Spongy, it was, covered with moss and lichens."

Blackie nodded. He knew those rotting old trees.

"Somehow," said Unicorn, "somehow, I drove my horn into that tree, into a crack or something, and I couldn't pull it out. There I was, stuck by my horn, while the humans gathered around me. I was helpless. I had to stand and listen while they decided what to do with me.

"The Count, he was friendly enough. 'Cut him free!' he ordered from his big horse.

"Then one of the barons spoke up. 'But my lord, he's caught, a wild unicorn. If you'd tame him, you'd become famous forever. Think of the songs and stories they'd tell about you.'

"Well, the Count wasn't for that. 'You can't tame a unicorn,' he said. 'It can't be done.'

"'Sure it can, me lord,' said a grizzled old huntsman. 'You'd tame him the way you'd tame a colt or a puppy. Geld him!'

"And he pulled out his knife, ready to trim me down."

Blackie gasped. He wasn't sure what Papa meant, but his tone of voice made Blackie's ears stand stiff, the hairs prick up on his mane.

"That's when I gave the lunge of my life," said Unicorn with a shiver. "I yanked free of that tree, knocked down that huntsman, and ran away from the whole crew. Then and there, I decided I'd had enough of humans. I loved the eating, loved the singing, loved warming myself at the fires in wintertime, but I wasn't letting them tame me. Not that way. It's not worth it for a pickle."

"But Papa," protested Blackie, "Grandpa never got gelded, did he?"

"He was just lucky," said Unicorn, trotting on. "Who knows what they'd have done if he'd stuck himself in a tree. Now, please, let's not talk about it."

A moment later, Unicorn spoke up again.

"You've seen today how the humans chase us. Sooner or later, some bowman will get lucky and you'll get an arrow in your side. Even if it doesn't kill you, you'll have a scar in your coat. Soon enough, you're all scratched and scarred like Grandpa. Best thing is to stay home where you belong."

Blackie said nothing. He thought of the radishes, the lettuce, the green onions he'd eaten.

"There's a whole world of gardens out here," he realized, licking his lips, "one after another. And the feasts in those castles. I wonder how you get into castles. I'll ask Papa when he feels better."

He trotted on a while, nodded. "When I go out into the world, I'll be careful. I won't go on hunts. I won't run my horn into trees. That way, I won't get gelded, whatever that is, but I will get to taste a pickle. Then I'll know what Papa's talking about."

CHAPTER FOUR

The River

Blackie woke, next morning, burping radishes. He ran to drink from the stream as Unicorn lifted his head with a groan.

"Ohhh, I feel . . . I feel like a turtle tossed by a fox! Why'd you let me eat so much? You know, I can't digest that stuff. Now, I'll have to sniff out some mint for my belly."

Blackie swallowed a mouthful of leaves. "Where we headed today, Papa?"

"Only a little farther," said Unicorn, limping to the stream for a drink. "We'll run around the town and take a look at the river. That'll be enough for your journey. Once you've seen the river, we can head home."

Blackie trotted past his father to the road. "The river, that's where they have the boats, isn't it, Papa?"

"Yes, boats," said Unicorn, looking up and down the road. "They're sort of like carts floating on water. The humans build boats in different sizes, you know. The great ships, you find them down at the sea. Some of those have twenty or thirty oars. On the river here, you'll see smaller boats, though a barge can stretch out considerably."

They didn't travel far before they found the forest cut away to long fields of gleaming grain, then the smaller plots of veggies. As they neared the stone wall around the town, they ran into clusters of women and children standing in the road. These seemed alarmed by the unicorns, yelling at them to keep away. Some threw rocks to drive them off.

"Strange," muttered Unicorn, "even for humans. Usually, they welcome us as lucky beasts. And where are the men? Shouldn't they be tending their fields?"

The only men they saw were a large band of guards standing at the town gate with their spears and bows. Many wore bits of armor, a helmet here, a breastplate there. As the unicorns approached, the men ran out, shaking their spears. A bell started to ring. Unicorn turned into a lane running between garden plots.

"We won't get near that bunch. Something's ruffled them up today."

"Was that the entrance?" asked Blackie, "the way you get into the town?"

"Oh, yes," said Unicorn. "That was the gate. You don't want to mess with gates before I explain them to you. Hasps, catches, latches, locks—There's so much human lore you'd have to learn before you could deal with gates. Otherwise, you'll get yourself trapped behind walls and never get out."

Blackie looked across rows of crops to see the roofs of tall buildings above the wall, a steeple sticking high in the air.

"Oh, Papa!" exclaimed Blackie. "You know everything about humans, don't you?"

"I know a few things," said Unicorn, stopping beside him in the lane. "You're looking at a town, Blackie. They've got more humans in there than you'd find in twenty villages. The City, though, if you ever get to the City, you'll find it twenty times bigger than this. The main streets in the City are wide enough for three wagons to pass at a time."

"Oh, Papa," said Blackie, staring at a tower in the wall where a man looked back at them, small at this distance. "I am seeing the world, aren't I?"

Unicorn nuzzled him with his big nose.

"You sure are, son. Once you see the river, you've had a good look at the world, good enough for any forest creature. Then you'll be happy to go back to our peaceful life. You'll enjoy the mushrooms and walnuts there and leave all this to the humans."

The only human they passed in the lane was a dirty boy whistling along with a string of dead creatures hanging from a stick over his shoulder, strange staring creatures shaped like ears.

The boy stared at Blackie, openmouthed. Unicorn pointed with his horn.

"Those things are fish. You've seen small fish in streams. Fish are creatures that live in water and never come out. No legs, all head and tail. They come in all sizes too. Down by the sea, I've seen fish as long as your leg."

"Fish," repeated Blackie, "live in the water like tadpoles."

The boy leaned the stick of fish against the hedge and scrambled after them. Blackie looked back to see the boy watching with imploring eyes. He folded his hands to sing to them as they trotted away.

> Holy beast, holy beast,
> heal my aches and pains.
> Show me where the treasure lies.
> Bring me sun and rains.

Unicorn stepped up his pace when the boy chased after, shouting, "Don't go, Unicorns! Stay with us. Cure our illness! Fight our enemies! Keep us happy!"

"See," said Unicorn, trotting around the bending lane. "That's humans for you! Begging, always begging. They all want something. They never think of what we want."

"What do we want, Papa?" asked Blackie.

"I don't know about you," grumbled Unicorn, "but I want your mother to leave me alone. Sending you out in the world at your age—that's asking for trouble!"

"But the wonders I'm seeing!" cried Blackie, leaping into the air. "So much to tell Mama!"

"Hold it down, hold it down," ordered Unicorn. "You don't have to tell her everything. You don't want to . . . to worry her. Just tell her that you had a good time with me, and you want to stay home from now on."

The lane ran into a wide path running along the riverbank. Blackie stopped on the bank, overwhelmed by the size and smell of the moving flood before him. To one side, he saw a big castle with flapping pennons. It was stuck in the middle of the river with a plank bridge passing back to the town. Swinging his head to the other side, Blackie followed the endless sheet of brown water flowing by in a great curve, shining and swirling and lapping up the bank. Three men rowed a boat upstream with a crate at the end.

"That's a boat, Papa!" cried Blackie.

"Sure is," said Unicorn, "a small one. You'll see lots of boats and barges if you watch the river for awhile."

"Oh, my," said Blackie, "this river, it's all water. Can I . . . can I drink from it?"

"Sure you can drink from it," said Unicorn. "That town gets its water from the river."

Sniffing the strong scent of the riverbank, Blackie waded into the squishy mud of the shallows and took a long drink of water. It tasted lightly of decay. He lifted his head, water dripping from his muzzle, and looked around. The wide, cloudy sky spread above the river with broad-winged birds swinging and dipping with shrill cries. Ducks floated in the water, rising and falling with the waves.

Blackie sighed with satisfaction. This was the world of humans, so different from the forest that he could only smile and stare until Unicorn nudged him.

"How about a dip?"

"What?"

Blackie looked over as Unicorn waved his horn. "A dip, a swim. Cool off in the water."

"In this river?" Blackie looked at the ducks bobbing up and down in the waves. "Oh, I don't think so, Papa. The river's so big—"

"Sure is," nodded Unicorn. "Biggest thing in the land. It flows from the eastern mountains to the sea below the City. Don't worry about water, Blackie. We unicorns are great swimmers. I've crossed this river ten times, once in wintertime. Now, that was a terrible swim, I promise you."

Unicorn shivered at the memory.

"Wind, cold, ice, you can imagine. Well, you can't, really. You've never seen ice. It's this hard white stuff, cold, freezing cold. It covered the water like a solid surface so I ran out over the river. It looked frozen all the way across, but the ice was thin in the center. It broke under me, dunked me in water so cold it burned my hide. I smoked like a chimney when I crawled out. It was a wonder I didn't freeze to death, but I had to keep running that day. Some baron or other was chasing me."

"Oh, my," breathed Blackie, grinning at Unicorn. "What adventures you had, Papa."

"There's adventures and adventures," grumbled Unicorn, kicking mud from a hoof. "Most of 'em are awful, but a swim feels good after a run on a day like today. I'm sweaty. My coat's filthy. Still, we better hurry before the humans come along."

Shaking his head, Blackie backed up the muddy bank.

"I think I'm ready to go home, Papa. I've seen enough of the world. Let's hurry back and tell Mama everything we've done."

"First, a little swim," said Unicorn, wading out into the water. "You gotta get baptized sometime. A dip'll pep you up. You'll meet old Mother River nose to nose. Come on."

Blackie sniffed at a pearly shell in the mud, then yelled at Unicorn who was up to his knees in the river.

"But Papa, remember what happened to Grandpa! Mama told me that he swam in a river where big crocs tried to eat him."

"Don't worry," Unicorn called. "There's no crocs here. Just remember to relax in the water. It'll hold you like a boat. Just kick along and keep your head up. It's easy."

Uncertainly, Blackie waded in a few steps, feeling the gritty bottom under his hooves. He watched Unicorn take another step into the river. He vanished under the surface. Blackie cried out, but Unicorn's horn reappeared a few feet downstream, followed by his head.

Swimming steadily, Unicorn pushed out into the current. He looked back, gasped at Blackie, "Come on in. It's fun!"

Blackie watched Unicorn doubtfully for a moment, then made up his mind.

"Here I come!"

Ears high, Blackie splashed out into the river, his hooves sinking into sticky bottom as the water rose up his sides, cooler and cooler the deeper he went. Holding his breath, he closed his eyes and plunged in when the bottom dipped under him. He sank below, shivering, as cold water squeezed about him. He heard a loud thrumming in his ears before bobbing up, sneezing. He snuffed water from his nose, kicking after Unicorn.

The river pushed him along with sunlight sparkling in his eyelashes. He lifted his nose to glance around for crocs and kicked steadily through the pulsing flow. He caught up with Unicorn and floated beside him, grinning at his father.

"This is fun, isn't it, Papa?"

"There they are," muttered Unicorn, sourly. Blackie looked back at the path.

Humans were running out from the town, gathering along the riverbank to point at the unicorns. One man blew a hunting horn that echoed over the river while others ran up with ropes and nets.

A woman in black hurried with a group of girls, their birdlike voices shrilling over the gurgle of the river. The woman passed out pieces of paper, and the girls squatted along the riverbank to sketch pictures of the unicorns.

"What do we do now, Papa?" cried Blackie. "Will they catch us?"

"Don't worry about that gang."

Unicorn's ears were back. He closed his eyes and floated at ease in the current, kicking now and then to keep his heading steady in the waves.

"If I can't outsmart a bunch of boobs like them— But it is a bother. I'm getting careless. We should have gone around the bend where they couldn't see us."

Blackie swam close to Unicorn and let himself float. He tried to relax in the river's cool embrace, winking as water splashed in his face, but couldn't help glancing at the crowd of humans following along the bank, talking loudly and watching him. Now, he was floating to the town itself where the wall ran down to the water.

Blackie was worried. "Papa, we're stuck here. We can't get out of the river with that wall there. Those people will catch us if we try."

Unicorn blew bubbles from his nose.

"Don't fret," he said, lazily. "We'll wait till nightfall to get out. The humans won't bother us after dark. They hate the night."

"After dark!" exclaimed Blackie. "We can't stay in this river all day."

"'Course we can," said Unicorn. "Not in the water, though. We'll run up on the island."

"What island?" asked Blackie, watching heads appear over the wall as they floated by. Ahead of him, he saw the bridge to the castle. Humans were running out on the bridge to lean over the wooden side to stare down at them. Floating under the bridge, they passed a pier

39

sticking out in the river where men were handing down oars to boats tied along its length.

Blackie turned his head to watch the boats when Unicorn said, "Oh, oh! I should have expected that."

"What is it?" questioned Blackie, rocking in the waves.

"Boats," snorted Unicorn. "Looks like they're coming after us. I should have known. They'll do anything they can to pester us."

"What'll we do, Papa?" squealed Blackie. "We're stuck out here in this water!"

Unicorn straightened to kick along in the current.

"Don't worry, Blackie. I know boats. Boats are skittish things in the best of conditions, and against a clever unicorn—Well, I'd rather take on a boat any day than have to fight spearmen on land."

Blackie glanced over to see the first boat setting out into the river as the humans cheered from the pier.

"Here they come, Papa! Will we have to fight them?"

Unicorn looked over his shoulder.

"I hope not. Just swim a little faster if you can. We'll stay ahead of them around this big bend."

Another boat had set out now, rowing hard after the first one. The humans on land were blowing horns and beating a drum. Unicorn was puffing, struggling to shove through the waves. Blackie kicked as hard as he could. He discovered that he wasn't streamlined like a fish. His big chest held him back. The boats gradually closed in on them.

Around the bank they swept. Blackie saw a green mass in the water ahead of them.

"There," gasped Unicorn, "just a little farther! We'll run up on that island!"

The boats were near enough that Blackie could hear the men huffing as they plunged in their oars. Ragged voices yelled from boat to boat.

"Stay back, Rafe Little! Them beasts is our prize!"

"That's what you says! They belongs to the man what catches 'em!"

"Dig oars, lads!" cried the first voice. "A couple more boat lengths, and we got 'em!"

"Blackie," ordered Unicorn, hoarsely, "Go deep when I say 'Dive'!"

"What?" gasped Blackie, sensing the boats right behind him.

"Underwater! Go down now! Dive, dive!"

Blackie obeyed, dipping his head to kick below the surface. Through the wavering light under water, he saw Unicorn's white form struggle down, down, his tail and mane foaming behind, then he suddenly shot up. The water roared in Blackie's ears, but he heard a dull knocking and thumping. He looked up to see Unicorn kick violently to pull his horn out of a shattered boat bottom.

By now, Blackie's chest was heaving from holding his breath. He let out a stream of bubbles as he followed Unicorn swimming off to the side. At the last moment, when his breath exploded out of him, Blackie stretched his neck and shot to surface, popping up to gasp in clean air. He sucked in breath after breath, paddling with his legs. He blinked in the sunlight to see the boats rock against each other as the men scrambled from the sinking boat into the other one, all of them yelling and cursing like mad.

Horns blew from the town. Humans screamed at them. "There they go!" shouted the humans on shore.

Unicorn swam as hard as he could toward the long, narrow island sticking up from the river. Blackie kicked after, panting. He looked over his shoulder to see the boat crammed with men row slowly toward shore, towing the flooded wreck behind.

Now, the unicorns swept down to the island's muddy shore, spotted with dirty yellow leaves. Blackie followed Unicorn into the speckled shade of thin green trees that ran down the spine of the island. They stood together, panting, kicking mud from their hooves as bugs whined about.

"That showed 'em," gasped Unicorn, sweeping Blackie with his tail. "Mess with me, will they? Once in awhile . . . you have to . . . to teach 'em a lesson."

"Oh, Papa," panted Blackie, "you saved me again."

Unicorn shook water from his mane. He stopped and sniffed. He drew back, frantically staring around.

"Snakes, I smell snakes!"

"Snakes?"

Blackie pulled in his hooves, looking anxiously at the mud.

"Make noise! Make noise." Unicorn kicked a tree. "Snakes keep away if you make noise."

"But what about the humans?"

"We'll keep an eye on 'em."

Unicorn kicked around in the trees while Blackie squeezed under the branches to look ashore. The boats that had chased them were gone, but more boats were rowing out from the pier, one after another. The men yelled from boat to boat, apparently planning a group effort. A lost oar floated by, bumped against the island, swung slowly around, and floated on as the boats pulled into the current, heading their way.

"Here they come again," called Blackie, "more boats."

"Oh, oh!"

Unicorn pushed next to Blackie. Through the thin screen of branches, they watched the boats bobbing toward them in a line.

"What do we do, Papa?"

"Well," said Unicorn, turning back into the trees, "we can either fight or run. You know that I never fight if I can get out of it, so we'll swim across the river."

"All that way?" gasped Blackie, staring across the water to the other side. "It's a long way over there."

Unicorn rubbed him with his nose.

"You can do it, Blackie. Just swim straight across. Leave those boats to me. I'll sink 'em all if I have to."

Blackie followed Unicorn into the water, protesting, "But Papa, I don't think I can swim that far."

Unicorn was up to his knees by now.

"Of course, you can, Blackie. Remember what I told you . . . unicorns are natural swimmers. Come on."

Shrugging, Blackie stepped after his father until the bottom gave way. He fell forward to be caught by the current. He thrashed a moment, poking his nose high to puff in air, then felt himself floating again. Kicking from his shoulders, he moved easily, so he aimed for the trees across the water and pumped along, rising and falling with each kick.

By now, the boats were rounding the island. "There they go!" shouted the men. "Let's get 'em!"

"Keep on, keep on!" urged Unicorn, dropping back between Blackie and the boats. Blackie tried to turn his head to follow Unicorn, but the waves caught him crosswise, tossing him till he focused on his own swimming, sucking in quick breaths and letting them out slowly.

His ears were high. He heard men yelling over the chop of the waves.

"Look out, boys! He's gone below! Watch your bottoms! Spear 'im when he comes under you!"

Blackie turned, pitching in the waves, kicking to hold his head up to see what was happening. Three or four boats had pulled in a half-circle. The men were leaning over, staring into the river with spears lifted to fight off Unicorn.

"Watch for him, watch for him! Oh, saints, there he be!"

The middle boat tipped violently, screeching humans tumbling backwards. Unicorn's wet head rose from the water, shoving the boat with his horn to roll it over. The far boards sank under the waves as men spilled out like kittens from a basket. Unicorn kicked furiously to shove the tilted boat into the flood as spears flew about him from the other boats, then he sank below. The boat rocked back, waterlogged, its sides barely above the waves.

Voices wailed as the boats paddled around, picking up the floundering crew. Unicorn's head emerged a few yards downstream, coughing and laughing. A spear splashed near him, but he swam after Blackie. Blackie turned back to his own swim and kicked steadily through the swell in the middle of the river.

By now, the current was pushing him downstream, so he concentrated on making headway. With half the river before him, he was tiring. The water sloshed and splashed. He couldn't hear anything until Unicorn swam up beside him, coughing.

"I hate fighting . . . but I've sunk . . . sunk two boats, today. I've got to stop . . . stop exerting myself like this!"

Blackie held his nose above the slapping waves in the middle of the river.

"You're a hero, Papa . . . a hero," he panted, kicking to stay in place. "Like Grandpa. You sank boats! You saved me again."

"Don't tell—" Unicorn stopped for a breath. "Don't tell . . . your mother! She doesn't need—"

He gave a deep sigh and lunged forward, pulling away from Blackie. Blackie watched Papa churn ahead to climb from the river on the far side.

Blackie took his own time, kicking and resting, kicking and resting, drifting south of Papa's landing place. As he paddled, he spotted the white form appearing and disappearing along the green shore, keeping abreast of him.

Unicorn was eating leaves from a bush when Blackie dragged up the sandy beach to the narrow path above the river.

"Took you forever to get here," Unicorn complained.

"It's my first swim, Papa. It's fun if you don't hurry."

Unicorn belched. "I don't know what I was thinking back there. Kick me if I ever suggest anything like this again."

Blackie sniffed the bushes Unicorn was eating. He shook himself vigorously and looked back across the wash. They'd been carried out of sight of castle and town. Both sides of the river looked green and empty from here.

A thought struck him. "Papa, aren't we on the wrong side of the river? Won't we have to swim back across to get home?"

Unicorn sighed. "You won't find a bridge downstream to cross on, not till you get to the City. We'll have to swim back across if we ever want to see the Nest again."

Blackie shivered, feeling panic sweep over him. Tired as he was, he knew he couldn't make it across the drift without drowning.

"Papa . . . I . . . I . . ."

Unicorn turned bloodshot eyes on Blackie.

"Don't worry, we're not going to try another swim today. We'll find a place to settle for a sleep. We'll paddle back across tomorrow or next day when we're rested. Now, we have to make our way back upstream to keep connected to the road home.

Blackie nodded wearily.

Swishing flies from his back, Unicorn walked slowly up the path, pulling leaves from passing bushes.

Blackie followed, his heart easing till he breathed normally. A half-mile up, they turned into a trail so they could circle around without being seen from the town. Trotting down a forest path that smelled of squirrels and foxes, Blackie relaxed until they ran into a shallow brook.

"Wait here," whispered Unicorn.

Blackie ate from low-hanging branches along the brook while Unicorn followed the course out of sight upstream. He returned a few minutes later, stepping through the water.

"Come on," he said to Blackie. He headed back upstream, keeping to the middle of the brook. "Walk carefully. Stay in the water. Don't step out or brush anything."

Blackie followed his father through the bubbling water. "What are we doing, Papa?"

"I laid a side trail for dogs. Those men are sure to be after us in an hour or so. I don't know how smart the humans are, but I don't want any dogs sniffing us out."

When Unicorn judged it safe, they crept from the brook and continued through the forest to the mossy edge of a deep stream running back toward the river. This place smelled good to Blackie. It had a patch of sweet leaves around the roots of a tree leaning over the stream where the water had washed away the soil.

They drank from the stream, enjoying the clean water after the muddy river, and turned to the leaves.

"See, son, I told you," said Unicorn, sniffing a stalk. "You swam that river with no trouble. The humans, well, you run into that type everywhere. Just keep with me, and I'll teach you how to handle yourself."

"You showed me how to sink boats, Papa."

"Oh, that was dumb of me." Unicorn yawned. "If I'd been more careful, the humans would never have seen us. That's how it goes out in the big world. You get careless for a moment and anything can happen. There's a rule about that, too."

The stream sparkled with light as the forest darkened. Stuffed with leaves, Blackie took a last drink and spread his hooves to sleep. He lifted his head at a faint sound ringing up the stream bed.

"Ting, ting . . . ting, ting."

"What's that Papa?"

"Whaaat?" said Unicorn, drowsily opening an eye.

"That noise."

"Oh," Unicorn listened, "that's church bells. Vespers down in the town, I guess."

"Vesperrrs," yawned Blackie, looking between branches at the shining sky above. "What's vespers?"

Unicorn took another bite of leaves.

"Singing, singing in church," he answered. "I remember up at Darr. Each evening, the Princess made me carry her to church on a silver saddle, and I—"

He belched.

"Would you believe? They made me stay outside with the horses. I don't mind horses, but they talk about nothing—gab, gab, gab—so I listened to the singing."

Blackie yawned again. He remembered something.

"Those girls, those girls with Aunt Josie . . . and that boy with the fish, they were all singing."

"If you call that singing—" muttered Unicorn. "Someday, maybe, you'll hear a choir, a group of humans singing together. Now, that's something to hear, almost as nice as the birds at dawn."

"Or the frogs in the pond," sighed Blackie, thinking of the Nest. "Croaking together each evening below our hill. Back with Mama, back home with Mama where we belong."

CHAPTER FIVE

Papa Lost

"Ting, ting . . . ting, ting . . . ting, ting."

Blackie heard the bells through his dream. He jerked his head, hitting an overhead branch that set leaves slapping his cheeks. Breathing deeply, he listened to the birds singing over the gurgling stream. He squinted at Unicorn through the gray light, tearing off branches beside him.

"You're awake already, Papa."

Unicorn raised his head, a spray of leaves hanging from his mouth. "'Course I'm awake. Who could sleep through all that noise last night?"

"Noise, what noise? Was it dogs?"

"No, it was not dogs," grumbled Unicorn. He paused. "I notice you don't ask how I feel this morning."

"Oh, how do you feel, Papa?"

Unicorn raised his voice.

"Done in, that's how I feel, wiped out, wasted, exhausted! That running yesterday and swimming. Down the river, over the river, under the river! Every muscle aches—my shoulders, my legs, my . . . my horn! My horn hurts from banging at boats to save you!"

Blackie lifted an ear. In the distance, he heard the bell ring again, the sound weaker this morning.

"There's that bell."

"More noise," complained Unicorn. "Bells, shouts, horns, drums—Those fellows were at it all night. Never heard such commotion. How could you sleep through it?"

"I was tired, Papa."

"Tired," sneered Unicorn. "You don't know what it is to be tired. So, how do you feel this morning?"

Blackie shook his muscles. He took a few steps.

"Good," he said, surprised. "I feel good, Papa."

"Typical," mumbled Unicorn, returning to the leaves. "Typical."

"But, Papa, that noise, last night. What do you think it was?"

Unicorn swallowed a mouthful. "Who cares? So long as humans aren't after me—"

Blackie ran to the stream, took a long drink. The light was brighter now, the leaves taking on color. He stepped back to Unicorn and ate hungrily. The pair of them stripped branch after branch.

Unicorn belched and sighed. "Guess we'd better tackle that river again."

"The river?" asked Blackie, looking up from the leaves. "Swim it today? You said we'd wait a couple days."

"I know, I did," said Unicorn, twitching his ears. "Last thing I need to do is swim a river, but I want to get it over with. If I don't have to battle boats, we could get back to the forest today."

Blackie was ready to go home. He was stuffed with things to think about, things to talk about. He wanted to see Mama, and he really wanted to feel secure again. He still trembled when he thought of those boatmen chasing them yesterday. If it hadn't been for Papa—

He realized now that traveling isn't a game like horn-wrestling deer. Here in the great world, anything could happen. Humans could shoot him for his hide or strap him to a wagon like a horse. He knew in his heart that he wasn't ready to face adventures, but he knew that he could swim the river.

He trotted to the path along the stream. "Let's go, Papa."

"Hold up," said Unicorn, stamping a hoof. "Don't run out headlong. Eat a good breakfast before you go. You'll need your strength to swim the river and run around that town, especially if the humans are watching out for us."

Blackie stepped impatiently about the path. "But you said you wanted an early start."

"Settle down now!" ordered Unicorn. "I need something in my stomach before I face that water."

"Well, I'm ready to go."

Unicorn insisted on eating before heading off. Blackie chewed a few more leaves, but the brightening day made him anxious. Once they'd crossed the river, he'd be glad to have breakfast, but he wanted to swim before the boats would be out.

"Ready, Papa?" Blackie asked for the hundredth time.

"All right, all right. You nag worse than your mother."

Unicorn sighed and turned into the path after Blackie. "Now, remember, we use our brains today. I don't want a repeat of yesterday. We keep an eye out for humans. No log bridges. No fighting. A quiet journey, peaceful, that's what I want."

"That's what I want, too," agreed Blackie, trotting down the path.

The morning smelled sweet with light forest odors and the fresh scent of the stream. The path was little used by the humans until it ran into the lane near the river where the smell of humans and horses was strong.

"Wait for me!" called Unicorn.

Blackie eased up, sniffing. Unicorn joined him to push through scratchy brush to the muddy point where the stream washed into the river. This place was obviously popular with humans. It was trampled and burnt over, scattered with ashes, fish bones, broken beer pots. An old shoe sole lay half-buried in mud.

Blackie ran to the riverside and looked out. The sky was washed with bands of pink. The river before him glowed with bubbles carrying glints of light along the shore. Blackie sniffed the river.

Now that he was here in the sour, muddy river smell, he was no longer eager to plunge in. He ran back up the stream for a drink of clean water.

Unicorn tasted ferns beside the point and nibbled a few grass stems. Blackie found some very nice leaves on a hanging tree branch, long and thin and chewy. Unicorn sniffed at the leaves.

"Umm, I'd forgotten these trees. Wish we had them near the Nest."

Unicorn took a deep drink of water and came back to the leaves. He ate a few mouthful and sighed.

49

"I remember running this path in the old days. Nice eating, but time's passing. We better get to it. You ready for your morning swim?"

"I guess so."

Blackie walked back to the point. He was no longer eager to swim, but the river lay between here and home. He looked out again, saw the pink fading from the brightening sky. The river sparkled as Blackie splashed to his knees in the water His hooves sank into the mud. He looked back.

"Come on, Papa."

"Hold up, not too fast!"

Unicorn stood with front hooves in the foam, scanning the far side of the river. He frowned.

"Something's wrong over there. I can feel it. It's like the countryside's uneasy, holding its breath."

"I don't feel anything, Papa. Let's go!"

Without waiting, Blackie pushed into the river till it embraced him. Shivering from ankles to neck, he kicked into the flow. He felt the water lift and push him with the slosh and splutter of the waves.

He looked back to see Unicorn's white form wade after him. Unicorn was yelling, but Blackie heard only a word or two.

"Watch out . . . careful—"

Blackie swam into the surge. He felt ready for the river this morning. He remembered thinking about his swim, last night, when he woke at a fox's cry.

"Riding on waters that hold you—it's fun!"

He swished his tail through the water and laughed. He reached into the swim with strong legs, holding his nose just above the surface and kicking as smoothly as possible. The river grew cooler toward the middle where a low fog cut visibility to a few feet. Waves splashed his nose. He kicked against the steady pull of the river until he heard something swimming toward him.

He slowed and floated, peering through curling fog. Something was kicking steadily, snuffing water out its nose. Silently, Blackie drifted toward it, watching nervously until he saw what it was. A large buck deer was kicking past him, followed by a doe struggling to keep up.

"Hi, there, deer!" shouted Blackie in relief.

The deer panicked at the cry. They choked and squealed in their hurry to swim away.

"It's me," cried Blackie, "the unicorn! I won't hurt you!"

But the deer were straining and splashing, pushing through the waves to escape this dark figure in the fog. In a moment, they were gone. Blackie had to look to his own course as he got confused in the choppy waves, not sure for a moment which side he was heading for. He kept his head, though, realizing that the morning glow should be to his side, and kicked toward the dark shore ahead.

His hooves touched sand before he expected it, an underwater bar curving against the current. Blackie waded across the bar and swam the last few yards to the muddy shoreline. The bank was too steep to scramble up. Blackie had to wade along the shore to a sandy path that ran up through bushes to a log smelling strongly of humans and fish. He stepped around the log and shook himself, looking back for Unicorn.

"Where's Papa?"

Blackie lifted his front hooves to the log and peered at the river. The sky was lighted now. Upstream, he saw a large tree limb float out of the fog, slowly rocking back and forth, but he didn't see Unicorn.

"Where is he? He was behind me when I swam out. Could the river have carried him off?"

Blackie listened to the river, the breeze, the birds. A fish plopped downstream.

"Papa!" he yelled, then caught himself. No noise! Papa had warned him to keep silent.

"How can I find him if I can't call?"

Blackie sniffed and listened. He tossed his head.

"So what do I do now? Wait here, or go looking for him? I'd better wait. He'll be angry if he comes along and I'm not waiting for him."

Blackie was hungry after his swim. He had bushes to nibble, but he couldn't relax without Unicorn. He kept looking up, raising his ears to listen.

"Oh, Papa, he'll run back and forth looking for me. He could get himself into trouble. Maybe I better go find him."

He stepped into the lane running along the river. "This is the way home, I think. Papa should be somewhere along here. Where else would he go?"

The lane followed the banks and beaches within sight of the river. Blackie passed a couple old fishermen with a net in the water. Beyond them, he heard running feet. He stepped into the trees and watched a dozen men hustle by with spears and shields, heading for town.

Now, he did worry about Papa. What if Papa ran into those men?

He came to a straggling collection of huts half-hidden in the trees. Wild-eyed dogs ran out at him, snapping their teeth. Without pause, he kicked the first dog. The others gave way, yelping and barking, and Blackie ran on.

By the time Blackie came to the town, he was trotting by fields he remembered from yesterday. He stopped and looked around. There were no humans working in the gardens this morning. Still, he felt nervous traveling alone. He felt lost, vulnerable without Unicorn.

Ahead, he saw the town wall and the bridge to the castle in the river. Humans were passing back and forth on the bridge. He saw only a single boat on the river.

A disturbing thought occurred to Blackie. "I don't know if I can find my way back to the Nest without Papa."

He'd been sure that he'd run into Unicorn on this lane, but what if he didn't? The road heading back to the forest, that'd be easy to find. But the paths they'd taken and that field where they'd had the run, could he find those?

"I don't know," Blackie thought. "There were lots of trails running into the road back there. If I miss the right one, I'll wander in circles. But I have to keep moving. Sooner or later, humans are bound to come out of town and see me."

In fact, he spotted a group of men around the river gate talking to the spearmen who'd run past him. Luckily, they didn't notice him until he dashed into the lane that ran along the town wall away from the river.

He heard their shouts as he ran past. By now, he felt weary, tired from the swim and anxious over Papa. He jumped a ditch, frightening up gray birds with long necks pecking at stinking sewage that flowed from a hole in the wall. He passed a carter who threw his stick at him, then turned with the lane at the end of the town.

Ahead, he saw the road running homeward from the main gate of the town. He heard an outcry as he neared. The gate was wide open. A crowd milled about. It was mostly women wrapped in shawls with children hanging onto them. A few men leaned on their spears.

Everyone stared up the road. Someone pointed as Blackie neared. Everyone turned to look at him.

Blackie jumped a hedge to avoid the crowd. He galloped down the strip through sweet-smelling bean bushes, then jumped a hedge into the road at the far end. He ran toward home, passing more women hugging each other and gazing up the road.

They pulled back when he ran by. Nobody challenged him. One woman cried after him, "Heal us, unicorn! Bring us peace!"

Blackie ran till he left the people behind. He slowed to a walk. The sun was bright now, lighting the hedges along the road. A few trees ran along ditches between fields. Mostly, he saw strips of gardens. Lonely as he was, he still felt hungry. He walked a few more steps, smelling the crops.

"Oh," he thought, panting, "This is the place to find Papa."

Blackie kicked open a gate and plunged into shoulder-high pea vines, scaring up birds that flew a few feet and dipped back to ground. Blackie swung his head to both sides, gobbling vines and blossoms and pea pods.

"Oh, Papa, why aren't you here?"

He ate till he was stuffed with peas. By now, Blackie was feeling thirsty. He jumped back to the road and trotted slowly past grain fields before reaching the open, chopped-over area. Running into the forest beyond, he turned up the first path that smelled of animals.

"I'm tired," he thought. "I can look for Papa after I've rested."

He walked a few yards up the path into the deep shade where he fell asleep, thirsty as he was. He was awakened by groans. He heard the clink of a bell, rattling metal, the "slop, slop, slop" of bare feet.

His black hide hidden in shadows, Blackie peeked around a tree trunk to see a man in a brown hood limp down the road with a small bell on a stick. A gang of worn men struggled after shouldering spears, shields, and axes. Three or four dozing horsemen rode by in dented armor.

Blackie jerked his head away when a cart followed, heaped with dead men. The horse smelled Blackie and turned its head, but the carter cursed and made it limp on.

A long file of wounded men hobbled by, leaning on spears and moaning. Some were supported by others. Three or four chanted wearily.

> We fought for our lord.
> We stood staunch and strong.
> We fought through the morning.
> We fought all day long.

The men staggered by, eyes down on the roadway. Their song trailed away to a whimper.

"What was all that?" breathed Blackie, when the stragglers were gone. "Those men have been fighting."

The stench of sweat and blood was rank in the road. Trotting on, his mind full of the gruesome parade, Blackie almost stepped on a dark heap in the road. The stink of pain and blood threw him back. It was a man, doubled up and gasping. Bugs buzzed about him while birds, black and silent, watched from a tree limb above. Blackie saw that the man's arm was gone, only a stump remaining in a filthy bandage.

Blackie shuddered. He stepped quietly around the man to trot up the road. He stopped. An instinct, deep inside, made him turn around and look again. The sight revolted him, but he silently crept back to the man. He leaned down his twisted horn. He touched the man's shoulder.

Blackie's body quivered as a jolt of power leaped from his horn into the man, who jerked and took a breath.

"Aaaah."

The man rolled over, groaning. He pushed up with his good arm, peered at Blackie, shook his head.

"I speared two of 'em afore they got me," he whispered. "Now, I got to get home."

Blackie backed away. The man took a step, wobbled against a tree, cursed, and limped after the rest of the humans. Blackie watched him stagger out of sight.

"I healed a man," said Blackie in wonder. "It really works."

The man's smell hung in the air after he was gone. Blackie turned away from the stink and trotted on.

"I don't think I like healing."

He felt dry to the bone. At least, he was back in the forest where trees softened the sunlight. Familiar smells of damp earth and green growth covered the smell of death. He trotted till he came to a shallow dribble of water crossing the road. He waded upstream to a rocky pool and drank.

Lifting his dripping muzzle, he widened his stance. He closed his eyes and slept with cool water running over his fetlocks. He woke suddenly out of a dream, whirling in the water with a splash, his horn lowered against an enemy.

"So there you are! Ran off and left me, did you?"

It was Papa, dirty and sweaty, his left side gouged with a bloody scratch.

"Papa, you're here!" cried Blackie, splashing toward him in relief. "I thought you were lost!"

Unicorn gave him a black look.

"Why'd you leave me in the river like that? You swam off like a fish, no concern, not a glance back to see where I was! You knew I was tired. I could have been swept all the way to the City for all you cared!"

"I'm sorry, Papa!"

Blackie jumped up to nuzzle Unicorn's nose, but Unicorn pulled away.

"I ran back and forth, looking for you! Up and down that path, smelling you here, smelling you there, but never finding you! All the time, I was worried, afraid! Anything could have happened to you!"

"I looked for you too, Papa!" Blackie wailed, tears running down his face. "I looked for you back in the river, honest. I waited on the bank when I got across, but you didn't come. I wanted to call, but you told me to stay silent. Finally, I just ran on, thinking I'd find you over here, but I couldn't find you anywhere! I couldn't!"

"Oh, well," grumbled Unicorn, "well, you were right to stay silent." He took a deep drink of water, shook his muzzle. "Here, now, let me look at you."

With a sigh, he inspected Blackie's coat, shook his head at the bent horn.

"At least, you're not scratched up. No one stuck a spear in you. Come on."

Blackie followed him down the stream. Unicorn moved heavily, limping along. He sniffed and looked carefully before stepping out in the road.

"So, how'd you find me, Papa?" whispered Blackie, walking on his father's wounded side. "I was afraid I was lost for good."

Unicorn cut in with a snort.

"How'd I find you? I used my head, that's what I did. How do you think we find things, we unicorns? We don't go running over the countryside like blind pigs. I sniffed out a fox who told me that his cousin had smelled you in a pea patch. Foxes keep up with things."

"And you're hurt, Papa, you're hurt! What happened to you?"

"What do you expect to happen when I'm bumbling around in daylight, hunting for you? Some human jumped out of the bushes with a spear."

"Oh." Blackie lowered his head. "I'm sorry, Papa. I was looking for you too."

Unicorn's ears went up. He listened for forest noises.

"Come along, we need to get home. These humans have mucked up everything here—armies marching back and forth, some sort of little war going on."

"I know, Papa." Blackie shuddered. "I saw them!"

"Come on, then. We've got to be extra careful the first few miles."

"Papa," exclaimed Blackie, stopping in the road. "Your side! I can heal you with my horn. It works. It works even if it's bent. I healed a wounded man. He got all better and went home."

Unicorn threw up his head with a snort.

"Oh, Blackie, don't you ever listen! What did I tell you about healing humans? Once you start it, they— Oh, what's the use?"

Disgusted, he headed on at a slow trot.

"Never listens, never listens. And you can't heal me! We unicorns can't heal each other. That's why Grandpa had to rest at home when he got torn up in his fights. I couldn't heal him."

"But you healed my head yesterday morning," muttered Blackie, stepping up to follow his father up the road.

"That was all in your mind," said Unicorn. "I didn't really do anything."

They traveled slowly. Unicorn's horn rocked up and down as he trotted. Blackie looked about, smelling deer and pigs in the forest. He saw only squirrels and birds.

Blackie thought of the dogs back on the path that morning. He'd kicked that dog that tried to bite him. Unicorn was right. There were lots of things in this big world he didn't like—biting dogs, warring humans. Back at the Nest, he could ask Mama about them.

Today, they circled around the villages. The fields were empty of humans, but dogs ran out to bark at them. Unicorn broke into a secluded garden where straggly vegetables competed with weeds. When the dogs ran close, he kicked out and they backed off, barking.

"Just ignore them," muttered Unicorn, turning back to the veggies. They ate seedy asparagus and turnip tops, radishes, and clover that had pushed into a patch of withered carrots.

Once back in the forest, they found a comfortable spot by a stream and took a long nap, waking when shadows darkened under the trees. They ate leaves for a few minutes before traveling on, circling more villages before the road narrowed into the deep forest.

They found the humans closed in their castles, this evening, with guards alert at the gates. A messenger passed them, running with his pouch, but they saw no peddlers or woodcutters on the road.

They pulled up at nightfall as birds quieted and smells grew heavy in the forest. Unicorn was footsore and gray with dust. He leaned against a tree while Blackie waded up a stream, looked for a stopping place. Blackie was tired himself, but he found a refuge on a bank above the stream screened by chewy bushes.

Unicorn sniffed carefully before he took a drink and started eating beside Blackie. He looked exhausted, his legs spread, his tail limp.

"You never told me," said Blackie, when he'd eaten awhile, "what happened to you this morning."

"What happened," said Unicorn, sourly, biting down on a bush and swallowing, "was that you swam off and left me in the river. I was more tired than I thought, got turned around in the fog. You were gone when I straightened out."

Blackie swallowed a mouthful of leaves. "Oh, I didn't know."

"Did it occur to you," demanded Unicorn, looking up, "that I could have been looking for you? I'd have found you if you'd only waited where you were. I smelled you by that log, found your tracks, but you, you'd run off somewhere. Finally, I just gave up and figured I'd hunt down a fox. By then, men were running everywhere with their spears."

Unicorn broke off a low-hanging branch. He pinned it under a hoof, tugging at the twigs. He chewed the leaves, then sighed.

"Well, I guess, this journey's been worth it if you've learned your lesson. You've had your adventure. You've seen what Grandpa went through every day of his life, the heat, cold, hunger, misery. I told you how I followed the roads for a couple years when I was young. At first, it seemed new and exciting—the gardens, the feasts, the cities and towns. Soon enough, I realized how wrong I was. I learned that I had to stay home to save my coat. This wandering isn't worth it! How often do you get yourself beat up, shot by arrows, clawed by bears, before you settle down and stay quietly in the forest where you belong?"

After thinking a moment, Blackie asked, "But what did Grandpa think of you then?"

"Oh," said Unicorn scornfully, "that old beast said I was wasting my life. He yammered on and on about the pride of the unicorn, the tradition of our ancestors. But I'd seen those horns up at the Shrine. That was enough for me. I'd learned my lesson. I turned my tail on it all, stayed happy at home, and never regretted any of it."

Blackie ate quietly awhile, then mused, "But the stories, Papa—Think of all we have to tell Mama, running that field, swimming the river, even . . . even healing that man. That was something!"

"Something," groaned Unicorn, drooping up his head, "yes, something. And having boats drown you and spears stab you—That's something, too. Just think of the arrows, Blackie, think of the spears! Think of that gelding knife!"

CHAPTER SIX

The Princess

Oh, how glorious it felt to be home again! Mama cried when she saw Blackie. She sniffed him over. She caressed him until her relief at his return made him feel guilty. He began spilling out his stories, telling her again and again about the villages he'd seen, the gardens, the river.

Unicorn had begged Blackie not to mention the sunken boats or the broken army on the road. Somehow, though, everything came out. They couldn't hide Unicorn's wound, so Mama got Blackie aside while Unicorn slept all afternoon. She questioned Blackie about his father until Blackie found himself describing the misery of the humans after their battle.

"They dragged along like moles above ground," Blackie explained. "Papa said it was a war between barons. We don't know what they were fighting about. We couldn't even tell whether we saw the winners or the losers."

"I wonder if it was your appearance," mused Mama, rubbing Blackie with her nose. "Humans react strongly to fabulous beasts. Some worship us. Others hunt us down to study us or keep us as trophies. No unicorns have been seen since Grandpa died, so all their concerns will be doubled and redoubled at the sight of you. Who knows what stories will run around the empire now? There are always humans claiming that the world is ending!"

"But Mama, we didn't do anything to them," protested Blackie. "We just looked at everything and swam over the river and came right back."

Mama sighed.

"That doesn't matter to humans. We may not be concerned with them, but they're fascinated by us. Look at all the banners with unicorns on them. Tell me the truth now, sweetheart, how did Papa get that wound in his side? He didn't get that from a brier patch."

Unicorn looked sharply at Blackie when Mama questioned him about the warring humans as soon as he woke up. He announced that he needed to check out favorite feeding spots and took off into the forest. Blackie stuck close to the Nest. The next few days, he grazed with Mama on the greens and herbs to be found on the midsummer hills.

The paths were shadowed by interwoven tree branches. Gullies and valleys opened to sunlight which brought on grasses and the wild berries of the forest. When Mama showed Blackie the crunchy roots of small trees and bushes, he learned that even a twisted unicorn horn is a handy device for digging.

A week or so after his adventure, Blackie was nibbling sweet vines hanging down a gully over a stream. That was when he told Mama of healing the man in the road. She wasn't surprised at his story.

"I know Papa says that healing gets people crazy," said Blackie, looking at her, "but the man was miserable. There were bugs crawling over him. I had to help him if I could."

"Of course, you did, sweetie!" cried Mama, throwing up her head. "And I'm proud of you! Papa's right of course. You can't heal everyone. Suffering humans are so hungry for relief that they'll suck out your soul to get it, but healing is what we do. It's a gift from the Lord. Unicorns are born to heal the sick like Saint Luke and fight dragons like Saint Michael. That's what it means to be a unicorn."

"But Papa won't heal anyone," said Blackie, kicking a stone into the stream. "Papa always says—"

Mama cut him off.

"I know exactly what your Papa says. You know, dear, I'm torn when I look at your father. One side of me loves how he looks. Most of the ancestors I know about were shattered at his age, ripped and scarred by claws and spears. Why, many were dead by then, but Papa's still alive and beautiful, more handsome than when I first met him. I'm joyful to have him with us, but I worry about the cost."

"What cost, Mama?" asked Blackie. "Papa's kept his coat. He's happy."

"But he's a unicorn," sighed Mama, "trying to live as a field mouse."

She stepped into the stream.

"All these years, he's fought down his instincts, held in his heroic blood. I'm afraid that some day he'll break out, let loose in some terrible fashion. You tell me he was battling boats in the river. That's not the Papa we know."

"But that was only to protect me, Mama," said Blackie, following her through the water.

"I know," said Mama, nuzzling Blackie's cheek. "Papa tries to be a good father. I guess I worry too much."

As the weeks followed, Blackie's stories got stale with repeating. The forest was swelling as the season rolled on, greening and darkening with tree limbs bowed under the weight of late summer's leaves. Mornings were hazy. Afternoons heated up until most animals crept along instead of running. Hidden birds sang low. Blackie brushed off so many bugs that he forgot he was doing it. He flicked his tail without noticing.

Filled with life, he ran from earliest dawn, racing down paths draped with vines and dewy spider webs. He jumped streams and splashed into pools to roll around and splash out again, then race away down fresh trails. On heavy afternoons, he grazed in clover beds even Unicorn didn't know about and napped in mossy bowers.

Some evenings, he found Unicorn in a good mood. Then Blackie could question his father about the mysteries of the human world—what makes boats go, how gates work, the horrors of butchery. Unicorn would relate some of his experiences before rebuffing Blackie.

"Why do you want to know such stuff? It's got nothing to do with you and me! Let me tell you about toadstools."

When he finally gave up at night, he stood beside Unicorn on the coolest hills. Unicorn twitched and snorted in his sleep. Blackie dreamed deeply till a sudden shower chased them back to the Nest where Blackie fell asleep again while Unicorn complained of water in his ears.

One morning, Unicorn caught Blackie before he could dash away for the day. "Come on, Son. How about a little run to the village? I haven't raided the gardens for a while."

"Can't, Papa," Blackie explained, dancing away. "I promised the fawns I'd play with them today."

"But you've never eaten blueberries," said Unicorn, licking his lips, "and melons, big, sweet melons. You squash a melon with a foot and suck out the juicy insides, seeds and all."

"Melons," Blackie repeated. "Sounds great, but I promised the fawns!"

Mama trotted around the tree, dragging fresh branches to spread on the floor of the Nest. She nodded at Blackie's words.

"Yes, dear, you go play with the fawns. I have a job for your father. Yesterday, I heard woodchopping around the twisty path. Those villagers are cutting trees again. They don't need to do that. They get plenty of firewood from the drops."

"Why do I have to stop them?" demanded Unicorn, tossing his head. "It's not my village."

"No, but this is your forest. The foxes tell me that woodcutting is moving in this direction."

Blackie jumped up and down. "I'll stop the villagers, Papa! I'm big enough! I'll stop the woodcutting!"

"Don't bother," Unicorn snorted. "Nobody has to stop those men! So they take a log or or two. That's not going to harm anything. The forest goes on forever."

Blackie shrugged. "Well, I'll see you, Mama! Bye, Papa!" He leaped down the path as Mama scolded Papa.

"No, you can't wait longer! You've got to do something! Those humans are spreading and sprawling, cutting trees every day and hauling them off on wagons. Someday soon, they'll cut so close that we have to move. Don't say I didn't warn you when—"

The forest smelled damp and sweet and green after last night's rain. Birds fluttered away as Blackie kicked out his hooves and jumped puddles. He ran through wet branches that made his eyes wink with sparkling raindrops. He paused for a bite of long grass in a sunny patch, pulling and chomping and shaking his ears, then ran over the hills to a small clearing.

The fawns were spread about an older brother, a yearling with a fork to his antlers, nibbling among vines and creepers on the side of a hill. Their heads swung around, ears flagging as Blackie leaped among them.

The yearling stepped out. He dropped his head, shook his horns, and snorted. Blackie lowered his horn, pawed the earth, and charged.

CRASH!

Blackie knocked the yearling back, sending him skidding through slippery leaves. The deer scrambled up and ran to the end of the clearing, whining.

"You didn't have to hit so hard! I was only playing!"

"I was playing, too!" shouted Blackie.

The youngest fawn, bouncy and curious, ran over. "Hey, Blackie!"

"Hey, Fawn! What you doing?"

"Eating vines."

Blackie shook his head at the tendrils the deer browsed on. "Too small, too small those leaves! Not worth eating. Let's run to the gardens. Papa says there's melons there, ripe and juicy. We can stomp 'em and eat 'em."

"No, no!" yelped the yearling, shaking leaves from his coat. "Not the gardens, not this late in the day! The humans will be out."

"Who's afraid of humans?" snorted Blackie. "I've traveled through their lands. I've seen their town. I'll take care of any humans who try to bother us."

"Blackie'll take care of the humans," repeated the youngest fawn. "Let's go with him!"

"We'll go tomorrow," said the yearling, turning away. "Early tomorrow, before humans wake up. It's too late, now. They'll shoot at us with their bows."

"I'm not scared!" said Blackie, stepping toward the trail. "Not me, I'm never scared. I'm going to the gardens now. I'll eat melons and blueberries and strawberries, big ones, all the things Papa's told me about. Come along. I'll protect you."

Flirting his tail, the youngest fawn scampered after Blackie. "Come on, guys. Let's go with Blackie. He'll protect us!"

The deer exchanged glances. The yearling protested again, "It's too late in the day!"

Another fawn ran over to Blackie. "I'm not scared! I'll go if you do!"

The others held back a moment, then gave up and followed in single file, the yearling at the rear.

Blackie led under trees that reached and rustled. Birds sang. Bugs buzzed. The earth was soft with wet leaves and twigs under hoof. The trail ran into the muddy road where trees were cut back. Brush grew thickly to both sides. Blackie ran boldly down the middle of the road, his heart thumping inside him. The deer paused, sniffed timidly, fanning their ears to listen.

"Come on!" called Blackie.

The fawns looked at each other. They followed Blackie toward the village. He trotted toward a carter dozing on a load of smelly hides as his horse plodded along. Blackie brushed by the wagon, sniffing man and horse as the deer slipped into the forest to thread through the trees.

"Hey, horse!" Blackie yelled.

The horse, half-asleep, jumped aside as though bit by a snake. She stretched her neck, spun in her tracks, and dashed off, smashing the cart against a tree. A wheel flew off. Hides and driver spilled out in a heap as the horse galloped up the road, dragging the shafts and broken boards behind her.

Astonished, Blackie watched the horse disappear around a turn. The driver rolled free of the wreck, cursing wildly. He grabbed up his stick and ran at Blackie, screeching.

"Beast of Evil! Hellhound! I'll kill you!"

Blackie gave him a glare and trotted into the forest, calling the fawns. He caught them a half-mile away, headed back to familiar ground. They skittered off when he yelled at them.

"Hey, guys! Come back! Come back! That was just a man with a horse! He won't hurt you!"

"How can you say that?" cried the yearling, poised to run, his tail up, ears out. "We heard him yell. Don't you know that humans shoot us! They chase us with dogs! We're going back where we belong."

"I'm not scared!" said the youngest fawn, running back to Blackie. "Blackie'll protect us! We've come this far. Let's taste those melons."

"I promise," insisted Blackie, "I'll protect you. Papa's taken me out among humans. I understand them."

"Oh, all right," said the yearling, reluctantly stepping closer. "If the others are going, I'll come along to lead them home again. Not on the road, though. That's too dangerous."

"The road, dangerous?" scoffed Blackie. "Not with me, it isn't! The humans won't even notice you, not with a unicorn along. If anyone threatens us, I'll knock him down. Come on."

The deer followed Blackie back to the road, the youngest fawn running happily along while the yearling lagged behind. They met more humans as they neared the village—women carrying baskets of greens and a red-bearded woodchopper shouldering his axe and a pair of three-inch logs.

That woodchopper! Moot! Blackie recognized the man from last spring. Moot was one of the men who'd tried to skin him when Papa had saved him from the villagers. To show off for the deer, Blackie charged Moot from behind and butted him down, knocking him into his own logs.

Blackie turned to the startled deer. "See? That's how I handle humans if they give me a hard time!"

Moot scrambled to his knees, swinging his axe. He threw it at Blackie with a shout. Blackie dodged the axe and ran at the man, kicking him till he crawled off, crying.

Blackie heard a yelp of pain behind him. He turned to see the youngest fawn stagger away with a bleeding slash in his shoulder where the axe had struck him. The other fawns had disappeared into the forest.

"Oh, I'm sorry!" cried Blackie, running back.

The fawn shied away. "I'm hurt! Look what he did to me! You said, you'd protect me."

The fawn stumbled off into the forest.

"Wait, wait," cried Blackie, "I can heal you!"

Blackie started to follow, then stopped. He looked at the axe. "Well, at least I can stop the woodcutting."

He grabbed the axe in his teeth and dragged it into the trees, hiding it beside a tree root and pulling a dead branch over it. He walked back to the road.

"I've come this far," he said to himself. "I'll run on to the gardens and get a taste of those melons. Then I'll come back and heal the fawn."

He trotted till he saw Moot angrily limping along, cursing to himself. Blackie slipped up behind the man and poked him with his horn. Moot shrieked and scampered into the trees, waving his arms.

Laughing, Blackie ran on till he came out of the forest. He passed the tree-cutting, sniffed the fresh stumps and withering leaves, and ran on to the fields. Blackie rose on rear hooves to look over the hedges and the fences woven from thorn branches. He saw humans working among gardens. Some picked vegetables while others scratched up weeds with hoes or knelt to pull at them.

A dog barked. Others joined in. Humans looked around, pointed at him. A man threw a spear that fell short.

Blackie galloped down the road, passing more humans. A crowd of children and dogs ran after him, barking and yelling. He galloped faster, thrilled with excitement, until he saw ahead of him the six-foot wall of sharpened stakes around the village.

A man at the gate heard the commotion. He ran out, holding up a spear to bar the way. Blackie didn't pause. He swerved around the man and jumped the wall, crashing down onto the grassy roof of a hut inside. He rolled off, dragging a swath of damp thatch with him, and splashed down into the stinking slime of a pigpen.

Squealing pigs jumped away as Blackie scrambled to his feet. Gagging at the stench, he shook filth from his coat. He kicked through the fence into the street. The pigs crowded after him through the hole. They ran off while chickens squawked and dogs barked.

Blackie looked down the street at the huts of the villagers and the gray church with its row of pigeons on the roof. He saw old women sitting in the sun with their sewing and young women gossiping under trees on both sides of the well. Babies crawled around their bare feet.

Everyone stared at Blackie a moment. They flew into a frenzy. Women screamed. Babies cried. Children dashed from all directions, picking up stones and garbage from the street to throw at Blackie as men ran around the huts with their hoes and hammers. Dogs dashed at him, barking and snapping.

Blackie reared, kicking front legs, then broke through the dogs. Humans jumped out of his way as he galloped to the end of the street where a spotted horse was tied to a fence post. The horse pulled back, screeching, but Blackie sailed over the wall to land outside in the trampled lane circling the village. Ignoring the howls behind, he trotted along the lane, looking over garden fences for melons, but seeing only grain plants until he came to a clover field.

Swishing his tail, Blackie jumped into the clover. He rested a moment to catch his breath, laughing at the memory of those pigs before digging into the green goodness.

"Umm, delicious," he thought, yanking up a mouthful, "but where's all the fruit? Maybe I should have come with Papa. At least, I wouldn't stink of pigs."

He had a few moments to eat before a dog ran up, yelping to the humans. Blackie ran to the fence and jumped into the next field. This one rested fallow, overgrown with weeds. He returned to the lane and trotted around the village, rearing to look into each field he passed.

Something smelled sweet behind a thorn fence. Blackie jumped over to find the blueberries Papa had mentioned. The berries were fat and tasty. Unfortunately, a boy was watching from a shaded corner to keep birds out of the patch. The boy yelled and ran over, shooting a rock from a sling as Blackie stripped branch after branch. Blackie yelped when the rock smacked his flank. The boy aimed another rock, so Blackie jumped the fence again and ran down the lane to the road.

Beyond the village, Blackie saw the castle looking dark, its moat stagnant, a shroud of blasted ivy hanging down the wall. Blackie trotted past the castle and turned into a new part of the forest.

Blackie roamed down strange trails. He sniffed everything—leaves, blossoms, toadstools, turtles. He nibbled tasty shoots along tree roots. He stirred up a wild cow, long-horned and hairy, which moved out of his path without speaking. Passing a stream, he drank, then rolled back and forth to wash off the smell from the pigs. He shook himself and ran down the path to the road.

The road was wider here, bridged over marshy spots with slippery logs that rolled under Blackie's hooves. The logs smelled of humans, cows, and horses.

Blackie stopped here, almost deciding to turn back home. He had seen the village and tasted blueberries. Still, having come this far into the world, it seemed a waste not to explore just a little further. Even Papa had traveled widely before giving it up and staying home. Blackie decided to go on for a while. Maybe he'd stay out all night and go home in the morning. He would be extra-careful, though, because these humans were a touchy lot.

He followed the road all morning, creeping into the forest when he heard humans. He passed carters with their horses and drovers herding cows and goats. Once, he heard wheels squeak loudly. He slipped into the brush to watch a pair of steers drag a huge wagon weighted down by a giant log.

Hearing bawling voices, Blackie hid behind a tree trunk to watch a thick human with a white beard lead a band of riders with shields and spears. The man rolled in the saddle waving a wineskin and bellowed out a song.

> Spanish ladies are handsome.
> German ladies are tall.
> Italian ladies are sprightly.
> My old beard's kissed them all.

He tossed the wineskin to the horsemen behind him who drank and sang along with him.

> My old beard's kissed them all!
> My old beard's kissed them all!
> Italian ladies are sprightly.
> My old beard's kissed them all!

The leader sang another verse

> Turkish ladies are timid.
> Flemish ladies are small.
> English ladies are eager.
> My old beard's kissed them all.

The song roared on as Blackie moved along the road until the forest fell away to grassy range with hills and bushes and small thickets of trees. Humans were everywhere, yelling and laughing and blowing horns.

"Time to get foxy," thought Blackie. He lowered his head and slipped from grove to thicket, thorn patch to bush, staying in shadows where his black coat melted in. No humans saw him, but Blackie saw everything.

He saw falconers with birds and huntsmen dragging packs of dogs who strained at their leashes and bayed at Blackie. The huntsmen shaded their eyes to stare toward him, but Blackie stayed still until they dragged the dogs away.

In a copse beside a stream, Blackie found a camp with battered carts, dirty tents, and skinny horses. Two Gypsies sat under a tree, fishing in a stream with strings. With their dark skin, mustaches, and gold earrings, they apeared different from other humans he'd seen. Blackie looked them over and passed on.

A few hills beyond, he found a paddock with horses eating grass, other horses tethered outside. Ragged grooms stood in a ring, yelling at a pair of men wrestling together. They clutched and butted each other while Blackie watched with interest.

"Clumsy, clumsy," he thought. He could show them how to butt.

Blackie pressed on till he saw big tents with banners in bright colors. He saw cooks sweating over steamy pots and turning spits over fires. Dead pigs and deer hung from trees. He turned his nose from the meat smell and ran on. Swinging around a grassy knoll, he heard more singing. Curious, he crept over the rise and peeked down.

At the bottom of the knoll, he saw saddled horses eating grass. A boy in a yellow suit scratched himself on a pile of bags near the horses. Halfway up the hill, a group of ladies in colorful dresses sat on a bright carpet, sewing with needles and petting small dogs.

A young man in a blue tunic knelt by the carpet. On his head, he wore a dirty blue hat with a feather. He had a lionskin over his shoulder. He plinked a round-bellied lute and sang in a high, quavering voice

> At the end of the world is a tower.
> A lady leans over and sings.
> She sings of her faraway lover
> and dreams of the present he brings.
>
> He'll bring her a bell made of silver
> that calls, whenever she rings,
> an eagle to carry her swiftly
> through clouds on strong beating wings.
>
> She'll follow wherever he wanders.
> She'll visit castles and kings.
> The tower is silent and lonely.
> She listens for silvery "pings."

"Not bad, Prince George," said a girl with curly dark hair sitting in the center of the carpet with the ladies around her. She wore a scarlet dress. She adjusted a purple hat on her head.

"Nice song, a little high for you."

She took a silver cup from a blond girl sitting beside her in a blue dress. "Wouldn't you say, Lady Jessica, that the Prince needs to practice more, get better voice control?"

The blond girl smiled. "The Prince sings well enough, my lady.

Blackie stiffened as the breeze carried a smell to him, an aroma that sank into his soul. It was his Princess! Blackie knew his Princess at once. All his life, he'd sensed that perfume in his deepest dreams, that smell sweeter than berries. The scent called him to her. He fought to hold back, but the scent dragged him, step by step, down the little hill.

Jessica saw him stepping toward them. She pointed, squealing. The other ladies stared open-mouthed as he neared the carpet while the tiny dogs scrambled from their laps to dash at Blackie, yipping and jumping off the ground in their fury. The Princess in the middle ignored everyone.

"Now, Prince George," she ordered, "I want you to sing that song you brought back from Castle Darr. You know, the one that starts 'The moon hung low one summer eve,' that song."

"But, my lady," cried Jessica, plucking at her sleeve.

Moving into clouds of perfume, Blackie stepped onto the carpet as the ladies rolled away from him. He bent his knees to stretch his neck around the Princess. He rested his head in her lap. She threw up her arms, screaming, "What's this, what's this?"

"I tried to warn you, my lady," laughed Jessica, reaching over to rub Blackie's nose. "He came over the hill. He's a unicorn."

"Well, get him off me!"

The Princess tried to push Blackie's head away with her red gloves, but he relaxed into her perfume with a sigh.

"What kind of Court are you," yelled the Princess, glaring at everyone, "letting a beast attack your Princess?"

Prince George had dropped the lute at the first cry. Now, he jerked out his sword and ran onto the carpet.

"I'll defend you, my lady!"

"Back off, Georgie, back off!" shouted the Princess, throwing her silver cup at him. "Don't wave that sword near me, you nitwit! I don't want blood all over my dress!"

"Oh!" said the Prince, dropping his sword. He stepped onto the blanket. He threw his arms around Blackie's neck to pull him away.

Blackie wouldn't move. Aware only of the Princess, he sniffed her perfume and rolled his head in her lap.

The ladies, clucking and crying, tugged at Blackie's mane to help Prince George pull him off, but Blackie dug his hooves into the carpet and held close to her body.

"Get this thing off me!" cried the Princess, struggling to push him away. "He's slobbering all over me!"

Jessica was laughing at her. "My lady, my lady, didn't you hear me? It's a unicorn!"

"It's a what?" screeched the Princess. "A unicorn?"

"Sure, my lady. Look at his horn, his tail."

"Oh, a unicorn?"

The Princess relaxed and took a look at Blackie. She touched his nose. "Get back, Georgie! Let me look at him."

The Prince let go of Blackie's neck and crawled away, panting. Everyone stared at Blackie. Blackie closed his eyes and relaxed in his bliss.

The Princess was doubtful. "Well, he does look like a unicorn! But he's black, not white! What do you think, Lady Katherine?"

An old lady in a gray dress let go of Blackie's tail. She moved around, bones creaking, and peered down at him.

"Jessica's right, my lady. He's definitely a unicorn. I guess, they come in different colors like horses. His horn's bent, that's all."

"A unicorn," said the Princess, nodding her head with satisfaction. "Excellent, excellent, I've been waiting all my life for my unicorn. I just hope, Prince George, that he doesn't run away like that white beast you brought Lady Dorinda."

"That wasn't my fault," protested Prince George, picking up his sword. "That unicorn would have stayed with her if she'd treated him right."

"Well, I'm going to keep this one." Gently stroking Blackie's ears, the Princess cooed, "Look how he dotes on me. He's a sweetie."

She bent her face to him.

71

"Don't kiss him!" cried another lady. "Look how dirty he is, how sweaty! You'll catch something, cow fever or something!"

"I will kiss him," declared the Princess. "My own unicorn."

She kissed Blackie above his horn. Blackie fainted at the thrill. All his weight fell on the carpet, pinning the Princess under him as the ladies shrieked in horror.

Lost in his happiness, Blackie didn't see Prince George jump to lift his head so the Princess could scramble out from under him. Instead, she straightened her skirt and eased Blackie's head back to her lap, laughing.

"What do you think of that, Kitty? I can knock 'em out with a kiss! Georgie, wake him up!"

"Wake him up?" exclaimed the Prince. "How do you wake up a unicorn?"

"Here, my lord," said Jessica, fetching a small pitcher of water. "Sprinkle him with water."

"Oh, yes!"

Prince George grabbed the pitcher and sloshed the water over Blackie. Blackie shivered and came awake to the glorious smell of his Princess. She was yelling at the Prince.

"Georgie, are you mad? Jessica told you to sprinkle the unicorn, not drown us! You've soaked everything!"

By now, the page in the yellow suit was running up to help. "Here, my lady, here's a towel! Shall I dry you off?"

"Give the towel to Lady Jessica, Cedric," commanded the Princess. "She can dry the unicorn. How does my hat look, Jessie? Is it wet?"

"The hat's fine, my lady," said Jessica. "Your skirt got most of the water."

"That's all right, then."

The Princess waved the page out of the way. Jessica knelt beside Blackie and began rubbing him with her towel. Blackie squirmed with joy, closing his eyes while his Princess whispered over him.

"At last, my own unicorn! And you'll stay with me forever. You won't be flighty like that white unicorn."

She looked up at the ladies. "Look how strong he is, how handsome! His poor twisted horn, I wonder what happened to it. Call up the Gypsies. They know how to doctor horses."

Blackie opened his eyes to see his Princess smiling down on him with her dark eyes. She scratched his neck and murmured to him.

"My own unicorn, I knew that you'd come to me one day. And you'll be faithful to me. You won't run away like that white unicorn. What a bust he was! All he wanted to do was stuff himself in the garden, not play with us. You'll live with me and pull my chariot, won't you? Shadow, I'll call you Shadow. You'll be my true friend, I know it."

Blackie weakly nodded his head. The Princess stretched her legs below him and scratched his ears. The ladies crowded around, patting him as the Princess sighed.

"Poor Shadow, how'd you hurt your horn? Did you bend it fighting a tiger or a rhino? What adventures we'll have, the warrior queen and her unicorn!"

She looked around. "Cedric, bring food, please. Shadow must be hungry."

The page boy brought up baskets and began spreading meat on silver platters beside them—cold chicken and tongue and beef. Blackie turned up his nose at the meat, but sniffed eagerly at beets and pickles and green salad.

"Where are the cookies?" demanded the Princess. "Did you eat all the cookies, Prince George?"

The Prince looked insulted. "Not me, I didn't touch your cookies!"

"You'd better not." The Princess stroked Blackie. "Lady Katherine counted them. I'm going to feed my unicorn on melon and cakes and cookies. The poor creature looks hungry, and he loves me, the only creature that loves me!"

"Why, Princess!" sputtered the ladies. "We all love you!"

"Love me!" cried the Princess. "You let this unicorn sneak up on me! What if it'd been a Hellhound? It could have grabbed me and carried me off before you lifted a finger!"

Cedric opened another basket. He reached among vegetables, cheese, and fruit, more smells that had Blackie drooling.

"No cookies, my lady," reported the page.

"Prince George!" yelled the Princess.

"So I ate a cookie or two, that's all," mumbled the Prince. "Ride to the cooks' tent, Cedric. Get more cookies. Hustle yourself for the Princess."

"Shall I, my lady?" asked the Page.

"Certainly not!" snapped the Princess. "You ate the cookies, Prince, you ride for more! Cedric can brush Shadow with my silver hairbrush while I feed him grapes. Have you ever tasted grapes, dear unicorn?"

Blackie shook his head.

"See, he understands me!" the Princess cried with delight, kissing him again. "Now, I have a true friend!"

Blackie wallowed in the smell of his Princess, her voice, the touch of her hands, and now the fruity sweetness of grapes! He had to take deep breaths to keep from fainting again. He felt ready to explode with happiness.

"How," he thought, "how could Papa give up all this to hide away in the forest?"

CHAPTER SEVEN

The Princess in the Forest

Blackie's tongue reached for the dripping slice of melon. Cooing to him, the Princess pulled the fruit away.

"No, Shadow, not yet. No melon for a naughty beast. Shadow must first swear obedience. Does my unicorn promise to honor and obey his mistress? Will he swear to love his Princess better than life itself, to serve her to the death?"

Totally at peace in his Princess's lap, Blackie nodded. The sweetness of melon blended with her scent.

"Well, then, beloved beast."

She squished the melon with her fingers. The juice and pulp dribbled down Blackie's throat. He let go of thought and sank into his senses.

"My lady, he's fainted again!" said Jessica, leaning near.

The Princess bent to kiss him on the nose. "He's not fainted, Jessie. He's just happy."

"But his head, isn't it heavy, my lady? Shouldn't I take his weight for you?"

"Jessica, Jessica," laughed the Princess, "if you want to hold Shadow, just ask for him. Don't snivel about it."

Blackie felt Jessica lift his head while the Princess scooted out from below, then Jessica edged her legs under him and lowered his head into her lap. He squinted his eyes to see Jessica's blue eyes smiling down on him while the Princess leaned close to scratch him under his chin.

"See? He didn't faint."

The Princess picked up the platter to feed Blackie more melon. She dropped slice after slice in his mouth. He chewed and swallowed with delight.

"How lovely it is, my lady," sighed Jessica, "that this unicorn came to you willingly."

"It's because he's young," said the Princess. "At his age, he's happy to serve me. That white unicorn was old when Prince George caught him. He was already crusty."

"He was just lazy!" snapped the old lady who had objected to Blackie. "But, Princess, what would your mother say if she saw you feeding that beast with your fingers? He could snap at you at any time."

Jessica patted Blackie's cheek.

"Don't worry, Lady Pru. This fellow's tame. He won't snap at anyone. You know, my lady, I think he's come to help you out of your troubles."

The Princess leaned back on her arms. "I'm sure he has, Jessica. Saint Jude has sent me the hero I need."

"Well," said Lady Pru, "he'd better be a hero, Princess. This is the morning the Council votes on your marriage. You have only five 'nay' votes on your side."

"No, no," said Jessica, shifting her legs under Blackie, "Lord Dreep will change his vote. I'm sure he'll support you."

The Princess stretched out beside them on a pillow. "Don't be silly, Jessica. The Council's sure to go along with Prince Vile. Vile's too powerful to resist, but now, I don't care."

She turned her head to grin at Jessica.

"What a surprise they're going to get! This unicorn changes everything. With the holy beast supporting me, more barons are sure to swing to my side. I already have the Heir of Darr sworn to me, along with Lady Thorn and Lady Amalia. That's the north and west. If Mother gives me back my magic bow, we can defend the City. Nobody will marry me then."

"Well, I wouldn't feed that unicorn by hand," insisted Lady Pru. "He may be tame, but you could catch a disease. It's unsanitary."

"Unsanitary!" hooted the Princess. She yawned and scratched thrilling fingernails down Blackie neck. "Don't you know that the unicorn's a healer? One touch of his horn could heal your swollen ankle."

"My ankle," sighed Lady Pru, "my ankle is my cross, bless the saints."

"The unicorn needs a treat," announced the Princess, lifting up on an elbow. "Feed him cakes, Jessica, until the Prince gets back with the cookies."

The page lifted a bowl of warm honeycakes from the basket. He pulled off the napkin covering it. The spicy smell came to Blackie as Jessica picked out a cake. His jaws opened. Papa had talked and talked about the pastries he'd eaten during his adventures—the cookies and cakes, turnovers and tarts. Now, Blackie was getting his taste of goodies.

"Oh, he loves his cake!" cried Jessica, reaching for another one. Blackie rolled the cake around with his tongue, nearly swooning again at the sweet spicy taste along with the crunch of nuts.

"Oh, Papa," Blackie thought, "oh, Papa!"

"Try him on berries," ordered the Princess.

The page handed bowl after bowl to Jessica, and Blackie discovered more thrills as she fed him blueberries and raspberries, currents and raisins.

"Now, I want a song," commanded the Princess, "a song for my unicorn."

The page jumped to grab up the lute. "What song would you like, my lady?"

"A song to soothe him. My unicorn needs his rest, poor dear. I'm sure he's been searching across the Empire to find me."

Cedric took up the lute and struck tender chords. The Princess stopped him. "Not that song. Sing 'Three Blessings.'"

As Cedric sang, the Princess leaned over to comb her fingers through Blackie's mane. Blackie closed his eyes and shivered with joy.

My lover gives me blessings three—
his ring, his sword, his company,
and I give him, most lovingly,
my heart, my home, my baby.

My heart, he may break,
my home, he may spurn,
but my baby will bind him.
He'll always re—

"EEEEEEAAGH!"

The song stopped dead at a shriek from the sky. The ladies screamed as Blackie jerked up his head, but the Princess grabbed his horn.

"Easy, Shadow, easy! It's only Prince Vile on his dragon. Ladies, ladies, sit still! We shall not let an enemy spoil my picnic."

Clucking nervously, the ladies moved closer to the Princess. Blackie lowered his head, his heart thumping in his chest. Off to the side, he saw a dozen knights run up with their shields to gather before spearmen while a squad of bowmen picked out their best arrows.

"Please, everyone," called the Princess, "stay calm! Prince Vile will keep the dragon under control. Pray, Cedric, finish your song."

Blackie didn't hear another note of the song. He turned his head as the wide-winged dragon circled the knoll. Prince Vile, a dark figure clinging to her neck, waved insolently. He guided the monster to flame down, burning a circle of sward from the flat below to settle into the ashes. The stink and smoke reached Blackie, who almost retched in Jessica's arms.

Coughing into handkerchiefs, the ladies scooted behind the Princess. She sat stiffly, arms folded, glaring at the monster snorting smoke across the hillside.

"Good news to the bride!" cried the goat-heeled Prince of the North, stepping out of the reek. "Princess, you must greet your husband with a kiss!"

The ladies gasped, but the Princess only held out the melon platter. "I have no husband, Prince Vile. Would you care for a piece of melon?"

"True it is, s-s-sweet lady," hissed Prince Vile, sweeping a bow below her, "you have no husband at this moment. You'll be happy to learn, though, that the Council has voted. In ninety days, three short months, I take you as my loving s-spouse. But for now—"

He turned glaring eyes toward the forest.

"Where are my Hellions? Where are my minions? I ordered my slaves to attend me here at this hour. When I give orders, as my bride will learn, I demand obedience!"

Blackie perked up an ear at the sound of hoofbeats.

Prince Vile waved a black glove with a blood-red ring on the pinkie. "At last, this must be my bullyboys!"

As the dragon swung up its head, Blackie watched a slim figure ride over the hill, the tail of his lionskin flopping with the trot of the old white stallion. He carried a basket covered with a red checked cloth.

"Prince George with the cookies!" exclaimed Jessica.

White-faced, out of breath, Prince George swung from the saddle to place the basket of cookies beside the Princess.

"Terrible news!" he gasped. "I just heard from the Council! The vote went against you, my lady, six votes to five!"

"Ah," sneered Prince Vile, looking coldly at Prince George, "the glittering lad, himself. No need to rupture yourself, dear boy, I've already given her the happy news."

He glared about the Court, his gaze settling on Blackie. "What a moving sight—the Princess, her lackeys, and this single-horned—Well, my lady, things will change after our marriage. I'll give you a pet that eats unicorns!"

The Princess kept her eyes on Prince George. "In the Council, Lord Dreep, how did he vote?"

"I'm sorry, my lady," said the Prince, shrugging. "I was told that Lord Dreep didn't show up to vote."

"Of course, Dreep didn't appear this morning!" snarled Prince Vile. "Lord Dreep's sworn to me now. You'll see him in a moment, my lady. I ordered him to attend me here with my guards. You, Princess, must be better escorted from now on. You'll find that I take good care of my possessions."

"Possessions!" cried the Princess, leaping up. Blackie scrambled off Jessica, jumping to his hooves while the ladies helped each other to rise. Jessica stood with the Princess. The other ladies squeezed together behind them.

The Princess glared back at Prince Vile. "You'll never possess me, you fiend! My father will pay back your silver, every ounce of it! When the debt is paid, we'll be free of you forever!"

"The Emperor pay back my silver?" Prince Vile burst out a nasty laugh. "Impossible! After a lifetime of borrowing, his Majesty's but a bankrupt. He even cadged silver for his coronation, and now—"

Prince Vile pulled off a glove, inspected the claws on his hand.

"After twenty years, his debt is due. Time has run out. The Contract requires that His Majesty settle this debt within ninety days. I leave it to your imagination, my pretty plaything, how many cartloads of silver the Emperor would have to come up with to settle a debt of that size!"

"No matter," cried the Princess, "it's not your day yet! We have months before your Contract is due."

"No, no, my Princess," sneered Prince Vile. "Not months. Weeks, fair lady, days, hours, minutes! I'll claim you as my own before you know it! The Contract stipulates that if the Emperor is unable to repay his debt to the very last copper, I get to select the chattel of my choice in repayment!"

"Not me!" screamed the Princess, stamping a foot. "I'm no chattel, you demon! I'm a human being!"

"Why, that was the very point the Council considered this morning," smiled the Prince. "You may read the Contract for yourself: *'Lender's choice among goods moveable, animate or inanimate.'* Lawyer-talk. It means, the Council agrees, that I get to seize anything I choose between earth and sky."

He giggled, shrilly.

"In this case, my lady, I choose a juicy bride with heir-right to the Empire! I'll marry you at the Cathedral door and carry you off to Vile. Once your spirit's broken, you'll love my burning mountain. But, ah, here come my guards! Someone will be punished for this delay."

Pounding around the side of the hill came three score riders in black capes with hooked spears and crossbows, their banner showing a silver-crowned skull upon a fiery mountain. A dozen hulking Hellions ran behind with their clubs.

"My bullyboys!" cried Prince Vile with satisfaction. "At last."

Blackie stepped before his Princess while the knights and spearmen moved closer to the blanket. The ladies inched back, except for Jessica who stood staunchly, squeezing the Princess's hand.

Panting and sweating, the riders streamed up to the Black Prince. The bullyboys spread to both sides to threaten the Court with crossbows while the Hellions grinned at Prince Vile, smacking their clubs against their palms. A falconer stood by with a great bearhawk on a T-staff. The hawk turned its head in its hood, its red tongue licking its curved beak.

Far behind galloped a pale lord, thin, hatless, his white hairs straggly and windblown. He fell off his horse at Prince Vile's feet. Prince Vile kicked him in the shoulder.

"You're late, Dreep! The raven ordered you to bring up my boys by noon."

Lord Dreep looked up, drooling with fear. "Pardon, lord, pardon! We had thirty miles to ride and little warning. We came as fast as we could!"

Prince Vile kicked him again. He turned to the Princess and spread his hands. "You see, my lady, he thinks that I'll listen to apologies. Soon, he'll know better. I demand obedience, a lesson my bride will learn."

Outraged by this leering demon, Blackie stepped forward till his horn was five feet from Prince Vile's belly. Vile lifted his nose with a sneer. "If this beast takes one more step toward me, I'll roast him for supper with garlic sauce."

The Princess stepped beside Blackie. She waved a haughty hand at the dark Prince. "Enough, Prince Vile, we've heard your threats. You may withdraw now. Pray leave me alone with my unicorn."

Prince Vile stared coldly at Blackie.

"What a crude specimen it is, Princess—twisted horn, off color! It does appear to be a genuine unicorn, however. Tell the Emperor that I'll accept the beast as my groom's gift. After all, my dragon must have her snack at the bridal feast. I'll save one haunch for our honeymoon."

That was enough for Blackie. He charged forward, smashing Vile in the belly to roll him, shrieking, down the knoll. Everyone stood frozen as Vile crawled to his knees, spitting with rage. He shook a trembling fist at Blackie.

"K-k-kill that unicorn!"

Prince George swung up his sword as the Hellions lumbered forward. The hawker yanked the hood off the bearhawk.

"No!" cried the Princess. She dashed forward, grabbed Blackie's mane, and swung to his back. Blackie spun on rear hooves as the Princess clutched his neck, shouting, "Run, Shadow, run!"

Blackie galloped up the hill, Prince Vile's shriek in his ears, "Kill, kill, kill!"

Crossbow bolts zinged around Blackie, but he was over the hill and running for a line of trees beyond the tents. In minutes, he was tearing up a trail in the forest.

Behind him, Blackie heard wings beating like kettledrums. He glanced over his shoulder to see the great hawk bearing down with steel talons. Up the narrow trail, Blackie ran faster and faster. Vines yanked at him. Branches clawed. The Princess clung tightly, her head pressed into his mane. Her hair fluttered, her hat gone.

The hawk swung easily around the curves in the path, its wings hammering in Blackie's ears. Blackie ran till his heart roared. His eyes were blinded with sweat. Without thinking, he leaped right as the path swung left around a massive oak tree. The Princess flew off as Blackie rolled through brush and saplings into a solid tree trunk that stopped him.

WHAM!

Swinging to follow the path, the hawk wavered after Blackie. It crashed into the oak tree. Blackie heard a thump as feathers sprayed. The hawk lay dazed and broken in the path.

Blackie lifted his head, torn, bruised, gasping for air. The Princess crawled over to him. She was bleeding from scratches on her neck and arms, but she hugged him, panting, "Oh, Shadow, that was wonderful!"

Blackie forced himself up on shaking hooves. The Princess leaned on him, her arms around his neck, listening to horses gallop up the path.

They heard a shriek from Prince Vile.

"Where'd they go? Where'd they go? I want that unicorn dead!"

The Princess pulled painfully onto Blackie's sweaty back. She leaned low on his neck as Blackie hobbled quietly through the trees. Behind them, they heard Lord Vile screech, "Is that my hawk? Strangle it, worthless bird, and hunt down that Princess! Kill that unicorn!"

Blackie limped silently through the forest. In case Hellhounds were following, he waded up a stream. When he thought they had gone far enough for safety, he stopped.

The Princess jumped down, her hands to her hair. "Oh, what I must look like!"

She knelt over the stream, wiping blood from scratches on her forehead and arms. She combed her thick, curly hair with her fingers and shook her head.

"I'm not fit to be seen."

She jumped up to face Blackie.

"It was worth it, Shadow! I'll never forget the look on Vile's face when you knocked him to the ground! You smeared him with mud and grass, the foul thing! Everyone's afraid of him, you know. With his dragon and his armies, he's won over most of the lords in the land. Those he can't frighten, he buys with silver. And now, he's got the due date of that Contract coming up! He thinks that he's won!"

She shivered.

"Why didn't Father stand strong? He started small, borrowing a hundred silver pieces at a time. It was easier than living on his private purse and building wealth through husbandry. Mama warned him that it couldn't continue, but he declared that he needed silver to rule the Empire, so borrowing became a habit."

She stood silently, her eyes cast down. Blackie stepped close to nuzzle her.

"No," she cried, throwing her arms about him, "I refuse to despair! Our luck's bound to turn! The Lord in Heaven won't permit evil to win. Why, look, Shadow, Saint Jude sent you to protect me! I'm sure that Father will think of something. He'll squeeze gold out of the Bishop, or something."

Blackie pressed his head against her as she brushed leaves and twigs from his coat. She knelt to pull thorns from his legs.

"Whatever happens," she said softly, touching her silver dagger, "I won't marry Vile."

She jumped up to scratch Blackie between the eyes. "Now, Shadow, this was supposed to be a pleasure trip, an outing free of the hot City, so let's enjoy ourselves. Show me your forest home."

Blackie cheered at that, a chance to show the Princess the secrets of his beloved forest. True, he had never traveled over this region, but he could smell his way through the hills and streams as though born here.

First, though, he stroked his horn over her cuts and scratches, shooting healing charges into the soft skin. She turned slowly under his horn, eyes closed, smiling brilliantly to the sky.

"Oh, Shadow, you are a holy beast. What a blessed day has brought you to me!"

He paused when her skin was perfect—moles gone from her shoulder, a pimple removed from her nose. She climbed to his back, and Blackie wandered through the paths to show off his forest, the spreading trees and the secret flowers, tiny yellow and white blossoms with leaves smaller than her littlest fingernail, along with birds' nests woven into thorns a foot above the ground.

"Why, where are the baby birds?" cried the Princess.

If the Princess wanted babies, Blackie would sniff out babies for her. He showed her squirrel babies chasing each other up and down tree trunks, hedgehog babies wrestling around the roots of bushes, owlets sleeping in a row on a stretching branch. On a rock near a marsh, Blackie found a tangle of baby snakes that lashed out with little fangs when he swung his horn near. The Princess stuck her tongue out at them.

Blackie carried the Princess deeper into the marsh where he sank to his knees in mud and his hooves made sucking sounds when he pulled them out. They sniffed the rich, rotting air and examined turtles and long-legged birds among huge ferns and reeds. Blackie swept away bugs with his tail while the Princess slapped at stingers and biters on her forehead and arms.

They crept up on a piglet nosing in the mud. The Princess leaned down and snatched up the pig by the tail. She tried to cuddle it, but it kicked and squealed until a great, hairy mama pig rushed out of the reeds with furious eyes. She chased them until the laughing Princess dropped the wriggling baby back in the mud, and they splashed up to higher ground.

"What fun," cried the Princess, "but I'm eaten alive! My neck's all bug bites! I need a bath!"

Blackie carried the Princess to a stream that ran like a small river. He trotted up to a wide pool and skidded to a stop, dropping his neck. The Princess shot over his head into cool, deep water.

SPLASH!

She coughed her way to the surface. "Shadow, Shadow . . . my clothes . . . my hair, soaked and stringy! I'll dunk you for this, see if I don't!"

She crawled up the bank, wiping water from her face. She ran at Blackie and pushed with both arms, trying to tip him into the stream. Joyously, Blackie pushed back and they shoved at each other till the Princess gave up, laughing.

Panting, she stripped off her wet gown and hung it on a branch beside the stream. She dived back into the water. She kicked to the surface, calling, "Shadow, Shadow!"

Blackie jumped in beside her, dousing her with a mighty splash. The Princess swam to him and gripped his mane.

She made Blackie tow her upstream so they could float back together, the Princess on her back with an arm under his neck watching sunlight glimmer through branches above. Holding her breath, she turned on her stomach to spy fish darting in schools and river crabs crawling over the sandy bottom.

Blackie looked with alarm when the Princess dived under him. She popped up on the other side and grabbed him with a hug. They rolled and raced until the Princess got tired and climbed out. Blackie followed, shaking like a dog.

"Stop, stop!" squealed the Princess. "Now, I'm dirty again!"

She settled on a mossy rock to wring out her hair, inspecting her reflection in the river. Blackie rubbed his nose against her while the Princess wailed, "Oh, I'm hideous! I'll never be pretty again! And it's all your fault, Shadow, dunking me like that! How dare you!"

She stretched out her legs and wiggled her toes. Blackie stepped back to the stream and took a long drink. He yawned and lay beside her on the rocks. She snuggled against him, singing a silly song.

My unicorn, he is so sweet!
I'm hungry.
It is time to eat.

"Oh, Shadow," she sighed, "if only I could eat grass and leaves like you. I'd stay out here forever, but now, I'm thinking of blueberries and cakes. What I'd give for a roasted turkey leg, yummm."

She laughed and leaned her head against his shoulder. She hummed in a low voice until she went quiet and slept.

Blackie turned his head to watch his Princess sleep, so pretty, even tousled with damp hair and bug bites. Ants ran over her. She twitched. A green worm inched down her arm.

Blackie stretched his horn around. Its bend reached a bug bite on her arm. He healed it with a touch and smiled. Even damaged, his horn was useful. Mama always said that blessings came from everywhere.

The Princess murmured in her sleep.

He reached for another welt, but the Princess twitched. She woke, sat up, and yawned.

"Let's do something! What haven't we done? Bears, I want to see bears."

She jumped up to pull on her damp clothes, reaching behind to tug at her gown. The back hung open, half-laced. She looked at her reflection again.

"I'm awful, just awful! No one must see me! We can't go back to camp till dark. Oh, how, they'll scold! Lady Pru will never get over it! Thank Heavens, Mother stayed back at the lodge to meet with the Council."

She tidied herself as best she could, then crawled on Blackie. He carried her up a path, calling for foxes until a red vixen peeped around a tree, barking softly.

"What you want? Why you with female human?"

"Oh, she's cute!" cried the Princess. "Call her over! I want to pet her!"

The fox vanished into the forest.

"Come back!" yelled Blackie. "She's a friend. I want to show her the bears. Where are the bears around here?"

The fox was gone. Blackie had to sniff his way to a bear wallow, a muddy hole with hair and tracks around. Nearby trees were scratched or polished smooth by bears rubbing against them.

Blackie walked softly, listening for rustling bushes or grunting bears. He found a cub playing in the dust of the trail. The Princess slipped off Blackie's back and walked slowly toward the cub, dangling a red ribbon. The cub stared and sniffed, sniffed and stared. The Princess caught him and tickled his fat sides till he squealed.

"Oh, oh!" thought Blackie.

That's when the mother crashed through the brush into the trail. She bawled with fury when she saw the Princess with her cub. She rose to hind feet, roaring. Blackie charged and knocked the bear on her backside. She blinked in surprise, lunged up again.

The Princess kissed the heavy cub. She set it down and raced for Blackie. She jumped to his back, and they trotted down the path.

"Oh, Shadow," murmured the Princess. "Why does this have to end? Let's stay in the forest forever."

Blackie slowed. He ambled down the path while the Princess yawned and played with his ears. Suddenly, she sat up.

"Shadow, what are you doing? You're eating!"

Absently chewing a wood cabbage, Blackie was startled.

"You pig!" she cried. "You stuff yourself while I starve! I missed my lunch to feed you! What can I eat?"

Blackie carried her to a blackberry patch but the berries were dried and seedy.

"I can't eat these," wailed the Princess. "I want a capon or a pheasant. Let's find servants to feed me."

She held up her hands. "Look, stained and scratched. I lost my gloves when we ran off and my shoes in the river. My gown's bedraggled, ruined. I'm filthier than a kitchen wench, and it's all your fault, you bad unicorn! You should be whipped!"

She pulled Blackie from the berries by his tail. He turned. She kissed his nose. "Come on, Shadow, kneel for me. I'm too tired to climb on. I know you're tired too, but you've been pigging out all afternoon. You've had luncheon upon luncheon. Kneel for me."

Blackie knelt for his Princess. She sat daintily on his back, and he stood with an effort.

"Now, carry me to food," she commanded.

"Human food," thought Blackie, "that's what she needs. Grass stems and leaves won't feed a Princess. The villagers, all those gardens—they'll have to give her what she wants."

Blackie traveled swiftly through the forest with the Princess dozing on his back. He kept alert, sniffing and listening at each new trail until she woke up and started singing in a low voice. He tried to quiet her but she couldn't understand, so he looked about carefully as he trotted out of the forest into the road where they saw the tower of a castle shining in the afternoon sun.

"Castle Shrems!" exclaimed the Princess. "What a good idea! Lady Bonnie is just my size. An hour with her hairdresser and her best gown, I'll look human again. And they'll give me dinner!"

Blackie started up the hill, but the Princess pulled him to a stop. "Hold up, Unicorn. Let's not go there yet. I want a moment by myself before I see anyone."

Wearily, Blackie turned to a forest trail. He carried the Princess to a grassy nook by a stream where he could drink. She slid down and hugged him.

"Oh, Shadow, sweet unicorn, I thank you! This has been the best day of my life. Alone with you, I could breathe for a change. You can't imagine what it's like—crowds of people hanging over me constantly, guarding, serving, watching. They suffocate me. I'm never alone. Even when I sleep, I have court ladies sleeping on cushions around my bed. A couple times, when I was a girl, Jessica and I ran off together. And one afternoon, I had adventures by myself at Castle Thorn. That was fun."

She smiled at the memory.

"What a golden day that was! I searched that castle on my own, found a bunch of lost boys and a treasure of crowns. That's where I found my magic bow. I shot a Hellhound with it. So much, so much, but as soon as we got home—"

She turned away, her voice tired.

"Prince George, that blabbermouth, told everyone what I'd done and Mother took away my magic bow. It was Georgie who got to carry the crowns back to the barons. I wasn't allowed to go, though I was the one who—"

She broke off. She turned back to Blackie and patted his neck.

"You stay here, Shadow. I want to walk upstream a few yards, just to feel what it's like to be by myself for a while. Truly alone. No one watching me. Wait here. I'll be back."

The Princess kissed Blackie and walked away. Blackie listened to her footsteps till he could hear nothing but the burble of the stream and the rattle of branches, the chirp and call of birds. He grazed on the grass till he heard a loud bird cry. He lifted his head, his ears up. He grew worried. She'd been gone too long. Did she know about snakes? He started to rush after, but held himself back.

"No, she told me to wait!"

Blackie forced himself to eat. He flicked flies with his tail. Time crawled by until he grew rigid with concern, staring up the stream bed with his ears spread.

"Shadow."

Blackie turned. The Princess walked around a tree. She'd tacked up the back of her gown with small thorns. She'd woven a crown of vines for her curls. Her dark eyes were bright.

"How do I look?"

Blackie let out his breath. She curtseyed to him. She held out a hand.

"Sir Unicorn, your Princess commands a dance."

She stepped up to him, took his horn in one hand, lifted her skirt with the other. She sang a little tune, drawing Blackie forward, back, around in a little dance. Blackie stepped nervously to keep off her bare toes. She let go and twirled around and around.

She stopped and curtseyed again.

"My thanks to you. Sir Unicorn. I've loved our afternoon together—the forest, the stream, the babies. I see everything more clearly, now. My prayers will be happier tonight."

She moved close to scratch his ears. Blackie lifted his head. He sniffed her scent. The perfume was gone, but her vital odor remained, the sweetness of the living girl.

"I'm ready to go back to the watchers and waiters. You'll protect me till I join the Court. Tomorrow, we'll go home to the City. You can stay with me until the Contract's due. You'll love the Castle, all the gardens, and I'll show you the City wall, the Cathedral, the sea. We'll have fun together, my last days—"

She shook her head.

"If we have to give in to Vile, I'll send you back to the forest. You'll be safest in the forest. You can hide from him there. He won't move against me for ninety days, but he'd have you poisoned if he got a chance. He'll never forget your horn. Unicorn horns terrify him."

She hugged Blackie and kissed him again. He took a step toward the path before them.

"Back to my duty I go," she said, "like a good girl. But now, when I'm on my stiffest royal behavior, sitting prim and proper in Court, I'll think of this afternoon when I could just be a girl playing with a friend in the forest."

She looked around with a smile. Blackie followed her gaze. The forest was healthy and alive, the grass springing up where they'd rumpled it. Bugs circled the stream, a squirrel peered around a tree trunk, brown birds flitted through the branches. The Princess hugged him again.

"When you're back in the forest, I'll send messages as long as I can. You can trust the Knights. Do you know Sir Otley? He's Captain of the Order, the fattest of them all. He loves me as much as he loves wine. And Georgie, Prince George is steady. He's a lot nicer than he acts sometimes, but then—"

The Princess sighed and stretched. "So am I."

She reached for Blackie's mane.

"Take me to Castle Shrems. The Baron and Baroness are about to receive royalty. How shocked they'll be. That makes me laugh! Those barons think they need months to prepare for a royal visit. I'll give them ten minutes."

CHAPTER EIGHT

The Lordless Village

Dust floated up from the weathered boards as Blackie's hooves rattled over the drawbridge to Castle Shrems. Blackie sneezed at the withered ivy hanging down the wall. The Princess jumped down to the drawbridge to stand, hands on hips, looking up and down the massive door.

"Strange. It appears they've removed the portcullis here. This outer door is new. Could it be they don't want people to look inside?"

She reached up both hands and yanked at the iron door knocker, so heavy it barely thumped. "Doorkeeper!" she shouted. "Baron, anyone, answer the door!"

Blackie backed off the drawbridge. He turned up his nose at the bitter grass around the moat. The surface of the water was spread with a slimy green growth that made him gag. Nothing moved, no bugs, no frogs. The only creature he saw was a lizard staring dully at him from a rock beside the moat. With a shudder, Blackie stepped back onto to the drawbridge.

"Come, Shadow!" The Princess gestured. "Knock on this door for me!"

The Princess stepped away as Blackie pivoted on the drawbridge. He swung up on his fore feet and smashed the door with rear hooves.

BANG!

The kick echoed. Black birds flapped away from the wall into the sky. Blackie kicked again.

BANG, BANG!

"Get away!" screamed a voice.

"Lord Shrems!" called the Princess, reaching to hold Blackie still. "Lord Shrems, it's me, Princess Julianna, come to call!"

"Get outta here! Die somewheres else! Leave us alone!"

The Princess frowned. "Open this door, immediately!" she cried.

"Get the door, Grubbo!" roared a voice inside. "Somebody needs to be killed!"

The gate jerked open on shrieking hinges. A shaggy Hellion glared out with small piggy eyes. When he saw Blackie, he cursed and swung up his club. Blackie charged through the gate and knocked the Hellion into a heap of garbage across the courtyard, the club flying away.

The Princess darted in after Blackie. She glanced around the courtyard at the whole gang of Hellions sitting on piles of dirt. They were covered with flies, their clubs scattered about them. They stared stupidly as the Princess snatched up a crossbow from a rack beside the door.

"A weapon!"

Two men ran out the inner door with spears. "Get them!" they yelled. The Hellions lurched to their feet with a roar, grabbing for their clubs.

The Princess braced the heavy crossbow on her forearm and snapped off a bolt that bounced through bones and chicken feathers and stuck in a dirt pile. The Hellions jumped back with a screech.

The Princess looked down at the crossbow. "Well, it's not magic, but it makes 'em jump."

She grabbed a quiver of bolts from a peg below the rack and whirled to scramble onto Blackie's back. She banged the heavy crossbow on his neck as the roaring Hellions lumbered toward her.

"Let's go!" she shouted.

The instant Blackie felt the Princess firmly settled, he raced over the drawbridge and down the lane toward the village. They heard the men yelling behind.

"Catch that girl! Nabs want her alive!"

Blackie heard one last cry as he raced around the turn in the lane. "Grubbo let the girl get away! Grubbo gotta go tell Nabs!"

At the end of the lane, Blackie found the village gate shut and guarded. A spearman dozed in a flimsy wooden tower above the gate, his head in his arms. He jerked up at their approach and stared as the Princess pulled Blackie to a halt.

"Look at this village, Shadow. Closed in, guarded during work hours. I don't like the looks of this."

Blackie sniffed the bushes beside the lane as the Princess jumped down to reload the crossbow. Charged with a fresh bolt, she balanced the weapon on Blackie's back. She ran her hands through her hair and straightened her gown as best she could.

By now, a dozen heads were peering over the wall. Blackie heard the men yelling to each other.

"Them's the ones! Them's the ones we're s'posed to watch for! We gotta catch 'em! Nabs is offerin' a reward!"

Blackie blinked at that, but the Princess picked up the crossbow. She marched toward the gate, her back straight, chin high, gaze bold and haughty.

"Open this gate!" she ordered in a loud, clear tone.

"What's she sayin'?" squealed an incredulous voice. "She wants us to open to her?"

The Princess swung up the crossbow. "Shadow, open this gate for me."

Blackie questioned in his heart whether this was a good idea, but his Princess had ordered it. He lowered his horn and charged the gate.

WHAM!

The gate fell flat, squashing two men standing behind it. Howling, they crawled out from underneath. The other guards fell back, shaking their spears as the Princess stomped over the gate, shouting at them.

"Down, slaves! Down, or I'll shoot off your noses!"

The men stood paralyzed, their mouths open.

She swung around the crossbow. "To ground! Grovel or die!"

The men gasped and dropped as one, falling on their faces before her. Other villagers, running up from the huts along the lane, stopped in their tracks.

"Hats off!" screamed the Princess. "Kneel to royalty!"

Old crones, workmen, young wives, children—they all looked at each other. Blackie stepped up beside her, trying to looking ferocious. Now, the people were staring at him in amazement.

"To your knees, you scruffy churls!" shouted the Princess. "Obey instantly, or be hanged! You first, you old ruffian!"

She jumped toward a man in a dirty white apron, a bit plumper than the others. He leaped back, throwing out his arms to keep from tumbling.

"But me lady," he squealed, "you're not allowed here!"

The Princess turned white with anger.

"I'd like to see who'd keep me out! I am Julianna, Princess and Heiress to the Throne of this Empire! I go where I go, do what I want, and woe to those who displease me! If you don't obey this instant, I'll burn this village and sell you all to the Turk! Down, dogs, down, down!"

Startled by her rage, Blackie backed away. The villagers cried in terror and fell over. Next moment, they were all stretched out on the ground, whimpering and flopping around like fish out of water.

Looking them over, the Princess nodded with satisfaction. She swung the crossbow to her shoulder and scolded the villagers.

"How dare lift your faces to a Princess, you worms? Don't you know I can destroy this village with a snap of my finger? In fact, it may be my duty to hang you all as an example to rebels everywhere. Beg for mercy, slaves, beg for grace before I unleash this mighty beast, this unicorn, to stomp you into jelly!"

Now, the howls really went up. The people wept and wallowed on the ground before Blackie's astonished eyes. He looked at the Princess, frightened at her fury. She winked at him.

He gasped, realizing, "She's not vicious. She's . . . she's pretending!"

Pretending or not, the Princess had the villagers under control.

"Gather yourselves together now," she ordered. "Come to your senses and take me to your priest. I must speak to someone with authority."

The villagers peeked up, uncertainly. She motioned them to their feet. One at a time, they crawled up, sweating and blubbering.

"You, fellow," the Princess said to the man in white, standing with hat in hand, "what do you mean that I'm not allowed here?"

The man looked down at his hat. As he spoke, Blackie recognized him—Bunly the Baker, the man who'd led the gang that tried to skin him last spring when Papa had rescued him.

"Orders, me lady," mumbled Bunly. "Orders from Nabs up at the castle. He says, we're not to let anyone inside our gates. Keep strangers out, he says. Don't give nothin' to nobody. Then, an hour ago, an order came down to hold you if we caught sight of you."

The Princess nodded, grimly. "So you take orders from this Nabs, do you? And what happened to Baron Shrems? He's the vassal who holds this barony. Where's your bailiff?"

"Run away, me lady," said a large woman in orange, who'd crept up beside the plump man. "When them Hellions showed up, they all skippered off somewhere."

"It's clear that something is wrong here," announced the Princess, resting the crossbow on Blackie's back. "Sadly wrong. It's good that we came by to straighten this out."

A boy wiggled through the crowd, shaking a finger at Blackie. "That unicorn, me lady, he's the one as let our pigs out!"

"And my axe," cried a red-bearded man, stepping up, "he knocked me down and stole my axe!"

Blackie recognized Moot, the woodchopper who'd thrown the axe at him. Blackie stepped forward, lowering his horn. The man jumped back.

"Don't bother me with your pigs and axes!" snapped the Princess. "I want to speak with the priest, now, and with your headman."

"Oh, the headman, now—" Bunly looked terrified. "Well, me lady, I . . . I . . . that is, with the bailiff gone and everybody, I'm afraid it's me."

"Well, lead us to the church. We can talk in peace there. Here, you, carry my crossbow. Shoot anybody that hinders me."

She tossed the weapon to Moot who caught it in shaking hands. The Princess walked haughtily down the lane with Blackie. Bunly hurried to keep up with her while the villagers, walking behind, chattered like starlings.

"She talks like a princess—don't look it though, so rumpled and wild. You never saw Lady Shrems with hair like that."

"And she don't wear shoes!"

"That can't be a unicorn! The unicorn's white. We've seen him in our gardens often enough."

The Princess stopped at the well in front of the church. Blackie stood beside her as the people sorted themselves out. The men stood in a half-circle before them while women and children filled the sides of the square. Older boys scrambled up in the limbs of the trees shading the well.

A baldheaded priest looked out the church door and ducked back in. The church bell began to ring, "Ding ding, ding ding!" Dogs barked. Chickens ran off, squawking, and babies started crying.

Bunly and Moot stood facing the Princess. Now, the priest scurried out from the church to join them, bobbing up and down before the Princess.

"Oh, my lady," he sputtered, "bless you, bless you! The angels bless you, the saints, the patriarchs, and . . . and . . ."

His speech ran down. He stood helplessly, eyes darting between Blackie and the Princess.

"Amen, Father," she said, politely, after a moment. "I thank you for the blessing, but to the purpose. No one has told me what's happening here, no one's answered my questions. I trust that you can explain about those Hellions in the castle and this Nabs."

"Nabs!" shivered the Priest. "Oh, no one will speak of Nabs. We're afraid, my lady. Since the dragon first flew in, we've been terrified."

"Dragonbait!" cried Bunly. "Nabs said, we'd be dragonbait if we said anything to anybody."

The crowd shivered at the mention of the dragon.

"You mean," asked the Princess, incredulously, "the dragon's here? Impossible! We saw her at the hunting fields this morning."

"She comes and goes," wailed the Priest. "We can't speak of her. No one must say anything!"

"No!" cried Moot, waving the crossbow in the air. "Please, please, me lady, we'd sooner speak o' the Death!"

"I'll speak," said a firm voice. A tall woman stepped through the crowd, people pulling away from her. She wore a woven green shawl over a faded multicolored dress. She smiled at the Princess and bowed low.

"Our Wise Woman," whispered Moot, dropping his eyes to the ground.

At her first words, Blackie felt drawn toward this Wise Woman almost as strongly as he was to the Princess. He smelled the hills and the forest in her, a life as sweet and comfortable as the one back home in the Nest.

The Princess nodded with approval. "At last, the first sign of respect since I've come to this place. So you're the healer here, the Wise Woman of this village. Well, tell me, what's with this 'dragonbait'?"

"Don't blame these people, my lady, please," begged the Wise Woman, waving toward the villagers. "Humble folks all, they led simple lives of plowing and planting until these Hellions showed up."

"Hellions!" Blackie nodded grimly at that word.

The Princess stamped her foot impatiently. "I've already seen the Hellions in the castle, but what in the world brings Hellions to Shrems? This place is nowhere. Why would Vile's butchers show up here?"

The Woman shrugged.

"We don't know, my lady. That makes it the more terrifying. It all started with a wedding at the castle. Someone in the train of Lord Pimple, the bridegroom, must have done something to bring them, for a band of Hellions took over the castle within weeks. That's when the dragon began flying in. That's when people began disappearing."

"My husband," cried a young woman, "my husband Jem. I haven't seen Jemmy since . . . since—"

She broke down weeping. The Woman stepped to her, put an arm over her shoulders as others cried out.

"Old Samwel and his boys—gone, gone!"

"And them girls gatherin' nuts out there!"

"When we asked about those people," said the Priest, hesitantly, "they . . . dragged us into the c-c-castle—me and . . . and Moot there."

He pointed at the woodchopper, who shuddered at the memory.

"They knocked us around and held us over the pit, that big hole they're digging—horrible! Then they . . . dragged us to Nabs."

Moot broke in.

"Nabs told us, me lady, he told us they'd leave us alone if we gave them bread and beer and three pigs a week. But any whisper 'o what's going on in there and they'd burn us out, burn the whole village and throw us all to the dragon."

"But what of Lord Shrems?" asked the Princess. "Didn't he fight them off when they first appeared?"

The men looked at the ground until the Wise Woman answered for them. "Lord Shrems disappeared, my lady, disappeared at the very beginning. We haven't seen him for eighteen months."

The Princess's jaw dropped at that.

"Eighteen months," she repeated slowly, "he was gone a year and a half and you said nothing? Your lord absent that long and you didn't report it to the Count? And you, Sir Priest, you didn't notify the Bishop?"

The Priest looked wretched, but Bunly the Baker spoke up.

"No, your ladyship, we learned something in that time. We found that we don't need a lord. We do better without him. No road work! No taxes! Everything we grow is our own—except for the pigs we give to the castle!"

The Princess gasped. Her face turned white. Her hands clenched to fists. Worried, Blackie moved close to her, touched her with his horn.

"Do better without your lord?" she shrieked. "Wickedness, wickedness! I hadn't expected anything this bad! This village must be burned indeed! I cannot believe, holy father, that you'd see heresy and rebellion in your parish and not run straight to your bishop! I'm shocked, shocked at all of you!"

The Priest dropped to his knees, sobbing. "B-but my l-lady, I pray about it!"

"All of you had better pray about it!" cried the Princess. "Pray on your knees for a week! I cannot stand here listening to this!"

She turned and stumbled toward the church, crying loudly, "Holy saints, angels above, please forgive these people! Send down mercy if it's possible!"

Blackie stepped after, staring in wonder as the villagers stumbled behind her, clinging together, groaning, beating their heads, and howling. The Princess stopped at the church door, unable to proceed. She turned, her face streaming with tears. She lifted her arms to the crowd.

"People, people, my dear people, you must be brought to your senses! Do better without your lord, you say? You do not do better! You do badly, very badly indeed! You're sheep without a shepherd, children without a mother. Look at this hand!"

She held up her gloveless hand, turned it to all sides. "Would my hand do better without its thumb?" She shook her head.

"Ridiculous question! Where would angels be without archangels, priests without bishops? Without our superiors looking after us, we're all slaves to vice and pride. We'd go to war over a clothespin if we didn't have order and degree. No prince, no peace—that's the way of the world. Why, look at me! Even I, a royal princess, must obey my mother and father, and if I ever marry—"

She stopped at that, swallowed, continued.

"So you see, for the sake of your eternal souls, you must obey your headman, who obeys the bailiff, who obeys the steward, who obeys Lord Shrems, who should have been reported at the first sign of his absence!"

She paused for a breath. "You must know that dutiful obedience brings peace and happiness, but there and there and there—" She pointed at nearby houses.

"What do I see? Hanging venison, the Baron's deer! And over there, a string of partridges! Look at that house—brand new wood! Someone's been cutting trees! These are crimes, crimes that get men hanged!"

The whole crowd was screeching by now, rocking back and forth in a storm of fear and remorse. The woman in orange wept, "I told Husband it was wrong! It couldn't last, it couldn't last!"

The weeping went on till Blackie got tired of the whole thing. He saw that the Princess had things in hand. He was thirsty. The crowd parted as he walked through them to the well.

Children gathered around him, petting his neck and sides. An older boy dropped the bucket inside and pulled up the rope with the bucket spilling cool water. Blackie took a long drink, watching the villagers wailing and weeping.

When the Princess thought it had gone on long enough, she held up her hand, shaking her head sorrowfully. "Dear people, dear people, how fortunate that I found you today. Your crimes are halted! I will lead you back to your duty."

She walked back through the weeping people and lifted the sobbing Priest to his feet. "Sir Priest, is this the way for a holy father to behave? Stop bellowing. Tell me exactly what happened when Lord Shrems disappeared!"

The Priest kept sobbing. He struck his chest and moaned, "My sins! My sins!"

The Princess turned to Bunly. She shook him by the arm. "I see that you were one of the ringleaders. Tell me what happened!"

Wiping tears from his eyes, Bunly stumbled over his words. He explained that no one had noticed when the Baron disappeared. It was harvest time. Everyone was busy in the fields. People assumed the Baron was off hunting or visiting the City. Then Moot, the woodchopper, decided that the Baron was gone for good.

"Yes!" cried Bunly. "It was Moot! Moot started it! He shot the first deer."

"Liar!" shouted Moot, drawing back a fist to strike Bunly. "Liar, I wasn't the first!"

"Quiet, fellow!" ordered the Princess, clapping her hands together. "Let Baker finish his story!"

When they realized that Lord Shrems was gone for good, the villagers stopped working in the Baron's fields. Then Moot started chopping trees and selling wood for building.

"But it was you that took over Baron's gardens!" accused Moot, poking Bunly. "It was you caught the fish in Baron's pond!"

Without taxes to pay or labor for the Baron, the village grew rich and shipped cartloads of produce to the river to sell on the barges. Men showed up from neighboring baronies to get work in the village. Bunly took on two apprentices.

"We planned to buy a Charter," Bunly explained. "We wanted to become a town ruling ourselves, so we started savin' money to bribe the Council."

"Oh," gasped the Princess, covering her ears, "you people are a showpiece, a very model of how wickedness works—one crime leading to another to another, down, down, down to darkest doom! No wonder Hellions appeared at your gates. Your actions invited the demons!"

"No, your ladyship," Bunly insisted, "it was the other way around. The Hellions appeared when Baron disappeared. We just took advantage of our freedom."

"Well, tell me about those villains," said the Princess, nodding her head in the direction of the castle. "What do they want?"

"We don't know. They stick to themselves, only come down to market once in awhile."

"Well, has anybody else visited the Castle since they came?"

"Only Six-Fingers the Brewer. He went up with a cartload of beer, but he never came out again. We've not seen hide nor tail of him, nor his donkey, neither. We never go near the Castle, now. The wives does the brewin' and gives the beer to Nabs when he comes to shop. Nabs brings a gang of bullyboys. They always come in groups, talk among themselves, buy what they wants—eggs, chickens, cheese—and they pay silver. Silver!"

Bunly reached in his purse, dug out a shiny sliver coin. "See that, me lady. Beautiful! I never thought I'd have a whole silver coin to myself." He kissed the coin and held it up to the sunlight.

"Let me see that coin!" demanded the Princess, holding out her hand.

"My coin?" groaned Bunly, jerking it back.

"Baker!" cried the Priest, "don't start trouble, now! For Heaven's sake, give the lady your coin!"

"Do I . . . do I get it back?" quavered Bunly.

The Princess snatched the coin. She looked at it in astonishment.

"This coin has Vile's face on it. Sacrilege! I must confiscate all such coins. Tell me, Moot, if that's your name. Where do they get this silver?"

Moot shrugged. "Must come in the wagons, black wagons with horses as dark as that unicorn there. They shows up every month or so. Comes at night, leaves by night, too, back to Vile or wherever they comes from. No one knows."

"Is that all? You hear nothing more from the Castle?"

"Oh, we hears plenty. Cries! Screams! That started as soon as the Hellions appeared. Then our cows and goats started disappearin', so we sharpened our spears and closed our gates. Now, we goes to the fields in groups and keeps everything under guard."

"But," Bunly insisted, "they always pay in silver!"

"If you ask me," snapped the Princess, "you'd be better off with honest coppers in your purse and your rightful lord in the castle."

She walked to Blackie and put a hand on his neck. "I see that I must carry your story to the Council. You, Baker, I'll take you with me. I need a witness to all these transgressions."

"Me?" cried Bunly. "Oh, no, the village needs me! Take Moot! He shot the first deer!"

"Not me!" shouted Moot, shoving Bunly. "You elected yourself headman! And it was you said we should capture the unicorn and sell him to the Hellions!"

"Capture the unicorn?" cried the Princess. "Crime after crime! Oh, you have much to answer for, but not just now. I'm hungry! Bring out your soup and sausages. I want a dinner, and I want it quickly!"

"Food, you want food?" asked Bunly, wiping his eyes.

"In twenty minutes," ordered the Princess. "I'm giving you twenty minutes to serve me a royal feast. With no lord to extend hospitality, you people have to do it. If you entertain me well enough, I'll reduce your punishment, though some crimes are hard to forgive. Watching your lord disappear without reporting it—that's surely earned every man in town a whipping."

Pale as a ghost, Bunly turned to the woman in orange. "Oh, Sarah, can you help me? Is it possible? Can you serve up a feast in twenty minutes?"

Sarah pushed him out of the way.

"Me lady," she said with heavy courtesy, "I'm wife to the Baker for all me sins. You want a feast, leave it to us. The women of the village will empty our cupboards and bring out our pots. You'll have hot stews, cold birds, smoked hams!"

"Excellent!" smiled the Princess. "That's the service I expect. But nothing criminal. No venison from the Baron's forest."

"No, never!" cried Sarah, turning to the crowd. "Wives and widows, you heard her. Bring your berries from the briars and beans from the vines. Bring whatever you got!"

Women ran in all directions.

"Don't forget wine!" shouted the Priest. "Wine for the Princess!"

"No wine for me!" called the Princess. "I drink water, only water on campaign."

"Water?" cried Bunly in amazement.

"Water," the Princess repeated, "it's my vow."

After watching the villagers bustle about, she turned to the Wise Woman. "Now, you, madam, I need to clean up. Do you have such a thing as soap?"

"Yes, my lady," smiled the Woman. "You just come home with me. I'll make you fresh as springtime."

The Princess looked at the Woman for a moment, then called to Blackie. "Let's go with this Wise Woman, Shadow. I'll clean up at her house, then we'll return for the feast."

CHAPTER NINE

Lost Horn

Blackie carried the Princess out the village gate after the Woman. They followed a lane past enclosed fields to the edge of the forest where they found a house with a thatched roof blooming with blossoms in a grove of trees. Flourishing gardens on both sides of the house sent up a smell that made Blackie's mouth water.

Smiling, the Woman pulled the door open for the Princess. "I'll heat water for you, my lady, so you can wash if you will while I clean your dress. Such pretty fabric to get all torn and stained."

"Do you have a hairbrush?" asked the Princess, sliding off Blackie. She stopped in the door to sniff. "Lovely smells, what is it?"

"Oh," said the Woman, "I was baking cookies when I heard the church bell. Are you hungry, my lady? The soup's hot in the kettle. I can give you fresh bread and berries, if you like."

"Well, I'd better save my appetite for the feast," said the Princess, entering, "but I can nibble a cookie or two. And give a handful to my unicorn."

"I like this place," said Blackie to himself, breathing in the odors. He was torn between entering for the cookies or running straight to the gardens. The Woman nodded to him, so he followed the Princess inside. A gray animal like an oversized dog rose from a carpet. It growled at him. The Woman clicked her tongue and the wolf pulled back under a table, watching with alert grey eyes.

Blackie looked around the room, clean and bright with sunlight pouring in the windows. He saw herbs hanging in bunches from the ceiling beside strands of onions and garlic. Bowls were stacked on counters and baskets in corners. A pot bubbled over the fireplace with spicy soup. Warm cookies spread on a towel on the table smelled of honey and nuts.

While the Princess peeked into pots on the shelf, Blackie ran to the Woman and nuzzled her apron with his nose. The wolf growled again as she placed a hand on Blackie's forehead and looked into his eyes.

"Damaged your horn, have you? Don't worry, young unicorn, that's natural at your age. You'll lose your baby horn soon. It'll drop right off. I'll rub some bone and muscle tonic around it to help the new horn grow in straight."

She began gathering the cookies, set a couple on a plate for the Princess, and placed the rest in a crock for Blackie. She set it on a low stool. He chomped with delight as the wolf stepped toward him, whining. Licking crumbs from his lips, Blackie thought of all the delicious food he'd eaten today. No wonder Unicorn had loved to travel when he was young. You don't find treats like this in the forest.

Meanwhile, the Princess had slipped out of her dress. The Woman examined the fabric before soaking it in a pungent cleanser.

"A stitch or two will make this good as new, my lady. I'll wash it and iron it dry. Here, smooth these lotions into your face. They'll clear up your complexion beautifully."

"Funny," said the Princess, looking at her arms. "An hour ago, I was covered with scratches. They seem to have gone away."

"Yes, my lady," said the Woman, smiling at Blackie, "they do that. May I suggest this rouge for your lips. It brightens your smile, and another of my specialties—"

She pulled the cork from an earthenware bottle on a shelf and took a sniff. "No, not quite ready. Sorry, my lady, this mixture needs to set another week. It's the heat, I suppose. Love potion has to be handled carefully."

"Love potion, really?" The Princess sniffed at the bottle. "Does it work?"

"Like magic, my lady."

The Woman bowed the Princess to a stool. She took up a hairbrush and began gently brushing the Princess's hair.

"About three years ago," she said, "I gave cookies steeped in potion to a young prince hunting a unicorn. I suspect they've changed his life."

"I wonder if they'd change Prince Vile," mused the Princess.

The Woman shuddered. "Oh, I wouldn't count on that, my lady. A demon like that responds only to poisons."

The Princess pulled around sharply. "So you've got poisons, do you, Wise Woman?"

"Oh, no, Princess," laughed the Woman, "not me. I deal with natural extracts, herbs and balms, salves and tonics. I can give you something to ease childbirth or sharpen your memory. Misery and death—I leave that to the dark sisters, or to lost souls like Prince Vile."

The Princess looked at her hair in a scrap of mirror. "It looks wonderful, Wise Woman, thank you very much. But tell me, what do you think those Hellions are doing inside Castle Shrems?"

The Wise Woman began threading a needle to repair the rips in the Princess's dress. "I'm afraid I can't answer that, my lady. Whatever they're doing, it involves digging. They've thrown up that pile of dirt you can see over the courtyard wall."

"A mystery," said the Princess with a sigh, "a mystery to explore, but no time to do it. Ninety days, I've only got ninety days left. Tomorrow, I return to the City to stir up the Emperor. He's got to do something fast."

Once his cookies were gone, Blackie pushed open the door with his horn. Outside, he ate his way through the long grass to the garden. There he found rows of tart and tangy herbs next to a patch of tender cabbage plants. He ate his way down the cabbages until the Princess and the Wise Woman came out.

The Princess looked prettier than ever, her lips bright, her skin glowing. Her dress seemed fresh again. A bag of tonics and lotions hung on a cord about her waist.

"Look what Blackie's into now," laughed the Wise Woman, "my poor cabbages!"

"Blackie," asked the Princess, startled, "is that his name? I call him 'Shadow.'"

"Shadow's a good name too."

The Wise Woman stood waving at the door as the Princess rode back to the village. Blackie sniffed her flowery new perfume as she raved about the Woman.

"What wisdom, what skill! Why, that Woman knows more about hair and complexions than any *estetista* in the City. Do you see my dress? Mended, cleaner and prettier than when Madame Mode designed it for me! And these shoes, look at my shoes, Blackie! Snakeskin! I've never had snakeskin shoes. The Elf-Queen herself would envy these shoes! Oh, wait till the ladies see them! They'll be all the fashion back in Court."

Blackie barely heard his Princess. His soul was full of the happiness of the last half-hour, a joy he'd remember the rest of his life. The cookies of the Woman— Oh, ho ho, those cookies! And the gardens, greener and tastier than any he'd ever seen! He couldn't imagine the Shrine itself having crunchier veggies than these. The very air about that cabin was sweet. The Woman herself, she seemed sent from Paradise to bring a trace of bliss into the world.

When she'd whispered to him that she knew Mama, he could only nod. Of course, she'd know Mama.

As Blackie carried his lady up to the row of tables in the village square, the humans looked with astonishment at the Princess, bright as a flower after the Woman's treatment. She smiled graciously, charming the clumsy villagers. They bowed and curtseyed as best they could, gesturing her to a rocking chair with clean cushions set on a quilt at the middle of the table.

Sarah, the baker's wife, spoke for the village.

"We've fixed up a throne for you, me lady. But first, Father Paul, our priest, asks wouldn't you like a short church service before the feast? He says we need a moment of repentin' and thanksgivin'."

"A good idea, Sarah," said the Princess, smiling, "a very good idea. I'm sure that we all have sins to repent—some more than others, perhaps. It's well that we pause for prayers. Please lead the way."

The church bell began dinging as Blackie carried the Princess across the marketplace behind Sarah and Bunly. The rest of the villagers crowded behind. The priest crept out the door of the church. He blinked at the sunlight and bowed to the Princess.

"Welcome, my lady, a thousand greetings to my humble chapel. Saints bless you and all the royal family!"

106

He rubbed his hands as they entered. "What an honor for us! Oh, the Bishop will hear of this! What a blessed day when your Majesty visits my church with the holy unicorn!"

"Well, Father Paul," said the Princess, holding her hand for him to kiss, "that's very good, I'm sure. I pray that the Bishop will be as understanding when he learns of your failure to report the disappearance of Lord Shrems. I suspect that he'll send the Archdeacon around for a little chat."

Father Paul's smile disappeared. Sweat popped out on his forehead. "Yes, yes, c-certainly, your Majesty, I . . . I can explain it."

The Princess gave a cool smile. "I'm sure that you can. Please hurry with this service. My luncheon is waiting on the table."

Father Paul jumped back with a swish of robes. "Oh, yes, yes, please enter, my lady."

The Princess tossed her head and walked into the dusky church. Blackie hesitated to follow, but the Priest urged him to follow.

"Please, holy unicorn, you too. It's a privilege to have the Lord's beast in my chapel."

Entering the dimness of the church, Blackie sniffed strong incense and the smells of generations of worshipping villagers. He walked through a shaft of light burning down from the high western window and stood by the Princess's chair before the altar. Murmuring villagers squeezed around, leaving a narrow aisle to the door for Cross and candle.

The Princess knelt as the procession passed. She rose, and the service began. Blackie listened to the Princess's voice in the songs that punctuated the kneelings and risings, the chants, the prayers, and Father Paul's sermon. The villagers sang heartily. Father Paul crowed like a rooster, his chest puffed out, eyes closed in his fervor.

Then the Cup was presented to the Princess. She took a sip. Father Paul hesitated, then offered the Cup to Blackie. Blackie smelled the sour wine, shook his head.

While the villagers straggled up to the priest for their wine, Blackie looked at the angels carved on the altar and the faded paintings on the walls. Finally, Father Peter declared the mass ended. He hurried to help the Princess to her feet. She gave her hand to the Priest to kiss.

"A privilege, Father Paul," she said graciously, "and a delight to receive the Cup from you. Would I could see such humble devotion at the Cathedral. I promise that I will speak to the Bishop. He'll be pleased to hear that you conduct a reverent Mass."

Father Paul wiped his brow with a smile of relief. "Oh, thank you, thank you, my lady. That should help a little, shouldn't it, with the disappearance and all?"

He bowed over and over till the small candle-bearer poked him in the side and handed up a battered book.

"Please, will my lady sign the church book?" begged Father Paul. "Such an honor! I always include the royal family in my prayers. From now on, I'll remember you, especially."

The Princess took the quill. Father Paul held out a small inkhorn as she inscribed her name in large letters.

Julianna, Feliae Caesar

"Hmm," she said, examining the pages of the book, "I see that Lady Shrems signed her name at Christmas and Easter up to, yes, eighteen months ago. Why did she sign so often? Are you collecting autographs?"

"Oh, no." Father Paul shook his bald head. "Lady Shrems likes to sign when she inspects the book for birth dates and marriages."

The boy passed a basket to Father Paul. The Priest took the basket. He looked hopefully at the Princess.

"Lady Shrems sometimes likes to leave something special, an extra gift if she approves the service. Would you, my lady?"

"Oh, I have no purse," said the Princess, grandly. "Coming alone like this, well—"

Father Paul's face fell.

"Oh, yes, of course. But your presence, my lady, that's the thing! Historic, it is, royalty setting foot in the church. We must get a carved plaque, wood or copper, if someone will donate it."

"Wonderful," said the Princess, passing back the quill, "well, now, perhaps the recessional? Everyone's waiting on us."

"Oh, yes, yes, my lady."

Father Paul uttered a swift blessing. Everyone began singing again. Father Peter bowed to the altar. He gestured to the Princess to follow the Cross in the procession. Blackie stepped behind the Princess as the boy in the corner began yanking at the bell cord. The ringing hurt Blackie's ears.

Blackie took two steps, twitching his ears. Suddenly, a thin man lurched out of the crowd on a crutch. He grabbed Blackie's horn.

"Heal me, heal me!"

The villagers roared a protest. The Princess turned in anger.

"What's this, fellow? Are you insane! Unhand that unicorn! This is church!"

Moot and Bunly jumped to pull the man away, but the man dropped the crutch to cling to the horn with both hands. He jerked Blackie's head back and forth, shouting, "Heal, heal!"

"Let go, Lame Alan!" screeched Father Paul. "Let go!"

Blackie twisted his head to free himself, pulling the man back and forth.

POP!

Blackie fell one way. Lame Alan fell the other, sprawling into the crowd which shoved the man back onto his good leg. Lame Alan stood for a moment, brandishing Blackie's twisted horn in his fist.

"I'm healed! I'm healed! It's a miracle!"

Dramatically, he threw up his arms and toppled over. Father Paul snatched the horn as he fell, kissed it, and set it in the alms basket.

"A holy relic for my church!"

Everyone was squawking. The Princess helped Blackie to his hooves, kissing his forehead.

"Oh, Blackie, you're hornless, now! Poor beast, does your head hurt?"

Blackie's head didn't hurt. It felt empty. He shook his forehead back and forth as the Princess dusted him off. She walked with him to the church door where the men had thrown Lame Alan out into the dirt.

"So sorry about that, Blackie," said the Princess. She pulled Blackie around the door stoop by his mane to kiss his forehead. "I'm sure that your horn will grow back like a deer's horn."

Blackie had known that he'd lose his baby horn. What an awkward time this was to lose it. He'd just met his Princess! How could he guard her without a horn?

Walking beside his Princess to the tables, Blackie looked back at the church door. Father Paul was standing outside in the sun. He held up the alms basket while the villagers lined up to touch the unicorn horn. Then the smell of the dinner drew Blackie's attention.

Stretching down the marketplace, the tables were piled with platters and bowls, pitchers and mugs. Boys, spaced every few feet to shoo off cats and birds, watched each new dish with eager eyes. Lame Alan hobbled to a bench at the end of the table that held the beer keg. He sat down and began telling his tale of the miracle.

"I tell you, I felt the spirit as soon as I touched that unicorn horn! It healed me through and through. Not leg-healed, of course, but healed in my soul, like I was Adam, running nekked through Paradise."

"None of that nasty talk, Lame Alan!" ordered Sarah, walking by with a vase of flowers to place before the Princess.

Lame Alan shook his head. He reached to fill his mug at the keg.

"No, ma'am, I don't mean nothing like that. I mean that when I touched that horn, I felt lighter than a feather, filled with Heaven's joys like a bubble in the Fountain up to the Shrine. I swear, if that horn hadn't broke off when it did, I'd have grown wings. You'd have seen me fly around that church singing the song of the angels."

"Well, you're no angel, Lame Alan! Stop swilling beer and stand up. The Princess hasn't set down yet!"

Blackie halted beside the quilt holding the throne. The women curtseyed to the Princess. Lame Alan took his mug and hobbled off to the well.

Standing erect behind her chair, the Princess looked hungrily at the steaming dishes of food. Blackie sniffed his own tray on the table beside the Princess. It was piled with barley, oats, and buckwheat, warm cakes, and a little heap of nutmeats from last fall's walnut trees.

"Oh, Papa," thought Blackie, "what a day, what a day!" He sniffed everything and took a bite of the nuts. "How right you are, Papa! Nuts are delicious."

He looked over to see the Princess still waiting while people squabbled for position at the benches. Women waved flies from the platters. Children snatched for chicken legs and got their hands smacked.

"All right, everyone!" called Sarah. "The feast is served!"

The people silenced. Bunly stalked up before the Princess's table and bowed low. He straightened with a pompous air.

"Since Bailiff has disappeared, Your Royalty, it falls on me to say a few words of welcome. Some might say that we stumbled a bit at our dooty, saints forgive us—"

He paused, throwing his eyes to Heaven, then looked back at the Princess.

"But, as you see, we do try our best to welcome you. Humble is our fare, yet well-baked. No spongy loaves from our ovens, no dried-out muffins. We're people of shop and soil, but from our hearts, we offers the works of our hands to your royal magnificence."

Bunly bowed. The Princess graciously inclined her head. The people applauded, and Bunly continued. "You've already met Father Paul, our priest, who lifted our spirits with his inspirin' service."

Bunly gestured grandly and the Priest bowed. Bunly answered the bow, straightened, pointed to Moot.

"At this time, it's my pleasure to reconize my fellow councilman, Moot the Woodchopper. Moot has some words of expression from the men of our village to inspire you of our loyalty and service."

Red-faced, Moot stepped out with the crossbow, which he had cleaned and recharged with a new bolt. He took a gulp of air and stammered.

"Madame P-P-Princess, your ladyship, I'm not much for t-talkin', but Bunly tells me I have to speak out for the village men. All I can say is that we p-promises to do better. No more shootin' deer and cuttin' trees—though they's goin' to waste with the Baron missin'. I'm sorry we attacked your unicorn last spring. We wouldn't 'a done it if Baker hadn't—"

Bunly broke in with a cry.

"Hold up, Moot! 'Nough said, 'nough said! All you has to do is tell her that she's welcome!"

"You're welcome, me lady," gasped Moot. He shut his mouth and backed away to hide himself in the crowd. Bunly turned to the women, squeezed along the left side of the table.

"And next," he continued with a wave of his arm, "'tis my honor to prescribe the women of the village, these livin' angels who cook our meals and nurse our babes. Speakin' for the fair sex, I give you Sarah, my wife. She cooked up the pork fritters in that brown dish over there—that dish, yeah, that one, hold it up."

Solemnly, Sarah held up the brown dish, turning it for everyone to see, as Bunly droned on. "We can't never forget what we owe to the ladies. Without them, life would be—"

"Yes, yes, Husband," Sarah put in, setting down the dish with a thump, "thank you, thank you."

She curtseyed deeply, drew herself up, and smiled upon the Princess. "Princess, dear Princess, your Majesty— As Husband says, I been asked to speak for the village women who cooked this meal that's gettin' cold while the men yammers away. We wishes health to you and yours, especially your mother and your father and any sisters or brothers you may have. Also, the blessin's of peace and holy forgiveness to one and all. May you enjoy your feast and take away good memories of our village. That's what I has to say."

She curtseyed again and folded her hands. Everyone looked at the Princess, who nodded briskly at Sarah.

"I thank you, Dame Sarah, for this warm greeting and thank all the women of the village for this lovely food. You, Master Bunly and Goodman Moot, I thank you both for this warm welcome. Father Paul, please say the blessing."

She bowed her head as the Priest started slowly praying. He gained speed as he spread blessings over the fields and crops, the pigs and chickens, the friends gathered here and the friends far away, the sick and the dying, Baron Shrems and his family, wherever they are, and the clergy of the Church, especially, the Bishop, which he had been thinking to notify about the missing baron. Slowing down again, he prayed Heavenly blessings on the Emperor and Empress in the far-off City, so filled with mercy to the poor of the land that he was sure they would forgive any inadvertent misdemeanors his flock may have committed.

He slowed even more on his final words. "And, lastly, dear Lord, bless this royal princess. We will pray for her forever and for this holy unicorn. Dark his hide, but noble his spirit, so good, so heroic."

As soon as he sang "Amen," everyone looked at the Princess. She straightened. She nodded to Father Paul.

"Many thanks, Sir Priest, a lovely benediction. No more ceremony, please! Everyone, I give you permission! Sit, eat!"

She dropped in her chair and reached for a pickled egg. The women moved in with their platters, Sarah first with her fritters. The Princess took a fritter and dipped it in sauce. Other women crowded around with their ham, bacon, chicken, and rabbit. The Princess refused a strange pinkish meat someone said was mole, but took small servings of blackbird pie, pigeon fricassee, and squirrel stew.

To sample as many dishes as quickly as possible, the Princess used a wooden spoon and a tray. When the women saw this, they ran to their homes for their own trays, but the men complained that the trays took up too much room on the tables. The trays wound up piled on the ground off to the side with dogs licking them.

Blackie chomped through his grain and nuts, then turned to salad, a huge bowl of greens with strong onions and biting red radishes, and, finally, to the cakes, spicy and nutty, warm from Bunly's ovens. The cakes weren't as good as the Wise Woman's cookies, but Blackie licked them right off the serving platter. He ignored the sad eyes of children who followed his mouth as he swallowed cake after cake. He finished them all, except for two cakes the Princess snatched for her tray. The Priest absently reached for a cake, but the Princess pushed his hand away.

"For the unicorn, Father Paul. Losing his horn like that—"

"Oh, yes, dear lady! Anything for the h-holy unicorn! I didn't mean—"

"Of course not, Sir Priest," said the Princess in a sweet tone. "Have some of these pears. I've never tasted pears this early in the season. They're delicious."

"Them pears is stewed by Barbara, over there in the checkered scarf," explained Sarah, hovering over the Princess. "She knows the secret of dryin' last fall's fruit. I've tried it, me lady, but my pears don't hold their flavor like Barbara's."

When he couldn't squeeze in one more bite, Blackie staggered to the well for fresh water. The children followed to pet him and touch the spot on his forehead where his horn had hung.

A thin girl stood outside of the group. She cried above the other voices, "Unicorn, will you help my grandma? She lies in the corner of our house. The Wise Woman says her herbs can't help Grandma anymore. Grandma's gone mortal, she says."

Blackie shrugged. Stuffed with dinner, he felt generous. He pushed over to the girl and nudged her with his nose.

The girl jumped with delight. "You'll come? You'll come heal Grandma?"

The girl led Blackie into a dark, smelly hut where Grandma lay twitching in a corner.

"Grandma," whispered the girl, hugging the old woman. "Grandma, here's the unicorn come to heal you."

Grandma woke up, coughing. "What's that? What's that?"

"The unicorn, Grandma," repeated the girl. "He's here to heal you."

"What, what, heal me?" coughed the old woman, rolling over to look up. "Dear me. Saint Helen, bless us all."

Holding his breath, Blackie leaned down to touch Grandma with his forehead. Nothing happened, no spark from his skin. He touched her again, concentrating. Nothing happened.

He backed off, sadly shaking his head. He couldn't heal. He'd lost his gift with his horn, but Grandma was feebly smiling.

"I . . . I do feel better, I do. The holy beast— Oh, that I'd live to see a unicorn! Grandpa, he'll be . . . flab-flabbergasted. I'll tell him . . . when . . . when I meet him up above."

Back in the bright square, Blackie noticed for the first time how many humans were scarred or bent, wrapped in bandages, propped on canes. They lay in doorways or hobbled around the table, helping the women clear away the dirty dishes while the Princess snoozed in her chair.

Blackie wandered up to Lame Alan sitting in the sun at the well. Blackie drank from the bucket while Lame Alan paused in his story of the vision of the horn.

"He healed her! He healed her!" shouted the children. "The unicorn healed Eva's Grandma!"

"'Of course, he did, me bareheaded friend here!" Lame Alan lifted his beer mug in salute. "I won't be forgetting that touch of his horn! It had a spark to it! Did I tell you what I felt when I touched it?"

By now, Lame Alan's tale had expanded until he described his soul being carried by angels at the touch of the horn. He soared through the air until he saw Saint Peter waiting before the Golden Gates to greet new arrivals. Saint Peter waved his keys at Lame Alan, stopping him at the door.

Lame Alan took a pull on his beer mug. He sighed and picked up his tale again. "The Gatekeeper shook his head to me, 'Alan, my boy—'"

Lame Alan broke off, nodding to his listeners. "That's the way the good Saint talks, familar-like, in his deep, deep voice.

"'Alan, Alan,' he says, shaking his head. 'What you doing up here, man? You're here too soon! You know, it's not your day yet. I got to send you back down. Unicorn or no unicorn, your job is to wander the earth reminding folks to love their neighbors. You're to tell 'em that what they gives to the poor down there earns 'em blessings up here. And, Alan, you're as poor as anyone, so what they gives to you—You tell 'em this! When someone gives you a pork chop, say, or a pot of beer, or even a couple of coppers, that person gets a ticket to Heaven, gets 'em inside these gates.'

"At that, the good Saint gave them golden gates a shake. He reached down his great keys and swept me off the cloud. I fell squealing till the angels spread their wings and flew after me. I looked back as they carried me down again and heard Father Peter hollering after me.

"'Remember, Alan, when your day does come, you report all the names to me! Bring 'em up! Bring 'em up, all them that opens their hand to you, the big-hearted, the givers, the gen'rous. I'll write their names in the Book of Life and throw the Gates open for one and all.'"

Some of the children started running around, waving their arms like wings and yelling, "Bring 'em up! Bring 'em up!"

"So I'm setting here and taking names." Lame Alan peered around the village, as Blackie took another drink. "They don't know it, but I'm a spy for the Saint. Bunly over there, does he toss me a loaf of bread or a doughnut? And Old Willa, does she sew up my shirt when I ask her? It's up to each one of 'em to earn their way into that Golden Book."

"Some of 'em—" Lame Alan shook his head, sadly. "I fear for some of 'em. The Innkeeper, I can't say that he ever unlocked the door on a frosty night and called out, 'Ho, friend Alan, you mustn't sleep in the cold doorway like this! Come in! Come in! There's room for you in the corner next to the fire. We got little left to eat tonight, but here's a big bowl of chicken necks!'"

"Oh, Lame Alan," scoffed a boy, spitting on the ground, "here you go tellin' lies. How'd you have time to get to Heaven and all that? You didn't hold to that horn no more than half a minute!"

115

Lame Alan regarded the boy with amazement.

"Why, young Hamen, how you talk! Don't you know that time stretches out in the world of the spirits? I can't tell you everything I saw in that half-minute. The angels flew up with their bright wings while the happy souls ran through the Gates, singing and jumping. The others crept away weeping. All the things I saw in that short time would amaze you."

"You think that'd amaze us!" said a woman, walking through the children to pet Blackie. "What'd truly amaze us, Lame Alan, is if we ever saw you turn your hand to do a little weedin' or hoein' to earn your keep. When I see you laborin' for your bread, then I'll know the end of the world is on us. Sure, you're crippled up a little, but they's plenty of jobs you could do. You're no better nor a Gypsy, settin' around tellin' lies like this."

When she walked away, Blackie heard Lame Alan lean down to whisper to the children. "There's one gets a bad report. Her name's blotted out of Saint Peter's Book forever."

CHAPTER TEN

The Princess Departs

Whisking away flies with his tail, Blackie stood over the Princess. She snored in her chair while Bunly darted from one end of the table to the other, hushing the humans removing the dirty dishes.

"Quiet, everyone, quiet! The lady sleeps."

The hush was unnatural, a hundred people tiptoeing around, whispering to each other while watching the Princess sleep. A fierce hiss met each nervous cough.

"Shhh! Shhh! Let 'er sleep!"

The Princess started. She opened her eyes. She yawned. The villagers backed away as she collected herself and straightened in her chair, rubbing her eyes. She glanced around for Blackie.

Blackie put his nose on her shoulder. She smiled up at him as Bunly began bobbing up and down in a pompous bow. He went into another speech as the Princess focused her eyes on him.

"Now that you're rested, dear Princess, you'll be ready for your entertainment. We know that you're used to pageants and parades. Back with the fine folk in the City, you got gleemen and minstrels, jugglers and such. We can't match that, o' course. All we has to offer is our rustic pastimes, the jig at harvest, the tale by the hearth. But we won't have it said that we didn't entertain you as best we can. First on the program—"

"No, no!" cried the Princess, jumping up. "No program, please! The sun's sinking in the west. I must leave for the camp before dark."

"But the program, Princess!" wailed Bunly. "You don't know what you're missin'! My song about King Mark and the maiden, and the educated goat that counts to up nine with its left front foot. That goat's been featured at fairs in three baronies! And we got Lame Alan's tale of the giant's hand that got chopped-off at the wrist and walks around on its fingers. Father Paul's choir will sing for you with pot lid and spoon accompnerment. You won't want to miss that!"

The Princess swept crumbs from her skirt and straightened her hat. "Oh, I know that I'm missing wonders, but it's impossible for me to stay. I must leave at once. I do want to thank everyone for this lovely picnic, especially Dame Sarah and the women. I'll not forget your feast, those fritters and that pink mole meat."

She shuddered.

"Oh, me lady," begged Bunly, "twenty minutes more, just twenty minutes! We want to do something for you. At least, give a look at the goat, please! I garantee you'll marvel at the goat!"

"No time, no time!" cried the Princess. She rounded her chair to Blackie, but he was frozen, his ears high. From the road outside the village, he heard hoofbeats. A blatting horn alerted everyone to riders.

The villagers cried out and ran in all directions. The Princess shouted, "Every man get his spear! Moot, my crossbow!"

The villagers vanished into church and homes as the sound of hooves grew louder with whoops and the jangle of chains. In a moment, the square was empty, except for Blackie and the Princess and the clucking chickens.

The Princess picked up the heavy crossbow from the mud where Moot had dropped it. She looked ruefully at Blackie's empty forehead.

"Well, so much for organizing a defense."

Blackie stood by the Princess, stepping nervously from hoof to hoof. His forehead felt naked as dogs ran up the street, barking at a string of riders galloping into the marketplace. Prince George rode at the lead with Jessica just behind, rising in her stirrups and waving.

"My lady, my lady, we've found you!"

In a moment, the Knights and Guards were tying sweaty horses around the beer keg at the end of the table. Blackie watched the horses with interest.

"At last," cried the Princess, tossing the crossbow onto the table, "you finally show up! Where've you been all day, Prince George?"

"Where've I been?" squealed the Prince, resentfully, jumping to earth. "Where haven't I been?"

"My lady," bellowed Sir Otley, pulling his dusty charger up to the table, "we rode from Hinch to Toll in four hours! I broke ten horses and a saddle strap lookin' for you. Every trooper in the country's out searchin' for you. The Empress is sick with worry back at the Castle, and the price of wine has doubled since you disappeared!"

"You didn't need to worry about me!" exclaimed the Princess. "I was protected by my unicorn, but you're just in time to escort me back to camp. These people have told me alarming news. Did you know that Lord Shrems is missing? His castle is filled with Hellions."

"And a dragon!" added Bunly, who'd reappeared as soon as he saw the riders were friendly.

"Hellions!" cried the Prince, clapping his hand to his sword. "What are they doing here?"

"First things first!" roared Sir Otley, looking up and down the table. "I need two good men to help me down! Is there any wine in this place?"

As the Princess explained about the castle, Blackie walked over to sniff the horses, keeping his ears back in a friendly gesture. He remembered what Unicorn had told him about horses.

"Smartest creatures you'll find, but don't have sense enough to enjoy their lives. Always ruled by humans. Born slaves, they are, born slaves."

Prince George's old warhorse stood shivering, eyeing Blackie as it tried to catch its breath.

"So you ran into Hellions!" scolded the Prince. "Oh, Princess, my lady, how could you run off at a time like this? You knew we'd be frantic. And Vile sending that hawk after you! We were sure you'd be torn down and carried off! Anything could happen to you alone in the forest!"

"I was not alone," said the Princess, coldly. "I was perfectly safe with my unicorn."

"I told them you'd be fine." Jessica hugged the Princess, then pulled back to inspect her. "You look beautiful, my lady, and your hair—What happened to your hat?"

The Princess touched a hand to her hair.

"Oh, Jessie, I met a wonderful woman, the Wise Woman of this village. I'll tell you about her later. She gave me these shoes."

"Well, young unicorn," drawled the horse, touching his nose to Blackie, "what happened to your horn? They take you to the vet, get you trimmed down? You gotta watch them buzzards. They'll take more than your horn."

Another horse nosed a blade of scrappy grass pushing through the mud. "Anything to eat around here? Any hay, any clover?"

Back at the table, the Princess was giving orders. "No time to talk, no time to drink. I must ride back to camp!"

"What camp?" exclaimed Sir Otley. "They broke up camp, m' lady, soon as you disappeared! The Court's headed down to Riverton. They're takin' the barges to the City tomorrow."

The Princess's eyes blazed. "They didn't wait for me?"

"My lady," said Jessica, taking her hand, "the threats, the demands. You know Prince Vile. After you escaped, he came shrieking out of the forest yelling at everyone! 'Where's my dragon!' he shouted. 'I'll burn you all! I'll blast you! I'll torch the world! I'll kill everyone!'"

"And they expect me to marry this?" The Princess shook her head. "Not for a mountain of silver! Well, mount up, everyone! Let's ride to Riverton."

"Sorry, my lady." Prince George looked down, kicking mud off a boot. "Can't ride till we rest the horses. They've run all afternoon looking for you. We wanted to find you before anyone else. Prince Vile put a price on your head, two hundred pieces of silver to anyone who brings him his bride."

"Only two hundred for me?" exclaimed the Princess, resting her hand on her dagger. "Is that all? I always knew he was cheap, the mingy thing. Sir Otley, mount up the men. Tired horses or not, I'm ready to ride!"

"What's wringin' her withers?" asked the old horse beside Blackie, looking up from the water bucket. "Don't she know we been runnin' all day? I'm sweatin' like a bumblebee in the rain."

The Guards trooped back to Sir Otley bearing beer kegs on their shoulders.

"Found 'em in the bakery!" shouted one.

"Under the donkey's straw," added another.

"Well, that's done it," said the horse. "Once they gets to drinkin', you can kick off your saddle for the evening."

"Oh, that thing," said Blackie, sniffing the horse's saddle. "I wish you would kick it off. I want to look at it."

"Yeah, kick it off, Steed," said another horse. "We want to see you do it again."

"You don't think I can do it?" said Steed. "Just watch this."

The old horse began sucking in his belly and wriggling his flanks. He reared and shook himself. Somehow, the saddle shook free and slipped over his rump. Steed kicked it away with a hoof.

"Ever see that before?" asked a brown horse, watching with interest. "Anyone can shed a saddle if you're strapped loose. Steed's the only one can do it with a proper cinch."

"That's 'cause I don't do it often," said Steed. He slapped a fly with his tail. "Let the humans know you can drop your saddle whenever you want, they'll cinch you till you can't breathe. That spoils the whole business. You got to use strategy!"

"I wouldn't let them put the thing on me in the first place," declared Blackie. "Why do you do it, you horses? Look at the harness, all those straps and buckles! Why do you horses put up with it?"

"Oh, we run off, now and then," said one of the younger horses, looking away, "but I don't know, seems there's—"

"There's no place to go!" snorted Steed. "Runnin's always good at first. You find new places to smell, new stuff to eat. Then a human sees you and they start chasing you."

"If they chased me—" Blackie stamped a hoof. "I'd just lose them in the forest."

"The forest!" scoffed Steed. "Who wants the forest? No hay to be found there! No oats, no baths, no rubdowns!"

"I don't like the trees," said the young horse. "You can't see to run. Only things in the forest is bugs and briers. Nothing to eat but tree leaves."

"Why, I eat tree leaves," said Blackie, "lots of them. And there's grasses and blossoms and wild grapes and mushrooms. Plenty to eat in the forest."

"I'll agree," said Steed, wisely, "the forest is better than the desert. You should see the ponies out west, scrawny creatures with legs worn down to stubs. They eat stuff you wouldn't walk on, spines and thorns that scar up their mouths till they look like pigs. And dumb, they don't know oats from thistle seeds."

"Well, I wouldn't stay in a place like that!" exclaimed Blackie. "When Prince George caught my Papa, they took him up to the mountains of Darr. The humans made him fight goats and pull chariots, so he ran away."

"You talkin' about old Unicorn?" Steed sniffed the bark of the tree reaching over the well. "I knew that beast up there. Laziest mount in the stable! If the humans took him out for a run, you'd never hear the end of it. Complain, complain, complain! And that Princess you hang around with, she was up there too. You better get away from her before she makes you fight goats."

"No, no," Blackie shook his head, "not my Princess, she wouldn't do that to me. She's wonderful. She just wants the best for everyone. Have you ever smelled anything like her?"

"Haw, haw!" chuckled Steed. "She's got you under her spell! I seen it before. Did she give you cookies? That's what did it to your sire. It was the Prince passin' around the cookies that time. Even gave 'em to a chicken named Junior. That rooster took to chasin' after her like a lapdog. Most unnatural thing you ever saw. A wonder he didn't end up in the pot."

"Here comes the hay wagon," said a horse.

"At last," said Steed, swishing his tail.

A Guard hustled up a couple villagers wheeling a cartload of fresh hay to the well. They tossed out the hay by armfuls and spread it on the ground for the horses.

"This is a start," said Steed, catching up a mouthful. He chewed and swallowed. "Throw in a bag o' grain, and I'll be ready to trot. After a three hour nap, o' course."

Blackie yawned, looking over at the Princess.

"All right, Georgie, you win," she said, shrugging her shoulders. "I'll give you an hour to rest the horses, then I'm heading off, guards or no guards. Anyone not ready to ride gets left behind. It'll be midnight, anyway, before we reach Riverton."

By now, Bunly was shooing the villagers from their hiding places, assuring them that the riders wouldn't hurt them.

"They're not Hellions," he insisted. "Sooner we feed 'em, sooner they'll be out of here. Bring your leftovers from the feast, more fodder for the horses."

Blackie told the horses that the men were bringing more hay.

"So you understand their speech," said Steed. "That's good. If you can talk to them, unicorn, tell 'em we want oats, too, and apples if they got 'em."

"Well, I can't really talk to them," said Blackie, sniffing the hay. "I know what they say to each other, but—"

More and more villagers crept out, looking suspiciously at the Guards. The women carried their half-empty bowls and platters back to the table.

"Oh, we need more than that for all these men!" cried Sarah, running up and down the table. "My fritters was ate up, but the rest of you— Jenny, Jenny, you had all that whatever-it-was left over! Bring that out, and bread, husband, more bread!"

The Princess turned away in disgust. "So now, they start eating. Come on, Jessica. Did you bring my make-up case?"

"Of course, my lady."

Jessica held up a leather case.

"Good. Grab a chicken leg and meet me at the church for repair work."

Jessica smiled at the Princess. "Don't worry, my lady. We'll fix you up on no time. Your complexion's beautiful today, glowing, and those shoes are fantastic!"

The Princess ran her hands over her hair.

"Well, it's good you showed up when you did, Jessie. Mama would have died of shame if she'd seen me before I met that Wise Woman. The Woman's got the secret of complexions. And these snakeskin shoes, they'll set the fashion for the Court ladies!"

"Lovely my lady!" cried Jessica. "Just lovely."

The Princess clapped her hands. "Hurry, Jessica, let's get to work! We leave in an hour!"

Blackie watched the ladies hurry to the church. He turned back to the hay.

When the Princess came out again, she had changed into a pretty green dress with a new hat and gloves. She still wore the snakeskin shoes. Her hair was brushed, her face clean, and she moved differently,

123

more restrained and formal. When Blackie ran to her, he smelled a fresh perfume. It was pretty, but too strong. It covered her own sweet smell.

She was just as bossy, though, calling to an old knight leaning against the table, "I don't believe for a minute you rode as far as Sir Otley claims. Sir Frederick, how far did you actually ride today?"

The knight pulled at his skimpy beard. "Oh, we covered ground, m'lady. 'Course, Sir Otley ordered a long break at the inn, and we did stop off at the wine shed near Scade. That's where I got my nap. Prince George was frantic to ride on, but Sir Otley insisted on a break. He claimed that you can take care of yourself."

"O' course, you can take care o' yourself!" roared Sir Otley, lumbering up with a handful of yellow flowers. "Didn't I train you myself?"

He bowed low to present the flowers. "My lady."

"Well, I don't want to be critical," said the Princess, smelling the flowers, "but it sounds like you did more drinking than riding."

Sir Otley lowered himself onto a bench at the table. He wiped his forehead.

"So I had a cup or two at that inn! Just wettin' my brain. You know my motto—'Can't fight without thinkin'; can't think without drinkin'!' It's military discipline! Besides, I was waitin' for news o' you, field intelligence. We'd 'a ridden ourselves down to skin and bones scourin' the country without intelligence."

"No chance of you riding yourself thin!" hooted Sir Frederick.

"Enough o' that, Knight!" shouted Sir Otley, slamming down his cup. "You go change the sentry at the gate and send a squad to hunt down more wine. This cask's dry!"

"Don't worry about wine!" snapped the Princess. "It's time to ride. Where's the Prince? I've got orders for him. And bring up Midnight. I'm switching to the horse."

Blackie tensed up, frowning from jealousy.

"Midnight!" he thought. "What does she want with a horse? I'm rested. I'm ready to run. After a feed like that, I can trot all night. I'm not letting that Midnight get near her."

The Princess turned as Prince George ran across the marketplace, sword in one hand, bowl of cakes in the other. He tossed the sword onto the table and bowed deeply.

"Fresh cakes, my lady, right out of the Baker's oven!"

"Bag them up," ordered the Princess. "We'll save them for later. It's time to ride, Prince. Are you ready for orders?"

Prince George bowed again. "I'm always ready for orders, my lady."

Blackie sniffed the warm cakes, watching suspiciously as a Guard led up a slim mare with a silver saddle. She was almost as dark as Blackie. She pranced up to the Princess, glaring defiantly at him.

"Well, pay attention," said the Princess. "We leave for Riverton, now. If the horses can make it, we'll stay at the castle tonight. But you, George, you and Blackie, I want you stay behind."

Blackie whipped his head around, dismayed. "What? She's leaving me behind?"

The Prince was protesting as well. "My lady, my lady, you know that Prince Vile's after you. You could run into an ambush without me!"

The Princess stiffened.

"Nonsense, Prince, I can look after myself! I have Sir Otley and the Guards. It's you that's going into danger. I'm giving you a perilous task and leaving Blackie to get you through it."

"This unicorn, Blackie?" said the Prince with scorn. "How can he look after anyone? He doesn't even have a horn."

"He doesn't need a horn!" snapped the Princess. "He's smart! If you do your job properly, he'll get you through it and bring you back to me."

The Prince sighed, hiking up his sword belt. "So what's this dangerous job you're giving me?"

The Princess whirled to Sir Otley. "Move everyone back, Knight. Give me room. I would speak privately to the Prince."

Sir Otley took a deep breath and roared, "Move your tails, people! Back off thirty paces! Give Her Majesty some breathing space!"

The Princess beckoned to Blackie and the Prince. "Come closer, Georgie. You, too, Blackie. No one must hear this."

Blackie leaned his head down, sniffing the Princess while she hugged him. Prince George knelt beside them, giving Blackie a sour look.

The Princess glanced around, whispering, "This is a critical task I'm giving you. I'd do it myself if I were free, but everyone's watching me. It could be days before I have another chance to escape by myself."

"So what's this serious job? What do I have to do?" demanded Prince George.

The Princess whispered even lower, "I want you to search Castle Shrems."

The Prince drew back. "What? Search what?"

"You know, Georgie." The Princess pointed. "Up there, that castle up the lane."

"But, my lady," protested the Prince, "you said the castle's full of Hellions."

"It is full of Hellions!" The Princess's eyes lit up. "Dozens of them! That's where I got the crossbow. But ask yourself, Georgie, what are Hellions doing here in Shrems, this little backwater? A crew like that, and they're restraining themselves, holding back. You ever hear of Hellions that weren't out burning and raiding and stealing pigs? There's a mystery here. Vile's up to something, and I want to know what it is."

Prince George shifted to his other knee.

"But Princess, this is nothing new. You know that Vile's bribing lords all over the Empire. They say, he's got troops at Mandor and Sloot and Mount Kurzon."

"Of course, I know that!" said the Princess, her voice rising. "But think, Georgie, think! Those are strategic points. They command rivers and roads. He has military reasons to send Hellions there, but there's no reason I can think of to station troops in Shrems—except for the digging."

"Digging?"

"Sure, just look at the castle, that dirt heap sticking up over the wall. The villagers tell me that the Hellions have taken prisoners. It sounds to me like they've got them digging in there, and I want to know why."

"Maybe it's a tunnel," suggested the Prince. "A secret tunnel to somewhere, maybe back to Vile."

"A tunnel to Vile!" repeated the Princess, scornfully. "A four hundred mile tunnel! Get serious! I want you to sneak in there and scout it out for me. Report back to me at Riverton. For now, though—"

She jumped up, called to Sir Otley. "Gather the men, Captain! Time to go."

"Yes, m'lady." Sir Otley pushed heavily to his feet. "Sergeant Grizzly, assemble the troops!"

The brawny Sergeant jumped to attention. "Humber, your bugle!" he shouted. When the bugler blew 'Assembly,' the men staggered up from all directions, emptying their beer mugs.

"Form up, men, form up!" bellowed Grizzly. "Stand to attention! Corporals, take a head count! Roust out the stragglers!"

The Princess nodded her head with satisfaction. She threw her arms around Blackie's neck. She rested her cheek against his ear.

"You be careful, sweet unicorn. Come to me as soon as you can. I wouldn't leave you behind, but you know your way through the forest. Prince George would get himself lost, and we don't have time to waste. When I see you again, we'll leave for the City. I want you to stay with me until the Contract runs out. You'll graze in the garden at our castle, and I'll show you everything."

Blackie watched sadly as the Princess said goodbye to Sarah and the Priest. She paused, looking from Bunly to Moot, standing there with the crossbow. She turned briskly to Grizzly.

"Sergeant, you're always looking for recruits. Here's a sturdy fellow for you, a crossbowman." She pointed at Moot.

"Oh, no!" Moot staggered back.

"Stand still, soldier!" roared Grizzly.

Moot stiffened. Grizzly walked around him, thumped him on the back.

"Crossbowman, eh? Well, we can use a few of them. You look like you can take a blow. Can you ride, soldier?"

"No, sir," Moot replied sullenly. "Never been on a horse in me life."

"Only one way to start. You go along with the corporal, there. He'll give you a mount and show you your place in formation. Make sure you keep up with the troops if you don't want to kiss the cudgel."

Moot threw himself to his knees before the Princess. "Please, me lady, don't make me a soldier!"

"You're enlisted now," she said. "I want to hear that you serve bravely."

The soldiers dragged Moot off, and the Princess turned to Bunly.

"You can thank goodwife Sarah, that I'm not sending you off with the troops as well, Baker. See that you listen to your wife in the future.

Stick to your ovens and stay out of trouble. If you keep the village safe, you may be forgiven when your lord returns."

Bunly cried out, gratefully, "Oh, my lady, I . . . I—"

The Princess stopped him with a hand. "That's enough! You know your duty."

She waved to the villagers. "Goodbye, everyone! I thank all the good women that served me. I'll remember your feast. I'll have prayers said for you at the Cathedral and do what I can to recover your lord!"

She looked around. Midnight whinnied for attention. Blackie frowned at her as the Princess gave him a last hug, then Prince George helped his lady onto the horse.

"Farewell, Prince," she called. "Take care of my unicorn."

Silently, Prince George saluted with his sword as the Princess wiped back a stray lock of hair on her forehead. She waved to the villagers and rode out the village gate ahead of Jessica and the Guards.

Blackie watched beside Prince George till his Princess was out of sight, then the Prince threw himself into her rocking chair. He frowned up at Blackie.

"So, Unicorn, she leaves me behind as usual. I knew it. She gives me every rotten job she can find. Now, it's a castle full of Hellions."

Blackie shook himself. "She's gone," he thought to himself, "and I'm left with this Prince. How'd I get myself into this?"

The Prince kicked the table.

"A hornless unicorn! I blame you, unicorn! It's your fault! If you hadn't knocked Vile down, I'd be riding with the Guards instead of staying behind to deal with a castle full of Hellions. I have as much chance of escaping that as I have of killing the dragon. Why'd you show up in the first place? Why didn't you leave me in peace?"

CHAPTER ELEVEN

Dragonfire

"Sooo, unicorn," yawned the Prince, rocking back in the Princess's throne, sword in his lap, boots on the table, "we've got a wait ahead of us. We'd better sleep while we can. Sir Otley says you never begin night action till after midnight."

Blackie brushed off flies as the village women crept up to remove the dishes for the second time. He turned toward Steed, licking up scattered wisps of hay in the street as Sarah warned the women to be quiet.

"Hush, now, goodwives, don't bother the lord. Let him sleep."

"No, no!" cried the Prince, toppling back in the chair. Blackie jerked around to see the man rock to his feet. He sheathed his sword with a snap.

"What am I thinking? We're wasting time! Come, unicorn, I want to visit someone."

Prince George strode past Blackie to the horse.

"Your saddle!" he exclaimed. "Who took off your saddle?"

"Anything wrong, me lord, anything wrong?" asked Bunly, running over with arms flapping. "Do these women disturb you? I'll run 'em off while you rest."

Without answering, Prince George grasped the saddle and lifted it to the horse. Blackie watched him buckle the straps, inspect them, and pull up on Steed. Blackie heard the saddle creak with his weight. The helmet, hanging to the side, clanked against the shield as Blackie followed to the village gate.

Bunly trotted behind. "Must you leave, me lord? We can bring more food!"

The children ran up calling good-bye to Blackie. A guard pulled the gate open for the Prince. The rest of the villagers watched silently. Only Bunly followed out into the road.

"I hope, me lord, you was happy with our service. We pray you'll put in a good word with that Princess."

Waving a hand, the Prince urged Steed into a trot. Bunly stopped after a few paces. He squealed after them, "It wasn't our fault . . . them Hellions . . . Lord Shrems!"

Blackie trotted behind, watching Prince George turn Steed into the lane around the village fence.

"Of course," Blackie thought, "the Wise Woman. This Prince knows where he's going."

The horse was certainly interested in the route. He swung his head back and forth in the bushy lane and slowed to sniff the gardens beside the Woman's house. Cawing, a crow flew up from the thatched roof as the door opened and the wolf leaped out. That stopped Steed so suddenly that Prince George lurched forward, almost tumbling off.

"Welcome, my lord," called the Wise Woman, appearing in the doorway. "I wondered if you'd call on me."

"Of course, I came as soon as I could," said the Prince, sliding to the ground. "I wouldn't visit Shrems without stopping by to say hello."

The Woman bowed gracefully with a smile. "Congratulations, my lord. Even here, we've heard of your great victory at Darr. Did my love-cookies help you capture the unicorn for your Contest?"

Blackie's ears flew up as Prince George answered, blushing. "Oh, yes, Wise Woman. The Unicorn became manageable with the first bite. All your tonics were splendid. I thank you for everything."

Sweeping her arm in welcome, the Woman stepped aside for Prince George to enter her cottage.

"Pray make yourself at home, my lord. What may I do to help you? Unfortunately, as I told the Princess, my latest batch of love potion isn't mature, but I have salves and tonics for many ailments."

Following closely behind the Prince, Blackie bumped into the man when he halted, staring at the Woman.

"Love potion—did you tell the Princess about that? What does she want with love potion?"

The Woman's smile widened. "What a charming lady she is! So intelligent, so pretty! I see why a young lord would be eager to serve her."

"Oh, er, yes, yes, of course," sputtered the Prince. "Tell me, Wise Woman, did she ask for poisons, sleepy drops, anything like that?"

"My lord!" exclaimed the Woman, shocked. "You know, the Princess wouldn't want forbidden drugs. She simply asked for what all young ladies desire—health tonics, beauty preparations, and, of course, a new pair of shoes."

"Shoes!" muttered the Prince, kicking at a toadstool beside the path. "Tell me, Wise Woman, do you have any sort of digestive compound? The main problem with knightly service is the feasts that come after days of skimpy rations. They wreck your system."

The Woman was quick to reassure him.

"Why, my lord, one could advise you to take it easy on feasts if you're not used to them, but don't worry. I have a perfect mix of herbs for you. Senna leaves and savory with a touch of ginger. You take it in warm water."

"Ginger!" exclaimed the Prince. He leaned forward, rubbing his chin. "How on earth do you come by ginger? That's rare, isn't it?"

"Oh, my lord, the sisters trade back and forth," said the Woman, leading into the house. "A little of this for a little of that. An old granny-wife often has balms and simples the physician has never heard of. While he powders rat dung for his bolus, she offers a soothing compound of ground roots and greens from the hills."

Blackie sniffed in the door when Prince George entered the house.

"Come in, Blackie, if you like," offered the Woman. "I've baked more cookies."

Blackie shook his head. He turned away and followed Steed to a lettuce patch where the horse bit up a huge mouthful. He swallowed and looked quizzically at Blackie.

"So, unicorn, these humans invite you into their houses, do they? What do they give you in there?"

"Whatever I want," said Blackie, nosing the lettuce. "Really, I'm not hungry now. Seems like I've been eating and eating all day. You know, this is the first day I've ever hung around humans. I haven't seen many gardens."

Steed looked from the gleaming vegetables to the grass beyond. "Hear the truth, youngster, from an old trooper. You're not going to find many gardens better than this one. A beast would do well to settle in here and never leave. Any day they want, they can put me out to pasture in a place like this."

"I wouldn't get comfortable, if I were you, old horse," advised Blackie. "We leave at midnight to investigate a castle full of Hellions."

Steed snorted. "Hellions, huh? They're the big stinkers, aren't they? The horse-eaters?"

"I wouldn't put it past them," said Blackie, shivering. "I've only seen them twice, but they were bad enough. And now, at midnight—"

Steed sniffed into a beet patch and chomped a mouthful of the red-lined leaves. He swallowed and grinned at Blackie.

"Listen to me, son, if you insist on runnin' with Knights, you better forget about midnight. Now's now, that's what matters. Here we are, up to our knees in the tastiest veggies you'll ever see. You got sunlight, a sweet breeze, and a cool spring to drink from. Plunge in and relish it all. Don't worry about what's to come—castles, Hellions, none of that. That's not here to bother us now. Leave midnight to midnight and take a bite of those little leaves over there. They'll set you straight."

Following Steed's advice, Blackie swung down his jaws and took a big chomp of the wrinkled green leaves Steed pointed to with his hoof. Blackie jerked away, his eyes watering at the tangy taste that choked him. His mouth puckered up. He breathed perfume.

"I thought so," said Steed with satisfaction. "That's mint. Strong stuff, mint. You get to thinkin' bad thoughts, just bite up a mouthful of mint. It'll straighten you out. You don't want to spoil a good place like this with bad thoughts. A horse could live happy here forever if there was a filly or two down the lane."

Steed went back to eating. Blackie tasted his way about the garden, settling down to chomp spinach, but he was so stuffed from the feast that he filled up soon. He walked into the grass and locked his knees. Thinking of the Princess, he closed his eyes. He tried to remember what she smelled like, but the taste of mint in his mouth made that impossible.

Bird calls from the trees covered the noises from the house. Blackie drifted off to sleep. He woke in darkness at the Prince's voice from the door. The Woman carried a lamp before Prince George.

"I wish you had a compound to soothe the Princess," the Prince was saying. "She's treating me worse than ever these days."

"I imagine that she's got a lot on her mind," said the Woman, softly treading through the grass. "Imagine if you were told that you had to marry a fiend in three months."

"Not me," said the Prince, firmly. "I'm not marrying anyone. You know that I won a beautiful duchess in the Contest. I could have married her and gained a great duchy, but I refused both. A warrior lives for sword and shield. Marriage only complicates his life."

"We'll see, my lord, we'll see," laughed the Woman. "You're young yet."

"Unicorn, where are you?" called the Prince, checking Steed's saddle straps by the light of the lamp.

"Well, here we go," thought Blackie. "Just when I'm feeling hungry again."

He bit up a mouthful of grass, stretched, and walked to the Prince. He poked him under the shoulder with his nose. The Prince jumped.

"Oh, there you are. Couldn't see you in the dark. It's almost midnight, time to check out that castle."

"Farewell, Blackie," said the Woman, rubbing his ears. "Give my love to your mother. And Prince, that pep-powder's strong medicine. Save it till you need it. It'll keep you up and alert for three days, but you'll sleep like a rock when you come down from it."

"I'll go easy with it." Prince George reached to hug the Woman. Remembering his rank, he drew back. He patted her shoulder.

"Thanks, Wise Woman, thanks for everything."

"Return when you can, my lord," she said. "I'm always here, ready to help."

A few minutes later, Blackie walked quietly up the lane to Castle Shrems looming tall in the moonlit sky. The horse thumped behind, snapping sticks on the path.

"Easy back there," whispered Blackie. "You're louder than a herd of swamp hogs!"

"I don't know why we're trampin' around in the dark," complained Steed. "My old eyes work best by daylight."

"Better get used to it," warned Blackie. "Once the Prince does his job, we're to take him on a midnight run. Thirty, forty miles further."

"Midnight run!" protested Steed. "You must be kiddin'. I already put in my day's march. I don't do double-duty any more, not at my age. Tell you what, young unicorn. You carry the boy while I go back to that garden."

Prince George rode silently until his spear got stuck in a low branch. They had to stop while he pulled it free, grumbling to himself.

"This time, she's got me tackling a castle crammed with Hellions! Why doesn't she simply order me to commit suicide? She might as well tell me to jump in the river and finish me off that way!"

"What's he spoutin' about?" asked Steed.

"About the Princess," said Blackie, "how she treats him."

"Oh, the fillies." Steed chuckled wisely. "Never tell a yearlin' how to deal with females. He gotta learn by experience."

Prince George smacked Steed with his spear. "Quiet, they'll hear us!"

Pulling up at the tree line around the moat, Prince George dropped to earth, still mumbling to himself.

"If that's not enough, she expects me to ride all night after searching this castle. I've already spent the whole day chasing back and forth after her. When do I get to rest? Not this week if she has her way, probably never."

Leaning the spear against a tree, Prince George paused a moment beside Blackie, listening for noises from the castle. Blackie perked up his ears. All he heard was Steed tearing leaves from a bush behind them.

The Prince put a hand on Blackie's shoulder. "This is a one-man job, Unicorn. You'll wait here with the horse till I get back."

He crossed himself, loosened his sword in its sheath, and crept off toward the castle. Blackie saw him pause on the drawbridge, looking along the wall to both sides. He disappeared into the ivy running up the stones.

Blackie stepped back to Steed and bit into the bushes. He chewed leaves while watching the dark castle. A sneeze burst out, then a tearing sound as the ivy pulled away from the wall. The Prince caught himself in the darkness and sneezed again.

"If they don't hear that—" muttered Blackie.

"What, what?" asked Steed, looking around from the leaves.

"Nothing," said Blackie as the dark form of the Prince appeared against the sky between blocky crennels at the top of the wall. "There he goes."

Steed nodded, swallowed a mouthful of leaves.

"Boy's got pluck, you gotta give him that. If he had good sense to go with it, he'd be a wonder. Can't count the times I've saved him from mantraps or snakes. Lucky, this castle looks on the smallish side. Shouldn't take him long to look it over."

"I don't know," muttered Blackie. "He's got to move slow and careful if he's going to get through this."

"Well, that's his business." Steed yawned. "I'm not searchin' any castles myself. What was that you said, thirty mile run tonight? If he thinks I'm gonna run all night— Oh, well, better catch a snooze while I can. What's gonna happen will happen."

Steed groaned, shifted his weight. He spread his hooves and snored where he stood.

Blackie wasn't sleepy. He nibbled leaves from the bushes and pulled up grass along the lane. Mostly, he just watched the dark castle and sniffed the cloud of scents around him—earth, trees, bushes, along with the odors of saddle and horse and the sour moat around the castle. A dog barked faintly back at the village.

Chewing a mouthful of leaves, Blackie thought of the Wise Woman's cookies and the lettuce in her garden.

"That Woman knows Mama," he thought. "Poor Mama, she doesn't know where I am. Oh, how she'll worry! I should have told her I was leaving. Of course, it's only been one day. It was this morning that—"

He felt a shock. All this had happened in one day! It felt like a month had passed since he'd run over the hills to see the fawns. He'd been so young then, and now, this horse, this castle, the Princess—

He took a breath. "What am I doing here? Where is that Prince, anyway? He's had time to search a dozen castles."

Blackie's hide itched. He rubbed against a tree trunk, listening intently, but the castle was silent. A dove moaned in the woods. Light clouds drifted across the moon.

"I don't have to stay here," he thought. "I can run home anytime I want to see Mama. What'll she say when she sees my forehead? Papa, he's going to start yelling again. He'll go on and on about me getting maimed. I hope he's not right. What if my new horn doesn't grow in? What if it comes in crooked like my baby horn? I could be ruined for life."

He pictured himself with his adult horn twirled and twisted. He groaned, then wrenched himself back to the present.

"That Prince, he's been gone forever. I better go see what's up."

Blackie left Steed snoring in the trees and stepped quietly down to the drawbridge. Brushing through ragged bushes, he walked along the moat. He stepped over low-growing vines and listened to the chirp of a bird and the raspy sighs of bugs. The moat smelled so rancid that he turned back toward Steed in disgust. He was almost to the trees again when a shriek shook the walls of the castle.

EEEEAAKKK!

Without thinking, Blackie bolted into a thorny bush. Trembling, he tore himself loose from the spines. He turned to see blasts of flame shoot above the tower, lighting the countryside with hideous flashes.

The castle was alive now, roaring, screeching, shouting. Bells clanged, horns blared, smoke and sparks billowed above the walls. A terrible stench spread to Blackie. He ran to Steed who plunged against the tether hooking him to the tree branch.

"Gotta run, gotta run!"

Steed's eyes were white, his mouth foamy. His whole body shook. He breathed in gasps, croaking out his fear.

"That stink, boy, I know that stink. I've seen the monster three times already, and that's too many for this old horse!"

Blackie coughed at the smoke. "What is it? What is it?" he gasped.

"It's . . . it's death!"

Steed reared and drove down his fore hooves, crushing the branch holding his tether.

CRACK!

The branch split from the tree. Steed kicked it loose and galloped off into the darkness, the branch bouncing behind on the cord.

Blackie spun around to the castle. He watched spear points glinting above torches. They rushed around the top of the walls from two sides. As they joined, Blackie saw a figure rise against the flames and hurl itself over the wall into the moat.

SPLASH!

Through the earsplitting shrieks, he heard rough voices.

"There he goes!"

"Shoot 'im, spear 'im!"

"Where is he?"

"Jump after 'im! Nibs wants 'is head!"

"Unchain Ole' Rosy! She'll finish him off!"

Backing off, ready to run, Blackie stared into the darkness below the castle wall, his eyes half-blinded by the flashes.

"Steed, Steed!"

It was Prince George, crashing through the bushes without hat or cape. He stank of smoke and moat water. He floundered up to the tree where he'd left the horse and flailed through the branches.

"My horse, my horse, where's my horse?"

He looked wildly at Blackie, lit up by a flash from the castle. "Save me, Unicorn! I've got to get away!"

He ran toward Blackie. Blackie shied away from the stink in the wet clothes, but the Prince raised his hands, imploring.

"Unicorn, you've got to carry me! The dragon's after me!"

"The dragon!"

Terror struck Blackie. He whirled to run, but Prince George jumped toward him, crying out, "The Princess, the Princess! I've found a way to save the Princess from that Contract! We can save her from that marriage!"

"The Princess—"

Blackie skidded to a halt in the lane.

"I'd do anything to save the Princess," he thought. "Even carry this fool!"

He braced his hooves as the Prince grabbed his mane to pull to his back. The man was a clumsy lump compared to the Princess's light form. Blackie waited for the Prince to settle himself, then galloped toward the road, wild thoughts in his head.

"The dragon! He says, the dragon's after us! My, my, this is bad! How many times has Papa warned me about the dragon? I don't even have a horn to fight with!"

"Faster, Unicorn, faster!" cried Prince George, slapping Blackie on the shoulder. "The serpent, here she comes!"

Blackie glanced back to spy the bat-winged shape flap into the sky over the castle walls. Soaring in an arc, the monster breathed a searing flame that lit hungry eyes glaring down.

Blackie lowered his head to race down the tree-shadowed road concealing them from moonlight. Prince George stretched flat on his back, hugging Blackie's neck. When they ran out of tree cover, the Prince rolled his head to look back.

"Oh, no, she sees us, she sees us! Run, unicorn, run, run, run!"

Heart pounding, lungs heaving, Blackie ran as never before. In and out of moonlight and shadow, catching the earth with his front hooves and throwing himself off rear. Foam ran from his jaws. Sweat sprayed from his sides. Branches scraped at the man on his back.

"Noooo!" cried the Prince. "Here she comes! Fire! Fire!"

Terror swept over Blackie. He thought, "Twice in one day! That hawk this morning—"

He dug in his hooves under a shaggy tree and rolled down the path, throwing the Prince into the bushes. The monster overshot them and blasted the forest just ahead.

Blinding flame splashed around, exploding sap in branches, flinging burning leaves into the sky. Fiery debris crashed down, stinging their hides, setting blazes to all sides.

"Oh, oh, oh!" cried the Prince, slapping sparks from his clothes as he crawled to his feet.

The earth was spinning when Blackie stood up. He panted for breath as Prince George ran to him. The man crawled onto Blackie, clutching his neck so tightly it choked. The unicorn crept blindly between trees, sniffing his way till his eyesight returned.

The dragon flapped around with a shriek, nosing the treetops for living meat. Blackie heard talons claw back branches as great jaws clashed together. Blackie squeezed against a tree trunk, holding his breath while the Prince choked in his sobs.

A deer ran from somewhere, squealing in terror. The dragon was on it like lightening, blasting the forest with a breath and crashing down through flaming branches to tear at the kicking carcass.

Blackie stumbled away from the screams, slamming Prince George against tree trunks. Grim and silent, Prince George clung like a wood tick till Blackie found a side trail he could limp along to get away.

Blackie trotted heavily until the path met a stream chattering over a stony bottom. He splashed up the stream to a glittering pool where trees pulled back under faint moonlight. Groaning, Prince George dropped into the water.

"My sword, my sword."

Panting like a wild thing, Blackie closed his eyes. He sucked at the water between ragged breaths, the picture of that blazing deer before his eyes. After a moment, his curiosity drove away the terror.

How had Prince George stirred up a dragon in the castle?

Blackie opened his eyes. Above the burns, the bruises, the total exhaustion of his body, he sensed the breeze in the branches, the gurgle of water. Prince George was moaning in the stream.

"My shoulders are burnt. My ribs are crushed! I've lost everything, my cape, my spear, my sword! My father's sword, lost in that moat! I'm weaponless, naked, naked!"

Blackie rolled into the steam next to Prince George. The water cooled the burns on his neck and flanks.

"Blessed water," he thought. "Blessed water. Thank the Lord for blessed water."

CHAPTER TWELVE

Chasing the Princess

Water dripped off Blackie's nose. He shivered in the shallows of the stream. Weary to the bone, his soul echoed the squeals of the burning deer. He had a thousand questions in his head if only he could get the Prince to answer them.

Prince George was wringing out his clothes in the bushes. He struggled to pull on wet hose while Blackie tasted a spray of leaves. Blackie's throat felt choked. He couldn't swallow. He munched the leaf pulp, sucked in drops of juice, and spat out the rest.

The Prince staggered toward Blackie, pushing off slapping branches with a hand. His other hand held his sword belt to the moon.

"This thing's useless. My shield, my helmet, the medicines from the Wise Woman—the horse ran off with them. My dagger, that's all I've got left."

"Funny thing," thought Blackie, "I've lost my horn, he's lost his sword. We're both defenseless. Any lion or bear could tear us apart."

The Prince stripped off the scabbard and threw it into the weeds. He strapped the belt around him.

"We can't rest here, unicorn. We'd better run on, get miles between us and the dragon. I don't think we can reach Riverton tonight, but the farther we get from here, the better."

With a sudden pang, Blackie thought of the Nest. "If I hadn't run away this morning—yesterday morning—I'd be safe at home where I belong. I'd be with Mama. I'd still have my horn."

"We have to hurry," sighed the Prince. "My lady waits for my report. It's true, unicorn. I can save her. I have the proof here in my purse. At least, that's still safe."

He patted the purse on his side. "No matter how tired we feel, we must hurry for my lady's sake. Without weapons, though, we have to keep our eyes open."

The Prince coughed hoarsely. He stepped into the stream beside Blackie. They splashed along together, sparkles of moonlight swishing away in the water.

"You'll have to guide us," whispered the Prince. "Try to find a trail we can follow. The dragon could be watching the road."

"Old Rosy," thought Blackie. He touched the Prince with his nose. The Prince yawned and threw an arm over Blackie's neck.

"You're as wet as I am."

Blackie braced his hooves. Prince George pulled up heavily. He slumped forward, arms around Blackie's neck.

"Head south," he whispered. "Keep the moon to your right. This way." He slapped the side of Blackie's neck.

Blackie sniffed his way into a trail smelling of badgers and squirrels. He trotted slowly through light and shadows. He felt exhausted with this weight on his back. Only his movement kept him awake.

An owl shrieked, pulling Blackie's head around. Behind his ear, he heard the Prince snort. Snort? The man was snoring, sprawled forward, sound asleep on Blackie's neck.

Blackie sighed, "Oh, well, let him sleep."

The Prince woke when Blackie slowed at a brook. The man coughed, mumbled something. He fell asleep again as soon as Blackie took up his steady pace. The moon vanished behind the trees, and the night grew darker. Blackie ran till his feet felt like stones. When he stopped at first light, Prince George rolled off, landing with a thump in the path.

"All right, Sir Otley," he groaned. "I'll keep going."

The Prince curled up where he fell. He went back to snoring. Blackie sniffed around, lifting his ears to listen to chirping birds. His head drooped. For a moment, he felt the ache in his shoulders and legs, the soreness of his hooves. His mouth was swollen, his skin burnt, but he was too tired to care. He leaned his hip against a tree trunk and fell asleep.

The next thing he knew something poked his side. Blackie tried to ignore it, clinging to his dream, but it poked again.

"Rise and shine, unicorn. Rise and shine."

Blackie opened slitted eyes to sunshine muted by the layers of leaves above. Prince George pulled back a five-foot stick he had lopped from a branch with his dagger.

"Hate to wake you, boy. I know how you feel. I'm stiff, too, sore as a boil, but we've got to run on to catch the Princess."

Blackie yawned. He rocked onto his hooves and shivered

"I'm starved!" cried Prince George, running his fingers through his hair. "What's to eat in these woods? Any villages around, peasants to plunder?"

Blackie shrugged. He didn't know this part of the forest. All he knew was that his head ached. His body was dry and sluggish. All four hooves felt tender.

He limped up the hill. The Prince stumbled after, calling, "Hold on, unicorn! Hey, let me ride!"

Blackie stepped faster. He wasn't hauling anyone today. For a cookie, he'd run off and leave this man to find his own way through the forest. Why stick around humans, anyway, if they insist on dealing with dragons and Hellions? It was vine and creeper season back home in the forest.

Blackie didn't cheer up until he found a stream with tasty grasses bending over the banks. He stopped for breakfast while the Prince kicked around in the bushes.

"Well, it's good enough for you gobbling leaves and grass. I can't eat that stuff. I've got to get real food! I'm going on. You coming, unicorn? You coming? Stay here by yourself if you want, I don't care!"

Prince George stumbled down the path, stopped, looked back. "You coming? I'm going on!"

"What a pest!" thought Blackie. "I'd better go with him. The Princess told me to look after him. She's right. He'll never find his way out of this forest by himself."

Blackie ripped off a last mouthful of grass. He stood for the Prince to crawl on his back. He set off slowly. Trying to ignore his sore feet, he picked up speed as his leg muscles limbered till he started to feel almost normal.

The path angled back to the road. Blackie trotted steadily until he started meeting up with families loaded with bundles and bags, many leading cows or goats down the road. Most humans fled into the forest at the first sight of Blackie. One group drew into a circle with bows and pitchforks.

"Ho there," cried the Prince, waving his arms. "*Pax, pax*! We're not enemies! You got anything to eat!"

"Has you seen a dragon?" demanded a grizzled man, lowering his bow.

"Did we see a dragon?" cried the Prince. "Saint Gabriel knows that we saw the dragon! That monster chased us down the road in a storm of fire. We barely escaped last night."

"That filthy worm!"

The man cursed, spitting on the ground. He said that the dragon had torched the village next to theirs. When his people heard that news, they'd taken to the road, headed toward the river with what tools and supplies they could carry.

"Some's hiding in the trees," said the man, "but I say, run to water when the dragon's about. Only thing she fears is water."

"You got any food," begged the Prince. "A loaf of bread would do me if you got it."

"What we needs," said another man, "is the unicorn. Ain't he supposed to drive off the dragon when she gets loose?"

"No unicorn around to protect us," said the first man. "Folks haven't seen the holy beast for years."

"Well, this is a unicorn." Prince George patted Blackie's neck. "He just lost his horn. Got it snapped off in church."

A woman pushed forward.

"Can he heal? I got this bruise on me shoulder, all swole up like a puddin'. It hurts terrible."

"I don't know," said the Prince. "Can you heal, Blackie?"

Blackie shook his head.

"Guess he can't heal without his horn," said the Prince. "Say, you folks got any food?"

"Nothin'," said the man, looking at the woman. "When the neighbors came poundin' on our door a-yellin' that the dragon was spittin' fire, we ran away without crust or crumb."

Blackie stepped forward to sniff the bags the people had dropped.

"Shoo, there," cried the man, clapping his hands, "get away from our stuff!"

Blackie kicked over a bag. Carrots and turnips rolled out. Prince George stared indignantly.

"You lied to me! You do have food!"

"That's ours, ours!" cried the man, pushing Blackie back. "Get away from here! Stop botherin' us!"

Prince George brandished his stick, but the men pulled together with their pitchforks. The children scampered around, grabbing up loose vegetables. The humans set off again, the bowmen trudging behind to keep Blackie back.

Prince George bent to retrieve a couple turnips that had rolled free. He took a bite of one and stuffed the other into his purse. Blackie sniffed at the purse, but the Prince pushed him away.

"Sorry, unicorn, I'd share with you if I could, but this is all I've got. You can eat grass and weeds."

Moving down the road, they found a village that had escaped the dragon. When the refugees streamed down the road, the villagers had pulled back behind their wall leaving their fields unguarded. They yelled at the travelers to stay away and shot arrows at them, but the fugitives stripped the gardens like a flock of crows.

On the far side of the village, Prince George pushed into a family sitting in the brush around a steaming pot of green beans and onions.

"Hey, there, scoot aside, make room. Stand up when royalty arrives!"

The mother bowed, frightened, as the children hid behind her skirt. The Prince touched the pot with his stick.

"Not done yet, huh? How much longer to cook? You got any bread? Oh, sit, sit. You may sit, I give permission."

To the children's dismay, Blackie sniffed out a basket of beans among their bundles. He rolled it around with a hoof till the lid fell off. He stuck his nose inside for a mouthful.

"Our food, our food!" cried the woman. "That's our rations for next week!"

"Me lord," protested a skinny boy, "don't let that donkey eat our beans!"

"Donkey?" cried Prince George, settling against a tree. "Can't you tell a unicorn when you see one? This is the beast himself, the holy beast. He lost his horn the other day, but he's strong as an ox. I've ridden him for a week without stopping, covered a thousand miles. You can pet him, if you like."

The children moved to stroke Blackie, but the mother wearily shook her head.

"Well, if he is a unicorn, he's too late. Our village was burned to the ground. I ask you, my lord, what's the use of a unicorn without a horn? There must be a curse on the land when the unicorn won't fight the dragon. He only shows up to eat up our food. Dark days, if you ask me, we're in the dark days the priest warned about! If the country don't repent, we're comin' to the End."

Prince George leaned forward on his knees to sniff the steaming pot.

"Don't worry, Mother. Everything's going to be fine. I've learned a secret that's going to make Prince Vile run home with his tail between his legs. The dragon'll be gone from the land forever. Happy days ahead."

The woman shook her head mournfully.

"I pray you're right, my lord, I pray you're right. But it'd take a powerful secret to scare off the Black Lord and his dragon. My man was took when the Count and his knights locked themselves in the castle. There wasn't room for the families, you see. Now, we got to go to my sister's down at Cogmill."

"Well, things are going to be different from here on, I guarantee it. You just wait." The Prince sniffed the pot again. "Those beans, aren't they done yet, Mother? You don't want to overcook them. Anything I hate is mushy beans."

The woman poked the pot with a spoon. "They'll take another half-hour at least. I don't hurry my cookin'. I always say, if a thing's worth doin', it's worth doin' right."

"Did it hurt him, Master?" asked a little girl. "The unicorn, losing his horn?"

"Oh, I don't think it did," said the Prince. He pulled off a boot and shook sand from it. "They told me it just popped off. Kind of startled him."

"Did he lose it fighting the dragon?" asked a boy.

"Well, he didn't actually fight the dragon." The Prince pulled off the other boot. He leaned back against the tree. "Not without his horn.

But when the dragon chased us, this unicorn outran the fire. That's a moment I'll never forget. Flames shooting down, trees blazing to both sides, we ducked under the dragon and got away."

"Ooh," breathed the children, their eyes as big as walnuts.

"And another thing he did," said the Prince, leaning forward again, "when the Black Lord spoke rough to us yesterday, the unicorn knocked him down. Butted him over like you'd slap a horsefly."

"Oh, I don't like that," said the mother, shivering. "Nothin' good can come from that. My grandmam always said you got to speak soft to the Bad Man. Speak soft and never look in his eyes."

"That's if you're not a unicorn," said Prince George. "He's born to fight demons. How long those beans going to take, anyway?"

The beans smelled delicious when the cooking was done. Blackie left them for the children. Prince George was right. A unicorn could find plenty to eat in the forest. These humans were stuck with the meager provisions they carried with them. Prince George ate a healthy share of the food, but there was still plenty to quiet the children.

Blackie was chewing tree leaves when the Prince stood to ride on. He thanked the mother for the lunch, assuring her again that things would get better.

"And children," he said, "I promise you that someday you'll sit at your fireside and tell your grandkids that you met up with a unicorn and a prince. Yes, sir, that's me, Prince George, the rightful heir of the Kingdom of Dacia across the sea. You'll tell 'em that you ate beans with the famous prince that all the songs are about, the prince that won the Contest for the beautiful Dorinda of Darr. And today, I'm off to meet with Princess Julianna and bring peace to the land."

"Oh, bless you, me lord!" cried the mother. "May it all come true as you say."

The children cheered as Prince George trotted off on Blackie. They waved goodbye until the road entered the forest. Blackie slowed under the trees to ease his tender hooves. Prince George didn't notice. He was starting to fret over what he could actually achieve.

"I know I can't fight the dragon," he told Blackie. "She's flying around loose, burning villages. I can stop the marriage though. Prince Vile will have to back off now and give up this mad claim to the Princess unless he completely ignores the law."

That sounded good to Blackie, so he limped on. They passed more fugitives on the road. Some had carts, some wheelbarrows. Most trudged along with the baskets and bags they could carry.

Tired as he was, this road didn't seem familiar to Blackie. Trees had darkened in the weeks since he and Papa had passed through on their outing. Bushes had sprouted out of recognition. Everything smelled different when they finally gave up at noon and pushed into the forest for a nap. Not until next morning, when they pulled out of the trees into the open fields before the river, did Blackie recognize the lay of the land.

Blackie grew watchful as he saw the turns he'd passed and the grove he'd hidden in as the shattered army staggered by. Except for a broken spear shaft by the side of the road, he saw no signs of those sad humans.

Dozing on Blackie's back, Prince George didn't notice Blackie's concern until they rode up to a mob of refugees outside the gate into Riverton. They found themselves surrounded by shouting men and screeching women banging on the closed gate to the town. That brought up the Prince, clutching his stick.

"What's going on here?"

Frantic humans clutched at him from all sides, begging for help. The townsmen had locked them out. No one was permitted inside without paying the entrance fee, three coppers a man and ten coppers a horse.

"They might as well ask for a bushel of silver!" cried an old man.

"We're starving at their very gates!" wept a woman with a baby slung to her back.

"Go home!" cried a sweating sergeant watching over the town gate with a dozen spearmen. "They's no room in here. Go back to your homes, you people! Back to your villages!"

"But we was burnt out!" bawled a man, waving a hoe in the air. "We got no homes. Dragon ruint everything!"

Women wailed above everyone, waving sunburnt arms in the air.

"Pity, pity, for the Lord's sake! Don't let us starve at your doorstep!"

"Step back, step back!" cried Prince George, directing Blackie through the heaving throng. "Out of the way! Royalty coming through!"

"Oh, me lord!" People reached out from all sides to clutch at him. "Charity! Charity!"

Prince George pushed them back with his stick as Blackie forced his way to the gate.

"Thirteen coppers!" cried the sergeant. "No entrance without the coppers!"

"But I'm a Prince!" cried Prince George, waving the stick. "A Prince with the royal party! This is a unicorn! We don't pay entrance fees!"

It was no use. Without sword or horn to prove their station, the sergeant refused to let them in without payment. Blackie shuddered at the miserable crowd pressing around him while Prince George argued with the man. Yelling in frustration, the Prince threatened to knock the guards out of his way. He had to give up when the gate stayed closed before them.

Grudgingly, he dug into his purse for a shining silver coin. At sight of the silver, the crowd began howling for alms, but the spearmen pulled open the gate wide enough to let Blackie slip inside. Blackie watched the guards shove the crowd back. They slammed the gate behind him as the sergeant gave Prince George a few coppers in change for the silver.

"A peasant, they treat me like a peasant!" grumbled the Prince, sliding the coppers into his purse. "How dare they demand dirty coin from me? They should see at a glance that I'm no roving knave! If I had my sword—"

The Prince complained as Blackie pushed through the street, swinging his head from side to side for his first look at inns, shops, and fine houses. The square before the big church with the steeple was packed with humans standing or sitting on the ground. Blackie saw painted statues of saints and a soup-line outside the door of the church. Black-robed nuns fed shabby humans from huge cauldrons.

"What if I do lack a sword and spear?" the Prince mumbled. "Any slave with half a brain could note my royal bearing and recognize blue blood when he sees it!"

Without guidance from the Prince, Blackie followed the crowded street through town to the bridge to the castle in the river. Once again, spearmen stopped them at the gatehouse.

"Stand aside, my man," cried the Prince to the sergeant of the guard. "I'm Prince George of Dacia, Knight of the Order, reporting to Princess Julianna in the castle."

"Oh, you be a prince, be you?" demanded the officer, looking skeptically at the Prince's disheveled condition. "Well, prince or no prince, they's no Princess in this castle. The royal party shipped out on barges two hours ago."

"They've left?" squealed the Prince. "Already? But I have important news for the Princess! She'll want to see me immediately!"

"Well, I can't say as to that, friend." The guardsman sat down on his bench beside the gatehouse door. "All I know is them lords and ladies is gone. The Princess wouldn't bide here while the dragon flies over the countryside. Soon as they told her the monster was out, she insisted they take to the boats and leave immediate."

"But who took her?" demanded the Prince. "With Hellions capturing castles and the dragon flying around, the river won't be safe."

"Oh, I'd say that she's safe enough," assured the guard, leaning his spear against the gatehouse. "The Duke hisself, Duke Rivers, took her in his own barge. They's most o' the knights with her and a strong band of archers with silver-tipped arrows. It's us left behind has the problems with this rabble tryin' to break in our walls. It's like bein' overrun by ants. Steward don't know what to do with 'em."

"Well, I've got to follow the Princess," the Prince decided. "I've got great news that can't wait. And food, I need food. All I had to eat this morning was a couple turnips and some beans."

The guard sat back on his bench.

"'Fraid I can't help you there, man. I don't let nobody through to the castle without a permit. And don't try to fake a pass. I can read writin'."

Wearily, Prince George patted Blackie's neck. "Let's find a tavern, unicorn. All I want is a quick meal to get back on the road."

Yawning, Blackie carried him away from the gatehouse. The Prince turned him down a muddy alley to a rundown area by the River Gate where aimless humans slept against warehouse walls. The workshops were locked. No coopers, rope makers, or boatbuilders were working today. Rank smells hung over the area.

"We should find something down here," muttered the Prince. "Hey, look, we're in luck, the Sign of the Unicorn!"

Blackie didn't think the dirty picture hanging over the tavern door looked anything like a unicorn, but he smelled food and beer inside. He followed the Prince into the dim room where he saw few customers, mostly old men snoozing on benches, empty cups marking their places.

"No animals inside!" cried a one-eyed man at the bar, lazily throwing dice by himself. "Where you think you are, man? This is a 'spectable 'stablishment!"

"Don't you know what this is?" The Prince pointed at Blackie. "This is a unicorn, fellow, the only unicorn you'll ever see. You better show him respect in a tavern named after him!"

"Unicorn is it?" The Taverner's eye sparkled in the light from a small fire in the grate at the corner. "Well, if he's a unicorn, where his horn?"

"He lost it in a fight. We were attacked by the dragon, man."

"Dragon!"

The word swept through the tavern, everyone jerking awake with a grunt.

"The dragon!" repeated the Prince. He dragged the biggest stool to a table and swept it clear of wooden mugs. Blackie stepped back as the mugs clunked to the muddy floor.

"Food!" demanded the Prince, sitting down. "Bread and bacon and a mug of your best ale."

"Oh, pardon, me lord," said the taverner, shuffling over the muddy floor to mop at the table with a dirty rag. He swept an exaggerated bow to the Prince. "Without seein' any hat or sword, I couldn't reconize me lord's rank. What I needs to know is does me lord happen to have the coppers to pay for his supper?"

"Pay, man?" cried the Prince. "We run the roads to save you from the dragon, and you talk of pay! I should cut out your tongue!"

He jerked out his dagger and stabbed it into the table. Blackie stepped beside the quivering blade, glaring at the taverner. The fellow moved back a step, shaking his head.

"No need for that, sir. Just show your coppers like a proper customer, and you'll get whatsoever you orders."

"Oh, here, if I must." Prince George reached into his purse and clapped down the coppers he'd received at the gate. "Now, bring bread and bacon for me, and apples for the unicorn. You got any eggs?"

The human straightened, a different tone in his voice. "Oh, you got coin! Well, that's different. Pardon, me lord. The town's full of freeloaders these days. A man's got to look after hisself."

He went after the food while a few of the old men scooted their benches closer to the Prince.

"Excuse me, your lordship," said one of them, bowing from his seat. "Could it be that you aksherly saw the dragon? Is the serpent so big and fierce as they say?"

"Fierce!" cried the Prince, leaning forward. "You ever seen a village set aflame in ten seconds? Old Rosy, the dragon, she sprays fire like a waterfall shoots water. We saw a stag, the biggest buck in the forest, roasted with a breath. She ate it in two bites, smoking. We saw that with our own eyes."

Blackie shuddered at the memory. The taverner came back with a mug of ale and a bowl of green apples. Blackie sniffed the apples. They were spotted and tart, but he dug in, chomping with relish. Prince George took a deep drink from his mug.

"Bring out my food, man. Hurry, hurry!"

"This dragon, me lord," asked another of the old men, dragging his bench closer, "does you have any idea what brings the monster down from the North? They say that the Princess what was up to the castle today is goin' to wed the Black Lord."

Prince George banged his mug against the table.

"That Princess isn't wedding anyone, not yet, anyway. Soon as we finish here, we're riding after her to put a stop to all these rumors. I know a secret that's going to blow Vile sky-high."

He tapped the side of his head. "That reminds me, Barkeeper, Barkeeper!"

The man scurried over from the fireplace. "Yes, me lord?"

"You got any lost hats in this place, anything that'd fit me? And swords, I need a sword if you've got one."

"Oh, we always got hats lost in bar fights." The man thought a moment. "No swords, though—a sword's worth real money—but I think we got a kind of a spear in the storeroom. I'll bring your food, then take a look-see back there."

151

The tavern keeper came back with greasy bacon, eggs, and half a loaf of bread. Prince George tore a chunk from the bread and gave the rest to Blackie.

"Bring water for the beast, too," he ordered, "and carrots if you got them."

The man brought Blackie a big bowl of warm water. Drinking from the bowl, Blackie watched the man disappear into a narrow door hung with dirty aprons next to the fireplace. The taverner returned with a six-foot boarspear and an armful of hats. He offered a choice to the Prince, who talked of ladies while waving a chunk of bread dripping with egg yolk.

"Now that Princess you're talking of, everyone with half an eye—your pardon, Barkeep!—anyone can see that she's the second most beautiful woman in the Empire. I've known her all my life. And the most beautiful of all ladies, Dorinda of Darr, why, I won her in the famous Contest."

The old men all nodded, eagerly following these claims.

"My lord," said the taverner, "here's them hats you asked for and the spear. The spear's free, if you want it, but a hat'll cost you two coppers."

"Now, what few people know," continued the Prince, reaching for the spear, "is that I also saw the ugliest woman in the world, Mother Hungry, up in the land of Obb in the western mountains."

"Oh, I don't know about that!" laughed one old man from his bench, leaning back with his hands around a knee. "We got some females here might dispute that record. You come back after dark on Sataday night, me lord, and see what's been let out for the evenin'."

Prince George jumped to his feet to get the feel of the boarspear. The shaft had a wicked spearhead with lugs sticking out ten inches behind the point to hold a wounded boar from driving up the shaft to get to the hunter.

"Ah, yes, this'll do," said the Prince, stabbing the spear through the air with a stamp of his foot. "It's a little short to tackle the dragon, but outside of that—"

He swung up the spear in salute. "I owe you, Barkeep. I'll kill a Hellion for you!"

"Kill a dozen of 'em!" cried the man on the bench.

"Kill 'em all!" said the taverner, tossing the hats on the table.

The Prince leaned the spear against the table and slumped into his chair again. He fumbled through the pile of hats, trying them on as he continued his story.

"Now, this Mother Hungry I was telling you about, she has long spidery arms to catch any man comes near her cave. When she catches a man, she feeds him garbage till he dies, then places his bones in a row with the skeletons of her other husbands."

As the listeners shuddered at that thought, the Prince tried on a stained gray hat. A dried-up little man on a stool wanted to know about Lady Dorinda.

"Pardon, me lord, could you tell us, that lady up to Darr, was she tall or was she short?"

The Prince got a far-off look in his eyes. "I'd say that she was tallish, about three inches taller than the Princess. Lady Dorinda smells of Purple Honesty, a rare flower of the west, and she sleeps in blue silk sheets."

"Blue silk sheets," repeated the little man, "oh, my."

The men grinned at each other, scratching their heads.

"Well, time to go!"

The Prince clapped a brown hat on his head, jumped up, and tossed the coppers from his change on the table. He seized the boarspear while Blackie took a last drink from the bowl. He waved to everyone in the tavern and stepped out the door.

"Well," he said, walking beside Blackie down the lane toward the gate, "with a hat and a boarspear, I'm transformed again. I didn't know myself with that old stick from the forest."

Prince George found the boarspear useful once the guards let them squeeze through the River Gate. This gate had fewer refugees than the North Gate, but they were more hungry. The Prince had to knock back a couple hooligans with his spear butt before the others saw fit to give them room to pass. They still yelled and threatened.

"The horse, let's butcher that horse!"

Blackie lowered his head to butt his way through them, as the Prince cried, "Horse? You're mad! This is a unicorn! Nobody butchers a unicorn!"

"Roast up the unicorn, then!" cried the men, rushing at Blackie.

"Ride 'em down, Blackie!" shouted the Prince. "Let's get out of here!"

He struck out with the boarspear while Blackie ran through the mob, rolling back humans with his head. They were through the crowd in an instant with only scratches from the fight.

Blackie ran three hundred yards before he slowed down, his heart beating like a hammer. He settled to a trot, his breath coming hard, sore hooves really hurting.

"Ho, ho," cried the Prince, shaking the spear. "That's the way to charge, old boy! There'd be a dozen dead if you had your horn! Why do they call you Blackie? They should call you Smasher!"

The fields around town had been stripped to black earth, everything edible ripped out down to roots. They pushed along the lane by the river until they entered the coolness of the forest. Blackie slowed, exhausted, and Prince George slid down to walk beside him, leaning on the boarspear.

Blackie was still horrified that humans would want to eat him. Prince George sensed his anxiety.

"I'm sorry you had to see that, Blackie. People get savage when they're hungry. In foreign lands, you even find cannibals, people who eat other people—the dark Africans across the sea, the blond Slavs at the end of the earth. They hunt down their neighbors and roast them medium-well with parsley and onions."

He absently ran a hand over his head. "Hey, my hat! I lost my new hat in the fight at the gate. I'm bareheaded again!"

CHAPTER THIRTEEN

The Prince's Report

Blackie trotted with the Prince down the lane along the river until they ran into rough territory. The bank was cut up by streams and gullies, ridges and swamps that set Prince George to complaining. He was sure they could catch up with the barges if they had a few clear miles to run.

It didn't help that much of the populace seemed on the move as well, stirred up by dragon attacks or local wars launched by barons taking advantage of troubled times to settle old scores. Many of the strays piled up at the river, seeking refuge or despoiling other travelers.

"We should get a boat," suggested Prince George, after Blackie sniffed out an ambush. "I've traveled in boats. They seem slow, floating with the current, but you don't run into these obstacles."

Blackie wasn't drawn to the idea of water travel. After watching Papa fight off boats last spring, they seemed skittish to him, unreliable things, more likely to flip over than to keep afloat. If it were up to him, he'd run at night when the humans were camped. A sudden thunderstorm whipping in from the west made that impossible, even for him.

Snug in the Nest back home, storms like this always seemed far away. Here on the road, they were exposed to crackling lightening and pounding rain. Blackie didn't hesitate when they splashed up to the broken gate of a small village. He ran straight to the shelter of the church across from the well. The church was full of women and children who spilled out the back door, screaming in fear when the strangers pushed in the front.

"Don't worry," called Prince George, wringing out his shirt. "We're not going to harm you. We just want to get out of the rain."

"Oh, Master," cried a trembling woman in a torn dress, "we thought the bandits was come again! They've rampaged through twice, taking everything we had. All that's left is for them to burn us out complete."

Blackie shook water from his coat as the Prince demanded, "So where are your men? Why didn't they fight them off?"

"Our men isn't fighters," explained another of the women. "'Specially, when the bandits comes stormin' in with spears and swords. Our husbands run off into the forest and left us flat."

Prince George looked around the crowded church.

"At least, I'm sure you women hid your food. You're too clever to run off without grabbing some bacon or bread."

"Nothing!" cried two or three women.

"It was the shock of it," explained another, "the yells and screams, everyone running in all directions. We was lucky to grab the babies as we run."

"And you have no food at all?" Prince George looked skeptical. "You better tell the truth. My unicorn can smell out a pea at twenty paces."

Blackie tried to sniff for veggies, but burst out sneezing from rainwater up his nose.

"We has nothing, Master, nothing," cried the woman, helplessly. "No one's tasted a mouthful since them bandits come through the first time. They emptied our bins, stripped our gardens, drove off our beasts. All the men is down to the shore now. They're tryin' to catch fish with pins on strings, but the rain has sent the fish deep."

"And where are the bandits?" asked the Prince, pouring water from his boots.

"Oh," said the woman, "there's a big camp of 'em down by Hog's Neck. The road turns with the river there, so them robbers has a good lookout to catch travelers by land or water."

"That's where the ferry used to cross the river," said another woman. "All's gone now. Overnight, it seems, everything's topsy-turvy."

Prince George pulled his boots back on his feet. He stood awhile, looking out the door. Blackie flicked his tail, realizing how hungry he was.

"Storm or no storm, I'm going out to graze. I'm not starving because these humans can't eat grass."

"Tell you what, goodwives," said the Prince, turning to the women. "Why don't you send a couple of your lads to call the men back. We'll have them round up their axes and hoes, whatever weapons they have, and take care of those bandits for you."

"Oh, oh," thought Blackie, wearily, "here we go again. I'd better get my dinner before the trouble starts."

With a shake of his head, he stepped out into the rain. Prince George called after him, "Don't go far, Blackie. We'll clear out those scoundrels when the men return."

The rain poured down on Blackie, making him blink. It ran down his ears and nose, over his shoulders and rump. Everything smelled of mud and water, but he found a strip of ragged grass along the village fence and tore at the spears. Much of the flavor was washed out by the rain, but he chewed doggedly, his ears half-deafened by the pelting rain and thunder.

He closed his eyes, eating without thinking, until the Prince slapped his wet shoulder with a hand.

"Ready to go, Blackie?"

Blackie looked at the village men shivering under the downpour, a handful of dripping scarecrows with pitchforks and sticks and a spear or two. As the Prince pointed down the road with his boarspear, they looked too frightened to do any fighting.

"Here's your chance, men!" the Prince cried heartily. "A bold assault and a quick victory!"

"How many does ye think we'll have to fight?" quavered one of the waterlogged villagers.

"Doesn't matter!" shouted the Prince. "We'll rush out of the storm like an army of a thousand. They won't last two minutes!"

"I hope so," gasped the man. "I know, I won't last for three."

Prince George told Blackie to bring up the rear in case anyone tried to run away. Blackie shook his head as the little band slogged along the river in the rain, dragging their weapons in the mud.

The lane ran up to Hog's Neck, a grassy little rise where a path swooped down to a gravelly landing place on the river. The Prince paused in the trees just below the Neck to gather his little force. He gave his orders in a low, husky tone.

"Now, we all charge in at once, screaming like Hellhounds. Blackie, your job is to stampede the horses while I take care of anyone that stands to fight."

"So we do the yellin'?" asked a man. "You'll do the fightin'?"

"You do what fighting you need to do," said the Prince, impatiently. "The main thing is to stick together! We charge as a group. There's few enough of us as it is, so we don't want to lose our momentum by scattering."

"Oh, I won't scatter," promised the man. "I'll stick behind you all the way."

"Right, then, everyone. Follow the unicorn. Run in on them when he starts to charge. Blackie, you lead the way."

Tired, wet, still hungry, there was nothing Blackie wanted less than to attack a camp of villains, but Prince George smacked his rump and sent him ahead of the band of villagers. Blackie limped up the lane past a guard sleeping against a tree in a soggy blanket, his bow in his lap.

A few yards on through the storm, he saw the shape of the river coming to a point. Running down the rise was a ramshackle collection of shacks and tents thrown together with a few board and scraps of cloth. A dispirited group of mules and horses lifted dripping heads to look at Blackie through the rain. A water-soaked dog jumped out to bark at him, "Woof, woof!"

"Run!" Blackie screamed, dashing wildly at the horses before they could see who he was. "Whips! Flames! Lightening! Dragons!"

He threw himself into the creatures, knocking over the first horses he came to. The others squealed and reared, pulling tethers free, scampering off into the storm.

Once the horses were gone, Blackie whirled and charged into the camp from the side, storming through tents and knocking over shacks. By now, the villagers were running in to whack shoulders and pound heads with their sticks while screeching like wildcats. Prince George stabbed two bandits who tried to fight back with spears.

It was over in a moment with most of the villains scattered into the storm. A handful lay moaning around the camp.

"Two or three to a man!" cried the Prince, kicking a raider who tried to crawl away. "Grab hold and toss them into the river!"

When the camp was cleared of the enemy, the villagers sifted through the debris to collect food and weapons. Prince George took charge of a small shield and a sturdy broadsword.

"Now, we're getting someplace," he said, whipping the sword through the rain. "Collect everything useful, men, all the weapons and the foodstuffs! Anything left over, throw it in the river. I don't want to leave a shingle for that gang to creep under."

Armed now with bows and spears, the villagers worked with a will. They collected meal and grain, turnips and onions. Pig carcasses hung from a tree. Four cows, tied above the riverbank, had escaped the flight of the horses. More important, they found fishing nets the villains had stolen somewhere. They wrapped them up with all their other loot.

An hour later, they splashed cheerfully back to the village, their arms full of booty. The cows mooed softly behind them as the men sang.

The river rises,
the river falls.
Seasons roll by.
The church bell calls.

Old men pass on.
The baby crawls.
The river rises,
the river falls.

"Now, we can fix you a dinner, me lord," cried a village woman, looking through the supplies carried by the men.

"I'm afraid not," said Prince George, looking regretfully at a pig on a spit over a sputtering fire. "Blackie and I are pressed for time. We have to catch up with the Princess's barge. I'll just take a handful of the vegetables to eat as we go."

Blackie was willing to wait out the storm, but the Prince was eager to travel on. He wrapped himself in a piece of sail canvas that had formed a tent, and they splashed back into the rain.

"Keep good guard in the future!" shouted the Prince to the villagers yelling good-bye at the village gate. "You're armed now. You can chase off any bandits who come along."

The rain continued. Travel was miserable through the muddy lane and running streams. Tired from the fight and still hungry, Blackie was bothered by his sore hooves. He refused to carry the Prince, so they trudged sullenly, side by side, Prince George gnawing an onion. Blackie snatched bites from the bushes along the path. Neither would call that satisfactory dining. Still, they were in better shape than the handful of bandits they found sloshing along the road. Those rascals dashed into the forest at their approach.

Watching them go, Blackie wondered if it had really been necessary to throw the prisoners into the river. He decided that Prince George must know how these things are done.

Slow and miserable as their progress was, it brought them to another river town before nightfall. Once again, the gate was shut tight against them. Prince George wanted Blackie to kick the gate down, but Blackie didn't feel like kicking anything. They had to wait in the rain for a boy to return from a lane with a string of rabbits over his shoulder.

The boy whistled for entrance. Blackie tensed to rush in when the gate swung back. Prince George followed closely behind, parrying spears as Blackie shoved back the townsmen pushing at them.

"Royal business!" cried the Prince. "Stand back in the name of the Crown!"

A rock struck him in the head, knocking him down as the men heaved together to hammer Blackie back. Blackie's hooves slipped in the mud. He felt himself rolling backward, too tired from his long day's travel to drive forward. Slippery hands heaved and hustled, pushed and pummeled until Blackie tumbled out the gate with Prince George thrown after. The gate slammed shut behind them. Blackie heard a cheer from within.

Blackie lay on his side in the muddy road, exhausted. Prince George sat up with a groan, rain washing blood from the cut on his forehead.

"My boots!" he cried. "Someone pulled off my boots in the fight. Now, I've lost everything again, hat and boots, spear and sword! I'm more naked than I was before!"

He put a hand to his head and groaned, "Oh, Blackie, I hope the minstrels don't hear of this episode."

The Prince tried to stand. His bare feet slipped from under him and he plopped down in the mud. With a groan, he crawled to hands and knees, shoved to his feet and rubbed his hands in the rain to wash off the mud. He hunched over in the downpour and looked down at Blackie.

"You look beat, old boy. Why don't you rest here while I go look for shelter? There's got to be a castle around here somewhere. Maybe I can stir up the lord to get my boots back from those bumpkins."

Certainly not. Blackie wasn't letting the Prince blunder off in the rain by himself. Blackie scrabbled at the mud to stand up while Prince George leaned against the gate. When Blackie finally got to his hooves, he swayed back and forth, sucking in his breath.

"Sure you're well . . . well enough to walk, Blackie?" gasped the Prince. "You could rest here while I go to bring help."

Blackie shook his head. He took a step, then another. He felt stronger once he started moving. He was in no shape to fight a dragon, but he could limp around the wall with Prince George.

This was another large town with tall buildings and a steepled church. The wall seemed to go on forever. They hobbled along in twilight until they found the castle half-hidden in the rain beside the river, a heap of dark walls and towers with spots of light from windows. They limped up to a gatehouse guarded by men-at-arms.

"Now, we're getting somewhere," said the Prince, trying to straighten his garments. He came to attention twenty paces before the gatehouse and saluted with his fist.

"Ho, the castle!"

Someone yelled back, "Who approaches Castle Garst by night?"

"George, Prince of Dacia, under orders of Princess Julianna!"

"Advance to be reconized, Lord Prince!"

Blackie followed the Prince up to the gate. Spearmen shoved it open. Sir Otley stepped out with a flaring torch.

"Ho, Prince, it is you! Still with the unicorn!"

The knight pounded Prince George on his back, then stepped back to look him over.

"What happened to you, m'lord? Where's your hat, your lionskin? You look like you been rolled in a barrel! It's good to see you, anyway. We worried about you. All of a sudden, there's troubles throughout the land—barons rebellin', the dragon burnin' to right and to left!"

"You don't have to tell me," said Prince George, his voice echoing as they limped through the murder passage, the gatehouse hallway open at the top so boiling oil could be poured onto attackers. "That dragon chased after us like a hawk on a hare. First, we got scorched by Old Rosy, then we got flooded in the rain!"

The passage opened onto the castle courtyard crowded with shadowy men and horses. Sir Otley waved his torch, scattering sparks to both sides.

"So you escaped the dragon, did you, Prince? You can thank your angel for that one. Not many outrun that monster once she's got their scent in her nose!"

Sir Otley reached a glove to rub Blackie's neck. "And you, unicorn, you must have missed your horn with that dragon burnin' down on you!"

"He's probably better off without it," sighed the Prince. "If he had his horn, he might have tried to fight. Is Her Majesty here? I have important news. I need to see her as soon as I get a hat and boots."

"Boots, Prince?" Sir Otley looked down and laughed. "Sure it is, you come barefooted in this weather! Don't worry, I won't ask what happened. You just wait here, my lord, and I'll check around. There must be an odd pair of boots somewhere around this gatehouse."

Prince George washed himself under a gushing drainpipe in the courtyard while Corporal Scrag, one of Sir Otley's Guardsmen, told him about the Princess.

"O' course, she's here, me lord. The rain caught us out on the river in them barges. When the lightening cut loose, we had to pull ashore at the first loyal castle we came to, so here we stopped at Garst."

When Sir Otley returned with an old pair of boots and a hat that was a half-size too small, Prince George insisted on going straight to the Princess. Blackie set his hooves carefully on the slippery stones as Sir Otley led them across the courtyard to the keep. Entering the hall, they heard music and voices. Blackie smelled a dank mix of food and wine, perfume, and smoke from torches and fireplaces.

Blackie heard a shriek of delight. "My unicorn's back!"

Wearing two shades of red, the Princess jumped up from her throne at a raised table on the upper end of the room. Lady Jessica was leading a circle of laughing children. They came to a halt as court ladies woke up on their benches. Lords and local worthies looked over from the food table across from the fireplace.

Blackie dashed over to the Princess. Laughing with joy, she ran out to hug him. She jerked back.

"Oh, Blackie, you're wet!" she cried, looking down at her water-stained gown. "Completely soaked! Why didn't you dry him off, Prince George?"

"We just arrived out the deluge, my lady," explained Prince George, bowing low before her.

"What have you been doing to my unicorn?" she demanded, walking around Blackie as he followed her with his eyes. "You've got him all scratched and muddy. Are those burns on his hide? He must be tended—cleaned and treated with the Wise Woman's lotions. You wouldn't show a mule in this condition."

Shaking in exasperation, Prince George shouted at her.

"Of course, Blackie's beat up! You'd be run-down, too, if you'd been chased by the dragon all day. We didn't get to glide along in barges! While you ate olives and raisins and listened to minstrels warble love songs, we battled bandits for ninety miles to get here, only to be thrown out of town when we arrived!"

The Court went deathly still. The Princess glared at Prince George, her hands on her hips.

"Who do you think you are, you shabby Prince, taking that tone of voice to me? Is this the way you greet your liege lady when reporting back from a mission? I'll have to find duties more suitable for a discourteous knave!"

"My lady, my lady," wailed the Prince, dropping to his knees before her, "if only you'd listen to me! I've made a discovery, one that will cancel Prince Vile's claim on you! I just want to explain it to you."

"Umph!"

The Princess lifted her nose, then turned back to her throne. She sat down, delicately spreading her skirts about her pretty brown boots. She took her little silver-framed mirror from Lady Katherine and inspected a curl hanging loose from under her hat.

"Sir Otley, see to my unicorn," she commanded. "Have his wounds treated. Bathe him and rub him down, then bring him back for his dinner. It seems that this Prince has something to say to me. I will listen to him."

"Come on, boy!" Sir Otley rumbled to Blackie. The knight tried to lead Blackie from the room, but the unicorn didn't move. Like everyone else, he wanted to hear Prince George's report.

Prince George spoke loudly over the whispering in the room, "You told me to search Castle Shrems, remember, my lady?"

"Of course, I remember," said the Princess, handing the mirror back to Lady Katherine. "I was curious about that dirt heap in the courtyard."

Standing stiffly before her, the Prince nodded. He gestured with a hand.

"I climbed the wall at midnight as you ordered, Princess, pulling up the ivy in the dark. It was dangerous, very dangerous—one slip, and I'd have broken my neck. The ivy kept tearing, dropping me back, but I kept at it until I reached the top and looked inside the wall. There, I saw dirt everywhere. It filled the courtyard and stretched between keep and wall as far as I could see. 'So where'd all this come from?' I asked myself."

"Yes, yes," said the Princess, impatiently, "get to it! What'd you find in there?"

"What I found was Hellions," said the Prince, lowering his voice. "Snoring Hellions curled up on the dirt pile and sleeping in corners along walls. I had to creep around them to search further. At first, I couldn't see anything. The whole place was dark. Stinking smoke poured up from a hole behind the keep. I almost fell into it, but the smell drove me back, the foulest stink I'd ever smelled."

"Must've been a privy," suggested Sir Otley, leaning against the back of the throne. "All them Hellions would really stink up a privy."

"No, no," the Prince explained, "this hole was wider and deeper than a privy, much deeper. It had ladders running down in it and a sort of crane thing leaning over with pulleys."

"Pulleys, you say?" asked the Princess, leaning forward.

"Yes, my lady, pulleys, you know. Hoists to lift heavy stuff."

She leaned back in annoyance. "I know what pulleys are. Go on. What did you do?"

"Well, the smell was terrible, a mixture of something burnt with something rotten. It was worse than the hot springs I smelled in the western desert when I hunted for Purple Honesty."

"Yes, yes," cried the Princess, "but what did you discover in the castle?"

While Prince George stretched out his story, Lady Jessica sent the Page to bring Blackie a drink of fresh water. Cedric set a basin of water on the floor before Blackie. He dipped his nose inside, his ears high to listen to Prince George's story.

"—right down the ladder into the hole," continued Prince George, dramatically. "I daren't carry a torch as the light would give me away, so I had to feel my way through the mud and dirt of tunnels going this way and that. I didn't have far to go. I came to this section dug out like a big cave. It was lit by an eerie fire in the corner that kept rising and falling, rising and falling. The smell was strongest in that area and I could hardly breathe in the heavy, choking smoke curling around the cave."

"Get with it, Prince!" cried the Princess. "What did you see!"

"I know what it was!" roared Sir Otley. "That light risin,' fallin'—must've been the gnomes at their forges, blowing up their fires with bellows as they worked. Did you hear the little people hammerin' away and singin'?"

"No, no," said the Prince, impatiently. "All I heard was a loud wheezing and snorting. I pulled my sword and crept toward it. There she was, the dragon, Old Rosy herself, surrounded by bones, asleep in this big pile of smeltings."

"Smeltings?" The Princess sat forward in her chair. "Just what was going on down there, Georgie?"

Prince George reached down to his waist. He patted his side, looked up apologetically.

"I'm sorry, my lady. My purse was stolen in my travels. I lost the samples I brought to show you."

"Samples of what?" cried the Princess, clenching her fists. "What did you see down there?"

"Silver!" cried Prince George, stepping forward. "Silver coins! What I discovered down there was a secret silver mine under Castle Shrems. Those Hellions had prisoners digging out the ore. They used the dragon's fiery breath to smelt out the silver from the ore. They had molds and everything. They coined it right down there in the mine and bagged up the silver in the opposite corner! The hoists were used to lift bags of coins to the surface to cart them away."

"Silver?" breathed the Princess in wonder. "That means—"

"It means, my lady," cried Prince George, throwing out his arms, "that you're free! Prince Vile has been cheating His Majesty. That silver he's been lending to the Emperor, it belonged to the Crown in the first place, most of it!"

The hall was in an uproar, everyone speaking to everyone else. Blackie was confused. He trotted after the Princess as she ran across the floor to Lady Jessica.

"Jessie, Jessie, remember our lessons, the Law of Underground Resources?"

"What was that, my lady?" cried Jessica, catching the Princess's hands.

The Princess shook with excitement.

"Brother John explained it to us. According to the Mineral Rights Agreement of 863, two-thirds of all physical resources discovered within the earth must be delivered to the Emperor upon pain of confiscation. If Prince Vile digs up an ounce of silver without giving the Emperor his share, it's ours, all of it! We owe Vile nothing!"

"That's what I'm trying to tell you!" shouted Prince George, jumping up and down. "The silver's yours! You have no debt, no Contract! You don't have to marry Prince Vile!"

"I'm free, I'm free!" sang the Princess, jumping around arm-in-arm with Jessica, as everyone applauded and cheered. Children, playing in a corner, ran over to hop around after her.

"No contract, no marriage, no Vile, no Vile!"

"But my lady," cried Jessica, stopping suddenly to pull the Princess to a halt. "All that silver couldn't have come from this mine! The Hellions only came to Castle Shrems a few months ago."

"Who cares?" cried the Princess. "If he's minting stolen silver now, that's evidence of theft—and the confiscation is total! All of it's ours! I'm sure the Council will accept that argument once Father offers the lords a share of the silver from the mine."

"But how do you think Prince Vile will take this?"

"Who cares? I'm free!"

The Princess turned to Blackie. Wet as he was, she threw her arms around his neck.

"Oh, Blackie, I've been so worried about you! All day, we've heard reports of the dragon terrorizing the countryside. I feared she'd catch you without your horn to defend yourself. I'm getting Mother to report Prince Vile to the Council! Imagine, letting his serpent loose to burn villages! That's almost as bad as stealing our silver!"

"Why, I can tell you about the dragon, too, my lady," said Prince George, eagerly, stepping beside Blackie.

"I must say, Prince George," said the Princess, smiling upon him, "I am truly pleased with you this time. You've handled yourself superbly in this assignment, exactly as I expect my knights to perform."

She turned back to her throne and sat down, warmly addressing the Prince.

"Now, my lord, please give us your whole report. And Blackie, come stand by me. I have a gift for you, something to make you whole again."

The Prince stood at attention before the Princess, looking importantly around the Court.

"Well, my lady, I was leaning over the bags to pick up some coins to show you when the dragon twitched in her sleep. I froze where I stood, but she let out a grumble. She opened an eye and shot sparks through the darkness. A guard in the corner woke up and looked around to see what was disturbing her. That's when I took off running!"

Now, Blackie knew the whole story. He nodded as the Prince described being chased through the mine, up the ladder, and off the wall into the moat.

"And that's where I lost my sword!" wailed the Prince. "My father's sword, dropped in the moat along with my lionskin. I've had bad luck ever since!"

"But what about the dragon?" asked the Princess, leaning forward again.

"Oh, that Nabs must have feared my escaping. He unchained the dragon to chase us down, and she did her best. She drove us for miles through the midnight forest, shooting fire at us, but we got away. And we've been traveling all day to bring you this report."

"Well, this will make a great song, my lord," said the Princess with satisfaction. "Your fame grows, lifting my prestige with it. And I shall not forget your courage. In fact, I shall honor you at this very moment. Kneel, Prince, kneel."

Blackie watched with pleasure as the grinning Prince sank to his knees before the Princess. She reached up for the sparkling necklace about her neck.

"Here, Jessica," she said, "help me take this off."

Jessica helped the Princess pull the necklace over her hair. As the court silenced, the Princess held up the gleaming golden strand with the dazzling red jewel. She announced in a clear voice.

"This necklace is my greatest treasure. It was sent to my grandmother by the Caliph of Granada and given me by my mother on my sixteenth birthday. In thanksgiving for my timely release from matrimonial misery, I hereby entrust this necklace to my friend and liegeman, Prince George, Heir to the noble Kingdom of Dacia, for the most important quest I've sent him on up to now."

His face as red as the jewel, Prince George touched the necklace the Princess held before him.

"As a sign of my faith in this noble Prince, I instruct him to deliver this necklace to the Eastern Shrine as an offering of gratitude to the Lord of All who has made possible my deliverance from this hateful marriage. Praise the Lord!"

At that, the cheering started again. Blackie shook his head. The poor Prince to be honored by being sent on another difficult task? These humans had the strangest ways. He wondered if he'd ever understand them. Prince George looked delighted as the Princess slipped the necklace over his head.

"Do not remove this treasure, my lord, until you donate it to the holy Fountain up at the Shrine."

Prince George touched the jewel at his throat. "I won't, my lady."

The Princess looked thoughtfully at the glittering jewel. "Perhaps you'd better hide it under your shirt when you travel, my lord. It'll be safest that way."

Prince George nodded. He tucked the necklace out of sight.

The Princess nodded. "To make sure you succeed at this quest, Prince George, I will permit you to continue riding my unicorn. For you, Blackie—"

She swung her attention to Blackie, watching with interest. "I've got a gift for you. Exactly what you need. Lady Jessica, get the bag."

"Yes, my lady."

Jessica knelt to pull a rough canvas bag from under the throne. She held the bag open while the Princess reached carefully inside, explaining, "I told the Armorer that you lost your horn. Look what he gave me."

With an effort, the Princess pulled out a foot-long steel blade attached to a curved metal plate with eye and ear holes. Straps dangled down, ending in buckles.

"This is a spike and frontal, horse armor that fits over your nose. You'll be more dangerous with this spike than you ever were with that bent horn of yours."

Blackie tilted his head, examining the thing. It did not look comfortable.

"Hold still, Blackie."

Lifting the frontal with both hands, the Princess eased the heavy plate onto Blackie's head. He tried to step back from the bruising metal, but she held him by an ear.

"Jessie, help me buckle it on. Stand still, Blackie! This won't hurt."

The Princess held Blackie while Jessica guided the frontal over his nose till it fit snugly. Blackie hated it immediately. The hard, heavy thing cut off half his eyesight. He had to swing his head sideways to see directly in front.

"Don't move," ordered the Princess. "Make yourself useful, Georgie. Hold the spike while we buckle the straps. That's it, Jessie—a little tighter, please."

The girls pulled at the straps until the frontal fit snugly, then the Princess jumped back with a grin.

"There you are, Blackie! The dragon won't want to deal with you now! My mirror, Jessie, let him see himself."

Blackie whipped his head around. The blade whooshed through the air. Jessica held up the mirror, and he looked at himself. He saw the gleaming steel of the blade and the bright eyes underneath. He was interested in the mirror.

"So that's a mirror," he said to himself. "You see yourself better than in a stream. That frontal does look fierce, but, oh, it's uncomfortable!"

"Well," cried the Princess, rubbing her hands together, "that's that. Now, Blackie, do you want your dinner first or a bath? We've got muffins, grapes, and cakes for you. Jessie, take him over for a snack."

"Come on, Blackie," said Jessica, walking with him to the tables along the wall. Jessica shooed away the buzzing flies feasting on the remains of the dinner. The children followed them, jumping away when Blackie swung the spike to peer at the food.

"How can I eat with this thing on?" Blackie asked himself.

As Blackie sniffed the platters, he heard Prince George asking the Princess for instructions.

"So, my lady, this quest to the Shrine, when do I leave? Do I travel alone or in company? How about expense money?"

CHAPTER FOURTEEN

Bad Luck Quest

The castle seemed to shake, next morning, under the thunderstorm booming outside. Entering the damp hall, Blackie snorted at the odors of dogs, food, smoke, and humans. He'd slept badly all night, dreaming and waking under the weight of the fronton. His nose was sore.

Prince George looked tired, too. He leaned back in his chair while the Princess addressed the Court after the benediction.

"Good morning, dear people. I hope everyone slept well. Again, our thanks to dear Baron Garst for his hospitality. Delightful!"

She bowed to the Baron, then turned bright eyes to Prince George. "Before the meal, one item of business— My lord Prince, after sleeping on it, I've decided not to have you deliver our Offering to the Shrine."

"Good," thought Blackie. He rubbed his itchy nose against the edge of the table. Prince George snapped to attention with a protest.

"But my lady—"

The Princess threw up a hand.

"It's not that I don't trust you, Prince. You're a skilled and faithful warrior, but Lady Pru reminds me that the necklace is a royal treasure. I was so thrilled at your news of the silver mine last night that I decided to send it on impulse. After taking time to think it over, it seems safer to deliver the necklace myself when the country quiets down. Next fall, I may be free to go on pilgrimage to the Shrine myself with a strong company to guard the Offering."

"My lady!" cried the Prince, throwing himself to his knees before the purple boots. "I swear, Princess, I won't lose the necklace! On my honor as prince and knight, I'll carry your Offering though fire and storm and heaving earth!"

"Don't be dramatic, Georgie!" snapped the Princess. "Get up and give the necklace back. I'll find another quest for you."

"Please, my lady, if I may?"

It was Lady Jessica, stepping beside the Prince.

The Princess spoke impatiently. "What is it, Jessica?"

Jessica spoke in a mild tone. "Why not give the Prince a chance, my lady? You can trust him. He's never failed you yet."

The Princess jerked up her head. "He certainly has failed me, Jessica. Remember the spotted horses? That was an embarrassment for all of us!"

His face red with anger, Prince George opened his mouth to protest again, but Jessica burst out, "That was years ago, my lady, and it was Gypsies that stole those horses! Who can outsmart a Gypsy when it comes to horses?"

The Princess turned to Lady Katherine, who leaned on the chair beside her. "What do you think, Kitty?"

"Why, of course, my lady," said Lady Katherine, slowly, "Prince George should have his chance. What's a ride to the Shrine compared to finding a silver mine? Think of his outrunning the dragon! Besides, as your Grandmother always said, 'A present given is better than three gifts promised.'"

"Well, Princess, I wouldn't trust him!" cried Lady Pru, standing stiffly by in her dark gown. "Not with your Grandmother's necklace, not with a royal treasure."

The Princess turned back to Jessica. "So you think that I should just send it off like that—a single knight to bear a fabulous treasure?"

Everyone looked at Jessica. She blushed and took a deep breath.

"You know how things go, my lady. I'm sure that an angel inspired you to send this Offering to the Shrine. Things will change if you wait, problems arise, details drag you down. You'll lose the blessed moment, and it won't come again. Today, you're moved to send the Offering, and the Prince is eager to take it. Also, you've got the unicorn to carry him through it."

"Well," said the Princess, thoughtfully, "you are right about that." She reached out to rub Blackie's neck.

"Blackie, do you want to carry the Prince on this quest to the Shrine?"

Blackie swallowed the cake he was chewing. He looked at the Prince, who silently implored him with clasped hands.

"Well," thought Blackie, "I've never seen the Fountain. Papa always said that the Shrine is the only place he'd visit again. Might as well go now. I'll see more of the human world on the way."

He nodded the spike on his nose.

"Then I've decided," announced the Princess. "Heaven has given me this notion of the Offering, so Heaven will guard its transmission. We'll pray for you, Prince. We'll wish you luck. Trust the unicorn in your travels. His good sense will get you through. Now, let's eat!"

She dropped into her chair. Two knights pushed her chair to the table. She shook out her napkin, stabbed a chunk of ham with her dagger, and talked as she chewed.

"I must train you in courtesy, Blackie. You're like a scratching dog. You keep eating while I speak. And you, Lady Jessica, contradicting me in public, that's discourtesy, too."

"But my lady," cried Jessica, "you tell us to speak our minds!"

The Princess spread a piece of bread with peach preserves. "Speak your mind, yes, Jessica, but your mind mustn't stray so far from mine. I don't want rumors of dissension in my Court."

Probably the greatest dissenter in the room was Blackie. He hated the thing she had strapped to his head. The fronton make it impossible to look straight at the grapes in his bowl. The angle of the spike kept him from reaching the fruit in the bottom.

"I'm sure it'll catch on branches in the forest," he said to himself. "The Princess meant well with this thing, but it's going to give me trouble."

He looked up from the grapes as Prince George jumped up from his chair and bowed before the Princess.

"My lady?"

The Princess held up a pickled beet on her dagger. "What is it now, my lord?"

"I believe, my Princess, that a knight in your Court should be as eager to serve as the wind. I am ready to leave at once."

Jessica gasped in dismay. Even the Princess protested, "But Prince, you haven't had your breakfast. You should at least wait until the rain eases."

Prince George jauntily waved a hand. "Rain is nothing to the lion in the field. When my lady gives an order, her knight obeys without delay."

The Princess stared at him a moment, then nodded. "As you wish, my lord. I do commend promptness in my officers. You may prepare to leave while the unicorn finishes his meal. Ask the Steward for whatever you need, including a proper pair of boots."

Prince George bowed again and ran from the room. The Princess stood to hug Blackie. He rubbed his cheek against her while breathing in her perfume.

"Oh, Blackie," she murmured, "how I long to keep you with me! I've only known you a couple days, but you're more important to me than anyone. However, we seem to be at a history-making moment. Not only my future, but the Empire itself is at stake now, so it's essential that we stay righteous with the Lord. Sending the Offering will thank Him for all the graces we've received, plus the thought of your quest will keep our minds on higher things during the troubled weeks ahead."

She kissed him and urged him to finish his breakfast. The humans around ate their meat and eggs while Blackie stuffed himself on cakes and fruit until he could barely lick up a blueberry.

By the time Prince George returned, Blackie was standing groggily against the back wall. The Court members leaned elbows on the table or slept with heads in their arms while the Page sang to the Princess.

My lady has the sweetest smile,
brighter than sun in the sky.
It thrills my soul
as she rides to me,
calling, "My love, hi, hi!"

My lady has the fairest hands,
whiter than clouds of the sky.
They break my heart
as she rides away,
waving, "Good-by, Good-by."

My lady has the sweetest scent,
lighter than wind in the sky.
It keeps her near
as she disappears,
leaving a tear in my eye.

The Princess saw the Prince approaching. She clapped her hands.

"Awake my lords! Awake my ladies! Prince George is ready to ride. We shall escort him out to his departure."

Blackie followed the Princess to the door downstairs, held open by guards standing at attention. The Princess paused, breathing in the damp air from the storm. Blackie stood with Prince George while lords and ladies of court and castle squeezed about them.

"Understand, Prince," said the Princess loudly over the splashing rain outside, "the only reason I'm sending the Offering by a single knight is to keep it secret. Our enemies might notice a larger company and attack them for the treasure. A good rider on a fast mount should be able to get through without trouble."

"I'll ride like lightening!" cried the Prince.

BANG!

A fiery bolt cracked down just beyond the castle wall. Shaking, Prince George let go of Blackie and straightened up again. With a nervous glance over his shoulder, he promised, "I'll be back before you know it!"

"We will swear you to the quest right here," announced the Princess, "before heading to the stables. May I see the necklace, please."

Prince George pulled the sparkling red stone from under his shirt on its gold chain. All the ladies whispered, "Ooooh!" The Prince dropped to his knees before the Princess.

A puppy ran from somewhere to sniff around Blackie's hooves. Blackie kicked it away with a foot. It yelped and ran off while the Princess placed her hand on the jewel and spoke in her most stately tone.

"Before the lords and ladies in this castle, I hereby dedicate this treasure to the Shrine of Our Lord, commanding my loyal knight, Prince George of Dacia, to carry the necklace as quickly as possible and to deposit it within the Fountain of Horns."

Prince George placed his hand on that of the Princess. Solemnly, he swore his oath. "On my honor as Prince and Heir to the Kingdom of Dacia, I will deliver this Offering to the Fountain in your name, Princess Julianna, and return to you as quickly as possible."

The Princess stepped back. He sprang to his feet, uncertain what to do next.

"Are you ready to depart, my lord?" questioned the Princess.

"I leave as soon as the unicorn is saddled."

"Saddled?" Blackie swung his head to look at the Prince out the eyeholes of the fronton. "'Unicorn saddled'—what does he mean by that?"

"Those who wish may follow to the stables," said the Princess. She walked to the door where servants waited with wide umbrellas. Most of the Court members turned back at the door, but the Princess, Jessica, and a handful of court ladies splashed through the downpour after Prince George and Blackie. They hurried around the courtyard to the stables.

The smell of straw and dung was heavy in the broad shed as the humans squeezed in after Blackie. Rainfall rattled on the roof.

Blackie glanced about the building at the stalls, hay racks, feed troughs, and buckets. Ropes and tackle hung from pegs about the wall. His attention swung to the horses shuffling about and tossing their heads. They whinnied uneasily as the humans squeezed between them.

Prince George signaled the grooms to bring forth a bulky saddle with dangling straps and stirrups. Two grooms lifted the saddle to Blackie's back.

"Easy, boy, easy boy."

Blackie wasn't having that. He reared and threw off the saddle, shoving squealing humans out into the rain. When the grooms brought the saddle back, he slashed around with the spike, driving them off.

"He's a wild thing, me lord!" cried the Head Groom. "Won't let us get near 'im!"

"Blackie, be reasonable, please!" begged the Prince with a glance at the Princess. "You must accept your saddle for this quest. I don't mind riding bareback for a quick run, but I need a saddle if I'm going to fight on your back."

Blackie shook his head, violently. He did not intend to be strapped up and loaded down like a packhorse.

"I think that saddle's too big for him," said the Princess, petting Blackie. "Try him with a lighter one."

"How 'bout a racin' saddle," suggested the Head Groom. "We got a couple racin' saddles here, not so coombersome as them big ones."

"But my gear!" protested the Prince. "A racing saddle won't have the hooks and straps I need for my armor and supplies."

"Nay, me lord, don't worry your head 'bout straps! A couple stabs with an awl, and I'll run through a dozen leather loops for you. You can hang on a whole kitchen and a washboard if you wants."

Blackie refused even the lightest saddle. He backed against the stalls, shaking his spike, until the Princess skipped over to him.

"Blackie, Blackie." She kissed his ear while scratching him under his chin. "What is this? You know the men have to saddle you for the quest."

Blackie took a long sniff of her scent and felt his objections melt away.

"Naughty unicorn," she chided, combing out his mane with her fingers. "Prince George can't ride bareback like a Bourrid of the desert. Not all the way to the Shrine. Once you're used to this light saddle, Blackie, you'll forget you've got it on. Trust me, you'll see."

Blackie wriggled under her touch.

"For you, sweet Princess," he thought, "I'd haul logs like a woodcutter's ox."

Once the Princess had quieted Blackie, the grooms saddled him in no time. They hung Prince George's new armor from thongs attached to the saddle, a helmet, shield, breastplate, and backplate. They added a rope and a blanket roll, and piled on bags of food. With bridle and reins hanging from his head, Blackie felt like a peddler's donkey.

"Can I ride with all that?" asked the Prince, standing back to inspect Blackie. "I don't think there's room for me with all that stuff."

"Don't complain, Georgie," chided the Princess. "Think of Blackie. He's used to running over the hills with nothing to hold him back. You're lucky to get any sort of saddle on a unicorn. And the glory, think of that! How many knights get to ride a unicorn on a quest?"

"In that case, my lady," Prince George saluted with his sword, "I'm ready to ride."

Lady Jessica handed the Prince a heavy purse stitched with the royal arms.

"This is money for your travel," said the Princess. "Use what you need for expenses. Donate the rest to the Shrine."

Jessica winked at Prince George and whispered to him, "My lady feels generous, Prince, now that the Crown has a silver mine."

Jessica helped the Prince buckle the purse at his waist. He informed the Princess that he was ready to leave. The Princess threw her arms around Blackie's neck.

"Oh, I'll miss you, Blackie! I hate sending you away so soon, but you'll carry the Prince safely through the countryside. And I know that you'll enjoy the Shrine. You'll come back to me stronger than ever."

Already, Blackie regretted the quest ahead of him. How could he enjoy anything with all the stuff piled on him? The straps chafed his chest and belly with every movement while the load weighed him down as much as another rider. But his Princess was still talking to him.

"Heaven be with you, dear beast. You know how I wish I could bear the Offering myself. Be good. Don't throw off your saddle. You must look after Prince George as you would me. Hurry back to me as soon as you can. And you, my lord—"

She straightened to extend a hand to Prince George. "Bless you, Georgie. I thank you again for discovering the silver mine. It was a miracle."

"A miracle, yes," muttered Prince George, "and I did it!"

The Princess frowned at him. "Of course, you did, though, it was me that noticed the dirt pile. I instructed you to search the castle. Let that be, though. You deserve the honor of your efforts. In fact, when we get back to the City, I'll entreat the Bishop to remember you with special prayers on . . . on . . ."

She turned to the Castle Chaplain, standing behind her in his sandals. "Yesterday, Father Stephen, what feast day was that?"

"Umm, umm," Father Stephen stroked his shaven chin. "Twenty-fourth of August, twenty-fifth—The Feast of Saint Louis, I believe. Yes, Saint Louis's Day, the Frenchman!"

"A Frenchman," said the Princess, thoughtfully, "oh, well, I guess, we can pray to a French saint. Saint Louis was a king after all, very appropriate."

She beamed upon Prince George. "So, annual prayers for you on Saint Louis's Day. What do you think of that?"

Prince George shrugged.

"Well, I'm glad I'm not forgotten, my lady. A little appreciation, that's all I ask. And prayers are always welcome."

"I'll pray for you, too, dear Prince!" cried Jessica, and the shivering Court ladies echoed their support.

"We'll start right now," said the Princess, turning to the Chaplain, shivering behind the ladies. "A prayer, Father, for their quest."

"Of course, my lady." The Chaplain lifted his Crucifix as the people crossed themselves. Blackie watched the blessing with interest.

"*In nomine Patre, et Filii, et Spiritus Sanctus.*

"Oh, Lord, we call upon Chistopher, Paul, Louis, and all the saints of Heaven. May they send blessings to these travelers to ward off demons and dragons and sinful desires of the heart. Bless us all, especially our royal lady, Princess Julianna, her lords and ladies, this holy unicorn and this loyal knight, Prince George. For these and all our mercies we thank you."

"Amen," echoed the people.

The Princess scratched Blackie above his spike, then reached down his side. "In your honor, Prince, I hold your stirrup for you to mount."

"Oh, my lady," cried the Prince, "you don't need to do that."

"In your honor—" she repeated, kneeling beside Blackie.

Blushing, the Prince pulled into the saddle. The Princess jumped to her feet.

"Join us back in the City, Georgie, as quickly as you can. As soon as the storm abates, we leave to await Prince Vile's response to your discovery. He hates being thwarted, you know. He'll be humiliated, furious. It's possible that he'll blame you for hindering his schemes, so be very careful!"

Taking a spear from Jessica, Prince George spoke loudly. "No problem, my lady, you'll see me in the City in three weeks. If I'm not back by September's end, you can have my head."

"Don't be silly," warned the Princess. "It'll take three weeks just to get to the Shrine. The important thing is to look after the necklace. It'd be a disaster if you lost it."

Nothing was left but for Blackie to trot out into the rain with everyone cheering. Prince George waved. He shouted that he'd see them all soon in the City. The cheers fell away as Blackie carried the Prince away through the gate passage and out into the flooded trail.

Travel was miserable this morning. Head down under the downpour, Blackie pushed along with hooves clogged with mud. Branches slapped at him while broken limbs in the lane tripped him up. The only creatures he saw were dark ravens flapping sullenly across the trail to croak at him from wet branches. Even the leaves he tore from scratchy bushes were soggy and tasteless.

The Prince was a heavy lump in Blackie's saddle, silent and glum. When they stopped for a break under a large tree that kept off some of the rain, Prince George gnawed a chicken leg and a piece of cheese. He watched Blackie try to crop grass stems along the lane, hampered by the spike that poked from his head.

"That frontal thing," suggested the Prince, "it's in your way. It's fierce and all, but I don't see how can you eat. Shall I remove it? I'm armed again, so I can do the fighting for both of us."

He stood up to reach for the buckle under Blackie's neck, but Blackie pulled back. The Princess had given him that spike. He'd kick off the saddle in a moment, but he was keeping the spike, no matter how he hated it. At least, he was armed against enemies.

As he'd expected, the spike caught on branches when he ran. It dug into the ground when he reached for a blade of grass. The Prince watched him rub the spike against a tree trunk to brush off a clump of mud.

"Well, keep the thing if you want. It's stupid, a bad idea, like this quest. Now that I think about it, I realize that the Princess should have kept us with her until she confronted Vile over the silver mine. That villain won't give up his dreams of power. He's sure to kick up a fuss about the Contract. The Princess will need every warrior she can get to support her, but she won't have us. Not after sending us off to the Shrine with this Offering."

Despite their complaints, the two struggled through the mud and mire on the river trail for two days. About the time the rain stopped, they swung north through a steamy forest road where clouds of bugs swirled through the heavy green of late summer to bite cheeks and necks and Blackie's broad flanks. Prince George tried to spread his new cloak to cover as much flesh as possible, but the fierce little stingers seemed to find their way under the cloth to raise welts the size of copper coins.

Even after the trail ran into the highroad east, their speed did not increase. Prince George didn't know which lords were loyal in this part of the country, so he had to circle most castles. A few days later, they reached the crossroad where the eastern highroad was guarded by the haunted castle of Mandor. Prince George remembered this castle from his previous travels. It stood gray and gloomy above a gibbet where a noose swayed in the wind.

By now, Blackie was hardened to the weight of saddle and man. His load was lighter, too. The armor had been lost while fording a rushing stream, and they'd eaten up their food. Provisions grew so thin that Prince George decided to beg hospitality, one night, at a shabby castle above a lake. He knocked once, twice. They heard a voice demand from above, "Who's down there?"

Blackie lifted his spike to see a hairy head look down from the wall. Prince George held up his arms and called back, "Peaceful travelers to the Shrine. We request quarters for the night."

"Peaceful travelers are ye?" The man looked suspiciously up and down the road behind them. "Hang on a minute."

A moment later, the gate swung open. A dozen dark-bearded men rushed out with spears and axes to surround Blackie.

"Ye sure ye're alone?"

Blackie didn't like the smell of these humans, but Prince George answered graciously.

"Certainly, we're alone. Just a wandering knight and his mount."

"Wanderin' knight, is ye?" sneered the biggest of the men. "Well, we'll just see how generous Lady Boggle be tonight."

"Oh, I'm sure that Lady Boggle will welcome me," said Prince George, trying to sound confident as he dismounted.

"Horses to the stable!" cried a man, pulling on Blackie.

"But this isn't a horse," said Prince George, trying to hold Blackie's reins. "This is the famous unicorn, a holy beast from the heart of the forest."

"Don't matter," said the man, jerking Blackie away. "Unicorns to the stable, too."

"Well, you better go with them," said Prince George, petting Blackie's shoulder. "I'm sure it'll be fine. You'll get plenty of hay and oats with the horses."

"Oh, sure," said the man, laughing nastily, "hay and oats, all he wants. Heaps of 'em!"

Blackie was tempted to fight off the men and stay with the Prince, but things happened so quickly that Prince George was whisked away before he knew it. Next thing Blackie knew, the men were stripping the saddle off his back, then they threw open thick gates at the base of the keep.

Blackie smelled a strong scent of horses as a man cried, "Here you goes, unicorn! Hay and oats down there." He slapped Blackie's rump and rushed him down a slippery ramp.

Scarcely had Blackie taken two steps when the gates were slammed behind him, closing out all light but a sliver of moonlight running up the crack in the middle of the doors. Blackie tried to hold back on the ramp but his hooves slipped on wet stones. Half running, half sliding, he hurtled down into a hot, squealing mass of horses squeezed so tightly together that they barely moved when he pitched into them. They shouted, though.

"Back off!"

"Stop pushing!"

"Make room there!"

Someone nipped Blackie in the side. He tried to jerk around, but the spike caught in someone's mane. He shook fiercely to free himself, but rumps and shoulders squeezed him from all sides. He was packed into a stinking, sweating crowd of horses with barely room to breathe. A chorus of protests rose up when he kicked out for space.

"Who's kickin'?" shouted a gruff voice over the cries. "Who's crowdin' me?"

A huge draft horse shoved through the crowd. He frowned down on Blackie over the back of a gray.

"You better suck in your breath, metalhead. I'll stomp you into mush if you squeeze me!"

"Why," cried Blackie, "why are you all jammed in down here? You don't have room to breathe!"

"They keep shovin' 'em down here," gasped someone. "More and more beasts everyday, with no hay to feed us. Just an armload of thorny branches now and then. We're starving!"

"Not me," said the draft horse, stomping a huge hoof, "I get first bites on all rations. That's the way it goes down here, right?"

"Oh, yes, yes, Perchy." The other horses tried to shrink away from him. "First bites is yours."

Blackie's mane stiffened. His ears were back, his spike up. "Well, I don't know about that," he gritted. "I may just take the first bites, myself."

He tried to squeeze around the gray to reach Perchy, but a chestnut stuck up her head before him. "No fighting, please," she begged. "It squeezes all of us. Horses get crushed against the walls."

"Not me," said Perchy, grinning evilly, "I does the crushin'."

"This is ridiculous!" cried Blackie. "I'm getting out of here! Move back, everyone. Let me get to that gate."

"No way out! No way out!" wailed someone. "They stuffs 'em in and stuffs 'em in, and nobody gets out."

Blackie tried to turn toward the door but horses blocked him from all sides, jostling, squeezing. Then Perchy got annoyed at being pushed. He shoved for space, knocking the gray into Blackie and Blackie into someone behind him.

"Oh, my ribs!" squealed a horse thrown against the wall.

Blackie had enough of this. It was time to get out.

"Hey, there," he snapped. "You, Perchy! Big boy!"

Perchy looked around, rocking the horses beside him. "Whadda ya want?"

"I heard about you. I heard about you before I got down here. They told me you were big."

"Big?" snorted Perchy, pulling his ears back. "I'm not big, I'm enormous!"

"Yeah," said Blackie. "Big and dumb, that's what they said. They're right about the dumb, but you don't look big to me."

"Don't look big!" growled Perchy. "I'll show you big!"

Eyes glaring through the dimness, he crushed over, trying to get to Blackie around the gray. The gray screamed in protest. Perchy pulled back to shove again, but Blackie pushed the horse after Perchy, opening a few inches into the crowd.

"You're not big!" yelled Blackie. "You're just puffed up, a fat, stinking gasbag!"

"No, no!" cried everyone, as Perchy threw his head high, roaring. "Don't make him mad!"

Perchy rose on rear hooves, kicking out and trumpeting. Blackie threw himself at the gray, shoving the poor beast into the space under Perchy's front legs. For an instant, Perchy was held high by the horse under him, half his space empty. Blackie used that moment to twist around and squeeze between the beasts behind him, accidentally scratching someone with his spike.

The horse yelped and moved over an inch. Then Perchy crashed down. Horses squealed, knocked to all directions, but Blackie was shoved toward the ramp. Wriggling between the nags, he dug in his hooves and pulled free, scrambling up the ramp toward that slit of light. Almost deafened by the horses squealing and crying behind him, he poked his spike into the crack between the doors.

"Now, from what Papa told me of gates, there should be a latch here!"

Blackie moved his spike up and down the slot.

The spike hit an obstruction. Blackie heaved up his head and the spike knocked back the latch outside. Blackie set his hooves to shove the doors, and he burst out into the moonlit courtyard.

"He's out! He's free!" cried the horses, scrambling up the ramp after Blackie.

"Let me outta here!" yelled Perchy.

"'Ere, now!" cried a groom, jumping up from a bench by the door, but the horses streamed past, knocking him down.

Blackie ran for the gate, the horses following blindly. They piled up before the great wooden door held by a heavy bar dropped into a pair of brackets. Guards grabbed for horses as Blackie threw up the bar with a mighty sweep of his spike. He pushed open the gate to dash over the drawbridge and stop, panting, under the first shadowy tree. He watched the horses run past him down the road.

The last horse, the gray, hobbled past Blackie, crying, "Wait for me! Wait for me!"

By now, the castle was astir with hairy men running out into the road screeching, "Was that the horses? Where'd they go? Who let 'em loose?"

Someone hollered, "Run 'em down, quick! They'll be scattered by mornin'!"

"Blackie, is that you?" whispered a voice.

Blackie whirled and sniffed. It was Prince George, crawling down from a tree limb.

"I can't believe it!" cried the Prince, hugging Blackie's neck in the shadows. "How'd you escape? Where'd you get all those horses? I didn't know where they'd taken you. I was afraid I was stuck here on foot, forced to hike all the way to the Shrine!"

Blackie stood for the Prince to climb on his bare back, then took off after the horses. Soon enough, he ran past wheezing nags voraciously eating leaves in the dim moonlight. Trotting past a big form chomping ragged weeds beside the road, he called, "So long, Perchy, you midget!"

Perchy didn't lift his head from the fodder.

"If I had a man or two," said Prince George, patting Blackie's neck, "I'd round up those horses and take 'em to town to sell for silver. We did that up at Cranch, the Heir and me. I never told you about that."

He rode in silence a moment, then burst out, "Oh, Blackie, I lost my spear back there and my helmet. The money for the trip, they've got that too. All I have left is my sword and dagger. I grabbed the belt as I ran. And the necklace, they never found the necklace under my shirt, though if that witch had come after me—"

He shuddered.

"I fear, Blackie, this is turning into a bad luck quest. You always run into problems on the road, but lots of quests go sour. It's not always feasts and flags, you know. Why did I talk the Princess into sending me off? My fame's secure. I don't need more songs and stories. I'd turn back in a minute if I hadn't promised her! And we're bareback again, bareback!"

"That's one good thing," thought Blackie, wearily. "At least, we've lost that saddle."

CHAPTER FIFTEEN

Gypsies

The countryside was turning from black to gray when Blackie woke next morning. He breathed heavily as the first bird calls broke the silence. Shivering in long, seedy grass next to a misty lake, he felt too tired to think of eating. He must have dozed off again, for birds were in full song when he fully woke up. Above the tweets and trills, he heard Prince George splash around in the rushes, trying to stab frogs with his sword.

Blackie reached down for grass as the Prince staggered back, dragging his rusting sword. "Not a frog," muttered the human, "not one of them. They jump in the water before I can get near."

Prince George sneezed suddenly, sneezed again and again. He caught himself and gasped, "Don't know why I feel so c-cold all of a sudden. Hope it's not a curse come down on me."

Blackie looked up as the Prince dropped into the wet grass, wrapping his arms around his chest. "I thought I'd had it, last night."

He sneezed once more. "That dreadful castle, that Countess! At least, I saved my sword."

Blackie felt battered himself, his flanks sore from the shoving horses, his nose bruised by the fronton. He almost dropped to sleep again, but Prince George's rambling kept him awake.

"Those hairy rogues, Blackie, they swarmed over me after they took you away. They poked me. They pinched me. Cackling like fiends, they dragged me up to that . . . that chamber with the beaky old crone on her filthy fur bedcover."

The Prince broke into a hacking cough. Losing his breath, he gasped, head down, till Blackie grew alarmed.

"The man's sick!"

Blackie stumbled over to rub the Prince with his nose. Prince George lifted a hand toward Blackie. The hand dropped.

"That Countess, Blackie—worst thing I've seen since . . . since Mother Hungry. Acted like her, too. They could have been sisters!"

Prince George kept talking between coughs, scraping out his story in a halting voice.

"I gotta tell you . . . tell you what happened! Get it out of my head once and for all. The old witch, she kept leering . . . leering at me.

"'What'cha got for the Countess?' she screeched. 'Come closer, pretty man! Gimme my present!'"

The Prince's voice turned anguished.

"Oh, Blackie, I had nothing to give her, nothing! Thank Gabriel, the necklace was tucked under my shirt. At least, she didn't see that. Running her fingers over me, she found my purse. I couldn't stop her. She scattered silver coins across that filthy fur spread on her bed.

"'What's this?' she yelled. 'My present?'"

The Prince beat his head, groaning at the memory.

"Oh, Blackie, she was horrible. First, she counted through the coins—'He loves me lots, he loves me not!' Then she jerked me to her. She rubbed her face against me, licking me, swearing over and over that she'd marry me. She promised to make me her C-Count. She'd send me out to . . . to raid the neighbors. She'd take their lands, and I could keep all the loot for myself.

"I'll never forget her shrieking, 'Stick with your Countess, big boy! You can have the plunder for yourself if you keep Mama happy at home! Wrap your arms around me, sweetmeat! Show me how ya loves me!'

"All the time," gasped the Prince, hugging himself, "All the time, those hairy guards were jumping up and down, pointing at us, screaming with laughter."

Prince George was shaking again, whimpering at the memory. Blackie pressed close to nuzzle him, trying to calm him. But the Prince pulled away.

"'Woo me!' she yelled. 'Court me! Sing to me like a cavalier!' Suddenly, she screeched with misery and jumped up on her bed like an ape. She grabbed a cracked mirror from under a pillow."

Prince George rocked back with a moan. He held a shaking hand in front of his face as though looking into a mirror.

"'My looks, my looks,' she wailed. 'I've lost my pretty face, lost my beauty! No one could love me like this! No, no, no, I must prink and primp, make myself pretty with paints and powders, my rouge, my rouge! Then you'll love me! Then I'll wear my silky red gown, and you'll love me."

Prince George fell back in a spasm of coughing that racked his whole body. Alarmed, Blackie tried to tell him, "Don't talk! Stay silent, please! Try to get control over yourself."

Of course, the Prince couldn't understand this. He finally choked down his cough and lay quietly a moment, wheezing, before picking up his story again.

"In the corner . . . cobwebby, dusty, her dressing table. Calling for candles, she hung the mirror on a nail over the table and commenced smearing paints on her face, making herself . . . uglier . . . if that's possible. The guards threw me back and forth, pounding my back and yelling, 'Ain't she a one! Wait'll you see her all decked out! She gonna burn you up like a comet, boy!'"

Prince George gave Blackie an anguished look.

"What could I do, Blackie? I had to get out of there, so I gathered up the silver coins scattered over that fur cover and gave them to the guards. I had just enough for two coins apiece. Once they'd bitten the coins and found them genuine, the hairy men bustled me down the stairs, whispering to me.

"'Naw, naw, me lord, you can't stay with that old Countess! She's low, Master, lower than a snake! You don't know! We could tell you stories, what happened to the old Count and all! You better get out of here while you can.'

"And the Countess, back in her chamber, I could still hear her yelling to me, 'Hang on, sweetheart! Fight back your passion till you see this goddess throbbin' with love! Hold onto your horses, baby! Mama's comin' home!'"

Prince George lapsed into silence, panting, shivering. After a moment, he gasped, "So that's it. I escaped without money, armor, food. What's the use, what's the use?"

He ran down, softly coughing. Blackie wobbled on his hooves, his head low in the grass as the frogs croaked about them.

"No wonder this human's sick. He caught some disease in that horrible place. Oh, my horn, my horn! I need my horn to heal him!"

An hour or so later, Blackie was awakened by a shower that spattered the lake and washed sweat and dirt from his coat. Prince George was drawn up in the grass, soaked, shaking in his sleep. When the Prince woke at last, he was flushed and sweating, too sick to move. Hoarsely, he complained that he was freezing.

"My throat's raw, too. I couldn't eat a thing, not even a spoonful of . . . of mole meat if I had it."

Shivering pitifully, he broke into a hacking cough. Blackie leaned over him, nuzzled him, but didn't know how to help him. The Prince rolled away, shivering. Blackie backed off. He drifted over to the lakeshore to eat the long grass while Prince George coughed himself back to sleep.

Blackie stuck with the Prince all morning. About noon, he left the shivering man. He walked around the lake to see if he could find anything for the Prince to eat. He watched bugs zooming over the water. He sniffed over a boat pulled up on the bank, but found nothing for the Prince, who seemed sicker than ever when Blackie returned.

All night, Prince George gasped and wheezed, wheezed and gasped. His deep, choking coughs kept Blackie awake. At dawn, next day, Blackie staggered over to smell the Prince, curled up like a caterpillar, reeking with sweat and infection.

Blackie touched Prince George with his nose again. He pulled back and looked carefully at the pale, shaking man. Blackie was frightened. What can you do for a sick man if you don't have a horn? He felt helpless, totally helpless. It was worse than being alone, feeling responsible for this man with no way to help him.

Blackie drew in a breath. "What if he gets sicker? What if he d-dies!"

Blackie grew still. His breath rasped in his throat. "The Offering, I'd have to carry it myself, but—"

He shook himself hard. "Stupid, stupid! I can't take the necklace. How'd I get it off his neck? If he dies, I'll . . . I'll run home to Mama. Oh, Mama, Mama, I wish I were home with you right now!"

How Mama would comfort him at home in the Nest! She'd nuzzle him and promise that he'd feel better. "You're going to grow up big," she'd say, "and have a long, long horn."

"No horn now," he whispered. "I have no horn at all!"

Blackie leaned forward to touch the Prince with his spike. Nothing, the spike did nothing. He touched the man on the arm and on the neck.

Prince George jerked and the blade scratched him. The man whimpered.

"I . . . I can't heal him," Blackie groaned. "I can't help him. I can guard him from wolves and bears—that's all I can do for him. Even if I could take the necklace, how would I find the Shrine? It's to the east, they say, the far east. But the east is all mountains. I wouldn't have any idea where to go."

Blackie sighed. He hobbled back to the lake. It was swept with broad bands of light by the breeze. Blackie drank. He lifted his nose to sniff the air and his ears perked up. He smelled cooking fires and horses.

Humans had ridden up! Fear struck him. "The hairy men from the castle! They'll find the Prince! I don't think I can move him."

Leaving the Prince rolled up in the grass with his arms over his head, Blackie trotted around the lake the way he'd gone yesterday. Smelling the fire more and more strongly, he followed a path through the brush until he could see over the bushes.

The first thing he saw was a green cart trimmed in yellow. Its walls were rounded up like a loaf of bread spilling over the baking pan. Half a dozen horses were staked to one side. Dark men in crumpled hats played cards before it. Beyond it, chattering women cooked fish over the fire while screeching children climbed up the rear of another wagon, one after another, to jump off into the grass.

A young girl with bracelets on her arms came out of the door of the wagon. Swinging her arms to jump, she looked up. She spotted Blackie. She stopped and pointed.

"Loose horse!" she sang out. "Loose horse, everyone, loose horse!"

All the Gypsies jumped up to look the way she was pointing. They moved toward Blackie. Skinny dogs ran from under the wagons, barking as women and children spread out to come at Blackie from two sides. The women yelled at the dogs to stay back.

"*Grastie, Grastie,*" the children called to Blackie, "nice *Grastie.*"

Blackie backed into bushes. The Gypsies stopped. An old woman yelled at the men. They lazily pulled ropes from a wagon. They limped close as the barefooted children circled further, trying to get behind Blackie.

Blackie lowered his head and shook his spike. The men froze.

"Better watch this one, Lazlo!" called a scrawny man with half an ear missing. "He'll stab you in your paunch!"

A large man with a wide mustache swished through the bushes in dirty boots. He snapped a long horsewhip. "Back, Ference!" he called. "Watch me snare this pigeon."

He stepped slowly toward Blackie, looping the whip.

"Easy, young *Grast*, easy. Hold still. Stay calm. By Mother Moon and all the saints, you're a treasure. Someone will pay handsomely for you!"

"This creature is a treasure indeed, my father!" cried an older girl running closer. Blackie saw her bold eyes, golden earrings, red slippers.

"This is the beast that Prince Vile seeks," she explained, "the unicorn! Look at his chest! Look at his tail!"

"Ah, the unicorn!" gasped Lazlo, stopping. "You are right, Lizetta, our luck has turned! Be careful. Don't alarm him. Do you have your medicines, daughter? We'll drug him and chain him to the wagon till we can sell him to Prince Vile."

"Chain me?" said Blackie, turning away. "I don't think so. Come along, you humans. Follow me to Prince George. Perhaps you can help him."

He trotted through the circle of children, shaking his blade when a boy reached for him. The children chased after, screeching like birds. Lazlo stumbled along, crying, "Unicorn, unicorn, come back, come back! We have treats for you, good things to eat—veggie pies, oats, barley!"

Blackie ran to Prince George, drawn up, sleeping. The children circled, yelling to each other, while Blackie stood over the man, swinging his spike.

The Prince lifted his head.

"Wha—, wha—, wha—! Leave me 'lone, Sir Otley, leave me 'lone."

Stepping around Blackie, Lizetta called with delight, "Look, my father, it's that Prince from Dacia. There's a reward for him too."

Lazlo trudged close with his whip. He threw his hands to the heavens. "Holy saints, what luck! The Black Lord will pay anything for the pair of them! For the man alone, we'll get a fortune!"

"Go ahead," urged Ference. "Cut his throat! Remember how he wanted to hang us back at Furland!"

Lazlo shook his head.

"No, no, no, the man's too valuable for that! Prince Vile wants him alive. The raven promises rewards for both of them and for the Princess. With two of the three, we can hold out for our great dream!"

"Then get to it, Lazlo," urged Ference. "The man's down. Let's catch the beast and finish the job."

The Gypsies all looked at Blackie. He watched them carefully. The young girl who'd first spotted Blackie ran from the wagons with a faded red blanket in her arms.

"Here, Sister!" she cried, tossing the blanket to Lizetta.

Lizetta caught it. "Good thinking, Sara."

Holding the blanket under an arm, Lizetta sauntered around the bushes as Lazlo and the men stepped toward Blackie. Blackie backed away, swinging his spike from side to side. Suddenly, Lazlo snapped his whip to draw Blackie's attention while Lizetta jumped from behind, throwing the blanket over Blackie.

All went dark for Blackie. He tumbled into a thorn bush, dragging the Gypsies with him. The shrieking children piled on him, wrestling him to the ground as he tried to kick them off.

"Ow! Ow!" the children cried in the prickly spines.

Blackie rolled to his hooves with a mighty heave. He threw off the Gypsies with the blanket except for Sara who clung to a rear leg like a leech. Lazlo ran forward, lashing the whip around Blackie's neck, digging in his boots to hold him.

"Don't resist, young beast, don't resist!" he panted. "Your father, the white unicorn, he's our friend! He visits our camp at the edge of the forest. We give him grain from the farmers, and he heals our sickness."

Kicking free of Sara, Blackie charged at Lazlo. The man leaped away from the spike. The whip fell to the ground and Blackie dashed free of the Gypsies. They chased after, howling like Hellhounds, but Blackie ran off a couple hundred yards. He turned to look back.

The Gypsies had stopped. The men helped Lazlo to his feet while Lizetta picked up the whip. They turned back to Prince George. Blackie heard Lizetta's voice over Lazlo's moans.

"Ference, Nabil, lift the lord carefully and bear him to the *vardo*. We will treat him with love as we would a fine *grastie*."

"Oh," panted Blackie, "those Gypsies are terrible. That Lazlo would sell the Prince for an acorn, but what can I do? The human needs care. He's too sick to lie in the grass. If only I had my horn!"

Off to the side, Blackie noticed Sara creeping toward him again with the blanket under her arm, the children following her.

"No, no, you don't!"

Blackie turned and galloped halfway around the lake. When he felt safe, he swished through damp bushes to the water for a drink. He ate lilies floating on the lake and worried about Prince George. No matter how he studied the situation, he could think of nothing to do but to leave the Prince to the Gypsies. With luck, he'd find a way to steal the Prince back once the man was healthy.

Blackie continued around the lake that afternoon, sniffing rocks and bushes. He waded through sticky mud at the marshy end to graze on low-hanging tree branches and tufts of coarse grass. Blackbirds flew up from tall horsetails in the water.

Blackie flicked bugs from his ears and yawned. When night shaded down, he stepped up the bank. He slept with frogs croaking about him.

Next morning was cool and foggy. As day came on, the fog cleared, but the sky stayed dim with heavy clouds. The breeze blew cool through the low, gray hills.

Blackie wandered around the lake, browsing on the long grass. By afternoon, he was back at the Gypsy camp, grazing on bushes a quarter mile from the wagons while Sara watched from the shade of a tree. Sara jumped up and ran near when Lizetta strolled out to talk to Blackie.

"I have news for you, unicorn, good news," said Lizetta, holding out a hand. Her heavy perfume came to Blackie. He took a step back. Lizetta smiled at him.

"Your Prince is getting better. My medicines are healing him. In a day or two, you may carry him away."

Blackie gave her a skeptical look.

"You must understand, dear beast," she continued, "the people have known this Prince for many years. In the past, we have helped him search for lost horses. We served him at the castle of Countess Amalia of Furland. We love him like a brother, but—"

Lizetta slipped closer to Blackie. She scratched him around the spike.

"You need care, yourself. You're covered with scratches, bruises. That blade, so heavy, so troublesome, it rubs the skin on your forehead. It must itch terribly. If you allow me, I'll remove it for you and put salve on your forehead. I'll give you a good bath, too, and a brushing. Let the people care for you. You can trust Lizetta."

Blackie wheeled suddenly and ran back around the lake. He stopped a half-mile away and shook himself to throw off Lizetta's perfume.

After that, the Gypsies left him alone to browse among the bushes. Only Sara came near, creeping as close as Blackie would let her. A couple of the scrawny dogs ambled out to sniff at his hooves. When Blackie tried to talk to them, they lifted their legs on the bushes and ran back to the camp.

Blackie felt himself grow drowsy. This waiting around was boring. He didn't need the turmoil of the last few days, but he was tired of watching Gypsies from afar. He had no idea how long it would take the Prince to get well. It might take weeks.

As the sun drooped in the west, Blackie grazed along the lake, watching the colors thrown over the waters by the setting sun. Yawning from boredom, it struck him that he could leave the Prince with the Gypsies, at least until the man recovered.

"Why hang around here?" he asked himself. "The human could be sick for a month. I can't help him in that wagon. I can't even see him. Why should I stick with this quest, anyway? It was Prince George that promised to carry the Offering, not me, and, now, he's stuck. There's no way I can get him out of the wagon. I might as well give it up and head home. He'll have to save himself."

Blackie stepped into the lake and took a long drink for the night. He shook water off his nose.

"But what would I do at home? Grandpa didn't stay home. He was always off fighting dragons. And Papa's boring. He doesn't do anything at all, just hangs around the forest eating mushrooms. I'd like to feast with the Princess, to play with her and carry her on rides, but not if she keeps sending me on quests like this."

Unable to make up his mind what to do, Blackie decided to stay a little longer to see what happened to the Prince. He went back to eating tree leaves until his ears caught the sound of singing. He looked under the branches to see the children walking down a path. Sara led them, singing as they came.

> Oh, onions make the soup.
> We chop, chop, chop,
> and drop them in the pot
> with a plop, plop, plop.

> The soup, the soup,
> the hot, hot soup.
> We drink up the soup
> from a big brown cup.

> And carrots make the soup.
> We chop, chop, chop,
> and drop them in the pot
> with a plop, plop, plop.

> The soup, the soup,
> the hot, hot soup.
> We drink up the soup
> from a big brown cup.

"Hello, unicorn!" called Sara. "We're gathering sticks for the fire. Night's coming on. It's cozy around the fire with a big cup of soup and a piece of warm bread."

She held out her hand. "We brought you a treat, a barley cake, hot from the baking pan."

Blackie sniffed the cake. It smelled good, but he was suspicious. He turned away his nose.

"Must be medicines in it," he thought. "Sleepy drops, love potion, something. Papa warned me about their medicines."

"Eat, eat," urged the girl, "is good."

"I can eat four of them," said a boy, rubbing his stomach.

Blackie shook his head and backed away.

"Look," said Sara, "I'll take a bite of the cake to show you how good it is. I'll nibble the plain side and leave the half with raisins to you."

Blackie shook his head. Why would they leave raisins to him? The raisins were probably soaked in poison.

He tossed his head and galloped back around the lake. At the upper end, he sniffed about for a comfortable resting place near the small stream bubbling into the lake. Stepping through shoulder-high rocks, he found a crevice hidden from the wind. It smelled of bear, but had a smooth, dry floor.

He ate stringy leaves beside the stream until the sun went down and the wind began to rise. He backed into the nook and leaned his side against the warm rock.

"The Prince," he thought, "I wonder how he's doing. Will I see him again?"

Tired as he was, Blackie slept through the night without dreaming until the rock chilled toward morning. He woke shivering. He turned in the narrow space and tried to sleep again, but hunger drove him out to the lake steaming with fog. As sunlight warmed the countryside, he browsed his way back toward the Gypsies.

The air was clear by the time he neared the Gypsy camp. Casually, he grazed along a chain of bushes with sweet leaves. He swung out to pass the camp and return to the path around the lake, but halted. He sniffed the path leading between trees.

Something was different here. He saw that the earth was disturbed. Blackie stepped forward and poked a dry bush with his spike. It was loose. He kicked it with a hoof. It collapsed into the earth.

Blackie looked down into a pit dug into the ground. It had been covered with sticks and bushes.

196

"What's this?" he cried, indignantly. "A trap? Do those humans really think I'd fall into this thing! They must think me a fool! I should run down and chase off their horses!"

Turning through the trees, he took a long look at the camp. One of the women was up, throwing sticks into the fire. Blackie trotted on around the lake to return to the marshy end. He had a quiet morning grazing on the grass, listening to bird calls.

"Unicorn, unicorn!"

Blackie turned to see who was calling him. Again he saw the girl, Sara, skipping along and waving to him. He looked around, warily. No one appeared to be following her.

"Oh, unicorn," she cried, throwing her arms around his neck, "good news of your Prince! He's better this morning, much better. He wants you to visit and keep him company for dinner. Uncle Lazlo says that he'll be able to leave in a day or two. Won't that be grand?"

"It'd be grand if I could believe it," said Blackie to himself. The girl hugged him and stroked his nose with her soft hand. He shook his head and snorted.

"Come along with Sara," she murmured, kissing him around the ears. "Don't hold back. Come along with me. Lizetta says that unicorns are drawn to maidens. You must give in to me. Listen to your heart. Follow Sara, follow, follow, follow."

She gently pulled him by his mane. Shocked, Blackie followed a step or two.

"She's pretending to be a princess," he realized. "She thinks that I'll obey her and go into that camp so they can chain me up. Well, I'll fool them. I'll go along with her a little to see what they're up to. I won't eat anything, though. I'm sure they have their medicines ready, brews to turn me into a pig or something. I do want to see the Prince. If he's well enough, I'll carry him off at once."

He took a step after Sara. Exultant, she threw her arms around his neck.

"I knew it! I do have power over you! Just relax, unicorn, and give in to Sara. You love me. You want to obey . . . obey . . . obey. Don't worry, I'll protect you and see that nothing harms you. Hold still. I'll ride you back to camp. It's far around this lake, and I ran all the way here."

"Here it comes," thought Blackie. "Put the unicorn to work. Well, she's light enough, so I might as well be a good beast for the moment."

Blackie relaxed. Sara jumped halfway up his back and wriggled up the rest of the way. She settled herself, crowing with delight, as Blackie lifted his head and trotted around the path.

"So handsome!" she cheered. "So strong! Such a high-stepper!"

They were soon at the Gypsy wagons. Lizetta hurried out to meet them.

"I've got him!" cried Sara. "I've tamed the unicorn!"

"So you have, Little Sister," agreed Lizetta. "As I told you, the unicorn always submits to a maiden. Ride him into camp, now."

Blackie stiffened as the Gypsies swarmed around him, rubbing his muscles, admiring his shape. Sara laughed proudly, calling Blackie to prance up to the fire. Hissing in a strange tongue, Ference pulled a clanking chain from the rear of his wagon.

"Oh, Uncle!" exclaimed Sara, "we don't have to chain up the unicorn, do we? He doesn't need a chain. I've tamed him, as you see."

"No, no, we won't have to chain the beast," smiled Lazlo, signaling Ference to toss the chain back in the wagon. "Now that you've tamed him, he won't want to escape. He can wander about the camp as he pleases."

Sara beamed as the Gypsies admired her unicorn. "He gave me no trouble. I caught him as you said, Sister. The unicorn wanted to come with me when I was kind to him."

"Now, you must take good care of him," advised Lizetta. "Groom him well and give him oats when you feed the horses. Not too much now. He's not used to that sort of food, but give him a good portion."

"Oh, I will, Sister," promised Sara.

She drew Blackie into the shade under the trees and began brushing him with a stiff-bristled brush. Blackie closed his eyes and relaxed under the strokes. He drew back when other Gypsies walked by, but they just smiled and continued on. About the time Sara finished brushing him, Lazlo came up to check on him.

"You see, Uncle," she said. "No chains are necessary. The handsome beast will do as we wish without drugs or fetters. He'll stay healthy that way, and you'll get a greater price for him."

"It appears that you're right," said Lazlo, scratching Blackie's neck. "Clean his hooves now and feed him with the other beasts. The Prince wants to see him when he's fed."

After all the talk about chains and drugs, Blackie was nervous about this feeding business. He watched carefully as Sara poured half a bag of oats into the wooden manger for the horses and then the rest into a bucket for himself. She tossed the empty bag into the door of a wagon.

Eating from the bucket was difficult with the spike, so Sara fed him his oats a handful at a time. Scarcely had he licked up the third handful than drowsiness swept over him.

"You look tired, dear unicorn," said Sara. "Would you like to run back to your sleeping place beyond the lake?"

Blackie nodded. Sara kissed him and waved to him as he wobbled off a few steps. He had barely passed the last cart before fatigue struck him. He slowly collapsed into the bushes. As he passed out, he heard Sara shout with triumph.

"See, Father, you don't need chains and traps to catch a unicorn! All it takes is a clever maiden."

CHAPTER SIXTEEN

The Chain

In his dream, Blackie struggled to throw off a huge centipede. It crawled over him with its hundred legs, pinching and plucking at him. From somewhere, he heard Gypsy voices speaking.

"So, the handsome beast has awakened at last!"

"I told you he would, Mother Teresa."

Blackie pulled away from the clawing legs. He shook awake with a terrible headache under his spike. The spike, the spike, where was the spike? Blinking in pain, Blackie lifted his head. The fronton was gone. He closed his eyes again.

"See?" said Lizetta. "As I told you, the unicorn is good as ever."

"Still, my granddaughter," said a woman's voice, "I would not have mixed more than a spoonful of the drug in his oats. Remember, he's not fully grown yet."

Someone pulled at Blackie's eyelid to look in his eye. Staring up, he saw an old Gypsy woman bending over him in a yellow shawl and beads. She shook her head as she inspected him.

"You might have harmed him with that much medicine."

"No, no," argued Lizetta, standing next to the woman, "he's a unicorn. Stronger, much stronger than any horse his size. I doubled the dose, and it knocked him out perfectly."

The Gypsies left him alone then. Blackie closed his eyes and tried to ease his head. Blinking hurt, breathing hurt, even twitching his tail was painful, and he couldn't move. Squinting his eyes to see what was binding him, Blackie saw a rusty chain holding his legs in a rigid embrace. He could only squirm and roll.

Looking slowly around, he saw horses tearing leaves from the bouncing branches of small trees behind the Gypsy carts. Chewing away, the horses watched him solemnly.

An old mare belched. "So, unicorn, what did you do get yourself chained up like this?"

Blackie took a careful breath. "They think . . . I'll run away . . . if they don't chain me."

"Why run away?" said the mare. She stripped the leaves from a branch and swallowed. "That'd be dumb. There's no place to go."

Blackie had to speak up at that. "What do you mean, no place to go? There's a whole Empire out there with forests, fields, gardens."

The mare nodded at the other horses.

"We know what's there, youngster. We've walked over it, mile by mile, but it's lonely out there by yourself. You're better off here with the herd."

Blackie tried to stretch, but the chain cut into his shoulders and legs. He had to settle back, sighing.

"How am I better off? My horn's gone. My spike's gone. I'm down to bare forehead again. I hate it! Chained up like this, a cow could push me around."

Groaning in misery, he let himself drift back to sleep. He jerked awake when hands, smelling of onions, clasped his head. Someone kissed him on the forehead.

"Here I am, unicorn! I couldn't come see you till now. I'm helping with the cooking."

Looking up again, he saw Sara smiling at him. She began wiping grit and sweat from his face with a wet rag.

"Ference says that I can care for you until we travel to Prince Vile. Isn't that lucky? I'll get you on your feet as soon as I shake out your chain. It's twisted all about you, cutting into your legs."

Kneeling beside him, Sara unwrapped the chain around his left leg. "You did this to yourself, unicorn, the way you jumped and kicked last night. You twisted yourself up till you couldn't move. Ease up. Let go. Roll over so I can free this last leg. Here, I'll help you."

Sara unwound the chain and straightened the links to the tree it wrapped around. "There, isn't that better? Now, you can stand up."

Blackie took a breath. He pushed to his hooves, his head aching worse than ever. The horses stepped back warily as Blackie stretched and shook hard. The chain clanked with each movement.

Blackie felt scraped and bruised. His head hurt, his neck hurt, but he was able to move in the bushes. He picked off leaves while Sara washed his back.

"We worried about you all night," she said. "Lazlo yelled at Sister for mixing so much medicine in your mash. It was a great trick, wasn't it, making you believe that we thought a maiden could control you?"

She laughed merrily.

"How we fooled you! It was funny to see you pretend to obey me! What a story that will make! The people will tell forever of pretty Sara and her unicorn. And you don't have to be ashamed, sweet beast. We trick all the *Gadjos*. The people live by wits and wiles, you know. Your Prince now, Sister Lizetta says he's a greater dunce than you. She has a hundred stories of tricking him. I'm sure that you'll never be as gullible as he is."

"The Prince," thought Blackie, "I wonder where he is. Do they have him chained up too?"

"It's good that you have this day to recover," said Sara, twirling around. "We're to travel tomorrow if you're well enough. We go north to the Portal to sell the pair of you to the Black Prince."

She picked up her rag to wash the rust from Blackie's coat.

"Evil as he is, I worry that Prince Vile will hurt you. Lizetta says he must value you to pay such a reward. Imagine, in return for the two of you, he'll give us the freedom of the roads! We can travel at will for five generations. No tolls, no fines, no jails, no gibbets. It'll be heavenly for the people. Lizetta says that the Black Lord will make you his pet. You'll run around his garden and eat strawberries while the people get rich from the *Gadjos*!"

Blackie groaned. His head felt worse than ever, but Sara laughed gleefully.

"And think of the husband Lazlo can buy for me—handsome, clever, totally under my spell! Lizetta says that I can have the gold chain from the necklace for my wedding, a treasure to pass down to my daughter."

"The Offering," Blackie remembered with a groan, "the Princess's necklace! Of course, these Gypsies would steal it! What can we deliver to the Shrine now?"

Sara leaned over again, staring into his eyes.

"Are you sick, Unicorn? I see pain. I'm afraid that Lizetta's medicines were too strong for you. Stay quiet, and I'll get Sister to treat you. She has remedies for the headache, you know—valerians, St. John's wort! You see, I'm learning the medicines, too. We'll have you healthy and happy in no time."

She jumped up and ran around the cart. Blackie stepped to the end of the chain, jerked against it. The rusty links hurt his neck. He backed up to ease the chain and stood, miserable. How he'd let the Princess down!

"And Vile," he realized, "these Gypsies plan to sell me to Vile!"

The old mare looked at him with amusement. "Look at you, unicorn, riled up like an old badger! What you been eating to get yourself colicky like that? You must have been at the stinkweed!"

Lizetta was back in a moment with a black bottle. She threw herself down by Blackie and popped the cork.

"Open your mouth, sweetheart! Lizetta says this potion will clear your head. Don't worry, it's only herbs, honey, and wine. Open up, take your medicine."

"Not me," thought Blackie, clamping his jaws, "I'm not playing your game! No more medicines for me."

He looked defiantly at her, breathing in and out through his nose.

"Oh, you want to play!" laughed Sara. She snatched up the wet cloth she'd used to wash him. She wrapped an arm around his head. Taking up the bottle in one hand, she pressed the cloth over Blackie's nose with the other hand.

Blackie couldn't breathe. He tried to shake her off. Sara flew back and forth, but she held his nose. Blackie's chest heaved. Sweat poured over his cheeks until his breath exploded out his open jaws. When Blackie sucked in air, Sara dropped the cloth and poured in the medicine from the bottle. She jumped back as Blackie choked and spat, but most of the nasty stuff went down his throat.

"Now, you'll feel better!" laughed Sara. "You'll see. I'll drop by later to check on you. I have to go help cook dinner."

She ran off, leaving Blackie with a horrible taste in his mouth. A moment later, Lazlo walked around the cart with Ference. Nabil slouched behind, sucking a straw. They watched Blackie for several minutes. Lazlo whacked Ference with the whip.

"I want you to take care of the unicorn."

Ference yelped and jumped away, whimpering, "But my King, the little one's doing a good job. The unicorn's healthy. Sister Sara knows how to care for *grasti*."

"She can wash him and feed him," growled Lazlo. "But you're in charge of holding him. If he escapes, I'll sell you to the Black Prince in his place!"

"Don't worry, Lazlo. The mother bolt will hold that chain."

The men walked off, leaving Blackie in misery. He and Prince George were to be sold to Vile. He didn't believe for a moment that demon would give him strawberries.

The horses stopped eating leaves to shake their heads at him. A young male said, "He must be a bad 'un to get chained up like that."

"I think he bites," said the mare.

Agonizing over the situation, Blackie sank deeper into his misery till he fell asleep again. When he woke, the sun was high. He was hungry. Without thinking, he reached out to snatch leaves, but the chain held him until he stepped back, easing the pull. Now, he smelled the smoke from the fire, the tree leaves, and the horses dozing together in the shade. The pair of dogs, watching from under a bush, grinned and licked their jaws when he shook himself. He realized that his headache had lightened. The misery of being chained was even deeper.

Late in the afternoon, Lizetta walked around to inspect him. Sara skipped behind with a bucket of oats.

"No medicines in this lot, unicorn," Lizetta said cheerily.

He sniffed cautiously until his hunger drove him to eat. Ignoring the horses jostling around, demanding their share, the girls admired him while he plunged his nose into the bucket. They took it away once the oats were gone. The horses settled down, and things grew quiet.

Rubbing his itchy forehead against the tree, Blackie listened to the whining bugs. He shook out his chain to ease it. The smells of fire and cooking came to him as the evening grew dark. Now, the Gypsies were talking and laughing. A violin took up a melody. A woman began singing.

Somewhere, the home that we're seeking.
Somewhere, the shading trees.
Somewhere, the fruit and the berries,
the swarms of honeybees.

Somewhere, the gardens are open.
Somewhere, the eggs are free.
Chickens run up for the plucking.
A barrel of wine rolls to me.

Somewhere, the Gypsies are dancing.
Somewhere, the song rises high,
and nobody weeps for tomorrow
or thinks of the past with a sigh.

Blackie's ordeal started early next morning. The whole camp was stirring before dawn. Dogs barked, horses neighed, humans clattered about and yelled at each other. Blackie tried to ignore them, but Ference came around the cart to poke Blackie with a stick.

"Wake up, unicorn."

The Gypsy walked around Blackie, straightening the chain. Blackie kicked at him and Ference jumped away. Nabil joined him. The two stood together, looking at the chain while Blackie glared at them.

"He's going to get away, I know it," said Ference, shaking his head. "The moment we unwind the chain from the tree, he's gone."

"No, he's not," said Nabil, spitting into the bushes. "Not if we keep a loop about the tree while we fix the end of the chain to the mother bolt of the wagon. That bolt will hold him to doomsday."

Blackie had to make a quick decision as the men moved around the tree to unwind the chain end. He could defend the chain where it was. It would be easy enough to drive them off. That would keep the Gypsies from traveling north to meet Prince Vile. How they'd hate that—to be stuck in one spot, unable to move.

On the other hand, it might be better to travel along. He could look for a chance to escape with Prince George on the road. No matter what Ference said, Blackie was sure that no bolt could hold him. The moment he saw Prince George healthy enough to ride, he'd break loose, scoop up the Prince, and dash away from these Gypsies. He might lose the necklace in escaping, but once he found another spike, they could get the necklace back from this bunch.

Even if he did intend to go along, Blackie didn't make it easy for them. He lunged back and forth. He kicked at the Gypsies and snapped with his strong jaws. They tried to trick him between them, one dancing in to draw his attention while the other loosened the end of the chain. By timing it right, Blackie could whirl around on the man at the chain and get in a good kick before he scrambled out of range.

This game cheered Blackie. He laughed to himself before the yelps and curses of the men brought Sara running.

"Bad Unicorn!" she cried. She grabbed Blackie's ear and held him down. Blackie relaxed. He wouldn't hurt the girl that fed him. As she directed, he backed peacefully into the shafts hooking him to the wagon. Seeing Blackie held down, Ference whapped him on the rear with his stick.

"Don't hit the unicorn when he behaves!" cried Sara.

Blackie glared at Ference, promising a good kick to pay the Gypsy back for that blow. Once Blackie was in position to pull the wagon, the Gypsies ran the chain through a ring under the big horse collar they pulled over his head. The other end of the chain was clamped to the central bolt holding the front axle to the cart. After they strapped leather harness about him, they went off to harness the other horses.

Sara stayed with him for a moment, full of delight.

"Now, you'll see how the people live, unicorn—new roads, new places, and *Gadjos* to trick. Travel keeps us alert and alive. It makes us sing."

When Sara ran off to see to her packing, Lizetta came around to see how Blackie was doing. Today, she wore a red hat on her head and a green shawl over her shoulders. She patted him and gave him carrots, then checked the chain to be sure it was bolted to the cart.

"I'm sorry you have to pull my cart, unicorn. We face difficult travel the next few days, crossing back trails to reach the Portal. We must stay off main roads in this journey—less chance of barons seizing you or Prince Vile catching us on his dragon. If we make a regular trade at the Portal, we'll have witnesses to avoid difficulties. That's better for everyone."

Blackie ate leaves while the Gypsies took their time getting loaded, forgetting this and changing that while constantly complaining and arguing among themselves. At last, Ference took his place beside Blackie and smacked out with his stick.

"Get moving, beast!"

Leaning into the harness, Blackie found that pulling a wagon was no fun. The cart rolled easily on the flat, clear trail until it hit rocks or caught brush in the wheels. On hills, though, the load dragged. Blackie had to dig in his hooves to haul it upward while the collar chafed his neck and the chain scraped at his chest. Even worse, when they crossed to the other side of the hill, the weight shoved down on him. He had to stiffen his legs and take choppy little steps to hold the wagon back from rolling over him.

The most frustrating thing for Blackie was the plodding pace of the horses. It took them all morning to go four miles. When Lazlo called a rest stop, the tribe settled in for hours. Smoke from a fire floated to Blackie cropping grass beside the horse harnessed to the next wagon.

"This as fast as you go?" asked Blackie. "Creeping along like this?"

"Creeping!" said the horse with a snort. "This is speeding for Gypsies. Who'd want to go faster, pulling carts up hills?"

"Oh," said Blackie, "I'm used to a real run. Forty miles in a day is nothing if I'm carrying my Princess."

The horse tore off a branch of leaves and chewed slowly. "Well," he said, swallowing, "don't know about a Princess, but we mainly amble along slow and easy. We stop at villages to pick up chickens and read futures. Travelin' with Gypsies ain't a bad life, but they'll sell you at the drop of a leaf. Buyin' and sellin', stealin' horses, and tradin' 'em off. You never know who's in the herd from week to week. It's hard to make friends if you're a Gypsy horse."

This roused Blackie's interest. "So you don't have any old-timers, horses been around for awhile?"

"Only old Vannar, the mare. She's been with this bunch since she was a colt."

The horse chomped up another sprig of leaves. He belched.

"Me," he said, "I've only been around since spring. Travelin' with the Gypsies, lemme tell you, it's easier than totin' the Peddler and his load. With the Peddler, it's push, push, push—hurry, hurry, hurry—and few oats or apples at the end of a day. I think Lazlo's tryin' to sell me now, so I act up when they come by to look me over. I kick out, act crazy. I even bit a logger the other day. I could smell the wood chips on him. Sure, they beat me for it, but it was worth it. No one's bought me yet!"

Blackie went back to his leaves, thinking of a horse's life.

"These horses, they never know what's what. Their master could trade them at any time. And what if they get a human that starves them or beats them, works them like an ox? Plus, their lives are boring—same thing, day after day. Look at all I've done this past week. Sure, I'm pulling a wagon today, but I might be running with the Princess tomorrow."

Next day, Blackie finally saw Prince George. They were following a leafy lane through an area of short, sharp hills. On one slippery rise, everybody had to get off to lighten the wagons. The Gypsies made Blackie stop halfway up the hill while Ference and Nabil pulled Prince George from the cart. Once the cart was empty, the Prince struggled upward with Lizetta supporting one shoulder and Nabil the other.

The way his head hung forward told the story to Blackie. "They're giving him medicines to keep him quiet."

As Blackie scooted down other side of the hill, holding back the weight of the wagon with braced legs, he thought of Prince George in the cart behind him. Drugged as he was, the man couldn't do anything for himself. Blackie made up his mind. It was time to rescue the Prince.

This was a long, tiring day. They covered few miles, but each step brought them closer to Prince Vile's Portal. That evening, they camped by a stream in a grassy valley between tree-covered hills. Blackie was chained to a tree as usual. By hunching under the low branches, he could swing his chain around the trunk to talk to the old horse, Vannar, eating grass up to her knees.

"Pardon me, Madam Vannar," said Blackie, politely bobbing his head, "could you tell me about these Gypsies?"

"No time to talk," said Vannar, taking another bite. "Can't disturb my dinner."

"But Vannar," Blackie appealed, "these medicines, is there any way to stop them?"

"Don't bother me, sonny. Been awhile since we got grass as good as this." Closing her eyes, Vannar reached down her jaws.

"Please, Vannar," Blackie persisted, "they tell me you're the old-timer, the only horse that's hung around these humans for awhile. You know everything."

Vannar swallowed her grass and frowned at him. "Knowin's not tellin'! You young'uns, you never stay around to learn anything. Here one day, next day gone. I know better than to mess with your problems."

"But wouldn't you like to know where we're heading? What if we're rushing into the dragon's jaws, wouldn't you like to know that?"

Vannar winked an old eye at Blackie. "My, my, young unicorn, don't try to tell me that stuff. You can't play a big trick on me. Last place Big Boots wants to go is anywhere near the dragon. He had enough of that three years ago."

Blackie spoke urgently. "But it's true, Vannar! You know that young human, the sick one they keep drugged. They want to deliver him to the dragon's master."

"Not my business, not my business. Leave me to my grass." Vannar stepped around slowly until Blackie found himself talking to her tail.

"It'll be your business if the dragon's hungry when we find her!" said Blackie sharply. "Which horse do you think Lazlo will give up first when Vile demands meat for his pet?"

Vannar ignored him. She twitched her ears and buried her head in the deep grass.

Blackie stepped back and mumbled, "Dumb old thing! Serve her right if she is thrown to the dragon!"

"What do you think, unicorn," asked one of the younger horses who'd been listening to him, "could we really be heading up to meet the dragon?"

"I know we are," said Blackie, nodding his head. "I heard the humans talk about it. We're heading straight north to her nest. And that dragon's got a big appetite. I saw her chase down a deer. She blasted it with a breath and pounced right on it. Vannar, there, she'd make about three bites for the dragon."

"Bad business," said another horse, nervously. "They got no call to take us near the dragon."

"Maybe so, but we can't stop it," insisted Vannar, looking around. "Just keep your head down, that's what I do. Stay to the rear of the herd. Try not to be noticed."

"Oh, yes," said Blackie, bitterly, "ignore everything. Hide away and wait for the dragon to sniff you out—that's the way you want to live!"

"But we're horses!" exclaimed Vannar. "How can horses fight the dragon? It can't be done. At my age, I don't fret myself over things that can't be done."

By now, the horses were all treading about, snuffling anxiously and whinnying to each other. Nabil walked around the wagon with his stick. The horses swung their heads to look at him.

"Now, what's this?" demanded the Gypsy. "What's stirred you up over here? Quiet down. Quiet down."

Nabil listened a moment, then walked back to the fire.

"What'd he say, unicorn?" asked the younger horse.

Blackie solemnly shook his head.

"He said that when we reach the dragon tomorrow, the dragon's bound to be hungry. She'll eat two or three of us at once."

"Two or three!" gasped an older horse. "Did he say which ones will go first?"

"No," said Blackie, "I guess they doesn't know. It depends on the dragon, which beasts look good to her."

A quiver ran through the herd. The younger horses shuffled around nervously, but Vannar stayed calm. "Nothin' we can do about it."

"You can run away," suggested Blackie, looking slyly at her.

"Run away! Are you mad?" Vannar turned around to glare at him. "Where do you think we'd go? Who'd tend us, inspect our hooves and our teeth? Who'd keep the wolves away?"

"No wolves here," said Blackie. "Any of you hear wolves last night? With all this good grass here, you'd live like carriage horses if you were free. No loads to pull, no roads to wear down your hooves. You should try living free awhile. That's how I live, and I love it."

"Horses don't run away!" insisted Vannar. "We never do it!"

"Just last week," said Blackie, nodding his head, "a whole herd of horses ran away from a castle I was visiting. A hundred horses, at least, and they were happy! They were free at last, no straps, no ropes, no chains! They had the best grazing in the land. Any of you eaten berries or mushrooms, then you know the delights of freedom. All you gotta do is say to yourself, 'I'm not taking it anymore. No sticks for me, no whips, no harness, no dragon!'"

"He's right," said a young horse, lifting her head. "I don't know why we stay with these men. It don't make sense."

"But think of wintertime," said Vannar, ominously. "Winter—white death! Wind, cold, snow, ice. Nothing to eat, no grass, no leaves. Big Boots takes us to the sunny lands in winter, down by the big water where it's warm and green. Left to yourselves, you'd never make it in wintertime. You'd starve away to nothing."

"Yes, unicorn," said another horse, "what about winter?"

Blackie shrugged his shoulders. "Oh, winter can't be that bad. If you can't make it on your own, just walk to the next village and pick out a new master. Find a good human who'll work you easy and give you hay. I promise you, he won't want to stir up monsters. If you stay with this Lazlo, though, you'll be dragonbait."

"But we can't run away," argued a horse. "They got us tied down."

Blackie snorted. "You kidding? You're horses, you're strong. You're not chained to a tree like me. Sure, a chain would hold you back, but those strings on you, give them a tug. You can walk right out of them."

"Oh, I don't think so," said the horse. "I've always been tied like this."

"Go ahead," urged Blackie. "Heave against that rope. It'll come loose."

The horse jerked against the tether. The peg slipped out of the damp earth.

"I'm free!" cried the startled horse.

"Sure," said Blackie, "see how easy that is? The rest of you, just pull loose like that."

Encouraged by Blackie, the horses started yanking out their pegs. One horse strained against his, but it wouldn't move.

"I can't get mine out," he squealed. "It won't budge."

"So," said Blackie, shrugging, "get a couple of your buddies to pull with you. You, there, grab that rope with your teeth and pull with your pal. Both together, now, one . . . two . . . three. Jerk it out!"

The horse jumped backward. "It's out! I'm free, too!"

"Stop, stop!" cried Vannar, swinging her head. "What are you doing? Are you crazy? Don't listen to a unicorn! You don't have any place to go! The Gypsies are good masters, you all know that!"

"My wagon's heavy," said a horse. "These hills are steep.

"And they beat us," said another, "and sell us off. They don't care who they sell us to, either. The unicorn's right! If I have to have a master, I'm picking my own. And I'm not getting near any dragon!"

"No dragon!" echoed the other horses, crowding around nervously, uncertain which way to go. Then Ference strolled around the cart to see what was disturbing the horses. His mouth fell open when he saw them stepping about freely.

"Hey, what are you doing over here?" he cried.

"Let's go!" yelled a yearling. She took off down the valley. Another horse followed. The rest looked at each other until Ference ran at them with his stick. That spooked the herd. They threw their heads in the air and galloped off after the first two. Only Vannar was left, crying after the others. Blackie listened with satisfaction as their hoofbeats died away down the valley.

"Lazlo, they're gone!" shrieked Ference, running back around the wagon. "The horses are gone!"

Now there was commotion among the Gypsy camp. All the humans rushed around the wagons, screeching and wailing, calling into the darkness for the horses to return.

Lazlo was furious at Ference. He beat the man with his whip handle, screaming, "I told you to check the horses! If they were flustered, you should have stayed with them!"

"But they weren't!" insisted Ference, dancing out of range. "They were just nickering among themselves. And how did they pull out their pegs? They never did that before!"

"*Bibaxt*," said someone, "bad luck, the Evil Eye!"

"No, it's the unicorn," said someone else. "*Narky* beast, put red ribbons on him."

"Too late for that, imbecile!" cried Lazlo. "Bring that lantern over here."

Blackie looked away as Lazlo moved the lantern over him and inspected his chain. "Well, the unicorn's safe at least."

"But what good's that?" cried a woman. "Our horses, our fortune, gone, gone! How can we travel anywhere?"

"Let me look at this unicorn," said Mother Teresa, limping around the cart in her shawls. The Gypsies stood near as Mother Teresa put a hand on Blackie's nose. She turned his head toward her and looked into his eyes.

"Oh, yes, an intelligent beast, always thinking. I'm sure, you know, this unicorn warned the horses about the dragon. He frightened them into running away."

"Well, what do we do now, Mother?" asked someone.

"Yes," said Lazlo, "do we stay here to hunt the horses, or leave the wagons and travel on without them?"

Mother Teresa nodded, "I will ask the cards."

"Ask them if the unicorn's to blame," said Lazlo, grimly. "If he made the horses run away, I swear by the moon that I'll chain the wagons together and make him pull them all!"

"At least, old Vannar's still here," said Ference.

"Shut up, Ference!" cried Lazlo, lashing out with his whip. "Whatever caused this, you could have stopped it if you'd stayed on watch!"

The squabbling Gypsies carried their lantern back around the wagon, leaving Blackie and Vannar in the dark.

"Now, see what you've done, unicorn?" cried the horse. "The herd's gone and the humans are upset. We're alone! I hate to be alone!"

"I'm sleepy," yawned Blackie. "I think I'll catch some shuteye."

"Sleepy!" squealed Vannar. "How can you be sleepy? We're alone!"

CHAPTER SEVENTEEN

The Nail

Vannar was furious with Blackie. She missed the herd. True, she'd never been warm to any special horse, except the colt, Swallow, but she needed the closeness, the crowding, the quarreling. Since she was the only horse remaining, Ference and Nabil had to ride her to hunt the others. Squeezed onto her back, they tried to push her into a gallop. She slowed to a walk after a mile and refused to go any faster despite their kicks and threats.

She was frazzled and blown when they rode back at the end of the day. She kicked feebly at Blackie, as Lazlo threw his whip at the men.

"Simpletons, fools, you call yourselves Gypsies? Not since Great-Grandfather's day have we lost a whole herd of horses! Oh, Saint Sebastian, what have we left? A unicorn and a nag!"

Lizetta bent to pick up the whip. She snapped it against a bush, exploding the leaves into fragments. "I told you, my father, to let me ride after the horses. These louts couldn't track a tortoise."

"But Lazlo, my King," protested Ference, backing away, "that horse is too weak to carry two of us! She's slower than a donkey. We'd have gone faster if we'd walked!"

"Then why didn't you walk?" shouted Lazlo.

Lizetta snapped the whip again.

"More to the point, my brothers, why didn't you steal fresh horses?"

"More horses, yes!" agreed Lazlo, slapping a hand against his thigh. "Why didn't you steal more horses?"

Lizetta tossed the whip to Lazlo. "Had I gone after them, I'd have brought back a hundred horses."

"Oh, not a hundred, daughter," cautioned Lazlo, rolling up the whip, "too many, too many. The *Gadjos* take notice when you steal more than a handful."

"But, Lazlo, the country's different now," Ference explained. "We didn't see any horses. None to buy, none to steal. The *Gadjos* we saw on the road were strays, hungry wanderers like ourselves. The only riders were bandits, and we hid out from them."

"Bandits!" Lizetta picked up a bucket. Tossing her head, she walked to the stream for water. "Who fears bandits? I'd have crept up on them and stripped them down to their shirts."

Laslo threw her an angry look. "That's enough from you, daughter."

Blackie swung around on the end of the chain to a patch of fresh grass. He ate cheerfully, listening to the Gypsies shout at each other until the whole tribe stormed around the wagon a few minutes later, Mother Teresa pulling Lazlo by the arm. Sara ran ahead to hug Blackie. He looked up mildly while Mother Teresa pointed a shaking finger at him.

"I warned you, my son, this beast is unlucky! Your daughter has been turning the cards. Three times in a row, she turned the Knight of Swords with the ten of spades! For the sake of us all, you must drive off the beast before he brings more woe!"

"Oh, my mother," cried Lazlo, "don't you know the value of this beast? Prince Vile swears that he will give us the freedom of the roads for five generations if we give him the unicorn and the Prince!"

"And you believe the Black Lord?" scoffed Mother Teresa. "Sell the Prince if you must, but send this beast out of our lives at once. The doom is upon us if you don't."

Lizetta took Mother Teresa's hand.

"But Grandmother, as I told you, it is too late to free the unicorn. The raven found us yesterday. The Black Prince knows that we've captured the unicorn. In truth, the raven tells us that Lord Vile plans to fly down on the dragon to inspect the beast."

Now, Blackie was alarmed. "Vile knows that I'm chained up like this?"

215

Ference spoke up, trembling with fear. "Listen to Lizetta, my King! Don't even think of releasing the prisoners! Remember the Prince's fury when we lost him the Grail? That would be nothing compared to his rage if we let these two escape from him."

"But the message is clear in the cards!" insisted Mother Teresa. "They instruct us to free the unicorn. It would be fatal to deal with Prince Vile. Much better we should hide in the forest as usual, find safety among the trees."

"Safety among the trees?" sneered Ference. "With the dragon hunting us? Let us not deceive ourselves, Grandmother. The dragon would sniff us out in an hour."

"Less than an hour," muttered Nabil. "Ten minutes at most!"

"In that case," exclaimed Lazlo, "we must run to the Shrine. No one can harm us there!"

Ference snorted again.

"The Shrine! What sort of reception would you receive from the Knights at the Shrine? Don't forget, Lazlo, they remember that you stole the Holy Grail from the Fountain!"

"I'll claim sanctuary!" cried Lazlo. "I'll beg forgiveness! I'll repent, crawl up the mountain on my knees if I have to! It's true, I am sorry that I stole the Grail. That was the closest I ever came to hanging."

Blackie shrugged. He went back to eating as Lizetta patted Lazlo on the shoulder.

"You must face reality, my father. It would take us days to reach the Shrine, but we may have only hours to react if the Black Prince flies down on the dragon. You must decide at once. Do we free the prisoners and run into hiding, or wait for the dragon and accept our fate?"

Blackie looked up again when Ference pointed his stick at him, shaking in anger.

"Look at him eat, the smug, sneaking thing! He turned the horses loose! I swear, Lazlo, he mocks us. He taunts us. Let me at him with my stick! I'll pound him like a walnut tree!"

"Pound me, will you!" thought Blackie, glaring back at the Gypsy. "I'd like to see you try."

"Oh, he's vicious," said Lazlo, grimly, "but I don't have to punish him. I'll leave that to Prince Vile."

"And the dragon, my son?" said Mother Teresa. "Have you forgotten the dragon? She's sure to be hungry when she arrives, and you, Lazlo, you're the fattest of us all."

With a cry of frustration, Lazlo struck a pose, closing his eyes with his hands clasped before him. Everyone watched him but Mother Teresa. She sighed and knelt to pray. Blackie bit up another mouthful of grass.

"I have decided," said Lazlo, suddenly, lifting his whip high. "We must split the family. Ference and I will run for the Shrine with the unicorn. The rest of you must hide the carts in the trees. Scatter out. Follow animal trails to cover your scent. Move quickly, people! We have little time."

A murmur swept through the camp. Mother Teresa started softly singing.

> The Gypsy scours the world like the wind,
> searching hill and plain
> for kin and comrades left behind—
> never to meet again.

Lizetta pointed to her wagon. "And the Prince, what of him?"

"I'll take him with me, of course. We'll take my big wagon."

"Then, I go, also," she declared. "I will look after the Prince."

"Me, too!" cried Sara, looking up from Blackie. "I will look after the unicorn!"

Blackie nuzzled the girl, as Lizetta said gently, "No, Little Sister. It is too dangerous for you. You must stay with the *vardo*."

Sara jumped up and down. "I want to go! I want to go! If you can go, I go, too!"

"Do as you're told, girl!" shouted Lazlo, suddenly angry. "Run, now! Help hide the carts! Make Vannar drag them to hiding, one at a time!"

Sara ran off, hissing curses under her breath.

Blackie chewed grass and flicked his ears while the Gypsies stripped Lazlo's big wagon of bedding and bags, clothes and cooking items. They tossed out the rusty tools, the horse doctoring supplies, the cards and crystals. In their place, the Gypsies loaded Lazlo's treasure box, the medicines, and most of the food in the camp. Lizetta's shawls and shoes

217

came last. When the wagon was loaded, the men lifted Prince George inside, limp and still. The door slammed behind him.

Nabil protested Lazlo's taking the food, but Lazlo insisted on it.

"You'll find plenty of rabbits and hedgehogs in the forest, but we'll be exposed in the lanes, running too fast to raid chicken houses. Hurry now, we must harness the unicorn."

Blackie backed to the end of the chain as the Gypsies walked around him. He glared at them. Lazlo snapped the whip.

"When I get his attention, you two switch the chain from the tree to the cart."

"The beast is too smart for that," said Lizetta. "He'll break away the moment the chain is loosened. What we must do, my father, is talk to him."

"Talk to him?"

Lizetta nodded. She walked up to Blackie and put a hand on his head.

"Oh, unicorn, I know you've been listening to us. You understand the danger. Naturally, you want to flee the Black Lord and the dragon, but think of your friend, the Prince. If you don't help us escape, the man will be taken. It's up to you. Will you pull us out of danger, Prince and Gypsies together, or will you let Lord Vile carry us off? If you agree to help us, we'll transfer the chain to the mother bolt of the cart so you can pull us away. If you don't, we'll all remain here to meet Prince Vile. What do you say?"

Blackie shook in frustration. All this was Lazlo's fault. The last thing Blackie wanted was to let these humans chain him to the wagon, but Lizetta was right. Prince George would be lost if he didn't pull them away from the dragon. Angrily, he nodded his head.

Lizetta whirled to the Gypsies. "Hurry, my brothers! With the help of the saints and the blessed unicorn, we have a good chance to escape."

Blackie allowed Nabil and Ference to back him between the traces of the wagon. He stood quietly while they buckled the harness around him. When the chain was clamped to the pivot bolt of the wagon, they stepped away.

"Yeah, the mother bolt!" they laughed. "That will hold him. That bolt would hold an elephant."

The men hurried off to complete the loading of the other carts. Lizetta stood at Blackie's head.

"You see, holy beast, everyone will be safe if you work with us. Vanner will pull the other carts to safety while the dragon chases after us. You must use all your unicorn strength to elude her. If you succeed, I swear to you, we will turn you loose with the Prince. You may take him wherever you desire to go. Trust Lizetta, you'll go free at last."

Blackie gave her a sceptical look as Lazlo rushed up in his old brown cloak, the other Gypsies hustling after. "The unicorn, is he ready to flee?"

"He understands, my father," said Lizetta, putting an arm around Sara. "He knows the danger if he doesn't obey."

Lazlo looked doubtfully at Blackie. He shook the harness and sighed, then turned to the Gypsies and spoke loudly.

"Once again, my people, the stars force us to separate. With cunning and luck, we'll survive to join together when we can. For now, farewell. May the saints watch over you."

The Gypsies crowded together, hugging each other and wailing, "Farewell, farewell! Take care on the road!"

"Oh, you be careful in the forest, my people! Saint Julian protect you!"

Sara ran to throw her arms around Blackie's neck. "Good luck to you, unicorn! I'll pray for you each morning."

Blackie shook his harness. He looked around for Vannar, harnessed to another cart, but the horse was ignoring everyone. Lizetta climbed in the door at the end of the car. Lazlo walked up beside Blackie. He shouted farewells and snapped his whip. Ference took his place behind the cart, and they took off, crushing the grass with their boots and wheels until they passed out of the valley into the leafy trail over the hills.

Fed and rested, Blackie easily pulled the wagon up the first long hill though the Gypsy's walking pace slowed and slowed as the rise steepened. At the top, Lazlo called for a rest. He walked around to speak a few words to Lizetta through the front window while Blackie ate leaves from a low-hanging tree limb. Ference leaned against the cart, pulling the stopper on a wine bag.

Blackie yawned, took a step to a fresh limb and pulled off another mouthful of leaves. He watched from the corner of his eye as Lazlo said something to Ference. They shook their heads mournfully.

Blackie swept off a deerfly with his tail. He took a casual step to reach a limb across the lane. He said to himself, "Time to get going."

He took one more step as though reaching to the next limb. Lazlo stepped back as the *vardo* rolled by him.

"Hold up, unicorn. We'll leave in a moment."

That was when Blackie burst into a gallop, dashing down the narrow lane. The men jumped back as the wagon swung out at them. Blackie heard their shouts as he dragged the wagon downhill through the forest, faster and faster as the rolling wagon picked up speed. Blackie heard the top of the wagon smash against a low branch and laughed to himself.

The wagon swung on the traces, bouncing from side to side as wheels hit rocks and fallen branches. It bashed against trees reaching into the lane. It banged down into a stream at the bottom of the hill. Blackie splashed through the stream and rushed up the next rise, buffeting the wagon against trees all the way.

Lizetta stuck her head out the window to yell at Blackie, but the side of the wagon struck a tree trunk and she flew back inside. Blackie dashed down that hill and up another, slowing as he tired from the frenzied pace that had left the Gypsies a mile behind.

By now, the wagon was a shattered mass of planks and panels scraping along on the chain. The front wheels were gone along with most of the harness, the roof, and the supplies stored inside. Slowing to a stop, Blackie looked back at Prince George held by a screaming Lizetta, clinging with her free arm to a strut that remained connected to a portion of the floor.

Spit flew out her mouth as she shrieked, "Are you insane, you stupid beast? You almost killed us! No wagon could stand this beating! It's a miracle it didn't turn over and crush us all!"

Rocking in her arms, Prince George bellowed out a song.

> Sway with the sea, roll with the waves,
> we sail on the ocean tide.
> Swing with the sails, speed with the winds,
> the ocean's arms are wide!
>
> Shake with the spars, cling to the sheets,
> we pitch on the salty brine.

Steer by the stars and gaze through the night
for a glimpse of hazy coastline.

Blackie stepped into the dust cloud rising from the wreck. He sniffed Prince George, who gazed up with love and reached to stroke his nose.

"Good old Blackie, uni-corny, give us another ride! Bump and bounce, shwing and shway, Blackie, Blackie, Blackie—"

The Prince didn't look sick to Blackie. Singing away there, he looked healthy as a hog, just drunk on medicines.

Blackie glared at Lizetta, who shrank away, stammering, "Th-the Prince was ill, you see. Poor man, I had to keep him on medicines. The fever, the fever—he's still . . . still out of his head."

Blackie saw all right. Just as he'd thought, Lizetta had been keeping Prince George knocked out on medicines so the Gypsies could deliver him up for the reward. At her throat, sparkling in the sun, Blackie saw the red jewel of the Princess.

Lizetta felt his eyes stare at her neck. Her hands flew up to the Offering.

"Oh, oh, this necklace! I was preserving it of course, keeping it safe for the dear Prince when he recovered. Why, he might have lost it, he might have—"

She broke down weeping, covering her eyes with her hands. "Oh, unicorn, you frightened me so. You ran like a wild thing, smashing the *vardo* against the trees. You could have killed us."

Pushing to her feet, she tried to pet him. "Let us be friends, sweet beast. I'll hunt for the grain bag and feed you oats."

Blackie stepped back to look at the wreckage of the wagon. He could see the chain running to the mother bolt that held the planks and floorboards to the front axle. Violently, he kicked at the bolt, trying to free the chain.

Lizetta pulled the Prince away from the hooves. The floorboards splintered under the blows, but the beams and axle merely bounced under the blows, fixed firmly by the bolt.

"Lemme help you, lemme help you!" cried Prince George, trying to shake free of Lizetta.

She clung to him, sputtering, "S-stay still, sweet P-Prince, stay still! He'll kick you! Watch out for splinters!"

Blackie stopped kicking. Panting hard, he backed off, dragging the sad heap of bolt and boards on the chain. Strips of leather hung from the sides. The two rear wheels wobbled behind.

"Hold on, good unicorn!" cried Lizetta, scrambling after him. "Don't destroy everything! Wait here for my people to catch up with us! We'll turn you loose! If we'd known that you wanted to run free—"

Blackie ignored her. He pulled around on his chain to nuzzle the Prince. The man threw an arm over him and tried to pull up on his back.

"Good old unicorn, faithful beesht! Let's ride like the wind. Where'sh my shword? Where's my shpear?"

Prince George looked around the wreck, seeing how little remained. Lizetta clung to his other arm, jabbering like a jay.

"Oh, my Prince, you're sick. You're ill! Don't leave me! Stay with your Lizetta! I'll care for you like a mother!"

"Here we go again!" thought Blackie. He lowered his neck and swept the Prince to his back, arms on one side and legs on the other. Prince George laughed and struggled, pulling on Blackie's mane and kicking to straighten himself. With a shout, he rolled off into the weeds.

"Whoops a-daisy!"

Lizetta tried to catch him. They tumbled down together. Laughing, Prince George crawled to Blackie and reached again for the mane to climb up.

"Does my Prince want to ride?" squealed Lizetta, scrambling to her feet. "Here, let your servant help you mount the unicorn."

Blackie stretched his neck to watch suspiciously out of the corner of his eye, but Lizetta seemed to actually want to help now. She ran to the wreckage and rolled over a leaking wine keg. She stood it on end by Blackie's side.

"Place a foot on the keg, my lord," she urged the Prince. "I'll help you up."

Lizetta held Prince George from swaying backwards as he lifted his foot to the keg. He hopped two or three times on the keg, pulling Blackie's mane, then lunged upward. Lizetta held him around the waist till he swung his leg over and settled into place, clutching the horse collar around Blackie's neck.

"Ooh, I'm up!" he cried in surprise. "Hi, Blackie, I'm up, I'm on! We can run like the wind!"

"Wait for Lizetta!"

Lizetta jumped to the keg and leaped up behind the Prince, throwing her arms around his chest to hold on.

"Don't pull me off!" cried the Prince.

Blackie staggered under the weight. His first thought was to knock the girl off, but he caught himself. Lizetta had the Princess's necklace. So long as he kept her with him, they had the Offering. Grimly, he decided that he'd haul the Gypsy all the way to the Shrine if that were the only way he could deliver the necklace.

He stepped forward till the chain tightened. Prince George dropped forward onto his neck while Lizetta leaned on the Prince.

"On, dear unicorn!" she called. "Remember the dragon! Save us all!"

"Oh, ho!" shouted Prince George, as Blackie trotted on again, starting slowly with the wreckage bumping and scraping behind. It caught onto trees and bushes, losing pieces here and there as he gathered speed.

It was a painful, tiring way to proceed. Blackie labored on, knowing that the Gypsies were somewhere behind him. If they had horses, they could catch him in no time, but, surely, he could drag along faster than they could climb these hills on foot. As to the dragon, he had to put her out of his mind.

The load scraped easily as Blackie ran downhill until the left wheel caught on the stub of a tree limb, jerking Blackie around. Prince George flew off with a cry, pulling Lizetta with him.

"Sorry, old boy!" called the Prince, pushing to his feet, while Lizetta squealed, "My dress, my dress!"

She was a sorry sight, her dress torn and dirty from the fall, her hair tangled, and the necklace—

She clasped her hands to her throat in panic.

"My necklace!" she shrieked.

"You mean," corrected the Prince, weaving from side to side while shaking a finger at her, "the Princess's fam . . . fam . . . famoush Great-Great-Grandma's—Where ish that necklash?"

They dropped to their knees to paw through the bushes. Blackie ate leaves while Lizetta gabbled nervously, combing through the brush.

"I was simply keeping the necklace for you, my lord. Around my neck, obviously, the safest place to keep it. You know, of course, I intended to return it the instant you recovered. I feared that some of those men might have been tempted, you know. Father Lazlo is faithful as the sun, but that Nabil—"

In the end, it was Blackie who found the necklace when the two stood in despair after combing the ground for a dozen feet around. Prince George shook his fist at Lizetta.

"That necklash was a royal treashure! If you've losht that necklash—"

Lizetta wailed, trembling with fear, "But it has to be here, my lord! It couldn't have flown away!"

That's when Blackie's sharp eyes spotted the glittery object slip through her dress to fall in the grass. She shrank back in alarm when he jumped toward her.

"It wasn't my fault!"

Reaching carefully with his horn, Blackie scooted the necklace toward Prince George.

"There it ish!" cried the Prince, peering down. "Blackie found it! Good beesht, good beesht!"

"Oh, I'll keep it for you, my lord," offered Lizetta, reaching eager fingers.

"No!" squealed the Prince, slapping her hand back. He bent uncertainly and snatched up the necklace. "I'll keep it meshelf!"

Standing, he held up the necklace and studied it with bleary eyes.

"Clashp 'pears to be broken, I'll put it in my pursh."

He fumbled about his waist.

"No pursh! Where'sh my pursh? No matter, I'll put it in my . . . my boot!"

"Your boot!" exclaimed Lizetta, jumping forward. "You mustn't, my lord! The necklace won't be safe in your boot!"

"Shafe enough," said the Prince, nodding his head. "Shafe enough with ten toesh to guard it, five toesh in thish boot—" He pointed down. "And five in thish boot."

He bent over and slipped the necklace into his boot. Blackie watched with satisfaction. Even Lizetta couldn't steal the Offering from a boot.

"Now, thish wagon," said the Prince, looking over the wreckage. Only one wheel was left, leaning uncertainly into the boards. "Not in the besht of shape, I'd shay. Needs a little toush-up to run properly."

He giggled. "A little 'toush-up,' get it?"

"Oh, my lord," begged Lizetta, "let's return to the people, get rid of this wreckage and pick up a good wagon. We can travel properly again."

"Travel properly?" repeated the Prince, suddenly serious. "You call it 'properly' to deliver Blackie and me to the evil Prince? No, no, there'sh no wagonload of shilver for you, this time. You can forget about that!"

"But, my lord, you didn't think we'd actually . . ."

Prince George cut her off. He turned to Blackie and began stripping off the harness, his voice clearing as he worked.

"Oh, I know that you'd do it. A wagonload of shilver? You'd shell us out for half a copper if it came to that! I don't trust you, Gypsy, as far ash I could throw that wagon wheel. But now, the unicorn and I can leave you behind. We have a necklace to deliver. You can turn back and join your band of shcoundrels. Make all the deals you want with the dragon. Just don't bother us."

Most of the straps and traces were tossed to the ground. Only the collar remained, secured to the chain by a brass ring at the bottom. Muttering to himself, Prince George began pulling the collar over Blackie's head.

"Once this is off, Blackie, old man, we can leave everything behind, chain and all."

"Oh, stop, my Prince, stop!" cried Lizetta, clutching his arm. "We mustn't lose that ironwork!"

"What, this chain?" protested the Prince. "Chain holds us back. We'll travel faster if we dump it. More comfortable for Blackie."

"No," begged Lizetta, "the mother bolt. We must not lose that bolt. It's valuable!"

The Prince turned to kick at the bolt on the axle.

"This bolt? It's worth little—a copper or two. I'm going to dump it all, collar, chain, and everything. That'll free Blackie to run."

Lizetta ran to him and seized his arm again.

"My lord, I'm serious! That bolt is valuable! It's . . . it's a treasure, more important than a hundred necklaces!"

"Oh, Gypsy," cried the Prince, shaking her off, "you've been shwallowing your own medichines! That bolt's a common piece of hardware, a bit larger than normal, perhaps, but ordinary iron. Any blacksmith can hammer out a bolt like that."

"Not this one, my lord!" cried Lizetta. "We must not lose it!"

"Why not?" The Prince rolled back like a drunken man. He stared at Lizetta with tired eyes. "Lose the chain, lose the bolt, lose it all! Blackie can run free, then. We'll go wherever we want!"

"I'm telling you, my lord!" Lizetta clasped his arm with frantic hands. "Please, please, we must preserve the bolt over everything! We must not lose that bolt!"

"You're crazy!" yelled Prince George, pushing her away. "Who cares about the bolt? The sooner we lose that thing, the better!"

"No, no, my lord, you don't understand!" wept Lizetta. "That bolt, it's the great treasure of the Gypsies! That bolt is the Nail!"

Blackie looked up, as the Prince repeated, "The Nail? What Nail?"

"The Nail of Christ!" Lizetta sobbed, trembling. "The Nail made to pin the foot of the Holy One, stolen by my ancestor to relieve the Lord's agony on the Cross. You know the story. The Gypsy tried to steal all four nails to stop the Crucifixion, but was able to get only one of them. That's why the feet of Christ were pinned together by a single nail—the Gypsy had stolen the fourth Nail! And there it is!"

She pointed to the dusty bolt sticking through the broken boards. Prince George shook his head.

"This thing? It can't be a Roman nail."

"Look at the Nail, my lord," begged Lizetta, kneeling to brush dust and leaf fragments from the strip of floorboard facing up. "Examine closely—no rust, no corrosion. The Nail is the great treasure of the Gypsies. Prince Vile, the Bishop, the lords of the earth, they've hunted for our Nail through the ages, but we have preserved it for a thousand years. Its hiding place is brilliant. The King of Gypsies keeps it in plain sight as the mother bolt of his wagon. No one has ever suspected."

Prince George dropped to hands and knees to study the bolt. Even Blackie stepped close to examine it. The Nail looked like an ordinary bolt about eight inches long, though the metal gleamed without a speck of rust once the dirt was brushed away.

"Look, my lord," said Lizetta. She spat on a twig and touched it to the bolt. There was a hiss and the moisture boiled away in a little burst of steam.

"My people," she said, "my people pray around the wagon. The Holy Nail, the sign of our love for Jesus, we must not lose it. We must carry it back to Lazlo as soon as possible."

"I'm not returning to Lazlo!" objected Prince George. "He'd sell me to the dark prince! No, no, I'll give this Nail to my lady. The Princess will know what to do with it!"

"The Princess, my lord?" Lizetta threw back her head. "My lord doesn't need the Princess! Surely, he can do better than that! Oh, the Gypsies know about that lady, so cold, so bossy, conceited. My lord needs a hot-blooded girl, one that will dance for him, steal for him, poison his enemies!"

Lizetta knelt before the Prince, embracing his knees. Stammering with anger, Prince George shoved her away as Blackie stared in amazement.

"My P-Princess can dance!" cried the Prince. "And sh-she's not c-cold! She's just— She's misunderstood! At least, she wouldn't . . . she wouldn't steal a necklace and sell me to Prince Vile! She cares for me!"

"Cares for you!" spat Lizetta, flaring up. "Oh, blind, blind! You *Gadjos*, you know nothing of love! All that Princess cares about is power! The world knows that she longs to be a warrior queen! She'd never cook for you, sing to you, nurse you back to health! She'll keep you a servant, a serf, a slave! Never will she kneel to you as I do!"

"Well, at least," cried the Prince, "she'd never drug me with medicines!"

He turned his back on Lizetta and stepped to Blackie, who was shaking his head, horrified at the Gypsy's lies about the Princess.

Who did this Gypsy think she was to abuse his sweet lady like that? The Princess was good. She was loving. She thought only of others. She perfumed the world, and all creatures were happy around her.

Perhaps the Princess had been a little abrupt with the Prince at times, but the human had his ways. Blackie had traveled with the Prince long enough to see that he required discipline. He needed a higher view to steer him into useful paths. Guided by the Princess, he could become a hero like Grandpa with songs and stories about his adventures. This Lizetta, she'd sell them both to Prince Vile. They'd wind up as dragonbait if she had her way.

Mumbling to himself, Prince George jerked at the chain, removing kinks so it lay as straight as possible.

"Come on, Blackie!" he cried. "Let's get out of here! Leave all these Gypsies behind!"

"No, no, my lord!" cried Lizetta, hanging on to him. "Don't leave your servant, your Lizetta! I'll be your handmaid, cook your food, clean your boots! Don't leave me behind!"

Prince George shoved her away. "Goodbye, Gypsy."

Grabbing the collar, he scrambled painfully onto Blackie, who stepped away from the wreck.

"My lord, look what I've got!" Lizetta cried in a tone that made Blackie look around. Lizetta was waving the frontal.

"I found this spear-thing in the wreckage! Let this show how Lizetta wants to help you! Please, don't run away from Lizetta!"

"Oh, give it here!"

Blackie stepped back to the Gypsy. Prince George reached down to snatch the frontal from Lizetta, but she sprang up behind him like a cat, wrapping her arms around his chest and resting her head on his shoulder.

"Bless you for taking Lizetta with you," she murmured in his ear. "I will serve you faithfully."

"And steal everything you get your hands on," muttered the Prince, slipping the straps of the frontal around his hand. The frontal scraped Blackie's neck as Prince George gripped the collar. He patted Blackie's cheek with the free hand.

"Come on, Blackie. Let's get out of here before Lazlo catches us. We'll find somewhere to leave her."

Blackie stepped to the end of the chain and set up the next hill, starting slowly, but quickening to a steady trot. The boards of the wagon bounced behind as Lizetta hugged the Prince. She sang in his ear.

The road before, the road behind,
the Gypsy sings like a dove.
No care has she, whatever she finds,
She's riding with her love.

Chapter Eighteen

Quarreling Companions

As they trotted through the forest, Lizetta jabbered in the Prince's ear, trying to convince him to turn back. "If we go back to the people, my Prince, Lazlo will return your sword. It's still in the *vardo* where he stored it. By my grandmother's head—"

"Could this girl really have a grandmother?" thought Blackie, sourly. "If you ask me, she hatched out of an egg like any old snake."

Blackie tried to stick to the center of the trail so the wreckage would drag as smoothly as possible, but the boards caught on another tree, jerking them off balance. Lizetta clutched the Prince. He rocked back, yelling, "You can swear by the heads of the whole Gypsy clan! I'm never going back to Lazlo! 'Once a fool, twice a fool'? That's not me!"

"But, my lord—" cried Lizetta. The Gypsy argued as Blackie backed up to kick the boards free.

"The necklace, you want it in perfect shape for the Fountain, don't you? You know that the Princess would not want you to offer a broken object to the Shrine. Lazlo could repair that clasp for you, an easy job for a skilled tinker like Lazlo."

Prince George ignored her. "Once we're running again, Blackie, drift back to the road. Now that you've got your spike back, you can keep us out of trouble. At least, we'll put more miles between us and the dragon."

Setting out again, Blackie trotted more slowly. He found that the boards skidded easily at this pace, merely knocking at trees instead of catching so often. Soon enough a root threw the boards so the wreckage wedged between tree trunks. Lizetta had to jump down to free it, protesting all the while.

"This is madness, my lord, dragging this debris through the forest. We must return to the people. Father Lazlo will free the chain with one blow of his hammer, and you can go wherever you wish."

When she was unable to shift the boards, Prince George had to slide off to jerk at the wreckage as well.

"Pull on that end of the axle, Gypsy."

Still arguing, Lizetta yanked at the end of the axle. "Has my lord thought about money? Lazlo will give us silver if we return to him, and a cart. Lazlo will give us a *vardo*. With a *vardo*, we can travel around the world. Dragging along like this is madness!"

"You're right, it's madness," cried the Prince, "madness to haul these old planks with us! Nail or no Nail, we should dump this chain, then we could run free!"

The Prince climbed back on Blackie. Lizetta grabbed his elbow and swung up behind him. She put her hands on his shoulders.

"But, the Nail, my lord, I've told you the story of the Nail. Promise me that we will not lose the Nail!"

"Don't promise her anything!" thought Blackie.

The Prince sighed, settling forward on Blackie's neck. "All right, Gypsy, I won't lose it. If there's a chance that the bolt is what you say it is, I have to hang on to it."

"More than a chance," murmured Lizetta, relaxing. "It is the blessed Nail itself."

"I hope so," groaned the Prince. "If not, my ballad will sound very strange."

> He rides the unicorn like a dolt,
> dragging a battered wagon bolt.

"Not at all, sweet Prince," cooed Lizetta. "The Gypsies know that the Nail is a holy treasure as great as the Grail itself."

The boards gave a jerk through the chain.

"The Grail?" muttered the Prince. "How dare you mention the Grail after trying to steal it!"

Lizetta fell silent at that. The boards bumped and banged as Blackie trotted along. Birds flew away at his noisy approach. Squirrels scratched up tree trunks.

Blackie stopped for a rest at a stream. Before he did anything else, Prince George strapped the fronton to Blackie's head. He stood back to admire the unicorn while Blackie ate leaves. The Prince stumped through the trees, looking for a stick to use as a club. He picked up a stone from the stream. He weighed it in his hand.

"Smooth," he said, "a good handful for throwing, but how to carry it? I have no bag, no purse, nothing, nothing."

Lizetta looked at herself in the stream. She ran her fingers through her hair.

"Not even a hairbrush! How do you expect your servant to live like a beast? No clothes, no shoes, no perfume. The Gypsy girl cannot live like—"

SPLASH!

The Prince dropped the stone in the stream.

"Who invited you along?" he demanded. "You kidnap me, drug me with medicines, then expect me to supply you like a queen! You can stop off any time you want, Gypsy!"

Lizetta gave the Prince a woeful look. "It's just that I'm hungry, my lord. Your servant's had nothing to eat all day."

"Good," said the Prince, reaching up on Blackie. "Think of it as a fast. Fasting is good for your soul."

"Please, my lord, please. We both need food."

Blackie grabbed a mouthful of leaves. He wasn't fasting. He chewed stubbornly as Prince George rubbed his shoulders.

"Sorry, Blackie, we have to go on. I know you're hungry, but humans need food, too."

Blackie pushed into a fresh bush and jerked off a sprig of leaves.

"I'm not moving," he thought. "Not till I've eaten. Who wears a spike on his head? Who carries a double load? Who's got to drag this rubbish? All they do, this pair, is squabble at each other while I choke on a horse collar. The Prince has done nothing these last few days but lie around in a wagon like a king. And Lizetta, I've never seen her do any work. She could give Papa lessons in laziness! So now they're worried about food? Good, this beast of burden is eating his lunch!"

Prince George patted Blackie while Lizetta tried to pull him by his mane. "Come along, beautiful unicorn. Surely, you remember the great burning dragon. We must hurry along to find food and safety as soon as possible."

Blackie ignored them. He thrust his nose into the leaves and chomped until the Prince threw himself down against a tree with a groan. The Gypsy knelt before him and patted his hand.

"Don't worry, my master. Lizetta will convince the beast to travel on."

She jumped up and scratched Blackie's neck.

"Unicorn, sweet unicorn, think of the treats that await when we find refuge—the fruits and greens and vegetables. When we find grain and honey, I'll stir up my mash for you, a delight for all hoofed beasts. Wouldn't you love such treats?"

"What I'd love," thought Blackie, winking his eyes, "is quiet. How is anyone safe in the forest with humans squawking away louder than magpies? The dragon could hear them a mile away!"

Lizetta shrugged and stepped back to Prince George, resting against a tree. She curled against his shoulder as he closed his eyes.

Blackie ate until satisfied for the moment. He belched and walked to the stream for a drink. Lizetta jumped up at once.

"Sweet unicorn!"

Blackie stretched and yawned. He set his legs for a nap, lowered his head slightly, and closed his eyes. He heard Lizetta sigh as he tried to relax. He began to breathe deeply. He didn't sleep. As weary as he felt, he couldn't let go. His mind was fidgety. He felt every ant walking over his hoof, every fly on his neck. He knew how hungry the humans must be. Somehow, he'd become responsible for the two of them, even the Gypsy.

Papa had warned him. Papa had told him over and over, "Stay away from humans! Whatever you do, don't let yourself get mixed up in their troubles. You'll be sorry if you do."

"Yeah, Papa," he thought, "look at me, now—hobbled, chained, worried about this pair. It's not my fault. All I wanted was to see a little of the world."

"Oh, yes, it is your fault," said Papa's voice in his mind. "You had to run away from the Nest, didn't you? So you met your Princess and she enchanted you. Didn't I warn you? Now, you're stuck with these humans!"

"I'm not stuck with them," Blackie argued back. "I could leave them anytime, but they're unarmed. They're defenseless without me. A rabbit, a mouse can survive in the forest better than they can. Anyone could snatch them up—a beast, a bandit, a baron. And the dragon's out there somewhere, hunting for us all. These two depend on me. I have the spike. I'm . . . I'm their protector!"

Prince George stirred. He lifted Lizetta's head from his shoulder and eased her down against the tree. He stood up and put an arm over Blackie's neck.

"Please, Blackie," he whispered, "we have to run on. You know that dragon's chasing us, plus Lazlo's after us. I'm still unarmed. Any rogue could shoot us now and get the necklace. Wake up, please. We have to go on!"

Blackie opened his eyes and snorted.

"That's a good beast!" cried the Prince. "I knew you'd see reason."

Lizetta jumped up to run to Blackie. "Faithful creature," she murmured, stroking Blackie's ears. "Lizetta will reward you. She'll groom you well when she steals a hairbrush."

Prince George kicked the boards around to straighten the chain and ease the drag. Walking back to Blackie, he grumbled, "I hate that Nail. It's going to get us all killed."

"No, no, my lord," said Lizetta, smiling at him. "The Nail is filled with the love of the Lord. It will bless us, so long as we keep it safe."

"It certainly doesn't stop hunger."

Blackie stiffened his legs for the humans to climb on. He began another difficult run. The path was rocky in the steep hills. The boards jammed regularly, choking him to a halt until Lizetta lifted the boards around the obstacles.

Travel like this was torture to a unicorn who'd grown up running the forest. Normally, he could slip through a wall of trees that looked impenetrable to the Prince, but to drag a splintering load that slammed against rocks and jammed up on roots—This was maddening.

After jumping down the hundredth time to pull the load free of tangling branches or vines, Lizetta begged Prince George to head back to the road.

"We need smoother going, dear Princey. The unicorn is choking up. That last jolt almost strangled him."

"We'll travel the road when we reach it," insisted the Prince, "though I'm having second thoughts about that. I'm sure the dragon has found your Gypsy camp by now. If she's flying along the road to catch us, she could spot at any time. Even with my sword and armor, the road was dangerous, but now—"

"Oh, the unicorn will guard us," Lizetta assured him. "Hero beast, he's born to fight dragons. He'll streak along the road like a comet!"

"So that's what they expect from me," groaned Blackie, plodding up the hill. "I'm to streak like a comet with humans on my back and a load dragging behind? Think again, Gypsy. I'm already staggering on my hooves."

He stopped in the trail, heaving for breath. Prince George opened his eyes.

"What's up, boy? Do you smell danger?"

Blackie's head was low, his ears down. Sweat ran from the fronton into his eyes. The Prince nudged him with a boot.

"Come on, Blackie. We've got miles to go before dark."

"Why, he's exhausted," cried Lizetta. She slipped down and walked around to feel Blackie's nose. She looked in his eyes.

"Poor beast, you've dragged those heavy boards so far! I tell you, my lord, Gypsies would never drive their animals like that. We'll have to walk now."

"Oh, sure, I can walk," said the Prince, yawning. He jumped down and stretched. "A good hike'll wake me up. I just wish I were walking off a dinner. Sooner or later, we have to find food. Let's go, Blackie. I'll lead the way."

Walking on, he ducked a low branch. Blackie didn't move. The Prince stopped, turned to look back.

"What's wrong with him?"

"I think, he's gone as far as he can," said Lizetta, scratching Blackie between the ears. "That chain's worn him down."

Prince George kicked at a root across the trail.

"We may have to leave those boards behind, Gypsy. You're the one who insists that we keep that Nail. I doubt if it's genuine, anyway. How could Gypsies hold on to the Nail for a thousand years?"

"Remember your promise, my lord," urged Lizetta. "No matter what, we're keeping the Nail!"

"No, I'm serious." Prince George bent to examine the bolt head sticking through the pile of boards. "Look at that thing. It doesn't look anything like a nail. It looks like any old bolt, wide head, flat bottom. I suspect you've been fooled. Some old Gypsy king probably sold the true Nail centuries ago and palmed off this fake on you. He must have thought it was funny, one of those big tricks of yours."

"No, my lord, this is the true Nail, I know it. On cool nights, you can feel the warmth in the metal!"

Prince George pulled at a loose floorboard sticking under the bolt. By holding the axle with a boot and wrenching up, he snapped off the board. He threw it aside.

"At least, I can lighten the load for Blackie."

Twisting and jerking, he ripped off a couple of the slighter boards, but the beams and axle held firm. One side board bent up from the peg that held it. He yanked on it, muttering, "If I only had a saw, a chisel—"

"Would this help?" asked Lizetta, pulling a wicked-looking knife with a five-inch blade from her sleeve.

Mouth open, Prince George stared her. "A knife! Where'd you get that?"

Lizetta shrugged her shoulders. "It's my sticker. I always carry my sticker. I'd feel naked without it."

"And you wait till now to mention it!" grumbled the Prince. "Give it here!"

Lizetta held out the knife. The Prince jerked it away and stepped to the wreckage. He dropped to his knees to get at the board more easily, squeezed the blade under the board, and began sawing at the peg. It was a slow job. The blade was sharp, but lacked teeth to cut through tough wood like the peg. Prince George paused to wipe his face.

"Don't break my sticker," warned Lizetta, leaning over to watch.

"I won't break it."

Prince George sawed away while Blackie ate bushes along the path. The man stopped now and then to see how deeply he'd cut.

"Lazlo has the proper tools for that job," commented Lizetta. "He'd slice through that peg in two minutes."

235

Prince George glared at her. Grimly, he chewed away with the blade till he cut through the peg. He tossed the board aside.

"Well, this'll help a little."

Lizetta stuck out her hand. "My knife, please."

Prince George weighed the knife in his hand. "I don't think so. It's not wise to trust you with a sticker when I'm unarmed."

He slipped the knife into the boot with the necklace. Lizetta looked furious for a moment, then covered it with a smile.

"No matter, my lord. I don't need a knife with you here to protect me."

Prince George stood, wiping dirt and sawdust from his hose.

"I'm here, all right. There are lots of places I'd rather be, but here I am. The load's lighter now, Blackie. You ready to travel on?"

Blackie nodded. Again, the humans crawled up on him. Again, he took up the trek, dragging the chain with the bouncing boards along the path.

Perhaps the Prince had stripped away a couple boards, but the load didn't feel any lighter to Blackie. The hills were high here, and he wasn't used to hauling loads. In any case, he was only able to drag up two or three more hills before running down completely. He came to a standstill, shaking, sweating.

"That's it," said Prince George, jumping to earth. "Blackie can't continue any further. He's done his best. We're going to abandon this rubbish."

"What are you doing, my lord?" cried Lizetta.

"Freeing Blackie," gritted the Prince, unbuckling the harness from Blackie's shoulders. He pulled the collar over Blackie's head and threw it aside with the chain. Lizetta ran over and grabbed the collar.

"The Nail! You can't leave the Nail!"

"I certainly can." Prince George wiped his hands on his shirt. "Now, Blackie can run."

"Go ahead then," said Lizetta, plopping down on the axle, the collar over her knee. "Run on if you must. I'm staying with the Nail."

Prince George looked at her in dismay. "You don't mean that you'll stay here alone!"

Lizetta glared up, arms folded tightly. "I do not leave the Holy Nail."

Prince George turned to Blackie. "What can I do? I can't leave her to the wolves, can I?"

Blackie tossed his head. He was tired of these delays. How long had they been gone from the Princess? She had told them to hurry back to her.

Prince George whirled back to Lizetta.

"Stand up!" he yelled. "I'm not leaving you behind! That old bolt can rust away as far as I care, but you're coming with us. I'll drop you off at the first safe place we find, but I'm not leaving you to starve in the forest."

Lizetta folded her arms tightly. She gave him a hostile glance and looked away. He stared at her a moment, then reached for her.

"I'll drag you along by your hair!"

Her eyes flashed up at him.

"You touch me, *gadjo*, and I'll curse you to blacken the sunshine! I'll freeze your bones with a spell! Your hair will fall out, your skin will crack, you'll grow old overnight!"

"You'd do that to me," cried the Prince, "when I'm trying to help you?"

Lizetta calmed her tone. "I told you, I am not moving. If my lord can find some way of removing the Nail, I'll go along with it. Until then, I stay here."

"So, stay behind!" Prince George turned to Blackie, throwing open his arms. "I give up on her. She can sit till she rots like an old shoe. We can't pull that rubbish any farther."

Blackie nodded. Prince George was right. The whole story sounded bogus to Blackie. He'd never heard of a Holy Nail. What if Lizetta had made up the story to hold them back until Lazlo catches them? If she had her way, they'd pull those stupid boards all the way to the Shrine.

"Dump them," he thought. "Lose them right here."

Lizetta jumped up. She reached for the Prince's arm. "My lord, you're a clever man. Use your brain. Think how to free the bolt from the boards. There must be some way to do it!"

"There is no way," complained the Prince. "How can I pull a bolt without tools? I could dig it out with your knife, but that'd take days."

"Why not harness the unicorn to the bolt?" suggested Lizetta. "Use his strength to pull it free?"

Prince George scratched his head.

"That might be possible if I could hook the wreckage to a tree or something. The chain's already attached to pull with, but the boards would need a powerful anchor to hold them down."

Lizetta thought a moment. "Could you burn away the wood, my lord? The Nail is iron. A fire won't hurt the metal, and the boards would burn away in no time."

"Sure, I could do that," nodded the Prince, "if I had a flame."

"Think, man!" cried the Gypsy. "You have my knife! Steel and stone—that's how you make fires, isn't it?"

The Prince turned away. "In theory, it is, but it's not as easy as it sounds. I've often made fires when I had the right metal and a proper flint. We'd lose time playing at fire-making."

Lizetta stood. "In that case—" She wiped her forehead and picked up the collar. "Help me, Saint Jude. It's up to me to save this Nail!"

Prince George walked to Blackie. He pulled up with an effort. "It's your choice, Gypsy. Come along, or stay behind."

Blackie twitched his tail, as Lizetta lifted the collar over her shoulder. "Wait for me!"

She started after Blackie, leaning against the heavy collar with the weight of the boards dragging in the dirt. Pieces of harness, still attached, trailed behind like a clutch of dead snakes.

Prince George slapped his head. "Oh, Saint Peter! You can't pull that load! It'll take you a week to walk a mile!"

"I won't leave it behind!" gasped Lizetta. "I must save the Nail!"

Prince George threw his hands up to Heaven. "Why do these things happen to me? The stupidest, stubbornest—"

He jumped off Blackie and ran to Lizetta, catching her by the shoulders. She screeched at him and tried to hold back, but he jerked the collar away from her. She grabbed it again and tried to hold on, but he pulled it free. She scratched at him, snarling like a wildcat. Both panted, glaring at each other.

Prince George threw the collar into the bushes.

"Now, come along, you! If I had any sense, I'd leave you to feed the wolves, but I'm stuck with you! You'll come along with us if I have to drag you every step of the way!"

"I won't leave the Nail!" she screamed. "You touch me, I'll bite off your nose!"

"That's it, Blackie!" cried the Prince, turning away. "We're leaving! She can fight off the beasts by herself. Let's go."

Prince George struggled onto Blackie's back, but Blackie didn't move. For the first time, he looked at Lizetta with admiration. She was tense, her teeth set, her eyes flashing. He saw something about this Gypsy that reminded him of his Princess. Sure, her perfume was musky as any wildcat, but she looked indomitable.

The Prince kicked his side. "Blackie, let's go!"

Doggedly, Lizetta picked up the collar again. She heaved it over a shoulder, holding it with an arm, and leaned against the chain to start dragging.

"See, my lord!" she panted. "I can pull it myself!"

Blackie glanced around at Prince George. He trotted to Lizetta. The Gypsy dropped the collar and threw her arms around Blackie, hugging his sweaty neck.

"Oh, noble beast, I knew you'd understand. You won't abandon Lizetta! Let the man go on by himself, puny thing! You and I, we'll save the Holy Nail together!"

The Prince beat his head with his hands.

"Oh, saints, give me strength! What can I do? I've vowed to hurry to the Shrine, but I'm stuck in these hills with a pair of—The unicorn won't pull those boards, and the Gypsy can't!"

In the end, it was Prince George who pulled the load. Complaining bitterly, he cut away the last strands of harness and tried to wrench off more boards. Blackie watched, grimly pleased, as the Prince drew the collar over his shoulder and glared up at him.

"Don't stand staring like a fat guildsman! Let's get on with it."

Blackie walked up the trail. He looked back at the Prince, bent against the chain as the boards dragged behind. Lizetta cooed to him.

"Oh, sweet Prince, so noble, so heroic! You'll be a legend to the Gypsies for saving the Nail in this wilderness."

As they hobbled along, Lizetta pointed out that Prince George made a good porter. He looped the chain short enough to elevate the front of the load, so it didn't catch on roots or vines. True, he couldn't trudge as quickly as Blackie could trot, but he wasn't choked up every few steps by the chain catching on something. They went almost as quickly on foot as they'd done on Blackie's back.

This pace gave Blackie a good rest. He walked easily, reaching every few steps for a mouthful of leaves, while Lizetta sang to herself as she caught up wildflowers and wove a pretty crown for her hair. Only Prince George moaned as the collar grew heavy and rubbed against his shoulder with each mile. He hated this task.

Worst of all, he learned that the load had a habit of swinging forward on descents to smack him on the calves of his legs. Repeated whacks developed painful bruises as hill followed hill until his legs ached. When Prince George unwound a couple feet of chain so the boards would scrape flat again, they dug against roots and tree trunks as they had for Blackie.

Lizetta cried out when she saw the Prince stagger under the burden.

"Oh, my lord, this load is too heavy for you, mighty as you are! Lizetta will help with the chain, now. The two of us will pull together. You'll see that a Gypsy girl is strong and hearty, not soft like a Princess who lies around on pillows."

"No, no," gasped the Prince, throwing the collar down beside a stream at the bottom of a hill. "We're stopping. I'm hungry. This is ridiculous, anyway, pulling all these boards for one nail. With a crowbar, I could pry it loose in no time."

Blackie agreed that it was ridiculous. They had traveled so slowly that the sun was already sinking. He'd browsed on leaves and herbs as he walked, but these humans hadn't eaten a mouthful all day. He looked with concern at the Prince, lying against a tree with his eyes shut while Lizetta shook dust from her dress.

"I guess, I'll have to find food for them," thought Blackie, sniffing tender shoots under a bush. "Humans are stupid, as Papa always said. There's plenty of stuff to eat here, but they won't even try it."

He poked Lizetta to signal to her that he intended to scout around for human food. She was kneeling by the Prince, trying to slip her hand into his boot without waking him. The Prince kicked out. She snatched back her hand.

Blackie shook his head. "These humans!"

He trotted heavily up the next hill. He stopped at the top and shook himself. How long had it been since he'd run free without humans holding him back? Talking, talking, always talking without listening to anyone else, no wonder they got themselves into such difficulties.

Sniffing the air, he ran on as darkness flowed over the land, bringing night sounds of breeze, calling birds, creeking bugs. Crickets! That was the sound of crickets. Papa had described that sound, the first signal that the frozen season lay weeks ahead. Winter was coming on.

Blackie sniffed the breathing forest with its smells of growth and decay. He settled into the night, another creature on the prowl, ranging along with deepened senses until the scent of smoke brought him to a halt.

A spark of firelight through the trees reminded him why he was running through this strange corner of the forest. He slipped off the path and crept up to the fire, hearing voices, smelling horses and humans.

He saw a small wagon in a clearing where the path ran into the road. A couple humans lay like bundles, firelight flickering over their forms. Two other men sat beside them talking, one of them plucking a fat-bottomed lute.

"No, no, the City's impossible," said the first. "If reports are right, Prince Vile's armies have surrounded it for a siege. We'll have to play castles and villages, the harvest festivals."

"Villages are well enough," said the man with the lute, "but villages don't pay. You collect your coppers in the City."

The men sat silent awhile. The first man spat into the fire.

"Don't forget, it was your idea to go to Darr for the birthing of the baby. We could have stayed in the City in the first place."

The other man strummed a ringing chord.

"You want to head toward the City, you go right ahead. You heard as well as me that all the Hellions in the world are throwing boulders into it. Even if you got past the walls, there's no feast in a war zone, no work for minstrels."

The talk made little sense to Blackie. He studied the camp for something humans could eat. He saw bags and baskets heaped on a blanket. They could be loaded with food, but—Oh, ho! Hanging from a tree was a large ham. Blackie could smell the salty odor, all cooked and ready to eat.

Blackie burst out of the dark between the men. They rolled aside yelling, "Beelzebub! The Fiend!"

Blackie jumped the fire and speared the ham with his spike. The cord snapped, the ham came free, and Blackie landed on a brown donkey standing in the shadows.

The donkey twisted away, kicking and squealing. Blackie slipped between trees, the ham riding heavy on his head. He laughed at the babble of voices behind arguing whether he was a monster or a devil.

"Horned he was like old Satan!" cried one. "And he stole our ham! You know that demons love pork, unhallowed meat."

By the time Blackie returned to the Prince and Lizetta, he was hobbling again. His neck ached with the effort of holding the ham high so it wouldn't fly off the spike. Even so, he kept bumping into low limbs that knocked it off his horn, so he had to stab it again and again to keep it on.

Juices from the ham ran down Blackie's nose, drawing night-flying bugs. Everything smelled of salty meat, blocking his nose. He could have stumbled into a bear or a pack of polecats without smelling them. Luckily, the trail was clear of threats, though he thought he heard something following awhile, drawn by the smell of ham. It scurried off when he looked behind.

Back in the trail, Blackie found the Prince and Lizetta sleeping side-by-side with their heads on a pile of leaves spread with one of Lizetta's scarves. She clutched the sticker in her hand.

Blackie crept forward not to frighten them, but Lizetta was awake in an instant. She pulled up like a tiger, ready to stab with the knife.

"Unicorn, is that you?"

Lizetta took a sniff of the ham and jumped up. "Ham! Food! Oh, blessed unicorn!"

Prince George snored on as Lizetta petted Blackie's neck, then jerked the meat off the spike. She ran a finger over the ham.

"This ham's filthy!" she exclaimed. "Stuck all over with dirt and leaves! What did you do, kick it down the path? I have to wash it off."

Lizetta ran to the stream to clean away the dirt while Blackie worked his neck back and forth to shake out the kinks from holding his head up so long. He walked upstream from Lizetta to take a drink and wash the meat smell from his nose.

Lizetta returned to the pile of leaves with the dripping meat. Holding the ham in her lap, she sawed off a slice with the knife. She lifted it to her mouth and bit off a bite, chewing with eyes closed.

"Ummm, ummm!"

She offered a ham slice to Blackie who shook his head violently. He walked away from the smell to sniff bushes along the stream while Lizetta tickled the Prince awake.

"Princey! Wake up, sweet Princey. Lizetta has something nice for you."

CHAPTER NINETEEN

The Spearhead

Last night's ham had revived the humans when they set out to travel at dawn. For once, they didn't quarrel. They petted Blackie until he was pleased with himself, too. Lizetta called him "clever beast" while Prince George chimed in with "trusty chum."

Lizetta even let Prince George borrow her sticker to cut chunks from the ham which they chewed while Blackie grazed by the stream. Seeing the humans laughing together made Blackie willing to cooperate. He agreed to pull the chain again, especially when Lizetta gave up her scarves to pad the collar where it chafed against his neck.

Prince George regretted that he had lost his lionskin. "That would have made you comfortable. If I were alone, old friend, I'd pad you with my shirt, but with the Gypsy girl along—Well, you see how it is."

Blackie didn't see how it was, but he nodded agreement. He got stubborn only when Lizetta suggested that he carry the rest of the ham on his spike. He'd carry humans, he'd pull loads, but he would not lug a hunk of meat on his nose. The fronton was burden enough. Lizetta had to take back one of her scarves to make a sling for the ham.

They headed east this morning at a steady pace. Prince George had decided they could chance the highroad if they were careful, so they traveled quietly, except for meals when they pulled off the road to grassy spots along streams. Blackie grazed in the sun while the humans sat in the shade, chewing ham and telling stories of their travels.

The Gypsy's tales dealt with tricks and thefts and evading pursuit after the tricks and thefts. Prince George told of the famous Contest in which he won the beautiful Dorinda of Darr by completing three tasks. His servant then had been Godfrey, an out-of-work headsman, who became the great Heir of Darr when Prince George turned Lady Dorinda over to him. The Prince had intended to marry Dorinda up to the point of winning her, but decided against matrimony at the last moment. Traveling with Prince George and Godfrey through their adventures had been the Seeker, a diviner who could find anything, and a strange boy from the western desert who hated the ice and snow of winter.

"His name was Aleet," said the Prince, yawning, "Aleet. He was the best bowman I ever saw, except for the Princess. 'Course she doesn't count because she shoots a magic bow."

"No," agreed Lizetta, "she doesn't count. This road we follow, the Gypsy knows it well, always passing back and forth to repair pots, tell fortunes, treat sick horses. My Great-Grandmother Florica crossed it once with a beautiful horse that could untie knots. Oh, that horse was a moneymaker! Great-Grandmother sold it two hundred and eleven times. Each time she sold it, the horse untied its tether and ran back to Grandmother. Finally, she sold it to an old witch who fed it rhubarb sweetened with honey. The horse was so happy with her that it refused to come back to the Gypsy. When Grandmother stole it away, it untied its knot and ran back to the witch. That was the last the Gypsies saw of it."

"Rhubarb and honey," thought Blackie. "Hmmm, I wonder what that tastes like."

"Is it true," asked Prince George, "that you Gypsies leave secret marks to show which villages are friendly and what castles to avoid?"

Lizetta smiled mysteriously. "The people have many secret signs. I've been watching for signals that might help us, perhaps steer us to one of our campgrounds. If we could find the traveling families, they could aid us in the quest. At least, we'd get better food than this salty ham. It makes my feet swell."

"Speaking of the quest," said the Prince, looking sternly at Lizetta, "I know, you stole the necklace again last night. It's time to give it back."

That set them quarreling. The Gypsy claimed that she took the necklace to keep it safe. She resented Prince George calling her "light-fingered." Blackie was glad when they set off again, Lizetta sullen and silent for a change.

For a few miles, this section of the forest was easy to travel with gentle hills and shallow streams. Trees grew scattered as the road wandered around standing water and sinkholes. The road passed into a reedy marsh where Blackie's hooves sank into the mud. The boards scooped up layers of sludge till Blackie could barely drag them along.

Prince George had to slide down into the mud to heave on the chain to dislodge the boards. They came free with a sucking sound, and Blackie could move forward a couple steps before getting stuck again as biting bugs swarmed around their necks and flanks.

"This part," gasped Prince George, slapping a deerfly on Blackie's back, "this part of the road . . . was frozen . . . when I passed before. Much better, much better."

"I recognize this place," said Lizetta, looking around. "The people call it Malyn's Mire. The people circle around it on that trail we passed two miles back. That lane sticks to high ground so our carts don't get stuck."

"An easier road and you didn't tell me?" demanded Prince George, stopping to wipe his forehead. His hand left black marks on his skin. "What are you up to? Are you trying to make us miserable?"

"You said you wanted to hurry, my lord," explained Lizetta. "That roundabout is much longer than the way through the Mire."

Sinking to his knees, Prince George bent to grasp the chain again.

"So this is how Gypsies hurry," he said sarcastically. "I guess, you'd argue that the fastest way off a mountain is over the cliff."

"But you don't ask for directions, my lord," protested Lizetta. "You bull ahead as though you're the one who's spent her life traveling these roads."

Prince George heaved on the chain again. Blackie dragged forward a few steps.

"Well, I do ask you now," gasped the Prince, shaking mud from his hands. "Whenever you see us blundering into disaster, don't hold back from warning me."

"Now that you request it," said Lizetta, loftily lifting her nose, "I shall."

"And to think," said Blackie to himself, watching a turtle swim slowly away, "I thought it was fun to carry the Princess into that swamp the first day I met her. I must have been mad!"

They reached dry ground a mile farther though the bugs followed until they found a clean stream to wash in. Prince George pulled the collar from Blackie as Lizetta waded out of sight upstream. Blackie rolled back and forth in the water and came to a rest with his nose on the mossy bank. The Prince stripped off his filthy clothes and lowered himself to the bottom with his head next to Blackie's.

Blackie breathed deeply, his eyes closed, while the stream washed away the mud caked on his legs. For a moment, he felt peaceful, the scrapes from the chain numbed by the cool water, his sore hooves eased.

When he relaxed, his nose slumped to the stream and he woke up snuffing and snorting. Now, he felt hungry. He pushed up quietly, trying not to drip on the Prince. He walked around a tree to shake off the water, returning for the tall grass leaning over the stream. As he chewed, he listened to Lizetta singing upstream.

> When Winter flies down from the mountain
> to frost the fields and trees,
> the Gypsy follows the honking geese
> to the land of sunny seas.
> She picks golden fruit from bushes
> and sleeps to the hum of bees.
>
> When she wakes, she leaps up singing.
> She dances on flashing toes.
> We clap wild hands to her whirling,
> forgetting about our woes.
> While the Gypsy is dancing and singing,
> Winter holds back his snows.

Prince George was sitting against a tree in his damp clothes when Lizetta returned, combing her hair with a three-pronged twig. They chewed ham while Blackie grazed between them.

"We have to find more food," said the Prince.

"Between us, that'll be easy, my lord," said Lizetta, tossing her head. "Soon, we'll reach settled areas with villages and castles. If the castles are friendly, you can introduce yourself. Remember the feast that Countess Amelia served us at Furland after you killed that great bear?"

"And if the castles aren't friendly?" asked the Prince, lifting an eyebrow.

"Then I'll visit hen houses and gardens by night. The clever Gypsy never goes hungry, you see."

"Always the thief," sighed the Prince. "You know, as a knight, I'm dishonored when I eat stolen food."

"You're allowed to capture food in battle, aren't you?" asked Lizetta.

"Why, of course!" said the Prince. "A stout seizure by arms, that's honorable, but this snitching and snatching, well, that's just wrong. I shouldn't be a party to it."

Lizetta threw out her hands.

"My Prince, I'm a Gypsy. Besides we Gypsies have permission to steal. Everyone knows that the Angel Gabriel set aside the Eighth Commandment in return for the Gypsies' attempt to save our Lord."

Prince George shrugged.

"I know you claim that's true. No one believes it though, so we better be careful in settled areas. They're dangerous for us without weapons. Even the unicorn would have trouble defending himself with this chain holding him back. Soon as possible, we have to dump these boards."

"You may do as you please with the boards, my lord," said Lizetta, "as soon as I recover the Nail."

Showing her willingness to share, Lizetta volunteered to take the next turn pulling the chain. A quarter-mile along, though, she began tempting Prince George to take her place by offering to reveal Gypsy secrets if he'd take the chain.

"The never-lose dice trick, my lord," she gasped, "worth . . . thousands of coppers to my father. Or the see-through . . . cards. Always know everyone's hand."

"Not for me, Gypsy, not for me," insisted the Prince. "I never cheat."

"What a fool," she muttered.

Prince George turned on her. "What's that you said?"

"I said," she panted, switching the collar to the other shoulder, "I need . . . a tool. A crowbar, a wrench. Any prying tool, or pulling . . . to yank out the Nail."

"Yes," said the Prince, "a good, heavy crowbar. I could jerk out that bolt with it and keep the bar for a weapon. I'd be formidable again."

Blackie took pity on Lizetta after a mile and let the Prince pull the collar over his neck once more. Soon after that, Prince George spotted the first castle they'd seen for days, a gloomy tower looming over the road. He stopped under a tree and waited for Blackie to catch up.

"I don't like that place," whispered the Prince, peeking out through the leaves. "No village, no banner. It has a Vile look about it, probably one of the Black Prince's outposts. He's scattered them around the Empire."

"Perhaps it's abandoned," suggested Lizetta. "Let's send the unicorn over to find out."

Blackie looked at her, startled, while the Prince frowned. "Blackie, why send Blackie? Why don't you go?"

Lizetta shrugged. "Well, if there's a garrison in there, they probably wouldn't attack a unicorn. If they did, he can run faster than we can."

"No, no," said the Prince, "I want you to go. I need the unicorn for the quest."

"But, my lord," argued Lizetta, "if the unicorn were captured, we'd be here to rescue him. Perhaps there are good people in there who'd give us food."

Blackie shook his head. He did not like the looks of that castle. He'd been captured twice already. He wasn't trying for a third time. He turned back up the road, pausing for Prince George to straighten the boards on the chain.

"The unicorn's right," said the Prince, straightening. "It's too much of a gamble for any of us to go to that castle. How could we rescue them without weapons? We'll just have to circle around and go on."

"But I'm hungry!" wailed Lizetta.

Without waiting, Blackie plunged into a narrow forest trail circling the castle. He trotted easily until the boards hung up on a root. Prince George had to get down to free them again.

"I'll pull the chain here in the forest, Blackie," he whispered. "I can handle it better than you can on this path."

"If we got help from the castle," muttered Lizetta, "you wouldn't have to deal with the chain."

The Prince shouldered the collar again. "If I abandoned the whole thing, I wouldn't have to deal with it either."

"Oh!" Lizetta sweetened her tone. "My lord is right, as usual. Of course, we must avoid the castle. Your Lizetta obeys your slightest suggestion."

She gave an exaggerated curtsy and followed Prince George up the path. Blackie walked slowly, sniffing the air and listening to the boards scraping along behind him.

They passed the castle without incident and returned to the road where Lizetta agreed to take another turn with the chain.

"After all," she pointed out, "it is the Gypsies who are entrusted with the Nail. At least, this road is smoother than the forest. The Gypsy is always glad to take her share in the toil."

"Good thinking," said Prince George, handing her the collar. "And don't insist on giving it back soon. You can drag it all day if it pleases you."

Lizetta gave him a wounded look. "My lord, it does not suit you to be sarcastic. Your servant desires to do her share."

Blackie trotted a few steps up the road to eat leaves from a bush as the couple squabbled behind him. The humans grew hungrier as the afternoon crawled by. Even with Blackie doing most of the pulling, they scratched along at a feeble pace until sundown when Blackie heard the sweetest sound in the world, the chime of a church bell calling to vespers.

Though he pulled the chain as usual, Blackie picked up his pace at the bell. Riding on Blackie, Lizetta straightened and called, "Look, my Prince, the unicorn is speeding up. He hears something promising."

Prince George was limping behind the load. He looked up wearily. "What's that? What's that?"

"I hear it too!" sang Lizetta. "A church bell! Good people! The Black Prince does not reign here!"

"Slow down, now, take care!" cried the Prince. "These could still be enemies of the Crown! We don't know their feuds."

"By the bell, they'll all be at church," insisted Lizetta. "Their food is ours!"

"At least," said the Prince, "let's drop the chain in case we have to run. We can come back and get it if we have to."

"No, no!" Lizetta urged Blackie on with her heels. "This is a friendly place. The Gypsy senses openhanded simpletons."

With Lizetta kicking him, Blackie trotted faster. The boards bounced merrily. Prince George broke into a shambling run to keep up. They hurried between fenced fields of mature crops up to the village gate where three or four armed fellows watched suspiciously.

"What have we here?" demanded the thinnest man Blackie had ever seen, leaning on his spear. "A Gypsy wench riding boldly, not stealing in the back door? The world must be upside down!"

"Why, good people," cried Lizetta, "we have nothing to hide! We are merchants seeking to trade our last goods before returning home."

"Goods," said the man, suspiciously. "I see no goods to trade. And what is the man doing running behind? Shouldn't the master be on the horse?"

Prince George stood panting. Tired and famished, he could think of nothing to say to men with spears, but Lizetta was glib. She slid down to earth and pointed to the load on the chain.

"Where are your eyes, my good man? Do you not see these fine boards? Any cart maker or carpenter would give coppers for boards like these."

"Boards!" laughed the thin man. "You seek to sell scraps like that to men who live in the forest? A few strokes with axe and adz give us boards enough to build a city."

Lizetta slapped her head in dismay.

"Boards, did I say? I must be confused, fatigued from our travel. Metal, I meant to say, metal. Look at this stout chain, twenty feet of good iron links, the strongest in the land. Your blacksmith would trade his hammer for metal like this."

"Well, now you're talking," nodded the man. "Iron is valuable."

Blackie lost interest in their talk. He turned to the clover growing beside the gate while the spearman weighed the chain in his hand.

"Our blacksmith could use sound metal like this. And you must be peaceful folks to travel through this country without arms. Aren't you afraid of bandits or dark riders?"

Prince George spoke up for the first time. "We have taken a vow, my good man. We're on a quest to the Shrine to pray for peace, so we travel unarmed as you see."

"Why, sir, that's madness!" exclaimed the villager. "No one travels without weapons these days. With all the troubles in the land, even religious brothers have armed escorts."

"And look, my lord," said another man, "your horse is smarter than you are. He's got that spear thing on his forehead."

"Do you think they could be correct, my master?" asked Lizetta, bowing to Prince George. "Could it be that you should get a sword or a spear to defend us?"

"Absolutely, my lord," said the thin man, vigorously. "Any traveler must arm himself. I don't know that you can find a weapon here, though. Our villagers have sharpened all their rusty blades for our own defense. We have few enough arms for these troubled times, but you should get yourselves a bow or battle-ax somewhere. I wouldn't set foot in the forest without my spear."

"Why, fellow, you seem serious about it!" exclaimed Prince George.

The villager shook his spear and nodded. "Indeed I am, sir. If you've heard what we've heard—armies on the roads, dragons in the sky, not to mention the beasts and bandits running through the forest—you'd think a score of stout warriors few enough to protect you. Our lord, Baron Mosse, keeps half our fighting men in his castle at all times, and the rest of us stay on alert."

"My man," said Prince George, clapping the villager on the shoulder, "you've convinced me. Take me to your blacksmith. Perhaps he'll buy my chain and I can find a proper weapon."

"Oh, well, there may be a problem there," said the man. "No doubt Smithy will want your chain, but coppers are short these days. It may be that he'll trade for something you can sell at the next village."

"I'm sure that my master can make a suitable deal," said Lizetta. "Why, he might trade a few inches of chain for a hot supper."

"Yes, a supper," said Prince George. "I hate to give up this valuable chain, but I am a bit peckish, as the city folk say."

"As to supper, sir—" The man sounded eager. "My wife could give you a supper in exchange for metal. If you're selling the chain, perhaps a couple links could come our way. Once the country settles down and peddlers are on the road, she can trade them for ribbons, you know, the trifles that women treasure."

"I don't know about that," said Lizetta, slowly. "My master is particular about his meals. Is your wife a good cook?"

"Good cook!" exclaimed the villager. "My Joanie learned to seethe and stew from her old mam, best cook in three villages. Why, Baron calls Joanie up to the castle to help out on feast days. Her pickles is famous. And you'd give a chain twice this long for one of her pigeon pies."

"Pigeon pies," said Prince George, wonderingly. "Tell me, fellow, what did she give you for supper tonight?"

"Tonight? Why, tonight it was cabbage soup, delicious stew simmered nice and thick with a bit of ham left from last spring's pig."

"Not ham!" cried the Prince with disgust. "I can't stand any more ham!"

"But, sir," assured the man, alarmed, "don't mind the ham! She used the smallest slice for flavoring you can imagine, a sliver you could see through and so mild, it tasted like toast! I promise you, master, you won't even notice the ham for the carrots and onions and cabbage and herbs."

"Well, take us to this smith," ordered Prince George. "If he can remove the bolt and release the chain, we may be able to trade for a supper, so long as it doesn't taste of ham."

"Oh, don't worry about that, sir," said the thin man, bowing. "Now that I think on it, the ham was only an old bone that she dipped in the broth for luck. Follow, my lord, to the forge, and we'll see about the chain."

Blackie was happily eating the clover outside the gate, but he felt he had to stick with the Prince. The villager led the way down the darkened lane, telling Prince George about Joanie's cheese. Blackie walked with Lizetta, sniffing the pigs and chickens beside the huts, as well as the garbage in the street. It was clear that there was plenty of food here for humans.

The blacksmith's forge held a low, flickering fire just inside an open shed. It reeked of the sulfurous stink of charcoal and metal. Blackie nibbled grass beside the forge as the villager pulled out a stool for Prince George to sit on.

"Smithy's at church with the rest of the folks. He'll be right back. Can I get you a cup of water or something'?"

"How about a cup of beer?" asked the Prince, leaning back on the stool.

"Beer?" The villager looked delighted. "Oh, master, you just wait! My Joanie's ale, tastiest dram in the barony! The brewer buys Joanie's ale on the sly to sell in kegs as his special brew. He admits that he can't match her recipe. She learned that from her old mam, too."

"This old mam," said Lizetta, licking her lips, "she must have been a good cook."

"Good cook," repeated the villager, "I should say so. Listen, Gypsy, that woman could roast a chicken so it tasted like pheasant. Half the village used to crowd around Saturday nights just to smell her cooking for the Sabbath. Joanie's mam knew ninety-nine recipes, and Joanie learned every one of em. When Joanie got old enough to wed, she had a dozen suitors standing in line, the richest men in the barony. She married them one by one, starting with the fattest, and worked down to me. Would you believe, each of her husbands ate himself to death within a month.

"I was number thirteen. Since the wedding, Joanie's been stuffing me like a butcher's pig, but I can't gain an ounce. I just can't. Men in the Sprat family always skinny, you see. Joanie says she don't know why she married me, but I was a challenge. You just wait, sir, for your supper. You don't get dry old bread from Joanie, no, no. Her bread's toasted in lard and slathered with butter an inch deep. Oh, my, I can't get enough of it!"

His eyes gleamed and he rubbed his hands together.

"Well, when does this blacksmith get back?" cried Prince George, hungrily.

Blackie looked up, startled at his tone. It wasn't long before the villagers came stumbling down the lane from church, calling goodbye in the darkness and hurrying to their homes.

"Ho, Smithy," cried the thin man, "is that you? We been waiting for an hour."

"What you waitin' for, Sprat?" said a deep voice. "You know that workday's over. It's time to put out the cat and latch the door."

"But I got travelers here with good, solid iron. They wants to trade off this fine chain for a weapon."

With an exclamation, the blacksmith bent to lift the chain to feel its weight.

"Good iron here, Sprat. I can always use iron, but I got no weapons. If they wants weapons, they has to go up to town and hunt down the armorer."

"Well, just give this chain a look, Smithy. See what you can do with it."

"Oh, I'll look at the chain, all right. Here, lemme light the lamp to see what they got."

Blackie blinked as lamplight blazed out the open door. The blacksmith, a stout man with broad shoulders and thick arms, held up the chain with hands as black as charcoal. He inspected the chain, link by link.

Blackie went back to eating grass. Prince George said, "And this bolt holding the chain at the end, can you pull it loose, Smithy?"

"Nothing to that," said Smithy. "Lemme get my gooseneck here. I'll yank it free in a jiffy. This bolt, sir, you want to trade it off, too?"

"Oh, no, man!" exclaimed Lizetta. "Just the chain, please. We need to hold on to that bolt there."

"Well, I got no coppers, but I could give you pots and pans for the chain. You can trade them off with any wife in the village. Tell you what, though, if you wants a weapon—This bolt, you got seasoned iron here. It'd make a biting spearhead if I'd hammer it out for you."

"A spearhead," repeated the Prince. "That's an idea."

"No, no, no!" insisted Lizetta. "We have to hide the Nail, not wave it around on a stick!"

"But look, Gypsy," suggested Prince George, speaking so low Blackie could barely hear, "remember your own rule of hiding things in plain sight. That makes sense. What better way to hide a feather than to stick it on your hat? It's so visible no one thinks twice of it. Same thing with your bolt."

"But not the Nail, my lord!" cried Lizetta. "That's sacrilege!"

Blackie turned away from the door to follow the ragged grass around to the back of the forge where it grew tall with seedy stems. All he heard from the other side were muffled voices and Lizetta crying.

Blackie ate peacefully till Prince George hunted him up a few minutes later and rubbed his muzzle.

"Well, Blackie, I'm off to Sprat's house for supper. The Gypsy says she's staying here to watch the Nail get hammered into a spearhead. Of course, she's upset at it, but I told her that the Nail can protect us as we ride along."

Lizetta ran around the side of the building. She tugged at the Prince's sleeve like an angry wasp.

"This is wrong, my lord, dead wrong! You know how precious the Nail is! To let the blacksmith, this churl, hammer it like an old horseshoe—that's sinful, desecration!"

"Quiet, Gypsy!" commanded Prince George. "Keep your mouth shut! Do you want everyone to know what we've got there? I wouldn't go shouting about the Nail if you want to keep it secret!"

"But my lord," pleaded Lizetta, "please, let me keep it as it is. I'll guard it with my life. You told me, yourself, how many weapons you've lost these past weeks, daggers, spears. Three swords, you said, not to mention all the armor. A Nail like this, a few inches of iron, you'll lose it before nightfall tomorrow. Either you're impossibly careless, or you've got a curse on you."

Prince George jerked up tall.

"I resent that, Gypsy! I'm not careless! Most of those arms were stolen from me! You Gypsies, you stole my last sword and dagger! I'll guard this new spear as I did my father's sword that he got from his father. I had that sword all my life until I lost it jumping into a moat to escape a castle filled with Hellions. And I haven't given up on that sword. Someday, I'll get back to Castle Shrems and find my sword again."

"Yes, I remember that tale," muttered Lizetta. "It fails to comfort me. I foresee that you'll meet another accident and lose this spear, too."

"Enough, Gypsy," ordered the Prince. "Come along. We'll see what supper Dame Sprat can serve us. I'm hungry enough to eat a boot if cooked tender and served with caper sauce."

They walked off into the darkness, Lizetta complaining in a shrill voice about the Nail. Blackie stretched. He walked into the light of the forge for a nasty-tasting drink of water from the barrel beside the anvil.

Smithy was kneeling on the pile of boards with his gooseneck, a long, curved pry bar. He looked at Blackie's fronton and shook his head.

"You're a funny-looking horse, you are. Where'd you get hooves and tail like that? I say, you have a wicked piece of iron on your noggin. I'd give a handsome supper to get me hands on that."

Blackie watched the blacksmith take a mighty heave on the bolt with the gooseneck. The bolt popped free with a squeal. Smithy tapped the metal with his tool.

"Solid," he mumbled. "Solid."

Blackie took another drink and went back to the dark grass beside the shed. The man grabbed the bolt with his tongs and set it on his anvil. He tossed a few piece of charcoal into the forge and took up a squeaky bellows.

Blackie chewed grass while the blacksmith spoke to himself.

"Never seen metal like this! Pulled out sweet like it wanted to be free of the wood. If it pounds out this easy, it may be too soft for a spearhead. It won't hold a sharp point."

Blackie swallowed a bite of grass. Sleepy, he closed his eyes and sighed.

BANG!

The hammer blow made him jump. Blackie whipped his blade around in the darkness. He relaxed as the blacksmith fell into a rhythmic hammering.

"At least," Blackie said, "we're rid of that chain. Whatever happens, we can run free tomorrow."

He coughed lightly, stretched, and went back to eating as the hammer banged on.

CHAPTER TWENTY

The Gypsy's Curse

A crowing rooster woke Blackie at dawn leaning against the side of the shed that held back the chilly breezes. Blinking sleepily, he looked around to see humans gazing at him.

"There he be, big as life," said an old man. "That, me boy, that's a unicorn!"

A tall boy spat in the grass. "Nah, nah, old man! That's not a unicorn. Unicorns is white!"

The humans drew back when Blackie stretched and walked around the forge.

"Has to be a unicorn with a tail like that."

The door to the forge was closed. Blackie couldn't get to the water barrel. The grass was cool and dewy so he moved to a fresh patch and dug in. When he looked up, the sun gleamed off vines hanging from the thatch.

"So here you are!" snapped Lizetta, sticking her head around the forge. "And you call yourself a holy beast!"

She rounded the shed before Prince George and Sprat. "You're the one I blame! A true unicorn would have saved the Nail."

"Morning, unicorn," said Sprat. He held up a basket. "I brought you some bread rolls for your breakfast."

Prince George pounded on the wide door, "Smithy, Smithy!"

Smithy staggered out from a side shed a moment later. Rubbing his eyes, he unlatched the door to the forge. Blackie hurried in to stick his nose into the water barrel as Smithy picked up an eight-foot staff with a long, gleaming spearhead.

"Here she be, me lord. A spear to do damage."

Prince George snatched the spear and shook it in his fists. Stamping out a foot, he made a thrust. He pulled back the spear to examine the head. He tested the point with a finger.

"How'd the head get so long, Smithy? Did the bolt grow as you hammered it?"

"Bless your heart, no," laughed the blacksmith. "That bolt didn't have the metal for a proper lancehead, so I hammered a link or two of the chain into a base for it. Take a peek, me lord. See where the bolt's brazed on? Touch that point, sharp as Granny's needle. You wouldn't think you'd get that edge from an iron bolt, would you? Them old smiths, they knew their metal."

Blackie took a roll from Sprat as Lizetta cried out, "But the metal of the bolt, you didn't defile it with base elements, did you?"

"De-file it?" said Smithy. "No, ma'am, I didn't use my file. I just hammered it out and welded it to a bit of chain metal. It sharpened up beautiful. Just a stroke or two with my emery and it was keen as a monk's razor. Tell you the truth, I'm sort of proud o' this spear."

Prince George thumped it against the ground. "Good and solid! Where'd you get a pole like this?"

"That was a bit o' luck!" chortled Smithy. "It was a flagstaff. Last June, Baron had old Carpenter turn out flagpoles for his banners, a dozen o' em. Before he could deliver, though, this war started, and Baron spent his coppers on arrows instead. The staff came cheap."

"Cheap, was it?" Prince George whipped the spear around. The spearhead whistled through the air. "Was there any . . . er . . . value left over from the chain?"

Once he finished the rolls, Blackie went back to his grass. Sprat followed to rub his back as Smithy reassured the Prince.

"Oh, sure, me lord. This job, pole and all, it'd be eight—" He scratched his head. "Now, let's see, nine coppers, if you paid cash. O' course, the chain, heavy as she was and iron in short supply, well, I'd owe you a dozen coppers over the spear if I had coppers to give. You look over in the corner, there. All them pots and things. Take your pick to fill out the bargain."

Prince George stared in disgust at the tinware in the corner. "What a stack of rubbish! Nothing in there worth an old stick, let alone five coppers."

"Let me look, master."

Lizetta squatted in the corner, running her fingers over the dented cups and pots and worn-out horseshoes.

"Nothing," she said. "Not a copper's worth in the lot."

"What'll we do?" asked the Prince.

"Why, we take the chain back," said Lizetta. "Those spare links will trade better than any of this stuff."

"Oh, no," begged Smithy, "don't take this metal from me! I can work off that iron for a month!"

"He's right," said the Prince, his spear butt smacking the ground. Blackie looked around.

"I'm not taking that chain! It's bad enough I have to bargain like a peddler. I refuse to touch that chain again."

Lizetta looked sharply at Smithy. "Well, blacksmith, bring out your treasure! I can see in your eyes that you're holding something back."

Blackie yawned and moved into the forge for another drink from the barrel. Smithy pulled off his cap. He ran a hand over his bald head.

"Sorry, missy, that's all I got. I can't give up me tools or bellows. The anvil and furnace, well, you wouldn't want them."

"In that case," said Lizetta, "it's got to be the chain."

She reached for the end of the chain hanging out of a wooden box.

"No, no, please!" Smithy ran back to his shed. "I . . . I do have something. It's not vallable, but it would be worth coppers if you could sell it."

"Let's see it," sighed the Prince. "We've got to get going."

Blackie lifted his head to watch. Smithy came out of his shed with a package wrapped in coarse cloth. He pulled back the wrapping. The light caught the face of a mirror in a wooden frame.

He shook his head, sadly. "I been keepin' this till I find a willin' maid to marry me, but the iron's more useful to me now."

"We'll take it."

Lizetta snatched the mirror and wrapped it back in the cloth.

"But Gypsy," cried the Prince. "What do I want with a mirror?"

"It's either the mirror or the chain," said Lizetta, bowing. "My lord may have his choice."

Blackie stepped between them. He tapped the mirror with his spike. This thing was light.

"Oh," said the Prince, "Blackie wants the mirror."

"Yep, yep, me lord," said Sprat. "That mirror's a rare creature. Only two of 'em in the land. Baroness has t'other one up at the castle."

"So we keep the mirror," said Lizetta. "And, Master Smithy, just dip into your basket and give us some of those apples and turnips you mentioned. With the meat pies and buns from Dame Sprat, we'll have food for a day or two."

"Oh," groaned Smithy, shaking his head. "I could spare turnips sooner than that mirror. I keep thinkin' it'll attract me a pretty wife, a gal that likes to look at herself in the mornin'."

"You'll have to buy a wife like any honest man," suggested Lizetta, looking at herself in the mirror. "Take your coppers to her father."

"That's what I did," said Sprat, "and I got me a wife among wifes!"

"Enough of this!" cried the Prince. He paused. "Oh, yes, Smithy, I do have one little job for you before we ride. Could you look at this necklace I have in my boot? Its clasp needs repair."

Blackie had time to finish the bread rolls before Prince George stalked out of the forge with his spear. He wore the Offering under his shirt again.

"Let's ride! By now, we should have reached the Shrine and returned. All these rumors of war—Who knows what the Princess has got herself into? I'm sure that she needs us."

Blackie stepped to Prince George and stood ready.

"A moment, my lord."

Lizetta spread her shawl on the grass and topped it with a scarf. She piled on the apples and turnips with Goody Sprat's meat pies, rolled up the food in the scarf, and placed the mirror package on top. She pulled all together in the shawl, tied it in a neat bow, and slung the lot over her shoulder.

"I'm ready to go, Princey."

Gripping Blackie's neck, Prince George swung to his back.

"Help me up, please," said Lizetta to the blacksmith. Instead of moving, he looked her over from her scarf to her slippers.

"Why don't you stay here with me, missy?" he pleaded. "If you married me, you could eat all the turnips you want. You'd stay toasty by my forge in the worst freezes o' winter."

"An appealing offer, Master Smith," said Lizetta, pulling herself up behind Prince George. "But I must find my people again."

"Don't forget this, my lord!" cried Sprat, handing the spear to Prince George. The Prince rested the spear across Blackie's shoulders.

"Now, we're ready for anything. Let's go, Blackie."

Sprat and Smithy walked with them to the village gate. Villagers poured from their huts to watch. A fat, cheery woman waved goodbye to the Prince.

"Come back to visit whensoe'er you can, me lord! The soup pot's always bubblin' on the stove!"

Prince George stared straight ahead, but Lizetta waved gracefully.

"Thanks to you, Mother Sprat!"

The guard at the gate this morning sat cross-legged on a stool, stitching at a jacket. His bow leaned against the planks. He stared up at the riders.

"Who you got here, Sprat? These the strangers came by, last night?"

"That they be," said Sprat, beaming.

The man stood, placed his sewing on the stool, and shoved open the gate. "Be careful, strangers. They's danger out beyond our fence."

"Go with God!" called Sprat.

Lizetta leaned back, kissing her hand to them. "A Gypsy blessing on you all, dear friends—full bellies, warm beds, and peaceful nights to enjoy them."

"Amen!"

Prince George kicked Blackie lightly. Blackie trotted toward the sun spreading a rosy glow across the east. The air was cool, but Blackie warmed up with his run. Without chain or cart to hold him back, he felt he was flying. He sniffed the morning air as birds fluttered up from the fields around.

In a short time, Prince George had to draw in the spear to pass under the trees of the forest. It was late in the morning before they rode out in another area of golden fields. Here, the people working the fields were fearful. They scampered away as Blackie approached until

Blackie ran down a trembling woman. She informed them that they were entering Cranch.

"Oh, oh," said Prince George, gripping his spear. "We've got to go easy in Cranch. Godfrey and I had a run-in with the Duke's riders."

"All the Gypsies know Duke Mark," said Lizetta. "He's as bad as any bandit. He strips every cart that passes through his lands."

They ate their dinner in a quiet corner of a field. Blackie grazed along the hedge while Prince George settled down with his meat pies and apples. Lizetta gnawed a turnip and listened to the Prince tell about traveling through Cranch three years before. His servant, Godfrey, had drugged the Duke's riders with sleepy drops and run off with thirteen horses.

"We sold the horses in the next town. Three silver ounces, we got for those horses."

Lizetta was delighted with the story. She smiled into the mirror.

"So, Princey, you've stolen horses in your time! I knew you were a Gypsy at heart. Too bad we don't have those sleepy drops."

"Oh, yes," Prince George nodded his head, "Duke Mark's men would catch me if they could. We'd better wait till nightfall to cross this duchy."

"Hide out, my lord, when we ride a unicorn?" hooted Lizetta. "Handsome Blackie can outrun any riders the Duke sends after us."

Soon enough, they ran into a roadblock around a curve, a couple miles up the road. Eight or ten toll collectors searched wagons with the drivers standing by. The man holding the horses shouted as Blackie turned across a field toward the forest. Most of the officers ran for their horses.

It wasn't much of a chase at first. Blackie trotted silently up a deer trail while the riders behind crashed into branches, cursed, and shouted. Then the forest ended, and they ran out into another broad field of grain divided into strips by hedges.

Blackie galloped down a long golden strip well ahead of the riders who emerged from the trees by ones and twos. They galloped after, blowing horns and whooping. At the end of the field, Blackie saw a bulging fence of vines woven over tall posts. Lizetta shrieked as Blackie charged up to the fence and leaped high, landing on the far side in a springy tree that threw them back onto a wagon full of ripe plums.

Blackie hit the side of the wagon and rolled to earth, but his riders squished down in plums. Lizetta grasped the side of the wagon and pulled herself free, gasping, while Prince George floundered through the juicy purple mess.

"My spear! Where's my spear?"

Blackie forced himself up on his hooves. Surrounded by the heavy scent of the plums and the buzzing wasps, he looked about the orchard. He saw men standing on folding ladders to pick fruit from upper branches while women and children picked from the ground.

Horns blatted across the fence, pulling the humans around to stare at Blackie. He lowered his head to slurp up a mouthful of sweet plums. He swallowed the seeds as Lizetta jerked at the Prince's shirt to get his attention. She pointed up in the tree where the spear shaft stuck out of the branches.

"Oh, there it is!" he cried. "Climb up and grab it, Gypsy!"

Lizetta was checking the shawl to make sure the mirror wasn't broken. Prince George had to stand in the sticky plums, grasping a branch to hold on to. He reached high to pull out the spear, rested the spear shaft against the ground, and vaulted down. He shook the purple pulp from his shirt.

"Nasty plums, sticky! I'm gummed up like a honeycomb!"

"The mirror's fine!" cried Lizetta. "We can ride on!"

Lizetta stepped from the wagon onto Blackie's back, holding the shawl with the mirror under her arm. She called the Prince to mount before her.

"Hurry, my lord! Those riders will cut us off at the gate!"

Blackie winced when Prince George pulled to his bruised back.

"Folly, absurdity!" wailed the Prince. "Only two wagons in the whole orchard, and we fall into one of them! I hope this doesn't get into my song. The way things are going, I can't tell if I'm hero or clown."

"Let's ride!" shouted Lizetta.

The Prince swung up his spear and leaned forward. Blackie trotted between trees, knocking down ladder after ladder as he passed. The fruit-pickers screeched at them while children threw plums. Dogs chased after, barking.

Ignoring the pain from his bruises, Blackie ran out the gate into the road as the riders came chasing around the fence. Blackie galloped away between the village and Castle Cranch where he saw the black flag of Vile flying above the Count's banner. With good road below him, Blackie pulled further and further ahead of the riders until he ran into another roadblock at the east end of the duchy.

"Let's take 'em!" cried Prince George, kicking Blackie's flanks from excitement.

"No, no!" cried Lizetta.

Blackie agreed with Lizetta. These troopers had their bows drawn and spears set. He swung into a side lane while the men ran for their horses to join the chase. Reaching the forest, Blackie galloped a couple hundred yards down the lane before stopping at Prince George's orders. Panting and sweating, he turned in the darkness of the trees to face the bright entrance to the woodland.

"Jump down!" Prince George ordered Lizetta.

"What, my lord?"

"Jump! We're going to fight!"

"Fight, my lord?" cried Lizetta, clutching her bundle. "No, no, surely we can outrun them, or trick them!"

Prince George pushed her off with an elbow. Landing on her bottom in the leafy path, she jumped up, protesting. When Prince George lowered his spear, she ran behind a tree to peek out.

Blackie gathered himself, heart beating, as the riders came tearing into the forest. Blinded by the darkness, they didn't see Blackie until he was on them, throwing over the first horses while Prince George jabbed with the spear, howling like a wild man.

Bunched up as they were, the horses crashed into each other, crushing riders and pitching them off into the forest. Blackie heard screeching and screaming as men and mounts were driven into the trees until those in the rear backed off and galloped away. Blackie kicked anyone that tried to fight while the Prince threw his spear at a bowman who shot from behind a tree. It was over in a moment, except for injured animals and wailing men limping away.

Lizetta ran out, clapping her hands and laughing with joy, "Oh, my lord, you showed them! You showed them! What a warrior! This fighting isn't as foolish as I thought!"

"Hurry, Gypsy!" cried Prince George, jumping to the path. "They'll regroup and be down on us in a minute."

He ran about picking up fallen arms, a sword, shield, and dagger to replace the ones he'd lost. Lizetta darted through the injured, cutting off purses with her sticker. She jerked a string from the neck of one groaning man. It held a copper coin.

Running to the Prince, who'd pulled onto Blackie with the weapons, Lizetta passed him the purses to hold while she pulled up.

"No, no!" he cried. "We can't carry this stuff!"

"Money, my lord, money! Let's keep it! Here, take your spear!"

She grasped the Prince's arm to pull up behind him. Blackie turned in the trail and ran deeper into the forest, his heart beating hard. Soon, they were buried in the trees where only bird cries could be heard. Blackie slowed to a comfortable pace. They trotted on until Prince George judged that they were free of Cranch.

He directed Blackie back to the road by a side trail. Blackie stopped for a rest at a stream crossing the path. His riders jumped down. Blackie took a long drink. He sniffed for leaves while Prince George inspected his coat for wounds.

"I don't think you're hurt at all, Blackie," he said. "I got only a couple of cuts, myself. We're lucky. That was a sharp little skirmish."

"Skirmish," thought Blackie. "If that's a skirmish, I'd hate to see a battle. Those poor horses! It wasn't their idea to chase us. The men should know better, but the horses, they just wanted to graze in the field."

He tore off a sprig of leaves and chewed as Lizetta dug into the purses she'd recovered. She sounded disappointed.

"Two dirty shirts—rags, I call them, not worth carrying with us. A dozen poor coppers, some dice, and a seashell. I can use the dice."

She held up the coin with a hole in it.

"That fellow had this coin around his neck. Ever see anything like that, my lord?"

The Prince turned the coin in his fingers. He glanced at it and gasped.

"Have I ever seen this? Oh, Gypsy, you can't know how this cuts to my heart! It's a sester, the coin of Dacia, my kingdom across the sea. I wonder where that fellow got it."

He looked at the other side.

"This could be the face of my grandfather with a hole bored through his forehead. The coin's worth little, I suppose, but to me, it's a treasure. I think I'll give it to the Princess."

Lizetta sniffed.

"That Princess again! I must say, my lord, your way of winning wealth doesn't appeal to me. I'd rather cut purses neatly and softly than bash around with spears and swords."

"Well, you can win a fortune in battle," said the Prince, throwing himself down in the leaves. "When Godfrey and I captured Lord Bann, I got five hundred silver pieces and a knife with a silver handle. Look at this sword I picked up this morning. It's dull as a soapmaker's spoon."

"I've got an idea, my lord," said Lizetta, throwing the empty purses into the trees. "The only thing we have of value is the mirror. You know how women love mirrors, but few can afford them. Why don't we divide the mirror into sections? By selling a half dozen small mirrors, we could buy food enough to get us to the Shrine without having to fight."

Prince George began sharpening the sword against a rock from the stream.

"Now, Gypsy, you're thinking like a tradesman. I thought you Gypsies always steal your way through the world."

"Please, my lord," protested Lizetta, "the people only steal to eat. We live without place or property, you know, hated and hunted by *Gadjos*. If they left us alone, we could live by our trades, telling fortunes, repairing pots, doctoring horses. As it is, the people must steal to survive. But now, with the mirror to sell, we can haggle for our food, unless you can capture more coins."

"Haggle," grumbled the Prince, trying the sword's edge with a finger. "I hate haggling. It's not royal!"

Blackie looked up, pulling back his ears.

"Not royal, my prince?" jeered Lizetta, packing up the mirror again. "So you're going to stand on your pride now? Look at you, stained blue with plum juice! What's royal about that? Be reasonable, my lord. Without money, we can't worry about what's royal. We have to steal or haggle if we want to eat."

Prince George groaned. "Oh, I guess, we live as we have to, but I hate it. It's degrading. This adventure has nothing heroic about it."

Lizetta snorted. "Adventure! My lord, we're struggling to survive. Look at the poor Nail, hammered to a spearhead. That's what's degraded, defiling a holy relic."

Prince George leaned back against a tree.

"Well, when we reach the Shrine as I vowed to the Princess, I'll gain fame for my quest. You have to expect struggles and reverses on a quest."

"But I'm hungry, my lord," moaned Lizetta. "And we've eaten most of Mother Sprat's dinner. Now, we smell of plums with none to eat. Look at the unicorn. He stuffs himself while my stomach's empty again. You know, we could have a feast in a cozy inn. We do have riches to spend."

"What do you mean?" asked Prince George, suspiciously.

She leaned toward him, speaking in a low, beguiling tone. "Why, sweet lord, that necklace you carry. Don't you think we're wasting a treasure to carry it so far, just to toss it into a fountain?"

Prince George grasped the necklace under his shirt.

"Don't even think it, Gypsy!" he spat. "I'd leave you to rot in the forest if I thought you planned to steal this necklace."

"Oh, I don't mean sell the necklace," she said in a soothing tone. "I know of your vow to carry the Offering to the Shrine. But look how large that stone is! A good gem-cutter could trim it down, make it even handsomer, and the offcuts, the scraps, would be jewels in themselves. No one would ever know. We'd have wealth for you to ride royally. I'm only thinking of your fame, my lord."

Prince George stood up. He stuck the sword in his belt.

"Enough of this nonsense. Come on, Blackie. I'd like to find a comfortable place to stop for the night."

Blackie sighed. He turned from the leaves. Still tired from the morning's skirmish, he'd like a good rest, but the Prince was right. He and Lizetta couldn't eat grass or leaves. How limited they were, these humans, needing rations specially grown for them. They had to travel from castle to village, never knowing the delight of a flowery clover patch. And when they did find food, they had to find ways to cook it.

By now, Lizetta was mounted behind the Prince, the two weighing painfully on Blackie's bruises as he followed the trail to the road and turned east toward the Shrine. All afternoon, they tried to stop at villages for Lizetta to buy food with the coppers they'd captured, but no one was friendly in this country. Every field had its watchmen, every gate its guards.

"Move on, move on!" was the cry, followed by rocks or arrows.

When Prince George speared a slow-moving hedgehog in the road, Lizetta stole a bit of flame from an unguarded hut and baked the fellow. She covered it with mud and built a fire on top. Blackie hated the smell of the meat, and the Prince complained of the taste.

"It's rank, too strong. That's what I get for eating prickly rats."

Lizetta sucked the bones as though eating pheasant at a palace feast.

Next day, Prince George perked up when he saw the tower of a castle beside a river. Behind the castle stretched a walled town with its toll gate guarding a bridge.

"Ho, it's Dorth, Dorth!" he shouted with relief. "A bridge to cross the river and food, good food! We'll be welcome here. I know the gateboy and the innkeeper!"

But the gateboy no sooner saw them than he blew a piercing whistle. Howls rose to the skies. The boy yanked open the gate to let a pack of dogs run through, huge hounds with black snapping muzzles and flopping white ears. They charged straight at Blackie.

"Boarhounds!" screeched Prince George.

Blackie turned from the road and galloped through scratchy brush to the riverbank. Gathering speed as he ran, he threw himself far out in the river. He smacked down into the chilly flow with a splash. He sank under, but rose to the surface with Prince George clinging to his neck. Lizetta was thrown off his back. She bobbed up downstream, choking and shrieking.

"The spear, my lord, the spear!"

Hearing the dogs baying behind, Blackie kicked through the surge and swirl of the river. On the east side, he waded through gravel to the narrow strip of sand under the bank. Prince George slid from his back, wailing, "My spear! I lost it!"

Blackie watched the Prince run downstream, shading his eyes, gazing into the sparkling wash.

"There it is!" The Prince pointed. "She's got it!"

Prince George waded back in the river to grab the end of the spear when Lizetta paddled near. He pulled her to him, sneezing and coughing. Shivering with hair plastered down, dripping clothes stuck about her, she looked like a hen caught in a rain shower.

The instant she felt land underfoot, Lizetta jerked at the spear, trying to pull it away from Prince George.

"The Nail!" she screamed. "The Holy Nail! You dropped it in the river, careless man, clumsy man!"

"I lost it when we jumped," the Prince explained, hanging onto his end. "I knew where it was. I'd have recovered it."

"Give it here!" she shrieked. She wrestled for the spear with both arms. "Let me have it, fool, *gadjo*! I can't trust you! You'll lose the Nail for sure!"

"There they go again," thought Blackie. He ran along the shore to a muddy cut in the riverbank and climbed it with two jumps. He had a moment to eat grass at the edge overlooking the river before Prince George scrambled up the bank, clutching the spear. Lizetta crawled after, screaming at him.

"Let's go!" panted the Prince. He reached for Blackie's shoulder. "I'm leaving her behind! She's mad, mad, claiming the spear is hers!"

"Kick the dotard, unicorn! Knock him down!" yelled Lizetta, throwing mud from her hands at Prince George. "Make him give me the Nail! He's sure to lose it!"

"Oh, they're both crazy!" thought Blackie. He shook off the Prince and trotted away through the trees, leaving both humans to chase after.

Once he reached the road again, Blackie galloped around a wide curve until the cries fell away. He stopped and shook himself. He browsed on yellow leaves from a bush beside the track until the pair caught up with him, snapping at each other like alley cats.

"So what if I dropped the spear?" grumbled Prince George. "You lost the bags and the mirror, everything you were supposed to hold!"

"How, by the saints, could I keep them?" cried Lizetta, slapping at him. "I had to save the Nail! If you had the brain of a tadpole, you'd have held onto your own spear. I could have cared for the bags then!"

"So now, we have nothing to eat!" shouted the Prince, shoving her away with a long arm. "Our food, our mirror—you lost it all! Worthless, that's what you are, Gypsy, just worthless!"

"Ooooh!" gasped Lizetta, panting in fury. She jerked out her sticker. "Call me worthless, will you? Well, *rom baro*, say that again! I'll cut you down to size! I'll slice your gizzard like an eggplant!"

Spitting with rage, Lizetta threw herself at Prince George. The Prince ran behind a tree. Blackie stood in astonishment, as Lizetta chased after, waving the knife and shrieking. She drove the Prince back around Blackie. He had to poke out the spear point to hold her off.

"Run, Blackie, run!" cried the Prince. He threw an arm over Blackie's back and hung on as Blackie trotted away, dragging Prince George's legs down the road.

"Let's go. Let's go! Here she comes! She's crazy!"

Blackie ran a few steps until Lizetta stopped. She threw out clawing fingers. Her eyes blazed.

"Wretched man, foolish man!" she cried. "You lose everything you touch—my clothes, my possessions, the *vardo*, the Nail! I call on the winds to pile up the curses! I curse you in waking and sleeping, in breathing and eating!"

"Oh, Blackie, let's go before she turns me to stone!" cried the Prince, pulling himself onto Blackie's back. He pointed at her, extending first and last fingers in the sign of the horns as he kicked Blackie.

"Go, go!"

Blackie threw up his head.

"It's too much, too much! I can't handle both of them! The Gypsy can take care of herself better than the Prince can, so . . . so . . . !"

He turned and galloped into the coloring leaves. Lizetta shrieked after Prince George.

"May your skin wither, your teeth fall out! May your eyes roll away, so you crawl down the road like a blind—"

CHAPTER TWENTY-ONE

Blessed Virgin's Day

Blackie trotted in silence, his mind on Lizetta. He barely noticed the bursts of red and orange on the branches. They were approaching the eastern uplands where trees had dropped their leaves. Limbs and branches reached bare and wiry. Bushes edging the road had turned brown or purple with tufts of white silk and dark sprays of seeds. Yellow leaves padded the road.

"I had to leave her!" cried the Prince, twisting on Blackie's back. "I had to! You saw what she's like—Venomous, vindictive! Can you imagine her screaming at me like that in the road? Over what, I ask you? An iron bolt, an old . . . old chunk of hardware. What could I do but leave her? Her presence, her whole being— It dishonors me to ride with her!"

"I don't know about dishonors," thought Blackie, "but I know you can't trust that girl. She's fierce as a hawk and clever as a fox. I'd watch out if I were the Prince. One way or another, she's going to come after that Nail!"

Prince George was shivering. "You heard her curse me worse than any witch! Thank Heaven, we're headed to the Shrine! The blessed waters of the Fountain remove curses."

Without Lizetta's help, Blackie felt the burden of the Prince on himself. Now, it was up to him to care for the man, to protect him, to find food for him.

"He hasn't eaten all afternoon. That's what makes him so jumpy."

The air smelled of seed pods and dust and falling leaves. A squirrel dashed into the road with an acorn in its mouth. It stared up at them and darted into the brush. Prince George stiffened.

"A squirrel! Give me a warning of such creatures, Blackie! I could spear that fellow for dinner."

Blackie saw nothing for a human to eat until they reached the next village. This place was empty—gate knocked in, doors hanging open, laundry hanging stiff on the lines. Even the mud in the street was dried hard.

The Prince tightened his legs on Blackie. He gripped the spear as Blackie stepped down the street.

"What happened here?" he whispered. "Is it the plague?"

Three dogs squeezed through a fence, thin dogs with hungry eyes.

"Dogs alive," muttered the Prince. "It's not plague, then. Rats survive plague, not dogs."

Waving off the dogs, he dropped to the street. He pushed back a door with the spear and looked into a hut. Blackie stepped around the side of the hut to sniff through a shattered garden to the rear. The dogs trailed Blackie, nosing wherever he looked for food. They eased close when Blackie kicked the brown outer leaves from a cabbage and ate the green inner core. They began scratching at the next cabbage in the patch.

Prince George came out of the hut with a musty gray blanket.

"No food there. The place has been looted, stuff thrown around. Only thing I found was this blanket, good for cold nights in high country."

He shook out the dust, tossed the blanket on a fence post to air, and went on to the next hut.

Blackie poked among empty chicken houses and pig pens. A brown hen watched from a housetop as the dogs sniffed avidly after him. Blackie heard chirping and fluttering behind a fence. He saw no gate or door, so he backed around and kicked.

BANG!

Boards went flying. Blackie pushed through the fence to find a yellowing tree in a corner of the lot. A cluster of small birds darted around to peck at spotty red apples on the ground below.

Blackie ran to the tree. The birds fluttered up in a bunch to settle in a row on the nearby rooftop. They cheeped at him with bobbing heads as he sniffed deeply, brushing wasps away with his tail. Eyes winking, tails wagging, the dogs sniffed the apples, too. They watched Blackie gobble apples from the lower branches, then began chewing half-rotten apples under the tree.

"Hey, Blackie, where are you?"

The Prince was yelling out in the street. Blackie trumpeted back, "Over here!"

Prince George popped his head over the fence. "Apples, good! I didn't find food in the houses, just a half-pot of honey someone left in the rafters. I almost got a hen, but I need practice with this spear."

They ate together in the sunlight, dogs chomping, birds chirping, wasps whining about. Prince George sat against the fence, cutting the apples into slices to dip into the honey pot. He fed the slices to Blackie, who closed his eyes to suck in the sweetness. Now, this was eating!

When the Prince took too long sucking his own slices, Blackie poked him with his spike. The dogs crept close, whining for their share.

The dogs stayed behind at the village gate when Blackie trotted on. Prince George held a blanketful of apples before him. Having nothing to slow them, no chain, no Gypsies, they reached the eastern crossroads by sunset.

Prince George stood in the middle of the roads, his long shadow before him. He pointed down the route heading south to Herne.

"A week's travel to the sea, Blackie. We could make in four days. You'd like it down there, warm and windy with the sea splashing up to palm trees and swooshing off the sandy shore. The sea, well, it's too big to describe, hundreds of miles of water with the surf and sails, the fish and mermaids."

The Prince had a faraway look on his face. "And the smells—the rich, salty sea and those white bushes, the jaz, jaz—whatever they are. They smell almost as good as Purple Honesty. You'll have to smell them for yourself someday."

Blackie thought of his Princess. "She promised to show me the sea."

Prince George spoke as though he could read Blackie's thoughts.

"I know the Princess promised to show you the sea, but you'd better leave that to me. She doesn't know anything about it. She never sailed out under the stars as I did. Jessica's story of the Princess sinking a heathen ship, well, nobody believes that."

Looming over the crossroads in the last rays of the sun, the dark castle of Mandor appeared lifeless but for vultures flapping up from the tower. A noose swung from the gibbet by the road.

"Vile had his claws in Mandor a long time ago," whispered the Prince. "It was bad when Godfrey and I rode by, but it feels worse now. The quicker we get beyond the Haunted Hostel, the happier I'll be."

Leaving Mandor behind, Blackie trotted into the twilight with Prince George dozing on his back. Blackie peered through the dusk to see the forest fall away and the road narrow to a single track with fields of thorn bushes to each side.

They stopped for the evening at a stagnant pond. Splintered tree trunks stuck up from the scum. Blackie sniffed for leaves he could stomach. Prince George lounged on the blanket, eating apples and talking about his sea voyage.

"Oh, I was sick on that boat! It was horrible—nothing but a pitching tub stinking of mildew and vomit. Those seamen squeezed sixty people into a space little bigger than this blanket. And the food? Those dogs wouldn't have touched it! We did have a battle, though. The Northmen came chasing after us in their dragon boats. We fought them with bows, sank three of their ships. That was enough for them. They paddled away smartly enough. It's all in my Song. I'll sing it to you, someday."

The Prince fell silent when night got loud. Half asleep, Blackie heard a howl in the darkness over the frogs and crickets. Prince George shifted restlessly in his blanket, hugging his spear. Blackie felt grateful for the spike on his forehead.

By now, he was used to wearing that fronton. It no longer felt clumsy on his head. In fact, he forgot he was wearing it except when he grew uneasy at noises in the night. Then he remembered the skirmish back at Cranch and felt big and bold.

Morning came, foggy, chill. Swathed in his blanket, Prince George shared apples with Blackie. He pulled the blanket over his shoulders and they trotted on. The road was straight and empty. They made good time, reaching the Haunted Hostel about noon.

Prince George jumped down to lean on his spear before the ashes of the burned Hostel, wiping his nose on his sleeve. Blackie's hide prickled. He gazed at the blackened hole in the brush. The air smelled foul with a touch of dragon stink.

"Even the chimney's gone now," observed the Prince. "The place was an inn, easy to get into, but the Devil to escape. The stairway went down to Hell over there."

He pointed. "After the fight, Godfrey nailed the doorway shut."

Blackie was relieved when the Prince mounted again. They trotted briskly until the air cleared. Prince George patted his shoulder.

"We'll get supplies at the monastery, Blackie, a half-day farther on. I don't remember any castles until Furland in the mountains. That's off the road to the north, another day's journey."

They met only one party of riders with a wagon. These pulled off the road and yelled at them to keep away.

The Prince shouted back, "We come in peace!"

An arrow thumped in the ground beside them, so Blackie decided to run on. Trotting steadily, they reached the monastery at dusk. They had no luck there. Though Prince George knocked at the gate with his spear butt, the monks refused to open their gate to late riders. A man looked over the top and ducked down again.

"Let me in!" shouted the Prince. "I demand entrance on service to the Crown! I am George, Prince of Dacia, under orders from Princess Julianna! I've been here before. Ask the Prior, he knows me. I'm a friend to Lady Amalia, Lady Amalia of Furland. Ask anyone about me!"

Even Lady Amalia's name didn't help. The gate remained locked, though someone threw a small loaf of bread over the top. To get away from the wind, they finally walked around to the south. Prince George stretched his blanket along the wall. He gnawed bread while Blackie ate the grass growing in patches beside the palings. They heard singing inside until the moon went behind the clouds. After that, all they heard was the cold wind whistling above the wall.

The monks who opened the gate, next morning, were full of apologies. "Sorry, my lord. We thought it was you, but we weren't sure."

"But I identified myself!" croaked Prince George, leading Blackie through a crowd of people to a big fire in the monastery courtyard. "I told the gatekeeper who I was. I'm not a wandering peddler or player! I'm royalty! I ride the unicorn on affairs of state!"

"Oh, the unicorn!" The monk looked at Blackie for the first time. "You're right, my lord, he is a unicorn. I didn't notice, the color, you know, and— Where's his horn?"

"That doesn't matter!" snapped the Prince. "Why did you refuse to receive me properly?"

Blackie edged up to the fire beside the Prince. He looked at the humans squeezed about him in the courtyard—mostly women in rags and children sleeping on bundles and baskets. A few old men glared when he pushed them away from the fire.

"Who are these people?" demanded the Prince.

The monk shrugged his shoulders. "Refugees, my lord, homeless folks fleeing raiders. They come from everywhere. That's why we couldn't open for you, last night. We can't chance strangers in the dark. We've had all sorts try to break in."

"You could have seen that we weren't Hellions," muttered Prince George, turning his other side to the fire.

"Of course, my lord," said the monk, patting Blackie. "But the whole country's in flames, you know. When Prince Vile called out his vassals to claim the Princess, our guards, a platoon of Saint Michael's Knights, rode off to defend the City. The loyal barons across the land have gathered their troops. They hold out in their castles, but the poor and wretched are caught in the middle. Where can they go?"

"So that's who you've got here," commented the Prince, glancing at the people around him.

"Oh, yes," said the Monk, "we take in as many as we can, feed them soup and bread, but we lack means to nurse all the sick and injured. Does your unicorn have the healing power?"

He looked hopefully at Blackie. Prince George shook his head.

"Not this unicorn, I'm afraid. Since he lost his horn, he's like any other creature."

"That's bad, bad." The monk took a breath. "We help as many as we can, but things seem to get worse every day. The dragon flames across the sky while raiders infest the countryside. Many fear that the end of the world is at hand. We pray for the return of the white unicorn to save us."

"If I could talk to them," thought Blackie, brushing off a spark from the fire, "I'd tell them not to count on the white unicorn. If Papa hears of this turmoil, he'll cling to the forest even harder."

"Well, brother Monk, when do you serve the soup?" asked Prince George, eagerly. "All I've had to eat for a day and a half was that bread."

"Come with me to the refectory, my lord. We can't have a fighting man like you getting weak from hunger. We live in charity with mankind, you know, but Prior fears the raiders. Each week brings news of another abbey or monastery overrun by bandits. Do you think you could stay around to protect us through the winter?"

"No, no, I can't stay," said Prince George, hastily. "I'm on a quest to the Shrine."

Blackie followed through an herb garden cleared neatly away to a lattice running up the walls. They stopped at a door into a stone building.

"You'll find more refugees up at the Shrine," said the monk, pulling open the door. "People have been passing for weeks since the troubles started."

He allowed the Prince to enter the building, but held Blackie from following. "You have to stop here, unicorn. No beasts allowed inside. The Prior forbids it."

"But he's a holy unicorn," protested Prince George.

"I'm sorry, my lord," said the monk. "Not even Balaam's ass could get in this door, and he could talk."

The Prince slapped Blackie on the shoulder. "Well, Blackie, you can go to the stables. I know you don't mind staying with horses."

Brother Monk coughed. "Sorry, my lord. There's no horses in the stables. When we ran out of room for the sick in the infirmary, we moved the overflow to the stables."

"Oh," said Prince George, "well, where'd you put the horses then?"

The monk turned his head from Blackie. He whispered in the Prince's ear. Prince George looked startled.

"You ate them?"

Blackie was horrified. He stepped back, bumping into another monk.

"Not all the horses," explained Brother Monk. "We kept the strong young ones, but with all these people—You see, we're running out of supplies. We have to feed them something!"

Blackie turned away in disgust. "These monks, they're supposed to be holy men! How can they eat horses? I hope the Prince doesn't touch that soup."

Blackie walked back through the garden to the crowded courtyard.

"Hey, watch that thing!" cried a large woman, pulling back from the spike. Blackie stepped back. He halted in surprise.

A chubby human in this crowd of broomsticks? What's she been eating? What's keeping her fat?

He pushed toward her, turning his head to sniff the bag in her arms.

"Stay back!" she cried, trying to pull away from him. "Leave me alone!"

Blackie smelled cakes. He couldn't mistake that smell, even with all these humans around. Blackie jabbed his blade into the bottom of the bag. The woman jerked away, but the blade tore through the cloth. Honeycakes spilled out.

Blackie caught up a cake in his mouth as the woman squealed, "Stop it! That's mine!"

Blackie chomped the cake. It was dry, but tasty.

"Food," someone cried, "she's got food!"

"Who got food?" demanded someone else. Soon, the whole crowd was yelling.

"Food over here!"

"She's hiding cakes!"

"Grab 'em, pass 'em out! Share, share!"

People dove for the cakes as the fat woman wept, "That's all I have in the world! All I have left! They're mine! They're mine!"

A man patted Blackie on the back. "Good beast, good beast! Sniff around. See who else is hiding food."

Blackie felt embarrassed with everyone petting him, calling to him, "Find the food, holy unicorn. Find who's holding out on us!"

Sure enough, when he sniffed carefully, he found beans in bundles and sausages in shawls.

"Oh," said a woman when he uncovered a turnip in her stocking, "I forgot it was there."

By now, the people had turned it into a game, crowding after Blackie, singing.

> Sniff it out, hunt it down,
> rubba-dubba-dub!
> Leave it to the unicorn
> to dig out all the grub!

Seeing Blackie sniffing their way, people who had hidden food brought it out before he caught them hoarding.

"Oh, it's only an old bit o' cheese I kept back just in case."

The food was collected on tables carried out from the refectory. By this time, the novices were bringing soup and bread from the kitchen. With Blackie's discoveries, the table was building up to enough food for a real dinner. Blackie sniffed around it, licking his lips. The people rubbed their hands together, muttering, "Oh, my! Oh, my!"

The Prior even gave permission for the monks to join some of the feast.

"It's Blessed Virgin's Day," he said. "It's proper for everyone to celebrate Our Lady's Day. With all these people to feed, we monks have shortened our own rations. It's a strain keeping up prayers while tending a flock of this size, but this spirit of sharing will inspire all of us."

"I'll share!" thought Blackie, sniffing the cheese. Then his conscience struck him.

All these muffins and cookies and cheese and grapes! Oh, the smell of the grapes from the vineyard, wonderful! But Blackie wasn't starving. He had grass and leaves to eat. Shouldn't he leave this food to the hungry humans?

Once again, he reminded himself that humans couldn't browse like other creatures. They'd starve in the finest clover patch, but there was plenty for him to graze on in the fields across the walls.

Most of the humans were focused on the hot bread being carried out on trays. Only a few children saw Blackie turn away from the crowd, carefully holding his blade up not to scratch anyone.

The gate was guarded by a monk and several novices muttering prayers on their stools. Blackie poked the monk with his nose. The man looked up, reaching for his staff.

"What, unicorn, you want to go outside? You sure of that? It's perilous out there, bless you. There's villainy everywhere."

Blackie nodded his blade, so the novices shoved up the bar. The monk dragged the gate open.

"Knock thrice when you want back in, holy beast, and we'll open up for you."

The gate slammed behind Blackie. He stood a moment, listening to the monks singing Grace over the dinner inside. Walking along the wall, he sniffed the air.

Far beyond the thorny wilderness, the air was scented with seed and harvest and the settling of earth after the long summer. Blackie turned from the path and walked along the hedges, sniffing for food. He heard small animals scurry away as he neared, birds flutter up from the fields.

Blackie walked through an open gate into a hayfield cut down to stubble. He found plenty of hay tufts tucked under the hedge. He whisked his tail and chomped at the hay as the darkness deepened and the ghost of a moon rose in the east. A "V" of flying geese honked over his head in a ring of clouds.

Blackie ate his way along the hedge as the night rolled on. When he got thirsty, he knocked at the monastery door for a drink at the well, returning to the hayfield where he found a family of deer browsing along the hedge.

The stag was too nervous to exchange more than a word or two before trotting off with the others trailing after. Blackie listened to the singing from the monastery and the scratchy call of crickets in the hedge.

Blackie's mind drifted to Lizetta, how different she was from the Princess. The Princess was royal and righteous. Everyone loved her. He was sure that she'd never sell anyone to Prince Vile.

For a moment, he wondered how Lizetta was doing. He snorted. Why worry about Lizetta? As slippery as she was, he'd better worry for the humans around her.

Blackie stepped to a fresh tuft of hay. Catching a movement out of the corner of his eye, he looked hard. A fox drifted across the field, its head held high.

"Hey, friend!" Blackie called to the fox.

The fox flashed him a glance. It whisked away into the shadows. Blackie sighed and yawned. He shook himself and relaxed until he fell asleep on his hooves.

When he awoke, he was thirsty again. He trotted along the hedge to the gate. Nearing the wall, he paused in the wind, which brought the smell of smoke and humans. He turned away, not wanting to face that crowd again. He felt calm and peaceful out here, so he moved around the corner out of the breeze. He yawned and swished his tail. His eyelids drooped.

The wind was cold when he woke again. Dots of stars spread across the sky to fade into the brightness of the moon. All was silent until a dog barked across the wall. Blackie stepped slowly about the monastery, pulling up clumps of dewy grass here and there.

An owl flew softly through the moonlight. Blackie shivered. Yawning, he turned the corner toward the gate. He stopped to sniff at a mint plant, the strong smell reminding him of the Wise Woman's garden, then a stink struck him, the smell of dirty men and dried blood.

His ears perked up. Ahead of him, moving toward the monastery, he heard a low stumbling and grumbling and the clank of metal against metal. Blackie crept down the shadow of the wall, watching a column of men crunch through the brush from the road. Moonlight glinted off hooked spear points. From this distance, Blackie smelled beer and sweat and old leather.

The men slowed as they neared the wall, clustering to left and to right. Breathing heavily and whispering together, they swung up their swords and axes and spears.

Blackie stepped closer, placing each hoof softly. He heard a hoarse command.

"Ladders forward, and keep it down! I don't wanta hear a squawk out of any bullyboy 'till we're cuttin' throats inside. And remember, use the nets on the unicorn. That one goes to the dragon!"

"I don't think so," thought Blackie, grimly drawing a deep breath. He heard the click of ladder legs on the wall. The first figures climbed in the moonlight.

Blackie charged at the shout, "Up and over! Blood and fire! Skive and skewer!"

Shouting and clashing weapons as they pushed forward to the ladders, the raiders didn't see the dark threat until Blackie was into them, crushing the mass of men along the wall with his charge. Blackie lost awareness in the violence. Caught up by instinct, he smashed down ladders and tore into flesh. Bodies broke as Blackie stomped back and forth. He stabbed with his spike and threw down raiders until those who could move were screaming in fear. Drunk with fury, Blackie heard only shrieks and howls as the raiders fought each other to escape.

The struggle ended in moments. Blackie came back to himself with a whimper. He was lying in a pile of dead, a screaming man pinned to his blade. Shaking with horror, Blackie jerked the spike from his victim and crawled over the wounded to vomit his guts out against the wall.

That was when Prince George came running from the monastery gate, spear in hand, leading men with clubs and torches. Stepping through the carnage, they murmured in awe at bodies thrown in heaps, the wounded crawling away.

"Look at 'em," cried someone, "twenty, thirty kilt, besides all them wounded!"

"Where's Blackie?" cried Prince George, dashing around with his spear.

They had to search through the dark to find Blackie. Prince George ran over when a torchbearer called out. Dropping the spear, the Prince fell to his knees to lift Blackie's head.

"All this blood, this blood," moaned the Prince. "He's wounded!"

"No, no." A monk examined Blackie by torchlight. "He's not injured at all. That blood, it isn't his."

The men standing around sucked in their breaths.

"Oh, the unicorn's back, for sure," declared a monk. "The dragon had better look to his wings."

"Oh, yes, Blackie, yes," murmured Prince George, holding Blackie's head to his chest, "your legend starts tonight."

While the men collected the raiders' weapons, the monks sorted out the wounded. Prince George and the novices helped Blackie to his hooves, gasping and trembling. They walked with him through the gate and over to the fire. The awed humans moved away to make room for him.

"Bring water," ordered Prince George, "warm water. I'm going to clean him myself, this blood, these . . . these bits."

Humans brought buckets of water and Prince George scrubbed Blackie with soft cloths. Everyone watched Blackie standing head down, his mind filled with the screams of the wounded.

Prince George removed the fronton to clean it inside and out, the blade, the straps, the buckles. Blackie tossed his head. He hated the thing now that he knew what it could do. Sure, he'd grown used to it, but the bulk of it, the weight, the metal! How could he go home to Mama with that thing on his head? How could he forget that choking man stuck to his forehead? He'd never be free of the horror.

The humans didn't understand. They kept praising him.

"There'll be fifty or sixty when they die," said someone. "What a hero! He saved us all."

A boy gazed at Blackie with shining eyes. "I bet he killed a hunderd!"

"We must pray for their souls now," said the Prior, walking over with a sloshing pail of wine. "Who knows what makes the poor things desperate enough to attack a monastery. They need all the prayers we can send. Even villains are created in God's image. Only the Unicorn, the holy beast, stands pure and unstained."

"If I could tell him the truth," thought Blackie, ruefully. "I'm as foul as the worst of them."

Prince George held the pail for Blackie to drink. The wine tasted sour, but it revived him.

"Now, my people," ordered the Prior, "we must organize to care for the wounded out there."

An old man spat in the fire. "Treat 'em like snakes. Knock 'em in the head and forget 'em."

"That's the way they'd treat us," sighed the Prior. "Surely, we can do better than that."

Blackie closed his eyes. His body was bruised and sore. He wanted to creep away to lick his wounds by himself. The wounded wailed beyond the wall as the nearby humans praised him over and over.

"Well, Blackie, we're not going to travel tomorrow," declared the Prince. "You'll be limp as a rag after your battle."

Closing his eyes, Blackie heard someone ask the Prince, "My lord, we collected all them axes and swords. Do you wanta pick out anything for yourself?"

"Bring me a good dagger and a shield if you've got one," said the Prince, offhand. "I've got a sword from a fight earlier today and my spear. With my luck, I'll lose the sword tomorrow, but I'm clinging to this spear no matter what. The head is made from the Holy Nail."

"So my lord," commented the Prior, "you've been around Gypsies. Every Gypsy coming along tries to sell me a Holy Nail. They must hammer them out by the hundreds."

"Oh, yes," sighed the Prince, "I've been with Gypsies. Come on, Blackie. Let's find a quiet place to sleep. I'll cover us both with my blanket."

CHAPTER TWENTY-TWO

Pilgrim's Rest

Blackie woke in darkness to the sound of singing monks. He ached to give up this quest and go home. His body was sore to the bone, his spirit just as weary. One thought ran through his head.

"I need a break from these humans. Papa, Papa, what are you eating this season? How I long to follow you around the forest! Mama, I want to empty my heart to you. I've so much to tell you."

His mind on the Nest, he limped between the rows of coughing humans to the center of the courtyard where the fire had burnt low. He found a shivering Prince George feeding it with dry leaves and sticks. A novice beside him held logs in his arms.

Another novice ran up with more logs. He dumped them on the ground. "Hurry, Anthony, we're missing prayers."

The boys ran off while Prince George arranged the logs on the fire. Blackie poked him with his nose. Prince George looked up.

"Good morning to you, Blackie." He leaned forward to warm his hands in the flames.

Blackie was ready to travel on. He nipped the Prince's jacket to pull him toward the gate. The Prince pushed him away.

"Hold on, Blackie. I want to see what he's done to my shield."

Last night, Prince George had outfitted himself with a new shield, breastplate, and dagger from the pile of arms gathered from the raiders. When he objected to the gaping boar's jaw on the shield, a monk had volunteered to scrape it down and repaint it for him.

"Make it a lion, rampant," the Prince told him, "my family crest."

286

Now, he held up the shield to the curling flames. "What's this?"

Instead of the lion he'd requested, the monk had painted the shield white with a stark cross in the middle, bright red.

"Where's my lion?"

"I had a vision, my lord," explained Brother Axius, nodding solemnly. "Everyone says that you carry the Holy Nail of the Gypsies. The Nail and the Cross, they fit together, don't they? That makes you sort of a holy warrior!"

"But the lion," protested the Prince, shaking the shield, "my crest! I'm famous for the beast. I killed lions in the desert. I've worn lionskins all my life!"

"Of course, my lord, but look," Brother Axius pointed at the design, "red on white—clean, isn't it? Attractive! And the Cross, our Christian emblem, how could you object to the blessed Cross?"

"But my lion!" wailed the Prince. "Why didn't you do what I wanted? I'm complaining to the Prior about this."

"Well, I think it's perfect," grumbled the monk, turning away. "You'll excuse me, my lord! I'm late for prayers."

As the monk scuttled off toward the chapel, Prince George threw down the shield with a clang.

"You see how it is, Blackie! Nothing goes right for me! Even my shield— I can't get them to paint it as I want! Why is everything so difficult? We've almost made it to the Shrine, and I'm still running into obstacles!"

Blackie nudged him with his nose, trying to urge him toward the gate, but Prince George turned his hands to the fire.

"Don't push, Blackie! I've got to get someone to repaint this shield the way I want it."

Exasperated, Blackie grabbed the shield by the arm-strap on the back. He dragged it toward the gate while a crowd of little boys scooted out of his way.

"Hey, where you going?" cried Prince George. "It's too early to leave! I haven't had breakfast, and my shield—"

"What's wrong with the shield, me lord?" asked a woman, sitting on a wheelbarrow stuffed with clothes, a baby on her lap.

"Everything's wrong!" burst out the Prince. "For one, the Nail was never driven into the Cross, that's what makes it holy! And for another— Oh, I don't know. I don't want to talk about it!"

Blackie dropped the shield at the big gate and looked back. Prince George was still complaining to the people as the fire leaped high, smoke blowing off to the side.

"I'm not going to wait around here," thought Blackie, nudging one of the sleeping guards with his spike. "I'll head east toward the sun. He can catch up when he feels like it."

"So, unicorn," yawned the monk, standing up from his stool and stretching, "you going scouting this morning? If you see more of those bandits, give them a kick for me."

The other monk looked up, blinking, while the first one shoved back the bar on the door with one hand.

"She moves easy this weather," he explained. "Shrinks up with the cold."

"Hold on, Blackie!" called Prince George, pulling his blanket over his shoulders. The Prince snatched his spear from a boy.

"I'm coming, I'm coming! Why are you in such a rush, this morning? I haven't even had breakfast!"

"It's that unicorn spirit!" cried an old man. "He tasted blood last night. Can't wait to hunt down more o' them villains."

Prince George hurried to Blackie as a bustle stirred the crowd—dark figures pushing through behind torches.

"The Prior," called someone, "Father Prior to say farewell."

The Prior hurried up with a handful of monks, his face red by torchlight.

"My lord, I'm told that you leave immediately."

"Apparently so," grumbled Prince George. "The unicorn's eager to travel this morning."

"Bless his heart." The Prior gestured to one of the novices following him. "We've prepared supplies for you, enough to get you to the Shrine, my lord. Will you please deliver this letter to the Knight Commander there? After the raid, last night, I'm asking him to send a squad of his troopers to protect us."

Standing in the gate, Blackie shook himself. He ached from his moonlight battle. He felt stale and cranky this morning, in no mood to hang around yammering humans. He poked Prince George with his nose. The Prince laughed, embarrassed.

"I see that the unicorn's eager to travel," said the Prior, stepping back. "Our prayers go with you."

Blackie flinched as the monks ran a light harness about his shoulders to hold the blanket, the breastplate and helmet, and the bags of supplies. Then a monk handed the spear and shield to the Prince. The Prior nodded approvingly at the Cross on the shield. He blessed the two of them with a short prayer while the crowd pressed around, stroking Blackie's neck and sides.

At last, the monks helped Prince George mount, and Blackie was allowed to limp out into the cold morning breeze. Shouts of farewell followed down the road. Blackie jogged along, ignoring the pangs in his head and the pains in his shoulders and sides. He blinked at a layer of frost sparkling on the brush beside the road.

Prince George rubbed his ears.

"Three more days, I figure three more days, and we'll be rid of this necklace. If I had any idea the quest would take so long, I'd have refused the Princess, no matter what she said. It's a miracle you weren't killed last night. I swear, if I'd lost you, I'd have given up and turned back to the City. After all, the Princess gave the quest to the pair of us."

Shivering in the breeze, Blackie barely heard the Prince. He trotted stiffly up the dark road, gazing at the low streak of red across the eastern sky. Sore as he felt at first, his legs loosened up after the first couple of miles. He limped steadily, watching the sun rise in layers of pinkish-gray clouds. In a short time, he began moving into foothills where brown and gold trees merged with green pines. The road roughened and narrowed with rises washed down to rock and dips where trickling streams chilled his hooves.

They rested on a sunny bank where squirrels whisked through the evergreens to gather pinecones. Blackie grazed on tasteless yellow leaves from bushes under the pines while Prince George chewed dried meat and bread.

"I think, I'll walk awhile this morning, Blackie. I can see that you're sore from tackling those bandits, last night. I have to say that you were terrific. Wait'll I tell Sir Otley! Everyone's heard of unicorns, of course, but the power, the ferocity! You have to see it to believe it."

Blackie twitched his ears. He kicked leaves away to uncover a few tasty stems as the Prince rambled on.

"This countryside was buried in snow when I traveled through with Godfrey, but I calculate that we're nearing the cutoff to Furland. I'd love to visit Lady Amalia again—the Empress's sister, you know—but we can't lose time getting to the Shrine. The Prior told me that Vile's uprising is turning into a general war. The barons are choosing up sides. Many are joining Prince Vile."

After an hour's rest, they traveled on. Leading the Prince around a long curve in the road, Blackie's ears heard a faint ringing. He alerted Prince George, who climbed onto Blackie and pulled up his shield with the spear ready. They backed into the dark pine boughs as the noise grew into clanging bells along with yelps and a "snap, snap, snap!"

"I wonder what this is," whispered the Prince. "It doesn't sound like a bear hunt."

Peeking from behind pines, Blackie saw men in robes stumble along the road ringing bells. Others carried crosses and banners. Behind them staggered a long line of humans, many stripped to the waist. To Blackie's astonishment, they paused every few feet crying madly while smacking each other with sticks or lashing out with leathers.

"Weep for your sins!" bellowed a tall friar on a donkey. "The end is coming! The end is coming!"

Blackie watched with horror as the parade passed by in an ecstasy of misery.

"Come on," whispered Prince George as the wailing faded away.

Confused, Blackie returned to the road, looking back at the humans, his ears high.

"Don't worry about them," said the Prince, patting Blackie's neck. "That's just penitents. You see penitents during any disaster. They think that scourging themselves will appease God's anger. Personally, I think it'd be better to beat on Prince Vile. This shows how widespread this war is getting. We'd better finish our quest and get back to the City as soon as possible."

Blackie trotted until late morning when he took a nap while Prince George said his prayers. Blackie felt more like himself after waking and sharing a loaf of bread with the Prince. He was starting to look forward to the Shrine. Papa had told him of the wonders up there, especially the food they served.

"Everything tastes good at the Shrine," Papa had told him. "It's the water, you know. I admit that the Fountain's morbid with all those horns, but the dinners make up for everything."

Gesturing with a piece of bread, Prince George drew Blackie's attention from his thoughts.

"Each spring, as long as I've known her, the Empress has talked about taking a pilgrimage to the Shrine. Something always seems to get in the way, though, wars, rebellions, trials, sickness. For some reason, the Court can never get free for the journey. I guess that somehow our quest takes their place. That's why the Princess thought it was so important."

Important or not, travel became difficult as the climb sharpened. Prince George had to slide to earth again so Blackie could struggle on without his weight. Leaning on his spear, Prince George toiled after the unicorn. They finally halted where the pine forest thinned away to rocky glens with tangled briers among leafless thorn trees. Small birds flitted back and forth through the brush. Weary from last night's battle, Blackie refused to move on until Prince George took the arms and supplies and carried them by himself.

The sun was bright. The wind blew cold. They trudged by a flock of sheep on a hillside. A black dog ran toward them, barking hoarsely. The dog had its tail high. Its eyes gleamed as it barked. Blackie looked at the lambs, fuzzy little things with bobbing tails. They ran back and forth and peered around their mothers. A lamb, Blackie remembered, that was what Papa had given to the wolves.

"If I weren't . . . a knight," panted the Prince, "I think . . . I'd like to be . . . a shepherd. Those fellows stay with their sheep all summer on the mountain. The dogs watch the flock while the shepherds sleep in the shade. At night, they sit around their fires, eating cheese and singing."

"Cheese," thought Blackie. "I wouldn't mind a chunk of cheese. Oh, how Papa loves cheese!"

Looking to both sides as he climbed before the Prince, Blackie saw jagged rock formations rising above twisted trees and thorn bushes. Hawks circled high on the wind. When they stopped between rocks for the night, the Prince built a small fire of crackling thorns while Blackie picked at the dry, chewy grass.

Blackie found his legs numb to the pain, next morning, so he let the Prince ride while he climbed up and up. He learned that he could keep going if he kept to a slow, steady pace in this tilted landscape. Persistence was the key to travel in the mountains, not speed.

In late afternoon, they passed a small castle with a few huts huddled inside a thorn fence. Dogs barked at them, but no humans came into view.

Blackie was exhausted. His back hurt, his ankles ached, his feet felt bruised. His mouth tasted like dust. The Prince slid off again. He limped behind in silence. They rested often, but pushed higher and higher up the road, now a narrow, rocky lane.

"Oh, to be a goat," thought Blackie, as the road curved and twisted, eventually climbing a shadowy crevice with walls towering ten times higher than the tallest trees of the forest. Painfully, he lifted one leg after another, pushing higher and higher as his chest pounded. Prince George limped behind, leaning on his spear shaft, panting too hard to complain.

At last, the mountains spread open to let sunlight pour down on a pool beside the road. Staggering close, Blackie saw the flashing stream that fed the pool in the shadow of a stone outcropping. Lacy white flowers swayed in the sunshine. Blue butterflies flitted about.

"Just in time," gasped the Prince. "I wondered when we'd find water in these mountains."

Blackie waded up to his knees in the pool. He lowered his nose and drank deeply. Instantly, he revived. The weight slid from his shoulders as the fatigue lifted. His feet stopped aching. He looked around, seeing everything sharp and bright. He watched scaly little fish dart back and forth in the pool.

Blackie whisked his tail. He nickered for joy as Prince George collapsed beside the pool. The Prince closed his eyes. He lowered his head into the water before pushing up with a yell, "Ho, that's fantastic!"

He plunged in for another long drink, then jumped up to hug Blackie.

"You know where we are, Blackie? Saint Raphael's Pool! I'd forgotten about it! You've heard of the Pool, of course. It carries a trace of the Fountain waters to revive pilgrims for the climb to the Shrine."

Restored by the Pool, Prince George hungrily attacked the last of his supplies while Blackie grazed on the flowers beside the water. Looking up at shouts down the road, they saw a small party of pilgrims drag themselves over the rocks, two women on mules and a handful of men leaning on spears. The pilgrims stopped, gripping their spears suspiciously until the Prince threw open his arms.

"Welcome, friends! Lord bless you in your travel!"

"Thank Heaven!" cried one of the men. "A Christian greeting!"

Blackie backed away to watch the humans stagger the last weary steps to the Pool. The men tore off cloaks and jackets to throw themselves into the Pool with outspread arms.

Prince George stepped forward to help an old woman down from her mule. She dumped a crying baby in his arms.

"Hold her a moment, sir, if you please," said the woman, sliding carefully to earth. The Prince held the baby like an awkward bundle while the woman knelt to scoop up water in a wooden cup. He looked ruefully at Blackie, who turned to ask the mules where they came from.

"Us?" said the closest mule, sniffing the flowers. "We come from the green land beside the big river. It's fair down there, wide and grassy, nothing like these horrible rocks. Bad humans rode up on horses. They burned everything, so we left to come up here."

"We had thirty in our party when we left," one of the men explained to the Prince while sipping a cup of Pool water. "Hellhounds jumped us one night and chased off the horses. After that, the other folks stopped at Castle Byre. They felt safe with the good Count, but our ladies insisted that we continue all the way to the Shrine. We know that the Shrine stands holy and secure no matter what happens in the world below."

"Did you see the dragon?" asked Prince George. "It chased us down the road at Shrems."

The man crossed himself. "No, nothing so bad as that, thank the Lord, but what we saw was plenty grim—the armies of Prince Vile marching out to attack the City."

"Attack the City!" exclaimed the Prince.

"Oh, yes," said the man. "Prince Vile plans to strike at the heart of the Empire. We watched from the towers of Byre as a dozen barons rode by, heading south. Must have been a thousand horse and foot passing the road that morning."

"A thousand men!" repeated the Prince. Blackie looked up from the flowers to listen.

"Yes," the man nodded, "at least, a thousand, my lord, one company after another. They kept passing all morning. The barons sent a herald to order Count Byre to join them, but the Count refused them flat like a loyal peer of the Empire, and the barons left him alone. Vile had them in a hurry, I guess. They didn't have time to attack the castle, but the herald cursed him right there in the road, a smoking curse that made a man shudder to hear it."

"Oh, bless the Count," said the Prince, shaking his spear. "I love to hear of a stout lord standing true like that. I pray that all good men will stick to their allegiance."

The man bent for another cup of water from the Pool. "Well," he said, standing up, "I wouldn't give two coppers for the castle once those villains return from the City. An army that size could walk right over it."

Prince George turned to Blackie. "Come on, boy. Let's hurry with our quest, so we can get back to the City. The Princess needs us for sure!"

"Oh, I'd stay up here where you're safe, my lord," advised the man. "If you saw all those axes and spears, you'd never want to leave the Shrine."

Strong and rested from the Pool water, Blackie easily carried the Prince up the rocky road. The sun was warm on his black coat. He leaped lightly when rocks rolled under his hooves.

Shading his eyes, Prince George scanned the heights above them. "Look up there," he cried.

Blackie tried to follow the pointing finger, but couldn't see anything at first, just rock walls rising to other walls. Then he saw them, dirty bugs on the cliffs, staring down at them.

"What's that?" he wondered.

"Goats, mountain goats!" The Prince sounded excited. "You know, they jump around the highest rocks. That must mean we're nearing the Shrine."

"Goats." Blackie stared up at them. Those were the goats that Papa had to wrestle up at Darr. Papa always said he wanted to corner a big ram somewhere that it couldn't jump away.

Prince George and Blackie watched the goats for a minute. They took up the climb again. Up, up, up, Blackie climbed, panting in thin air until the road flattened and edged around a precipice. The sun was sinking in the west with shifting layers of rose, purple, and blue that froze Blackie to the road, staring in awe until Prince George urged him to hurry before it got dark.

"We've got to press on while we can see," panted Prince George. "Footing's treacherous up here. We need to find refuge before the light's gone!"

Glancing over his shoulder, Blackie followed the Prince into the deep shadow behind a wall where the rock fell away to a black drop-off to his side. They climbed slowly here, step by step, squeezing against the cliff away from the chasm.

Blackie set each foot carefully, reaching ahead in the darkness as the icy wind tried to blow him over the side. His nose and ears were frozen, the spike on his head an icicle. He heard the Prince cough over the wail of the wind.

"This must be . . . Frenchman's Fall," gasped the Prince. "A mile down, they say, but Pilgrim's Rest . . . just ahead. I think, I hear the dogs."

At that, Blackie heard the barking over the wind, a deep "Ruff, ruff, ruff!" His hooves struck flat surface. He saw a spark of light through the dusk and followed the ghostly shape of the Prince across a broad shelf where a hut pressed against the side of the mountain, a pale cross cut in the wood of the door.

Big dogs, shaggy and strong, rushed out of the darkness to jump on them, panting, licking their faces. Prince George pushed them off.

"Don't mind these guys," he gasped. "They don't bite. They're just mad that they have to stay outside while we go into the Rest."

The hut door opened. Cheery light poured out, showing a bearded man in a long robe looking out at them.

"A unicorn," he said wonderingly, staring at Blackie. "A blessed unicorn."

"Greetings to you, old Hermit!" cried the Prince, pushing by the man. "You got shelter tonight for a couple of hungry travelers?"

The Prince passed into the hut while Blackie paused outside. He sniffed the dogs, strong and rank. The dogs smelled him back. One stuck a cold nose under Blackie's tail.

Blackie turned to look back over the shelf as the dogs panted about him. He saw only the faint afterglow of sunset fringing the mountains. He listened to the wind, then ran to the hut and shoved inside.

Blackie stood with his tail to the door, sniffing the overwhelming odor of fire and humans. The thin Hermit, brown and barefooted, laughed and scratched Blackie under the chin.

"Praise the Lord, young unicorn! Saints' blessings, you're a beauty! Strong unicorn stock—big ribs, good hooves. You've got your grandpa's shoulders."

The Hermit held out a worn and dirty hand to Blackie. The hand smelled of smoke and wood chips. Blackie sniffed the bony knees and toenails, then turned to the fire, squeezing between benches crowding the floor space.

The Hermit chuckled. "It is a mite cluttered in here, isn't it, boy? No pilgrims, though, lucky for you. Sometimes I have fifteen, twenty people squeezed in here. Here, let me give us some room."

He piled baskets and bags along the wall. He opened the door to heave out a couple benches, clearing a space where Blackie could stand comfortably. The dogs whined outside and cold wind blasted in until Hermit slammed the door again.

With one flank warm, Blackie turned the other side to the fire. He stepped closer, drawn to the bright, dancing fire after the dark winds of the mountain. A spark snapped out. It burned his shoulder. He jumped back.

"Watch out, young unicorn," cried the Hermit. "Don't scorch yourself! Here, my lord, take my stool."

Hermit pulled a stool from the corner beside Blackie. Prince George carefully leaned the spear down the side of the room. He tossed his armor into a corner and sat down with a sigh, stretching his boots to the fire.

Even without the benches, the hut was tight quarters. Once he was warm, Blackie sniffed the wood stacked beside the fireplace. He frowned at an axe leaning against the woodpile.

"Don't like axes, do you, boy?" said Hermit, patting his shoulder. "Don't worry. No one's going to harm a holy unicorn in my house."

Prince George bent forward on his stool before the flames, his elbows resting on his knees as Blackie sniffed around the walls. Blackie stuck his nose into pots on shelves. He smelled cloaks hanging on pegs by the door. He paused at a narrow desk under the window to sniff the stiff pages of a Bible that smelled of generations of human fingers.

"You're hungry of course," said Hermit, watching in delight. "Sorry, my lord, the bread's gone, eaten by a big party of pilgrims headed up this morning. I gave the last crusts to the dogs. I do have apples, though. I'm sure the unicorn won't say no to a few autumn apples."

Hermit lifted a bag from a peg on the wall. He rolled a dozen apples across the floor to Blackie.

Blackie sniffed the apples. These were dry and shrunken, but still held a hint of sweetness. His mouth filled with seeds and juice as he chomped apple after apple.

"Apples again!" complained the Prince, frowning at the wrinkled fruit. "We've been living on apples the last few days. It's pathetic! I don't see how you survive up here, Hermit, eating garbage like this!"

The hermit chewed his apple philosophically.

"Oh, I eat what the Lord sends me. Supplies have been sparse this year with all the troubles below. It's as much as I can do to scrape up a morsel for the pilgrims passing by. Some days, we have to get by with stone soup."

"Well, if you can eat stones," said the Prince, picking the freshest apple he could find, "you'll never go hungry up here."

The Hermit leaned back with his arms behind his head.

"Things'll get better at Michaelmas. Lady Amalia always sends up a few hams. I can get a rousing stew pot going with a bit of ham, some peas and onions. Ah, how that smell fills my cabin!"

"Please don't talk of food you can't give me," begged the Prince. "The worst thing about starving is remembering past dinners."

The Hermit shook his head.

"Why, that's no way to look on it. I thank the Lord that folks somewhere can feast on caviar and pheasant. At least, we have firewood tonight—now, that's a blessing! I'm not sure that I wouldn't rather be warm than fed."

"I hate having to make choices like that," grumbled the Prince. "Why can't I be a little warm and a little fed? I could get by with that."

"In that case, my lord," laughed the Hermit, "eat more apples. Heaven knows, they're small, but they're better than stones. So, Master Unicorn, would you like a rubdown? You're probably sore after that climb."

"He's not the only one," groaned the Prince.

297

Hermit crawled around, spreading smelly rags before the fire for Blackie to lie on.

"Rest here, young unicorn. I'll give you a good rubdown, boy. The Lord washed the feet of his friends, so I can comfort a unicorn."

He brought a towel from a dark corner and knelt over the unicorn. Blackie closed his eyes as the Hermit started rubbing his shoulders.

Blackie's skin itched where the towel scratched. Something bit his side. It bit again. He threw his head around, trying to scratch the bites with his blade. Chewing an apple, Prince George nodded thoughtfully.

"Fleas up here. I should have known."

"Oh, a flea won't hurt you," said Hermit. "Our little brothers, they just want a meal like the rest of us."

"I'm sure they'll feed well before this night's over," said the Prince, flinging his blanket down beside Blackie.

Blackie yawned. Hermit spread an old cloak over him and tossed a couple more logs on the fire. Blackie closed his eyes as Hermit sang in a low voice.

> Sleep in the arms of the Lord, oh sinner,
> sleep in the fleece of the Lamb.
> Sleep for the long, weary day is over.
> Sleep till the glorious dawn.
>
> Sleep till the trumpet signals the morning.
> Sleep till the roll is called.
> Wake then, wake up to live forever,
> forgetting the hunger and cold.
>
> Rise up, dance through the beautiful garden,
> sing through your tears of joy—
> all of your loved ones dancing around you—
> dancing and praising,
> singing and blessing,
> blessing and praising the Lord.

Blackie twitched when a flea bit his flank. He took a long breath. He slept.

CHAPTER TWENTY-THREE

The Fountain

The crackle and pop of the fireplace woke Blackie in the cold gray of early morning. He opened his eyes to see the Hermit on his knees, tossing sticks onto the fire. Blackie stretched, wrinkling his nose at the heavy smell of humans in the air.

"This'll warm us in no time!" called the Hermit, cheerily. "How about breakfast? No fat bacon or cakes on the menu, but we've got apples."

Blackie was ready for apples, but Prince George groaned when he sat up, running his hands through his hair.

"Not apples again—my bowels can't stand it! I was dreaming of thick slices of toast with melted butter and honey."

"Bit colicky, are you?" asked Hermit, passing over a cup. "Here, my lord, bless you, a splash of wine. Just the thing for a bad belly."

Blackie stepped to the water bucket while Prince George slurped at the wine. Hermit filled the cup again. Suddenly, the Prince's belly heaved. He retched. He ran for the door, and Blackie heard him vomiting outside as the dogs barked around him.

"Ooh, Blackie," said the Prince, sticking his head back in. "Let's go. Sooner I get to the Fountain—"

Blackie refused to be hurried. He chewed his apples while Prince George shivered in his blanket by the fire. The Hermit leaned back on his stool, toes stretched to the flames.

"Is this your first visit to the Shrine, my lord? What a treat you have ahead of you! It'll be warm up there, I promise, always lovely, and the feast—Well, who'd think that bread and wine could be so filling! That's where I get my stores. Pilgrims heading down drop off a bag or two of bread, plus a jug of wine. Of course, pilgrims climbing the other way leave off supplies they don't want to haul up the stairs. A few days ago, a group heading up left a couple bags of apples. One way or another, I usually have something for the hungry. I share whatever the Lord provides."

The Prince bit reluctantly into a wrinkled apple.

"Well, Hermit, if you've got Paradise a mile above, why do you live here in the cold? I wouldn't stay ten minutes in this freezing shack if I had a choice like that."

"Why," cried the Hermit with a laugh, "this is where the Lord placed me! You'd be amazed how many pilgrims crawl by, hungry and wasted. They need help to make it up that last leg to the Shrine."

Prince George pulled on a boot. "But Gabriel's Pool," he said with a yawn, "doesn't it refresh them?"

"You'd think it would," said the Hermit, tossing a small log onto the fire, "but some are so blind they don't see the Pool, while others, they just toss it off. You can always reject the offer of Grace. I remember one Gypsy—"

"Don't talk to me of Gypsies!" snapped the Prince, stomping down the foot inside his boot. "I've lived with Gypsies. But you, you must have been a mighty sinner to get stuck on this rocky shelf."

The Hermit chuckled.

"Oh, we're all miserable sinners. Life here does have its rewards. I love to see some crusty old scoundrel jump up from the Fountain, crowing like a rooster! I watch them run down the mountain filled with salvation—old men turning somersaults, women hopping like crickets."

Prince George scrambled to his feet. "You hear him, Blackie? Why hang back for apples? There's a feast for us a mile above, and I'll finally get rid of this necklace."

The Hermit pounded the Prince on the back, laughing.

"That's the spirit, young warrior! You've got a thrill ahead of you, your first taste of the Fountain! And unicorn, you'll see the horns! What a sight that is—the horns of your ancestors in the blessed waters!"

By now, Blackie was eager to see the Shrine. He swallowed the last apple, took a gulp from the water bucket, and squeezed by the Hermit to the door.

"Wait for me!" cried Prince George, grabbing his spear. Pulling a cap on his head, he left the rest of his arms in the corner. The Hermit had promised to watch over them until he returned.

He paused at the door. "You're sure my sword is safe?"

"Don't worry about that, my lord. We never see villains up here. They can't stand the holiness of the Shrine."

Blackie shook himself in the blue-grey of dawn as the dogs leaped about. He looked over the ledge at mountain peaks rising from shadows.

Even with the blanket wrapped about him, Prince George shivered in the wind. "It's freezing out here."

The Hermit bowed. "'Tis the day the Lord has made."

"It's too windy to wait, Blackie!" cried Prince George, pointing to the stairway winding up the mountain. "Let's not hang back!"

Blackie trotted toward the steps as the Hermit called, "Lord bless you, young unicorn, and you too, my lord! I'll pray for you."

"Thanks for everything, old Hermit!" yelled the Prince, following Blackie, his spear shaft clicking on the stones. "I'll bring you a jug of wine."

Blackie heard the Hermit's last words as he rounded the stairway. "You'll see, my lord. One sip of the Fountain, that's all it takes!"

"Hold up, Blackie," called the Prince. "Don't be in such a rush. You've got to save your strength for the climb. This stairway'll be hard going, even for you."

The Prince was right. Blackie quickly discovered that stairways are not designed for unicorns. All his weight fell on his rear knees which began to pain after a hundred steps. Climbing behind, Prince George was silent except for his heavy breathing.

The air grew brighter as Blackie climbed, the steps more clear to sight. He could see chisel marks where the stairway was hacked from the mountain. The initials of pilgrims were scratched into the rock, along with crosses chipped into the stone.

Prince George read messages begging for prayers. "It's like . . ." he panted, "the road to Obb. There, it was . . . advertising jingles. Here, it's prayers. Look at that one."

Eleven set out, but
seven remane.
Pray for the soles
of our brothers slayn.

Writ by Thomas,
son of Thomas
of Gelly

Blackie realized that he was no longer shivering. As sunlight strengthened, the wind grew gentle. Even the rock seemed to soften, his hoof-beats changing tone as the stairway steepened. By now, though, the altitude had grown intimidating. He sensed the height as a physical presence, the mountain leaning to push him toward the drop-off. He pressed his inner side against the rock and fumbled for steps, striving to place each hoof securely.

Over his thumping heart, Blackie heard the Prince climbing behind, panting and moaning, "Almost there . . . almost there . . . almost there . . . almost—!"

As the stairway rounded the rock to the broad ledge of the Shrine, the fear fell away from Blackie. Ahead, he saw the great Hand carved from the tallest crag, its fingers reaching black against bright dawn, the Fountain waters bubbling from the wound in the palm.

Sunstruck after climbing through shadows, Blackie blinked as his eyes adjusted to the light. Prince George dropped his spear to throw an arm over Blackie, his other arm high to shade his eyes.

They limped together toward the Fountain, their ears full of the song of the pilgrims around.

I lift up my eyes to the mountains.
That's where I find my help.
My aid must come
from the Lord reaching down.
He lifts me above myself.

"We're here, Blackie," breathed the Prince. "We're here."

Half-blind, they stepped over the heel of the hand to the shimmering waters of the Fountain that flow down the mountain to the streams below and on through the river to the sea. Blackie bowed his head to the water. He stopped, staring at the sight Papa had described so often during quiet evenings back at the Nest.

Sparkling water swirled through a hundred unicorn horns, blackened and broken, strewn with the offerings of princes and kings. Blackie saw gold piled in coins and caskets, bracelets and chains, loops of pearl and gleaming gems of all colors.

The light of the sun rising through the fingers above beamed down to strike the waters, reflecting the rainbow of colored jewels over the world in the reds and yellows and purples of dawn. Blackie was aglow in this glorious light. Unicorn would blaze like a star.

With a cry, Blackie thrust his head into the Fountain. A shock threw him back on his haunches.

"Blackie!" gasped Prince George. "Your horn!"

A monk, standing by, intoned, "He has raised up a horn for his people."

Startled, Blackie shook his head. The straps on the fronton broke away as the spike flew off into the piles of crutches and bandages around the fountain. Glancing about him, Blackie saw the splints and casts, eye patches and hearing horns tossed away after the healing of the waters.

He turned back to the Fountain. Mirrored on the surface of the water, he saw his new horn, a yard of gleaming ivory spiraling out to a point. He whipped his horn through the air. He felt the power of a full-grown unicorn.

"It just . . . just sprang out!" breathed Prince George.

Blackie took a deep breath. He shivered. This horn, so mighty, it frightened him. He didn't feel different now, except for a new sense of bulk about his thighs and shoulders along with the weight of the horn. He certainly didn't feel grown up, adult, ready to take on the burden of the unicorn's life. Those shattered horns in the Fountain, what did they show but the struggles, the suffering of his ancestors?

"Mama, Mama," he thought, "I'm too young for this!"

A wave of sympathy for Papa swept over him. No wonder Papa hid out in the forest! Papa had climbed up here. He'd seen these horns, cracked and broken in the battles of the ages. Their message was plain, and Papa had backed away. He'd chosen to hide in the forest to preserve his horn intact. One horn at least would be left in its purity.

Blackie became aware that Prince George was pulling on his mane. "Come, Blackie, let's watch the dawn from the top of the world."

Blackie swung his horn away from the Fountain and moved with the Prince to stand at the rim of the ledge, watching the dawn brighten the world with sunbeams cast through the fingers of the Hand. The long, probing rays lit up the mountains of the west, rolled over the gray desert, where water was rare, and gleamed on the green lands in the center of the Empire. Grandly, the light spread over hill and valley, field and forest, from the great sea glowing in the south to the dark smudge of Vile in the north under its smoky shroud.

By now, men were approaching, shaven men in worn robes with tattered red crosses that mirrored the Prince's shield. The men bowed to Prince George. He broke into a wide grin and jumped to shake their hands.

"Sir Sebastian, Sir Andrew, I'd hoped to see you up here!"

"Welcome, my lord, welcome to the Shrine!" cried the Knights, returning his smile. "You arrive at last! We've known for weeks that you were headed up with the unicorn. We thought you'd be here long before now."

"Blackie," cried the Prince, turning to him, "these are my comrades, the Knights of Saint Michael! They guard the holy places of the Empire. I've told you how I rode with them at Furland."

He turned back to the Knights. "Tell me, Sir Sebastian, how'd you know we were coming?"

"The messages, my lord, we've had messages about you. In fact, we've been waiting for you to—"

Sir Sebastian broke off as an older Knight walked up. The Cross on this man's robe was more worn than the others. His eyes were deep, his face lined and scarred.

"Our Commander, my lord," said Sir Sebastian, bowing, "the Protector of the Shrine. He can tell you better than I what is happening."

"You are welcome indeed, my lord Prince," said the Commander in a deep voice, "and the unicorn, as well. What a thrill for us to see the holy beast returning in this form, a dark warrior for a troubled age. We have prayed for this moment!"

"Yes, my lord," said Prince George, patting Blackie's shoulder, "this beast is a fighter. A few days ago, he destroyed an army of raiders by himself. We had many to bury."

"That's the true unicorn!" cried the Commander. "We pray for peace in every age, but Satan sends warfare instead. It's a blessing that the unicorn returns to lend us aid."

As the Commander gazed upon him, Blackie turned warm, thanking his dark coat that no one could see him blush. He didn't like the attention, but grew interested when the Commander spoke of Grandpa.

"I had the privilege of following the old unicorn into battle. He was a fearsome sight, I can tell you, breaking the shield wall as we followed to victory. And you, my lord, I've heard of your valor. In fact, we've waited for you to lead the relief forces. We have a letter for you from Her Majesty, the Empress. It will explain what is happening."

He gestured to Sir Sebastian, who pulled a worn scroll from his purse. Prince George unrolled the letter to read the Empress's elegant script.

Castle Royal
Saint Ursula's Day

To be held at the Shrine of the Fountain for
George, Knight of the Order,
Prince and True Heir to the Kingdom of Dacia.

My lord,
I'm sure that you've heard, by now, that the City is under attack by Prince Vile. That rebel Prince denies our possession of the silver mines you discovered (and many thanks to you for that, dear boy!) Prince Vile stands by the Contract, insisting on his claim to the Princess.

We have gathered our barons and armed the Commons of the City. The Heir of Darr is collecting the lords of the North. Unfortunately, due to the speed of the rebellion, which the Dark Prince has been preparing secretly for years, our loyal lords are scattered and without rule.

Please gather the powers of the east and hurry to our aid. Especially, bring the unicorn. We need his might. Tell him that I long to see him. I knew both his father and his grandfather.

Princess Julianna sends her love to him and also to you. Despite our warnings, she has climbed to the tower with her magic bow. She is keeping the dragon away from the City. The desert boy, Aleet, is with her.

Prince George looked up, anxiously.

"Blackie, the Empress needs us! Prince Vile has rebelled like a foul traitor. He threatens the City with his armies. The Princess is in danger! He continues to claim her as his bride!"

Blackie jerked to attention, his horn quivering with alarm.

"My lord, my lord," said the Commander in a soothing voice, "I'm sure that you can rest for a spell in the Shrine. You need time to recover from your journey. Whatever's happening down there will take weeks to develop."

"But Commander," cried the Prince, "the City was already under siege when Her Majesty wrote to me. How long has the letter been waiting?"

The Commander turned to Sir Sebastian, muttered orders, and the Knight ran off. The Commander turned back to Prince George.

"Now, Prince, "he said, pulling up his sword belt, "in a case like this, we must make haste slowly. You know that you can't fight the enemy by yourselves. The Empress instructs you to gather an army to break the siege so the first thing we must do is to write to the barons of the East to call out their clans. When they reply, we'll start down the mountain with two hundred of my troopers. Even that will take time for we must go carefully. The downward climb is a neck-breaker for horses, too narrow and slippery to hurry."

"But then, once we've gathered the army," asked the Prince, looking about for his spear, "what's the best route to the City? Last time I came East, I sailed to Herne and took the roads from there."

"I suspect that shipping will be cut off by now," said the Commander, rubbing his beard. "The Northmen, sons of Satan, they'll block the sea routes for sure. We'll have to keep to the roads. As horsemen, we prefer solid land, anyway."

"But what can I do now, what can I do?" cried the Prince.

"I suggest," smiled the Commander, "that you finish reading your letter. What else does the Empress say?"

"Oh, yes, my letter."

Flustered, the Prince shook out the scroll and held it up to his eyes again.

> *Care for yourself, dear Prince. Watch for Hellions as you near the City. The siege is very heavy. We pray for you and the unicorn. May the Offering you deliver to the Shrine bring peace to the Empire. God bless you*

The letter was signed with the Empress's seal.

"Oh, the Offering," cried the Prince, clapping his hand to his shirt to feel for the Necklace. "I'd forgotten the Offering."

"Indeed," said the Commander, nodding, "while you enjoyed the dawn, we have prepared for the Donation Ceremony. The Abbot of the Shrine awaits you at the Fountain."

"I suppose it's time, Blackie, to get rid of this," said the Prince. He pulled the chain of the necklace over his head.

The Commander saluted the necklace, sparkling brilliantly in the morning sun.

"That is a treasure indeed, my lord! Magnificent! A privilege to see it at last. And now, if you're ready, Prince—"

"Er, yes, of course, Commander." Prince George patted Blackie's neck. "Here, Blackie, hold up your horn. The unicorn must carry the Offering."

Sighing, the Prince slipped the necklace over Blackie's horn. "Such a struggle to get this up here! Come, Blackie. Let's finish our Quest."

The Commander bowed. "May I lead you to the Fountain, my lord?"

"Here, my lord," said a Knight, handing over the spear, "your weapon."

Prince George swept up the spear to Order Arms. The Nail gleamed in the bright sun as they marched back to the Fountain, Blackie holding his horn high.

By now, the area was crowded with pilgrims running to see the Donation. The Knights of Saint Michael had formed to the left of the Fountain while the monks of the Shrine were gathered to the right.

As he stepped along, Blackie's eyes crossed, watching the glittering stone swing back and forth on his horn. They neared the Hand, and the Knights came to attention. The monks began singing.

307

We gather as one at the waters,
the prince on his knees with the churl.
The merchant and priest
share the Lord's feast.
The joy spreads over the world.

The Abbot, a wrinkled man with a long, white beard, was praying on his knees at the Fountain. Two monks helped him to his feet. His voice rolled above the waters as he bowed to Blackie.

"Oh, holy unicorn, it is a joy to receive you at the Fountain. It has been too long since the blessed beast visited the Shrine."

Blackie nodded his head in reply. As he bowed, the Offering slipped from his slanted horn.

"Oh, no!" cried the Prince, jumping for the necklace. It slid between his fingers and splashed into the Fountain. It settled between two of the horns. There was a stir of dismay, but the Abbot lifted his hand with a smile.

"No matter, my lord. This little accident saved you all from my tedious speech of welcome. It is more important that we pray that this gift brings peace to the Empire. Please, let us kneel to the Lord."

Blackie bowed his horn as the humans knelt for the prayer. The Abbot turned and lifted his hands to the Fountain.

"Heavenly Father, you promise us peace. Let not our hearts be troubled, neither let them be afraid. As ever, though, in this fallen world, we find our lives filled with worries and anxieties. May we accept the peace you offer in the spirit that you give it—to face each day with courage and confidence, faith in our hearts and a prayer on our lips. As the widow offers her mite and the Princess her treasure, let us dedicate our love and labor, our care and concern, until the spirit of peace spreads like the dawn and the world is again the Paradise you created. The Cross shall then stand without bloodshed and the unicorn shall carry a horn unstained. In Thy name, we pray."

The Shrine rang with the blessing of the Trinity.

"Blackie," whispered Prince George after the Amens had faded away, "didn't you think the Necklace was a little light? Could Lizetta have chipped some of the stone away while she had it? I forgot to examine it after I got it back from her. What will the Princess say if she sees a shrunken stone when she makes her pilgrimage to the Shrine?"

Blackie shook his head. He didn't know, and he didn't care. The necklace was delivered. It glittered nicely among the horns. He was glad to be done with it. The thing had caused trouble since the Princess gave it to them, and now with the incense of the Shrine around him, he refused to worry about anything.

"Well, Prince," said the Abbot, walking into the garden beside Blackie, "it's a joy to have you and the unicorn join our love feast. We've longed to see you since you recovered the Grail from the Gypsies, three years ago."

"I'm sorry, Father Abbot, but we must rush through our meal," said the Prince, looking up at the sun to check the time. "My duty calls me back to the City as soon as possible."

"Oh, my child," murmured the Abbot, looking upon the Prince with love, "you must stay with us for days. You'll learn there's no need to hurry. The sun rises as the Lord smiles and sets as He nods. We worship at the Lord's pace and work at our own. Be at ease."

Although Prince George was eager to hurry, Blackie felt comfortable already. He closed his eyes to relish the breeze filled with intoxicating smells from the garden—the grass, lusher and greener even than the Wise Woman's lawn, the trees and bushes bending with glowing fruit.

Prince George quieted as food was served. Sitting beside Blackie at the end of a long table, he realized how hungry he was after the long climb to the Shrine. Pilgrims arranged bowls of fruit and fresh vegetables down the table. The Abbot took up a loaf of bread and began breaking off chunks to fill trays as another monk passed a pitcher of wine. An old Knight at the other end of the table was splitting a small fish for platters passed back the other way.

As they began to eat after the blessing, Blackie found himself famished. He'd never tasted such juicy fruit, such crispy vegetables, fresh from tree and soil. Of course, he skipped the fish, but the warm, crunchy bread was a meal in itself, and he sucked wine from a bowl placed on the table before him.

Remembering Mama's warning about Papa's drinking, Blackie took only a few reviving gulps before turning to a bowl of Fountain water. Somehow, this simple meal seemed more satisfying than any he'd ever eaten, perhaps because of the joy of the humans about him, smiling and talking and laughing together.

"I'm sure, there's no need to apologize for the simplicity of our feast," said the Abbot, gesturing at the platters around the table. "Fish, bread, and wine we have in plenty as they multiply at the Shrine, so Brother Chef serves many dishes of fish stew and bread pudding. Other than that which grows in our garden, we have what pilgrims carry up to us from below. A few weeks ago, we received supplies from a great wave of pilgrims from all over the Empire—refugees, mainly, driven from their homes. Most will stay with us until things settle down below."

"We saw a party, yesterday, that seemed to be heading home," said the Prince.

"I expect they were warriors," said the Abbot, "healed by the Fountain and returning to their charge. We get many such."

Chewing a piece of fish, Prince George asked about the horns in the fountain.

"We receive the horn whenever a unicorn dies," answered the Abbot. "It's been forty years since a new horn was delivered. Father Anselm, I believe, was Abbot at the last Dedication."

As the meal continued, the air filled with music, laughter, and talk of all kinds from the fools' jest to the doctors' philosophy. His mouth full of peaches, Prince George chuckled when the Abbot joked about the speech they'd missed by the necklace dropping so abruptly.

"Oh, I promise you, my lord, I had much to say. I'd have spoken for hours on the generosity of the Princess and your heroism in delivering it, not to mention the symbolism of a unicorn carrying the Offering on his horn. I'd have come up with a hundred good quotes in Greek and Latin and thrown in a phrase or two of Hebrew. Oh, I'd have kept preaching until you had to throw a bag over me to shut me up!"

He roared with laughter as Prince George begged for the speech.

"Write it out in Latin, Father Abbot. I'll take it back it to the Princess. She'll put it in the Cathedral Library. Preachers will quote your wisdom forever."

Chuckling, the Abbot pulled the rind from a melon with his fingers. He piled the fruit on Blackie's plate. "Oh, my lord, preachers don't need my ramblings. They have the Gospels and the writings of the fathers. Better they spend their time praising the Lord and sharing their own feasts."

Blackie agreed fully. There couldn't be too many feasts like this one. This was a moment to relish. He'd carry this memory through life along with his horn.

"*Carpe diem*," murmured Prince George. "That's what the Princess always says, '*Carpe diem*.'"

"A song, my lord!" cried the Abbot. "After traveling so far, you must open your heart and sing for us."

"Me, sing?" squealed the Prince, blushing. "Oh, Abbot, you don't want to hear me sing. Back in Court, they shut me up when I try to join in."

"But you're not at Court!" laughed the Abbot. "Here, we share our love and joy. When you sing for us, you sing with the angels, right, unicorn?"

Full of delight, Blackie threw up his horn. He trumpeted until Prince George jumped up.

"I'll sing! I'll sing! But what should I sing?"

"Open your heart, Prince!" cried Sir Sebastian from down the table. "Open your heart and let it out."

"Uh, uh—"

The Prince ran his hands down his tunic. He could think of no song worthy of this company until Blackie swung around and touched him, shooting out a spark from his horn. Then Prince George threw out his arms and sang the song in his heart.

We beg for the blessing,
The aid of our Lord
in the grit and grime
of the road.

We long for the smile,
the touch of the Hand
to show us that
we're not alone.

And then, the flash—
the light, the warmth,
the heat and light
of the Word.

We throw back our heads
and stretch up our arms
and sing out the Grace
of the Lord!

"Good," thought Blackie, listening to the humans join the Prince's song. "Prince George deserves his happiness. He's traveled long and hard to get here. He's loyal, this man. He never gives up. 'Georgie,' that's what the Princess calls him, he's . . . he's a good human. He's a friend."

He sighed.

"If only everyone could visit the Shrine and share this joy. Mama, she belongs here, and Papa—Well, he knows, he's been here. But the Princess has never climbed the mountain. I've got to bring her up as soon as I can. Oh, how she'll love it! If I know her, she'll make a show of her pilgrimage. She'll arrive in style!"

He imagined the Princess climbing barefooted up the stairway with trumpets blowing. She'd probably have Jessica climbing behind, bearing golden slippers on a cushion for her lady to wear about the Shrine.

"Who else belongs up here?" he asked himself. "Surely, surely, that desert boy, the one the Prince talks about, and the Heir of Darr, the Prince's friend. Lizetta and Lazlo, now, that's a pair that need the holy waters if they'd ever truly repent. As it is, I wouldn't trust them near the jewels in the Fountain. Prince George tells me that Lazlo waded into the Fountain with his boots on to steal the holy Grail!

"Other creatures—I'm sure that the beasts of the forest would love the Fountain waters, too, the birds, the deer, the foxes, all the lonely, the suffering—"

Struck by the misery of a world that needs blessing, Blackie spoke out the words he'd heard in the prayers of the humans.

"Deliver us, Lord, please deliver us."

"Amen," said the Abbot, smiling at him.

Toasting, singing, laughing, few humans noticed Blackie pull away from the table. He trotted back to the Fountain for another look at the horns. This time, he spotted the ancient bowl of clay, half-hidden under the jewels.

The Holy Grail, blessed by the lips of the Lord, now returned to its resting place. Blackie gave a long sigh. He closed his eyes and stood in a happiness greater than his childhood joy at dancing through the forest in springtime, greater than nuzzling Mama.

What was different, now, was the awareness. Here, he knew who he was, what he was, where he was. He bathed in the love pouring through the Fountain.

Even so, tears winked from his eyes when he looked again at the broken horns, the relics of his ancestors who had died fighting to preserve this peace. The tragedy of life was before him. Why did dragons burn through the sky when the Grace of the Lord flowed from the Fountain? Why were unicorns doomed to fight them?

"I could stay here all my life," Blackie realized. "I'd eat the bread and drink from the Fountain. I'd be safer here than even Papa down in the forest. I'd protect my horn and sing with the pilgrims. Now that I've tasted the fruit, I'm surprised that Papa ever left this garden."

He looked at his own horn gleaming white in the waters over the horns, perfect, unblemished. He peered deeper into the waters.

"I wonder which of those horns is Grandpa's."

Blackie examined the horns closely, scanning the lengths, the spirals, the points on those that still had their tips. Each of them was notched and cracked, scarred by battle.

A twisted smile came to his face.

"In a way, I have to admire Papa. When you think of it, he's sort of a backward hero. He struggles as hard to avoid battles as these unicorns did to fight them—and I don't know if I blame him. Fighting's terrible! I learned that at the monastery. If Papa hadn't hidden out in the forest, I'd be seeing his horn on top of the pile, broken like the others, broken as mine may be some day."

Blackie shivered at the thought, then lowered his horn to the Fountain.

"Blessed horns, I salute you. For myself, I intend to keep my horn for a long, long time. I have much to do with it, starting with freeing the Princess from her tower."

He trotted back to the edge of the Shrine and looked again over the land below, shining under the morning sun. "There it is, the Empire. My Princess is down by the sea."

He took a deep breath. "Hold on, my lady, hold on! I come to rescue you!"

After a long look, he turned away.

"I wonder what apricots taste like on the branch. I'd better enjoy them while I can."

CHAPTER TWENTY-FOUR

Down the Mountain

Despite Prince George's impatience, it proved impossible to collect the lords with any speed. Blackie was forced to stay in bliss for weeks longer.

The first obstacle was the letter to the lords. Prince George assumed he could dash off a note in twenty minutes, but it proved hard to frame his letter. He had to promise honor, promotion, and booty to those who came forward against the threat of punishment for stay-at-homes.

Wandering by the table with his back filled with singing children, Blackie shook his head at Prince George scribbling away at sheets of parchment with ink-stained hands. The knights around the Prince offered suggestions and criticisms that only seemed to muddle him more.

Once the message was completed at last, it had to be sent to the scribes to be copied by hand with extra copies for the files.

"Files!" cried the Prince in dismay. "What do we need with files—all these scripts and scrolls? We'll have to drag a wagon with nothing but documents."

The Commander shrugged. "That's the way it's done, my lord. Since the Devil invented attorneys, no man's word is sufficient. Everything has to be backed up by paperwork."

Blackie snorted and dashed off to the greensward where pilgrims danced in circles. While he swayed to the music, girls looped chains of yellow, orange, and red flowers around his horn.

"Let's go see the horses!" cried the boys, tugging at Blackie's mane.

The children helped each other onto Blackie's back, and he set off for the pasture, but someone ran by with the news that an angel had flown in to drink at the Fountain.

"Around, unicorn, around!" yelled Blackie's riders. "Let's go see the angel!"

Blackie galloped back across the Shrine, but the angel was already off on its errands, leaving humans standing in silence. A woman whispered to Blackie, "It smiled at me."

Playing with the children, Blackie forgot about tomorrow. Golden days at the Shrine, they were enough for him.

At last, the heralds were sent down the mountain with the letters. A few days later, the replies began to return. Only two of the lords were ready to march at once. The rest had excuses. The stars were wrong. It was late in the year. Their fighting men were sick or needed for harvest.

Some barons feared that neighbors would invade their lands if they sent off their troops. Others simply refused to budge. Several didn't answer at all.

Blackie got an inkling of all this when he trotted up to the table for a pre-dinner snack of strawberries and cream over Shrine bread. Prince George was holding another conference with the Abbot and the Commander.

"I'll send another letter," insisted the Prince, "stronger than the first! I'll force them to recognize the Empress's orders."

The Commander snorted. "Well, that's not going to work. Your message was clear enough, my lord. The thing to do is to pick one of those holdouts and make an example of him. That'll stir out the rabbits."

"But Commander," objected the Abbot, "surely, you can find a peaceful way to reach these barons. Remember, Prince Vile is the enemy, not these lords. They're simply frightened and vulnerable."

"Nonsense!" roared the Commander. He thumped the table with his fist, startling Blackie. "They're lazy as Greeks and twice as slow! They expect others to do their fighting while they lie back in their lands. Just burn a castle or two! They'll come around! That's my advice."

Blackie backed away as the Abbot cried out. "My lord, you can't do that! Surely, there's something you can do without burning castles!"

"Can we send down an angel?" asked the Prince.

"I wish we could," sighed the Abbot. "Those holy spirits would convince anyone, but they fly on the highest orders, speak only to saints."

"You've got to do something, Prince," insisted the Commander, "something quick and dramatic. Otherwise, we'll hang around here all winter until the City falls."

"Well, Blackie," said the Prince, walking away with a hand on Blackie's shoulder, "looks like it's up to us. We leave tomorrow with the troopers. Once we're off the mountain, we have to think of some way to stir up the barons, douse them with Fountain water, or something."

"Tomorrow?" thought Blackie, turning away in dismay. "So soon? Only one more day here? What shall I do with my time—play with the children, talk to the horses, search out old-timers to tell me stories of Grandpa?"

As it turned out, the children found Blackie standing in the Fountain gazing at the horns. They called him away to eat pineapple, a fruit they'd just discovered. It was all jolly to Blackie. He ate pineapple and listened to the singing and trotted around the garden with the children to collect seven-leaf clovers. Finally, he lay down in the green pastures with all the little heads resting on him and let the prayers wash over them.

It was only next morning, watching the troopers lead their horses to the stairway, that he started to feel nervous.

"What if I fall on the way down?" he thought. "The pilgrims say it's snowing below. That stairway was bad enough when dry. It'll be impossible if it's icy."

He ran to the Fountain for a drink, but its assurance lasted only till he faced the stairs again. At that point, he welcomed the aid of a sergeant and half a dozen troopers who strapped a harness about him.

"Thing is, unicorn," explained the sergeant, "your basic shape isn't fitted for climbing down stairs. You can barely see the steps below you.

"Don't worry, Blackie," said Sir Sebastian, overseeing the move. "We're used to hauling horses up and down the steps. This harness gives the men something to hold to. We can't have you slide away, can we? You'd roll down these steps like a bowling ball and knock off everyone below you!"

It was a slow descent for Blackie with humans holding back his weight and guiding him to plant his hooves on the steps. The troopers were shivering and sweating as they edged around the narrow turns with the frigid wind whistling up at them. It was such a job that the men had to switch off twice on the way down.

Prince George pushed in to help on the bottom stage, gripping the harness as he backed step by step down the stairway. Nervous as he was, Blackie noticed that the Prince was unusually silent. When they reached the Hermit's ledge, he pulled away in dismay. The Fountain's effect was wearing off. He began complaining about the degradation of doing groom's work.

"Oh, that Shrine's wonderful of course, but you forget the distinctions of rank! A peasant will plop down next to a prince as though they shared the same blood. Next thing you know, I'll be polishing boots like a scrub boy."

He stood with Blackie while the men unbuckled the harness to carry back to the Shrine for the next group of horses. Except for the wind which felt bitter after the warmth of the Shrine Blackie felt easy enough on the rocky shelf. He watched the wild-eyed horses as the Fountain waters wore away and they realized that they were back in the world of snowstorms and icicles. The humans shooed them into a stockade set up against the mountain and poured bags of Shrine bread into a feeding trough.

The Commander spoke to Prince George. "So you'll stay here, my lord, to guard the horses, while we bring down the next bunch? This job always takes all day. It's a painful process, shifting the mounts, but they come down healthy and ready to ride. They do hate moving into winter, though!"

Prince George shivered in his blanket. He said nothing until the Commander climbed off with the sergeants and grooms, then he burst out with worries.

"Why did we wait so long? The siege at the City, the Princess in danger—somehow, we've lost the autumn. I wasted weeks sending letters to barons who just ignored them! It's hard to think clearly up there! You get bewitched by the Fountain. Everything seems under control. Now, I see the perils ahead of us! How thoughtless I was! How foolish to feast and sing while the Princess fights the dragon without me!"

The Prince seemed in no state to be useful so Blackie followed the horses into the stockade for his share of Shrine bread. Most of the horses were eating eagerly from the trough, their backs to the wind. One dark-brown nag kept shivering to herself.

"Cold again!" she said loudly. "Cold down here! Ice and snow! Oh, I told you what was going on! I warned you when I saw them coming for us. Didn't I tell you that they'd drag us down the mountain? They're gonna run us hard! Same old story, loadin' us up to face spears and arrows. We're in for it, now. You'll see!"

"Oh, shut up, Maudie," said another horse.

"Yeah, Maudie, why worry about it?" said a third horse. "We can't do anything about it. Keep fretting like this, and the food'll be gone before you get a bite."

"I'm not gonna eat," declared Maudie. "I know what they're up to! I'm not gonna eat a bite! That'll show 'em!"

The horses snickered at that. "Sure, Maudie, you show 'em. You show 'em and show 'em, and keep showin' 'em till the bread's all gone."

Blackie ate quietly in his corner of the trough until he accidentally poked a gray and white horse with his horn.

"Hey, watch that thing!" cried the horse. "What you doin' here anyway? You don't smell like a horse!"

"That's right!" cried Maudie, stepping around to glare at Blackie. "Who let that critter in here to stab folks and eat our feed? I say, let's drive him off!"

"That's okay with me," said Blackie, tossing his horn. "It's too cold here. I'm going inside where it's warm."

"Inside?" cried Maudie, looking about. "Inside where? They got a warm stable around here?"

Blackie backed from the group of horses and walked to the gate.

"Look!" cried Maudie. "He's gettin' away!"

She followed after him, crying, "Where you going? Why do you get to go out?"

She whinnied her protests as the guard opened the gate for Blackie. Blackie ran around to the Hermit's hut. He knocked on the door with his horn while the sniffing dogs twined about his legs. The Hermit didn't seem to be home.

Blackie looked around the shelf for the Hermit, found him setting up tents on the sheltered end of the ledge. Glancing at Blackie, the Hermit dropped the stone he was carrying to weigh down the edge of a tent against the wind.

"Oh, Blackie!" he cried, running over. "Bless the Lord, how you've grown! You're eight inches taller at least, and you've got your horn! It's beautiful, magnificent! Another miracle of the Shrine!"

The Hermit rubbed Blackie's nose and examined the horn. "Perfect, perfect."

Blackie tugged at the Hermit's cloak. The man nodded. "Sure, you can shelter at my house. We don't have wood for a fire, but you'll be out of the wind. I have plenty of bread from the Shrine, though. They're hauling down bags of it."

The Hermit opened the door to the hut, holding back the dogs while Blackie stepped inside. Prince George was kneeling at the fireplace, trying to start a flame with empty bread bags. He struck at his dagger with a flint and sat back on his heels.

"Ho, there, Hermit! Your wood box was empty when I came in. I figure we can burn these bags. There's a pile of them outside your door."

The Hermit bowed to the Prince. "God bless you, my lord. It's good to see you again. Go ahead. Burn all the bags you want. I send them back to the Shrine to refill, but they have plenty more up there."

The Prince struck at his dagger while the Hermit hauled benches out to clear a space for Blackie. Once lit, the bags flared up with smoke and the smell of toasted breadcrumbs. They never fully heated the hut, but Blackie was comfortable out of the wind. He lowered himself onto the Prince's blanket below the smoke level and chewed bread and carrots carried down from the Shrine.

Once the horses were moved, the leaders of the Army squeezed into the hut to discuss the route to the City. They all agreed they must hurry.

"Time's passing!" insisted the Prince. "We have to ride at once. I don't know how long the siege has gone on, but I wasted weeks in that quest. Sadly, we don't have leisure to hustle these barons. We'll have to ride with the lords who are willing to fight."

"I guess, you're right, my lord," agreed the Commander. "It sticks in my craw to ignore those holdouts, but a worker at the task is worth ten shirkers in the tavern. The question I have is what path we should take. Hermit, here, tells me that the sea route from Herne is definitely cut off."

"Since time's the issue," declared Prince George, "we should sweep along the highroad like heroes. Let Vile see the rescue coming up behind him. That'll cool him down."

The Commander questioned the wisdom of an open attack. He wanted to move across country under cover of the forest.

"I know that a direct assault would make an exciting episode in your Song, but it seems to me that a surprise attack is our only chance to defeat the villains with our small army. Besides, we'll find more food in the back country. The main roads have already been ravaged by the enemy."

"But the time!" cried the Prince. "Now that we're on the road, we don't want to lose weeks bumbling around cow paths!"

"Another problem with back roads," added Sir Sebastian, "is that we'd be too well hidden. Her Majesty's letter tells us to gather friendly forces as we march. How will our allies find us if we stick to the trails?"

Sir Anthony scratched a flea bite on his leg.

"Friendly forces, certainly, Prince, we do want to meet them, but what if we attract the dragon as well? That's one meeting we want to avoid!"

"My lords, if you permit me—" said the Hermit, throwing the last bag on the fire. "I don't see why you worry about the dragon. The unicorn's got his horn now. The Lord sends the holy beast to kill such monsters."

They all looked at Blackie. Blackie looked away, lowering his ears.

"Here we go again," he thought. "Of course, they count on me to fight the dragon. I'd attack in a minute if I could catch her on the ground, but horn or no horn, I can't fly into the sky after her. I don't know how Grandpa did it."

By nightfall, all the horses had been moved down from the Shrine. The army was ready to move. There were no stairs to deal with next morning, but the steep mountain trail was only slightly better than the stairway. Digging his hooves into an icy patch, Blackie thought he could use that harness. Still, they descended carefully enough that no horses had been lost when they camped that night near the road north to Furland.

The troopers were leading the last horses into camp when Prince George found Blackie grazing on withered brush between snow-powdered pine trees.

"Ho, Blackie, you up for a run? We need to scout the forest around the camp."

A run seemed attractive. Blackie hadn't stretched his legs for days, but he halted when he saw a trooper follow the Prince with a saddle over his shoulder.

"It's the lightest saddle I could find," explained the Prince, rubbing Blackie's nose. "Going up against Hellions, I'll need the support for mounted battle."

Shaking his head, Blackie backed into the long, sweeping pine boughs.

"Not again, Blackie," begged the Prince, stepping after him. "Please be reasonable. I'll ride easier with the saddle, plus I can strap on my armor and our bags of supplies."

"No," thought Blackie, tossing his horn, "we've been through this before. I'm not letting you load me up like a mule. It's bad enough I have to carry a human. I'm not toting that saddle, too!"

The trooper set down the saddle while Prince George tried to convince Blackie to accept the thing. "It's for the Princess, you see."

Blackie raised a skeptical ear.

"Don't you remember what she told you?" the Prince insisted. "She wants me to be properly equipped. Look at me, a knight in her service. I have to wear freezing armor. Just touch this helmet and breastplate. They feel like ice in this wind. You don't hear me complain, do you? A warrior does what he must to fight effectively."

Blackie didn't know how to respond to this. Certainly, he'd take the saddle if his lady strapped it on with her sweet hands, but he refused to believe that she wanted him to wear this heavy thing. She'd ridden him herself without a saddle. The Prince could do the same.

He shook his head until the Prince waved the saddle away. Blackie stepped forward. Prince George scrambled on his back, grumbling.

"Stubborn as a mule! If only I had a dram of the Wise Woman's potion!"

Pleased with himself, Blackie trotted through the pines as the Prince muttered, "Now, I'm sorry I bragged to the Knights about you. I told them how loyal you are, how faithful. It's that horn, I think. It's turned you into a real prima donna."

Once Blackie learned to angle his long horn to avoid the swishing boughs, he trotted cheerfully through the pines despite icy flecks stinging his nose and ears. Everything smelled of pinecones and needles. The sticky sap on the pine bark brushed off on his coat, perfuming him like a Yule log. He smelled squirrels everywhere, but bear scent was faint. Those beasts were hidden away in their winter dens.

Since Blackie could see better in the dusk than any man, Prince George let the unicorn pick the path as darkness crept from the shadowy trails to the snow-covered treetops. Blackie made a complete circuit around the camp without smelling danger on the trails. Turning back with cold hooves, he skidded to a stop when they heard a hunting horn from behind.

Prince George backed him between heavy boughs that sprinkled snow on them. "Take care, Blackie. They ride openly, but—"

Prince George pulled up shield and spear as Blackie saw a file of men ride toward them, the lead man blowing a horn.

"Who goes there?" shouted the Prince.

The riders halted in a clash of metal. Someone yelled back, "Who are you? Give a name to yourself!"

"I asked you first!" insisted the Prince. "Do you serve the Crown or Prince Vile?"

The answer came instantly. "We spits on Vile! We're men of Furland sent by the Countess Amalia, bless her heart. We seeks the Army of the Shrine under the famous Prince of Dacia."

"How do they look, Blackie?" whispered the Prince.

Blackie sniffed carefully. The men smelled all right—no chains or bloody whips that he could smell. He nickered softly to the Prince.

"Welcome, men of Furland," called the Prince, urging Blackie forward. "I am the Prince you seek. Our camp is just down the road with bread and bonfires to welcome you."

The Furlanders greeted him with cheers as the horses stepped closer.

"Prince George, ho, me lord!" shouted a deep voice. "By the saints, it's good to see you again! I'm Sandor, Master of Foresters to the

Countess Amalia. I lead ninety of the best bowmen in the country to join your army, all mounted and ready to ride."

"Oh, Sandor, Sandor!" cried Prince George in sudden recognition.

"See, lads!" cried Sandor to his men, pulling up beside Blackie. "I knew he'd reconize me! He's a terrible fighter is this Prince. I seen him tackle a giant bear with nothin' but a ten-inch dagger. We had to drag the beast off him—three hundred pounds, it weighed if an ounce!"

Sandor peered at Blackie's silvery horn. His tone dropped to awe. "And it's true, me lord. You do ride the unicorn! My lady tole me you did, but—"

"Well, Sandor," asked Prince George, turning Blackie to ride toward the camp, "how's the Countess? Are the Eastern lords loyal to the Crown?"

"My lord, the Countess sends you a gift," said Sandor, unstrapping a large roll from his saddle. "A cloak made from the hide of that very bear you killed."

"A trophy!" cried the Prince, shaking out the cloak. The stench of bearskin and tanning solution rose up. Blackie sneezed as the Prince drew the heavy fur about him. "Just in time! This is a worthy replacement for the lionskin I lost at Shrems."

"And it's warm," added Sandor, "perfect for this weather."

Riding up the road to the army, the men talked of the Countess while Sandor's horse sniffed Blackie. The horse snorted. "Never seen anything like you, stranger. Where you get that nib on your nob? Must get in your way somethin' fierce. You got any notion why they runnin' us around the countryside in this weather? They givin' us anything good to eat?"

Blackie ignored the horse to listen to Prince George question Sandor. "So the Seeker's back with Lady Amalia? Last I heard, he was taking refuge at the Shrine. I looked for him up there, but no one knew where he'd gone."

"Old Seeker missed the seein'," explained the Furlander. "He says he loved the Shrine—no man's wretched in that holy place! But he warn't needed there. He's used to housewives askin' him to find their lost spoons and stockin's, workmen askin' about lost nails. He was just settin' out to wander the Empire again when he 'seen' the Black Prince sendin' out his army o' Hellions. That's when he made tracks for Furland Castle. He feels safe with the Countess."

"Too bad he didn't ride with you," said the Prince. "I'd like to question him about the City."

At that moment, the horse spoke sharply to get Blackie's attention. "What's the matter with you, unicorn? I asked you a question. I swear you don't listen better than an old bull ox. Did that bodkin pull out your brains?"

"Sorry," said Blackie, politely. "I was just thinking of something."

"Ho, ho, ho," chuckled the horse, swinging a hip against him. "I know what's on your mind. You got a filly somewhere, a female unicorn. I know you young bucks. You always sniffin' after the fillies if they don't geld you young."

"Geld me!" Blackie shuddered. "No, no, it's nothing like that. I was just wondering if they'd have enough bread to feed us all at camp."

The horse's ears went up at that. "Bread, they feedin' you bread? My, my, ain't you fancy! Only time we get bread is when the baker burns a batch, or puffs it up so it don't have flavor."

"Well, this bread is delicious and never gets stale. You can only get it at the Shrine, so it fills the heart as well as the belly."

"I'm up for that," said the horse. "I hope they shares with the livestock. Forage is terrible in the forest this time o' year, nothin' but rusty old roots and twigs. I don't mind tellin' you, my heart sank when they started draggin' out the saddles for this ride."

"Tell me, horse," asked Blackie, "did you ever meet an old stallion named Steed? Steed carried the Prince when I first met him."

"Steed?" whinnied the horse. "Oh, he was a one, all right! Old Steed had an eye for the fillies, but he's so full of lies you can't believe a thing he tells you. He told us he used to travel with a unicorn like you. A big thing, colored white and lazy as a toad. He said, that unicorn would shy at a quarter-mile run."

"Lazy!" exclaimed Blackie. "Papa's not lazy—well, not really. He's . . . he's just peaceful. He likes the quiet life."

"Now you're talkin'!" exclaimed the horse. "That's what I like—the quiet life. But these humans—"

Rounding a turn with the campfire glowing ahead, Blackie brushed against a tree. A branch slapped snow over him. He shivered.

"Times like this, I think Papa's smarter than me. He holes up for the winter, warm and cozy in the Nest."

Blackie said goodbye to the horses at the fires where the Knights welcomed the troops from Furland. The horses were led off to the stockade, the stallion calling loudly, "Where's the bread? Where's the bread?"

The Furlanders had brought supplies from the Countess, so Blackie and Prince George shared their dinner. Blackie skipped the ham and venison, but gobbled turnips and apples along with Shrine bread.

Sandor told the officers that the Countess had sent her own messengers throughout the east urging the barons to bring their troops to join the army. Many of the lords had refused to help, fearing raiders if they left their castles, but two barons, Lord Sherbs and Lord Blaggin, were marching a couple hundred men to join them at the cutoff.

"Good hunters, they are, skilled at bringin' in bear and deer and the wild goats o' the mountain. They love the Countess and serve the Empress with a good heart."

"That's the kind of men we want!" cried the Prince, sitting down on a tree stump. "Experienced foresters who serve willingly. They're the men to hammer Vile's blackguards!"

Blackie turned his cold side to the fire as Sandor asked how big was the army that Prince Vile had mustered around the City.

Prince George threw up his hands. "Who knows? All we've heard are rumors and guesses."

"From the Seeker's account," said Sandor, "they's plenty o' wicked lords about the Empire. If they all obey Vile, he'll have hordes under his command."

"Don't worry, Hunt Master," insisted Sir Sebastian. "Those scoundrels will desert Vile at the first clash of arms. A sinner, you know, will betray an evil master as soon as a true lord."

"Yes," agreed the Prince, wrapping his bearskin about him, "most of the bandits raiding the country are runaways from Prince Vile. His bullyboys are too handy with noose and whip to suit those rascals."

"I hear, though, me lord," said a Furlander, "that Vile's armies fight for the promise o' loot. The City's a treasure house for wretches like them."

Blackie turned away to the next fire where troopers were singing quietly. The humans welcomed him by scooting aside to make space before the crackling flames. A man tossed a blanket over him, so he slept as well as possible, though he woke up through dreams of the dragon.

Snow was falling when Prince George collected him early next morning to scout ahead of the army. A shivering groom held the spear and shield while the Prince fed Blackie a few chunks of Shrine bread from a bag.

"Remember, Blackie," said the Prince, giving him the last of the bread, "we're scouting today, not skirmishing. We're the eyes of the army. We have to stay out of fights to bring the news back to the troopers."

Blackie nodded. That was all right with him. His hunger for adventure had vanished with the midnight battle at the monastery. True, he wanted to save the Princess, but those shattered horns in the Fountain had impressed him deeply. He'd save her by scouting quietly if he could.

The day was gloomy with heavy clouds above the trees. There was little wind. Big snowflakes drifted slowly to whiten trees and melt on the road. Prince George bent low in his bearskin as Blackie trotted briskly to get the blood flowing in his legs. Blackie smelled the usual road smells until they reached the forces of the barons waiting for the army near the lane to Furland. There, he smelled the strong scent of goats, along with men and horses.

"Yes, my lord," Baron Blaggin told the Prince, looking proudly at the herd, "we're drivin' three hundred goats to feed the troops. Nothin' like a fat goat roasted over a slow fire with lard and herbs—good meat for good men."

"I'm sure it's good meat," said the Prince, scratching his head, "but the pace! We have a hard ride ahead of us. We can't drag along like goatherds."

"But my lord," said Baron Sherbs, pointing to the bowmen standing around, "we're mountain men, foot soldiers. We only have horses for officers and supply wagons."

"Oh, ho, that's a problem," admitted Prince George. "I'd hoped to reach the City in a week."

The barons shrugged.

"That's the way it is, my lord," said Baron Sherbs. "You'll find riders down on the grassy plains, but horses are rare in these hills. They're costly to keep. We hear that the Countess had to strip her country to find mounts for her men."

Blackie watched Prince George stamp around in frustration. "We can't take months to march across the Empire! I'm sure the Empress expected us weeks ago."

"Here we go again," thought Blackie, "more problems."

He left the men talking and wandered down to look at the goats. Goats were strange creatures, restless and noisy, sniffing over the hillside. He was astonished at the stuff they ate—thorns, bushes, branches. The goats looked curiously as Blackie walked closer. A big ram rushed out, tossing his horns.

"Hey, brother," said Blackie, stepping forward, "How you doing? What's up with you?"

"Big as you are, big as you are," bleated the goat, "I'll take you on! These nannies are mine, mine, mine—get it, buster?"

"Sure," said Blackie, looking mildly at the bristling creature. "I don't want your nannies. I don't want anything. I'm just trying to be friendly."

"Move on, then!" yelled the goat, jumping forward. "Make tracks, bucko! Hit the road if you don't want a pair of horns up your butt!"

"Anything you say, goat. Don't get worked up over nothing."

Shaking his head at the stupid thing, Blackie walked away through soldiers cutting boughs to make shelters, chopping wood to build fires. The humans looked at him with wonder, called to him, petted him. One man pulled his knife from his belt and leaned close to cut a chunk from Blackie's horn. Blackie knocked him away, indignantly.

"Just a slice," begged the man, waving his knife, "a little slice o' horn for luck. Come on, unicorn. You won't miss it."

Blackie looked at him with disgust and passed on. At the other side of the campground, he found a dozen supply carts. The carters greeted him warmly.

"Ho, unicorn, ho, boy, we heard you was here!"

One carter had his bandaged arm in a sling. "Can you heal me broken flipper, unicorn?" he begged. "I tripped over me boots dancin' drunk at harvest festival. It's been four weeks, now, a whole month. Me arm's not gettin' any better. It's got a bad color to it and hurts more every day."

Blackie paused. He remembered what Papa had said about healing people—once you start, they won't let you stop. But the carter leaned forward and whispered, "I got oats, unicorn. Give you a bucket of oats to heal up me arm."

"Oats, well, that's different," thought Blackie. "A man with oats should have a good arm."

He nodded, and the carter called out, "Hey, Archie, give me a hand here."

Another carter stood up. "Sure, Ritchie."

Wincing, Ritchie held up the arm so Archie could strip off the filthy bandages. The arm was twisted and purple.

Ritchie explained, almost proudly, "Me fingers is swole up like sausages, ye see. Can't move 'em."

Blackie touched his horn to the arm just below the elbow. He twitched as a spark shot to the arm, and the bone twisted back into place.

"Eeeee!" shrieked the carter, jerking away. He looked down, panting, as the purple faded from the skin, leaving it as brown as his other arm.

"Saints bless us, Ritchie," breathed Archie. "Looks like it did the trick."

"I can . . . I can move my fingers again." Ritchie flexed the fingers on the damaged hand. He swung his arms around and yelled, "Yahoo! I'm healed! No pain, no pain at all!"

Another carter ran around the cart, pointing to his neck. "Unicorn, unicorn, I got this goiter!"

"Back off, Larry, back off!" insisted Ritchie. "This unicorn is going to eat his oats before he does anything else."

"But me goiter!"

True to his word, Ritchie filled a bucket with crunchy oats. He kept everyone back while Blackie ate it. Archie offered him a bucket of beer. Blackie took a taste, sour, pungent, but it warmed the belly. He ate his supper while the carters passed the beer bucket around and Ritchie showed his arm to everybody.

"You could see it was dyin' away!" he declared. "Dyin' there on the stump, but the unicorn, he healed it up like Judgment Day. If you ask me, his healin's better'n the Shrine Fountain, lots better'n the Fountain! Just 'Snap!' and me arm's good as new."

By the time Blackie finished his oats, he had a line of men complaining of headaches, sprains, and something called "the runs." Archie and Ritchie took charge, questioned each man about his malady and demanded a copper coin for Blackie's services. Full of oats, Blackie went along with it cheerfully, touching heads and throats and other organs. He didn't like treating festering sores, but the pus dried when the horn touched them. The men were so grateful that even that wasn't so bad.

The men had all been healed by the time Prince George came by to check on Blackie. "You all right here, Blackie?"

"Oh, we takin' real good care of him, me lord," said Ritchie, saluting.

Prince George looked him over. Blackie seemed comfortable with the carters, standing by the fire under a blanket, bathed and brushed. He'd eaten his oats, as well as peas, pears, and the nutcakes the troopers had given him.

The Prince nodded, "Well, all right then. If you need me, Blackie, I'm over with the officers under the banners. We leave with the vanguard at dawn."

"Don't you worry 'bout the unicorn," said Archie. "We're used to carin' for our horses."

"Horses, yes," said the Prince, looking around. "Let's have a look at these horses."

Ritchie and Archie took the Prince behind the carts where the horses were gathered in a makeshift corral. Prince George shook his head at them.

"Small, aren't they? Are they trained to saddle?"

"Well, they'll take a rider if needs be," said Archie. "Mostly they pulls carts, drags logs, plows fields."

Prince George walked around, counting the horses. "Looks like you got eighteen here. That's good. Not really warhorses, but we've got to use what we've got."

"You don't want our horses, me lord!" exclaimed Archie in alarm.

"Don't worry, man. You'll get them back after the campaign."

"But our carts—they's useless without horses!"

"Might as well burn 'em for firewood!" cried another carter.

The Prince shrugged. "Sorry, friends. We need horses for the soldiers. We all have to sacrifice to keep the army moving."

Looking at the weeping carters fondling their horses, Blackie decided he might as well stay with the officers tonight. He walked with Prince George to their pine shelter.

"I'll send a couple spearmen to guard those horses," said the Prince. "Those carters will run off with them if we don't watch out."

Blackie thought of the oats and nutcakes the carters had given him.

"Those humans are going to miss their horses," he said to himself. "At least, their broken arms and goiters are healed."

CHAPTER TWENTY-FIVE

Campaigning

The horses stamped around next morning while the carters wept over them, brokenhearted at giving up their beasts.

"The plowin', next spring, what'll I do?"

"Me wife can't carry them furs to the fair on her back!"

As Prince George approached to inspect the mounts, Archie hugged his horse like a sister. "Poor old Em'ly, sixteen years in the family! What'll they do to you now? Will anyone remember to watch your bad foot?"

Full of questions, the horses turned to Blackie. He tried to explain what was happening, but they couldn't understand. Finally, he shrugged. "Don't worry, don't worry. There's plenty of clover and oats where you're going."

"But why?" whinnied Emily. The other horses echoed her. "Why do these humans pull us away from our masters?"

"I guess," said Blackie with a sigh, "it's the lead human of the herd. This is what he wants."

"Oh," he groaned to the Knights' horses, grazing at the edge of the field, "I don't like this! I feel sorry for the poor things. They don't know what's happening to them."

A stallion whisked him in the face with his tail. "Who says you're s'pposed to like it? Trouble with you, boy, you spend your life on detached duty. You have no idea what it's like trottin' in column with the army all day, followin' orders every minute of your life. Scoutin',

332

now, scoutin's good duty if you're young and strong, but it gives you wrong ideas of a horse's life."

Blackie looked over to Prince George who was lifting Em'ly's head to look into her mouth. Archie had an arm over the horse.

The Prince shook his head. "This mare, how old is she?"

Archie kicked the ground. He scratched his head. "Don't know, me lord. We stopped countin' at twenty-two."

"No, no!" Prince George pushed Em'ly aside. "We can't use such horses! They'd break down at a run. Nags, jades, I've never seen such poultry! The Gypsies have better horses than these."

"But my lord," the Commander insisted, "we can't refuse them all! We've got to mount our troops."

"It's no use putting men on hacks." Prince George pointed to the youngest horses. "We can take these three, that one, and those. The others, send them back to the carts, and bring up the next bunch. Let's get on with this."

Blackie was cheered when Em'ly was returned to her master. Archie wept with joy while the men losing their horses cried with envy and anger. All in all, it was a miserable business. Blackie thought less than ever of humans when he saw the whole day wasted in wrangling over the beasts. He felt dirty when he carried Prince George to headquarters at the end of the day.

The Prince shook his head at the Commander, standing to receive him. "You know, my lord, I insisted on inspecting the horses myself to stop the bribery. Turns out, none of these horses is much good."

The Commander shrugged. "That's why officers take bribes, my lord. You can still turn away the worst horses, but you keep the troops happy. They think they have a little control over their lives."

"You know, that's not sound, Commander. It's dishonorable! The consuls of Rome were kings of bribery in their provinces, but they didn't permit peculation in the ranks."

"Peculation, my lord?"

"You know what I mean."

That night, the carters brought the Prince a load of hay.

"It's not a bribe, me lord!" Archie protested. "It's for the holy beast. We've got to leave half the carts behind tomorrow. We don't have enough horses to carry the hay."

Prince George looked at Blackie and nodded his head. "Thanks, my man, we can use it if it's surplus."

"Oh, it's surplus, all right. It's surplus!"

Blackie happily ate the hay pitched down to him. Prince George frowned when he discovered a barrel of beer under the hay, but the officers lined up with their cups.

"For morale, my lord," said the Commander at the head of the line, "the troops' morale."

As hungry as he felt, Blackie ate like he would devour the whole heap of hay at once.

"Don't eat too much, boy," warned the stallion, chewing on the other side of the heap. "You'll make yourself sick."

"I know, I know," said Blackie, "but I can't stop. I've been hungry since we left the Shrine."

"Well, you'd better take care, young unicorn. Travelin' with the army's no picnic."

Blackie tried to take care, but the army moved so slowly that he kept falling asleep on the road. In order to move as many troopers as possible, the officers had decided to double them up on the strongest horses until they could find more mounts. Not only did the horses creep along with two men on their backs, but they rested twice as often which drove the Prince wild with frustration.

"A gaggle of geese would walk faster than this army!" he complained at the Headquarters camp. "The Huns rode eighty miles a day. These clodhoppers don't cover twenty! It'll take us weeks to reach the City at this rate!"

"Oh, Prince," said the Commander, warming his hands, "we don't do so badly. With the Lord's help, we'll do better tomorrow."

"How?" cried the Prince. "Donkeys run faster than these plowhorses! The men would march faster on foot."

"True, my lord, we're slower than the Guards you're used to," said the Commander with a shrug. "But most armies ride farm horses. We just have to get the best out of the beasts."

Dropping onto a barrel by the fire, Prince George held his head in his hands. "I don't think they have a best. Slow and slowest—that's all you'll get from them."

"Don't worry, my lord," assured the Commander. "We've got a secret weapon. You're sitting on it."

The Prince looked down. "Wha . . . what?"

The Commander pointed. "The barrel you're sitting on. Water from the Fountain. Now that you've screened the nags, we'll dose them with holy water to give them speed. Just a sip or two in their regular drink, and they'll run like racehorses. Nothing to a unicorn, of course, but a steady pace for horses."

Prince George straightened up at once. "Oh, yes, Shrine water, good thinking. That'll keep them running. I think, my lord, I've had enough beer. The Princess drinks water on campaign."

"We always carry Shrine water for injuries," explained the Commander. "Don't need it this time with the unicorn to handle sick call."

Blackie felt dismayed. Sick call, they name it! Once again, he saw the humans depending on him, expecting miracles. They want him to scout ahead all day, then stay awake at night to treat injuries. It had been a mistake to heal those carters in the first place. Papa was right—sometimes, you have to hide your talents.

"Now they call on me to heal every saddlesore and chilblain in the army. It's not fair."

"Me lords, if you permit," someone called. It was Ritchie, leading up a limping man. They pulled off their hats to the officers, as Ritchie pointed to the man's foot.

"If it please your lordships, Perse, here, cut his foot choppin' wood. The axehead flew off. If we could borry the unicorn for a moment to heal him up?"

"Sure, sure," said the Master with a gesture, "you can take him. We don't need him now."

"Don't need me," thought Blackie sourly as Ritchie pulled him away from the fire by his mane. He shivered as Ritchie petted his nose.

"Just touch your horn down there, unicorn, right there on that bloody gash. Good. Hold on, man. He'll heal you in a trice."

Blackie swung his horn to the foot. The soldier sighed as the wound closed up.

"Oh, unicorn, much better, much better. Now, can you heal me boot? It's sliced right through the leather there."

The army next day had a good run. Dosed with Shrine water, the horses trotted all morning despite an icy rain that turned the trail to slush. Blackie ran ahead of the army until his hooves grew numb and his legs felt frozen to his thighs. He jogged along with head down, blinking icy drops from his eyelashes.

They reached St. Catherine's by dusk. The monks welcomed Prince George with soup and hot drinks. Blackie enjoyed a couple pitchforks of good hay and a rubdown from the novices while Prince George looked over the refugees for men who could carry a spear. He found twenty likely men, armed them with weapons collected from the raiders Blackie had destroyed, and mounted them on the few horses the monks had not eaten. Next day, they moved on to find fifty spearmen under Baron Chine, waiting in a valley along the road.

The Baron waved happily as Blackie trotted up to his fire. After the greeting, Baron Chine rattled away like an innkeeper.

"No, no, my lord Prince, I wouldn't miss this action. My neighbors are holed up like rabbits, afraid to ride out. Even Count Bork's staying home though his lordship could call out two hundred as easy as a dozen. Me, I figure on the rewards for loyal peers. Plenty of bad barons have thrown in with Prince Vile, so the faithful will share their lands after they're killed. You'll put in a word for me, won't you, my lord? Just a hint to the Empress, if you will, that I'd be grateful for the long fields of Baron Styge. That'd be most satisfactory, unless she cares to award me the whole barony."

Blackie walked to the horses sniffing for dripping grass spears scattered among the brush in the field. Ignoring Blackie, the horses stared warily at each other. They were all strangers, so there was some jostling over status, but the humans pulled out the troublemakers and the rest settling down to graze.

Blaring horns disturbed the camp a half-hour later. Men grabbed spears as another group of riders sloshed into the field. Prince George ran to find Blackie, but it turned out to be Baron Gorse bringing his men to the army. He explained that his neighbor, Lord Chine, had convinced him to join up.

"Yes, me lords," he said, rubbing his hands before the sputtering fire, "he promised me the big reward. I'm puttin' my bid in for the lands of Lord Swart that sits empty while he runs around with Hellhounds and dragons. When Chine told me you had a unicorn to do the heavy fightin', that convinced me!"

Another baron trailed up an hour later, so the lords decided to rest where they were and continue toward Mandor, next morning. As it turned out, they gave up on sleeping before midnight as the cold rain increased till it soaked the blankets and smothered the fires. The men would be miserable whether huddled under trees or shivering on horseback, so everyone took a big dose of Shrine water, and they pushed out on a night march.

As usual, Blackie splashed ahead of the army on scouting duty. The rain washed away odors here, so he had to peer through the drizzle as best he could. At least, they'd left the dark pines of the high country behind. With only scattered branches and the few brown leaves remaining in the lower forest, Blackie could spy through bare tree trunks while Prince George dozed on his neck, wrapped in his warm bearskin.

Any raiders or bandits must have been hiding in their dens. Blackie saw no humans until dawn when Prince George pulled up at the haunted hostel. After the officers came up, Prince George rode slowly about the blackened ashes, telling once again the story of the hostel. Sensing the curse on the site, the horses stepped nervously.

Sir Anthony made the sign of the Cross. "I remember you showing us this hostel three years ago. Good thing you burnt it down, hateful place."

"Oh, I'm not the one that torched it," corrected the Prince. "I thought of burning it, probably should have done it, but we just tried to sanitize the inn. Lord Godfrey bolted down the door over the black tunnel."

Sir Anthony cleared his throat.

"Rain or no rain, my lord, the army can't ride much further this morning. Why don't I stay on guard against Hellions bursting out of the ground while you search out a stopping place a mile or two further on? Something on high ground with dry wood for fires, if you can find it. More weather like this, and we'll have a sick army. Your unicorn will have to work overtime to heal all the colds."

Blackie snorted grumpily as the Prince agreed, "Good idea. But keep watch, Brother Knight. Who knows what could rise out of this cesspool!"

Clouds were heavy, this morning. There was no glimpse of the sun as Blackie splashed through low spots in the road. Everything was soaked and dripping. Blackie's hooves were clogged with mud, his mane plastered to his neck. He blew out steam with every breath.

"Keep your eyes open, Blackie," said the Prince. "Visibility's low, so you'll have to pick the campsite for the army. It must be wide enough for six hundred men and high enough to keep us out of the runoff. As for shelter, looks like it'll be bearskins and cloaks today."

"Oh, for the Shrine," thought Blackie, shaking water off his horn. "Why didn't I stay up there? This lower world is miserable enough at any time, but it feels worse after the joys of the Shrine. There's no rain up there, no snow, no mud! A crust of bread by the Fountain is better than a feast down here, and you don't have humans pestering you to heal them. If the Princess had been at the Shrine—and Mama—I'd have stayed there forever."

Though he circled the open land for an hour, Blackie was unable to find proper shelter for the army. He finally had to settle on a thorny field rising a foot or two above the flood.

"Pathetic," complained the Prince, kicking through the prickly burrs. "Totally inadequate, but I guess this place is as good as we'll find in a downpour. The troops won't be happy. I swear, I'd rather have a snowstorm than a miserable rain like this."

The complaints were loud when the exhausted army straggled up through the mud, the horses even more bitter than the men. "You trying to kill us off, unicorn? Do you hate us? You must have hunted hard to find this mudhole—nothing to eat here, nowhere to sleep!"

Prince George told the men that this was the best to be found. Blackie just shrugged and closed his eyes. He dropped to sleep where he stood in the mud and woke about midafternoon, shivering to find the rain turning to big sloppy flakes of snow that splashed white on his coat.

Everyone was coughing and sneezing and complaining. Prince George roused the army to travel on for better shelter. They splashed off through a half-foot of cold mud to push as far as possible before the tired horses ran down again, despite their dose of Shrine water.

The army was alone on the road this day. Blackie saw no bugs, no birds, no beasts, just the file of tired riders passing scattered trees under a flat gray sky. They plodded a pitifully few miles before darkness came on. Sir Sebastian picked the camp site this time, but it was no better than Blackie's field this morning. At least, the drizzle gradually stopped and the troopers were able to raise the officer's tents, though the scrappy trees provided little fuel for fires. Prince George shook his head at the troopers trying to light piles of wet thorns.

Blackie sniffed out a chain of gray leaves creeping under the brush. He had eaten only a few mouthfuls before being called away to heal a score of coughing, feverish spearmen and a bowman from Chine who'd fallen onto his own arrows. Blackie was not surprised, next morning, to hear that a dozen men had slipped off in the dark to head home.

"They even left their horses," a sergeant reported to the Commander.

"Of course, they did," said the Commander. "We can watch the horses, but no one can stop an unhappy man from sneaking away in the dark."

Sandor slapped his boot with a whip. "If I had dogs, me lords, I'd run 'em down in twenty minutes."

"Let them go," advised the Commander. "Remember Gideon's army. We want only hearty souls, those eager to face the enemy."

Whether eager to face the enemy or not, most of the soldiers were unhappy about another muddy ride this morning. The Knights' troopers saddled quickly after bugle call, but the barons' men hung around their smoky fires, spitting and complaining.

"They need discipline," said Prince George, frowning at a squad of men leaning on their spears while watching one man saddle his horse. "Sir Otley would whip this rabble into shape in no time!"

"Turn me loose on them," begged Sandor. "I'll get 'em riding."

"What they need," suggested Sir Sebastian, "is sergeants. Promote the biggest of them, give them cudgels, and pay them double to keep the troops movin'."

"That's an idea," said the Commander, "but it's easier to just give them Shrine water. A half-cup for each horse and man, that'll hustle them along."

Prince George turned to Blackie, who tossed his head, spraying icy drops from his horn. "We'll head out, now, and wait for the army down the road."

"If you please, my lord, look for real shelter this time," begged Sir Sebastian. "A good night's sleep would cheer us all."

The Prince shrugged. "Well, we'll find villages when we turn south, but I don't want the men too comfortable. I'm afraid we'd never collect them if they got settled into huts. We have to push along. Speed, speed, speed—that's what we want!"

"The Shrine water will help that," promised the Commander. "We'll keep moving as long as our barrels hold out."

Blackie braced his legs for the Prince to mount. Sir Sebastian handed up shield and spear, and Blackie headed back to the road with Prince George.

"God bless you," called the Commander.

"Oh, Blackie," wailed the Prince, pulling his bearskin around him, "this army is slower than snails! The Knights are ready enough, but these mountain men, you'd think they weren't eager to knock heads. I don't know if we have enough Shrine water to keep them moving."

Blackie poked along to stay fairly close to the army. Happily, the day got more comfortable as the wind changed, blowing away the clouds. A bit of sun warmed the air and the water began draining away.

The road continued empty until they came to forest again, scattered shrubs first, then more and more trees until the riders were closed in by gray trunks and bare branches. The only creatures Blackie saw was a family of deer that crossed ahead of them, looking back with upright ears.

By noon, they reached Mandor. Prince George swung to ground before the closed gates of the castle.

"This place still looks empty. We better make sure there's no enemies inside to take the army by surprise."

Spear in hand, Prince George roamed around the castle while Blackie sniffed moldy leaves along the moat. He was glad when the Prince returned.

"No sign of anyone. Let's ride on. With luck, we'll reach Cranch before nightfall. With this army behind me, I can settle some scores there."

Just beyond the castle, Blackie passed the eastern crossroads to Herne. They didn't pause this time, but continued west through the forest. Blackie trotted over broken limbs and slippery leaves in the trail. Bare branches rattled above. Occasionally, Blackie could snatch a mouthful of dry yellow leaves, just enough to rouse his hunger. Otherwise, he saw nothing worth eating.

At sundown, Blackie began looking for the next camp. He found a hamlet hidden back in the trees, a dozen huts abandoned by the woodsmen living there. The huts provided shelter for the officers, but the men had to scatter among the trees. At least, there was plenty of wood in the forest, so the troopers huddled around blazing fires. Now, Prince George began complaining that the fires would attract attention.

"The flames stand out in this leafless forest like bonfires in a hayfield. The dragon could spot us a mile away."

Blackie was more concerned about the lack of food. Bread was short among the men and all the oats were gone. The rotting leaves on the ground weren't worth eating. He tried digging up roots with his horn, but the muddy roots were dense and chewy. He might as well eat sticks.

He went to sleep hungry and dreamed of hayfields until Prince George woke him at midnight.

"Blackie, wake up! There's a hunting party lost in the forest. We've got to bring them back."

Blackie yawned, shivering in the wind as Prince George led him to a stump to climb on.

"They say there's twelve or fifteen men with them. If it was only five or six, we'd leave them behind, but a dozen makes a platoon of cavalry."

Though a sergeant pointed out the direction the men had gone, Blackie lost the scent in the maze of deer trails among branches so low that Prince George had to dismount and blunder after him in the darkness.

"Slow down, Blackie, slow down. Where are you? Oh, ouch!"

Prince George simply couldn't keep up in the dark. His spear caught in branches, slowing him down, and he snagged himself on sharp stubs. He gave it up when he fell into a stream. Blackie had to lead the Prince back to camp, holding to his tail. Prince George rolled up in his bearskin in the Commander's hut, leaving his wet clothes hanging from the spear before the fire while Blackie took off alone to find the lost men.

Running easily, Blackie ranged in a wide circle through the forest to pick up the scent of soldiers. When he smelled a patch of leafy bushes sheltered under a rocky bank along a stream, he stopped for a late meal.

Once he caught the scent, Blackie had little trouble sniffing out the troopers. They'd lost their way at dusk chasing a pig that pulled them down a path until it disappeared into thorns. When they gave up on the pig, they'd blundered about in the darkness until they exhausted themselves. They settled around a fire that Blackie could smell a half-mile away. The humans were snorting and coughing in their sleep when Blackie trotted up, their tired horses tied to branches.

A dozing guard screamed when Blackie poked him with his horn. Waking suddenly, the soldiers tumbled over each other, grabbing for weapons until they recognized Blackie. They shouted with relief.

"Thank the Lord! It's the holy beast come to save us!"

The men crowded about Blackie, petting him, hugging him. "Take us back to our mates, dear unicorn! We was afeard we'd be left behind!"

"No, no," said a deep-voiced man with an axe. "'Tis better to wait for dawn. Even with the unicorn, we'd wear ourselves out stumbling around the dark forest at night."

Blackie nodded at that, so the men relaxed about him. Blackie healed their scratches and bruises while the axeman chopped more wood for the fire. Blackie positioned himself upwind of the fire to keep watch. The men settled around him like chicks about a hen, curling as close as they could to sleep peacefully.

Blackie listened to the wind whistling, the fire crackling, the branches clicking above. He slept lightly, waking at a sneeze from a sleeper or a howl in the distance, but the night passed peacefully.

The men rose at dawn, tired and complaining. The axeman hushed them fiercely. "Stop that bellyachin'! I don't want to hear it!"

"But Calder," cried a man, "we're hungry!"

"So you're hungry! I'm hungry, too, but no man can gripe when the Lord sends a unicorn to save him from his own foolishness!"

Calder got the men in order to follow Blackie at a good pace toward the camp. By the time they reached the huts, the army had departed. Prince George waited by a declining fire with two spearmen. The Prince jumped up when he saw Blackie.

"You found them. Good, I thought you would."

"O' course, he found us," said Calder. "He's a tower of strength, this unicorn."

Prince George looked Calder up and down. "So you're an axeman? What's your name?"

"I'm Calder, me lord, Calder the woodchopper."

"Well, Calder, I like a good axeman. Can you handle your tool?"

Calder brandished his axe in one hand. "To be sure, me lord, I'm a master with the chopper! Set me to the tallest tree at daybreak, and I'll give you logs and firewood by noon."

Prince George nodded approvingly. "I like your spirit, man. You remind me of someone I know. Well, seems to me, we better ride on while we can. The army camped here all night, so there'll be no forage around here. I've got a couple loaves of bread and some goat meat, a mouthful for every man, but we'll have to find feed for the horses on the trail."

The men cheered at the mention of food, but the horses grew restive at the smell of the bread. Blackie had to calm them, promising that they'd find food shortly. Once the humans had eaten, Prince George surveyed the men.

"Calder, you'll be my sergeant. I'll ride on Blackie at the column head. You take the tail and keep the men moving. I don't want stragglers to hold us back."

"There'll be no stragglers!" promised Calder, grimly patting his axe. "I promise you that, me lord."

Prince George pointed to a couple men in green and brown. "You bowmen, don't I recognize you from Furland?"

"Oh, yes, me lord, from Furland, that's us!" cried one. "We saw you at the great shoot-out when you killed the granddaddy bear."

The other nodded vigorously, wiping his nose on a sleeve. "I helped pull that monster off of you."

"Oh, yes, I thought I knew you. And the rest of you spearmen—You, there, where's your weapon?"

The man looked down, stammering, "Oh, me . . . me lord, the spear got lost last night. It stuck in a tree as I rode along, just sprung out of me hands, and I couldn't find it in the dark. I still got me dagger, though."

He waved his dagger in the air. Prince George laughed shortly.

"Lost your spear, did you? Most captains would whip you for that, but I've lost a weapon or two, myself. I'm sure we'll find a spear for you soon enough."

Blackie stepped to the Prince while the men mounted their tired horses. Prince George paused and turned to the troopers again.

"One last thing, keep an eye out for the dragon. If you see her, don't try to fight. Just scatter in all directions. Hide near water, if you can, and wait until she's gone to assemble again."

Blackie set off slowly when the men were mounted. After running all day and night on little food, Blackie was exhausted. His body felt heavy, his hooves sore. Just holding up his head to keep watch was an effort. He slipped on leaves and lurched against trees, drawing yelps of protest from the Prince.

This was a slow, painful ride. The column was often stopped by cries. "Horse down!" "Man off!" Blackie would wait, sleeping on his feet, until the word was passed up the line to head off again. Once, Blackie was pulled around by the shout, "Unicorn, unicorn, injured man!"

Blackie had to trot by the shivering horses with frothy muzzles. He found a spearman who'd fallen off his horse onto the broken stub of a limb sticking out into the road.

Prince George jumped down and directed the humans to hold the crying man so Blackie could treat the injury. Tired as he was, Blackie found it difficult to heal the bleeding wound. Just placing his horn on the man's shoulder didn't help. Blackie had to wake enough to force the healing spark.

Prince George urged him, "Do it, Blackie, just do it! We can't dilly-dally in the road. We haven't even reached Dorth."

Annoyed, Blackie took a breath and strained. He felt the jolt of healing power.

The spearman jerked in his breath. "Yes, oh, yes, me lord! The holy beast has done it! I'm healt, healt! Even the boil on me neck don't hurt."

"About time," mumbled Prince George, leading Blackie back to the head of the file. "I swear, any more delays, I'm leaving them behind."

They mounted again. Blackie followed the road across a stream where a small furry animal scuttled into the brush. Half awake, he settled into a steady trot until he started at strange smells near a fork where a lane entered the road. He paused and sniffed into the trees.

Prince George woke up, grasping the spear. "What is it, boy? What do you smell?"

Hidden in the wet brush a few yards off the road, Blackie found three empty wagons. Scattered about in the brush were clothes and bits of harness. Prince George kicked through the litter while Blackie sniffed a broken crock beside a wheel wrapped in dry vines.

"What is it, me lord?" asked one of the bowmen.

"Looks like raiders took a couple families here," said the Prince, picking up a wooden spoon. "Probably refugees. But these wagons—"

He kicked the side of the closest.

"Look, Calder, there's brush here and grass for the horses to eat. Knock this wagon apart for me. It'll make a rousing fire. I think we'll camp here where the horses can graze. We'll get snug for a good rest before running on to catch up to the army. You, Blackie, sniff out a fat deer for dinner."

CHAPTER TWENTY-SIX

Hunting

Before Blackie could protest, Prince George shooed him off into the forest with the bowmen from Furland. "A good, fat deer, Blackie, you know what we need. Once we're fed, we'll catch up with the army in no time."

Blackie obediently trotted up the trail ahead of the bowmen until they came to a cross-path, a mile up the lane.

"This is the place," whispered one of the bowmen. He settling himself on a log behind a screening branch where a few late leaves flapped in the breeze.

"You take cover over there, Milo. Now, unicorn, all you gotta do is make a big circle upwind from here. Chase the beasts down that there path."

Blackie trotted off, repeating to himself in a tired voice, "A good, fat deer—a good, fat deer."

He circled off to the left as instructed, then turned to thread through the trees over twigs and wet leaves. Almost immediately, he found fresh scent. Hearing the soft snuff of a deer, he turned away from the path. He could make out the deer's outline, bedded down in a pile of leaves under a patch of saplings. It lay motionless, achingly aware of him, holding its breath until the dark figure passed by without noticing.

"Here goes," thought Blackie, and rushed straight into the saplings. The deer exploded into flight, a large doe flipping her tail as she jumped through the trees in the direction of the hunters, a small, brown fawn scrambling behind. Blackie stopped, panting. He felt sick at heart.

346

He barely had time to sniff the bed of the deer, scented with the warmth of their bodies, before he heard the shouts of the men. "Here she comes, Milo! Shoot, shoot! Oh, too bad, the little one got away!"

Blackie limped down the path to find the men standing over the doe. She bled from arrows driven into her chest and belly. She kicked a little and rolled her eyes.

"Horray, unicorn, horray!" cried the humans, waving their bows. "Look here, dinner on the hoof! What a tracker you are! I told 'em it wouldn't take you no time at all."

Blackie stared at the doe, horrified. "What have I done? The deer, my friends. I helped the humans kill this mother!" He jerked around, shuddering, and ran back in the trees.

The men yelled after him, "Unicorn, where you goin'? Come back! We wants you to carry the meat!"

Blackie ran further into the forest where he could weep without smelling the doe. "That poor creature!"

He stood among dry grass under a sheltering hill. He couldn't eat a bite. Everything stuck in his throat. A little stream trickled merrily beside him, but his thoughts were filled with horror. He could imagine the humans at work back in camp, singing as they gutted and flayed, butchered and broiled.

A family of deer came down a path to drink at a pool downstream from Blackie. First the buck, looking warily to all sides, then another doe and two fawns. Blackie stood stiffly, watching them drink. They lifted their heads, sniffed the wind, and moved on, the buck leading the way up the next hill.

"I drove that doe to her death," Blackie thought. "What would those deer say if they knew that?"

Blackie stood in a cloud of misery, unable to move, unable to think. He shivered with cold, his mind filled by that doe lying in the dirt. Over and over, he repeated, "I'm sorry, I'm so sorry."

The soldiers were waiting impatiently when Blackie finally returned to camp that afternoon. Prince George stalked up and down the trail, calling to him.

"Where've you been? We've been ready to travel for hours. I want to make Cranch before dark."

"The sooner we leave this place, the better," thought Blackie, moving upwind of the fire to escape the smell of blood and flesh. The men threw dirt on the ashes. They mounted to ride. Blackie turned his eyes from the packets of meat tied to the saddles.

Prince George hustled them on this afternoon, seconded by Calder, who shook his axe and threatened laggards with a pounding. It was too cold to stand in the wind, so everyone moved stiffly into a riding column with Prince George and Blackie a quarter-mile ahead.

Blackie's muscles loosened once he fell into a steady trot, and his senses sharpened. The road they followed was a stinking mess of trampled mud, chewed bushes, scattered trash. Any blind creature could tell where the army rested, watered, cooked its meals. Prince George pointed out the track of another group of horsemen joining the army from the north just before the bridge at Dorth.

Across the bridge, Blackie and the Prince found weeping townsmen laboring to reset the great gate pulled from the wall when the army broke through to strip the homes and sheds of supplies. Most of the workers ignored them, barely reacting when Prince George rode up, except to give Blackie a startled look.

A tall man in a blue cap walked up to them, wiping his hands on his jacket. He squinted his eyes at Prince George.

"You looking for an army? They headed west before noon. If you looking for anything else, you might as well give it up. There's nothing left to take."

"So what happened here?" asked the Prince.

"What do you think happened?" cried the man. "That army cleared us out, that's what, took everything we had! Food, horses, blankets—they spread out like cockroaches and looted every house, stole everything but the dirt on the floor."

Prince George looked down the street. He could see women collecting bits of furniture, kitchen pots, and bedding thrown out into the dirt.

"What about Baron Dorth? Didn't he sic his boarhounds on them?"

"The Baron!" cried the man, indignantly. "Baron did nothing. He just set behind his castle walls and watched us get stripped bare. Baron admitted afterwards to the headman that he was afraid to send out his boarhounds. That lot would have cooked 'em up like turkeys. They'd as soon eat a dog as a duck. 'Course, they gave us a paper for the Crown to pay back everthing they took, but what good's a paper? What do we eat this winter? How do we plant, next spring, without seed for the crops?"

"Surely," suggested Prince George, "surely, if the Baron escaped the pillaging, he'll help you get through the winter."

The man stared at him like he'd lost his senses.

"What you thinking, man? Old Baron empty his storerooms for us? That's not gonna happen. Traffic goes one way to Castle Dorth—straight from our fields to Baron's belly. Oh, no, more of 'em!"

The man gave a jump at the thump of horse hooves on the bridge. The tired troopers straggled across the bridge and pulled up along the road. Calder rode over to the Prince.

"Ho, me lord, any rations for us here?"

Prince George pointed to Castle Dorth. "That castle's full of food, but I can't think of any way of getting to it."

"Well," suggested Calder, "can the unicorn knock down the door for us?"

"Oh, no," thought Blackie, pulling back, "not for anyone! I'm not breaking my horn on those planks."

Prince George gave him a regretful pat. "I'm afraid not. The unicorn's a mighty warrior, but he can't knock down castle doors. We need another way in. If I had Gypsy medicines, I could offer the Baron a drink, but I don't have anything."

"So, me lord, we have to ride on hungry?" asked Calder.

"Yes, sir," said the tall man, "you just ride on. And tell any other soldiers to stay away. Nothing to eat here at Dorth but rats and roaches, and I suspect we'll see few of them now we been looted."

"Well, that's a bust," said Prince George to Calder, riding back to the men waiting expectantly along the road.

"What you find, me lord?" cried one the spearmen. "Any grub in that town?"

Calder shook his head at the riders. "No, boys, the army got to 'em first. That town's scoured clean down to the pigsties."

The troopers sent up a cry, but Calder turned away, shrugging his shoulders at the Prince. "Well, me lord, you can't expect to feed hearty if you foller six hundred hungry men."

"I guess not," said the Prince, thoughtfully. "You know, I'm thinking that we should leave the road, take to the trails again."

"But, me lord," protested Calder, "you know how slow we go on them trails. How'd that help us with anything?"

"Look." The Prince scratched a line in the dirt with the Nail. "Here's the road we're on. A hundred miles or so, we meet this north-south road and turn towards the City, but if we angle southwest from here—"

He drew a line crossing from one road to the other. "We save a couple days' ride and wind up ahead of the army. Surely, we can find food out in the countryside."

"Sure," said Calder, growing interested, "out there, the unicorn can hunt down more deer for us. The army's grown so big it's sure to gobble any food along the road, but the forest's just a big game preserve for us. We have men enough to keep off bandits, but not so many that we have to spend all our time feeding 'em."

"Oh, no!" thought Blackie in alarm. "Not more hunting! I'll sniff out gardens for them, if we find such, but I'm not chasing any deer. I do hope we turn off the road, though. The stink here would kill a polecat."

The troopers protested the idea of leaving the road, but Prince George warned them that they'd starve on the road.

"You see already that the army's like a flock of locusts, eating up everything ahead of us. If we cut across country, we're sure to find fresh meat."

"No bread, though," objected a spearman. "Meat's heavy rations without bread, not good for me guts."

"But Donal," Calder pointed out, "if we stay on the road, we'll have no meat and no bread. I like something in me belly, even if it is all meat."

The other men looked doubtful, but no one said anything against the idea.

"So there it is, men," said Prince George. "We ride across country, living off the land, and catch up with the army above the City. Also, we'll be safer from the dragon. It's a lot easier for her to spot a big army on the highroad than a small company in the trees."

"Well, I don't like it," said Donal. "I get beat up on them narrow paths. Every swingin' branch takes a smack at me!"

"This time, though," said the Prince, walking to Blackie, "we won't be riding in the dark. Riding's always rough at night. We'll travel by daylight."

Only the Prince seemed enthusiastic about heading off into the forest. Even Blackie saw problems in guiding this bunch through the trees. For one thing, these humans had no instinct for the field. If they'd watched where they were going in the first place, they wouldn't have gotten lost. And now, they wanted to hurry. They expected him to nurse them along at top speed—impossible on game trails.

Sure enough, the men began complaining as soon as Blackie turned down a forest path to angle southwest. He brushed between branches as Prince George flattened on his neck to pass through the trees.

The cry went up immediately. "Slow down, slow down! It's too close here, no room for horse or man!"

Blackie ignored the cries and concentrated on following the trail, which turned out to be fairly comfortable. It passed hills at their lowest point and crossed streams over shallows. Still, there were plenty of clawing briers and tangling vines to hold back the riders, while waving branches whacked them often enough to keep them awake.

Blackie slipped easily through the path, but the horses tired quickly and had to stop to rest. Hungry as they were, they paused to sniff around every leafless bush along the trail. All in all, the squad made little progress before dusk came on and Blackie had to hunt for a stopping point with water and grazing for the hungry horses.

Sitting at a flickering fire in a protected gully, the soldiers unwrapped their packets of venison for dinner. Blackie moved up the hill where he could watch for trouble without smelling the meat too strongly. He chewed twigs from a broken branch.

"Leading meat-eaters to fight Hellions," he said to himself, "this isn't going to get any better. If it weren't for the Princess, I'd turn my back on them right now. Back at the Nest, I play with deer, instead of killing them."

They traveled peacefully next day, but that evening, Prince George started pestering Blackie again.

"You know we ate up our deer meat today. You've got to hunt more food for us, Blackie. How can the men fight if they're hungry?"

Blackie shook his head. If the men wanted meat, they could hunt it down for themselves. The Prince kept after him.

"Blackie, you've got to help me feed these men. It's only fair. You can eat grass and leaves, but these men have to have meat. It's meat that gives them the strength to keep going."

Stubbornly, Blackie tried to ignore him. He reached down and bit a withered leaf from a vine. Prince George slapped him on the neck.

"I'm disappointed at you, Blackie! Here we are, pushing as hard as we can to rescue the Princess. On a march like this, everyone has to sacrifice for the good of the army. What would the Princess say if she knew you refused to cooperate? You know she's in danger. She's looking for us to show up and drive off the enemy. We're already weeks behind schedule, and now you hold us back even more!"

Shaking his head, Prince George stumbled into the lane, dragging his spear. Blackie looked after him, feeling terrible.

The Prince was right. They were riding to save the Princess. The soldiers were slow enough as it was, but hungry humans would be even slower. They needed meat. In summertime, they could eat the fruits and vegetables they grew, but the forest had nothing they could stomach in winter. Deer, though, were his friends. How could he betray his friends?

He took another bite from the vines. The leaves tasted bitter in his mouth. Look at him, feeding while the humans went hungry. Didn't the Prince share his carrots and cakes? Hadn't he'd given Shrine bread to Blackie until it was gone? How could Blackie let the Prince starve when the forest was full of game, easy to find if you were a unicorn?

Blackie looked at all the soldiers working together to set up camp. Two guards sat in place watching the trail while other soldiers piled springy branches to keep sleepers out of the mud. Calder was chopping up a dead tree for the fire. Only Blackie was off eating by himself.

Blackie took a breath and sighed. If he had to do it, he'd better do it quickly so he didn't have to think about it. He walked over and nudged the Prince, who nodded and told the bowmen to follow Blackie into the forest. Leading the humans, Blackie tramped up a path, sniffing the air. A mile beyond the noise, he caught the fresh scent of deer to windward. He stopped, sick at heart, as the humans squeezed close to him.

"What is it, boy?" whispered the bowman. "You smell a beast out there? Here we go again, Milo. Spread yourself and notch your arrow. He'll run down the meat for us."

Struggling to keep his mind clear, Blackie crept up a narrow trail that circled the deer scent. Once he felt himself beyond the deer, he turned through the trees, stepping lightly across crawling roots and crunching twigs.

"Okay," he thought, pausing beside a fallen log. "This is good enough. Let's get it over with."

He kicked the log with a thump that knocked off bits of wet bark. He kicked it again, then jumped over it and rushed between the trees, crashing through bushes to make as much noise as possible. He didn't see the deer, but he heard the bowman shout.

"Here, he comes! Ho, good shot, good shot! I'll finish him off with me knife!"

Blackie stopped at the deer's cry. He turned away, panting. He paused on the path. He trembled at the cheers. What had he done?

These humans were hungry. They had to eat something. Heaven knows, there's nothing to cook up in the winter forest, no berries or greens or mushrooms. Why, Blackie could barely sniff out a mouthful for himself. When you think about it, humans are lucky to be able eat meat. There's always plenty of meat in the forest. The foxes eat it.

"I wish I could eat meat!" he declared before gagging at the thought. Who could stand the smell of the cooking, the singed flesh, dripping juices?

"No, no, I wouldn't eat that stuff, not if I was starving!"

Blackie was sorry for the hungry humans, but hunting deer, those delicate runners, his friends? He couldn't do that. Deer are different from most animals. You can talk to deer, play with them. Hogs, now, they're just a lot of filthy squealers. He wouldn't hesitate to chase hogs for the humans. The problem is that hogs are rare in the forest. You seldom see hogs except in muddy swamps, though deer are everywhere. You find deer on every hillside, eating the same stuff you do. It makes sense for the humans to eat them—that's their rations.

"But not me!" cried Blackie in anguish. "I can't hunt them! I'm not going to do it—chase does and fawns to the shooters, watch them get stabbed by sharp arrows! No, no, I won't do it! No matter what, I won't be part of this hunting!"

But again, trotting back toward the camp, his mind swung to the Princess. "The Princess, my Princess—these soldiers are riding to save her! They have to be strong to fight, and meat, the meat gives them strength. Am I failing the Princess if I don't help them hunt?

"I can find the deer quickly so the humans don't waste time blundering about in the trees. They're so clumsy, poor things. A rabbit, a field mouse catches scent better than they do! The only time they smell food is when it's roasting over the fire. I've seen Prince George walk ten feet from a hidden deer and not see it."

He shook his head violently, torn by the choices before him. All in all, it was a messy business getting mixed up with humans. Life was much simpler in the forest with creatures that ate properly. There, he didn't have to hunt or fight or run around at night.

"Unicorn, unicorn!"

Now, he heard humans again, calling him back to their business. Well, the Princess, the Princess—he had to keep her in mind. So long as he focused on saving the Princess, he couldn't go wrong, even if . . . even if— He shuddered again, thinking of the hunters wanting to load bleeding deer on his back. He stiffened at another thought.

"There's the dragon, of course. That's what I'm against! Fighting evil, the cruelty that enjoys pain, that's different from hunting for food. Humans are meat-eaters, even my Princess too, bless her. That's the way God made her. I can't do anything about that. And deer are stupid. If they weren't, the humans would never catch any of them. So the humans plant gardens to grow vegetables, then the deer sneak in to steal veggies and the humans shoot them for dinner. Round and round it goes. But the dragon, she's different. She'd burn up the world just for fun.

"Me, I'm a unicorn, and unicorns kill dragons. That's our fate. If I have to feed humans to do it, I guess that's my choice. I'd rather hunt hogs than deer, but I'll do what I must."

Back at camp, Blackie smelled the roasting meat before he saw the troopers. Most of the soldiers were asleep, wrapped in their blankets on their beds. The deer meat, chopped into chunks to roast faster, was tended by guards who watched the fat crackle and drip with hungry eyes.

That meat kept the men happy next day. The riders saw no settlements yet, though the trail had signs of regular travel. Expecting to meet the south road at any moment, Prince George called on Blackie to bring in another deer, so they'd have rations in hand when they reached the army.

Blackie hated the idea, but he'd talked himself into the notion that his hunting advanced the rescue of the Princess. He sullenly led the bowmen into the trees while the others made camp.

Prince George called, "Bring back a fat one!"

"A fat one!" Blackie grumbled. "He always says that. I'm not going to pick and choose my victims like a poulterer weighing chickens. The first deer gets it, whatever it is."

This time, deer seemed to be scarce. He did smell a couple fawns lying motionless in a bush. He ignored them. They wouldn't even make a snack for the men. Finally, after sniffing and circling for an hour, he discovered a big buck, but it refused to run in the right direction. It ran nearly as fast as he did, darting this way and that, and finally crashed off into the brush under a fallen tree that caught Blackie's horn in a forking limb.

That's when Blackie smelled the bear in a hole under the tree. He stopped, panting, to sniff at the dark slit barely seen through the scratchy bushes crowding the tree roots. Blackie smelled the bear strongly, but heard nothing, as he turned his head to listen.

"Well," he thought, "men can eat bear meat. I'd rather give them a bear, anyway, dumb old thing. I don't know if I can chase it over to the men, but the first thing is to roust it out of this stinking hole."

Blackie stepped through the bushes, the smell growing stronger as he squeezed toward the opening. He stretched his neck and poked his horn into the darkness. The horn hit something soft. He poked again. Nothing happened though he heard the wheeze of the bear's breath.

"That thing's asleep," he said to himself. He stepped out a hoof so he could thrust more deeply and gave the bear a sharp jab.

"Whuff!" grunted the bear

Blackie felt it shudder under his horn, so Blackie jabbed harder. This time, the bear growled and rolled a little in its den.

"Time to wake up, big guy!"

Blackie stabbed forward. He heard the bear suck in air. It twisted violently in its hole and surged outside, roaring. Blackie fell over his hooves as the bear's small, blinking eyes focused on him. The bear rose high, shaking its head, then tore after him on four great paws, bawling loudly.

Blackie rolled back, scrambling to his feet to dash away with the bear roaring after him. Blackie galloped up the trail as hard as he could run. He jumped a stream, hearing the bear crash through the branches just behind him.

"I hope those humans are ready for this!" he thought.

Up the hill he raced, pulling away, as the bear was puffing now, tired after its long nap. Blackie ignored the waiting bowmen. He raced the shortest distance to the camp, galloped up to the campfire, and leaped over the heads of the men turning to stare at him. The men scattered as the bear barreled in on them. Shrieking in terror, the horses yanked their tethers free and dashed away to all sides.

Prince George reacted quicker than anyone. He grabbed up his spear and set the butt under a boot. The bear rushed at him, the only man standing in its path, and hurled itself onto the Nail. The Prince leaped aside when the bear was speared, staying well away from its claws.

The bear went down, rolling into the fire with the spear stuck in its belly. Blackie pulled up on the path, hearing shrieks and yells. He smelled ashes and burnt fur as the soldiers came after the bear with their spears, stabbing from all sides.

Once the bear was dead, Calder stood laughing off to the side, leaning on his axe. "'Tis a perilous move, my lord, sending the unicorn after meat! I suppose he'd bring in an elephant if we had such monsters in this country."

"He's scattered all the horses," complained the Prince, tugging back and forth on the spear to yank the Nail from the bear. "We'll never find them in the forest. Blackie, you're going to have to round them up for us."

Calling back the horses was easy enough, as the creatures gathered in groups, but it took so long that the forest was dark before Blackie found them all. Back at the camp, the humans had butchered the bear and roasted the meat over their fire, leaving most of it hanging in the smoke so they would have meat for the next few days. Blackie stayed upwind with the nervous horses, trying to explain why the bear had attacked the camp.

"Well, it's good they killed the big scratcher," said a young horse, sniffing the bushes around her. "The fewer of those monsters around, the happier I am."

"Yes, but if two-legs would just eat proper," said an old mare, "we'd all be better off. Such stories I've heard of their animal-chases—the crashes, spills, heads banged, legs broken. They can grow good feed if they put themselves to it. This chasing deer and running bears, none of it makes sense to me."

"Far as that goes," said another mare, "why go riding off across the countryside in the first place? I was cozy back home with my little shed and patch of pasture. I had the garden to sniff about in wintertime, and my master gave me dry grass when it snowed."

"Yes, unicorn," asked the old mare, "what are we doing out here, anyway? I've never been gone so long from my mistress. When do we go home again?"

How could Blackie explain the situation to the horses? Telling them about battles and dragons—that wouldn't make them happy. He just shrugged and said, "Oh, you know the humans. They're always up to something."

The old mare wisely nodded her head. "Oh, they are, they are, you can't say no to that. We all know the way horses disappear. Some nag's set up happy one day, draggin' a plow, pullin' a wagon, then next day, she's gone. Maybe a new horse in her place, maybe not, but it's all the humans' doin'. Never settled, never satisfied, they are."

"Blackie, Blackie!"

It was Prince George stumbling around in the dark, stirring up the horses again. Sighing, Blackie walked through the trees to the Prince.

"Oh, there you are," said the Prince, rubbing his nose. "Do me a favor, will you? Just take a scout around the camp, check that everything's okay. We've set guards, but you know how they are. Some men get more sleep on guard duty than they do when dismissed."

Blackie snorted agreement. He slipped into the darkness to circle the camp a couple hundred yards out. His ears were up and he sniffed carefully. Finding no tasty grasses or enemies, he came back to sleep by the horses, waking only when a distant rabbit shrieked under an owl.

Mounting went smoothly, next morning, as the men were fed and the horses rested. Weather continued cold, though rising sun cast cheering rays through the tree limbs.

"We need to move faster," Prince George told Blackie. "I didn't leave the highroad to dawdle like this. I thought we'd reach the south road by now."

Blackie did his best to keep the troopers moving along the trails, ranging ahead to find the widest and most direct paths. He sniffed for forage, too, so the horses could pause for a bite, now and then. Horses ran more happily with frequent snacks. They tired less, so the rest stops were shorter. With the humans chewing their smoked meat, there was no need to hunt before they came to the highroad.

To the Prince's relief, there was no sign that the army had passed by the road. Prince George scratched his head, undecided whether his small group should scout down the road or wait for the main force to catch up.

Though anxious about the fate of the Princess, he had to admit that the long ride was shaking down the men into serious fighters. They complained less as they set up and broke camp, and each man looked to his horse and weapons. The bowmen pretty much knew their task, but Prince George worked an hour each evening with the spearmen, teaching them to support each other in battle.

He showed them how to mass their spear points when facing horsemen and to fight dirty when confronted by infantrymen, doubling up on single foes and stabbing in the back when possible.

"Eyes open! Eyes open!" he shouted. "No time to daydream in combat! Watch for weakness—the man that hesitates or swings wide! Move swiftly, shouting your war cry. Fierceness doubles your strength!"

He matched the spearmen in pairs and had them practice with reversed spears while he walked around, critiquing their form.

"Points low, points low, and watch your grip! Hey, there, Jinks, don't slide back on the spear! Use the length, but keep it under control. And watch your footwork! Keep your balance to move in, move out."

Calder watched, nodding approval. "Good training, me lord. Most of these hayseeds never faced an arrow-shower. They inherited their spears from their grandpas, use 'em to poke up the fireplace."

"Oh, the men will be okay," said the Prince, wiping his brow. "Better than the rabble following Vile, I'm sure. It's the horses I worry about. Takes serious training to make a warhorse."

If Blackie could speak, he'd tell the Prince to be very worried about the horses. The steadier the men became, the more jittery grew the horses. Not only did they sense the shift in their riders, but they hated forest travel, the long runs, strange smells, poor food. Most of all, they feared the closeness of the trees.

"You can't see here!" complained a young mare. "No fields, no pastures to look across, just trees. How can the herd stay safe? A wolf pack could climb your tail before you know it."

"What I hate," said the oldest mare, "what I hate is that everything changes so quick. No time to settle down, get comfortable, learn the points and paths of the land. Back home, I knew every inch of the countryside. I could smell my way home in the dark."

There was a chorus of agreement.

"You got it right, girl," said a gelding. "Everything's the same out here, trees and more trees, but nothing's familiar. I hate it, too!"

CHAPTER TWENTY-SEVEN

The Spy

Much as the horses hated the trees, they found it worse when they began to run into settlements again. Prince George was afraid to alert the enemy that the army was approaching, so he made his little force sneak around any village or castle that looked threatening. The hungry horses protested when they were held back from hayfields and gardens gone to seed. It was all Blackie could do to keep them moving through the fringes of the forest.

The only castle that seemed friendly flew the banner of Baron Balser. Lord Balser was a distant cousin to the Emperor. He had spent his summers in the City while Prince George grew up. Vague, harmless, the Baron was one lord that wouldn't join Prince Vile.

Leaving the troopers hidden in the trees, Prince George spied on the castle from the edge of the forest for a couple cold hours, sending Blackie to sniff for villainy around the empty village. To Blackie, it appeared that the villagers had moved peacefully inside the Castle walls. He smelled no burnings. He saw no hanging corpses or signs of looting. Only the brooding stillness spoke of fear.

The Prince took up his spear when Blackie returned. "Well, everything looks innocent here. The people have pulled into the castle. We saw girls walk to the pond for duck eggs, escorted by spearmen. It's just what you'd expect the way things stand. If the Baron's loyal, we may get news of the siege."

Mounting Blackie, the Prince guided him down the lane between village and castle, waving vigorously to the men on the castle wall who gathered as soon as the pair showed themselves. Before Prince George could identify himself, the castle folks waved their bows, yelling, "Go away! Go away, or we'll shoot!"

"Well, Blackie," said the Prince, setting his spear across Blackie's back, "this is as friendly as it gets. At least, they didn't shoot first."

Blackie half-turned, ready to run as Prince George stretched his empty arms and shouted, "Ho, the castle, I come in peace! Tell Baron Balser that George of Dacia wishes to speak with him, Prince George of Dacia!"

"Get away from here!" bellowed a hoarse voice. "The Baron don't care if you're the Prince o' Darkness! He don't talk to no one!"

"But look closer!" called the Prince. "I ride the unicorn! Surely, his lordship would welcome the holy beast!"

"The unicorn!" cried voices from the castle. Bows were lowered. There was a burst of chatter. Blackie relaxed a little. He waited quietly, listening to the commotion from the castle until the speaker shouted again.

"Baron Balser agrees to speak with Prince George. You can come forward to the drawbridge on the unicorn."

"So we've made it as far as the drawbridge," said Prince George, patting Blackie's neck. "That's halfway into the castle."

As Blackie walked around the moat, the drawbridge thumped down. The portcullis scraped up on its chain. A dozen spearmen ran out, looking nervously about. The little Baron followed, leaning on a cane. He peered up at the Prince.

"Prince George, it is you! You're alive, my lord, still alive!"

He bowed as Prince George dropped to the drawbridge. "Of course, I'm alive, Baron. Did you think I was dead?"

Baron Balser shrugged his shoulders. "Oh, my lord, we hear such stories these days. You know, armies marching, castles burnt. Do you come from the City? Is the Empress still holding out?"

"Oh," cried the Prince in dismay, "I thought to ask you. We're returning from the Shrine. We've heard no news for weeks!"

Lord Balser looked at Blackie with wonder. He put out a hand to touch Blackie's horn.

"And you do ride the unicorn! What a wonderful beast! Is it true he's a healer? Can he heal back pain?"

"Certainly," nodded the Prince, "he can heal anything. But tell me, my lord, what do you hear from the City?"

The Baron bent slightly, holding his hand above his hip. "Such pains I've got here, unicorn, beside my spine. I wrenched it a year ago, still have to lie flat in a wagon when I travel. I get shooting pains up and down my leg when I stand. Can you heal it for me?"

"Oh, go ahead, Blackie," urged Prince George. "Heal him up. Show him your power."

Blackie touched his horn to the Baron's spine, squeezed out a healing charge.

"Oh!" gasped the Baron, straightening. "A miracle, a miracle! The pain's gone. I haven't stood without pain for months."

"Now, Baron," said the Prince, "the news. What's happening in the war?"

"Oh, blessed relief," said the Baron, swinging his body to left and right. "I can ride again and play golf, that Scottish game. I haven't sat my horse since a year ago Christmas."

"But the news!" demanded the Prince. "What's happening in your region?"

Lord Balser threw his cane into the moat. It bounced on the ice as his voice grew serious.

"All I know, my lord, is that things appear dark, very dark. Passing travelers tell all sorts of tales. Some say that Vile's on the verge of capturing the City. Others say that Saint Michael has flown in to drive him away. We do know that a horde of Hellions has taken over Castle Croy down the road. No one knows what they're doing there, but they appear to be setting an ambush for someone."

"An ambush, is it?" said the Prince slowly. "I think I know what that's about."

"But now, you're here, my lord!" exclaimed the Baron, bowing over and over. "You're alive and well and riding a unicorn. You'll have our prayers when you ride on. I'll give you a cask of wine to take with you."

"Oh, Baron," cried Prince George with a laugh, "I want more than a cask of wine! I need supplies for seventeen men and all the fighters you can spare. Looks like you've got hearty fellows here who'd love to spear a Hellion."

The spearmen, who'd been listening to the talk, looked alarmed. They backed across the drawbridge. Baron Balser sputtered his protests.

"No, no, my lord! I've declared for peace in this war! I'm standing neutral! I refused the Black Captain when he demanded entrance and turned away Sir Frederick, who rode up with a letter from the Empress. I tell 'em all that we're quiet people here. We just want to be left alone."

"Left alone!" shouted the Prince. "Do you think Prince Vile will leave you alone after you refused his Captain? You've sealed your doom! Dragonbait, that's what you are! Dragonbait, unless you help us defeat him!"

"No, no" squealed the Baron, covering his ears, "I can't hear this! I'm a noncombatant! The Bishop says that everyone has to spare noncombatants. It's good to see you, Prince, and the unicorn. Sorry, I can't help. Good luck in the fighting. Send me a letter if you save the Empire!"

He scurried back in the castle, calling his men to follow. One spearman hesitated, asking Prince George, "Is it possible, me lord, that the unicorn can heal the headache?"

"No healing, no healing!" shouted the Baron. "Come along, Wat! Raise the drawbridge!"

The man whispered to Prince George, "Tell you what, me lord. If your unicorn can heal me headache, I'll come with you. It's me sinuses that bothers me!"

"Certainly, he can heal you," promised the Prince. "Do you have a horse?"

Bart nodded his head, wincing, "Sorry, me lord, it's the pain. I get the headache ever morning in this cold weather."

He took a breath and whispered. "If you heal me, I'll show you the horses. We hid 'em in the forest with the cows. They wasn't room for beasts when the people come into the castle."

The Prince clapped Wat on the shoulder. He pulled back when the man cried out from his head pain.

"Don't worry, man," promised the Prince. "Show us the horses, and we'll heal your headache forever."

"Hey, Wat!" cried a voice from the wall, as they walked off the drawbridge. "Where you think you goin'?"

"I'm going off with this Prince!" Wat shouted. "I don't wantta be dragonbait like the rest o' you!"

"You crazy, man! You think a unicorn can save you? You runnin' right up the dragon's jaws!"

"Maybe so, but I'll go down fighting," replied Wat. "And I'll have a clear head when I do it!"

Blackie heard an exchange of oaths across the drawbridge, the sound of a scuffle. Five more men ran across before the portcullis clanked down.

"We're for you, too, me lord!" one cried. "We don't want to be burnt with the castle! We'll take our chances with the unicorn!"

"Welcome, men!" cried the Prince. "Welcome to anyone with the guts to fight! If you have aches and pains, the unicorn will heal you when we get those horses. Let's bring up my troopers and ride to the forest to round up the beasts."

Sure enough, Baron Balser's men led the Prince to a herd of horses and cows in a small pasture far back in the trees. The first thing that Calder did was to knock the fattest cow in the head and truss it from a tree to butcher.

Blackie watched grimly. At least, with beef to eat, the humans wouldn't be after him to hunt deer. He didn't stand long, gawking at the slaughter. Prince George pulled him back to the road to scout out Castle Croy.

"We have to be careful here, Blackie," said Prince George, rubbing his neck. "Castle Croy's said to be full of Hellions. I need to get a count of the enemy. I've been expecting Vile to pull something like this. He knows that the army can't pass by a strong force that could strike it from behind. On the other hand, I don't want to lose time besieging Croy while the City's in danger."

Snow began to fall again as Blackie trotted down the road, big, wet flakes that melted on his coat as they speckled the leaves under the bare trees. Blackie shook them off his nose as he sniffed for ambushes in the forest.

The next castle they came to was a burnt pile of ruins. Lord Balser's men had told the Prince that the Hellions from Croy had swooped down on Punge, one night, capturing the castle in a rush before ravaging the unsuspecting village. Luckily, the humans that escaped had brought the word to Baron Balser, who'd immediately ordered his people into his castle.

Punge Village was torn apart like other plundered places, but this had been a hasty job. The Hellions had left the place a shambles, ripping and hammering everything they saw, but had abandoned a shed stuffed with good hay. Blackie ate there for an hour while Prince George walked about with a crock of pickled peaches under his arm, sucking the fruit with juice dripping from his fingers and spitting peach pits into the street. He returned to Blackie holding up a couple white sheets.

"Look what I found in the priest's house. Camouflage! No one will see us if this snow continues."

The snow did continue, cloaking the treetops and spreading over the forest floor. It chilled Blackie's hooves as he crunched down the road, belching from all the hay he'd stuffed down. By the time he spotted the castle tower on the hill, the fields around were white with snow outlining the furrows, stubble sticking through.

"There it is," whispered Prince George, slowing Blackie to a walk. "Castle Croy. I'd better cover you with a sheet."

Blinking snowflakes from his eyelashes, Blackie stared through the snowfall at the dark walls of the castle. They were spying from an apple orchard where rows of snow-topped trees led to the castle. Scattered branches poked up blackly through the white on the ground. The wind had risen to sift snowflakes under the sheets, stinging Blackie's ears and cheeks. All was silent but the hiss of blowing snow and the crunch underfoot when Blackie shifted his hooves.

"We have to move closer," breathed the Prince. "I can't see anything from here."

Blackie nodded his horn. He stepped through the trees to the hedge around the orchard, piled with snow like a long, narrow strawstack. Prince George studied the castle walls through a hole in the hedge where the gate had been torn away. Blackie looked uneasily up and down the lane outside the orchard.

Blackie did not want to be jumped by Hellions. He'd only glanced at the brutes that first afternoon with the Princess, but Prince George and the troopers had talked about them for hours last night.

A soldier who had joined up along the road claimed to have seen a squad of Hellions run by at night. Seven feet tall they stood, hulking giants bred by Prince Vile to boss his slave gangs. Rumor spoke of hundreds of Hellions riding Hellhounds as Vile's shock troops. Once the dragon burned away major resistance, the Hellions crashed through the armies of northern lords to round up captives for Vile's slave pens.

"I hear, they's spawned from monsters!" claimed Calder. "They gets their size from Northmen and their strength from trolls."

"Maybe so," said Prince George, shaking his spear, "but remember, men, Hellions are mortal. A spear in the gut, an arrow in the eye—you'll bring them down! If we catch them by surprise, they'll flee like rabbits."

"How many, me lord, how many Hell . . . Hellions do you think there'll be in Castle Croy?" asked a quavering man.

"Eighty, ninety at least," said the Prince. "It'd take that many to ambush our army. But don't worry. We've got the unicorn on our side. If Blackie can fight a dragon, a few Hellions will be no problem to him. I'd worry more about Hellhounds."

A bowman looked up from restringing his bow. "Has you ever seen a Hellhound, me lord?"

Prince George nodded. "Indeed, I have. Up at Thorn two years ago, the Princess shot a Hellhound carrying off a child. It was big as a horse with four-inch fangs, but it went down to steel."

"Four-inch fangs," repeated the bowman. The men shuddered and fell silent.

Blackie was shivering. "From the cold," he told himself. The sheet had afforded a bit of protection when the Prince first draped it over him, but it was wet and frosty now. It stuck to his hide, letting in the chill. Spying was frigid work, anyway. Trotting through the snow to get here had heated him, but standing and watching, well, this was a job he'd like to leave to someone else.

"Saint Christopher, it's cold!" muttered Prince George. "I need to get out of this wind. Blackie, you stay here and keep watch. I'm going back to that orchard shed. Let me know if you see anything."

Blackie watched in dismay as Prince George trudged back through the snow to close himself in a shack at the corner of the orchard. The long spear stuck out of the crack between frame and door. Looking down, Blackie saw their footprints in the snow. What a giveaway! Any Hellion patrolling outside would see the tracks where they walked, where they stood, where Prince George was hiding.

"He might as well fly a flag over the place," thought Blackie. "Now, I have to keep alert to make sure he doesn't get trapped in there."

Spying by himself was a lot lonelier than standing with the Prince, and now, worrying about footprints, Blackie hesitated to move. But he was still too far away to see much of the castle. It could be filled with a hundred Hellions for all he knew. On the other hand, they could have taken off. What if they were gone? What if the castle was empty? What if he was freezing himself for nothing?

"I'll scoot closer to the castle," he thought to himself. "Get a good sniff of the place. I'll know in a second if there's Hellions in there."

He looked back at the orchard shack, uncertain whether to leave the Prince unguarded while scouting near the castle.

"Oh, who's to hurt him?" he thought. "If anything shows up, I'll get him out of there in a moment. I'm just moving to the end of the field."

Even covered by his sheet, Blackie felt exposed as he stepped between the apple trees. He looked around to all sides, saw nothing move. Glancing down at the ground, he was startled to see fresh prints in the snow ahead of him, odd footprints, a series of single steps with something scraping through the snow beside them.

Curious, Blackie followed the tracks to a clump of bushes across from the corner tower of the castle where the icy moat swung around to the gate. Creeping close, Blackie caught a whiff of man-scent. The snow before the bushes was flattened where a human had dropped to his belly to slide underneath.

"He's hiding like a bear," thought Blackie. "What's he up to?"

Moving gently to make only the softest crunch when he stepped, Blackie eased up on the hiding human. Sticking from under the bush, Blackie could see a trembling foot wrapped in wet rags. He smelled sweat and fear.

Blackie took a sudden step, leaned down, and pressed his horn into the middle of the man's back. There was a spasm of hands and knees as the man tried to roll, jump, and run all at once, but couldn't move under the horn. He went limp, gasping in fear, "Aw . . . aw . . . all right, you can eat me!"

Blackie held him silently a moment, then stepped back. Breathing harshly, the human jerked his head around to look back at Blackie.

He stared up at Blackie in his sheet, not comprehending, then his eyes widened.

"The horn . . . the nose . . . it's the unicorn, the black . . . unicorn!"

The man's eyes squinted. He began weeping, snot running from his nose. He crawled backwards to embrace Blackie's legs sticking out below the sheet.

"Oh, unicorn, bless you, bless you. You come to save me!"

Blackie could see him clearly now, a thin man with bright eyes and a sparse beard wearing an old green hat. The man pulled a long stick from the bush, a crutch with a curved armrest at the top.

"Don't you . . . don't you remember me?" sputtered the man. "I'm Lame Alan from Shrems! Back in church there, you healed me, or rather, didn't heal me when I broke . . . broke off your horn. By accident, you remember, that was an accident! Not my fault, not my fault at all!"

Oh, yes, Blackie remembered Lame Alan. What an embarrassing moment that had been! This human had grabbed Blackie's baby horn in church and wouldn't let go till he snapped it off. Now, Lame Alan was rolling around, gibbering in the snow with Castle Croy only a few yards away across the moat.

Blackie stepped backward, pulling free of the human to trot back into the trees, but Lame Alan followed on his crutch, trying to keep a hand on Blackie's back.

"I'll come with you!" whispered Lame Alan. "Do you have an army here? Did you bring the Guards? Last I saw, you was running with Princess Julianna and those knights."

Half-walking, half-hopping through the snow on his crutch, Lame Alan followed Blackie through the orchard to the shack in the corner.

"What you got here?" asked Lame Alan, leaning on his crutch. "This is just an old basket-shed for the orchard."

Ignoring him, Blackie slipped his horn in the crack in the door and pulled it open to find Prince George sound asleep, wrapped in his fur cape and sheet. The Prince jerked awake as the wind poured in on him.

"Oh, it's you, the Prince!" cried Lame Alan, peering in the door. "Now, I'm sure we're saved!"

"Who's that?" demanded Prince George, whipping his spear about. Lame Alan fell over. Crouching in the snow, he made an attempt at a bow.

"Don't you remember me, Prince? Lame Alan from Shrems village, Father Paul's church? I'm Lame Alan, Lame Alan."

Prince George frowned down at him. "I remember you! You broke Blackie's horn!"

"That's me, that's me!" squealed Lame Alan, nodding his head like a pump handle. "Lame Alan, the storyteller! But you know, my lord, I didn't aim to break any horn! I just wanted my leg healed, but unicorn, oh, blessed unicorn, I've thanked you a million times for not healing me. If you'd done it, they'd have marched me off with spear and shield like the rest of them. You saved my life by not healing me. A crippled foot's a blessing when the whole land's at war."

"Well, what are you doing here, man?" whispered the Prince. "And keep your voice down! Noises carry out here in the snow."

Lame Alan looked around, nervously. Wrapping his shawl about his shoulders, he lowered his voice to explain.

"Why, you see, my lord, after Shrems was burnt in the fighting over the silver mine, I had to wander from village to village looking for refuge. But the whole country's shut down, towns burnt or closed up behind walls, no vagrants allowed. Finally, I came here to Croy where Tad the Innkeeper promised to put me up for awhile. I hoped to stay all winter if I could, telling stories for my keep, but the Hellions stormed in during the middle of night when everybody was sleeping. They didn't get me 'cause I was tucked into the haystack behind the inn."

"Make it short, man!" interrupted Prince George, shuffling his feet. "Tell me about the Hellions in the Castle."

Lane Alan bowed and went on with his story.

"Oh, the Hellions, well, they didn't catch me. When the shouting woke me up, I burrowed into the haystack like a bedbug. Didn't peek out all day. By then, the townsfolk was all killed or captured. There was Hellions whooping around everywhere, but I crept into the storeroom at the inn and rolled out a barrel of beer to my haystack. I been hiding and drinking ever since."

Blackie's ears perked up when Lame Alan mentioned his haystack. More hay to eat! That was good news.

"Tell me about the Hellions," demanded Prince George. "How many are there, man? How big are they?"

Lame Alan crossed himself.

"Saints guard us, me lord, you don't want to talk of them savages! They're big enough, and hairy and ugly. You'd know a Hellion when you saw one. They got two or three hundred of them in the castle. Not all Hellions, of course. Sixty or seventy Hellions, but the Captain—that's the commander—he's got crossbowmen with him and spearmen. Those spearmen, now, they're as scared of the Hellions as anyone, but they gotta fight for them."

"So it's a small army in there," said the Prince, slowly.

"Oh, yes, me lord, they're all hiding in there to ambush some folks traveling down the road to the City. They say that the dragon's going to fly in and help them do it."

"The dragon!" cried Prince George, jumping up and banging his head on the low roof of the shack. "Ouch!"

Bending, he stepped out, rubbing his head.

"I didn't count on the dragon, but the rest of it, the Hellions, the ambush, that's exactly what I expected. Our army riding down from the north—these villains aim to hit us by surprise. Now that I know what they're up to, they're the ones to get surprised."

"Well, you'd best be careful, me lord," warned Lame Alan. "That Captain, he's got a raven watchin' the road, an old raven that can talk."

"Crepitar!" growled the Prince. "Has to be Crepitar! I know that raven. I've had trouble with him before."

He stopped. "One more question, Lame Alan, what about Hellhounds? Does this Captain have any Hellhounds with him?"

Lame Alan shook his head vigorously. "No, no, that's one curse we're spared, thank Heaven. Hellhounds would have sniffed me out in no time."

Suddenly, Prince George grew suspicious. "How do you know all this, Lame Alan? You're awfully well informed for a man that hides in a haystack!"

Lame Alan spread his hands, looking innocent. "Why, the deserters, you know, the spearmen that run away from Vile, they tell me things."

Prince George looked interested. "Deserters, are there a lot of them?"

"A few of them," nodded Lame Alan, "twelve or fifteen, I'd say. Problem is, they're as lost as any man without a lord. A bunch of them hide around Croy village, and I run into them all the time."

"Hmmm, I could use more spearmen. But the Hellions, what do they do in the castle? Just hang out and wait to fight?"

"Why, no," said Lame Alan, shuffling his foot in the snow, "they dance."

"Dance?" exclaimed Prince George, looking surprised.

"Yep," said Lame Alan, waving a hand, "every night, they get drunk and hop around for hours. That's what they love best, next to bashing folks with clubs. They gather the army into the courtyard right across the wall there, gets the drummers drumming, and make the men all clap and sing while they twirl and dance and has a high old time."

Blackie shivered. He was hungry again, tired of listening to this talk. But Prince George repeated slowly, "Every night, you say? The whole gang is packed in there, dancing and singing?"

"You just stay here," advised Lame Alan. "Wait till dark, and you'll hear such a caterwauling as if Hell broke open. Guess they feel safe with the town under control and the raven watching the road."

The Prince stepped from the shack to look around the countryside. "I must say, Lame Alan, you're a braver man than I thought, hanging around town with Hellions next door."

Lame Alan shrugged. "Who can walk in all this snow, my lord? Crippled as I am, I'm stuck here—plus I'm gathering material."

"Material? What do you mean, material?"

"Why, this war is the legend of the ages. Songs'll be sung forever and stories told about this war. A man that's seen Hellions firsthand, and—if ye please, my lord—unicorns, why, that man's set for life. Folks'll line up to hear my tales. I'll have free beer forever."

Prince George looked at Lame Alan with approval. "Lame Alan, you surprise me again. That's enterprising of you. Who'd have thought you'd have the good sense and courage to collect material like this? It's lucky for us that you do, since we have real information to work with. I thank you."

"You wouldn't care to take me with you now, would you?" asked Lame Alan, hopefully, as Prince George mounted Blackie.

Prince George reached for his spear, leaning against the shed. "It wouldn't do you any good, man. We'll be returning to Croy at nightfall. Just keep spying in case anything changes. And take a scout around town to collect those deserters. Tell them I'll give a pardon to any man who fights for me. They'll get rewarded when peace returns."

Lame Alan bowed on his crutch as Blackie carried the Prince out to the road.

"So there's a haystack at Lame Alan's inn," thought Blackie. "I wonder if there's oats there too."

He put the matter out of his mind when a swishing branch poured snow over his neck. Back with the troopers where beef bones bubbled in a soup pot, Blackie was not surprised at their horror when Prince George announced they were to attack a castle full of Hellions.

"No, no, me lord," cried a bowmen, "they's just a handful of us! It'd be suicide!"

"He's right!" cried another. "Let's wait for the Knights and the others to ride up and help!"

"That's the point!" exclaimed the Prince. "The raven's told Prince Vile that our warriors are riding to fall on the siege forces at the City. That's why he's placed these villains here to ambush the army. If we can shatter these ambushers tonight, the army can move through without delay and rescue the City in a day or two."

"But Prince," asked Calder, "do we really have a chance? You say, they're holed up in a strong castle, outnumbering us ten to one, not to mention three score o' Hellions. Won't this just sacrifice us without helping anybody?"

"That depends on how we fight 'em, Calder," said the Prince. "I have a plan to even the odds."

Looking up from a chewy bush, Blackie had to admire the Prince, planning this risky attack so confidently.

"Tonight," Prince George went on, "when those Hellions are dancing and singing with all those spearmen and crossbowmen packed around them, we're going to douse them with heavy rain. Now, here's what I want you to do. You all have bags, don't you, the empty bags from the supplies you brought from home?"

"O' course, we have bags," replied Calder.

"Yeah," said another man, sadly, "too bad they're all empty."

"Well, I want every man to search down the streams in the area to collect rocks, rocks like this one."

Prince George held up a round stone, slightly smaller than his fist.

"See this rock? I'd say it weighs a good pound. I stopped at a stream on the way back and picked up a dozen like this in no time. I want each of you to fill a couple bags with rocks, then rest up all afternoon. We'll eat our beef at dusk before we ride to Castle Croy."

There were bitter complaints at the orders, even a threat of rebellion from Lord Balser's spearmen, but Blackie and Calder supported the Prince, so the men finally spread out to search the streams for rocks. Prince George insisted on inspecting the bags when they trudged back with their rocks. He dumped all stones that looked too small for the job and sent the men to find bigger ones.

The afternoon passed quickly for Blackie who foraged on rough brush about the camp, his mind on the haystack back at the village. Before he knew it, Calder was counting the men to make sure that everyone was assembled, the horses were saddled, and the bags of rocks tied on.

"What do we do about these cows?" asked Calder, pointing to Lord Balser's herd.

"We move them to another hiding place in the forest. We'll leave them for the army passing by. Those troopers will be hungry when they get here. If we're lucky, we can capture more supplies at Croy, but an army of that size needs a lot of meat."

Walking slowly ahead of the riders and the cows, Blackie was disturbed at the noise they made. The cows mooed, the riders muttered, and the rocks clicked in their bags with each lurch of the horses. Even after they left the cows in a little valley where dry grass poked up from the snow, Prince George kept turning to hush the riders. Soon they left the deep forest for the fields around Castle Croy.

"We'll stop in the orchard," he whispered. "I want to check with Lame Alan, if we can find him."

He had the men dismount under cover of the snowy trees and told them to rest while he consulted with the spy.

"The spy!" whispered one of the men. "We have a spy on our side? This Prince is more organized than I thought."

"Oh, yes," agreed Calder, "his lordship has everything under control. If every man sticks to his duty, we have nothin' to worry about, nothin' at all."

"Nothin' but a castle full o' Hellions," muttered a bowman. "Nothin' at all."

CHAPTER TWENTY-EIGHT

Capturing Croy

"The dragon, here, now?" screeched the Prince. "Are you sure of that?"

Blackie's heart stopped in his chest. He turned his gaze from Lame Alan, shivering behind the bushes, to stare at the castle across the moat. Its towers and walls were faintly lit by firelight from inside the courtyard.

"Oh, yes, my lord," whispered Lame Alan. "No one could miss that great worm! She flapped in just after you left today. I heard the sentries talking. The dragon's gonna lead the ambush to wipe out your army. Appears your army's closer than you thought."

"Well, where's she nesting, do you know?

"Sounds to me like she's up there on that central tower. That's where the screams came from."

The thought of the dragon filled Blackie with fury. He listened angrily as Prince George asked, "So the dancing— Do you think the Hellions will dance tonight?"

Lame Alan was quick to assure him. "Oh, yes, my lord, I heard the guard say this'll be the last party for awhile. It's an extry-big feast, he said. Lots of 'em won't be dancing after the ambush."

"He's right about that," said Prince George, grimly. "We'll go ahead with our attack despite the dragon. She'll be as surprised as the rest of them. Could be, she'll fly low enough for Blackie to get at her."

Blackie nodded as Lame Alan wished them luck. The man backed away on his crutch.

"You won't see me tonight. I can watch the fighting from the other side of the field."

"Well, what about those deserters?" asked the Prince. "I need as many spears as I can get."

"I found the bunch of 'em holed up at the inn, my lord. I told 'em what you said. They're not happy about fighting Hellions, but they're willin' to listen to what you has to say. I wouldn't mention the dragon if I was you."

Prince George walked with Blackie back to the soldiers resting under the trees. The humans were shivering as the wind grew colder, but Blackie was hot at the thought of the dragon. So near, that monster, and so wicked! He'd seen her carry Prince Vile through the sky. She'd chased him down a country road. She even dared to attack the Princess in the City. She'd lived long enough!

His horn felt heavy on his forehead, but Blackie had to hold back while Prince George sent Calder to talk to the deserters at the inn as the rest of his men rested in the nearest huts.

Blackie stalked back and forth, whipping his tail about, until Calder returned with a dozen men who wanted to see the unicorn. Once Blackie calmed himself enough to heal their colds and bruises, they agreed to join the Prince. Prince George sent them off to gather stones like the rest of the men.

So Blackie had to wait, nervously pacing through the cold, dark evening. Finally, at midnight, Prince George was ready to move. By then, the party in the castle was a frenzied brawl. Blackie could hear the hammered drums, wild screams, and raucous laughter from the end of the orchard. Prince George ordered the troopers to draw close around him.

"Men," he said, "I have bad news for you. I learned from my spy that the dragon's in Castle Croy."

He paused as the men gasped in horror, then rushed to reassure them. "I can also tell you that the monster's asleep now, bloated with meat and bones in the highest tower. We don't need to worry about her. By the time she wakes up, we'll have broken Prince Vile's ambush. Our target is the Hellions jumping around behind those walls. You can hear them squealing over there. Do they sound like a disciplined fighting force to you?"

"They sounds fierce to me," said someone.

The Prince shook his spear. "They may sound fierce with their screaming and yelling, but they're nothing but a drunken rout, a herd of hogs ready to butcher. We'll wash them down with heavy rain. With luck, they'll get to fighting each other in the dark while we slip away unharmed. So men, stay cool and organized, work together, and we'll all survive to tell this story around the bonfire."

With the attack at hand, Blackie couldn't stand still to listen. Nervy, sweaty, he pranced about in the snow. He took deep breaths, trying to calm himself, then gave up on the Prince's speech and trotted through the trees to look at the Castle.

Bonfires and torches outlined the walls and towers of Castle Croy, shaking from the drums and shrieks within. Blackie could see the guards along the top of the walls. Standing with their backs to him, they jerked back and forth with the singing. They waved beer mugs and joined the obscene chant howled by the dancers.

> Death to plower, planter, reaper!
> Death to mother and child!
> Death to kneeler, prayer, sleeper!
> Peace and order go wild!
>
> Drink to stabber, slicer, smasher!
> Drink to fire and flood!
> Drink to butcher, burner, basher!
> Drown the world in blood!

Blackie rocked back and forth, switching his tail and tossing his horn as the song broke down to a roar of cheers and curses, then started again with shouts of "Drink, drink, drink!"

> Drink to the dragon!
> She hunts from the sky
> and burns up the City,
> the steeples so high!
>
> Drink to the master!
> We'll chop him a head!
> All who aren't drinking—
> the Prince wants them dead!

377

Blackie became aware of men crunching softly through the orchard to arrange themselves along the moat on both sides of him. He heard their shaky breaths and the clink of rocks in their bags. By the flaring lights from the castle, he saw the bowmen notching the arrows.

Prince George passed behind with a cheery whisper, "Hold on, men. Wait for my signal to let them have it. Arrows first, then rocks. They won't know what hit them."

Stepping to Blackie, the Prince scratched his ears, whispering, "Come on, Blackie. I want you directly in front of the drawbridge."

Blackie's heart was beating fast. His breath came short as he held himself down to walk quietly with the Prince, the crunch of their footsteps lost in the tumult behind the walls. Calder was waiting at the drawbridge.

"Your squad arranged?" asked the Prince.

"Oh, yeah," whispered Calder, "every man waiting the signal to cut loose."

"How about the men you found in the village?"

"They seems steady enough. They hates the Hellions worse than anyone."

Prince George rested his spear on Blackie while he opened his own bag of stones. He leaned forward to hug Blackie's neck.

"Hold on another moment, Blackie. I can see that you're ready to fight. I hope the men are as eager. Remember, don't charge till they're packed on the drawbridge."

Panting now, Blackie trembled with excitement, his ears up, his tail stiff.

"God bless you, me lord," whispered Calder.

"God bless us all."

Calder and the Prince ran back to their squads. Blackie heard the shout, "Bows up, men . . . fire!"

His heart surged within him as bowstrings twanged. He saw the watchmen outlined by the fires throw out their arms and topple inside the walls.

"Now, the rocks!" cried the Prince. "Hurl them high!"

Lined up and down the moat on both sides of the castle, the men dug into their bags. With grunts and gasps, they sailed the weighty stones over moat and walls to smash down onto the revelers packed in the courtyard. Blackie heard screams of pain amid the singing and shouting within. More rocks flew into the air. The troopers threw as quickly as they could dig missiles from the bags.

"Rain, heavy rain!" shouted the troopers, gleefully emptying one bag and taking up another.

By now, the singing was stopped. Blackie heard different cries from the castle—shrieks, curses, shouts.

"Clubs, clubs! Out and at 'em! Smash 'em! Bash 'em! Kill 'em all!"

The bags were empty before the drawbridge thumped down. Feverish with excitement, Blackie backed up a few yards to give himself room to pick up speed. Prince George and Calder were hustling their troopers into formation beside the lane, spears to the center, bows to the flanks.

Everything seemed to happen at once. To get at their attackers, crazed Hellions crawled like spiders under the portcullis creaking up on its chain. The bowmen snapped their bowstrings, and the leading Hellions, stuck with arrows, tumbled, screaming, into the icy moat. Then the portcullis was up. The yowling mob of Hellions shoved across the drawbridge, waving their clubs.

That's when Blackie charged. He had room enough to reach full gallop before smashing into the Hellions wedged in the gate like a blacksmith's hammer crashing down on a walnut. Shrieking Hellions flew off the drawbridge on both sides.

Blackie blacked out as he drove under the portcullis. Only later, the awed troopers wiping guts and blood from his hide told how he tore around the courtyard stomping and stabbing panicked spearmen and Hellions until they locked themselves into the castle keep.

"All we had to do stab 'em on the run," laughed Calder, "and finish off the wounded. Must 'a been forty, fifty lying around with broken heads from the rocks and you brought down at least that many more. Them crossbowmen—ho, ho, ho!—them poor souls crowded up to the walls to shoot down at us. That's where the dragon caught 'em when she came swooping out of the sky."

"What a sight that was!" shouted a bowman, jumping up and down. "Woken suddenly at midnight, Old Rosie didn't know friend from foe. She came burnin' down and toasted the fighters hanging around after we scampered away to safety!"

"Yep," added Calder, "best thing is that we saved the villagers, what was left of 'em. Once the dragon flew off, them villains chased the prisoners out of the dungeon, probly thinking you'd wear yourself down stomping on them, too. But the Prince had tackled you long before that. You shook him around some, but he got you to follow us back to town when the dragon started screaming from the tower."

Blackie tried to understand what they were saying, but all he felt was horror at the stinking gore on his coat. Trembling with exhaustion, he gagged at the smell.

Prince George trudged up, leaning on his bloody spear. "What are you men doing talking? I want you to search the village, find food for these poor people. They're starving."

"We was just telling the unicorn what he did," explained Calder. "He's like stunned, he is, doesn't even know how he knocked them Hellions around."

The Prince threw his arms around Blackie's neck.

"Blackie, Blackie, you're a wonder, but we need you to snap out of it. We didn't lose many, but there's a dozen wounded men that need healing. Most of those villagers are in bad shape, too. The Baron, Baron Croy, he's shrunk down to skin and bones. You better come with me, now. I've got warm water for your bath and soup for you to drink."

Soup, meat soup! Blackie shuddered at the idea. Prince George hastened to reassure him.

"Don't worry, Blackie. The village women don't have any meat for the soup, just dry peas and barley and onions they dug up for a quick boil with a carrot or two. It'll be cooked in a few minutes. We'll clean you, then you can have a mouthful of soup to revive you before getting to the healing."

"Veggie soup," thought Blackie. He took a deep breath and followed numbly as Prince George held his horn to lead him along. Blackie stayed awake while being scrubbed, but passed out when put to the healing. He'd barely restored Lord Croy and three or four of the worst cases before falling asleep with his horn on an injured man. Prince George had him stretched out on straw and covered with quilts.

Blackie was still asleep when the Hellions burst out of the castle at dawn. Barely a dozen had survived to drop from the wall like apes and scuttle across the ice on the moat. A bowman shot one of them, but Calder's spearmen didn't try to stop the rest of them. The soldiers pulled back with their spears and jeered the fleeing monsters.

"Run, rockheads! Run, ye scum! Come back this way, and we'll pound ye again!"

Prince George found Blackie sleeping at the inn with the wounded. Blackie felt stiff and weary when the Prince guided him down the street to the moat. He sneezed awake at the foul smell of the Hellions.

"That's it, Blackie, sniff 'em well," advised the Prince. "We've got to follow the villains to keep them out of mischief. Calder and the boys will guard Castle Croy until the army catches up."

Shivering in the crisp, cold air, they followed the outsized tracks a mile or two until it became clear that the Hellions were "skedaddling," as Calder put it over a blazing fire when Blackie and Prince George returned to the inn.

"Let 'em go! Let 'em go!" squealed Baron Croy, trembling in his big chair by the fireplace. "You don't want to st-st-stir up that bunch!"

"But they's a dozen more fighters for Prince Vile," argued Calder. "We should kill 'em all."

"They're a dozen panicked Hellions," said Prince George, taking a warm mug of ale from the thin, shaking innkeeper. "Think of the tales those monsters will carry back to the siege. When Vile's villains hear that the unicorn's coming after them, they'll be as skittish as squirrels. They'll see Blackie in every shadow."

"But what do we do with the wretches up in the castle?" asked a spearman, heaving one of the Hellions' great clubs onto the fire.

"Leave them alone," advised the Prince. "Let them starve there till the war's over. They're no threat to anybody. If they knew it, they outnumber us still, but after last night's battle, they'll be in no mind to try their luck against us."

"'Specially not against the unicorn," said the spearman, grinning at Blackie, who was eating hay from Lame Alan's bed in the corner of the room. Lame Alan sat on a stool by the fire with a beer cup in his hand, while Baron Croy clutched the arms of his chair and stammered like a nannygoat.

"Yes, yes, yes, let . . . let them freeze in there. My hall, my ch-chambers—filthy, polluted by their very presence. I won't set foot inside those walls till it's fum-fumigated! I want the B-Bishop, himself, to bless the place!"

The men nodded over their beer cups, but looked up when a half-dozen troopers rushed in, calling, "Me lords, masters, look what we got!"

Blackie glanced up from his hay as Calder shouted, "Was you born in a barn? Shut the door, there! You're letting in the weather!"

"Look, me lord! I shot it!"

A bowman held up a bending arrow with a huge purplish-black bird on it, stuck through the muscle of a foot-long wing. The bird flapped its good wing, croaking feebly, "Hurrrts . . . hurrrts."

"By the saints," cried Prince George, jumping up, "that's Crepitar, Prince Vile's spy-bird!"

"Crepitar!" exclaimed Lame Alan, pushing up to examine the bird.

"Why'd you bring that thing in here, Duff?" demanded Calder. "Wring its neck. Toss it on the garbage heap."

Crepitar squawked loudly until Prince George said, "No, no, we can question him, learn Vile's intentions. Crepitar can tell us how near the army is."

"Better question it quick, me lord," said the bowman, wrinkling his nose at the bird. "I think it's done for. It was flappin about the drawbridge countin' the dead when I picked it off."

"Probly looking for a meal," growled Calder. "Them ravens is nothing but short-necked vultures."

"Here, give me that bird," ordered the Prince. He pulled on his gloves and took Crepitar gently under the breast. "We have to remove that arrow. Snap it off for me, Duff."

"But me lord," protested the man, "that's the last of me arrows. I shot 'em all away, last night."

"Oh, I'm sure there's more arrows around town."

The Prince gently stretched out Crepitar's injured wing. "Now, as close as you can to the feathers, break it cleanly without hurting the bird."

"Hurrrts . . . hurrrts," croaked Crepitar. He squawked loudly and pecked at the Prince when the arrow snapped. Twisting the arrow slightly, Duff pulled the shaft from the wound.

Prince George carried Crepitar to Blackie, chomping in another mouthful of hay. "Blackie, touch this bird with your horn, will you? Heal him up for me."

"Me?" thought Blackie in disgust. "Heal a bird? What will you ask for next?"

As ordered, he swung his horn to the raven and squeezed out a healing charge that set Crepitar squawking louder than ever. He beat at the Prince with his wings, trying to escape. Prince George slapped his head with a glove.

"Quiet, bird, quiet! You'll obey if you know what's good for you. I remember you from Darr—lying to the Princess about my Song! You're lucky I don't wring your neck and toss you in the stewpot."

Crepitar drew in his head, glaring sullenly as the Prince pointed a finger at him.

"You know what I'm talking about, Crepitar. You've been lying and spying since you hatched. Speak up, now! Tell the truth for once. How far off is the army? How many soldiers ride with the Knights?"

Crepitar looked away. He clamped his beak shut, flirted his feathers, and closed his eyes.

"Just look at him," said Baron Croy, bitterly, "Evil thing. I'd toss him to the cat."

"Why, that's an idea, my lord!" cried Prince George. "Innkeeper, where's your cat?

Crepitar's eyes popped open. "Aaawk!"

"Sorry, me lord," said the Innkeeper. "Cat run off when the Hellions came through."

"No problem," said the Prince. "I'm sure there are hungry cats in every alley of this town. How about it, Crepitar? You like to share a cage with a big old tomcat?"

"Aawk, aawk," croaked Crepitar, shaking his head. "No caaats, no caaats."

Prince George stroked his back with a finger. "Of course not, Crepitar. We don't want to hurt you. Be a good bird for once in your life. Tell us what we want to know. How far away is the army?"

Crepitar glared at the Prince, then glanced around the room. He thrust up his head, pulled his neck back. "Arrmy," he muttered sullenly, "two daaays away, two daaays."

"Well, now you're talking, Crepitar." Prince George smiled down at him. "You're going to tell us about Prince Vile's army, how big it is, how many Hellions he's got with him. But first, you must be hungry. What would you like for a snack?"

Crepitar looked up suspiciously. He looked around the room again, lowered his head, and whispered, "Corpsesss."

"C-corpses!" shuddered Baron Croy. "What a revolting bird."

Blackie looked at the raven with disgust.

"Well," said Prince George, shrugging his shoulders, "what do you expect? These birds are carrion eaters. What else would you eat, Crepitar?"

"Eggses," hissed the bird. "Creptah eat eggses."

Prince George called to the innkeeper, washing pots over at the bar. "Say, host, do we have any eggs?"

"Sorry, me lord," replied the man, turning over a pot to drain, "no eggs. What chickens wasn't carried off by them villains is froze to death. How about a bit o' deer tongue? The bowmen brought in a couple deer this morning."

Blackie took a drink of water from his pail. He'd eaten enough hay. He didn't like this raven. He thought he'd take a quick look around town to find someplace for a nap.

Out in the street, he found himself the object of wonder, almost of worship. The troopers called to him, petted him, and tried to get him to hang around the shops and huts where they lodged. Wandering further down the street, he was surrounded by townsfolk, who stopped weeping or working on their houses to gather around Blackie in a growing crowd that followed him from block to block.

Blackie heard the voices behind him.

"He killed all them Hellions, last night," declared a man. "Stomped them into jelly!"

"Look close, Stevie and Kevin," a mother said to her children. "You'll tell your children that you seen the unicorn, the mighty beast that saved us."

"Why didn't he save Papa too?" whimpered the little boy.

"Oh, unicorn," offered a goodwife, running out with an apron filled with withered apples, "last autumn's fruit, hidden from them villains! Eat as many as you wants."

Blackie was chewing the first apple when he heard the cry, "Unicorn, unicorn!"

It was a priest running through the people. They stepped back, crossing themselves.

The priest clasped his hands and bowed to Blackie. "Oh, holy creature, Angel Gabriel sent you to answer our prayers. Last night, you saved us from the villains. Now, we need your healing horn for the suffering townsfolk. Please come to the church to save lives."

Blackie sighed. More humans demanding help. Did he have nothing to do, but fight Hellions and heal humans? His horn already felt tender on his head, but he followed the priest, the townspeople streaming behind.

At the door to the church, the priest held back the crowd so Blackie could walk freely between the rows of invalids. The sickroom stench was overwhelming—sweat, blood, infection—but Blackie stepped from person to person, forcing the healing that closed wounds and eased fevered foreheads. Some humans opened their eyes in relief and moved paralyzed limbs. Others closed their eyes to rest from painful spasms.

Voices cried in joy as Blackie worked his way down the last row. A group of still forms lay in the corner. The priest pointed to them, but Blackie shook his head. The priest bowed with a sigh, made the sign of the cross over the dead, and followed Blackie to the door.

Many of the humans Blackie had healed followed with tottering steps when he left the church. He had only a second to smell the clean air before other humans surrounded him, pulling his attention to their aches and pains. It seemed that every human had some ailment to complain about from hair loss to ingrown toenails.

Blackie staggered back to the inn where the guard held back the crowd with his spear. Blackie crept to the fireplace, shivering, his horn low from fatigue.

"Oh, what's the matter, boy?" murmured Prince George, following him. He sat on the end of a bench and stroked Blackie gently. "Poor, poor Blackie, what we've put you through. Just look at your horn. Back at the Shrine, it was so beautiful. Now, it's cut and scratched from fighting. I'm afraid, it'll never be the same again."

His horn scratched! Blackie's thoughts jumped to Papa, back home at the Nest, so proud of his own perfect horn.

"Ah, Papa, I've failed you already!"

Blackie spread his legs and lowered his head. He slept a moment, wracked by a dream in which he ran endless roads after a picnic basket. On waking, he tried to remember his dream. He gave it up as more humans crowded into the inn shouting, "Ho, the unicorn, there he is!"

It was the vanguard of the army, Sir Anthony and a squad of Knights from the Shrine. Eager voices began telling the newcomers of last night's battle as everyone gathered around Blackie, petting him, praising him.

"We kept an eye out for ambushes," Sir Anthony told Prince George, pulling off his cloak. "But that gang in the castle—If you hadn't killed those Hellions, they'd have jumped us for sure. I wouldn't want to face that dragon."

"She flapped away after the battle, last night," said Prince George. "I'd love to see Vile's face when he learns how she blasted his crossbows."

The innkeeper bustled about with pots of beer for the riders. "Drink up, lords. The villains carried off me wine, but the beer barrels was hidden under the hay."

"Well, I have good news for you, my lord," said the Knight. He took a drink from his pot. "The army's in strength to relieve the siege. When we reached the crossroads to turn south, we met seven hundred mountaineers marching down from the north under Godfrey of Darr."

"Godfrey!" shouted Prince George.

"Oh, yes, my lord, the mighty Heir, himself. Lord Godfrey brags of your travels together. He'll be here in a couple hours. He leads troops from four or five border baronies, Ballow, Groot, and Thorn, as well as his own Darrmen. They lack horses, to be sure, but with the Heir leading them, they march as fast as our troops can ride."

"Thank the Lord!" exclaimed the Prince. "Now, we're an army indeed!"

Sir Anthony crossed himself. "We're close onto two thousand men, my lord, and more riding in every day. With you leading on the unicorn, we'll make short work of Vile's minions."

Prince George shook his head. "Vile still has the dragon."

Sir Anthony shook his head. He shouted over the noise of the men crowding into the inn.

"Don't worry about that dragon! The Darrmen have dealt with the dragon before. They carry silver arrows to pierce her hide. Any case, I heard from the townsmen, my lord, that you put her to good work, last night."

Prince George nodded vigorously, patting Blackie on the shoulder.

"Oh, you should have seen that, Knight. Old Rosie was slow getting into the fight. By the time she flew down, we'd pulled back into the darkness. She was so frantic to kill that she burned her way around the wall and cleared off most of the villains still fighting. We figure there's only a hundred or so still holding the castle."

"But you say that the Hellions got away this morning?" asked Sir Anthony.

"What's left of them did, a dozen or so. Think of the shock to the Hellions in Vile's army when they hear that the unicorn's coming after them. That's news to sink through their thick skulls!"

By now, Blackie was surrounded by soldiers and knights, all reaching to pat him or touch his horn. He felt a sting as someone pulled a hair from his tail. He swished his tail irritably and tried to swing his head around. Finally, he gave up and pushed through the crowd to the door.

"Don't leave us, unicorn!" cried voices, but the guard opened the door for him. Blackie stepped out into the cold air to find that it was starting to snow again. He stood a moment, twitching his ears, then walked around the alley to the paddock behind the inn. It had a broad, open shed, stuffed with horses eating the last of the hay.

Looking through the fence, Blackie recognized many of the horses, the broad-shouldered mounts of the knights hungrily eating their hay, along with assorted nags snorting at each other. Seeing him, they hushed a moment, perking their ears, until someone recognized him. Then they crowded close to ask what the two-legs were up to.

"Hey, unicorn, how many more horses they gonna squeeze in here? We're crowded already."

"They gonna let us rest a spell, or they gonna run us out again?"

"My feet are sore—when they gonna clean our hooves?"

Blackie asked the horses about old Maudie, the mare he'd talked to up at the Shrine.

"Oh, that one," laughed a gray nag, "she got so snappy and sulky, they left her behind."

"Left behind?" demanded a young mare. "You mean if you snort and stamp around, you can get out of these campaigns?"

"Not if you have a master like mine," said a brown gelding. "If I tried that, he'd lay on the whip."

"Ho, Unicorn!"

A boy from the inn hustled up, shivering in his apron. He ran to Blackie and reverently patted his side.

"They want you down at the gate, great beast. They're planning to take the castle."

"What do they want with me?" thought Blackie, walking through the alley with the boy. "They know I can't knock down stone walls."

A hundred knights and soldiers were assembled at the corner of the town wall facing the castle. In the middle was a mob of townsmen armed with shields and spears gathered after last night's fight.

Wearing helmet and breastplate, Prince George was talking to Sir Anthony and Baron Croy just outside the gate. The boy hugged Blackie and ran to his squad while Blackie limped to the Prince.

"Oh, there you are," called Prince George. "We've decided to capture the castle before Godfrey arrives. We need you to break through the wall for us."

Blackie stopped. He pulled back his ears and stared at the Prince like he'd lost his senses.

"Oh, I don't mean knock it open, of course," laughed the Prince. "I know you can't smash through walls, but those rascals in the castle don't know it. Trapped there in the castle, they'll believe anything. After seeing you toss Hellions around, last night, they think you're as strong as an elephant. We figure they're so frightened that if you appear to assault them, they'll yield without fighting."

Blackie looked at the grinning men, then nodded. Tired as he was, it was worth an effort to capture a castle without casualties.

"Okay, boys," Prince George called to a dozen grooms waiting with ropes, "harness him up!"

Blackie stood numbly, as the grooms swarmed about him, pulling a big collar over his head and tossing straps over his shoulders.

"You see, Blackie," the Prince explained, "all you have to do is act like you're frantic to rip into the castle. Run at the ropes. Strain to knock down the walls while the boys hold you back. Put on a good enough show, and they'll surrender while they can."

Blackie took a long breath. This was the dumbest idea he'd ever heard. He'd seen lots of craziness from the humans, but for them to think that he could shatter stone walls—That didn't make sense!

"Don't worry," the Prince assured him, "I know it'll work. You just play along with the trick."

Blackie stood wearily while the grooms looped ropes through brass rings on the harness around his chest and shoulders.

"Unicorn's ready!" Prince George called to Sir Anthony.

"Call the troops to attention!" shouted Sir Anthony. The trumpets blew, the drums rattled, and the men fell in at attention, the Knights in perfect order under their flapping banner, their spearmen and archers in exact lines.

Sergeants on both sides of the field bawled at their soldiers, "Dress up your lines like the Knights! Spears at the proper angle!"

Calder and his little band tried to imitate the Knights. When the trumpet blew and the order went out, "Forward, march!" they straggled behind the marching troopers to the tapping of the drum.

Trembling in the saddle, Baron Croy rode behind Prince George, who walked with Blackie and the grooms holding the ropes. The Baron called nervously to the Prince, "Now, you're certain, my lord, we won't have to fight? After weeks in the dungeon—little food, no wine—I can't take it! I can't face a battle!"

"Don't worry, my lord," the Prince reassured him. "The unicorn'll do all that's necessary."

Blackie limped along with the grooms fanned out behind him holding the ropes. These humans didn't seem to understand that this was just a show. They kept yelling to each other, "Run back when he tackles that tower! There'll be stones a-flyin' when the wall crashes down like Solomon and Delilah!"

The thought made Blackie weary. He shivered as they marched down the lane toward the castle. They halted a hundred yards from the drawbridge.

The Prince whispered to him, "Get ready, Blackie. Pull against the ropes like we're holding you back."

Blackie did his best to appear fierce, lifting his horn and pacing heavily, but he broke out coughing. Sweat rolled down his neck. By the time the troopers had spread out before the castle, the defenders had climbed to the roof and windows of the towers, yelling threats, but not yet shooting at them.

Prince George gazed about the army filling in the area up to the moat. The trumpets and drums fell silent, everyone standing at attention.

"Looks like we're ready to go."

The Prince stepped over to Blackie, as Baron Croy called, "Good luck, my lord! I'm out of here the moment they draw bowstrings!"

"All right, Blackie," said the Prince, rubbing Blackie between the ears. "Remember, now, I want to see you put on a show. When I give the word, you charge out to shatter those stones. Just prance and jump and froth at the mouth like a lion. Act like you'll tear that tower to pieces! You're furious, savage, a wild beast carrying death and destruction!"

"I'll give it my best," thought Blackie. He tossed his horn and ran against the ropes to warm up.

At the drumroll, Sir Sebastian stepped forward as herald. There was a pause. Everything silenced until Prince George yelled, "Bring forth the unicorn!"

"I'm on, now," thought Blackie. "This better work. After the battle last night, I couldn't fight a three-legged mule."

Everyone watched him stalk along, the boys following step by step as though holding him back.

"Remember, Blackie," called the Prince, "rage, fury, wrath! Pretend it's the dragon before you, the fiery dragon!"

"The dragon!" Blackie jumped at that. "Oh, if it were the dragon, I wouldn't pretend! If I ever catch that evil thing on the ground, nothing will stop me! I'll charge through fire and fangs! I'll tear open her belly!"

Picturing the foul serpent in his mind, he threw himself forward, dragging the grooms across the field.

"Hold tight!" shouted Sir Anthony, waving his sword. "Hold the unicorn! By the laws of civilized warfare, the castle must be given its chance to yield before the holy unicorn knocks it down and crushes everyone in it!"

Twenty spearmen threw down their weapons and jumped to help with the ropes. With four and five men on each line, Blackie threw them around, leaping, straining, kicking earth from the ground in his struggle to hurl himself at the gate tower and knock it to pieces.

"Hold him back!" yelled Prince George.

By now, everyone was shouting, swords beating against shields, trumpet blaring, drums pounding. Cupping his hands to his mouth, Sir Anthony bellowed above it all.

"Men of Castle Croy, you see the mighty unicorn before you! Your doom is upon you! Accept mercy at once! Surrender or die!"

Fearful screams rose from the castle. Terrified men threw their crossbows and spears from the walls. The drawbridge crashed down. The portcullis dragged up, and the defenders crawled out on their knees.

"We yields ourselves! Hold back the unicorn! Don't let him eat us!"

Fatigue grabbed Blackie at this point. He collapsed in a heap as Prince George dashed across the drawbridge to round up the prisoners and capture the castle. It was a complete surrender. Within five minutes, Baron Croy's banner flew high over the gate, and the cheering soldiers were released from their formations to straggle back to their billets in town. Blackie lay on his side, totally exhausted.

CHAPTER TWENTY-NINE

Healing

Blackie lay crumpled on the ground, sobbing for breath. Calder knelt over him, wiping foam from Blackie's muzzle with his cap.

"Good boy, good boy, you was perfect! Even knowing you was putting it on, you scared me worse than the Devil in the Corpus Christi play."

Prince George walked out to him, rolling up Vile's black banner to present to the Princess. "How's he doing, Calder?"

Calder looked up. "Don't worry about this beast, me lord. He's fine, just wore down after killing Hellions, last night. It's a wonder he could jump around like that."

"That's Blackie," said the Prince, looking down fondly. "He always comes through."

Baron Croy ran up to bend over Blackie. "Dear me, Prince George, I've never seen anything like this unicorn, never in my life! Thunder and lightning's nothing to him! He's a tempest in himself! Oh, my saints, am I glad he's on our side! I'd hate to have that horn charging down on me!"

The Baron insisted that Blackie be carried to the hall inside the castle. "I know it's not fit to receive him, but he deserves any honor I can give him. And you, my lord, what can I do for you? You captured the castle single-handedly. I'm sending a letter to the Empress to tell her so."

"Well, not single-handedly," said the Prince, blushing. "After all, we have two thousand men in the army."

"Not last night, you didn't," insisted the Baron. "You saved me from my own dungeon with a dozen men and a unicorn. What a deed that was!"

By now, a squad of soldiers had gathered about Blackie to carry him into the castle. As they started to lift him, Blackie feebly shook his horn.

"He wants to walk," said Prince George, waving them away. "Just help him onto his feet. He'll make his own way. That's how he is."

Shivering from exhaustion, Blackie wobbled through the courtyard on his hooves. He took one halting step after another, every bone aching in his body. Rampaging around this morning after charging last night—he felt like he'd never run again.

The soldiers had to help Blackie up a short flight of stairs. Baron Croy called for wine and honey to revive Blackie. The Baron looked bleakly around his ravaged hall. "If you can find anything in this mess."

Ashes, sticks, bones, shards of glass, and broken pots covered the floor. Staring through tired eyes, Blackie saw piles of trash and dirty rags in every corner. Benches were overturned, tables chopped up for firewood, nooses hanging from the beams. Even the tapestries on the walls were shot full of crossbow holes. Everything smelled of blood, beer, and vomit.

"No wine, me lord," reported one of the Baron's men, running up from the cellars, "and not much food. They got a dozen porkers hangin' in the storage room and a few barrels of beer."

"Any wheat, barley, anything the unicorn could eat?" asked the Prince.

"Nothing, me lord. Looks like they lived on beer and meanness."

"Well, check around the stables. See if there's hay. In the meantime, send those prisoners in here. Put them to work scrubbing everything. I want the bodies burned and the chambers perfumed before nightfall. Get a priest in here with a gallon of holy water. This castle needs blessing from top to bottom."

"Have them start over there, my lord," said the Baron, pointing to the fireplace end of the hall. "Clear the garbage and bones out of there. Let's get a good fire going."

There was a stir from the stairway, and the Knights marched in, followed by a shuffling line of prisoners bound by ropes.

"Hey, Baron, we've brought your cleaning staff. How's Blackie?"

"Poor beast," said the Baron, patting Blackie's head, "he's about to pass out from fatigue."

"Bless the creature, he did a great job out there." Sir Anthony slid his sword into his scabbard. "He scared even me."

He turned to four men carrying a wooden box slung on a pair of spears. "Set it down right here."

"My treasure chest!" exclaimed the Baron, clapping his hands together. "Is my crown in there?"

"We didn't open it, my lord," Sir Anthony said. "It's just as we found it."

The Baron fumbled with the hasp on the treasure chest as Prince George knelt by Blackie and shook him gently.

"Well, old boy, you've got to snap out of it for a moment. We've got more wounded to heal."

Exhausted, Blackie bleated out, "Leave me alone! Leave me alone! Heal them yourself."

Prince George understood his tone of voice. "I know you're tired, Blackie, but we have a hundred sick and injured with the army. It would have been worse if you hadn't scared these rascals out of the castle. Just one more sick call, and you can have a long sleep."

Blackie sighed and tried to rise.

"Give us some help here," ordered the Prince. The spearmen ran to lift Blackie.

"Look, my crown's gone!" exclaimed the Baron, pawing through the chest. "But this silver—I didn't put all this silver in here."

"Must be Vile's silver," said Sir Anthony. "That's how he bribes the lords."

"Well, at least, I made some profit out of this," said the Baron, pouring silver coins from both hands.

Sir Anthony reached down and picked up a silver coin. He weighed it in his hand.

"If you don't mind, my lord, I'll relieve you of a dozen of these. We need silver arrowheads for the dragon."

Soldiers began carrying litters of the injured to the far side of the hall. Prince George helped Blackie stumble across the rubbish to the first wounded soldier. The man had dirty bandages about his head.

"Oh, thankee, thankee, unicorn," he said, as Blackie took a deep breath and concentrated on pumping up his energy for the healing.

While Blackie healed his way through the injured, Prince George dashed to the doorway of the hall, jumping and whooping. He threw himself on a tall Darrman, who grinned back at him.

It was Godfrey of the Axe, Heir to the Duke of Darr, famous from all the songs about Prince George. On arriving at Croy, the Heir had hurried to the castle to pledge his service to Prince George as General of the army.

"It's been years since I've seen you, Godfrey!" cried Prince George, pounding the Heir on the back. "And you're a father now! How's Lady Dorinda? How's the old Duke?"

"They're well, all well!" shouted Godfrey with a laugh. "Thanks for asking, my lord! You can imagine what a time I had to get the Duke to stay home when I rode off with the barons. He swore that he'd bump along in a cart if he had to. He wanted his share of the fighting."

"So now, you're here with seven hundred men," smiled the Prince, offering Godfrey a cup of wine. "You arrive just in time for the big assault on Vile's army."

Godfrey took a deep drink. He pulled back the cup and shook his head.

"Sorry, my lord, I didn't actually bring seven hundred. I had to leave half my clansmen to hold the border, but I do have three hundred Darrmen, mountain men, all veterans, the best fighters in the Empire, and another two hundred from the barons."

"No matter, no matter!" exclaimed Prince George. "If you were alone, Godfrey, your axe would double our strength. Now, present your barons to me, if you please. I welcome all loyal lords."

Staggering from litter to litter with his healing, Blackie lost track of their pleasantries. He concentrated on keeping erect as he poured his healing into the pitiful cases before him. When he finished the last of them, he tried to crawl off to a quiet corner, but Prince George brought Godfrey and the nobles about him.

"So the unicorn's a hunter, is he?" asked Godfrey, leaning on his huge executioner's axe.

"No one understands the forest like Blackie," bragged Prince George. "He knows every grasshopper and vole in the wilderness.

He can round up more deer in an hour than we shot all morning at Furland."

"Those were the days, my lord!" exclaimed Godfrey, nodding his head. "We rode from one end of the Empire to the other in that Contest, free as birds of the air. What adventures we had!"

The Prince grinned at Godfrey. "So tell me, Godfrey, is Lady Dorinda as pretty as ever?"

"My lady's still the beauty of the land," said Godfrey, proudly, "and what a mother! So careful with the boy! She won't even let me give him a tin axe to chew on."

"Oh, yes, your child," said the Prince. "I should have asked about the little Heir."

Godfrey laughed. "He's a lively one, he is. Already weighs over twenty pounds. I can't wait for you to see him."

"My lord," said Neeve, Godfrey's captain, "about the hunt? Can we take the unicorn?"

"Sure, sure." Prince George waved his arm. "Blackie, you don't mind bringing in a few deer, do you?"

"Oh, no," thought Blackie. He shook his head, "I'm not getting into that again!"

"You won't?" demanded the Prince, surprised. "But Blackie, we're counting on you. The army needs food. You don't want us to turn to horsemeat, do you?"

"What?"

Now, Blackie was horrified. He'd put that horse-eating out of his mind since Saint Catherine's.

"I've told you again and again, Blackie, we're an army. The men can't fight without eating, and in winter—" Prince George shrugged. "They have to eat what they can get. If we camped by the river, they could eat fish, but here in the forest, well, you see how it is."

The Darrmen gave Blackie a bucket of sour wine to revive him. They let him sleep into the afternoon, but woke him up about two o'clock in a bitter mood. The humans insisted that he had to go with the bowmen, so he dragged himself to his hooves to run out over snowy hills, furious at the humans who couldn't supply themselves without pulling him into this filthy game. But what else could he do? He couldn't let horses get butchered. They were his cousins. But he wept for the very beasts he had to chase.

He hated the soldiers, so cheerful about the whole thing. They pressed around him in the lane, blessing him, petting him, before dropping behind when the lane narrowed into animal trails beyond the noise of the camp.

"Good luck, unicorn. Happy hunting!"

Blackie wanted to kick the bowmen spreading out to wait for the prey. Instead, he stormed over the hills to drive in the deer he found, along with a herd of wild, shaggy cows with a bull that tried to fight him. Tossing the bull and chasing it toward the huntsmen relieved some of his anger. When he heard the shouts of the shooters, he turned away from the killing and returned to town by another path.

Soldiers were everywhere in the village, drinking beer, wandering the street, talking to girls while sergeants patrolled with clubs in pairs to stop fights and protect the townsfolk.

Grumbling under the pats and hugs of soldiers as he walked the street, Blackie smelled a strong whiff of bread. His nose led him to the bakery, a big hut with a fence around the yard. Spearmen stopped him at the gate.

"Sorry, Unicorn. The bakery's off limits."

"That the unicorn?" called someone inside. "Let him pass."

The guards stepped back. Blackie trotted around the hut to a double row of beehive-shaped brick ovens that spread a delicious heat.

"Ho, Blackie!" someone called. It was Calder, sitting on a bench with a couple of his men in the steam and smell of the baking. Men in dirty aprons were kneading dough on tables and feeding round loaves into the ovens on long wooden shovels.

"Prince put me in charge of the bakery," explained Calder. "We got the town baker here and army bakers from Furland and Darr. We're turning out a hundred loaves an hour for the army. Give him a taste of our bread, Hob."

Hob was an old man with a squint in his eye and hands as brown as the loaves he was shaping. He tossed Blackie half a loaf of warm, crusty bread, the best thing Blackie had eaten for weeks. Blackie cheered up as he chomped the bread, switching his tail back and forth. He opened his mouth for the rest of the loaf.

"So, what do you think?" asked Calder, grinning at him. "That bread's Hob's own creation, two-thirds oats from Darr and the rest ground acorns."

"I knows how to wash out the acorns," Hob explained, grinning at Blackie. "Raw acorn'll pison ye, but if ye washes 'em over and over after grindin', ye gets a meal that makes a prime loaf."

"Yep," Calder leaned back with his beer cup, "Hob knows all about bread. He can bake a loaf from anything. Give him a taste of your carrot bread, Hob."

"Aw, that's nothin'," said Hob, rubbing his chin. "You should 'a seen the tricks of me old master. That man had a rare gift for bakin'. He were caught by the elves, one night, and put to bakin' little loaves for the Elf Queen from flower seeds and honey. He told me that the trick was keepin' 'em from burnin', tiny as they was."

"My aunt saw an elf one time," said Calder. "It squeezed under the door before she could catch it. Did your master get a reward from the Queen?"

"O' course, he did," nodded Hob. "She gave him one wish for his troubles. He could wish for anythin' so he used his wish to get hisself a young wife. Oh, that were a mistake, I can tell you. The Missus were so lively that she ruled his shop with a stick. We 'prentices had to step lively."

Blackie yawned. Relaxing in the yeasty warmth of the ovens, he closed his eyes. The men's voices faded into a dream of chasing deer around gigantic bread loaves. He had to drive the beasts on when they tried to snatch mouthfuls from the loaves.

Blackie slept long into the night. He woke while the army was still asleep in the quiet village. The bakers were packing firewood into their ovens to burn down to coals for the morning's baking.

"Go back to sleep again, Blackie," advised Calder, sleepily. "The bugles won't blow for hours."

Blackie tried to sleep, but he was too restless to relax. He ate a couple more loaves of bread and watched the bakers unload a cart of firewood to stack against the rear of the hut.

"You know, Blackie," said Calder, yawning, "I thought, last night, to set up as a baker when the war's over. This seems a cozy life in winter with the heat of the ovens and the smell of the bread. But who could stand the hours? The Baker has to be up bakin' when good Christians is sound asleep. No wonder he sees elves."

The flaming ovens soon had the bakery warm again. Blackie ate bread and listened to stories until the bugles blared in the streets to rouse the army. The bakers shouted goodbye when Blackie stepped out to the street. The sergeants were going from hut to hut, rousting soldiers who'd settled in with the townsfolk. Down at the assembly field beyond the gate, the Knights were standing by their mounts, ready to ride, while other companies collected their soldiers two and three at a time.

Waiting with the lords, Prince George was complaining to the Heir. "We're already an hour behind schedule, Godfrey. I don't call this military discipline. The Princess would be furious at this delay."

"It's not the army that's off, my lord," said Godfrey, stretching. "It's your schedule, not realistic. These men aren't trained and ordered like Roman legions. You've got a collection of clansmen from two score baronies. It'll be a wonder if they march by noon."

"I wish they were Romans," said the Prince, rolling up his chart. "The Roman cohorts ate as they marched and slept on their shields. They wouldn't even call this lot an army."

"Well, it'll be a couple hours at least before we march. Do you want to call the lords together for a parley?"

"What's to talk about?" growled the Prince. "Last night, we agreed to march at dawn!"

"Well, my lord, come back to your tent at least. You can stay comfortable until we ride."

Blackie followed down the hill to the banners and tents where the lords sat around the fire in their chairs. Prince George lounged in a field throne Godfrey had given him. It had a red cushion and a lion carved on the back.

"It folds up," explained Prince George proudly. "Like those ladders in that plum orchard at Cranch, remember, Blackie? We carry it in a box."

Blackie warmed himself at the fire, half-listening to the humans argue with each other.

"The bigger the army grows," grumbled the Prince, "the slower it gets. I hate these parleys. They just take up time. Every little baron has to give his speech, and they never agree on anything. If I'm General, I want to command."

"Well, my lord, that's leadership," said Godfrey, sharpening his axe on a stone, "convincing the peers to action."

"That's not leadership!" exclaimed the Prince. "Leadership is heading a cavalry charge into the spear-line while arrows fly like hailstones."

Godfrey snorted. "How many generals lead charges today? Leaders count supply wagons and keep records."

"Well, records must have their uses, I guess," said the Prince, settling back. "The Romans kept records."

Turning around before the fire, Blackie thought of the Romans. From what he'd heard, they were a strange folk who made their captives fight lions. Prince George had told him a story about the Romans capturing a unicorn to fight in their games. When the lions refused to fight him, the Romans sent in spearmen to prod them on, but the unicorn jumped up in the seats and carried off the Emperor on his horn.

It all seemed a waste of time to Blackie. Why would Romans want to make animals fight? Why keep records of that sort of thing?

Everyone looked up as a messenger galloped up to the fire and jumped down from his horse. He bowed to Prince George.

"My lord, my lord . . . Sir Sebastian, he needs the unicorn!"

"If he needs him, he can have him," drawled Prince George, waving a hand. "Blackie's always ready to help. What's up?"

The messenger wiped an arm across his face. He panted as he talked. "Fallen oak tree . . . two miles down . . . road closed. They need the unicorn to . . . to drag away the tree."

"Why, I can handle that job!" cried Godfrey, jumping up from his chair with his axe. "I'll call a dozen of my Darrmen. We'll chop that tree to firewood in twenty minutes."

"Oh, let Blackie handle it," said the Prince. "He'll tug it away with one jerk."

But Blackie was gone. As soon as he heard "needs the unicorn," he was running down a lane away from the army. He galloped into a field where the snow lay in even rows, jumped the fence at the far end, and trotted down a deer path through the trees.

Once he was beyond trumpet calls, he stopped and shook himself. No humans here. He felt free, free of the talk and stink and bad water of the camp.

"I can get a drink, here."

Blackie jumped a fallen limb into a stream, crunching down through the ice. He shook freezing water from his legs and bent his neck for a drink, gulping the water a cold mouthful at a time.

"Oh, good drink," he said, "fresh and clean. No taint of bucket or barrel, no goatskin taste. Yuk! I've had enough of that army. The bread was good, but the rest of it— I won't drag logs like a mule!"

Blackie turned into a woodcutter's trail running parallel to the road. He settled into an easy trot that carried him far beyond the army in a short time. Still grumbling about the army, he was startled by a pair of deer jumping out from a thorny clump of bushes, a third deer following. Blackie watched them with a smile.

"Run free, dear brothers!" he called. "Run free! No arrows will stab you, no fires roast you! Just feed and be happy in the forest!"

That brought him to a stop.

"Food!" he said. "What do I eat now? I can't get a dinner in this forest!"

The forest wasn't appetizing. It was all white and black, snowy hillsides with bare tree limbs sticking up. Blackie saw nothing he wanted to eat. Roots and twigs and tree bark—Blackie could chew that stuff if he had to, but he couldn't live on it like the deer did.

"I'm not even going to try. I'll look for more humans, perhaps a peaceful village. When spring comes, I can live in the forest, but now—"

He turned down the next trail leading back to the road. Running out ahead of the army, he reached the road before it got scuffed up by marching soldiers. The trees weren't chopped away for firewood here. The earth didn't smell like a toilet.

He trotted comfortably, listening to the click of bare limbs in the wind until he thought of the Princess. What would she say about him running off from Prince George?

"I'm not deserting him," Blackie insisted. "I can scout better on my own, move faster than dragging along with those slowpokes. I'll check the trail for ambushes. Could be I'll catch the dragon on the ground. I'm sure to find—Hellions!"

He wrinkled his nose at a strong sniff of the brutes. He'd forgotten those Hellions escaping down this road yesterday morning. Here, their smell was mixed with humans and a donkey. Trotting around a curve in the road, he found an overturned cart. Black chunks of charcoal were scattered on the snow along with donkey bones, splashed with dark red blood. Ravens fluttered up from the bones as he approached. They squawked at him from tree limbs above.

Gagging at the smell, Blackie turned into the trees to pass the scene. Trotting on, he smelled the Hellions, closer now after they'd taken their time to eat that donkey. His mind went to ravens.

"Crepitar, I wonder where he is. Nasty birds, those ravens. That bunch, at least, didn't seem to be spying for Vile, just enjoying their horrible feast."

The next smell he came to was human, children, a bunch of them. He smelled at least five boys, a girl, and a dog. The dog came first, running up the road to bark at him. Blackie kicked at the dog. It ran away howling.

"What about these children?" Blackie asked himself. "I can't slow down to help anyone. I want to catch the Hellions, give them what they deserve!"

He stopped, startled. It seemed that he'd made up his mind without noticing. He was set on catching those Hellions. Was that what he really wanted to do?

Walking slowly around the bend in the road, he smelled the children more strongly, but didn't see them until they jumped out from behind trees with sharp sticks for spears.

"Kill the unicorn!" they yelled. "Kill him! Prince Vile pays silver for unicorn horn!"

Blackie pulled back, astonished, as the grubby children ran at him, led by a redheaded girl in a man's cap.

"Children . . . sell me to Vile? Don't they know I'm a holy beast, a healer?"

Blackie jumped away as they threw their sticks at him. He dashed between the trees and galloped up the hill, the dog barking after him. He heard the children shouting in high voices as he looped around and trotted back to the road where he found a doll in the snow.

"One of those little demons had a doll."

Blackie turned the doll with his horn. It had knotted brown hair and a smile stitched in red yarn.

He left the doll where he found it and trotted on. A mile further, the road widened upon joining with another trail. Blackie smelled traffic here. Men and horses had stamped the snow into frozen slush. The Hellion smell was gone at this point.

Blackie came to a halt, unsure if he wanted to continue. Where to now? He could turn back to the army or continue forward. Blackie decided to trot on a few more miles.

"I've had enough of deer hunts and sick calls. I'll fight if I catch the Hellions, but I won't obey any orders."

He began passing small groups of travelers who ran into the forest on seeing him. He trotted by empty villages. One or two had been abandoned intact, though most were knocked to pieces. That sight was becoming familiar to Blackie, the streets littered with furnishings and clothes, farm tools broken and rusting.

Rats looked up from shattered pots and baskets. They watched with gleaming eyes as Blackie sniffed around for food stores, bags of nuts hanging from cracked roof beams, half-rotten cabbages buried in straw. The rats held back, squeaking, while Blackie ate what he could. They poured in the moment he left.

Blackie stayed away from the castles on hills. He knew that the barons loyal to the Crown would be low on food, while the others would grab him as a prize for Prince Vile.

Dusk was creeping through the trees when Blackie found a siege in place at Castle Bales. The castle had a good position on a hill over a frozen lake, but the besiegers had surrounded it with a bulwark of boards, loose doors, and wagon beds. Blackie caught an archer sitting on a log by the lake, but didn't know what to do with him.

The man squirmed under Blackie's hoof, yelling threats. "Lemme me up, foul beast, lemme up! I'll show ye when I get holt o' me bow!"

Turning aside, Blackie stomped on the bow to break it, but it bent like a tree branch. Blackie grabbed it up in his teeth and ran off with it. He dropped it behind a bush down the road and turned to look back at the smoke from the fires around the castle.

"The army will have to clear that up when it marches by. I can't save everyone."

The snow was beginning again, first drifting flakes, then a steady fall that freshened the layer on the tree limbs. It was early evening now, the forest darkening by the minute. Blackie moved out of the trees into a scrappy wasteland of untended fields coated with snow.

Tired and depressed, he walked slowly until horn calls swung him around. Across a broad field, he heard shouts and the hammering of arms. Curiosity drew him into the field, but he stopped himself with an effort.

"No, no, I promised myself, no battles today. I'll fight for the Princess, but these little frays, I'm keeping free of them."

He heard a bellow and watched a mule scramble into the rutted road with a wagon bouncing behind. Men in ragged jackets chased after it. The wagon lost a wheel on a rock. The men grabbed the mule's halter and dragged it to a stop.

Blackie ran on despite the mule's bawling. Darkness shrouded the countryside, but Blackie kept trotting through the snow. The road rounded a hill and Blackie saw the fire of a burning village. He heard dogs howling out in the night.

Blackie moved silently toward the village, his dark coat powdered with snow. At the gate, he saw a row of weeping women standing on beer kegs. A man in a helmet sat on a horse, surrounded by spearmen. He held a parchment up to the light of a torch.

"This document, signed by Prince Vile, gives me claim to all holdings of the traitor, Lord Gammel. Since your husbands continue to serve this Lord Gammel with spear and shield, I'm hanging you high as an example. The folks of this Barony need a lesson in obedience."

Blackie was close enough to see nooses rising from the necks of the women to the gatepost above.

"This one," thought Blackie, "I gotta stop."

Blackie didn't bother to charge. He shoved through the spearmen to knock their leader off his horse. The horse ran for the hills, stomping over its master as the women wobbled on the barrels, trying to stay erect.

Blackie whirled to deal with the open-mouthed spearmen. They stared at him a moment, then fled, dropping their weapons and running across the field after the horse.

As they ran, men and boys came yelling out of the darkness with homemade spears and knives. They caught some of the runners and dragged them down, then turned to cut the women free. Limp with shock, the women could barely stand, but the men held them up while children gathered about, hugging their mothers and crying.

"Oh, blessed unicorn!" shouted a woman, throwing herself on Blackie. She pulled back and looked closely. "You are a unicorn, ain't you, with that horn?"

"We was prayin' with the Baron up to the chapel, Peggy," said her husband, reaching an arm over her shoulders. "Then Tolly noticed the fire. Why didn't you send someone to warn us?"

"We was caught by surprise," said Peggy, pulling the noose off her head. "They came sweepin' in with their torches and rounded us up afore we could run. But why you talkin' here, man? Put them out them fires before the whole village burns!"

The men and women ran to save the village, leaving the bodies of raiders bleeding in the snow. Blackie saw a big-eyed girl hanging behind to watch him. She held a twisted hand to her breast. She drew back as Blackie stepped forward, but he touched his horn to her hand, healed it with a spark, then turned into the darkness and crunched off through the snow.

The children shrieked after him. A woman cried, "Who was that, who was that?"

"Saint Eustace, it was," answered a hoarse voice. "The holy Saint, it had to be, takin' the shape of a unicorn."

"Come back, Saint Eustace, come back!"

Blackie felt a surge of satisfaction as he trotted back to the road. He'd done a good deed, helped the humans, and escaped without getting caught up in their troubles. If they had food to give him, he might stay around, but those people looked as hungry as he was, hungry enough to eat anything.

"That horse," he said, "it better stay away from those humans."

Blackie shivered. Tired and hungry as he was, his sturdy coat couldn't keep out the cold.

"Time to get out of this wind."

He passed another abandoned village. Up a lane just beyond, he saw a spot of red light. It turned out to be a lamp over the gate of a large building with windows faintly lit.

Blackie stopped for a moment, stamping in the icy lane, while he considered whether he should take a chance on this place.

"That red lamp—" he thought. "Surely, it means these people are all right. I can't see villains putting out a welcome light."

He grew more uncertain as he trotted closer. The wind blew a strange smell to him, rank and putrid, while Blackie heard a noise that stopped him, a wail of hopeless suffering. Out of the gate trudged two men in white robes carrying a dark figure on a stretcher. Without noticing him in the darkness, they passed around the building, chanting a prayer as they walked.

"They're praying," Blackie thought, shivering in the wind. "That's a good sign."

He waited until the men returned, then moved forward, crunching lightly through the snow. Startled, the men stopped to peer at his dark form against the white background.

"That horn—!" gasped one, dropping the stretcher. "It's . . . it's the answer to our prayers, the unicorn!"

"Oh, thank the Lord!" cried the other. "The healer has come."

To Blackie's astonishment, they burst into tears and rushed forward to embrace him. Blackie smelled that putrid stink on their robes.

"Oh, you're just in time, just in time!" they cried, stroking him and talking at the same time.

"Come inside, unicorn. We have food for you."

"We've lost so many!"

"Bread, hay, whatever you like! And work, the Lord's work!"

"Oh, yes, the holy labor of the Lord."

Blackie moved slowly as the men urged him. He wasn't sure about this place. He was hungry and these men sounded genuine in their welcome, but the smells and the cries increasing as he neared the door were enough to drive anyone away.

One man held the door for him while the other gently pulled him forward by his mane. Blackie stuck his head into the great hall and saw a frightful sight. A smoky fire in the center of the room lit up rows of straw pallets stretching from one end of the wide floor to the other. Shivering figures tossed on the pallets, coughing, gasping, wailing, cursing. Men in white ran from one patient to the next, offering drinks, wiping foreheads, praying over those at the point of dying.

"As you see," murmured one of the men with Blackie, "the Death has come to us, the curse brought down by the sins of the world. We can do so little to stop it! Half our Order has died already, and the rest of us—We'll work until we drop unless your virtue can stop the disease."

"Oh, oh."

Blackie's heart sank in his chest. He turned to dash back out that door. He knew, of course, what these friars wanted, what humans always wanted, but he was weary already. He needed rest himself, and he saw hundreds of suffering humans about the room.

"This is just the men's chamber," explained the friar, pulling Blackie inside. "The women lie next door. We accept all who come to us, you see."

"Give him bread, Brother Matthew," suggested the other man. "The holy beast needs sustenance for his work."

"Oh, of course, of course! I'll be right back."

Brother Matthew moved off, stepping carefully between the pallets, stopping to straighten a man who'd rolled off his bed.

The other friar patted Blackie, suggesting, "If you could begin at once, dear unicorn. So many are dying. The Death starts with a wheezy cough, then the fever. The poor souls are gone within a week, some in a day. Villages are emptied when the plague strikes."

"Oh, why did I leave the army?" thought Blackie, staring around. "I'd drag a hundred fallen trees rather than face this horror. But what will happen when the army catches up? This area's infected. The soldiers will all catch the disease. I can't heal the whole world!"

"Of course, you can't heal all of them."

Gently stroking Blackie, the Friar echoed Blackie's thoughts.

"Not tonight, dear unicorn, there are many, so many, and you're tired yourself. We'll guide you to the very sickest, the dying. Tomorrow, when revived by a good rest, you can finish the job. What a blessing you are, bringing hope to the hopeless, peace to a warring world."

"Oh, what can I do?" thought Blackie, taking a deep breath of stinking air. "I'm stuck now. Serving humans, that's my doom. The more I try to avoid it, the deeper I fall in. Papa escaped, but not me. Maybe it's for the best, though. If I can stop the sickness now, Prince George and the soldiers may be safe when they ride by."

So Blackie started on his horrible work, guided by the friers from pallet to pallet to stretch his horn to the most racked and wretched in the room.

The worst part was the distress of those he passed by. Those just touched by the Death were still strong. They could sit up as he moved toward them, their eyes glittering, teeth shining. They cried out when

Blackie stepped past to the blind and drooling who weren't even aware of his presence until flooded by the power of the horn.

"Why not me?" screamed the others. "Me, me, me! I'm suffering, too! I'm dying, can't you see?"

They grabbed for his horn, his legs, his tail, shouting in protest as the friars pushed them away them with promises that the healer would return. They burst out with curses and fell back, coughing, spitting blood, choking on their fear and fury as Blackie labored through the hospital to save as many as he could until he fell asleep against a cold wall in the women's chamber, totally drained of spirit.

The friars eased Blackie onto a bed of straw. They washed him with warm water, dried him with rags, threw on blankets to keep him warm. Leaving him shuddering in his dreams, they dragged themselves through the chambers of the hospital to serve warm soup to the revived while assuring the rest that their healing would come. The Lord had sent his unicorn. No one would be forgotten.

CHAPTER THIRTY

Reunion

Brother Simon hustled into the hospital wiping his hands on a dirty towel. He beamed upon Blackie, standing exhausted over a litter. "Good news, Holy One, your friends are riding by! Brother Malachi says that South Road is packed with soldiers."

"At last," groaned Blackie, shaking sweat from his mane. He needed a break. These days of healing had been the worst of his life.

"The friars," he told himself in wonder, "they're the true heroes. Day after day, they treat these bleeders and sneezers, wailers and weepers! How can they stand it? I can't take it! I don't eat. I don't sleep! I've lost thirty pounds since I got here."

He sighed and moved to the next litter.

"Aw, unicorn," croaked the man, reaching up a thin arm, "here you is at last. You bin passin' me up, passin' me up while I suffers. I thought you'd never get to me, and you come too late for Susie over to the women's side. She's gone without me so much as holdin' her hand."

Blackie leaned down his horn. When the healing struck, the man gasped, "Oh!" He tried to push to his feet.

"Not so fast," cautioned Brother Simon, holding him back. "Stay still till you clear your head. You need rest before you try to walk."

The man settled back and stroked Blackie's knee.

"Remember me, unicorn, remember me when you travels on. Big Dave, the butcher o' Brade. Stop by me shop when you pass through town. I'll give you the best dinner you ever et, though . . . though it won't be Sue what cooks it."

"All these names," thought Blackie, lifting his horn. "Big Dave, Susie, Bessie, Ann. How can I remember them all?"

"Isn't it wonderful?" cried Brother Simon, rubbing his hands in delight. "What a miracle to actually cure sickness! All these years I've cared for patients, held them, soothed them, prayed over them, but few of them, such a pitiful few, ever recovered. Now, with you here, we've cleared the room all but this corner over here. Just imagine, hundreds of people running home because of you, unicorn. They'll make our hospital famous. Donors will come forth, rich donors! We can build a new chapel!"

Shaking his head, Blackie staggered to the next litter.

"Don't give me the credit," he thought. "I hate this job! I'm leaving as soon as I'm finished. These friars spend their nights with crocks and cripples, not me. I'll be out of here as soon as the Prince arrives. I'll never come near a place like this, not if I can help it."

To the last moment, the friars kept carrying in stretchers. It seemed to Blackie that it'd go on to doomsday. At last, though, Prince George ran into the hall, crying his name.

"Blackie, Blackie!"

Blackie swung about to see the Prince jumping beds to get to him, only to jerk back with a squeal, "What happened to you? You're foul! You stink!"

He stared at Blackie in disgust. "Look at you! Snot, spit all over your coat! Horn black with filth! Why'd you run off like that? I was worried about you! I had to ride a horse the past couple days. After you, it was like riding a tortoise!"

"The Unicorn, my lord," cried Brother Simon, signing the Cross, "he's doing the work of the Lord! He's a saint, an angel on four legs. He healed the sickest of the sick. He stopped the Death."

"The Death!"

Prince George fell back, stumbling over a bed. He jumped up, frantically brushing at his bearskin. The Heir and the Commander had followed him into the room. They all backed away, repeating, "The Death? The Death?"

"I didn't realize," gasped Prince George, "it was the . . . the Death."

"It had every sign of plague, my lord," beamed Brother Simon. "The brothers were dying about me. We were sure we'd all be wiped out, but then Saint Jude sent the unicorn."

"Splendid, Blackie, splendid," said the Prince, holding a dirty handkerchief to his nose. "Let's get out of this nauseating place. You need a bath!"

"The army needs you, unicorn!" bellowed the Commander. "We've got our own sick and injured to care for. We haven't had a proper sick call since you ran away."

Blackie rolled his eyes. "Sick call! Here we go again! That's all they think I'm good for!"

"So, friars," said the Heir, looking around the room, "the unicorn healed all your patients? That's good, good. We can use this hall for our headquarters. We'll burn those filthy litters. We'll scrub the walls with vinegar and herbs. It'll be good as new."

"Uh, Godfrey," said Prince George, shaking his head, "don't you think we'd better move along to the next castle? The soldiers won't come near a hospital that's had the Death in it."

"Don't worry, my lord!" cried the Heir, cheerily. "If anyone gets sick, Blackie can cure them."

"No, no," insisted the Prince, edging toward the door, "we don't want to hang around a hospital. The smell would sicken a tanner. Let's find someplace healthy to set up. Come on, Blackie."

"Just these last cases," said Blackie to himself, limping to the dark corner. "I promised to finish the job."

To free himself from the Hospital, he moved quickly between the litters, swinging his horn from right to left. He touched this man and that before reaching the last patient, a huge lump on a double-pallet, so large he had three flimsy blankets stretched over him.

"That's a big one," said Godfrey, walking with Blackie while Prince George hovered near the door.

"We found him in the road," said the Friar. "Took six men to haul him in."

Eyes closed, Blackie leaned down with a sigh and emptied himself of healing power.

"Stop!" yelled Prince George, dashing toward him. The blankets flew back. A Hellion sprang up with a roar, catching Blackie toppling

411

over. Brother Simon leaped forward to grab the huge arm around
Blackie's neck.

"Unhand that unicorn, you fiend!"

"Oonicorn good!" roared the Hellion. "Mardoc likes oonicorn!"

He set Blackie back on his hooves and gave him a smacking kiss on
the forehead.

Godfrey stopped his axe in mid-swing. Blackie lifted his tired head
to stare at the Hellion, who looked around with a goofy grin.

"Mardoc hungry. Got any bones to chew?"

"You mean," asked Brother Simon, letting go of the brawny creature
and stepping back, "you're not attacking the unicorn?"

"Mardoc loves oonicorn," said the Hellion, stroking Blackie with a
great hand. "Oonicon make Mardoc well."

Brother Simon crossed himself. "Bless the Lord, the monster's
redeemed! Another miracle of the unicorn."

Prince George leaned on his spear, watching through narrowed
eyes. "I don't think Hellions can be redeemed. I'd knock him in the
head and forget about him."

Brother Simon reached for Mardoc's hand. "Come, Mardoc, there's
bones in the kitchen, piles of them. And we have work for you. If you're
truly reformed, you can carry the litters for us."

They watched the friar leave with the Hellion, the monster
slouching tall over the man.

"Well, Prince," said Godfrey, resting his axe on his shoulder, "did
you know the unicorn could heal souls like that?"

Prince George shook his head, walking beside Blackie. "A Hellion
saved? I don't believe it. I think that Mardoc saw himself surrounded.
He just pretended to reform."

The Heir held the door for Blackie and the Prince. Blackie took a
breath of cold, clean air and shivered.

"If Mardoc is redeemed, my lord," said Godfrey, "we should recruit
him for the army. We could use another point man to lead the charge
beside Blackie."

"Leave the fighting to me," thought Blackie, swaying from fatigue.
"Let Mardoc drag the logs."

Out in the road, they held a quick conference. They'd heard there
was a castle a few miles ahead, but had no report yet on its condition.

Godfrey suggested they haul Blackie there on a wagon, but the Prince pointed out that the horses were already tired from the march.

"Let's stop right here," he said. "Put up the tents and let the troopers camp in the field. Blackie needs fresh air. Didn't you see how he was sweating in there? That place got to him, feverish, poisonous. What he needs now is apples and honey to give him energy."

"I've got raisins," said Godfrey, "plenty of raisins. We had a bumper crop of grapes up at Darr last fall."

Blackie eased his hunger with a bucketful of raisins, but he felt drained from inside out. His horn felt tender, his legs clumsy. He stumbled when he tried to walk, so Prince George had a cartload of straw spread under a canopy. They helped Blackie down to the dry bedding.

While the troopers set up the tents, Prince George knelt beside Blackie to wipe his horn with a handkerchief.

"I missed you the last couple days, old fellow. I'd rather patrol ahead with you than hang back at the pace of the wagons. It's boring to creep along with the army. And look how thin and drawn you are! Those friars worked you too hard!"

"But he stopped the Death," said Godfrey with wonder. "You ever hear of anyone stopping the Death?"

"Thank Heaven for that," said the Commander. "That plague would have run through the troops like the cruddies."

"So Blackie," said the Prince, standing as solders set up his throne, "we want you to rest up, get healthy. We have work for you, but it can wait till tomorrow. The horses need healing. Don't worry. It's not plague with them. Just ordinary complaints—cracked hooves, sprains, gripes from bad food and water, that sort of thing."

"Now, it's horses I'm healing," thought Blackie. "At least, they'll be cleaner than humans."

"I think we'll rest here a couple days," said the Prince, signaling a boy to him. "This is a good spot to prepare our assault on Vile's army before the City."

The boy bowed to Prince George.

"Run to the Quartermaster," ordered the Prince. "Tell him the unicorn will treat the horses tomorrow."

Blackie lay limp. Over his heavy breath, he heard Prince George speak to the officers. "Without news from the City, we don't know the situation there. We may have to go straight into battle from the march, so let's use this break to sharpen our spears and rest the horses."

Blackie thought of Mardoc the Hellion. What a start he'd had when that monster had jumped at him! Mardoc did seem to be redeemed. Is it possible that his horn could reform villains? Could it change Prince Vile?

For the first time in days, Blackie had a long, peaceful sleep, but the horses, next morning, were a woeful sight. They were penned in separate groups—bone and muscle problems in one pen, hoof ailments in another, the diseased fenced off by themselves. The sick horses were frightening—thin and balding, weeping, coughing, sweating, spewing. Some kicked about, wild and anxious, screeching at anyone that came near. Others lay senseless with eyes closed, tongues hanging out, dragging in painful breaths that shook their bony sides.

The grooms helped as much as they could by keeping the horses in order so Blackie could get to them. They soothed the nervous and held the hysterical, but it was an anxious, tiring job to treat them.

Prince George brought Blackie a bucket of milk and honey to invigorate him when the healing left him tottering. He had to pause after each horse, horn down, breathing hard, to pull himself together before stumbling to the next nag. Grooms held him when he staggered while laying his horn to the shoulder of the beast to pour out a strong charge for such a large creature.

Prince George stayed with Blackie for the first dozen horses before running off to a parley. Blackie was left to the horses and the grooms.

By the time he was done with the job, Blackie felt as feeble as the horses he was treating. The grooms helped him over to their fire. They threw an armload of hay into a manger and let him eat while washing him with warm water. They rubbed him well and threw a blanket over him. He went to sleep with his horn resting in the hay.

Hours later, a sergeant shook him awake. "Prince wants you, unicorn. Over by the tents."

"We got him cleaned up and ready to go," said the head groom, patting Blackie's rump. "He's a different beast than he was last night."

Blackie hobbled through the camp with the sergeant. Everywhere he looked, he saw soldiers sleeping, cooking, sewing clothes, tossing dice. They ran to him from all sides.

"You remember me, holy unicorn!" cried a man waving an arm. "Little Burt, the bowman with the leg broke twice. It were swole up big as an eggplant an' more purpler. Look at this leg now!"

Blackie felt a sting at his mane. Another stolen hair. He swung his horn around, knocking away the humans.

"Back, you rogues!" cried the sergeant, hammering out with his stick. "Leave him alone! The beast can't breathe for you squeezin' around!"

The soldiers shouted in protest. "We wouldn't squeeze him! We love the unicorn!"

"Well, pray for him then!" yelled the Sergeant. "Don't climb all over him!"

They marched through the camp to cheers and blessings. They found Prince George and the Heir talking to the officers before the tents. Prince George paused to give Blackie a hug.

"Sorry, old fellow, about this morning. I know how tired you were, but those horses needed you. It's a struggle to keep the nags healthy in wintertime. Now you can relax at the fire. We've got a big dinner on its way."

Blackie walked to the bonfire with the Prince and the Heir. Blackie moved close to the fire, shutting his eyes and panting.

"We're planning our approach to the City," said the Prince, patting Blackie's shoulder. "I've volunteered to lead the vanguard."

"Noble as ever, my lord," said the Heir, leaning on his axe. "I argue, Unicorn, that we should run straight into battle from the march. Charge right in swinging axes before the villains have time to react. That's the way to break through a siege."

Blackie opened his eyes, throwing up his horn.

"This Heir's a man for me!" he thought. "Charge ahead, get the thing over with—that's the unicorn way."

"You're the same as ever, Godfrey!" said the Prince, clapping the Heir on the back. "I used to think that way, but now I'd rather move carefully. Check out the situation, you know. Look for the weak spots. Cunning has helped as much as courage in my battles."

"Whatever you decide, Prince, you can count on my Darrmen. Give the word, and we'll chop through those Hellions like a hot knife through butter. And if the dragon shows up, why, look at this!"

He showed his axe to Blackie. "A silver coating to my blade! That'll slice old Rosie's neck if I get near her!"

Blackie admired the axe, a wide-bladed executioner's chopper, but he was skeptical about the notion of slicing dragon necks.

"Has this man ever seen a dragon?" he asked himself. "It's easy to talk of slicing necks when you're snug by the fire, but it's different when the serpent's blasting down at you from the sky."

"Look now, Blackie. "Prince George scratched around Blackie's horn. "I have veggies for you and honeycakes! Lord Brand sent wagonloads of turnips, parsnips, and onions. They're stewing in the kitchen, right now, with a dozen oxen roasting in a pit. It's a regular soldier's feast!"

The words seemed strange to Blackie. Feasts had come seldom since leaving the Shrine. He'd eaten scraps of this and bits of that between chasing deer, fighting Hellions, and all that dreadful healing. Mostly, he'd nibbled the scarce leaves and dry stems he found in the forest. Calder's hot bread, now, that had seemed a feast.

As he watched, the bakers came running in from the ovens with huge trays of steaming cakes, fragrant with walnuts and honey. That scent would make you cry for peacetime when every village smelled of cakes and cookies and Blackie had only warts and flea bites to heal. With a moan of satisfaction, Blackie chomped into the cakes, gobbling oozing, nutty sweetness. He felt strength flooding back in him.

"How about a bucket of milk to go with your cakes?" asked the Prince.

Blackie was licking his lips when a sudden roar went up. The officers whirled to stare at the troops along the road who'd begun cheering and shouting, clashing swords against shields as the cake tray spilled to the ground.

"What's that?" cried Prince George. He snatched up his spear and ran toward the cries. Blackie followed, the Heir jogging behind with his axe. They ran around a group of horses bucking against their tethers to see the whole army jumping and screaming like madmen, hats and gloves flying into the air. Bowmen shot wild arrows to the sky. They shouted warnings as the arrows zoomed back down to thump in the ground.

"What is it?" shouted the Prince, running beside Blackie.

"It's peace!" cried a spearman, weeping on his knees. "Peace has come! The war's over!"

"What?" shouted the Heir. "Peace, already, after we marched four hundred miles in frozen wintertime?"

Blackie stood panting by the road while the Prince sang along with a great song swelling over the camp.

> Praise God who sends the sun and rain.
> Praise Him who gives the grape and grain.
> Praise Him who comforts when we weep.
> Praise God who watches while we sleep.

After a dozen rounds, the song died away, only to be picked up down the road and work its way back to be shouted out with greater fervor by those nearby.

"Hold this, Godfrey!" Prince George tossed his spear to the Heir. He pulled up on Blackie and grabbed the spear again. "Come, Blackie. Let's go see what's happening."

Blackie tossed his head about, looking in wonder as they trotted through the singing, weeping army. Whole companies of troopers swayed together, arms over their comrades' shoulders. Other soldiers stood alone, breathing the words like a prayer. A wild-eyed man waved his arms to the skies, shouting in a high voice, "Beat your spearheads into sickles, your swords into plowshares!"

Barons ran up to the Prince with questions, but the Prince trotted by. "No, my lords, sorry. I don't know what it means, either. I'm riding to find out."

"Lord bless you, Prince!" the barons shouted after him. "Saints smile on your battles!"

Passing the companies of spearmen, they began riding through strange groups of walkers. A pack of penitents singing a solemn hymn, barefooted, bareheaded, were followed by a lord in a white sheet tossing coppers to a snatching crowd of beggars.

"Pray for my sins, dear brothers! Pray for my sins!" he cried tossing another handful of coins.

"That was Lord Blackheart," said the Prince in wonder. "He's shaved his head."

They rode through a bedraggled troupe of minstrels and players, tossing instruments and costume bags into the air. When they saw the Prince, they flourished their cloaks, singing out, "Alms for the artists who bring your fame! Remember us, Prince! We celebrate your deeds in song and story!"

A player ran to Blackie, brandishing a huge unicorn tail made of yarn. "I'm the man that plays the rump! I get all the laughs!"

"It's the General!" cried another group of soldiers. "Prince George!"

Clustering around Blackie, they stroked him from all sides. They reached to Prince George's boots, his bearskin. They broke away when Godfrey galloped up at that point, riding a horse that came up to Blackie's shoulder.

Prince George pushed away the last of them, commenting sourly, "All those songs and stories, Godfrey, they've become a bother! People won't let me alone now."

"You're famed, my lord," smiled the Heir. "You're lauded. I told you in the old days that you'd be a hero."

"You didn't warn me that I'd be pestered and plagued wherever I go. How can I ride with mobs swarming about me?"

Beyond the players, Blackie saw a rainbow of flapping banners. He heard the singing of priests riding slowly on their mules amid a cloud of incense. Prince George doffed his hat as a statue of the Virgin was carried by. Blackie stood gazing until he got a whiff of a sweeter perfume.

Swinging up his head to look over the priests, he saw his Princess riding Midnight in a cloak of white fur with a white hat, her magic bow sticking up over her shoulder. Filled with sudden vigor, Blackie rose on rear hooves, trumpeting as the Prince clutched his neck to hold on.

"Blackie, what's gotten into you?"

The Princess rose in her stirrups, waving both arms. "There you are, Blackie! Georgie, Prince George, have you heard the news? I won the war! I saved the Empire! I'll be a warrior queen for sure!"

She pushed her horse through the priests, waving frantically. "Down, Georgie, down! I must ride my unicorn! You've had him too long, you slug, you snail!"

Sputtering indignantly, Prince George dropped to the road. He reached for his hat, fallen into the slush, as the Princess swung onto Blackie with a great sweep of skirts and furs. She threw her arms around Blackie's neck, burying her face in his mane.

"Oh, Blackie, how I've missed you! It's been months since I've seen you!"

She settled back to adjust her skirt as Lady Jessica rode up on Butterball, a pretty red scarf about her neck. The other Court ladies trailed behind.

"Welcome, Prince, welcome!" cried Jessica. "It's so good to see you, my lord! And the songs about you, more a hero than ever!"

Red-faced, Prince George bowed to the ladies as the Princess crowed with delight, "Jessie, Jessie, look at Blackie! He's two hands taller than he was, and his horn—it's longer than my arm!"

"He's a mighty unicorn to be sure," smiled Jessica.

Blackie swept his horn around to watch his Princess shake her head at Prince George.

"Prince, Prince, I'm ashamed of you! Didn't the Empress write for you to hurry to our aid? Here you are at last, weeks late, months late! Oh, I know you from old! You've been feasting your way across the countryside! You've lived high in castles while Vile attacked the City. You've been treating this campaign as a pleasure tour!"

"Pleasure tour!" gasped the Prince, his face red.

"Yes, pleasure tour," repeated the Princess. "Without your help, we had to drive off the enemy ourselves with a handful of lords and our loyal commons."

"Slanders, lies!" cried the Prince. "There were no parties! I'll have you know we had to fight our way across the countryside without supplies. We had sickness among the men."

"So that's the way it was!" cried the Princess. "Of course, you're short of supplies! Bad planning! Organization, logistics, according to the Romans, that's the sign of good leadership. That's why I've got a wagon train following a few miles back."

"But, Princess," asked Godfrey in amazement, "where did you get supplies? We heard that Vile's army had starved the City."

"Oh, yes, yes, we were down to cooking rats and shoe leather," nodded the Princess, "but the harbor opened to ships the moment the siege lifted. Supplies poured in from friends and allies eager to support

419

us. The problem was gathering wagons, but nothing's impossible to the resourceful. Had I been as slow as you, we'd never had made it here."

"We hurried as fast as we could!" protested the Prince, jamming his hat on his head. "I'd like to see you try to collect troops from reluctant barons and keep them fed them in wintertime!"

"No matter, no matter!" cried the Princess. "You'd have gained honor had you hurried, but I won the war without you. When the dragon burned about the City, it came down to Aleet and me. I fought off the monster with my magic bow while you lolled around the countryside. But now, where do we go to celebrate my victory?"

Godfrey spoke up again. "Our headquarters is in the field back there, my lady. We'd be honored to receive you there."

"Oh, Godfrey," cried the Princess, beaming at him, "grown so great, I didn't recognize you at first! 'My lord Heir,' I must call you now. How's dear Dorinda and your son? How I long to see that young lord!"

"They're splendid, my lady," grinned Godfrey, bowing in the saddle, "splendid! Thank you for asking about them."

The Princess sighed, adjusting her hat. "Oh, Godfrey, too bad you're not chopping heads these days. With all these bandits and rebels about, we need your axe more than ever!"

"You can be sure, sweet lady, I'd willingly swing my axe for you," replied the Heir with another bow. "But Lady Dorinda, she's expects me home as soon as possible. She only let me ride on campaign to save you."

"Oh, I must find time to visit your lady!" cried the Princess. "I can't wait to see your baby."

"Come visit whenever you can, my lady," begged the Heir. "You're always welcome at Castle Darr."

"I'm sure I am," she said, urging Blackie closer to hold out her hand for Godfrey's kiss. "I've heard wonderful tales about you, my lord, holding the border against Hellions, and, now, riding with your Darrmen to rescue us. If we had more lords like you, Prince Vile couldn't have started this rebellion in the first place!"

"But you must realize, my lady," insisted the Heir, "the army wouldn't have got this far without my lord Prince. He's the leader who gathered these barons into an army. He scouted our way on the road. He captured Castle Croy in the teeth of the dragon."

"The dragon!" echoed Jessica, drawing in her arms.

"The dragon was at Croy?" asked the Princess in surprise. "So that's what happened to her! She disappeared from the siege three weeks ago. Once she was gone, we were able to stop the fires and break the siege."

"It was all Prince George, my lady!" insisted the Heir. "He charged on the unicorn, killing Hellions by the dozens, and chased the dragon away. Lord Croy, himself, told me the story. The castle surrendered after Prince George drove across the drawbridge. Why, I'm sure that the Hellions fled the City when they heard that Prince George was coming after them."

"Georgie, this is news!" cried the Princess, pulling off her glove to squeeze the Prince's hand. "This explains why the Hellions gave up the siege so suddenly. So many of Vile's men had died of the plague by that point that the rest just melted away. I determined at once to ride out and meet the army to release your men. There's no need for them to continue to the City when they have their own families to care for."

"So thoughtful," Blackie said to himself. "She always thinks of others."

"My lady, your hand's cold," said Prince George, "you must take shelter in the tents."

The Princess shivered. "Tents, Prince? Have you no better place to receive me?"

"At least, you'll be out of the wind, Princess. Or would you rather settle into a hospital? Blackie healed the patients, so it's empty, and it's big enough for all your Court."

"Even better, my lord," suggested Godfrey, smiling, "why don't we return to Castle Croy. It's only a few miles back, and her Majesty can witness the scene of your victory."

"Excellent!" cried the Princess. "I must examine the castle you captured, Georgie. You may ride Midnight to escort me to the castle. And Godfrey, I promise to ride up to Darr as soon as the rebuilding starts. The City's battered now. You wouldn't believe how horrible it is."

Prince George tried to mount Midnight as ordered, but the horse pulled away from him.

"I don't want the man," she snorted, "clumsy, heavy lump. You take him, unicorn. I'll carry my lady."

"But the Princess wants you to carry him," insisted Blackie, as grooms ran to hold her steady.

The horse continued protesting, but settled down once Prince George was in the saddle.

"Follow me," said the Prince, grumpily, turning Midnight back up the road.

By now, the companies of the army were standing at attention as the Princess rode past. Prince George led the way while Godfrey followed with Jessica, then the ladies and Guards and the rest of the Court. Trumpets blew, banners fluttered. Blackie pranced along with the Princess smiling and waving to the troops, who broke into frantic cheers, all but the Knights of the Shrine, who kept their discipline and stood proudly at attention.

Blackie was happier than he'd been since leaving the Shrine. The war over, no more fighting, and his Princess come to him—what a turn of events! The possibilities made his mind whirl. He could tour the City with his lady to see the ships in the harbor and the Cathedral. After that, he could run home to Mama in the forest. He could even head back to the bliss of the Shrine. He could do anything!

Joyfully, he glanced around at his Princess—thin and weather-beaten now, but beautiful, more beautiful than ever with her curly hair, bright eyes, and that brilliant smile. She leaned over to kiss his ear.

"Blackie, Blackie, how I missed you! I'm so relieved to see you unharmed. Up in that tower with my bow, I was filled with worries about you. And when the dragon flew away, I was afraid that she was after you. Such stories we've heard. Tales of you and Georgie, of Gypsies, witches, all sorts of strange adventures. I couldn't rest until I saw you again."

She rubbed Blackie's cheek. "And Blackie, I declare, you look splendid. So tall and rangy and handsome, but these cuts—"

She touched a spear gash in Blackie's neck.

"A scar or two is becoming to a fighting beast, but no more of them! You've earned your fame, now you can relax. We'll take our time returning to the City. The place is a mess anyway, half burned, half ruined. The lords on the Council are totally out of hand. Those rascals voted to keep all that silver from Prince Vile's mine for themselves, but Mama overruled them. That wealth is to be used to rebuild the Empire."

She laughed and waved to the shouting Darrmen. "Look at me, talking politics already! We must enjoy our reunion before thinking about our troubles. Let's relish this peace while we can."

"Georgie," she called, turning to Prince George, "Did you hear that Lady Memling had triplets! I haven't seen them yet, but Mother says they're precious. She's agreed to be godmother."

CHAPTER THIRTY-ONE

The Feast

The Princess rode briskly to Castle Croy, commenting on the countryside all the way. She paused at the burned village where Blackie had saved the women on the barrels and stopped before battered Castle Bales where the local lord stood waving with his liegemen about him. The barricades had been shoved back, but still surrounded much of the castle.

"My dear Lord Gilbert," called the Princess. "I knew I'd find you loyal."

The Baron walked up to Blackie and saluted. "Oh, m'lady, it was a near thing! Old Stook was gobbling up his neighbors to both sides. I'd be a goner by now if the Prince's army hadn't ridden up when they did."

"So, that's what happened," nodded the Princess. "Same old story, I've heard it a hundred times. Prince George, I trust that you dealt with Count Stook as you passed by."

Prince George shrugged. "I didn't want to delay in saving the City, Princess, so I detached a troop to chase him back to his castle and hurried on."

"Send a herald to the Count, my lord," ordered the Princess. "Tell him that I expect him on his knees at the City gate within thirty days. Judgment is coming to all these villains."

"But what about Combe and Nage?" cried Baron Bayles. "Stook still holds both baronies! Lord Combe escaped to Lady Moyne, but Stook's ruffians threw Baron Nage off his castle tower."

"Oh, they did?" asked the Princess, slowly. "In that case, Prince George, don't bother sending a herald. I'll deal with this situation, myself."

She patted her magic bow.

"The Empress permits me to bring correction when necessary. Please attend me at Castle Croy, Baron. I want to talk to Baron Combe and Lady Moyne. It may be that I need to capture Castle Stook before I release the army."

"But Princess," protested the Prince, "your mother wouldn't want you to endanger yourself. You have dozens of lords eager to fight for you."

The Princess tossed her head. "Why should they have all the fun?"

Turning Blackie, she trotted on, leaving Prince George talking to Baron Bayles. Jessica had to gallop Butterball to catch up, calling to the Princess as she neared.

"My lady, my lady, you know that Prince George is right! Her Majesty didn't send you off to start your own little wars in the countryside"

"I'm not starting anything!" cried the Princess. "I'm righting injustice when I see it, exactly what a warrior queen should do."

"It looks like you're feeding your own heroic legend," muttered Jessica.

The Princess rode silently until Blackie raised his ears at a thumping sound over the horses. She turned to Godfrey, riding beside her at that point.

"What's that I hear, a bass drum?"

"I understand, my lady, that it was captured from the villains at Castle Croy just ahead. The Hellions had many drummers for the dancing."

"I like that drum. I think I'll take it with me."

The Princess looked about with eager eyes as Blackie carried her into Castle Croy. "So this is the castle Prince George captured. Godfrey, where was the dragon during the battle?"

Godfrey pointed with his axe. "That tippy-top tower, my lady. Where you see the banners. Baron Croy said that she swooped down on the crossbows from there."

The Princess laughed. "Don't you suppose, Godfrey, that it was Blackie who did the fighting here? I'm sure Prince George rode him like a true knight, but I doubt if he captured this castle single-handedly. What do you think, Jessica?"

She looked back at Jessica, who walked behind, leading tired Butterball by his reins. Jessica spoke up, pertly.

"All I know is what you told me, Princess. The City would have fallen if the army hadn't frightened off the Hellions. Since Prince George commanded the army, he gets credit for saving the Empire, doesn't he?"

"Something of the sort," said the Princess, jumping down at the door. "But don't tell him that, Jessica. Georgie's head is big enough already. And you, Godfrey, I'm pleased with you, too. The pair of you did an excellent job. That's what I'm reporting to the Council."

Pulling off her gloves, the Princess walked around Blackie to give him a big hug. He sighed with pleasure, closing his eyes.

"It's a joy to ride you again, Blackie," she declared. "No other mount carries me so smoothly. But I have to leave you now. I must inspect the castle and get Baron Croy's report on the Hellions. You will escort me, Lord Godfrey. And you, Lady Jessica, you wait here to inform my lord Prince, when he arrives, that I give him the honor of organizing the feast."

"Feast, my lady?" Jessica exchanged looks with Godfrey.

"The traditional feast, of course, Jessica. Isn't it customary for the general of an army to throw a feast for visiting royalty?"

"Well, yes," Jessica admitted, "but that's in peacetime. Under the circumstances, you know, the war and all—"

The Princess let go of Blackie with a sigh.

"Of course, I don't expect Georgie to come up with a magnificent gala, birds flying out of pies, that sort of thing. Just a modest banquet for a hundred or so. Tell him to take his supplies from the wagons."

She paused as Godfrey pulled open the castle door for her. "And, Jessica, once you've instructed the Prince, please see to my chamber. Have my trunks brought up from the wagon. Make sure that nothing's lost."

Jessica curtseyed. "Yes, my lady."

"And now, Lord Godfrey, I want to see the Hellions' clubs."

The Princess walked into the castle for her inspection tour. While the ladies and lords flocked after her, Jessica seized Blackie's mane to pull him to a cracked bench beside the wall.

"Hold still, Blackie."

Blackie looked about in surprise as Jessica clambered onto his back from the bench. She grasped his mane.

"We have orders for Prince George, Blackie, and we need to hurry the wagon with my lady's trunks. She plans to rest here a few days, so we must make her comfortable."

Blackie shrugged and trotted back over the drawbridge. Jessica was lighter than the Princess and much quieter, not always twisting about to call to others or point things out.

Back on the road, they found the army breaking up. The Darrmen still waited for orders from the Heir, though other companies had returned to their campgrounds to chop wood and cook their dinners. Crowds of soldiers had left altogether, trudging north up the road with their few possessions on their backs.

Jessica waved to captains she knew. Once they were free of the army, she sat back, singing "My Lover Gives Me Blessing Three."

A couple miles outside Croy, they saw Prince George trotting toward them on Midnight. Seeing Jessica, he cried in surprise, "Oh, Jessica, you ride the unicorn!"

"Yes, my lord," replied Jessica, blithely, halting Blackie beside him, "the Princess sent me to locate her trunks. She has orders for you, too."

Prince George groaned, pulling Midnight to stand still. "What is it, now?"

"Why, she's giving you the honor of preparing tonight's grand feast at Castle Croy."

Prince George threw his arms up in the air.

"Oh, Jessie, she hasn't changed a bit, not one bit! After I raise an army and lead it across the Empire, she claims that I've been on a pleasure tour. Now, she wants me to organize a feast!"

Jessica smiled at the Prince, stroking Blackie's mane. "But you know, my lord, it's an honor to be the Marshal of the Feast."

Prine George shrugged. "That's an honor for stay-at-homes, midnight-drinkers. A fighting man gets his honor from action."

"My lord Prince," said Jessica, touching his shoulder, "the Princess respects you. Do you know that she's sponsoring a contest for the best song about your triumphs? All the minstrels are singing of you. That shows how she admires you."

Midnight sidled away, sniffing, as Prince George reached over to pat Blackie. "But she doesn't tell me that. She gives me snubs and sneers. Imagine claiming that I'd feasted my way across the country!"

Jessica laughed. "She's teasing you, my lord. I suspect she doesn't know how to deal with you as a great warrior. Despite her magic bow, there are more songs about you and the unicorn than there are about her."

"You think," demanded the Prince, incredulously, "that she's jealous of me?"

"Not jealous exactly," said Jessica, pulling Blackie back to Midnight. "She fears that your fame will puff you up like a frog. After all, you're not a poor prince anymore. You're a victorious general, a hero. You lead great lords in the army. That could go to your head. I assure you, my lord, the Princess admires you. Do you know that the Empress plans a celebration when you return to the City? There'll be a parade and honors and a special mass at the Cathedral."

"Oh," said the Prince, blushing. "I hope they don't get carried away with it. I don't need a lot of swank. I just want to be treated with a little respect."

Jessica took his hand. She patted it like a mother. "Don't worry, my lord. The Princess loves you in her way. She honors you now by making you Marshal."

The Prince jerked back his hand. "Making me work, you mean! I'll be counting spoons in the kitchen while Godfrey and the others stroll around the castle I captured."

"Prince, Prince," cried Jessica, frowning, "don't you see that she learns of your heroism this way? When the Heir talks of your courage, she hears the truth of your victories. If you showed her the captured arms yourself, it might be considered bragging."

"But we've burned the Hellions' clubs!" cried the Prince.

"That's not the point!" snapped Jessica, turning Blackie down the road. "Just accept the honor she gives you and be happy. I'll see you back at the castle. I have my own duties to perform."

"Please, Jessica," begged the Prince, "hurry the food wagons along! If I'm Marshall, I need to get busy with this feast."

Blackie soon passed into the forest, meeting only stragglers from the Court party. Jessica spoke to the humans that they met, a thin friar shivering on a mule, three nervous maids in a cart. Blackie looked warily at a swaying wagon, covered by an old canvas, but it was only a pair of blacksmiths following the horses.

Blackie jogged wearily under lazy snowflakes while Jessica sang.

> The fire burns warm and merry.
> The stew pot bubbles low.
> Baby sleeps within her crib.
> Oh, why do I have to go?
>
> The wind blows sharp and bitter.
> The road is clogged with snow.
> I turn once more to see behind
> the window's happy glow.
>
> But duty calls me hither,
> to rest where I don't know.
> I'll dream of the cozy fireplace
> where the stew pot bubbles low.

They rode several miles before they came to the wagons trundling along, the carters sleeping on their loads. The wagon train was led by a squad of nodding guards commanded by a young knight, Sir Callow of Pineheart, who galloped up, waving, when he caught sight of Jessica.

"Sweet Lady Jessica," he called, "these are perilous lands! Why do you ride without a guard?"

"Oh, I'm well protected, my lord!" laughed Jessica, patting Blackie's shoulder. "Look what I'm riding!"

"Ah!" gasped the knight, staring at Blackie. "The unicorn!"

"Yes, certainly." Jessica patted Blackie's neck. "My lady permits me to ride the holy beast on her service. With the unicorn to guard me, I fear no threats from lovesick boys or bandits."

The knight pressed his horse close to Blackie, reaching for Jessica's hand. "Oh, I'll be a bandit, sweet lady. I'll steal your heart if you'd let me."

Blackie pulled away from the horse as Jessica snatched back her hand with a giggle.

"No, no, you naughty fellow! You've already stolen my ribbon. How much did you pay my maid for that token?"

"Oh, my lady," cried Sir Callow, opening his arms, "think what I'd pay for a kiss."

Shaking a finger at him, Jessica stepped Blackie toward the wagons. "Stay back, stay back. I'd hate to have to report you to my lady. I must find her wagon to deliver her trunks to her chamber."

Sir Callow pressed close as they passed the guards and the leading wagons. "Don't ride away, sweet Jessica. Say a word, my lady, one word, and I'll have my father speak to the Empress. We can marry in the springtime."

Jessica turned her head from him. "Not so, young swain! You must carry your honey to other ladies. I have no time to think of marriage with my duties to the Princess. Is this the wagon? Ho, there, Kroker, wake up!"

The carter on the wagon seat shook awake. "Uh, uh, that you, Lady Jessica? We there yet?"

"Scoot these carts aside, Sir Callow," ordered Jessica. "I must hustle this load to Castle Croy."

"Oh, dear Jessica, must you leave me so soon?" cried the knight. "Ride along with me for awhile. I haven't seen you for days."

"Move the carts, please," insisted Jessica, waving her hand. "The Princess's load must pass. And send the food wagons forward. You can't hold them back for the slowest rig in the line."

The road was too narrow for the Princess's wagon to pass at this point, so Jessica had to ride with Sir Callow till it widened. The knight sighed to Jessica while his horse looked at Blackie with interest.

"I've seen few horses as big as you, stranger. You some kind of monster? How fast do you run?"

"I'm not a horse," explained Blackie, "I'm a unicorn. You ever hear of unicorns?"

The horse shook its head. "Nope, never, 'course I've never been stuck on guard duty before, either. I hate this dragging along. I'm used to running with the chargers, but they've got me creeping with the nags. Have you been out on campaign?"

Blackie snorted. "It's been nothing but campaigning since I left home last summer. Have you seen the City?"

By this time, they'd come to a little clearing where the carts could pull aside. Blowing a kiss to Sir Callow, Jessica trotted off with the luggage wagon.

The Knight shouted after her, "Please, sweet lady, save me a dance at the feast tonight!"

With the wagon creaking behind, Blackie held himself to a walk, moving along with half-shut eyes. Jessica hummed happily until they rode into Castle Croy where she made Blackie wait in the courtyard while she hurried into the castle to find boys to carry in the hatboxes and trunks. A moment later, she ran back in a fluster.

"Oh, Blackie, I have to hurry! Things are totally out of hand here. That chamber's not fit for a scullery wench—scribblings on the walls, trash on the floor! Everything stinks of Hellions. The Princess gave me her scent bottle to perfume the room, but we have to scrub it out first. I have drapes to hang and carpets to lay before we can look to the dresses. What a mess!"

She kissed him on his nose and dashed back into the castle. Blackie looked around.

"That place stinks of Hellions. I'm not going in there. There must be a stable around here, somewhere."

Sniffing for horses, he trotted around the courtyard. In a corner to the rear, he found an open shed smelling comfortably of straw and manure. Forty horses chomped on hay, switching their tails back and forth. A dog stood and yawned as Blackie pushed between Midnight and the old warhorse, Steed.

"It's you again, Sir High-and-Mighty," snorted Midnight. "Do you lower yourself to visit horses? Don't they pamper you with oats and barley?"

She kicked at the trough. "Look at this stuff they call hay—straw, stems, weeds. I'm not eating this fodder! I swear, we had better rations during the siege when they fed us on shoestrings and rags. I want real hay, something with leaves in it!"

Steed threw up his large head to jeer at her complaints. "Look who's snooty, now! If you ate shoestrings in the City, why turn up your nose at good field hay?"

"Not me!" cried Midnight. "I never stomached such fare! My mistress fed me on cake and biscuits!"

"That ain't the way I heard it," Steed chuckled.

"So, horse," Blackie asked Steed, "how'd you get here? Last I saw you, you were running away from Castle Shrems at midnight."

Steed winked an eye at him. "I knew where I was goin', young unicorn. When that monster burned up the sky, I high-tailed back to my stable in the City. Who could guess that she'd follow me home? We had hard times durin' the siege, I can tell you."

·"Terrible times," groaned a sorrel in the corner. "The humans took most of us and . . . and—"

"And killed 'em!" declared Steed, stamping a hoof. "Killed 'em and ate 'em! Might as well come right out and admit it. The humans knocked those ponies in the head and dragged 'em off. It was terrible, but everyone was starvin'. They didn't feel a thing."

Midnight looked scornfully at Steed. "I wouldn't talk about such things. It's in bad taste."

"Well," said Steed, "the unicorn brought it up. And why hide the truth? The young 'uns got to know the facts. We only survived because humans preserved us. The knights looked after me."

"Well, me, of course—" Midnight drew herself up. "The Princess made sure that I survived. You see the braids in my mane? She braided each and every one of them."

Steed's ears perked up. "I thought that other female braided your mane."

"The blond one, Jessica," nodded Midnight, "she did, but the Princess told her to do it. It's the same thing."

"Listen," said Steed, nodding wisely, "if that Princess got hungry enough, she'd send us all to the butcher. Don't matter to me. At my age, I could stumble down the next hill and break my neck. I just hope the dragon doesn't catch me. Gettin' barbecued alive, that's not for me."

Blackie lifted his horn. "Lots of unicorns get killed by dragons. We sort of expect it."

"That's because you're stupid!" cried Midnight with a shudder. "You go running after dragons. Saint Francis knows I'll carry the Princess wherever she wants to go, but I'd dig in my hooves if I caught her chasing a dragon."

Thinking of dragons, the horses got quiet in the stable. Blackie closed his eyes and slept. It was dark before Cedric the Page came to wake him up with a torch.

"Oh, there you are, unicorn. You're to come inside for the feast. Hurry, they're ready for the benediction."

"What's the boy saying?" Midnight poked Blackie with her nose. "Is it feeding time? Do they want me?"

"Nope, just me," said Blackie, yawning. He followed the Page through the great door. Cedric set the torch in a sconce, straightened his hat, and led Blackie to the castle hall. It smelled of paint and vinegar.

Blackie saw a collection of tables covered with newly-washed cloths. The Princess sat at the center of the head table in Prince George's field throne. Torches blazed around her, lighting her rose-colored gown and hat wound about with a string of green holly. Her magic bow hung from a hook at the side of the throne.

Prince George stood across from her, holding his spear like a marshall's staff. Looking critically around the room, he watched the humans move aside as the Page led Blackie toward the table. He bowed to the Princess.

"Here's the unicorn, my lady."

Smiling, the Princess stood to reach a hand to Blackie's nose. "Oh, Blackie, look what Prince George gave me! This throne, it folds up for travel! So thoughtful, isn't it?"

She patted the tablecloth beside her throne. "You stand here, Blackie."

Blackie stepped beside her, and the Princess lifted her voice. "Sir Marshall, the unicorn's present. We are ready for the blessing."

The room silenced as Prince George thumped the spear loudly against the stones of the floor. "My lords, ladies, and gentles all, silence for the Provost!"

A chubby man in green robes stepped to the center of the room, the priests and deacons forming a line behind him. The buzz of voices quieted as he lifted his crucifix. Heads bowed as the priests chanted.

In nomine Patris, et Filii, et Spiritus Sancti,
Amen.

"Traveling the world on His holy mission," pronounced the Provost, "our Lord told His apostles to bless any home they enter, saying, 'Peace be to this house.' Following the instruction of my Master, I bless this Castle Croy with holy peace. May Satan and his works be banned from these walls. May gentle words be spoken here, and may the happiness of our Lord's own home with Saint Joseph and our Mother Mary enter here. I pray the blessings of the angels and saints upon this castle and on the company assembled here this evening and forever."

The Provost strode grandly around the room, making the sign of the Cross on each door and wall of the hall. Returning to his place before the Princess, he concluded his prayer.

"For the royal family, we thank you, O Lord, particularly for this blessed Princess, and for all the lords and ladies who remained faithful through the late troubles. We thank you for this holy unicorn who shines in his blackness like the mystery of our Lord's grace to sinners. Lastly, Lord, we thank you for these viands that nourish our bodies for the labors of our days and ask your blessing on all who partake of our feast."

The priests sang again, ending with a rousing "Amen." They returned to their end of the table as the noise in the room boiled up louder than ever.

Prince George thumped his staff. "Let the feast be served!" He tossed his spear to the Page and hurried to the kitchen to prompt the food service.

The Princess turned to Baron Croy, sitting to her right. "Your castle, my lord, transformed! It was such a wreck when we rode in today that I feared we'd have to put off our feast. Now, it looks presentable."

"We owe that to your servants, my lady," said Baron Croy, looking about with pleasure. "They stormed through my castle in a frenzy of cleaning and painting. It almost looks like home again."

"It was due to Prince George, my lady," said Jessica, standing before the Princess to serve her. "He organized the cleanup, as well as the feast. I'm honored to have helped him."

Blackie watched Prince George march from the kitchen with a parade of cooks in clean aprons bearing platters of roasted birds, venison, pork, and beef. They spread out before the Princess. Blackie reeled back as the meat smell hit him.

"The feast is served, my lady," announced Prince George with a bow.

While the meat was portioned out, Blackie turned his head to sniff the Princess's perfume. Taking this as a sign of affection, she rubbed him under his jaw.

"I love you, too, Blackie."

Blackie turned back to the food after the meat platters were carried down the wings of the table. Now, the waiters were bringing steaming bowls of cabbage, onions, parsnips, and turnips, along with baskets of bread and pots of pickles. The Princess loaded his tray with all the things he liked.

"More of this, Blackie? More of this? Surely, you'll want some of this."

Blackie was happily eating pickles and cabbage when Prince George hurried back to see that everything was to his lady's satisfaction. The Prince looked hungrily at the platters as the lords and ladies stuffed themselves. The Princess smiled at Prince George over a duck leg.

"Excellent work, my lord. I knew you could tidy up the castle for our feast this evening."

"Tidy it?" protested the Prince, wiping crumbs from the table with a napkin. "I practically had to rebuild it! I recruited every carpenter, plasterer, and painter in the army and put them to work while collecting the kitchen staff to turn out a meal. If the people weren't so thrilled at the prospect of peace, they couldn't have done it. As it is, we just dumped the trash out the windows and closed off the ruined parts of the castle."

"But you did it, my lord!" cried the Princess. "You brought off another difficult task! I give you all the credit."

"It was scarcely the job for a prince." Glancing down the table, Prince George ran back to the kitchen for refills.

There was little talk for the next hour. In the wake of the war, the humans dealt seriously with such a feast. They didn't start telling stories until the dessert was served—puddings and cakes, cheese, nuts, dried fruits, and raisins.

Blackie ate as much as any dozen humans while listening to his Princess tell of stinging the dragon with her magic bow.

"I'd like to have seen that," said Godfrey.

"Oh, yes," laughed the Princess, rubbing Blackie about the ears with her free hand, "once that monster tasted my magic arrow, she stayed well away from the Castle. She couldn't even fly up at night since her burning jaws gave her away. Aleet watched one way with his poisoned arrows and I watched the other. We kept her back from the heart of the City, though she burned her way around the fringes. All of Saint Ornac is gone and Saint Paul's and the Beefmarket, but we held

Bay Avenue from the Castle to the Quay. The Cathedral was saved, too."

"Thank the Lord for His mercies," intoned the Provost from down the table. "Amen."

"But my lady," asked Godfrey, "you were cut off from supplies all those weeks. How could you survive?"

The Princess took a sip from her silver goblet. "Why, we lived on horse flesh and pilchards."

"Pilchards, my lady?"

"Yes, pilchards." The Princess held up fingers about three inches apart. "Little fish, sardines, you know. When Vile's villains cut off the countryside, we still held the beach and the bay. Of course, the pigeons and rats were eaten, first thing."

"Rats, you ate rats?"

Prince George, walking up at that moment, made a face.

"Yes, rats," repeated the Princess. "When you're hungry, a fat rat with onion sauce is just the thing. After the rats were gone, we turned to the pilchards which were running in the bay. For weeks, we ate fish, nothing but oily fish from breakfast to supper. I swear, I don't want to face another fish till I'm forty!"

She wiped her mouth with her napkin. "I'm still belching fish breath!"

"But you remember, my lady," said Jessica from down the table, "the Wizard says that eating pilchards saved us from the Death."

"Nonsense, Jessica!" The Princess threw down her napkin. "That's his crazy theory. Those of us who ate the fish survived the plague, so he decided it was the fish that saved us. What would Euclid say about that? Bad logic! You could read Galen from one end to the other without finding a mention of pilchards! No, no, it was the prayers in the Cathedral. While the Hellions were cursing and killing like demons, our clergy sang prayers day and night. That's what saved us from the villains, that and my bow, of course."

"Speaking of bows, my lady," asked Godfrey, "how's the desert boy?"

"Oh, Aleet," said the Princess warmly, "he's fine, fine. He hates this cold weather, of course, so I left him to guard the Castle in case the dragon flew back."

"Not a proper Christian, that boy," snorted Lady Pru, down the table to the Princess's left. "Refused to eat his fish, even on Friday. He was always begging for cheese."

"Ah, yes, cheese. Would you like some cheese, Blackie?" The Princess leaned to the block of cheese with her knife.

Blackie chewed a sticky chunk of cheese while Godfrey said in a thoughtful voice, "Aleet always loved his cheese. 'Cheesies,' he called it."

"Well, he's certainly a wonderful bowman," said the Princess, taking a slice of cheese on her knifepoint for herself. "I never saw anyone use the wind like he does. My bow, of course, hits where I aim in any breeze, but his poisoned arrows would whirl on a draft and still hit the chink in an armor. When the dragon last attacked the castle, we shot together at the serpent. My arrow stabbed her in the eye, but his caught that black tongue as she opened her jaws to blast fire. That's when she fled north with the Hellions beating their gongs and yelling for her to come back."

"I guess, we missed the real fighting," said the Heir, filling his cup from a wine pitcher.

"You certainly did," said the Princess, nodding. "We had battles, I tell you, battles! Two hundred Hellions at a time storming the wall with a thousand spears behind them! Flames, arrows, flying stones filling the sky! Everyone cursing and screaming and hacking away like madmen—that was real fighting!

"Up in the tower, I pulled my bowstring till my fingers bled while Knights and City folk battled side-by-side in the streets below to throw back the villains. Nobles and guildsmen, peddlers and 'prentices, even seamen from the ships and prisoners from jail, all fighting together like comrades, if you can picture it. Father called for his armor and mumbled about heading to the shield wall."

Godfrey swallowed a handful of dried cherries. "You must have lost many of the knights I met three years ago."

"Oh, yes." The Princess's voice grew sad. "We had terrible losses. Every church and hall is still filled with wounded. We have stretchers running down the lower corridors of the Castle."

"The unicorn can help out there, my lady," said Jessica, serving almond cake to the Princess. "Prince George says he's a mighty healer."

"Oh, yes," thought Blackie, sourly, "let the unicorn do the dirty work."

But his heart jumped when the Princess smiled at him. She reached scented fingers to rub his neck.

"You're wonderful, Blackie. I'm sure you'll be happy to help us. Why, Jessica and my court ladies worked night and day to nurse the wounded."

"Oh, I did, my lady," said Jessica, nodding. "I saw the saddest cases."

Blackie sighed. Of course, he'd help the Princess. The Lord gave him healing power, so he had to help out when he could.

"Sir Otley was among those I nursed," said Jessica. "He was crushed in his armor. I held his hand when he died."

"Sir Otley!" cried Prince George in distress. He had returned with a group of waiters to fill the wine cups. "My old friend, he's dead?"

"Yes," said the Princess, sadly, "Uncle Otley. He led me around on my pony when I was a child."

"How did he die?" asked the Prince, wiping away a tear. "He always joked that he'd drown in wine like that English king."

"He went sword in hand like a hero!" exclaimed the Princess. "The enemy broke through near the Shambles. The wall was weak there—not the outer wall, of course, that'd been breached long before, but the inner wall thrown up with stones and debris from ruined buildings. The enemy kept breaking through our defenses, but we built back-up lines to hold them off. It was a regular siege!"

"Oh, to have been there with my spear!" sighed the Prince.

"Well, you weren't!" snapped the Princess. "You were dawdling about the countryside while we fought off the Hellions. Anyway—"

She wiped her lips on a napkin.

"It was Saint Anastasia's Day. Sir Otley heard that Hellions were attacking the inner wall that was held by oldsters and boys who could barely lift their spears. On his way to the battle, he saw blacksmiths patching armor in a shed, so he shooed them along with their hammers and fire pots to throw at the Hellions. Those villains got their fill when they stormed up that morning, but the Knight got his sword stuck in a Hellion's eye hole. The demon tumbled back off the wall, dragging Uncle Dudly with him. He wouldn't let go of his sword so the Hellions stomped him to death, his weapon in his hand."

"Clinging to his sword," said Prince George with a sigh. "A noble death. It'll sound good in his Song."

"Saint Anastasia, now," asked the Heir, "she's the lady that turned monk, isn't she?"

"I don't think she became a monk," said Jessica. "She couldn't, could she, my lady? She just disguised herself in monk's robes to preserve herself from one of those Roman emperors."

"She should have gotten herself a magic bow," said the Princess, stretching her arms. "That'd keep 'em off."

"Who else was lost beside Sir Otley?" asked Godfrey.

"Oh, many, many of name."

Blackie grew sleepy as the Princess went down the list of knights he'd never heard of. He caught himself dozing, horn down on the tablecloth, so he pulled away from the feast and staggered out in the corridor to find a quiet place to sleep. The steamy lower floor was crowded with cooks and servers, entertainers, and Guards peeking in the door for leftovers—too much activity for Blackie.

Wearily, he mounted the stair, almost unconsciously following a faint odor that became stronger on the next floor. It led him to a door guarded by a spearman dozing under a small lamp hanging from the wall. The Guard jumped up as Blackie approached.

"Is that you, unicorn? Princess sent you up? She knows you're here, o' course. All righty, then."

The Guard threw open the door. Lowering his head, Blackie walked into the Princess's chamber, smelling strongly of perfume over the vinegar on the walls. A lamp over the dressing table lit up the room. A fire flickered in the fireplace against an inner wall.

Dully, Blackie stared around at the trunks piled with colorful gowns, the shoes and boots set around corners, the table littered with shiny bottles and brushes before a mirror hanging under the lamp. He stepped to the bed, spread with bright, puffy comforters. He let himself fall into the pillows. He slept.

CHAPTER THIRTY-TWO

Pursuing Papa

"Oh, Blackie, here you are! Everyone's looking for you."

Blackie felt someone plump down on the bed beside him. A soft hand stroked his nose. He opened his eyes to see Jessica leaning over him, pulling lightly on his mane. The chamber was cold and dim with only one small flame licking up in the fireplace.

"Come quickly, Blackie!" she urged. "Everyone's looking for you all over the castle. There's a surprise for you downstairs, a wonderful surprise!"

Blackie yawned and stretched, his body still weary.

"What is it now?" he groaned to himself. "If humans left me alone for an evening, that'd be the best surprise."

"Come on." Jessica pulled his mane again. She let go when he clumsily scooted across the bed and toppled onto his hooves.

"Hurry up, Blackie! You'll be delighted, I promise you!"

Taking a last look at the shoes in the corner, Blackie followed Jessica out into the hall where the guard rubbed his back for luck. Yawning, Blackie stepped awkwardly down the stairs.

Jessica tripped before him, singing out, "I found him! I found him!"

"Here he comes!" cried Lady Pru, on watch at the hall door. "Lady Jessica's found the unicorn!"

By torchlight in the hall, Blackie saw that the tables had been pulled back. The broken pots and garbage from the feast were swept into corners where dogs snarled at each other over the bones. All the humans were squeezed around the Princess in the middle of the room, looking over each other's shoulders at something he couldn't see.

"Stand back!" cried Jessica. "Stand back! The unicorn's coming through!"

The murmuring crowd pulled back. Jessica ran ahead, calling excitedly, "I found him, my lady! He was asleep in your chamber."

The Princess waved to Blackie. "Oh, there you are, Blackie! Look who's come to visit you!"

The room fell silent. Someone called out, "Blackie, sweetheart, you're so beautiful!"

Blackie gasped, stumbling in surprise. It was Mama, limping up to him. Mama looked worn and worried, smaller than he remembered, but just as loving. She rubbed him with her nose and kissed his wounds.

"My poor baby, so many scratches and scars! And you've lost your sweet little horn. Oh, how many months since I've seen you—"

The Princess followed, stroking Mama's mane with delight. "It's the female unicorn, rare, very rare. She hasn't been seen for generations. This is an event for the chronicles."

Blackie pressed his nose against Mama. He sniffed her warm, earthy smell. Tears streamed down, as memories of her milk in the Nest flowed over him.

"Oh, Mama."

"My baby!" she cried. She pulled back a step to look him over. "I don't believe it—you're bigger than Papa already! And your horn, it's as long as Grandpa's! How do you feel, sweetheart? You look thin. Are you eating enough?"

Blackie was crying now. "Oh, Mama, I'm sorry I ran away, so sorry! A million times, I've wished I could go back to tell you goodbye. I know you must have worried!"

"Worried, love?" Mama tossed her head. "I was terrified! I thought those scoundrels in the village had caught you! I sent Papa over to see if you were there. He saw humans guarding both gates with their spears, so he knew you'd been through. He questioned foxes for miles around. He heard that you'd been chased by the dragon and that you were traveling with Gypsies. I knew then that you were having adventures. But you were young, Blackie, far too young to go off by yourself. You should have stayed home for the winter. Now, look at you! How did you get your adult horn so quickly?"

"It was the Fountain, Mama. I went up to the Shrine with Prince George."

"Oh, the Fountain. Of course."

Mama stepped close to nuzzle him again. "When you disappeared, I guessed that it was your time to go into the world. Your Papa didn't believe it, though. He never got over your leaving."

"Poor Papa!"

Blackie rubbed his nose over Mama's shoulders.

"Yes," said Mama with a sigh, "Papa was sure that something dreadful had happened to you. He went on and on about you. 'Blackie wouldn't run away from home,' he said. "My son's too smart for that. I showed him the world, told him all about it—how wretched it is out there, dangerous, unhappy! I taught him to enjoy life in the forest, our safe, comfortable life.' That's what he kept saying.

"But I knew, Blackie, I knew you had to go. You're a true unicorn. Too soon, though, too soon!"

Blackie drooped his head. "I missed you, Mama. Every minute I was gone, I kept missing you."

Mama rubbed his muzzle. "I missed you too, sweetheart. But you're young. You'll enjoy your adventures, see new lands, fight foes. One of these days, you'll meet your Princess and serve her. I hope she's a good human. Who knows what an evil one could get you into."

"Mama!" Blackie jumped away. "I've already met my Princess! I've got to introduce you."

Mama rocked back. "Your Princess already, Blackie? Oh, sweet daffodils, you're but a baby!"

"She's wonderful, Mama, beautiful!"

"I'm sure she is," sighed Mama. "I knew you'd pick a pretty one. Your Papa had his troubles that way."

"Over here, Mama, this lady, over here!"

Blackie led his Mama toward the Princess, who had settled back in her throne to watch them together. Mama ran up to Jessica, standing by the throne, and sniffed her chest.

"Lovely," she said.

"Over here, Mama!" called Blackie, pointing his horn to the throne.

Mama looked at the Princess, who held out a hand, smiling. Mama breathed deeply.

"Her smell, Blackie, her smell! She's a mountain flower!"

"That's perfume," said Blackie, happily. "It's Purple Honesty. Prince George got it for her."

Mama looked at Prince George leaning on his spear. "This must be the Prince I've heard so much about. While I traveled the roads to find you, I heard the humans sing about him."

Mama sang a bit of a song. Her voice set Jessica and the Princess laughing.

> Mother Hungry's husbands
> are stacked along the wall.
> She left a space for another man
> to sit among them all.
>
> The Prince, he picks a flower.
> It grows on high, high hill
> and fills the air with sweetness—
> once sniffed, you smell it still.
>
> The Gypsy Girl is weeping.
> Behind iron bars she sleeps.
> She waits for the Prince to save her,
> and down the hill, he leaps.

"That noise," cried the Princess, "she's singing!"

"Of course," whispered Jessica, "all mothers sing to their young."

Blackie shook his head at the song. "That song's all confused, Mama. The Gypsy girl, Lizetta, she was bad. She tried to steal Prince George's spear."

"I wish unicorns could speak," said the Princess with a sigh. "I'd love to know what she's singing about."

The Princess jumped up to give a tug at Blackie's mane. "Blackie, we're forgetting our manners! Your mother must be hungry after traveling to find you. We must feed her."

"No, no, I can't eat yet!"

Mama shook the humans off. She straightened, threw up her head, drew in a long breath.

"Blackie, sweetheart, I have something sad to tell you. There's no way to say this gently, but . . . but . . . your Papa's gone."

"Gone, Papa?" said Blackie, his heart dropping within him. "Papa? You mean . . . dead?"

Mama shivered. "I don't know, maybe. If he's not dead now, he soon will be. I tried to hold him back, sweetheart, but he wouldn't listen. He insisted. He had to go. He was frantic! He dashed off without waiting to hear more! Why, oh, why didn't he wait for the whole story?"

"Papa ran off?" gasped Blackie. "Where'd he go?"

Seeing the unicorns so disturbed, the Princess hugged Blackie while Jessica put an arm over Mama.

"Don't be upset, Mother Unicorn," whispered Jessica. "Whatever it is, we'll find some way to help you."

"The saddest thing in the world," said Mama, shaking her head. "Someone told Papa that Prince Vile had captured you. Papa got it in his mind that Vile planned to throw you to the dragon, so he set out to save you."

Blackie was astonished. "Save me, Papa? He left home?"

"Straight through the forest," sighed Mama. "Headed north. I tried to hold him back. I told him to stay calm—it was just a rumor. But he dashed around the villages. When he didn't hear more about you, he ran off to Vile to rescue you from the dragon."

Blackie's legs gave way as Mama nodded. He fell to the floor, moaning in horror, "Oh, Papa, Papa!"

"Blackie!" cried Prince George, dropping his spear and running to the unicorn. The Princess threw herself down to hold Blackie's head on her lap. She looked up at Jessica.

"What do you think, Jessie? What's she telling him?"

Jessica was crying. "I don't know, my lady, but it's sad. Look at their eyes."

"Oh, if I'd only brought the Wizard!" cried the Princess. "He could translate for us."

"Mama," gasped Blackie, scrambling to his hooves with the Prince's help, "who told Papa I was captured by Prince Vile? Who'd tell such a lie?"

"It was a bird," said Mama, "a raven."

"A raven!" cried Blackie. "Crepitar!"

"Yes, that was the one," Mama agreed. "When you left, Papa asked the birds and beasts about you, but all he heard were bits of news. Winter was coming on by then, so he gave up on finding you and turned to checking out food stores. When he saw the raven, he asked it about grasses in the valleys around, but the bird spoke of you. He said that you'd been chained to a wagon and driven up to Vile."

Blackie snorted. "Well, I was chained for a day or so, but I didn't get close to Vile. I'm not that stupid."

"The raven said you did. He claimed he saw you turning a mill-wheel in Vile's slave camp."

"That liar!" cried Blackie. He jumped into the air, knocking Prince George back. "Bird of evil! He was spying for Prince Vile a couple days ago and one of the Darrmen shot him. I healed him, Mama. I healed that foul bird with my horn!"

"Where's he now?" asked Mama, looking around. "We can question him."

"I'm afraid not," groaned Blackie. "A soldier told me he escaped. The very evening we caught him, he picked the latch on his cage with a claw. Such a wicked creature! Prince Vile wants revenge against me, and, now, he's getting it through Papa!"

The humans stood listening, looking from one unicorn to the other.

"I don't know what they're saying," said the Princess, "but it must be terrible, whatever it is. She's got Blackie stirred up."

"But I don't understand, Mama!" Blackie exclaimed, staring at Mama. "Why would Papa run to Vile to save me! He never leaves home!"

Mama smiled sadly.

"He'd never leave, sweetheart, except for you. Your father loves you, you know, and he blames himself. He thinks that he's failed you. If he'd taught you properly about the dangers of the world, you'd have stayed home in the forest. You'd have never run off. You'd have never been in danger. Why, he was so disturbed when you disappeared that he forgot about berries for a month."

Blackie took a long breath. He looked at the humans watching with concern and shook himself.

"You know what I've got to do now, Mama. I've got to go after Papa. I've got to try to stop him from going to Vile. If he gets himself captured, I've got to rescue him."

Mama stiffened. She looked anxiously at him.

"Are you sure, son? Don't you think that's exactly what Prince Vile wants? He doesn't care about your father, hidden away in the forest. Oh, sure, he'd torture a unicorn for the fun of it, but it's you he's after. You travel through the world. You oppose his schemes. You threaten his dragon. The only reason he'd trick Papa into running to Vile is to pounce on you."

Blackie nodded, sure that she was right.

"I know, Mama, I know. But for Papa's sake, I have to go. All those years in the forest have made him soft, feeble. He's eaten too many berries, too many mushrooms. He wouldn't have a chance against the dragon. Me, though, I drank from the Fountain a few weeks ago. I'm powerful!"

Filled with determination, Blackie reared into the air, trumpeting. The nearby humans fell back at the blast. Blackie came down with an echoing thump.

The Princess applauded. "That's my unicorn!"

"I can take on the dragon, Mama!" Blackie cried. "You should have seen me fight! I threw Hellions around like puppies! What I can't do is let Papa run into Vile by himself. I have to go after him."

"If you go to the fiery mountain," insisted Mama, pushing up to him, "I'll go with you. I can't let you go into that cursed kingdom alone. You could be swallowed up there. I'd never know what happened to you."

Blackie shook his head. "No, Mama, you can't go with me. Vile could capture us both! Besides, you'd hold me back. I'd have to watch out for you instead of concentrating on the enemy."

"But, don't you think, son," Mama cried, "that it's already too late? It's been a month since Papa left home. I doubt if he'd last three days on the road as wild as the country's become. I saw horrible things while traveling to find you."

Blackie lifted his horn. "I have to go, Mama!"

Mama wept. "Just when I've found you again!" She rubbed against him, sobbing.

The Princess petted her as Blackie rubbed her with his nose.

"Don't cry, Mama. Papa won't actually go into Vile. You know Papa. I'm sure that he charged out with noble intentions, but it's a long way up north. Don't you think that he'll hole up in a warm tavern somewhere, or settle down in a castle? Lords will welcome him with cakes and cookies. Once he gets to feasting, he'll decide to wait until spring. I'll probably find him sitting before the fire in some abbey, listening to the monks sing."

Mama smiled slightly, but shook her head.

"I don't know. From what I saw, there's little to hold anyone on the road these days. The Empire's shaken with hunger and misery. I never expected the dreadful things I ran into. I'm afraid to have you out on the road, let alone Papa."

"I'll be careful, Mama."

For a moment, Blackie tried to think what to say to her, then realized he must simply leave.

"Goodbye, Mama. I'll bring Papa back, if I can."

He placed his horn on Mama and shot her a healing jolt to cheer her up. He turned to push through the humans.

"Be careful, son!" cried Mama, following toward the door. "Come back to me! I love you."

"My lady," cried Jessica, following Blackie. "He's leaving us!"

The Princess ran after Blackie, Prince George just behind. "Blackie, hold up! Where are you going?"

She caught him at the door and threw her arms about his neck to hold him back. He stopped a moment, eyes closed, breathing in her beloved scent. Reluctantly, he shook himself loose to trot down the steps to the door.

"After him, Georgie, after him!" ordered the Princess, stamping her foot. "That female's sent him off somewhere. I don't want him running around the Empire by himself!"

"Yes, my lady." Prince George scooped up his spear from the floor. He hurried back to his chair for his bearskin and shield.

"Wait, Georgie!" cried the Princess, running to her throne. "Take this, too! You might need it!"

Grabbing the magic bow hanging over the back of her throne with the arrow clinging to it, she tossed it across the room.

Prince George dropped the shield to catch the bow. He looked at the Princess in amazement. "Your bow, Princess? Are you sure?"

She waved him away. "Take it, Georgie! Take it! And stay with Blackie wherever he goes. Make sure he comes back to me!"

"I will, my lady. I promise!"

Prince George threw his fur cape over his shoulder. He scooped up the shield with his spear hand. He ran to the door.

"Goodbye!" shouted the Princess, waving both arms. "The Lord be with you! And don't lose my magic bow!"

Jessica caught the Prince at the door. She had wrapped up a packet of bread and cheese in her red scarf.

"Here, Prince, take this, and my purse, all the money I have! You'll need it to travel."

"Thanks, Jessica, thanks!"

Prince George threw her a grateful look. He ran out into the wind as a guard threw open the door. Pulling the cloak about him with one arm, he clutched the rest of his load under the other.

"Hold up, Blackie! I'm coming, I'm coming!"

He paused a moment to swing the bow over his shoulder and the shield to his back. He strapped the purse to his belt and tied the scarf about his waist. Snatching up the spear again, he splashed through freezing slush at the foot of the drawbridge. By the light of a campfire, he saw Blackie far ahead of him, kicking an empty keg down the road.

Blackie was totally miserable. How joyful he'd been to see Mama with his Princess and the other humans he loved. Now, he was alone and headed to Vile, that filthy kingdom of woe.

He kicked the keg again.

"No one goes to Vile! No one but Hellions and the dragon! All you find up there is suffering and death—and Papa!"

He glanced at the campfire where drunken soldiers were singing loudly.

> The fair maid of Holder
> grew bolder and bolder.
> She carried my coppers away.

"Papa, oh, Papa!" Blackie cried. "What made you think Vile could catch me? I'm not that dumb! I'm a yearling now, strong and smart and holy. I can take care of myself."

Waves of loneliness swept over Blackie as the song went through verse after verse.

> I followed to seek her
> though weaker and weaker,
> to kiss all my suffering away.

Blackie stabbed his horn into the mud.

"I'll search for you, Papa! I'll rescue you if I can, but why, why would you trust a raven? No fox would ever trust a raven!"

He jerked out his horn, tossing a splat of mud over his shoulder, and took up a slow trot north. The song followed around the turn in the road.

> The fair maid of Holder
> grows older and older,
> digs holes to hide coppers away.

> The same earth she digs in
> holds me for our sweet sin
> till we meet on that last Judgment Day.

"Blackie, Blackie!"

Someone smacked Blackie's flank. Blackie jumped around, horn ready to stab. Prince George fell away, throwing up his hands with the spear.

"Hey, Blackie, didn't you hear me call? Where you going in such a hurry?"

Blackie snorted. He turned to run, but the Prince dropped the spear to grab his tail.

"Blackie, please," he panted. "Princess insists! She orders me! I have to stick to you . . . wherever you're going . . . take care of you."

"You take care of me?" Blackie thought, resentfully. Then he shivered with relief. He felt warmer. The Prince, his friend— He wouldn't be alone like . . . like Papa!

Another thought struck him. "How he'll slow me down! Hunting food for the man, cooking—all that waste of time—and he'll talk, jabber, jabber, jabber, the way of all humans! I'd do better running alone to get the thing over with."

"So where we going, Blackie?" asked the Prince, patting his back.

"Well," Blackie decided, "if the Princess insists, I'll take him as far as he goes. He'll drop off when he realizes where I'm headed. For awhile at least, I won't be alone."

"You sure you want to run off like this?" asked the Prince, picking up the spear again. "Can't we return to Castle Croy for supplies? It'd make everything a lot easier."

"There it is again," thought Blackie, tossing his head. "Wait up, slow down, take a rest—that's why we poke along so! Humans talk about travel instead of doing it."

Shaking his head, Blackie turned up the road. Prince George pulled his bearskin about him and trudged along with Blackie.

"If I were you, Blackie, I'd wait a few weeks. It's horrid traveling now with the hills melting around us—water draining, everything sloppy with more cold weather ahead of us. In springtime, travel would be a pleasure, plus the forest would be green to hide in if we got into trouble."

Prince George was right about the slushy roads. As though to tease them, spring had crept in for a moment, the winds swinging south with smells of far-off plantings, but the countryside was soaked and icy. Since Blackie insisted, they slogged late into the night. When they stopped, Prince George slept under a broken cart. Blackie stood beside it, his tail to the wind.

The skies cleared next morning, and the sun beamed hot enough that Prince George rolled up his bearskin and tied it to Blackie's back. A handful of birds flitted through the trees, singing songs that reminded Blackie of other seasons.

For a few miles, they traveled with a company of soldiers from Thorn, a barony just below Darr. Their baroness, Lady Thorn, was a staunch supporter of the Princess, but her troops saw no reason to hang around once the rebellion was over.

"We'll get our families through the last weeks o' winter," explained the headman. "They need us at home to hunt food and chop wood. We'd stay with the army if we had a chance for booty, but this peace puts the freeze on that."

When the soldiers began hinting that Blackie should round up a fat deer for them, Blackie quickened his pace and carried Prince George ahead.

Prince George protested. "Those fellows seem like fine chaps. I wouldn't mind sharing some venison with them."

The warm wind was softening the snow, melted it faster. Dark patches of mud and rotted leaves appeared on exposed hills. Streams of cold water ran down the road, pooling in low places. Blackie trotted with an effort, half-wading, half-splashing, which left both of them chilled and dripping.

They stopped early in an abandoned hut that held a few dry logs in the woodbox. Prince George struck a flint against his dagger to touch off a sulky little flame in the fireplace. While it smoked, Blackie went outside to nip short green blades around the south side of the hut.

As the evening darkened, he squeezed back in the door to eat his share of a crusty loaf of bread from Jessica's packet. The Prince leaned against the wall in his bearskin, twanging the string of the Princess's bow.

"Now, Blackie—" Prince George aimed the bow across the room. The arrow struck a knot in the wood. It shook itself free and zoomed back to the Prince. He caught it in the air, clapped it back on the bow.

"We need to have a serious talk. I want to know where we're headed so suddenly. Did your mother send you on an errand?"

"Oh, oh," Blackie thought, perking up his ears and nodding. "I knew this would happen. He won't like what I have to tell him."

Prince George leaned the bow against the wall and poked at the fire with a stick.

"Obviously, we're headed north now, and we'll reach the Crossroads in a day or so. Do we turn there? Are we headed back to the Shrine?"

"Oh, the Shrine," thought Blackie, shaking his head, "how I wish we were going there! I could use more of that blessed peace."

"Not the Shrine," mused the Prince, "well, do we turn east . . . or west?"

Blackie shook his head with each suggestion.

The Prince tossed the stick in the fireplace, stretched, and lay back on an elbow, considering the possibilities. "So we're going north. Well, there's all the baronies up there, Groot, Thorn, and the great Duchy of Darr. I've told you about Darr. If we stopped there, I could see my godson. How about that?"

Blackie shook his head again.

"So you mean that Darr's out?"

When Blackie nodded, the Prince yawned.

"Well, the only place beyond Darr is the vast waste of Vile. Nobody goes there, so we must be going to one of the baronies. Is it Thorn?"

Prince George seized on the idea of visiting Thorn. "So, it's Thorn, is it? I know Baroness Thorn very well. In fact, I led an embassy up there, two years ago. That's where the Princess found this magic bow. If we go there, the Baroness will throw us a real feast."

But Blackie snorted, "No," and shook his head again.

Prince George looked perplexed. "It's not Thorn? I thought you meant—Well, there are other baronies up there. I don't know why you'd want to visit them in wintertime. It's sure to be freezing up there. Some of them may be dangerous, those that threw in with Vile during the war."

Blackie nodded his head at that. Prince George scratched his head and shivered.

"If I didn't know better, I'd think you're trying to tell me that you plan to go to Vile. Nobody goes to Vile, nobody but—"

The Prince sat up in horror when Blackie vigorously nodded his horn. "You don't mean— Not Vile! I'm not going to Vile!"

Blackie nodded more positively.

"But why," cried the Prince, jumping up, throwing out his arms, "why would anyone go into Vile? That's where the Gypsies tried to take us, remember? Are we . . . are we an embassy, delivering a message?"

Prince George got more and more upset as Blackie shook his head at each suggestion. No, he wasn't carrying a message, he wasn't scouting the place for an invasion, he wasn't trying to kill Prince Vile.

"I'd go for that," nodded the Prince, "if I could get in range with this bow. Even if they slew us afterwards, it'd be a glorious feat worth a hundred ballads, but entering Vile for no reason? No, no, that's ridiculous!"

Prince George tossed another stick on the fire and sat back. He thought a moment before bursting out.

"A test of courage, is it, a rite of passage? You have to enter Vile to prove yourself a worthy adult? That, I could understand. It's crazy, but in a way it makes sense. I'm sure you'd never go into Vile for no reason, but I can't imagine what. How I wish you could talk!"

Blackie gave up. How could he explain to this human what amazed even him—that Papa, who'd spent his life hiding among spring greens and mushrooms, would throw himself into caverns of fire to rescue a disobedient son. No one would accept that, no one who knew Papa! If Mama hadn't told him, Blackie wouldn't have believed it himself.

By now, the winds had cooled down. Blackie shivered restlessly before the dying fire while Prince George tossed in his bearskin, muttering to himself.

"Well, I'm not going into Vile, that's for sure! Even the Princess wouldn't expect that. If it's some beastly initiation, some rite of passage for unicorns, I'm sure that Blackie's supposed to do it alone. It'd be cheating to take a knight with him. But why else would he go there? Why would anyone go into Vile?"

CHAPTER THIRTY-THREE

The Storm

Blackie had an uncomfortable night in the hut, drifting in and out of nightmares while Prince George whimpered in his sleep. The Prince's distress frightened Blackie. It showed how terrible Vile's kingdom must be.

All his life, Blackie had heard whispers about Vile's horrors, but he'd never thought about them. A healthy young unicorn doesn't dwell on such things. Now, though, the Prince's reaction made him ponder the little he'd heard of the burning mountain with its Hellhounds, its brutal guards, its slave pens, not to mention the dragon. That evil worm was a perfect symbol of Vile.

What he'd seen of Vile was bad enough, the Hellions with their clubs, the crossbows, even the Black Prince. That lost soul was responsible for the miserable war they'd gone through. Blackie saw the suffering and destruction caused by the demon on all sides, so what in the world was he doing now, running into those torture chambers up north? He must be mad!

Mad or not, his duty was clear. Papa had run into Vile for him, so he had to follow Papa. The question he wrestled with was whether or not he should take Prince George with him. Clearly, the Prince hated the idea. He only traveled with Blackie because the Princess had ordered him to.

"What kind of friend am I," Blackie asked himself, "dragging this human into danger, probably to death. I can't do that! I'm not Vile! If Vile had a friend, he'd throw him to the dragon to hear him scream, but that's not me. I must look out for the Prince—and for Papa if I can."

Blackie shook with anxiety.

"Oh, Papa, I fear for you! Vile's sure to catch you! You're dragonbait! How could you ever escape with that coat of yours? Your whiteness will shine like a beacon through the ashes of Vile. The Hellhounds will drag you down on sight. You won't live to face the dragon. You could be dead already, and I'd never know. I can't lose Prince George, too."

Blackie knew what he had to do, but how could he explain it to the Prince?

"If he understood my speech, I'd tell him that this is a job for me alone. Since he doesn't understand, though, I'll have to slip away from him. Tomorrow or the next day, while he's sleeping or talking, I'll step behind a tree. He won't know I'm leaving till I'm gone. That's what I have to do."

That thought relaxed Blackie. He was breathing deep breaths, almost asleep, when another thought popped into his head.

"But the Princess told the Prince to stick to me. He knows where I'm going. No matter what he wants to do, he'll obey orders. He's stubborn. He'll follow me into Vile the way I trail after Papa."

He coughed and shook out his shoulders.

"Even worse, our chances of being spotted are doubled if we enter Vile separately. If the Hellions see one of us, they'll be alerted to the other one. I have to stop him. I'll have to kick him in the head or break his leg. For his own sake! Then the Princess won't expect—"

Blackie caught himself with a sob.

"What am I thinking? I've gone mad! Now, I'm kicking my friend so he won't help me do something I don't want to do in the first place! Oh, these midnight worries! They twist you around till you don't know where you are. I gotta stop thinking, relax, relax, get some sleep."

Struggling to relax kept Blackie awake. His thoughts got wilder and darker until he dropped off just before dawn. He woke an hour later, tired and heavy, his eyes scratchy, a bad taste in his mouth.

"Oh, what a morning," groaned the Prince, pushing open the door. Sunlight streamed in. "Sunny, warm. I'd hoped for a blizzard. I prayed for snow to pile up against the door, to cover the roof, to bury us so we couldn't move."

Blackie hobbled outside. As miserable as he felt, the smell of the thaw cheered him. Wide stretches of earth appeared on sunny hillsides through shiny black tree trunks. Even the thorny bushes glowed with life, many sparkling with red seed pods. Green stems peeked up along the road.

Blackie chomped on scattered shoots while Prince George ate the last bits of bread. The Prince shook out Jessica's scarf and wrapped it around the cheese.

"This is the end of our food, Blackie. I'll hang onto it till later. We'd better get started if we're going to Vile."

The shoots lost their flavor at that. Blackie felt tired again. He gave Prince George a bleak look and nodded.

The Prince took a long breath. "I'm sure we'll find food before long. At least, I've got the Princess's bow. I can shoot game if we see anything."

He leaned the spear against a tree and went back in the hut. Blackie looked around. "I can run away now, leave him behind!"

He took a painful step and groaned, "Not today. Today, I don't feel like running anywhere."

Prince George came out, swinging the bow over his shoulder. "Hold still, Blackie."

The Prince leaned the spear against Blackie's neck and crawled on his back. He took up the spear. Blackie trotted wearily on.

The track was muddy with water flowing over low spots. Tired as Blackie was, they covered a few miles, pausing at a village where humans greeted them warmly and crowded around to ask the Prince about kinsmen in the army. Unhappily, these people had no food to give him. They were living on fish caught in streams and the few winter birds snared in bushes.

"They's no deer anywhere," reported an old man leaning on a stick. "Hunted out, all hunted out when the army passed through."

Blackie wriggled guiltily. He'd noticed that deer scent was missing from the hills.

"Folks is eatin' pine bark and worms," said the man. "Tastes terrible, if you asks me, but they'll eat anything. It'll be weeks afore the yerbs appears in the forest again. The hunters goes deep into the forest, but folks says they's meetin' hunters comin' in from t'other side. Everythin's gone until the country greens up again, but we got weeks o' snow and ice before spring."

They didn't stay long. Blackie healed an old woman with the itch and a gabbling boy whose eyes didn't focus. The boy had fallen from a tree, hunting birds' eggs last summer.

"If the army hadn't picked the countryside clean," commented Prince George, looking back at the villagers waving after them, "they'd serve us cabbage and sausages, fresh bread and old wine. There's be nuts and apples and pears from the harvest. The church would be full of song."

"Why talk of such things?" grumbled Blackie to himself. "My hooves are frozen from icy roads, but I don't chatter about bonfires to make myself miserable."

Despite himself, his mind turned to springtime. He recalled the peapods and spinach and tender carrots he'd enjoyed a few seasons back. Running into Vile, he might never see another garden. He'd never picnic again with the Princess. He felt bitter, and he knew who to blame.

"Papa should know I'd never let Vile catch me! How could he think I'm so stupid? Could it be that he's jealous of my fame? He always claimed that he doesn't care about songs and stories. 'Fame's but a bubble in the river,' he said. 'It floats away before you know it.' What if he's changed his mind? Raiding Vile will make him a hero to be sure, but it pulls me after him!"

Caught up in dark thoughts, Blackie trotted into an ambush. He smelled the bowmen at the last moment and leaped off the path, almost dumping the sleeping Prince.

"Hey!"

Prince George grabbed for Blackie's neck as the unicorn slid down a muddy gully. They splashed up a stream. Once safely away, Blackie jumped to the bank and climbed the hill to circle around the bandits through criss-cross shadows thrown by bare branches.

Back on the road, Prince George sat up straight again.

"What'd you see, Blackie, a bear? Give out a warning before you dive off hills! You nearly dumped me like an old sack of grain."

They stopped to rest at an outcropping of stone sticking up among dry strands of ivy. Blackie browsed on sprouts near the road while

Prince George pushed through the stones to sit in the sun. The Prince jumped back with a cry.

Blackie glanced over to see a brown-banded snake glide over the stone and vanish into a crack. Prince George thumped the rock with his spear, gazing carefully to all sides.

"That was an adder!" he cried, his voice hoarse. "I almost sat on it."

He sat on another stone to nibble a tiny bite of cheese.

"You know," he said in a faraway tone, "the Bourrids of the desert eat snakes. They say that snake meat tastes like chicken. If I'd been quicker, I could be broiling that fellow now."

Sighing, he wrapped the rest of the cheese in the scarf.

"In any case, Blackie, the snake couldn't kill me, not while I'm with you. If it bit me, you'd just heal me with your horn. Tell me, do you think you could heal yourself if you got snake-bit?"

Sniffing for forage around the rocks, Blackie shrugged. He'd wondered about that before. He did seem to heal faster from cuts and scrapes than these humans did, certainly quicker than horses. That was lucky, as the horn on his head was too long to reach most of his body. He could touch a leg if an adder bit it, but he'd be out of luck if it got him on the shoulder or belly.

"Well," sighed the Prince, tying the scarf about his waist, "no use roasting lost snakes. I might as well dream of eating summer's strawberries."

He stood and stretched. "Come on, Blackie. We won't get to Vile by resting here."

Traveling the forest road, that afternoon, they ran into more hungry people, wanderers without homes.

"We was burned out," said a straggly-haired woman with a pushcart piled with old clothes and blankets. Two women and an old man hobbled after her, followed by half a dozen thin children carrying armloads of sticks. The children dropped their loads and ran to stroke Blackie's sides.

"It was the fightin', you know, between Baron Creeb and them other lords. Seems like they all went to it at the same time, ridin' back and forth to whack at each other and burn their villages. We stayed with the monks till the monastery got torched—that's where the baby died."

"Where are you heading now?" asked the Prince.

"That baby," said the woman with a faraway look in her eyes. "She was a one to eat. Always crying for food."

"But where are you going now?"

"Where we're goin'? Oh, they tell us the fightin's finished back at Creeb. The village is gone, but the fields is still there. The monks gave us a bag o' seeds. If we can hold off eatin' 'em, we can plant and start over. I don't know, though. The children is awful hungry."

"Well, here, this is all I have."

The Prince unwrapped the scarf from his waist. He looked mournfully at the yellow cheese. Blackie smelled the savory chunk as Prince George tossed it to the woman. Catching it in both hands, she let out a sigh. The children clustered around, squealing with joy, their jaws open like baby birds. The woman pinched off small pieces of cheese and poked them out for the children to suck.

"Oh, me lord," she cried, "how can I thank you?"

"Try to hold onto your seeds if you can."

Prince George fastened the scarf about his waist and swung back on Blackie. They turned up the road.

"I've got to stay away from people," moaned the Prince. "They're too pitiful, their stories too sad. Now, I'll have to eat tree bark myself."

Happily, though, they arrived at Castle Minch by evening where they were hosted by Count Basham, a staunch supporter of the Emperor. During the war, the Count had defended the villages in his county. Once the pressure lightened, he'd moved down to the Barony of Minch, abandoned by a vassal who'd marched off to support Prince Vile.

Lifting his wine cup to Prince George after an excellent dinner of fish, roast duck, and lamb stew with dumplings, the Count spoke of raising gibbets along the road to show that he was serious about stopping bandits.

"I've got to bring order to this place," he explained. He lifted his wine cup to the Prince. "Years ago, Baron Minch stopped paying his tribute. I let it ride, hoping he'd come to his senses. I was too busy to deal with him, anyway, fighting off the wild Boyles who swarmed down as soon as the rebellion started. I'm sure you've noticed, Prince, that every blackguard and villain in the Empire got stirred up by Vile's threats and bribes. Now's the time to stop them, I say. Hang 'em today and enjoy peace tomorrow."

"Who are these Boyles?" asked Prince George, scooping up the last drops of stew in his bowl with a piece of bread. He reached over for a cookie from Blackie's bowl. Blackie stood beside him with big bowls of milk, millet, and cookies on the table, and a tub of loose hay to his side.

"This is the way to live," thought Blackie, munching a mouthful of grain. "Papa would have stayed at this place all winter."

The Count held out his wine cup for a refill.

"Ah, the Boyles," he sighed, "lordless men, a tribe of ruffians who hold the ragged lands south of the river. Every generation or so, they boil over and have to be hammered back. It's almost a sport, it is, gathering the barons, riding up into the hills. The Boyles scatter to the caves in the heights while we burn their fields and huts, then they wait us out till the next time they fly down on us.

"For years, we've talked of mounting a real campaign. After their raids this year, I'm ready to clear them out once and for all. I'll set up a strong baron who'll keep the hills quiet. If you and the unicorn stop by after harvest, I'll show you some real hunting."

Prince George took another cookie and leaned back in his chair. "Next fall, that's another story. Who knows where we'll be then. For now, I'm on a mission up north. I've got a godson in Darr that I've never seen."

"Oh, a godson," chuckled the Count. "Well, m'lord, he won't miss you for a month or two. Why not stay with us through Lent? We'll move back to Castle Basham then. Anyway, you don't want to travel north. The worst of winter is to come. My bones tell me that the winds are changing again."

"I've traveled in winter before," said the Prince. "Back during the Contest for Lady Dorinda."

"Oh, yes, Prince, my lady traveled up with the Princess for that occasion." Count Basham shook his head in wonder. "After winning Lady Dorinda with three deeds of honor, you turned her over to your squire, the Headsman. Don't know how you could do that. Lady Dorinda has stayed overnight at my castle. She is a fair lady!"

Blackie perked up his ears. This was interesting. Prince George had often talked of Godfrey, but had not said much about Lady Dorinda.

"Well," mumbled the Prince, "you know Darr, so far away up north. I have my duty to the royal family down in the City."

"But, my lord," persisted the Count, "I know, you're still young, but this wandering knight business has to stop sometime, doesn't it? And Lady Dorinda sleeps in silken sheets. I've seen them. They'd be cozier in winter than a blanket on the ground."

Prince George looked over at Blackie, his face red. "Oh, I don't know, Count. Many knights go questing their whole lives, riding about in search of fame."

"True, true," nodded the Count, "but not if they're offered a great Duchy—especially with a goddess like Lady Dorinda thrown in. And now, the Heir has a fine son! What more would you want than that?"

"Well, you know, Count, some prefer the traveling life, the adventure, seeing something new every day. Some knights love that."

The Count leaned back with his wine cup.

"I'm sure, you're right, my lord. Some warriors do like it. Those knight errants ride by now and then, all beat up and scrawny, old before their time. Mostly, they've got a wild look in their eyes. And they're lousy—we have to boil the bedding when they ride on. That's not the life for me. I'm for a settled life, myself. That's why I get upset at these rebels and raiders. They destroy everything, bring misery to peaceful folks. I beat them back, so we can live quiet for a spell."

The Prince took a couple more cookies.

"The unicorn and I," he sighed, "we don't get to rest often. It's a treat to visit you, my lord. A good meal and a soft bed—even a wanderer likes to relax once in awhile."

"Glad to have you, my lord," smiled the Count, "and don't worry about a thing. We've got plenty of hot water if we do have to boil your sheets when you ride on."

After the feast, Blackie spent the night under an overhang in the paddock outside the stable. These horses were used to strangers. Once they saw that Blackie was quiet and friendly, they returned to their concerns about the storm they could smell in the air.

"Just a few drops, just a shower," said a brown and white mare.

"What d'you know about it?" snorted a yellow stallion. "Winds like this don't bring showers. Listen to that!"

They all moved restlessly as thunder boomed in the west.

461

"Sounds like a serious storm to me," said a bay, "what do you think, unicorn?"

"Unicorn—is that what it is?" asked the mare. "I didn't care to ask."

"Of course, he's a unicorn," snorted the bay. "Only creature you'll see with a horn like that. I passed a big white unicorn on the road, a few days ago."

"You did," asked Blackie, eagerly, "a white unicorn? What'd he say? Where was he going?"

"Didn't say anything to me. He was moving right along, taking up more room on the road than he needed to."

"How long ago was it?"

"I don't know," yawned the bay. "He just ran by. He'll get himself soaked if he's out in a storm like this one."

The bay had no more to offer. Raindrops started bouncing off the courtyard and hammering the overhead. The horses rustled around, talking of storms they'd endured in the past.

One gelding was moaning, "You just watch, this rain won't stop my master. When he sets himself to ride, nothing holds him back—not rainstorms, snowstorms, sleet! Why, he'll ride me out when there's an inch of ice on the trail. I've fallen twice. It's a wonder I haven't broken all four ankles and my tailbone!"

"Well, I can't stop for a little rain," said Blackie. "I'm chasing that white unicorn. There's no time to waste if I'm to catch him."

"That big guy?" scoffed the bay. "You're not going to catch him! I saw him days ago, and he was hustling right along. Better stay here till the storm stops."

Prince George was of the same opinion when he checked on Blackie, next morning. He wiped his face and shook rainwater from his bearskin.

"No use traveling in this kind of rain," he said. "Streams'll be flooded, so we'd be held up at the first brook. At least, the warm spell's holding on. It's not turning to snow yet."

"What'd he say?" asked the bay.

"He says the streams will be flooded," answered Blackie. "We need to run after that unicorn, but he doesn't think we can get through."

The gelding nodded his head.

"He's right, youngster. I don't know how many times my master's ridden me out into storms. We'd wade a couple streams, then hit one that's too wild even for him. Then we're stuck in the middle of the weather. Instead of waiting in shelter for things to calm down, that human's kicking and yelling in the middle of the storm, frantic to get on."

"Come back to the hall, Blackie," begged the Prince. "They've built up the fires. More cookies coming up in few minutes."

"I don't know what to do!" Blackie told himself, watching the water sweep across the flagstones. "Could Papa keep going in this storm?"

A shout rang out, a bell clanged. The horses became alert, jostling around as men ran by with spears and shields.

"What is it?" yelled Prince George to a man splashing by.

"Trouble down at the pike! Someone breakin' through the gate!"

"Oh." The Prince turned back to Blackie. "That's none of our business, Blackie. Come on, let's go back to the hall."

Blackie nodded. "Guess that horse is right. It'd be dumb to run out in a storm like this."

"Unicorn, unicorn!" someone shouted. A dripping man dashed out of the downpour waving a spear. "Bring the unicorn!"

"What's going on?" demanded Prince George.

"A monster, me lord! Broke right through the gate! The guards got it surrounded. They callin' for the unicorn to come down and finish it off."

"A monster, is it?" cried the Prince. "We'll be right down! Wait'll I get my bow!"

Prince George ran up to the hall while the human begged Blackie, "Please, unicorn, come along. The Count told me to bring you!"

The horses, stepping around nervously, poked Blackie with their noses. "What's he saying, unicorn? What's going on out there?"

"He says, they've got a monster out there."

"A monster, oh, no!" cried the bay. "Monsters are terrible! You remember the giant hog of Legman Slime? That was a horse-killer!"

"Well, goodbye, horses," said Blackie. "I might as well take a look at this monster. If I'm lucky, I won't have to fight it, not with the Prince bringing a magic bow."

He plunged into the downpour, snorting as water snuffed up his nose.

The man jogging beside him shivered in the rain. "They say it's huge, unicorn, like a giant crab!"

As they neared the crossroads, Blackie heard dogs howl and men shout. A trumpet tooted. The man with Blackie pointed to a group of excited spearmen running back and forth, then dogs dashed up to Blackie, barking wildly, shaking water from their coats.

"Ho, there, the unicorn, the unicorn!" shouted the men, as Blackie trotted through the dogs. "He'll drive that monster out of there!"

"Bring him to the Count!" yelled someone, and the man directed Blackie to Count Basham.

"Here's sport for you, unicorn!" called the Count, pointing with his dripping sword. "'Pears to be a giant spider! It came swarmin' up from the south this morning and jumped over the gate. We cornered it over in them wagons. You chase it out, and we'll finish it off."

In a field near the meeting point of the roads where a stone tower guarded the tollgates, Blackie saw a mass of broken carts and wagons piled up like a scrambled haystack. Men and dogs circled the wagons at a respectful distance. As Blackie watched, a cart flew through the air, crashing down near the dogs. They jumped away, yelping.

"Don't know what it is, but it's fierce!" said the Count, wiping his face. "If the wagons were dry, unicorn, we could burn it out, but you'll have to root it out for us. Don't worry, though, the thing's small. Nothing to a dragon."

The men looked expectantly at Blackie, so he moved toward the wagons to get a better look. Stepping through broken wheel spokes and shafts, he tried to sniff the monster, but the rain had carried off the scent. The stacked carts in front of him shook violently. Blackie moved back, looking for Prince George, who came running through the rain with his spear and magic bow.

"What have you got here?" shouted the Prince.

The Count waved to him. "The watchmen say it jumps like a spider. Whatever it is, we got it trapped under them wagons. It howls like a wolf and flings wagons about. Unicorn's going to chase it out for us."

The Prince ran over to Blackie, panting.

"You . . . you be careful, Blackie. A bite from a spider that big could poison an elephant. Don't try to fight it. Just draw it out till I can get a shot with the bow."

He pulled the bow from his shoulder. Once the Prince lifted the arrow from the bow, the string snapped taut. Prince George notched the arrow.

"Shouldn't you use your spear, m' lord?" asked the Count. "Your bowstring won't be much good in the rain."

"Oh, this bow's magic," said the Prince, peering through the raindrops for a target. "It hits what I aim at, wet or dry. Go ahead, Blackie. Chase the monster out for me."

"How'd I get into this?" thought Blackie, stepping through the circle of barking dogs. Nearing the wreckage, he heard something huffing and moaning behind the wagons. He heard a clatter of wood as the thing moved about.

"I'll just charge in and see what happens."

He stepped forward. The dogs followed, staring at the wagons. Blackie heard a loud grunt and a cart flew at him. He charged under the cart, hearing it smash down behind him, then clambered onto the overturned wagons that cracked and rolled under his hooves.

He got a glimpse of a frightened, blinking eye and sucked in a noseful of stink that threw him back into the splintering mass of wheels and sideboards. Carts flew aside as a terrified Hellion leaped out in a mighty spring that brought him right down on Blackie.

"Oonicorn!"

With a grunt, Blackie relaxed into the shattered wood when he saw it was Mardoc, hugging him in a sticky embrace. Mardoc was howling and kissing Blackie with wet smacks when the magic arrow struck the Hellion in the shoulder.

"Oonicorn save Mardoc!"

"Hold up!" cried Prince George, catching the bloody arrow as it flew back after jerking free from Mardoc. "Hold up! That Hellion's tame!"

"Tame?" shouted the Count, running forward with his sword. "A Hellion? Are you sure, my lord? I never heard of such a thing!"

Prince George slapped the arrow against the bow to stop it squirming in his grasp. It stiffened and he clamped it back on the bow.

"Oh, yes, last I saw Mardoc, he was helping the brothers in a hospital."

By now, the Count's men had pulled off the dogs. The spearmen stared in disgust at the squatting Hellion, who peered at them over Blackie's back.

"What a horrible thing!" they muttered. "A livin' nightmare!"

"Okay, Mardoc!" called Prince George, walking forward. "You can stand up, now. Nobody's going to hurt you."

The spearmen stepped back when Mardoc hunched up on his big feet. Bent in pain from the wound in his shoulder, he whimpered like a hurt puppy. Blackie rolled to his hooves, shaking splinters from his coat. With a sigh, he reached up his horn to heal Mardoc's arrow wound.

"Mardoc," snapped Prince George. He frowned as the wet Hellion crowed with delight, stroking Blackie with a great fist, "What are you doing here? We left you working at the hospital."

"Mardoc not like 'spital," whined the Hellion, looking guilty. "Ever'one sick there. No one drink and dance at night."

Prince George shook his head.

"Mardoc, Mardoc, you didn't have to run off like this. You should have asked for another job. You could haul logs for timbermen or pile stones at construction. Construction workers love to sing and dance."

"Heavens, yes," said Count Basham, stepping close to feel Mardoc's biceps. "The problem is keeping 'em at work. And now, with war damage everywhere, a worker like you has his pick of jobs."

Mardoc twisted his face into a hopeful grin. "Mardoc work with oonicorn?"

"Oh, I don't think so," said Prince George, pulling Blackie away by his mane. "The unicorn has another job now, but I'm sure our friends here can find you work with folks who love to drink."

"No problem with that," promised the Count, reaching up to pat Mardoc's shoulder. "I can put you to work in the quarries. You'll like the stonecutters, Mardoc. Hell-raisers to a man, if you'll pardon the expression."

The Hellion raised to his full height, howling, "Mardoc want stay with oonicorn! Mardoc loves oonicorn!"

Eager to get along, Blackie pressed his wet shoulder against Prince George. The Prince caught his meaning and scrambled onto Blackie's back.

"Sorry, Mardoc, the unicorn has his own work to do!"

Blackie trotted up the road, splashing through the muddy runoff. Prince George shouted over his shoulder, "Thanks for the feast, Count! We'll see you when we pass by again!"

The Count's farewell was covered by Mardoc's wail. "Goo'bye, goo'bye, oonicorn! Mardoc loves oonicorn!"

CHAPTER THIRTY-FOUR

The Duchy of Darr

"Well, we've sunk to the bottom, now!" complained Prince George, glancing back at Castle Minch. He wiped cold rain from his face and pulled his bearskin about his shoulders.

"Stupidest thing we've done yet. We could have feasted in comfort for a week and traveled on with a mule load of supplies. Count Basham would give us anything we wanted, but no, off we go again with empty bags."

"At least, our bellies are full," thought Blackie. "Who knows if Papa has anything to eat."

Though the storm had thinned down to a drizzle, Prince George grumbled for an hour. He stopped only when a flock of geese flew under the clouds in a wide, honking "V." He hastily swung the bow from his back. The string snapped taut as he snatched the arrow. The flapping birds were out of sight by the time he was ready to shoot, but he loosed the arrow down their wake, shouting, "Go, go, go!"

The arrow returned in a moment, pierced through a heavy goose with a hanging head. With a shout, the Prince caught the goose in his glove.

"Now, that's what I call magic! Here's dinner!"

Shooting the goose cheered him so much that he hummed to himself as Blackie continued north. Blackie didn't like the weight of the dead bird across his shoulder, but it was good to see the Prince in spirits. The Prince's mood carried through the evening when they shared the campfire of a squad of soldiers heading home to Groot.

Blackie sniffed about the dripping fringe of the forest while the soldiers shared their beer and oatcakes with Prince George in exchange for strips of greasy goose flesh. As the wind sharpened after dark, Blackie came back to the fire where the soldiers were asking the Prince about his adventures.

"Oh, yes," he responded, staring into the flames, "most of those tales are true. I did discover the mine, you know, where the dragon was melting ore for Vile's silver coins. I didn't get any of the silver myself, but the Empress plans to use it to rebuild the country after the war."

"You should 'a grabbed a bootful o' coin for yourself, me lord," said a Grootman, tossing a goose bone onto the fire. "Fifteen, twenty ounces of silver, you could buy a few acres o' land with a tidy house to raise a family."

One of the other soldiers corrected him.

"Naw, Levi, the Prince don't want a family for hisself. He sworn to his spear like a warrior, right, me lord? You never rest for nothin', do you?"

Prince George shivered. "Seems like that, my man."

In the last hours of the night, the rain turned to sleet, smothering the fire and freezing everyone. The sleet stopped before dawn, but earth and trees were covered with sparkling ice crystals, covering Blackie's breakfast of scattered grasses and shoots. Coughing and moaning, the soldiers huddled under stiff blankets, waiting miserably for the ice to melt under the gray light of day.

Blackie refused to hang around. Blowing steam from his nose, he prodded Prince George with his horn until the Prince dragged to his feet, complaining to the heavens. He beat his bearskin with the spear shaft to loosen the ice, shook it off, and mounted. The Prince had to bend his head under branches pulled low by the weight of the sparkling casing.

Blackie warmed as he moved. The blood flowed to his legs and heated him. He bit thawing shoots as the ice melted about him. They didn't seem to have been spoiled by their ice-bath.

What Blackie dreaded most about this leg of the trip was the river-crossing. Old Steed had told about swimming the northern branch of the great river with chunks of ice scraping at his hide. This time, however, Prince George paid coppers from Jessica's purse for a couple strong-armed men to row them across the water in a pitching ferryboat. The men asked if they should blindfold Blackie for the crossing, as they did horses.

"No, no," said Prince George, "the unicorn understands boats. He'll be a good passenger."

Blackie may have understood boats, but he didn't like them. He braced his legs as the ferry shuddered in surging current, telling himself that this was better than swimming through ice.

"Is it true, Boatmen?" asked Prince George, swathed in his bearskin so only his nose stuck out. "Did Lord Godfrey set up this ferry system?"

"Oh, he's a far-sighted ruler," said one of the watermen, resting on his oar while his partner pulled to keep the bow on line in the drifting water. "Would you believe, this ferry tripled the trade to Darr before the war. Someday, the Heir says, he's goin' to build a bridge here and make us toll collectors."

Blackie hopped off the instant the boat scraped into mud on the north side of the river. He stood a moment as the ground rocked under him, then ran a few feet up the bank, sniffing for green sprigs.

Leaning on his spear as he hobbled up the bank, Prince George was thankful for the ferry. "Best coppers I've spent the whole trip, Blackie. You can't imagine how bitter the water feels this season. Even in summer, my knees ache from the cold and exposure I've had during winter travel."

North of the river, the road climbed slowly through the foothills of the mountains. The wind grew colder. Snow started to blow again, and Blackie had to nibble crusty buds on low fir trees along the edge of the forest. Prince George rode with the bow in his hand, looking hopefully for a goose or squirrel for breakfast, but all he saw were the black crows that greeted them with harsh cries.

"Breast of crow is good in a pie," he said, "but I don't fancy them roasted."

All in all, it was a cold, hungry ride until they reached Castle Helme next day. A vassal to the Duke of Darr, Baron Helme welcomed them properly, kneeling bareheaded at the gate to his castle.

"Greetings, my lord!" he exclaimed, kissing Prince George's hand. "We've been awaiting you. A messenger rode by from the Heir, telling us to expect the General of the army that drove out the rebels from the City."

"Oh, er, yes, I did something like that, my lord," said the Prince, motioning him to rise.

"And the unicorn!" Lord Helme bowed to Blackie. "What a treat to welcome the holy beast! This season is a time of wonders, hosting two unicorns in a month."

"You've seen another unicorn?" asked Prince George as Blackie perked up his ears.

"Oh, yes, my lord, the great white unicorn, the one rarely witnessed."

Lord Helme crossed himself and rolled up his eyes.

"His appearance, it was a miracle. My Baroness—Lady Sharon of Mildor, you know—she has a putrid throat that had worn her away. She couldn't eat a thing. She'd lost thirty pounds before the unicorn appeared, but he healed her at once when we promised him a feast. A touch of that horn and she leaped up, calling for luncheon. A miracle!"

"So where was the unicorn going?"

"The unicorn? Apparently, he was headed to Darr, my lord. You can imagine how disappointed we were. We wanted him to stay a month, but he only stopped by that single evening. Even the feast couldn't tempt him to linger. He ate his dinner, then shook his great head and continued north. Nothing could stop him."

"Well," said the Prince, looking at Blackie, who was struck with amazement that Papa would leave a feast, "it's obvious that something's going on. Now, we find the white unicorn traveling the same road we're on. Are you following him, Blackie? Do the two of you have some private quest I don't know about?"

The Prince's guess was uncomfortably close to the truth. Blackie didn't know how to answer, so he looked fixedly at the Baron, who nodded his head.

"I think it's a change in the heavens. My star-man says that remarkable things are happening in the spheres. He thinks it's the second Golden Age."

As Blackie shivered, thinking of Papa running toward Vile, Prince George suggested they get out of the wind. Lord Helme bowed again.

"Many pardons, my lord, for holding you outside. Enter, please. My castle's yours. Call for anything you desire."

Blackie hurried across the courtyard, the men following, talking politely.

"You won't remember me, my lord," said the Baron, "but I met you three years ago at the Contest. I was the gentleman that returned your hat when you dropped it while dancing with Lady Dorinda. You thanked me most graciously."

"Of course, I remember you, Baron," muttered the Prince.

In the hall, Blackie trotted to the fireplace where a large woman in a pink gown rose from a chair to greet him. "Oh, blessed unicorn, how pleased I am to see you! How fortunate you came today! My throat doesn't feel at all well. Could you . . . could you?"

She drew back the woolen scarf wrapped about her neck and rolled back her head so he could get to her flabby throat. With a shrug, he touched her with his horn.

"Oh," she cried, shaking her head around, "much better, much better! No one knows, unicorn, how I suffer with my throat. It's the planets, you see. My sun's in Libra, a bad aspect to Venus, so I choke up at a draft. I'm in misery half the year. Physician tells me to take cinnamon and pepper for it, but those spices are impossible to get. I have to sip turpentine in a spoon, one part to three parts of water, and suffer, suffer in silence."

By now, the Prince and Baron had reached the fireplace. Lady Helme curtseyed grandly to the Prince, throwing an arm to her chest.

"My lord," she gasped, "your unicorn has saved my life! My throat was afire this morning! I sat here, weak as a worm, till he touched me with his healing horn. Now, I can talk again, thanks to the holy beast. The white unicorn brought relief, a couple days ago, but I'd lapsed badly, badly. Now, I feel passable again."

"I'm pleased, my lady, at your recovery," said the Prince with a bow.

"Oh, it's not recovery!" cried the Lady. "We may never expect recovery, my lord, but a moment of relief, even that's a blessing. If only the unicorn could stay with me for a year or two, give me treatments four or five times a day, then I might recover, but these little therapies—Well, all I can say is that I'm grateful for a moment's relief."

Baron Helme grasped her hand, turning to the Prince.

"You see, Prince, my lady's a Christian martyr, a model to us all. She suffers in silence like a saint. The Heir told me himself, when he rode by on his way to the army, that it's my duty to stay with her. He took thirty of my bowmen with him, but left me to tend my lady. Most gracious of him."

"You know, my love," whispered Lady Helme to the Baron, "I think I could take a little food now, perhaps some light soup if it's not too hot."

"Of course, my dear," said the Baron, patting her hand, "and Prince George, I'm sure that you're hungry. Luckily, we had word that you were coming, so the birds are roasting in the kitchen. I'm sorry that it's wintertime. If it were summer, we'd have a real feast. We can at least satisfy the unicorn, I believe, as we have plenty of grain and fodder, or bread and cakes if he prefers. I'll have my people draw up the tables, if you please, and start the meal. Our storerooms are running low with the war, but we have enough to carry us to spring planting. It's poor fare for the season, but it's nourishing!"

At the signal, serving men began pulling up tables before the fireplace. Prince George excused himself to go to the private room to wash up, but Blackie followed the preparations with eager eyes.

One of the servers slipped him a couple dried carrots which made him even more hungry as he smelled the platters being arranged on the table. When the Prince returned, Blackie had to wait through the seating at the tables and the benediction before digging into the bread, grain, and vegetables set before him.

No one ate more eagerly than Baroness Helme. She complained about her poor appetite while consuming half a pigeon pie, a duck, and a platter of fish with onions. Prince George kept up with her the first hour, but fell behind on the dried fruits and cakes. All the while, the Baroness talked with her mouth full.

"I haven't seen you, my lord, since the Contest at Darr. Who can forget the feasting and dancing there, with Princess Julianna herself staying in the Northlands for weeks! What a treat that was! I must say, though, my lord, that I was shocked at the minstrels' songs of those days. The ballads about the Contest are so deficient in details. Why, none of them mentions me, though I had a completely new wardrobe for the occasion!"

"I've noticed that, my lady," said the Prince, winking at Blackie. "Shocking."

"You know, my lord," continued the Baroness, "I thought it a tragedy that you didn't take Lady Dorinda for yourself. That would have been perfect for us all. Now, I must say, the Heir is a thoughtful neighbor. I hold nothing against him! You'll be happy to know that Lady Dorinda has recovered totally from her childbed, and the baby, Lord Bruce, he's healthy as a horse from what I hear. Of course, she never visits me. She spends whole weeks with Lady Thorn, next door, but never finds an evening to call on me, despite all my urging and invitations. Well, I think I understand why. She's afraid of catching my bad throat!"

Blackie turned his attention to his food. More and more, he was learning to tune out the human chatter to think of his own problems. When should he slip away from Prince George? A feast like this is a wonderful treat, but Papa's getting away from him. And now, Lady Helme began begging the Prince to stay till spring.

"Since you're here, my lord, you must have a regular visit. There's so much to see around Barony Helme, even in this weather. And the heavy snows will return soon, the bitter cold. Why don't you stay with us all winter, rest up until Easter? Then the minstrels would have something to sing about!"

She paused to swallow a honeycake, then continued, spitting out little crumbs.

"Despite the war, you'll find few castles as well supplied for pleasure as this one, I assure you. We have beautiful music and maidens to dance with— And my throat, the unicorn would have time to heal it properly."

Prince George began making apologies for his early departure, but the Baroness bore him down.

"Oh, what I forgot to tell you, Prince, is that the Heir will be here tomorrow! That's what the latest messenger reported. Lord Godfrey has left the army with a small company to head home. He's eager to return to Lady Dorinda, of course, but he especially desires to escort you through Darr. We'll request that he stop off with us a few days. If you're here, I'm sure that he'll agree to stay."

"Well, I don't know," said Prince George, looking uncertainly at Blackie, who was perplexed over what to do. Waiting for the Heir would hold him back longer, but the Prince—

"If I wait, I can leave the Prince with the Heir. They're old friends. They'll want to be together. Surely, in the hubbub of hospitality, I can slip over the border by myself. Vile's just beyond Darr. It'll be easy."

Blackie nodded his horn, so the Prince cheerfully accepted the offer. "I thank you, my lady. I will stay until the Heir arrives. That will please everyone. I certainly don't want to leave your gracious entertainment."

"Perfect!" she cried, rising up, then sank down in her chair, gasping, "Oh, oh, oh!"

"My dear, my dear!" exclaimed the Baron, grasping her hand. "I'm afraid you're exerting yourself! This is too much excitement for you."

"No, no, my lord," she whispered. "Just one of my spells. This . . . this one strikes me lower in the body, a bilious attack, a cramp, the gripes. If only the unicorn could . . . you know!"

So Blackie had to give treatments to her belly. While they awaited the Heir for the next day and a half, Lady Helme required frequent treatments on various sections of her body. In between his medical duties, Blackie listened to the singing in the hall and ate hay outside in the stables with the donkeys left behind when the Heir rode off to the army. The donkeys asked about the horses who'd carried off the troops. When Blackie had nothing to report about the mounts, the donkeys ignored him, except to complain that he ate more than his share.

Late the second day, the Heir rode in with a great blare of trumpets. The donkeys grew excited as the horses were led in, two and three at a time. To everyone's dismay, several beasts from the castle were missing, and most of those returning were in bad shape.

Blackie took it on himself to heal the worst of the horses, which raised him in everyone's opinion. Even the mules stepped back for him when he moved along the mangers, though he politely deferred to Hannah, the old donkey in charge. She thanked him for his attentions before turning to the survivors to learn what had happened to the lost horses.

As darkness fell, Blackie walked around to the castle keep. Inside the hall, he found Prince George and the Heir eating goose and fish with the barons and knights. Godfrey was laughing about a platter of baked eel Prince George had shoved away with a sniff.

"Try it, my lord, it's good," urged the Baroness, but the Heir roared loudly, thumping the table with his knife. "My lord Prince had a famous encounter with an eel in the lower river. As he pulled it into the boat, the eel went for his snout!"

"Well, I'm not afraid of this fellow," said the Prince, wrinkling his nose. "I just don't like the taste, too bony, too fishy."

"Please, give it a try, my lord," begged the Baroness. "I'm sure that you'll like the way my cook prepares it."

Later, Prince George asked Blackie to touch him with his horn. "The aftertaste—that eel! I can't get it out of my mouth."

Blackie gave the Prince a spark from his horn. It healed a wart on his elbow, but didn't remove the fishy taste. Next morning, Prince George was still complaining about the eel when they mounted to ride to Darr so the Heir visited the kitchen before they left and returned with a wrinkled piece of root.

"Here, my lord, chew on this."

Frowning, Prince George lifted the thing in his fingers and sniffed it. "What is it?"

"Horseradish."

Prince George had the rank taste of horseradish in his mouth all day. He claimed it tasted better than eel.

The road through Darr had been vastly improved since the last time Prince George had visited. They made excellent time up to Darr Town. Godfrey sent a couple spearman ahead to alert his people, so the streets were crowded with townsfolk waving scarves and hats while cheering the Heir and the soldiers.

To the Prince's amusement, the Heir felt he had to make a speech on returning. He jumped onto a bench outside the inn, lifted his arms, and waited for the applause to trail off.

"My dear people," he called, "greetings to you!"

"Blessings on you, me lord!" shouted the crowd.

"I bring good news! The war is over! We didn't have to fight! The very appearance of our heroic Darrmen was enough to cause the enemy to break off the siege."

Tremendous cheers at this news went on for several minutes.

"The best of the story," shouted Godfrey, "is that no one was killed but Edric the broom-maker who fell off his horse!"

"My husband!" shrieked a woman.

"And, of course," Godfrey added, hastily, "the bereaved widow is entitled to three silver coins in compensation for her loss!"

The cheers for this were broken by another cry, "You can kill my husband for two coins!"

Blackie heard an explosion of hoots and laughter before Godfrey spoke again.

"I've ridden ahead with twenty men to prepare for the return of our soldiers. They'll be home in a week. At that time, the Duke will declare a holiday so our families can unite in peace. I'll provide cider and wine from my own stocks to celebrate their return, and we'll thank God for His blessings."

The cheering continued even louder. Godfrey started to jump from the bench, but stopped. Again, he held up his arms to quiet the shouts. He pointed to Prince George and Blackie.

"As you see, my people, I bring guests. Here you have the famous Prince, George of Dacia, whom we thank for graciously granting me the heart and hand of my lady, Dorinda."

After another storm of catcalls and applause, the Heir went on, "I'm sure that you've already noticed our other guest. This is the famous black unicorn whose mighty deeds have done so much to defeat the schemes of our evil neighbor. As part of our festival, we'll hold a clinic, so all our sick and injured can profit by his gift of healing!"

There were even louder cheers at that. Jumping from the bench, the Heir said to Blackie, "I hope you don't mind healing a few aches and pains. The people will remember your easing a toothache more that anything else during the festival."

"I'll run on before that happens," Blackie promised himself as he carried Prince George through the cheering throng to the castle.

"Why, Godfrey," the Prince shouted over the commotion, "these people love you! No one cares that you were just a starving headsman that I discovered in the forest."

"They love me because of that," said the Heir, waving back to the crowds. "Everyone likes the story of a poor boy who makes good. And of course, little Brucie puts the seal on it. As old as Dorinda was before her marriage, the people feared they'd never see a proper heir to the duchy."

"Yes, she was—what?—twenty-four, twenty-five?" asked the Prince.

"Oh, yes, practically a spinster," agreed the Heir. "But she's a different woman since we married, more beautiful than ever! You'll see. There's the castle on the hill!"

Having heard the Prince's stories of the Contest, Blackie was interested in everything about the great castle of Darr with its surrounding barrier of spiny northorns looking savage without the concealing leaves of summer. Why, Papa had carried Prince George up this very path in the first task of the Contest! As they entered the castle gate under the heavy portcullis, Blackie looked up at the platform from which Lady Dorinda had thrown her golden ring into the thorns.

Godfrey pointed to the platform. "Remember, my lord, Prince Vile landing up there on his dragon?"

Prince George nodded silently, his heart full of memories.

Though the townspeople were turned back at the gate, the courtyard was packed with castle folk and gentry. Bells rang. Trumpets blew. Limping out the castle door came the Duke of Darr in a great fur cloak, looking shorter and older than Blackie had imagined, but beaming with a gap-toothed grin. Towering above the Duke, thin and gaunt, came the Duchess carrying the bright-eyed child, Brucie, who waved a small, wooden axe. Hurrying last of all, tucking a strand of blond hair under her headdress, came Dorinda of Darr, said to be the most beautiful woman in the Empire.

Demurely casting down her eyes, Lady Dorinda curtseyed low before her lord. Godfrey swept her up in a passionate kiss.

"Ooh, ooh!" squealed Lady Dorinda, struggling to free herself, her face as red as if sunburnt. "My lord, my lord, not before company—and Prince George of all people!"

"That's my bonny girl!" shouted Godfrey, giving her a clap on the bottom before grabbing the baby and lifting him high in the air. The boy wriggled and laughed, kicking knitted booties under his skirt.

"Welcome back, me lord, welcome back!" roared the Duke, bowing to Prince George. "Too many seasons has passed since you visited us, and, now, you ride this black unicorn, the mighty beast we hear so much about! Did you know that the white unicorn has been visitin' us? He left us the day before yesterday!"

"Only two days ago?" cried Prince George, sliding off Blackie.

"Yep, just before we heard you was comin'. He galloped up through the storm, all beat up and shaky from the ice. He stayed around long enough to recover, then ran on at the thaw."

The Duke took Prince George's arm and walked with him to the castle hall, everyone following. To the Duchess's alarm, Godfrey carried the squirming baby in one arm while he embraced Lady Dorinda with the other.

Blackie followed, sniffing Lady Dorinda's scent. He recognized her perfume, the same Purple Honesty the Princess wore, but the effect was different. He missed the hypnotic bouquet of the Princess. Inside the hall, Blackie looked at the high ceiling with its tattered banners while the Duke talked about Papa's visit.

"Seein' the unicorn was like old times. The larder's run down from the winter, o' course, but we fed him oats and hay, dried peas and apples and cherries. He still refuses to heal anyone, but he seemed happy to hang around, eatin' as much as any three horses, till somethin' stung him into motion, and he trotted away to the north."

The Duke pulled off his hat and rubbed his bald head.

"Don't know where he was goin'. Nothin' up there but the Citadel and the border. He seemed to know where he was headin', though, and he was determined to get there."

"Lord Godfrey, please," begged the Duchess, reaching for the baby, "don't you think I should take the child? You're getting him too excited for his nap."

"What, my son?" cried Godfrey. "I haven't seen him for weeks. He'll be forgetting his daddy if I don't play with him awhile."

"He won't forget you, my lord," said Dorinda, fondly taking the baby and kissing his red cheeks. She gave him to her mother, who carried him away quickly, then addressed Prince George.

"It's so good to see you, my lord. As you see, many things have changed since the Contest."

"Many things, many things!" sighed the Duke, settling down in his chair. "And me knees most of all! I can't get around the way I used to. Was a day, I'd go ridin' out before the army with sword and shield, but now, I just set in the rockin' chair before the fire."

"And that's where you belong, father," said Dorinda, firmly. "Man of your age should have his rest while the young lords go off on campaign. We need you at home to hold court and keep things in order."

"But you say, my lord," cried Prince George with concern, "your knees are giving you problems? Why, that white unicorn could have healed you. He helped Lady Helme, after all. But don't worry, this unicorn, here, is a healer, too. He'll be glad to remove any aches and pains you may have."

"Oh, really, me lord," asked the Duke, "your unicorn does heal? What a blessin' that is! That white unicorn, he wasn't interested in anything but food, so no one thought about the healin'. I figgered that he'd lost his powers, or somethin'. D'ye think this one'd give me some relief now?"

Prince George rubbed Blackie's ears. "He'd be glad to do it, my lord. He loves to be of service, don't you, old man?"

Sighing, Blackie stepped close to the Duke, who pulled up the skirt of his robe to expose his hairy legs. As Blackie touched each bony knee with his horn, the Duke kicked out with a cry.

"Thank Heaven, thank Heaven, I haven't felt this good for years!"

He jumped to his feet and strode back and forth, lifting his knees and stomping his feet.

"Why, feelin' like this, I can ride out as soon as I'm armed! I'll deal meself with that traitor Ord who refused to answer when we called out the barons. I been waitin' for you to come back, Godfrey, to handle that little job, but soon as I saddle me horse—"

"No, no, you're not saddling any horse!" cried the Duchess, running back into the room to grab the Duke's arm. "You're not going anywhere till we know that the healing will last. I know your knees from way back. It'd be like that left knee of yours to give out on the road, so you'd have to be carried home in a cart. Let Lord Godfrey deal with Baron Ord when he's ready."

"But dear—" cried the Duke.

"Don't you 'dear' me!" she insisted. "At your age, you have to take care of yourself before you break down completely. You may have good knees now, but your heart isn't what it was, and everyone knows about your kidneys."

"Me kidneys is perfect!" declared the Duke. "When the unicorn healed me knees, he healed me innards as well."

"We'll see about that. When you can climb the stairway without stopping twice to catch your breath, then we'll think about you riding again."

"See what you escaped stayin' single, Prince!" laughed the Duke, settling back in his chair while the Duchess ran back to see that Lord Brucie was resting quietly. "A married man don't need a liege lord. He gets orders enough in his own home."

"Well," Prince George said a little enviously, "Godfrey seems to be comfortable enough with his married life."

The Duke rocked back with a yawn.

"True enough, true enough, but they's few wives like Dorinda. You find another Dorinda, Prince, you better snap her up. You can't keep givin' away beautiful ladies forever!"

"Well, the Prince already has his eye on a lady," grinned Godfrey, "and she's highborn enough for anyone."

By now, the lords had to move aside so the servants could set up the tables before the fire. A squire began pouring cups of wine for the lords while a kitchen boy brought a basket of oatcakes for Blackie.

"Eat up, young unicorn, eat up!" cried the Duke. "Since the Citadel held out against the Hellions, Darr wasn't ravaged like them other duchies. You don't have to hold back on anything here. If you can hang around till the early crops comes in, you'll think you was feedin' at the Shrine!"

"Oh, we can't stay that long," Prince George insisted. "A good dinner and a rest, then we'll hit the road after the other unicorn. We want to catch him before he enters Vile. That's right, isn't it, Blackie?"

He looked at Blackie, who nodded as the Duke declared, "Don't worry about that, Prince. That unicorn won't go into Vile. He loves the easy life too much. One sniff o' the burnin' mountain, and he'll run back to his comforts like a blacksmith threatened with soap. If I was you, I'd just wait here with us. I guarantee, you'll see him back at our gate in a day or two."

Blackie had to shake his head at those words. He wished the Duke were right, but Blackie feared the worst. Of course, Papa might weaken. If the food was good enough, he'd hang around the castle a day or two. But if he was convinced that his son was in danger, Papa's unicorn blood could drive him into anything, even into the flaming jaws of the dragon!

481

And now, only two days behind Papa, they had a real chance of catching him. Blackie would stay for the feast tonight to build up his strength. He might even heal the toothaches and bad knees of the people as the Heir had promised, but he had to run north tomorrow. If he moved quickly enough, he had a real chance of catching Papa and getting him home in one piece.

The ladies went off to watch Lord Brucie sleep while Blackie ate oatcakes and dried apples. He listened to Prince George try to talk Godfrey into launching a raid into Vile.

"Impossible, Prince!" protested Godfrey. "I don't want to stir up that hornets' nest. And I owe my clansmen a good rest when they return home. After that, we have to think of spring planting. It might be different next fall when our storerooms are full again, but now, my soldiers are worn down from this recent war. I can't hold them to another campaign so soon."

"In that case," said the Prince, "it'll be just Blackie and me, as planned. We'll slip in on the quiet and catch the unicorn if we can."

"You know, my lord, I'd go with you if I could," said Godfrey, ruefully. "I'd love to ride free like the old days, but my lady would never forgive me for leaving her now."

"How about me?" cried the Duke. "I'll go with you. After all, Godfrey's taken over most o' me duties! If me knees are healed, I can set a spear with the best o' 'em!"

"No, no, my lord," laughed Godfrey, "the Duchess would skin us alive. You think the dragon's fierce? That'd be nothing to your lady's wrath if she heard your suggestion!"

CHAPTER THIRTY-FIVE

Road's End

Blackie quivered in the blast whistling across the narrow lane crawling up the ridge of the mountain. He looked ahead where Prince George was pointing.

"That's it!" shouted the Prince over the wind. "Castle March, the Citadel! Look at the size of that fortress!"

Castle March stood across the central spur of the mountain range dividing the Empire from Vile. This Citadel was built over the road so that the route entered the walls on one side and exited on the other, giving control of traffic to the Captain.

The Heir had explained back in Darr Town that no vassal held the Citadel. It was commanded by a knight at the appointment of the Duke with a band of paid guards, changed twice a year to prevent border fever.

"Double pay, they get, to sign up there," Godfrey told them. "With no town, no village, nothing to spend their coppers on, the men dream of saving their pay to buy pigs or set up a mill. But it's so boring, the Captain tells me, that they get to gambling. Most of them stagger home as poor as when they went up."

Blackie could not get his head around this gambling. He'd often seen humans turning cards or throwing dice, but it made no sense to him. He could understand why frontier duty was boring, though. Nearing Castle March, he saw only a few strips of cultivated earth stair-stepping down the southwest side of the mountain. When it warmed in a few weeks, they'd be planted with the hardy vegetables that could survive in this wind, but the task would occupy only a few of the men. The rest would have to amuse themselves however they could.

The portcullis was down as they rode up to the Citadel. A tall sergeant peered through the bars. "Name, rank, and reason for passage!"

"Prince George of Docia, scouting north to the border."

"Prince George," the sergeant repeated, signaling for the portcullis to rise, "we've heard o' you, me lord. And you got another unicorn with you. I never in me life saw a unicorn before Sunday. Now, this makes two of 'em in one week. Must be a conclave o' unicorns up north."

Blackie's ears went up at the mention of Unicorn.

"Is it the white unicorn?" asked Prince George, eagerly. "Is he still here?"

"Oh, no, me lord, he left three days ago. He rested overnight to warm up, but he wouldn't stop for more than a day. He kicked at the north gate 'till Captain said to let him go, then he ran off like he knew where he was headed."

As the portcullis creaked up on its chain, more guards came out to look at Blackie. They clustered around, patting his muscles, touching his horn.

"I bet this unicorn could whip the white one in a fight," said a red-bearded spearman.

"I'd give you five to one on that," said the Sergeant.

"Tell me, Sergeant," asked the Prince, watching the portcullis descend behind him, "who's Captain here these days?"

"Why, Sir Burly it is, to be sure, a mighty man o' Rhudd."

"Sir Burly!" exclaimed the Prince, walking past the inspection booth with Blackie. "I knew a Sergeant Burly back in the Guards. He was a mighty man in those days."

"One in the same," said the Sergeant, waving off the examiners reaching for Blackie's bags. "Lucky man, he got promoted for valor. What with this war killin' off so many knights, the Empress wanted a trusty man up here, so they dubbed him with his sword and sent him right up."

"Take your arms, me lord?" asked a guard, saluting the Prince.

"You can hold my armor, man, and get your groom to look over the unicorn. He needs a good rubdown. Blackie, I'll go meet the Captain. You can join us for dinner once these men tend to you."

"We'll take good care of the beast, me lord," promised the Sergeant. "'Tis a rare task to groom a unicorn. Doin' it twice in one week is a treat."

"A hundred to one, we see a third unicorn within a fortnight!" cried the guard.

Prince George gave up his helmet and shield, but he carried the bow and spear as he walked off with the Sergeant. The soldiers led Blackie to the broad stables, empty now, except for two horses, a few mules, and a dozen donkeys.

"Well, looky what we got here," blurted one of the donkeys, looking impudently at Blackie. "Another single-horn. Their mama must a' been half mountain goat."

"Shut up, ass," said the largest horse. "That's a unicorn. You saw the white beast that stopped by the other day."

The mules stared Blackie up and down.

"So these fellas come in black and white, does they?" said one. "What I want to know is will this beast carry a load? Far as I could see, that white unicorn was worthless, running alone without pack nor saddle. What's the use of a quatterped trottin' over these hills if he don't carry his load?"

"Don't know why you're concerned," said the horse, shortly. "The fuss you make when they load you down! I'd be ashamed to act that way if I was a pack animal."

"Why, you gotta make a fuss," said the mule, yawning. "Two-legs'll take advantage if you don't throw off a load now and then. Awhile back, they tried to load me with chairs, hard, bumpy things with legs stickin' out all directions. I wouldn't put up with that. Chairs is loadin' for a cart, not for a beast with any self-respect."

Tired from the climb, Blackie stood with head down while the men tossed coins to see who got to groom him. Once the rubbing started, he let the babble flow about him while he considered how he could sneak into Vile. It seemed impossible from the road they'd been following, so exposed and vulnerable.

Another man walked in with pails of musty grain. He scattered one pail into the manger for the donkeys and mules, then set the other bucket before Blackie. The mules put up a screech at that.

"Not fair, not fair! How's he get all that supper when we gets only a mouthful? Who carried them grain bags up the mountain in the first place?"

Blackie had only chomped his first mouthful when another man stuck his head around the door.

"Unicorn groomed yet? He's wanted in the mess hall."

The man rubbing Blackie tossed the towel into a basket. "Oh, you might as well take him now, Higgin. He got the beasts in an uproar."

"Come on, unicorn," said Higgin, picking up Blackie's bags. "They got better chow for you up in the hall."

The mules were yelling as Blackie walked into the courtyard, "Hey, spread the rest o' that bucket over here!"

The hall in the Citadel was smoky and dim. The walls were undressed stone with arrow-slits above a shooters' platform that ran around the room. Baskets of arrows and fist-sized stones stood under the slits. Rows of shields hung on pegs along the walls.

Stools were placed around a long table before the large fireplace where figures, outlined by the flames, tended the spits and pots hanging over the fire. A group of soldiers knelt on the floor at the corner of the fireplace, throwing dice with sharp exclamations, while other soldiers, bundled in cloaks and blankets, lay on benches lined down the room, their heads on clothing bags for pillows.

Prince George was sitting at the center of the table before the fire. Beside him sat a big knight, who pushed to his feet when Blackie walked near. The knight patted Blackie's shoulder with a heavy hand.

"So this's your unicorn, me lord? Brawny beast, he is. I like that. And his horn's got scratches and scars from combat. That white unicorn, ugh, he was too primped and polished for me. None 'o the weals and welts that shows a veteran—and weak? He barely made the climb up here. That beast was exhausted! Stood at the door, pantin' like he'd run a horse race. Then the crazy puppy insisted on headin' off into Vile! I warned him that he wouldn't make it."

Prince George lifted his wine cup to Blackie. "Well, Burly, this unicorn's tough enough, I can tell you. The things he and I have been through—You wouldn't believe them all. Come on over here, Blackie. We've got supper for you."

Sir Burly walked with Blackie to the table. "O' course, everyone's heard you been runnin' with a unicorn, Prince. They sing the wildest songs about you."

"They're probably true," said the Prince, setting down his cup. He reached up to rub Blackie's nose. "This unicorn and I, we've had a wild time this year, fighting our way through bandits and Hellions. One day, we'd escape the dragon chasing us through the forest, then shake off Gypsies the next. Blackie here, he's as proper a unicorn as you'll ever see. He's ready to take on the dragon any chance he gets."

"That's what I likes to hear!" cried Sir Burly, thumping Blackie on his back. "Now, you're describin' a real unicorn! What's he want to eat, me lord? We eats rough up here on the border, but he can have anything we've got."

Prince George leaned back in his chair. "Well, he doesn't eat meat, you know. He likes fruit and vegetables and bread. He'll eat muffins, cakes, cookies, that sort of thing."

"I fear that we're short 'o fruits and veggies," replied Sir Burly. "They're hard to get holt of up here, you know. But we has dried peas and bread. I'm sure the cook can bake up a tart for him with a bit of dried fruit. Does he like beer?"

Blackie ate his supper while Prince George studied a large map stretched over the table. Sir Burly leaned beside him, holding a candle over the small trails running through the mountains.

"That's another of 'em, me lord," said Sir Burly, tracing a path with his thick finger. "Smuggler's trails. I sets out ambushes every once in a while, but I don't have men enough to close 'em all. I has to keep most of the troops guardin' the castle."

Prince George scratched his head in wonder. "What in the world do they smuggle out of Vile? Do they have anything up there a merchant would want?"

"Oh, you'd be surprised, me lord. They carries out jewels and weapons, drugs and poisons, that sort of things. It's a rare prize when we captures a smuggling crew, I promise you. That's the reason a knight would agree to come here in the first place. As Captain, I gets a third o' any booty we capture. Two or three good hauls and I can set up as a gentleman—fix up that crumbly old castle they give me and pick out a wife, a proper lady who knows how to use a napkin."

"Why, Burly," said the Prince, astonished, "I'd never imagine you for the smart life. Here, you're dreaming of a lady with style and fashion!"

Sir Burly choked on his cup, spitting wine over the table. He turned red as a brick. He hastened to correct the Prince.

"No, no, me lord, you know better'n that! I'm not a teacup and saucer man, never will be. But I do want to live decent and comfortable. I've served the Empress long enough to know how a lady behooves herself. That's what I want for meself."

"Well, bless you, Burly!" cried the Prince. "Good luck to you! I used to think that men should stay in the rank they're born to, but I've seen too many nobles turn traitor the past few months. Now, I honor any loyal man who rises on merit."

"Oh," said Sir Burly gloomily, "there's lots of lords hates it, Prince. I hear the whispers behind me back. They say I'm a jackdaw in borrowed feathers. I never paged a day in me life, you know, never was a squire. They just had me pray over me sword in the chapel one night, then jumped me up to knight the next mornin'."

"Don't let anyone distress you over that," urged the Prince, patting Burly on the shoulder. "If the Empress chose you for promotion, I'm sure you deserve it. Look at the Heir of Darr! He shows us there's more to gentle life than knowing the right spoon. Serving in good faith, having a true heart, that's what's important."

"What's important—"

Those words rang in Blackie's head. He knew what was important to him. He had to get on with this mission, shake himself free to catch Papa before he got rounded up by Prince Vile's patrols.

"I'm on the very doorstep to Vile," he said to himself. "Why am I hanging around these humans? I've eaten now. I should get on my way without wasting more time."

Tail waving, Blackie backed away from the table. The men looked up at him.

"What is it, boy?" asked the Prince, rising to follow him. "You need to go out?"

Sir Burly lifted his eyebrows. "You got him toilet-trained, me lord?"

"Toilet-trailed!" exclaimed the Prince. "Listen, Burly, if anyone tries to tell you that the lion is king of beasts, just tell him you've seen the unicorn! This beast knows everything we say. He speaks to animals and birds. I'm just starting to learn all his powers."

"Look," said Sir Burly, "he's pointing to the door with his horn. He wants to go out."

Rubbing his chin, Prince George watched Blackie. "No, no, I can tell you what he wants. He doesn't like lounging around. He's ready for action. He wants to make a midnight run of it."

"Oh, no!" cried the soldiers, "you can't do that, me lord!"

"Not wise," said Sir Burly, soberly, "not wise. These mountains is treacherous enough by daylight. Stumblin' around in the dark, you'll break your neck for sure. What you need to do is get a good night's rest, then run on at dawn if you must go. I'll lead you to a likely trail and turn you loose."

"That sounds sensible to me." The Prince turned to Blackie. "What do you think, old man? You've seen what these hills are like the last few days. You don't want to try a goat-path in the dark, do you? We'd break our necks."

Blackie shrugged and turned back to the table. Much as he hated it, he knew that Sir Burly was right. He could see better in the dark than humans, well enough for familiar forest paths, but he wouldn't want to chance it down these twisting mountain trails. If he crippled himself, he couldn't rescue anyone.

Prince George sat down again, taking up his wine cup. "So, Burly, did you hear that Sir Otley went over the wall?"

Tired of the stuffy room, Blackie left the men talking and went back to the stable to sleep. The animals looked up at him drowsily, asked a question or two, and settled down quietly. Of course, the mules complained, next morning, when men came down with a lantern to take Blackie to the hall for an early breakfast. The soldiers pulled a light harness over him. They loaded him with supplies while he gobbled two loaves of bread and a handful of raisins.

Prince George came in then, shivering and coughing. "What time is it, Burly?"

"I figger it's after five in the mornin', me lord. Sun'll be risin' about the time we gets to the head o' the trail, then it's up to you. You sure you want to keep on? That's a mighty dodgy path you're travelin'. Things only get worse across the border."

Prince George stretched and looked at Blackie. "What do you say, Blackie? You still determined to cross into Vile?"

Blackie vigorously nodded his horn.

"There's your answer, Burly. 'Sir Burly,' I should say. Sorry, knight, I keep forgetting to call you by your proper rank."

"I keep forgettin' it, meself," muttered Sir Burly. "Guess I'll pick it up as I goes along."

They left twenty minutes later with a dozen archers, four spearmen, and the chaplain of Castle March. This north end of the castle had twice as many defensive walls and towers as the south end. The men led their donkeys and mules through the murder passage, which smelled of rancid bacon grease. As they mounted outside in the wind, Prince George asked about recent attacks.

"Not bad, me lord, not so many as we feared," Sir Burly answered. "We was prepared for 'em. The Heir sent me thirty extry men, and I keep 'em on alert. Once in awhile, we skirmish with raiders out on the trails, but they was only one determined assault on the castle. We saw the Hellions comin' a long ways off, so we was ready when they got here."

"So you had a peaceful time of it," said Prince George, walking Blackie up the road beside Sir Burly's mule.

"Pretty much," said the knight. "O' course, just as you'd expect, a couple messengers showed up with threats and promises. Prince Vile offered to make me baron if I surrendered him the castle. He promised I could keep half the money from traffic tolls, too. Tolls goin' up tenfold, they said, once he becomes Emperor."

"I suppose," suggested the Prince, "they threatened to throw you off the mountain if you didn't go along with it."

"Somethin' like that." Sir Burly laughed harshly. "I told Vile's herald that I'd chuck him over the wall, black flag and all, if I ever saw his face again."

"That's why the Empress knighted you!" exclaimed the Prince. "She knew you'd stand faithful under pressure."

Exposed to the wind on the bare track they followed, the men bent in their saddles against the gusts. Blackie looked down the mountainside. He felt like a fluttering leaf on a branch. One good blast could blow him out into the rolling fog below.

Mountain peaks rose from the mist as far Blackie could see. Still shadowed to the west, they glowed purple and gold to the east as the sun climbed over the far-off Shrine. Ahead, the Kingdom of Vile was walled off by gray pinnacles sticking up like sharp teeth.

They rode silently through swirling clouds until the road narrowed to a single wagon-track. The Chaplain rode first in line, holding up his bronze cross. The men-at-arms rode in pairs, the archers clutching silver-tipped arrows. Breathing hard in the thin air, Blackie's heart beat faster. He assured himself that it was only the altitude.

Every half mile or so, they crossed a ledge or platform just wide enough for wagons to pass. Blackie noticed scattered bones and the dark ashes of dead fires. One ledge had a message scraped into the rock. Prince George read it aloud:

PRAY WHILEST YE MAY
THE END IS NIGH
6.3 MILS

"So the border's six miles away?" he asked the knight.

"Yes, me lord," said Sir Burly. "They's a small station right on the crossin'. We keeps it manned durin' peaceful days when trade goes back and forth. Times like these, we pulls back to the Citadel and collects tolls there—what tolls gets paid."

The men swung from their mules with a rattle of arms. Sir Burly walked to the east end of the ledge and thumped his spear against the rock.

"Well, this is where you sets off if you insists on goin'. I wouldn't advise it, me lord. That white unicorn, his bones is probably in the rocks down there, breakfast for the vultures that sails through the mountains."

Blackie looked down at the tangle of ridges and ravines gleaming gold under the rays of sun piercing the mountain peaks. Prince George drew his bearskin tight about him.

"What do we do from here on, fly?"

"No, you has to climb down there if you wants to avoid the Hellions at the border station." Sir Burly pointed behind a jagged row of boulders. "That's the best o' the smuggler's trail."

Stepping through the rocks, Blackie saw a stony path threading down the side of the mountain to a slit of stream bed headed roughly the same direction as the road.

"That's our best trail?" The Prince's protest echoed Blackie's thoughts. "We'd have to turn mountain goat to travel that hairline."

Sir Burly patted Blackie's flank.

"We hike or ride donkeys on off-road patrols, but I figure this unicorn's nimble enough for a little rock-climbin'. Now, you gotta tread careful in this territory if you don't want broken bones. Take your time goin' downward and keep an eye out for ambushes. It's no-man's land from here. You'll find Vile's patrols on the hunt for smugglers and escapees. Keep a good watch for Hellhounds, too. They don't spare man or beast."

Prince George turned to Blackie and looked into his eyes. "What do you say, old man? We can still turn back at this point. Once we're down in those rocks, it'll be too late to run home."

Blackie swallowed. His mouth felt dry, but he was determined. If Papa could make it across that border, well— He took a breath and nodded his horn.

"Here you goes, then," said Sir Burly. "Father Tim, let's start 'em out with a prayer."

"Aye, me lord," said the chaplain, pulling back his cloak. Father Timothy lifted his crucifix. The humans knelt on the cold rock while Blackie dipped his horn.

"Oh, Lord," said the priest, "we stand at the end of your goodly kingdom, facing a new day with its struggles and temptations. Watch over us in our journeys, especially this Prince, your faithful servant, and the holy beast. Keep them in the safety of your Grace as they venture into the cursed land of the enemy, and please, oh, Lord, bring them back unharmed. Bless us all and bring us into your salvation.

"*In nomine Patre, et Filii, et Spiritus Sanctus.*"

"Amen," chorused the men.

"Amen," Blackie whispered with a shiver.

The men pushed to their feet. Blackie sniffed around the trailhead for sign of his father while Prince George thanked Father Timothy for his words.

"My lord," said the priest, hesitantly, "if you would permit, I'd . . . I'd like to accompany you and the holy beast on your journey into Vile."

Blackie looked back in astonishment while Prince George gaped at the priest. "What? You want to go with us?"

"Well," the Priest knotted his hands, "I mentioned to Sir Burly— I thought I might be useful in those unclean paths, carrying supplies, you know, or holding off demons while you pass."

"Oh, good Father," cried the Prince, exchanging looks with Blackie, "many thanks for your offer! You'd be more than useful, I know. You'd be a blessing, but we can't accept your help. Your donkey— Once we pass the mountains, no donkey could keep up with the unicorn."

"Oh, right, right." The priest lowered his gaze. "I just thought I'd ask.

"That's what I told him," said Sir Burly, shifting his weight. "Plus, the more o' you there are, the more chances o' gettin' caught."

"That's right, too," said the Prince, spreading his hands. "You see, Father? It's just impossible."

The priest shrugged.

"Yes, yes, of course, I'm sure that I'd be in the way. It's just that I see you entering the great battle— Like the saints, you know, good versus evil. I'm tempted in my everyday life like other men, but to confront naked wickedness, that's something else. I understand, though, if you can't take me—"

"Don't worry, Father!" cried Sir Burly, pounding the priest on the back. "I promise that you'll have problems enough back at the castle tryin' to keep the men from killin' each other."

"Oh, yes, of course," said the priest. He pulled the leather thong from his neck with the bronze crucifix.

"In that case, then, would it be possible—? Could you accept my cross as a gift? It might help in those cursed tracks."

Father Timothy held out his crucifix. "I know the unicorn has his holy horn to protect him, but you, my lord—Well, this cross has been blessed by the Bishop."

Prince George looked up his spear shaft at the Nail, gleaming in the morning light.

"Thank you, good Father, your offer touches me, but I have my spear, you see, and it carries its own blessing."

"Take the cross, me lord," advised Sir Burly. "Where you're goin', you can't have too much armor against villainy."

"Well," said the Prince, "since you offer—Thanks, Father, I'll be glad to accept your cross."

Prince George bent his neck. Father Timothy lowered the chain about his neck. He gripped the Prince by the arm, a tear glistening on his cheek.

"Be of stout heart, my lord. This cross will carry you through the Pit itself if your path leads there."

"Oh, the Pit!" muttered Prince George. "Well, let's hope—"

"Farewell, my lord!" roared Sir Burly. He pushed the Priest aside to grasp the Prince's hand. "We hears all these terrible stories about Vile, but it can't be so bad as folks say. I bet three months' pay you comes back with the unicorn as sound as you goes in."

Blackie took a step down the trail. He looked back at Prince George, who was watching a bird circle in the sky. The Prince shook himself.

"Well, I guess, we better get started."

"Goodbye, me lord!" chorused the men, and Blackie lurched down the narrow trail, setting his feet carefully among rolling stones. He heard the click of Prince George's spear against the rock behind him.

"Oh, here I go," Blackie thought, "and I've still got the Prince with me. I was supposed to leave him behind, but I . . . I didn't do it. I guess I didn't want to. Maybe down below there when we get to the border, maybe."

Blackie had other things to think about when the path leveled off at the stream bubbling around dark stones. Patches of green leaves with tight little buds showed up here and there on reddish stems against the gray walls rising on both sides.

Blackie snatched a mouthful of leaves as the Prince swung to his back. The taste of the leaves reassured Blackie considerably.

"Let's go, boy," whispered the Prince, and Blackie walked northward through the icy stream.

He saw little sign of travel along the stream except for a couple arrowheads rusting in the water and a battered skull, face-up in the water with small gray fish darting in and out of it. Blackie stepped over it carefully.

A few yards farther, he left the stream at a little waterfall where the track circled a mound of rocks, then returned to the stream a few feet higher on the other side. They were traveling through a deep gorge with ridges rising far above their heads. Blackie had an uneasy sense of hostile mountains leaning out with armloads of stones to slide down on travelers.

When the stream disappeared again, Blackie had to climb a slope of loose rocks. The trail faded away at a rift where the gorge split into ravines rising left and right. Blackie sniffed the damp rocks lining the channels while Prince George sat on a rock to eat a sausage from the supplies packed at Godfrey's castle.

"Seems from the map that the trail splits here," said the Prince, gesturing with the sausage. "I guess we could go this way or that—both lead into Vile."

The smell of the sausage was stronger than other scents, so Blackie gave up sniffing to graze on the patches of green among the rocks. Prince George looked up and down the rocky walls.

"Lonely place, isn't it? All I've seen since we left Sir Burly is a couple birds."

Without human speech, Blackie couldn't tell the Prince of the snake sunning itself on a rock above his head or the mountain goats looking down from the crags. Along the trail, Blackie had smelled various creatures, including a large cat of some sort. He hadn't smelled Papa.

"I figure we've gone two or three miles," said the Prince, digging into a bag of oatcakes. "It's slow travel in these rocks, but we've only got three or four more miles to Vile. We should go as far as we can before dark, then get a good rest to tackle the border tomorrow."

Blackie stepped to the Prince for his share of the oatcakes. He might have to face the dragon tomorrow. He wanted a peaceful dinner today.

CHAPTER THIRTY-SIX

Hellhounds

"The question is," whispered Prince George, pulling his spear into the deep shade behind a boulder a few miles up the track, "do we back up and try the other trail, or push by this outpost?"

Blackie pricked up his ears at the clamor from the watchmen at the border. The voices would drop to a rumble, then rise to a roar echoed by the mountain walls around as though Vile's border guards camped in the trail were holding a contest of some sort—wrestling or dwarf-tossing.

The Prince shook his head in exasperation. "How, by the saints, do any smugglers get by those rascals squatting in the middle of the trail? They've got the pass plugged up."

Blackie's impulse was to charge through the guards. If Prince George didn't insist on slipping into Vile without notice, Blackie would run over this bunch and keep going, trusting to his speed and power to get through. But the Prince was probably right. The moment the villains realized that someone was trying to break into Vile, they'd turn the evil Kingdom upside down to catch them. Best to be cautious while they could. Still, time was running on. They couldn't reach Unicorn by hiding in the rocks.

From the looks of the mountains around Blackie, it appeared that rain stopped at the border. The sparkling freshets that poured from the mountains on the Darr side were cut off here as though a notch had been gashed across the countryside. Green stems turned to brown thorns. Instead of snatching bites of tasty grasses from crannies along the canyons up to the border, Blackie turned in disgust from the bristles and brambles spreading through the boulders.

Creeping offroad was painful for Prince George, too. Blackie's tough hide protected him from thorns, but the Prince snagged his skin with each movement. As they slipped closer to the guard camp, Blackie heard little gasps of pain as the spines dug in.

"This won't work," whispered the Prince. "Back off, Blackie. I've got an idea. Let's swing over to the other side of the trail. The wind's coming from that side."

"What's he thinking now?" wondered Blackie. "The windward side? Does he want them to smell us?"

Pulling back was more painful than creeping forward. Despite the Prince's care to move slowly, Blackie saw bloody scratches appear on the Prince's arms. The man had to stop at each step to pull out snags that dug into his skin.

While Blackie watched the camp, Prince George scuttled across the trail and hid in the rocks on the other side. Blackie waited till the Prince was settled, then followed quietly.

"Watch out!"

The Prince jerked back as a large, gray snake whipped up its head before him. The snake glared without blinking, swaying on its body until the Prince poked out his spear. The serpent lunged at the Nail with curved fangs. It jerked back as if hitting something horrible. Violently shaking its head, it pulled down and flowed away into the thorns. Blackie watched the red triangles running down its back.

"So it's snakes, now," whispered Prince George. "What else are we going to find?"

Prince George watched the briers more carefully as he pushed through the rocks before Blackie. Following the mountain wall, they stepping quietly around the largest stones until a frenzied bawling broke out as they crept upwind of the guard post.

"Hear that?" gasped the Prince. "That's a Hellhound! Keep a good lookout, Blackie!"

Prince George dropped to his knees, digging into the pouch at his waist for his fire-flint. Blackie's ears flew up in question. After glancing at the Prince striking the flint against his dagger, he turned his attention to the guards, yelling to each other up the trail.

"Yo, there, Fetty, the Hound's smelled something out there!"

"So what? It's just another runaway. Let 'im starve in the mountains!"

"Oh, yeah, so you can report me for neglect? Not on your life. Send a couple searchers to run 'im down!"

The Hound at the camp howled wildly as Blackie lowered himself into the briers to watch two skinny men dragging short spears down the trail. Prince George sweated beside him, hissing to himself as he snapped the flint against the steel to direct sparks into the layer of dried thorns and leaves on the rocky ground.

"A spark, a spark! Burn, blast you, burn!"

"Hey, you, up there," cried the searchers, leaning on their spears in the path, "come out, you filthy scum! It'll go worse for you if we have to sniff you out! Dig yourself into a hidey-hole, and we'll turn the Hound on you! You'd make two bites for that beast!"

"Ah," whispered the Prince, blowing on a tiny flame licking up from a spark. He fed it with leaves till the fire leaped into the briers and started to spread. It crackled through the brush as Prince George crawled back from the flame.

Smoke wafted to Blackie's nose. Prince George sneezed.

"So there you are, Turdhead!" hollered one of the searchers. "Might as well come on out. You can't get away from us!"

"What's that?" cried the other, catching sight of the smoke. "Brush fire! Wildfire! Save your butt! Every man for himself!"

The searchers dashed back down the trail, waving their spears as the wind caught the fire and flung it through the dry brush like a roaring wave. It leaped and snapped, burning out snakes and lizards that scuttled through the camp where the men went mad.

Backing frantically down the trail, Blackie and the Prince listened to the guards scream as the Hound leaped against its chains and howled.

"Move it, curse you, move it! Outta my way!"

"Save the arrows!"

"Watch the beast, he pullin' loose!"

"Yaaah, he got Fetty!"

Shuddering at the shrieks of the men, Blackie and the Prince ran out of the smoke as the fire rolled away from them. Prince George doubled up, coughing hoarsely until Blackie touched him with his horn to heal the cough and the scratches.

Prince George sat on a stone. He fanned himself with his cap.

"That was . . . that was a Hellhound," he wheezed, running a hand through his hair. "It turned on them. They must have had it chained."

Blackie nodded, groaning to himself. "That's what we have to deal with in Vile."

Blackie ran across the border for a deep drink of water from the last stream in Darr. He made his way back to wait by the Prince until the heavy smoke cloud lightened to drifting fumes.

"Might as well go on," said the Prince, standing and stretching. He mounted. Blackie set off slowly, treading gingerly over blackened ash. The fire had burnt down to cinders though debris still flamed here and there. Blackie tried to step lightly as smoldering seed pods burst under his hooves, stinging his fetlocks, raising fumes that made his eyes burn.

The smoke set the Prince to coughing again. He shook on Blackie's back.

"I should've thought—" he gasped. "Should've thought a . . . better way to chase off those knaves!"

The fire had burned to a rock barrier where the trail ended in a swirling cloud of smoke. Sparks kicked up around Blackie's ankles as he circled in frustration, staring through teary eyes to peer out their next move.

Prince George hissed at him, "See an exit anywhere, a path? We can't stay here!"

Finally, Prince George had to jump down into the sparks to search out the trail passing between the biggest rocks and up a dusty rise that twisted through a smoke-filled fissure. Struggling to hold down his coughs, the Prince peered through the haze.

"Perfect place . . . for ambush," he whispered. "Do you smell danger?"

Smelling nothing but smoke, Blackie shook his head.

Prince George stepped out of the sparks onto a boulder. Fighting to catch his breath, he pulled the magic bow from his back, coughing.

"I'll . . . I'll ch-check it out!"

He notched the arrow and shot it up the path. The arrow whisked out of sight, curving between smoky walls. A moment later, it returned with a pair of gray snakes pierced through the middles. They twisted wildly on all four ends.

Prince George jumped away from the slashing heads with a screech. He lost his balance and tumbled off the boulder into the smoking rocks. The arrow followed, holding out the furious snakes until Blackie knocked it away with his horn.

"Oh, oh, oh!" coughed the Prince, blindly beating the air with his arms. "Are they gone? Are they gone?"

The arrow resentfully shook off the snakes in the rocks. It slowly returned and hung just out of reach while Prince George struggled to stand. Blackie braced himself as the shaking Prince clung to his neck, trying to steady his boots below him.

"My back!" moaned the Prince. "I'm banged, bruised, beaten! What a scare! I don't frighten easily, but snakes in my face— No one could take that!"

Holding onto Blackie with an arm, he grabbed the arrow and shook it. "Stupid thing, you know I didn't want snakes! Where's my hat?"

Prince George lowered himself to the boulder. He sat with head down, gasping. "Wha . . . What are we . . . d-doing here, Blackie? I didn't want to come to this horrible place! It better be w-worth it. If we don't find your father—"

While Prince George moaned to himself, Blackie scouted further up the path. Rounding a corner, he joined a flow of cold wind that blew away the smoke. The air wasn't what you'd call fresh. It had a rancid tang, but it didn't burn his lungs. He paused to listen for howls or voices, heard only a croaking bird in the sky.

Blackie shivered. He felt tired already. His eyes were runny and sore, his ankles scorched, his tongue swollen.

"Blackie, Blackie!"

The Prince lurched out of the smoke, leaning on his spear. "Oh, th-thank the saints, we're above the smoke here. I'm kippered like a mullet. Remind me not to set any more fires in Vile."

"It wasn't my idea," thought Blackie.

Coughing, Prince George pulled off his bearskin and shook out ashes. He threw it around his shoulders. He lowered himself to a rock.

"Gotta rest a minute."

He bent forward with his chin in his hands, elbows resting on his knees. He fell asleep. Blackie looked down at him, thinking, "This is the moment. I could leave him right here. He could get back to Darr in minutes. There's nothing to stop him except for . . . except for that Hellhound."

Blackie raised his ears, listened to the wind.

"That monster's loose in these mountains. What if it's hiding nearby? It could dash down the instant I leave, snatch him up and carry him off. What would the Princess say? I . . . I don't think I should leave him alone. Maybe I'll find a safer place to leave him a little farther along. Where'd those villains go, anyway?"

Blackie walked a few steps up the path, sniffing for tracks. The dust and pebbles were undisturbed. No ruffians had scrambled up here today. They must have escaped by some other trail, probably a path with a stream.

"Oh, water—"

As soon as Blackie thought of water, he felt how thirsty he was. The fire and smoke had dried him out like toast. He was hungry too, cold and hungry, but it was water his body craved. All he saw about him were spiny brown bushes and rocks.

Didn't Vile have any water? Blackie thought of the sparkling stream back over the border. He had not seen a drop of water on this side, nor anything green, no buds, no stems, no leaves. All he saw were scratchy brown vines and briers. Nothing to eat or drink.

He knew little about this place. Humans didn't tell stories of Vile. It was unlucky even to mention it, so Blackie had heard only muttered comments about the misery here—the burning mountain, the dragon, the pit. Of course, he knew that the Archangel Michael had raided the place to rescue captured saints, but he'd never heard a proper travel story like Prince George's tales of crossing the western lands with the wandering people there, the Bourrids.

All he knew was that Vile was always described as the center of evil—a festering sore infecting the Empire from the north. He felt sick at heart already, cold and miserable after his fiery introduction to the place.

He walked back to the Prince, coughing in his sleep, and touched him with his horn.

"I'd planned to leave him behind," Blackie thought, "but somehow, he's still with me. I knew this would happen. It's desperate enough for me to break into Vile alone, but now, I've got to look after this man. If I'd slipped in by myself, I'd have dashed through those guards and run up here without all this fuss and fire. Bringing a human complicates everything."

Prince George did not sleep long. As Blackie watched, the Prince twitched until an arm slipped from his knee. He fell forward in panic, striking out with both hands as he awakened.

"Snakes, snakes, what happened to the snakes?"

Blackie had forgotten the snakes, but they were certainly on the Prince's mind. The man jumped up, staring around. He poked the spear through the rocks along the trail. When he didn't see any thick, squirming bodies, he shuddered and pulled his bearskin close about him.

"Let's go on, Blackie. I dreamed . . . I dreamed those snakes were slipping up on me. Somehow, they blamed me for the arrow."

Prince George looked nervously up the trail ahead of them.

"Don't you wonder, Blackie, how that arrow found those snakes so quickly? I wonder if it dipped into a snake pit, a n-nest of the horrible creatures like they have in Egypt. No wonder those villains didn't run this way. I wouldn't have come this way myself, if I'd known that snakes were hiding in our path."

"Oh, nonsense," thought Blackie, shaking out his coat, "I never heard of a snake pit. That arrow was looking for whatever it could find. It just happened to fly across that pair of the snakes."

Blackie stood for Prince George to mount, then stepped off, sniffing about sharply. His sense of smell seemed to be returning. He couldn't sense the full world of odors yet, but he thought he could smell a nest of snakes or a spring of water, if there were such a thing.

They were climbing between cracked plates of gray rock tilted in all directions. The path went from flat, scooped-out surfaces where Blackie could trot a few yards to the crumbling edges of layers where he had to set each hoof carefully to avoid slipping. The wind didn't help either, blasting between rising slabs. When blocked behind walls, the wind whooshed and wailed, as though crying out for the misery of the world.

Gradually, the trail climbed the cracks between ridges until they broke through to level countryside. Blackie saw peaks rising around a wide, forbidding tableland. His eye was caught by the huge swelling in the center of the flat. Smoke poured from the crater at its heart to be seized by the wind that blew to the end of Vile, unchecked by hill or trees.

"The burning mountain!" whispered Prince George.

Blackie wanted to know more, but the Prince pulled in his bearskin and fell silent. Blackie could spy nothing indicating direction—no guidepost or sign, not even a road. The path they had followed through the mountains melted away to this cold, forbidding plateau.

Open as it was, he should be able to see for miles and miles, but the smoke from the mountain blended with dust in the wind to a general haze that obscured details. All appeared an eerie monotony with the dirty gray of the plain merging with the sooty murk of the sky to deaden the senses like a nightmare.

Blackie felt Prince George shiver on his back. The Prince leaned forward on Blackie's neck to seek physical contact. Thankful for the Prince's warmth, Blackie trotted toward that smoking hump, scanning the plain to both sides for shapes or movement. He saw less and less as the sun sank in the west, leaving garish reds and purples that hung in the haze beyond nightfall and veiled the sight in a feverish afterglow.

Once the great red ball dipped below the horizon, the wind increased till it sliced like a blade. Blackie limped to a stop from fatigue. Prince George rolled off his back to scrunch low against the blast, struggling to untie a bag of oatcakes with frozen fingers. Blackie sniffed the icy surface of the land. He nibbled at the scrappy matting of tiny branches and vines. It was about as nourishing as the frozen froth on a swamp.

Calling Blackie to lie down with his back to the wind, Prince George fed Blackie a couple oatcakes, then wrapped the bearskin about himself and curled up against Blackie's belly. They shivered together as sunlight faded. The sky never completely darkened. Flames deep in the burning mountain cast a glare against the haze that seemed to shimmer from one end of Vile to the other.

Despite his thirst and hunger, Blackie dropped off into troubled sleep for a few minutes. Stirring suddenly, he yawned and lifted his nose to sniff the air for any change. He opened his eyes, gritty with fatigue, and looked about, but saw only the glowing haze to all sides.

Lowering his head again, he spotted something shine a few feet away. His eyes snapped open. He stared at a clear, steady light four or five feet away, filtered by the mat of vegetation.

Lifting his head, Blackie couldn't make out what it was. He poked Prince George with a hoof. The Prince grunted in his sleep, "Yeah, yeah, 'nother drink, please."

Blackie poked again. Prince George shook awake, reaching for his spear.

"Wha . . . wha . . . what is it? The Hound?"

He sat up, swinging the spear. Both saw it then. Gleaming from the end of the staff, the Nail shone with a bright, sharp light.

"The Nail!" gasped the Prince. "It blazes like the sun!"

They gazed in awe, slitting their eyes to gaze at its brightness until Prince George collected himself. "That light, we've got to cover it! Any villains out there could see that shine from miles away."

Blackie looked around nervously as Prince George pulled an empty oatcake bag from his belt. He drew it over the Nail with trembling hands. The bag muffled the light except for a tiny spark shining through a hole in the cloth. Prince George twisted a fold in the bag to cover the hole, then wrapped the bag twice with a woolen cord and tied it tightly.

"Well, that proves one thing," sighed the Prince, gently placing the spear across his lap. He straightened his bearskin and settled back against Blackie. "Lizetta told the truth once in her life. Shining like that in an evil place, this has to be the genuine Nail of Christ. Prince Vile's been trying to get his claws on the Nail forever. Now I'm responsible for it. Something else to worry about."

"I hope we're not delivering it to him," thought Blackie, lowering his head again. "What a haul for Vile if he captures us—two of his enemies, plus the Nail! Catching Papa would finish the job."

The Prince yawned again.

"This means I've got to be extra careful. I've had bad luck with weapons since I met you, Blackie, weapons and hats. It started when I lost my father's sword at Shrems, then that second sword and the boarspear. All my arms—this shield's just a pick-up from the Monastery. And now, I've got treasures to worry about, the Princess's bow, this Nail. It's too much, too much."

Blackie frowned at the muffled Nail.

"So the thing lights up? What good is that? You can't heal wounds with it. If it gave off a real fire to keep us toasty in this wind, it'd be worth having. But a shining thing you've got to keep in a bag, that's just a bother. I'd give it back to the Gypsies. They hid it properly when they had it."

Thinking comfortably of his own horn, so definitely useful, Blackie drew himself up to sleep the rest of the night when a howl out in the darkness made him jump.

"The Hound!" breathed Prince George, pushing to his knees. "It must have seen the Nail!"

"No," thought Blackie, "it caught our scent. It's hunting tonight!"

To complete their distress, another howl rose up and another, shrieks of pain and terror echoing each other like the cries of anguished demons. Blackie leaped up, spreading his ears to locate the cries.

"It's a pack!" cried the Prince, crawling to his feet. "A pack of Hellhounds, and they're after us! Getting closer, too! We've got to run for it!"

"Run for it?" thought Blackie. "We'll break our necks! I can barely see to walk in this horrible place!"

With shaking fingers, Prince George unwrapped the string from the Nail. He jerked off the bag and the Nail flashed out.

"Now, we can see! Stand still, Blackie! Let me mount!"

Tossing the empty bag aside, the Prince leaned the shining spear against Blackie's horn and scrambled around in the light. He grabbed for his shield and the food bags as the howls neared to a half-mile away.

"No time!" cried the Prince in despair, dropping the bags. He scooped up the shield, pulled the bow over his shoulder, and leaped onto Blackie.

"Blessed Saint Michael, help us now! Go, Blackie, go!"

He caught up the spear as Blackie took off. The spear light flashed around like a torch, lighting the dark mat under Blackie's hooves, but falling off a few yards away. It blocked Blackie's night vision. All he could see beyond the swinging circle of light was the sullen glow of the mountain to his left.

Blackie lowered his horn and galloped across the flatlands for the nearest mountains, using the fiery crater as a marker to guide himself. Hugging Blackie's neck, Prince George held out the flaring spear. It whipped back and forth with the hoofbeats.

As long as Blackie kept up the pace, the howls fell behind, but he ran into a stony area in the foothills where he had to slow to swerve around boulders and jump low rocks. Struggling through this rough ground was doubly hard at night where the spear gave only a few yards' scope for Blackie to choose his path. In no time it seemed, stones bulged and vaulted around him until he ran to the end of a rocky hollow where he had to backtrack to seek a way around. By now, he was panting and blowing, sweaty despite the cold wind.

"Hold up, Blackie!" gasped the Prince, jerking Blackie's mane. "Let's stop before you wear down."

They halted a moment, shivering in the cold wind billowing up the hollow. The tired Hellhounds were largely silenced now, but yelps and yawps told Blackie that they were coming.

Prince George slid to earth and wedged the spear butt into a cranny that held it erect, the light shaking in the wind.

"We'll make our stand here."

While the Prince drew the bow from his back, Blackie swept his eyes over the cracks and facets in the walls around. This appeared to be a good place to fight. The rocky bowl allowed an approach only from the front. Thank Heaven, the Hellhounds couldn't get at them from the sides.

"Where are they, Blackie?" cried the Prince, notching the arrow. "Give me an exact line on them."

By now, Blackie could hear the panting hounds scratching through the rocks. Ears high, he aimed his horn directly at the oncoming pack. Prince George lined up the bow with the horn and snapped off the arrow. It darted into the shadows beyond the light.

Seconds later, they heard a shriek of pain, and the hounds set up a fearful howling. The arrow zoomed back before the Prince, blood glistening over half its length. Prince George grabbed the arrow, shook off the blood, and set it to the bowstring again as the yelping hounds came rushing into the hollow—great shaggy forms with eyes and fangs flashing in the spearlight.

TWANG!

Prince George shot the arrow into the foremost beast. It crashed into a stone with a shriek as Blackie threw himself at the next leaping hound, driving his horn down the open jaws and rolling the beast over its tail. Hurling the heavy body off with a swing of his neck, Blackie rose to his haunches to smash the snapping monsters with fore hooves as Prince George stabbed out with the flashing spear.

Moments later, the surviving hounds scuttled away yelping, tails between their legs. Blackie got a glimpse of two large pups whining in their rear before the pack vanished into darkness, leaving four dead in the light of the spear.

Blackie stood panting, head down, blood running darkly from his horn. He looked at Prince George flopped against a rock. Gasping for breath, the Prince looked pale in the spearlight, his own blood running from gashes on his arms and shoulders. The arrow bounced in the air before him, eager to be off again.

Prince George waved a tired hand at Blackie. "That was close, old boy! If they'd . . . they'd got us down, it'd be all over!"

Blackie had tooth marks up and down his horn and a couple serious bites on his right side. He could do nothing about these, but he limped to Prince George. He touched the human's wounds with his horn. The Prince closed his eyes with a deep sigh of relief.

"Thanks, Blackie."

A moment later, he opened his eyes again and smiled wryly at Blackie. "You know, I'd do the same for you if I could."

Blackie nodded, then saw the Prince's eyes widen, looking over Blackie's shoulder.

"What's that?"

Prince George threw himself forward, groping for the arrow as Blackie whirled to see two pairs of eyes gleaming down from a tall rock behind him.

CHAPTER THIRTY-SEVEN

Underground and Above

Blackie lay under the shining spear in a corner of the cave where Prince George huddled around the fire with the old men. Blackie could barely lift his muzzle from the rocky floor. He was shut away from sunlight and air in a stony chamber that stank of roasting Hellhounds turning on spits over the charcoal fire. He hated this cavern closing him in as much as he'd hated the flatlands above.

At least, the raggedy men were happy to serve him, bringing water to drink and to wash his wounds. A springy, loose-limbed lot used to squeezing through the crevices of their rocky world, they had a pale, big-eyed look as if they'd given up daylight forever. The only cheer in the atmosphere was the spear, burning against the side of the cave with its bright, clear illumination.

A boy offered Blackie a tray of small, plump breads. "Buns, unicorn? You give us meat, we give you buns."

Blackie took a bun in his jaw. It burst into crumbs when he bit into it. The boy grinned, delighted.

"Crunchy buns," he explained. "Baked dry for storage."

Above the smell of roasting hounds, Blackie caught the scent of strong drink as the headman, Vurm, pulled out a goatskin. He offered it to Prince George, who sniffed the mouth of the bag.

"Drink, drink, my lord!" whispered Vurm. "Straight from Vile's vats. This'll shake you up. It's got a bite to it."

Prince George lifted the skin to his lips. He took a sip and winced. With a laugh, Vurm reached over and struck up the bag, sloshing drink down the Prince's throat.

"A real draft, that's what you need after your battle last night!"

Blackie sneezed at the stink of the liquor. Prince George collapsed, kicking out his feet. Vurm chuckled. He took a deep swig from the bag and passed it to the next man in the circle. He looked at the Prince, shaking with coughs, trying to catch his breath.

"That's what the Hellions drink, me lord. That's what we're up against!"

Blackie had to force himself up to step over and touch Prince George with his horn before the human could stop coughing. The Prince finally caught his breath. He sat up, wiping tears from his eyes. "You sure that's not tanning solution?"

Vurm offered him the goatskin again. "Another nip, me lord? Second drink scours out your bowels."

Prince George pushed it away. He wiped his eyes. "No thanks, man. I'd keep that to poison rats. Tell me more about Vile's castle."

As Vurm explained the layout, the Prince pulled out his dagger and drew a cone shape in the dust on the floor.

"You're telling me that Vile's castle runs around the north side of the mountain where it's cooled by the wind while the dragon pit's here to the south, where it gets the heat."

There was a murmur of assent. Vurm nodded his head. The boy pattered over to the Prince, who took a couple buns from the tray.

"Well, then, where are the slave pens?"

The heads swung back to Vurm, who pointed to the east and west sides of the mountain.

"The pens is stuck on the castle like wings, see? The dark prince wants his prisoners close so he can get to 'em easy."

"That's the layout, eh?"

From his corner, Blackie snorted impatiently. He gestured with his horn when Prince George looked around.

"Oh, yes, Blackie wants to know about the unicorn. Has anyone seen a white unicorn running around here?"

The men shook their heads.

"No unicorn," said Vurm. "We never seen a unicorn in our lives till we seen this one killin' hounds, last night. What a sight that was!

There's nothin' in Vile can stand up to Hellhounds 'cept for the dragon."

"So," asked the Prince, "does anyone know where the dragon is at the moment?"

The men looked at each other. Vurm lowered his voice.

"Far as we know, she's still in her pit under the mountain. Been there for days, folks say, since she flew up from the south. By now, she's got the mountain rumblin' over her, set to boil over. The black prince is furious at her. He blames her for flyin' away from his armies and losin' him the war."

Flicking his ears, Blackie stepped halfway to the fire to listen as the Prince questioned Vurm more closely. The spilled drink masked the smell of the roasting hounds.

"So let me get this straight. Prince Vile blames the dragon for abandoning his armies and losing the war?"

"You know how he operates," said Vurm, scratching an arm. "He blames the dragon, blames the officers, blames the soldiers, blames everyone but himself. And he punishes everyone, the cowards that run off instead of fightin', the traitors that betrayed him at home. His Hellions is busy roundin' 'em all up for trial. No one found innocent yet."

Prince George jumped to his feet. He shouted in fury, rolling the raggedy men back.

"That villain should blame himself! He's the biggest traitor of all! He started the war to force his claim on the Princess! He bribed those lords to rebel against the Crown!"

The raggedy men froze, hands to their ears as they listened in all directions.

"Hush, my lord, please!" Vurm begged, twisting in alarm. "You'll alert the—"

"Searchers," whispered a man, pointing off to the side. "I hears searchers! Sniffin' and snuffin'. Creepin' from that direction!"

"Disappear!" hissed Vurm. "Disappear!"

Blackie stretched his ears to listen about. He heard nothing but the raggedy people whisking through the cave. They grabbed up bags and baskets. Quickly, they wrapped the roasting hounds in their own dogskins and stuck spears through the bundles to heave them along As they vanished through holes in the wall, the bun boy dashed through the cave, closing each hole with a piece of slate and rubbing it over with dust until it looked like part of the wall. He threw more dust over the fire.

"Come, now," he whispered, pointing toward a slit at the rear of the cave. "The unicorn's too big for the mole-holes. We have to stick to the tunnels, but don't worry, I know the rocky ways better than any old searcher."

With that, Blackie went running on the strangest journey of his life. He squeezed after the raggedy boy through twists and turns of cracks and crannies with no sense of any direction. All he could smell was dust and stone while the rock hanging above took his breath away. He sensed the crushing weight. It felt like it could smash down at any moment.

Half the time, he was blind. Prince George lumbered ahead with the Nail-light shining and shading with the forks and bends as they zigzagged through the rock. They ducked under stony spikes hanging from the ceiling. They threaded through giant needles sticking from the floor. Up crystal ramps they climbed to slide down shadowy chutes where Blackie had to hold back in the dark until the others could stand away from his leggy landings.

As a creature formed to run to the horizon, Blackie hated this world of bumpy shadows. His horn banged walls when the Prince swung the spear around turns while his sides hurt from scraping corners.

Holding up a hand to still them, the boy stopped in a chamber to listen. The cave was silent as though noise had ceased to exist. Blackie could hear his heart beat. His breath wheezed in his lungs.

"I told you," said the boy in a normal tone, "we're safe here. We've escaped all the searchers in the world. They won't find us here. They give up after a trap or two."

"I didn't see—" said the Prince. His voice rang hoarse in this stony confine. He started again more quietly. "I didn't see any traps as we ran along."

The boy wiped his nose. "You wouldn't see 'em, would you? What's the good of traps if you can see 'em? If you're not with me down here, things happen to you. The ceiling gives way of a sudden, squashes you flat, or the pointy stalks drop down to stab you. We don't make it easy for searchers to sneak around here. Remind me to show you the snake pits."

"Really," squealed the Prince, "you have snake pits?"

"Oh, sure," said the boy, "the floor lets go underneath you, and you slide down into the fangs. I'll show 'em to you, if you want."

"No thanks," cried the Prince, stepping back, "not necessary! I'll take your word for it."

He swung the spearlight around the chamber. "Where are we now?"

The boy stretched and sighed, then came alert again. "Come along with me. I'll show you a secret."

Blackie followed the humans into another twisting tunnel, trying to stay to the center of the space so he banged himself as little as possible.

"Are you allowed to show these secrets?" asked the Prince, nervously stretching out the spear. "It's not one of these things where you bury everybody that sees them, is it?"

The boy laughed. "Don't worry, me lord. You couldn't never find this place by yourself, not if you crawled around for a hundred years. Come on."

The boy darted through the rock into a side passage. Prince George shrugged at Blackie, then stumbled after the boy, his boots clattering on the stone.

Blackie followed wearily. His shoulder muscles were tired, his hooves tender from running on hard rock.

They descended a glittery channel. Gleaming flecks threw the light back from the spear, giving the appearance of a royal progress.

"How the Princess would love this adventure," whispered Prince George, flashing the spear around.

Blackie felt a guilty twinge. "Oh, yes, the Princess!"

He hadn't thought of the Princess since he'd entered Vile. Now that he considered his lady, he knew how eagerly the Princess would throw herself into this fantastic tour through badger holes. She'd love to explore a secret underground world.

"Up on the surface," thought Blackie, "under the sun, I could defend her against anyone, but down here—"

"The Princess would be a queen down here," panted the Prince. "As clever and sly as she is, she'd fit right in. Probably not even get herself dirty."

"Look, look!" cried the boy, stopping in a vast cave where the Prince's spear gleamed over a lake of still water. "Drink—pure drink! Clean!"

Gleefully, he ran down a rocky spit reaching into the lake and threw out a stone. It arced over the lake.

SPLASH!

Ripples spread. Water swayed, sparkling up the point where the boy stood, then quieted, quieted.

"Go ahead," urged the boy, whirling around. "Drink all you want. We hold all the water in Vile down here, water enough to last to eternity. We haul barrels up to the surface to trade for goods to smuggle across the border."

Blackie felt dry from the run. He stepped down the point, but the Prince held him back by his mane.

"Where does all this water come from?"

"It's always been here," said the boy with a shrug. "Up above, they don't get rain enough to cut a channel. A shower that soaks away in minutes, that's about it. They catch a few drops in cisterns, but they has to buy their drink from us."

"I can't believe Prince Vile would leave all this water to you," said Prince George, splashing his spear butt through the lake. "Why doesn't he dig a well to get it?"

"He doesn't know where to dig," chuckled the boy, squatting down at the rim of the lake. He plunged in a hand and drank from his palm.

"Good water, cold, cold!"

Wringing his fingers, he wiped his hand on his shirt. He jumped up and ran to a pile of tools against the cave wall. He came back with a bucket.

"Here, unicorn, I'll give you a drink."

He scooped the bucket full and heaved it before Blackie. Blackie sniffed the bucket, then dipped in his nose, taking a drink of icy water that made him shiver. He lifted his nose to breathe and drank again.

"Well, it's all right, I guess," said the Prince. He drank a cupful of water while the boy explained how the lake was concealed.

"It's funny," he said, laughing, "watching 'em bumble around underground, tryin' to find us. It's not just the hooks and snares, the deadfalls and tumblin' floors that stops 'em. There's miles of holes and tunnels twistin' around and turnin' back on themselves, runnin' out and startin' over somewhere else."

He filled another bucket for Blackie.

"'You see, we change the passageways constantly—wallin' up here, openin' new holes there. Even when they catches our people and tortures 'em, that don't help. A week later, everything looks different. Anyone that don't belong down here gets lost in a nightmare, creepin' up and down without end, round and round and round. And if they really bother us, we hold back on their drink. Let 'em dry out a couple months, then triple the price for a barrel of water. That brings 'em around."

"So Prince Vile can't even control his own country," said the Prince thoughtfully.

"No, me lord, and it drives him crazy," said the boy, carrying the bucket back to the corner. "That sort of villain, always plottin', always schemin', they suspects the worst against themselves and brings it down on their own head. Even the dragon— You knows that old Vile, the Prince's daddy, he was killed by his own dragon."

Blackie looked up as Prince George cried, "No!"

The boy nodded, tossing the bucket back onto the pile of tools.

"Oh, yes, me lord, true as tales. You see, the dragon got stabbed in a fight with the unicorn of them days. It didn't kill her right away, but she got all tetchy and feverish. When Old Vile tried to stir her up with his stick, she turned on him. This Prince Vile we have now, he threw his brothers to the dragon to reward her for that job."

Prince George held his spear high to look out over the waters. Blackie couldn't see the far side of the cavern. The gleam faded off into darkness. The Prince tossed his spear to the boy and pulled the bow from his shoulder. The bowstring tightened as he notched the arrow.

"Let's shoot out the arrow, see what she finds."

SPRONG!

The arrow shot out over its reflection, a wave bouncing behind. Prince George lowered the bow and leaned to listen. Slow seconds passed. A couple minutes later, Blackie heard something smacking on the water.

SPLISH, SPLISH, SPLISH!

"Here she comes."

The arrow flew back stuck in a long, wet oar bouncing over the surface of the lake. The arrow dropped the dripping oar in the Prince's hand, twisted free of the wood, and flew back to the bow. Prince George lifted the oar into the spearlight to examine it.

"Look we've got here."

With his finger, he traced a carving of Christ walking on waters. The Prince crossed himself.

"Look, Blackie, the Lord in his majestic works. Oh, this is a wonder, happily found, happily found. A good omen, Lord bless us."

At the very point of the rock running into the lake, Prince George held the oar blade upright while the boy piled rocks around the base of the handle to hold it firmly. The Prince pulled the bronze crucifix from his neck and carefully hung it down the end of the oar by its leather thong.

"This'll be a holy place at the base of Vile," he said, kneeling before the cross.

The boy dropped beside him. "My people will pray here."

As the humans prayed, Blackie listened to the silence about him. He sniffed the purity of rock and water. For a moment, he sensed a peace spreading through the heart of the stone. He shivered.

"Prince Vile won't sleep easily tonight."

Blackie turned, ready to go. He had more than enough of the stony weight pressing down on him. He wanted sun and sky and space to run. He prodded the Prince with his horn.

Prince George looked up at him. "Oh, the unicorn's ready to leave. What do you say, my boy, can you get us back to the surface?"

The boy leaped to his feet.

"Whenever you're ready, Master. I'll lead you up without running into the searchers."

Taking the spear, Prince George flashed it over Blackie. He reached a hand to stroke Blackie's horn.

"Poor Blackie, your horn's getting knocked around by all this rock, isn't it? I'm sorry, old beast."

Blackie nodded. "Well, Papa," he sighed to himself, "this is what you always feared—my horn scratched and scarred like Grandpa's. I can't help it."

The boy talked in a low voice as they climbed.

"Nothin's easier, Master, than takin' you up if you want to go. Me, I'd stay below until the Mountain cools down. She's been heatin' up for days. If she blows, it won't be safe to roam around the surface. We don't go up when she gets to rumblin' and spittin'. We wait until the dark prince flies off on the dragon. The guards pull back to the mountain then, and we opens a hole or two to look around. If we don't see hounds, it's safe to come out. That's the time we move about. The traders set off for the border to bring back the grain and cloth we can't find here while the rest of us gather cactus pods and roots."

"What in the world do you have to trade with?" asked the Prince, leaning on his spear to rest muscles tired from all the climbing.

"Ho, ho!" chuckled the boy. "You'd be surprised, me lord. Let's just say that the castle's leakier than Vile knows. He puts his slaves to laborin' like gnomes in his mills and workshops, but he can't hold onto the output. None of his minions will refuse a bribe if they're not under an officer's eye. In fact, we could smuggle twice as much as we do if it wasn't so tricky at the border."

Blackie heard Prince George breathe hard as he climbed. Even Blackie felt the strain in his legs. They must have gone deeper than he thought.

"I wonder what time of day it is? Underground here, you have no way to tell."

They twisted around another passageway with the spear light bouncing off the walls. Prince George was puffing.

"How much . . . much farther . . . do we climb, boy? We can't afford to lose any time. We must do . . . something . . . while we're here. Our Princess expects it. If we can't find . . . find the unicorn, there's the dragon to kill or prisoners to rescue. If I get in range of Vile, I'll pick him off with my bow. The death of the tyrant, what a s-song that'd make!"

The boy stopped and held up his hand. He listened a moment, then whispered, "We're almost there, me lord. Why don't you wait with the beast while I scout the outlets ahead? I'll pick up a bag of crunchy buns for you to take with you, too."

Sighing, Prince George leaned against the side of the cave while the boy padded off through the dust. The air felt colder here. Blackie sensed the reek of the mountain in his nose. His mood had changed as they neared the upper surface. Now he felt reluctant to leave the security of the cave for the bleak desert outside.

"There's no comfort anywhere in Vile," he thought. "Even the snowy fields back home are better than this place."

In no time, the boy was back with a bag of buns. "The way out looks open at the moment. I didn't see any Hounds or guard patrols."

Prince George took up shield and spear. The Nail dimmed as they walked toward the exit from the cavern. Outside, the air was cold. They stood in a rocky cleft looking out on the rising sun reflected off the western hills in a narrow band of red shifting through dreary purples and grays to the black sky above. As they watched, it flashed a golden burst before choking behind the smoke and ash from the smoldering mountain across the plain.

The boy crossed himself and turned back into the darkness of the cave. "Saints bless you, Master. Good luck with the Hellhounds."

"Goodbye, boy," called the Prince.

Blackie stepped out into the morning frost. The cold wind seized him. He gasped and shivered as the Prince clutched at his bearskin. The light on the spear was gone. Blackie scanned the countryside. Nothing moved but wisps of dry stems blown by the wind.

"How bitter it is," grumbled the Prince. "All frozen over. And we're exposed out here. The dragon could pick us off like a hawk on a hare. What should we do, Blackie, wait until nightfall to sneak along or ride out like heroes?"

Blackie trotted forward. It was the only way to go. Scary as the mountain seemed this morning, smoking like a huge, smouldering trash pile, it had been scarier last night. He looked back at Prince George.

The Prince limped through the rocks, the wind catching his bearskin. He pulled up on Blackie, tucking the fur around him. He grasped the spear. "Well, old comrade, we're here at last. Let's get this over with."

He reached down to rub Blackie's neck. "Whatever happens, Blackie, this is an epic quest. The minstrels will sing our song through the ages. We'll have a story to tell Saint Peter when we see him. Ready, boy?"

Blackie trotted over the frozen mat of vegetation with the wind in his ears and the stench in his nose, a mixture of smoke and rotten eggs. Now, he could see the mountain clearly, a dark cone sticking up from the plain, chopped short at the top where the black smudge spewed into the wind.

Wrapped in his bearskin, Prince George slumped into a snorting sleep. Blackie felt exposed and alone. The further he trotted from the cave, the more vulnerable he felt. Sure, he could see for miles out here, but any watcher could see him as well. No spying raven or dragon could miss his dark form.

Blackie slowed his pace to save strength in case he had to run. Prince George woke at once.

"What is it, boy? What is it? Are we there?"

The Prince straightened up, sneezing at the fumes. He looked ahead.

"Oh, Blackie, we've been riding for an hour, but that mountain doesn't seem any closer. It's bigger than I thought, much bigger. And the sun, you can't see the sun at all, though the wind is warming up."

"That's true, I guess," thought Blackie. He lifted his nose to sniff the air and sneezed.

Prince George was right. The air was warmer. The run had lifted Blackie's spirits a little. True, this was in no way a cheerful place and he was fearful about Papa, but the dread he had felt underground was eased with the daylight softening the earth. By noon, the tableland was transformed. The surface mat had thawed to a soggy tangle of tiny leaves and wormy little stems dotted with bright flowers.

Stopping for a break, Prince George looked around the countryside while chewing on crispy buns. Blackie pressed his mouth against the surface to nip cold strands in his fore teeth. He sucked at drops of mossy water collected in shallow depressions. The sips soothed his dry mouth, but didn't really settle his thirst from the run.

Bugs appeared suddenly, buzzing around Blackie's eyes. While Prince George swatted at mosquitoes, Blackie watched a small bird chase a white butterfly. It flitted after the butterfly and batted it to earth with a wing, then gobbled it down.

A couple hours later, the birds and insects disappeared as the earth cooled under weakening sunlight. The moisture dried away, and the sun drooped below the cloud for a final burst of garish light before darkness took over. The wind chilled though the earth couldn't freeze as the mountain swelled ahead, flaming as sunlight faded. By now, they were deep into the filthy smoke cloud with its sulfurous smell and gritty ash. The Prince's spearhead flashed like lamplight through the murk.

"Oh, yes, we've got to stifle the light again," muttered the Prince. He pulled the empty bun bag over the spearhead and tied it with a thread.

They were close enough to the mountain that Blackie could see fairly well by the flames shooting up from the crater. Nothing that he saw could cheer him. The turrets of Vile's castle stuck up on the far side of the jagged mountain cap with the dark walls of the slave pens below. On the near side, a stream of fiery rock spilled over the crater into smooth waves of silvery gray running down to the flat. A rumble shook the earth.

"Now's the time to turn back," he said to himself, "if we're ever going to do it."

"Do you hear that noise?" whispered the Prince. "Only Vile would live in such a terrible place. How can we possibly approach it?"

"I'd ask those humans," thought Blackie.

To his left, he saw a dark speck creeping toward the mountain. He couldn't make out what it was at this distance, but it was too small to daunt him. Slowing to match its approach, Blackie felt his hooves sink into the ash.

The oncomers drew close before a flare from the mountain lit them up for Prince George to notice. Blackie could see them clearly by then, two bony horses slogging along with some sort of wagon and a smaller beast trotting behind.

"Oh, oh," muttered the Prince, pulling his bow and notching the arrow. Blackie tensed for action, then relaxed when he saw who it was.

Though the cart was but a box of boards roughly hammered together, Blackie recognized the wheels and the shape of the driver bending forward in misery, his head down in his arms. Blackie snorted to calm the Prince.

"Lazlo the Gypsy!" he thought. "Who else would be riding up to Vile's Mountain?"

"It can't be!" gasped the Prince. "Lazlo? What's he doing here?"

Awakened by the voice, Lazlo leaped up with a squeal. He stared at them, jerking around a crossbow.

"S-Stay away!" he quavered. "I'm armed! I'll shoot! You better leave me alone!"

Blackie's impulse was to give Lazlo a good kicking and knock his wagon apart. He hadn't forgotten the Gypsy chaining him up as a prisoner.

"And here we meet again," he thought with a start. "Exactly where he planned to bring us. This must be fate!"

"Stand away! Stand away!" Lazlo shrieked, waving the crossbow. "I'm King of Gypsies! I carry an important gift to the Black Prince! He'll be furious if you delay me!"

"Oh, shut up, Lazlo!" snapped Prince George, lowering the bow. "Why are you sneaking into Vile like this?"

Recognizing them by the flames from the mountain, Lazlo shouted with delight. "My lord, Prince George, is that you?"

He stood up in the wagon to see better. "And the unicorn, the holy beast, he's with you too! Oh, bless the saints and martyrs, you've come to save us!"

Bursting into tears, Lazlo scrambled down from the wagon. He wobbled up to the Prince's knee, blubbering and drooling in relief.

"Sweet Prince, my lord, how I've prayed for you! Oh, forgive me! I know I did wrong to hold you when you were sick, but here you are when I need you! I find you just in time to rescue my daughter!"

He threw himself down before Prince George and hugged his boot.

"Forgive me, forgive me, dear Prince. Look at me! You see a humble sinner come alone to this terrible place to sacrifice himself. Oh, yes, I'm a reformed man. I've come to redeem Lizetta. I planned to give myself for her, father for daughter, but now—"

He lurched to his feet, rubbing his hands together. "Now, you and the unicorn have come with your might, your strength, your holy power! You can shatter Vile's walls and release his prisoners! You can save Lizetta!"

"Well," said the Prince, swinging the bow to his back, "we're here, anyway. What's all this about Lizetta?"

Lazlo shivered. He pulled his cloak about him and lowered his voice.

"Oh, my lord, it wasn't my doing! As you remember, the people fled in different directions when the dragon came flying after us. Not finding me, the monster chased after you and Lizetta. It caught her near Cranch, riding a stolen horse. I blame the unicorn. If he hadn't run off with my *vardo*, none of this would have happened in the first place."

"What a lie!" cried Prince George indignantly. "If Blackie hadn't carried me away, you'd have both of us in Vile's prison. Anything that happened to Lizetta is your fault, Lazlo!"

By now, Lazlo was weeping. "My only news of my daughter was a message from the raven. I don't know if she's still alive. I can only pray for her and try to recover her if I can."

"Well, Lazlo," said the Prince, jumping down into the ash beside the Gypsy, "at least, you've got some fatherly spirit about you. I wouldn't have thought you'd sacrifice yourself for anyone."

"Oh, yes," sighed Lazlo, "the burden of the Gypsy. Always blamed for everyone's troubles, misprized, misjudged, never given credit for his good intentions."

Prince George cut him off. "Yes, yes, I admit I may have been wrong about you, slightly wrong perhaps. Where is Lizetta being held?"

By now, Blackie had sniffed his way to Lazlo's cart. Here he smelled a terrible stink that had nothing to do with the burning mountain. Something was warm and alive in there. He poked his horn over the side of the cart. A fierce yowl went up like an angry cat. Blackie jumped away.

"Lazlo, Lazlo," cried the Prince, "what do you have in your cart?"

"In . . . in my cart, my lord?" stammered Lazlo. "Nothing, it's nothing."

Prince George crunched over to the cart. The goat tied to the rear stepped up to sniff at his bearskin.

"I heard something crying. What is it? What have you got in here?"

Lazlo looked about wildly. He caught his breath as Prince George reached inside to a large basket covered with blankets.

"Oh, my lord, please leave it alone. The cry, it's my— It's a parrot! A parrot, my lord, only a parrot."

"A parrot?" questioned the Prince.

"Yes, yes," cried Lazlo, throwing out his hands and speaking quickly, "it's a parrot for Prince Vile. I'd hoped he'd be willing to trade for Lizetta. A tropical bird, you understand, with bright colors never seen in Vile. I'd show it to you, but we mustn't disturb its basket. It's snug in there, warm, cozy, out of the cold wind. It's hungry, though, that's why it cries. It's calling for bread crumbs."

"That's no parrot!" insisted the Prince, shoving away the goat nibbling at his bearskin. "That sounds like a baby!"

"By my sainted grandmother, my lord, it is a parrot!" exclaimed Lazlo. As the flame spurted up from the mountain, Blackie saw sweat glisten on his face. "Parrots are mimics, you know. A parrot can squawk like a donkey, a monkey, a child."

"Well, give us a look, then!" cried the Prince, reaching into the wagon. "I've haven't seen a parrot since I sailed to Herne. And Blackie's never seen one. So bring out your bird, Lazlo. Let's take a peek."

The thing in the wagon didn't smell like a bird to Blackie. He'd swear that the wail was human.

Prince George pulled at the blanket on the basket. A small fist shot up. An angry little voice cried, "Daddy, Daddy!"

"Watch out!" screeched Lazlo. "He bites!"

CHAPTER THIRTY-EIGHT

The Burning Mountain

"Lazlo," cried Prince George, shoving the goat back with his spear butt, "what are you doing with this baby?"

Lazlo took a step backward. He kicked the ground with a dirty boot. "Nothing, nothing by the saints, my lord. It's just an . . . an orphan child I ran across. It was lost, hungry. I couldn't leave it behind."

Blackie sniffed at the wagon. Despite the acid smell of the mountain, he could tell that the baby seriously needed changing. Still, there was something familiar about this screaming infant.

"Stealing babies again, are you, Gypsy?" demanded the Prince. "Didn't the Bishop warn you about that? And whose child is this?"

Prince George held up the hem of the blanket before his eyes. In the next flash of the mountain, he examined the coat of arms stitched on the corner.

"What's this?" he mused. "That's a goat, I think. It's the arms of Darr crossed by—What's that, a headman's axe?"

He gasped. "It's Godfrey's! Lazlo, you've stolen Godfrey's baby! This is the heir of the Heir of Darr—my godson!"

"Oh, oh, oh, my lord!" howled Lazlo, beating his head. "What could I do? What could I do? You can't imagine Prince Vile's fury when I failed to deliver the unicorn! The Prince caught up Lizetta in his rage! He carried her off to his castle, swearing to throw her to the dragon if I didn't bring him this child in her place. He wants a hostage to force the Heir to open the border to him."

"Oh, Gypsy, Gypsy!" exclaimed Prince George, throwing back the blanket, "you're determined to be hanged! First, the Holy Grail, then me and Blackie! Now, it's Lord Godfrey's child! How can you ever make up for crimes like these?"

Horrified at Lazlo's wickedness, Blackie snorted his agreement. Lazlo looked guilty for a moment, then burst into tears.

"But . . . but my lord, don't you see? I only took the baby for Lizetta, my daughter, my child! How could I leave my daughter to the Black Prince without trying to save her! Crepitar, the raven, told me that this was my last chance! What could I do? I didn't want to steal this baby. I hate the child. But I had no choice, you must see that! I'd do anything to save Lizetta!"

Blackie looked skeptical while Lazlo wept.

"Oh, please, my Prince, look how I'm sacrificing myself—throwing myself into Vile's clutches! Everyone knows that he's the lord of lies, the king of treachery. I don't believe for one second that he'll keep his promise to me. Even if I give him what he wants, he won't free Lizetta. He'll have me to torture along with her. But I have to make the effort. That's why I borrowed the baby—to trade for Lizetta. It's my last hope."

Blackie tossed his horn in the air. What a mess this had turned into! Rescuing Papa was hard enough. Now, they had to deal with Lazlo and Godfrey's baby, as well as Lizetta, wherever she was!

Prince George was questioning how Lazlo had got here. "Tell the truth, Gypsy, how'd you sneak across into Vile? We're told that the border's been sealed since the beginning of the war."

"Oh, my lord." Lazlo looked down. "We Gypsies, you know—"

"I know," said the Prince, grimly. "You Gypsies can out-smuggle the smugglers. This time, Lazlo, you've done it. You've finally gone too far. You've got Prince Vile furious at you on this side of the border for failing him over and over while you've got the Heir on the other side hunting you for stealing his baby. This time, you won't escape punishment. Nothing can save you, nothing!"

Lazlo threw himself down into the ash, clutching at the Prince's knees. "Please, my lord, my Prince, you can save us if you will, save me and Lizetta, both of us! Why else would the stars have brought you here?"

"Up, Lazlo, up!" cried the Prince, exasperated. "Stop whining about the stars! Make yourself useful as a nursemaid, if nothing else. This baby needs changing! And feed him! Get him to stop crying."

"Oh, yes, certainly, my lord," mumbled Lazlo, pushing to his knees. "I'll just get . . . get milk from my goat."

"What do we do now, Blackie?" wailed the Prince. He pulled the baby from the wagon as Lazlo picked up a bucket and called to the goat. Wrapping the baby in his bearskin, Prince George tried to comfort it against his shoulder, but the boy kicked and screamed.

"I don't know anything about babies!" the Prince screeched, helplessly wrestling with the infant. "What do I do with it?"

Blackie stepped up to the screaming child and placed his horn in the little hand. The fingers clutched the horn. The crying stilled as Blackie sent gentle pulses to calm the baby's loneliness and fear.

"Once again, I thank the saints for your powers, Blackie," whispered Prince George, cuddling the quiet child. "Nothing makes a man feel more useless than a crying baby."

"Maaaa, maaaa!"

Now, the goat was tossing her head as the mountain spouted fire. Bleating, she backed away from Lazlo, crawling after with the bucket.

"Hold still, stupid thing! You need milking, anyway."

"Hate this place. Hate this place!" bleated the goat. "I want to go back to my kids, my friends, the tasty thorns of home!"

"What's next?" thought Blackie, stepping to calm the goat with his horn. The nanny stood reluctantly while Lazlo fumbled with its udders.

Clumsily, Prince George rocked the baby in his arm. As Lazlo spurted goat milk into the bucket, the Prince croaked out a lullaby in a scratchy voice.

> Papa holds his baby
> and the night creeps by.
> The old lady laughs.
> The old men sigh.
>
> Outside the window,
> the dark birds fly.
> Papa holds his baby
> and the night creeps by.

Trying to pour a stream from the bucket into a glove with a fingertip snipped off, Lazlo sloshed half the goat's milk onto the ground.

"I . . . I can feed the child now, my lord."

Prince George dumped the baby into Lazlo's arms. "Here, take it."

Lazlo pulled blankets around the baby and let it taste a drop of milk. It sucked eagerly at the glove as Prince George walked back and forth, trying to think out the situation.

"First thing is to get this baby back to its parents. I could never face Godfrey if . . . if—"

"But what of Lizetta?" demanded Lazlo, bouncing the baby up and down to burp him. "My daughter, my treasure, think of her! I taught her everything I know! She's beautiful as the moon and a master thief, worth a hundred silver pieces to any groom. But she's worthless to me as Prince Vile's prisoner, and—"

The baby started wailing again. Prince George cut off Lazlo's complaint.

"Enough, Lazlo, we know how you feel about your daughter. Now, here's what's going to happen. You're going to feed this baby, then take him straight back to Darr. No arguments about it, no excuses! I don't care how you do it. This baby goes back to its parents! If you can steal a baby out of a castle, you can sneak it back in. Blackie and I, well, we have to continue to the mountain anyway. If we come across Lizetta along the way, we'll rescue her. We'll save her if we can, I promise you, Gypsy."

"But what if you don't come across her? What if you don't see her?" squealed Lazlo. "What then, what then?"

Prince George swung the bow to his back and looked about for his shield. Blackie trotted over to stand beside him.

"If we make it to the mountain," said the Prince, pulling the shield up his arm, "Vile's going to be shaken to the core. As slippery as Lizetta is, she can escape in the commotion if she wants to. Don't be surprised, though, if she chooses to stay. Knowing Lizetta, she's probably bewitched Prince Vile. I wouldn't be surprised if he doesn't make her his queen."

Lazlo halted. His eyes widened in the firelight as he held the baby to his chest. His voice changed to a wistful note.

"My Lizetta, Queen of Vile! Just think of that! The wealth of Mulciber in her hands—the silver, the gold, the jewels!"

Prince George poked Lazlo with the spear butt.

"Forget it, Gypsy, do you hear? Turn this cart around now! If you don't carry this baby back to his father, Blackie and I will do it. We'd love an excuse to turn back. You could travel alone to the burning mountain then. I'm sure you can explain to Prince Vile why you failed him again. You know how he'd welcome your excuses."

In the glow of the mountain, Blackie saw Lazlo turn pale at that suggestion. Blackie tensed as Lazlo's eyes shifted to him. He jumped aside as the Gypsy clawed for his horn. Lazlo dropped to his knees again, shouting over the screams of the baby.

"Unicorn, unicorn, holy beast, I appeal to your conscience! You travel the world doing good deeds. What deed could be nobler than rescuing the poor Gypsy girl from wicked Vile? And you, my lord—"

Waving the screaming baby in one arm, he reached to the Prince with the other.

"I forgive everything you've done to me! I'll give up my claim to the Nail if you'll only save Lizetta. She's all I have left in the world!"

"Enough, Lazlo!" cried the Prince, shaking ashes from his bearskin. "You're wasting our time! Your task is to return this child to his father. Leave Vile to us."

Wearily pulling up on Blackie, he pointed the spear at Lazlo. "I promise you, Gypsy, we'll save your girl if it's possible. We don't know what we have to face over here. Truth is, I wouldn't give two coppers for our own chance of escaping. But if we run across Lizetta, we'll bring her out with us."

Hugging the baby, Lazlo pushed to his feet. He waved as Blackie turned toward the mountain. He shouted after them.

"Since you swear, my Prince, that you'll rescue Lizetta, I'll return the baby as you ask. And I'll pray for both of you—may the saints give you victory! Also, my lord, when you do see Lizetta, tell her to bring the jewels! Remind my daughter that her father waits for her, for her and the jewels—diamonds, especially, and emeralds, rubies!"

As they trotted away, Lazlo's shouts rang in Blackie's ears.

"Tell her to leave the clothes, leave the shoes! We can steal more finery, but she should bring all the rubies she can carry, bags of them!"

Ahead of them, the mountain roared, drowning out Lazlo's cries. It flung fiery rocks into the air. Now, Blackie truly felt despair.

527

"How can we ever rescue Lizetta?" he asked himself. "All I wanted was to stop Papa from entering this terrible place. Now, we're in the heart of Vile with no sign of Papa, and now, we're expected to rescue the Gypsy, too!"

Catching his mood, the Prince patted his shoulder, trying to reassure him.

"Now, now, Blackie, don't get upset. I promised that we'd save Lizetta if we run across her. Unicorn's still our target. Once we find him, we're running for the border, no matter how many prisoners Vile holds. I'm hoping for a simple in-and-out job."

"What have we ever done that was simple?" groaned Blackie. "Everything we do seems to get complicated."

After a quick glance to make sure that Lazlo was dragging back toward the border, Blackie turned to study the outline of the mountain by the flames ahead, trying to figure the best angle to approach the horror. It was easy enough to see where not to go, the lanes where the blazing glop spilling over the side made passage impassable. It was harder to figure where an approach might be possible. It all looked hopeless at this point.

Blackie shook his head, coughing in the foul air. This close to the mountain, the wind was heavy with smoke and ash, a taste of the choking fumes they'd run through if they continued toward this downwind side of the crater.

Even the earth under Blackie's hooves had changed. The gusts had heated the surface while spreading ash and cinders in a crackly scurf that coated his legs with grit. Blackie hated the whole malevolent mound spewing filth and fire. Caught in the smoke and stink, he couldn't remember what spring was like back in the green forest.

Prince George shook with deep coughs on Blackie's back. He drew in a wheezing breath.

"How . . . how can anyone breathe in this poison?"

Blackie swung his horn around and shot a healing charge through the Prince's leg to clear out his lungs. Gratefully, the Prince bent to rub his neck.

Blackie plodded on through the ash, eyes stinging in the smoke. The haze thickened until all he could see was the hectic flush of flames ahead.

"Enough of this!" cried the Prince.

He drew in his spear, sweeping ash from the shaft with his glove. Snapping the thread around the bun bag, he jerked away the bag to free the Nail. Brilliant light flashed around them, driving back the worst of the fumes.

"Look, Blackie, look!"

From the corner of his eye, Blackie saw Prince George pointing down at the ground. Running ahead of them, spaced about a yard apart, they saw a row of deep hoofprints filling up with ash.

"Papa!" cried Blackie, joyously.

The Nail cleared enough of the smoke from the air that Blackie got a hint of last summer's familiar scent—Papa, hot and sweaty, galloping hard as though determined to get through this nightmare before waking.

Prince George leaned forward with excitement. "How long, Blackie? How long since he ran along here, an hour, a day?"

Blackie couldn't guess how long it would take the mountain to cover all trace of a running unicorn, but it hadn't been longer than an hour or so. Apparently, Papa had angled in from the south while they'd swung east through the caves. Now, they had a clear track to follow. Despite the smoke, they weren't running blind.

Cheered by the sight of Unicorn's tracks, Blackie picked up his pace. He cantered up Papa's trail toward the sullen glow of the crater, but the mountain seemed to become aware of them. It came awake with threatening grumbles that build up to a blast.

The mountain roared. Flames surged high. Blackie rocked back under a burning hail shaking his head frantically to throw off sparks while sweeping his tail over his hindquarters. Yelping with pain, Prince George cowered under his shield, kicking burning clinkers from his legs.

"Ooh, ooh, ooh! Blackie, this is terrible! Battle wounds are bad enough, but to be peppered with fire—horrible!"

"Papa went through it!" cried Blackie, galloping through the fiery ash that burnt his hooves to his knees. He tried to blank the pain from his mind, thinking only of Papa charging through flames to rescue him.

"This horror would be worse for Papa, poor pampered Papa! How could he face this—and alone?"

The heat grew fiercer as the mountain towered above. Again, the mountain roared with rage.

"Here it comes again!" shouted Prince George, whipping his bearskin over Blackie's rear.

The Prince lunged forward, throwing himself high onto Blackie's neck to brandish the shield over their heads. Blackie closed his eyes, as the mountain heaved with a burst of flames that spattered the earth with burning rocks.

Fiery hailstones banged down on the shield. Prince George threw them aside. He reached back to jerk the burning bearskin from Blackie, shake off the debris, and roll it tightly to smother the flames. The stink of smoldering hair and skin came to Blackie with the sulfurous gasses from the blast. The Prince used the underside of the cloak to sweep scorching cinders from Blackie's legs as Blackie hopped about in pain.

The Prince looked with dismay at the smoking scars dotting Blackie's rump.

"Oh, Blackie, I know this is torture! If only I had a healing horn to soothe you!"

"The Nail," cried Blackie, "use the Nail."

"What?"

"The Nail, the Nail!"

Blackie tapped his horn against the spear.

"The Nail? It doesn't— Oh, I don't know."

Prince George drew in the spear shaft and touched the gleaming light against Blackie's burns. Blackie sucked in his breath with a sigh.

The Nail didn't heal wounds as the horn did, but it did numb pain. Howling, Prince George jumped down into smoking cinders to run the Nail over Blackie's haunches and legs, hopping around as his own boots scorched on the surface. Blackie touched the Prince with his horn and stood quietly as the Prince scrambled back on to escape the embers, kicking out his boots to shake off sparks.

"Oh, those Gypsies!" cried Prince George. "I'm sure they knew that the Nail could stop pain. I bet they've used it forever with their medicines, but they never said one word about it."

Picking up speed again, Blackie looked ruefully at Unicorn's hoofprints, half-buried by the last eruption.

"We'd better hurry before Papa's footprints are gone."

The Nail protected Blackie's feet from torment as he trotted on, stepping as lightly as possible over the smoking earth that glowed with red-hot fragments. The mountain rumbled and shook, stoking up for another burst. The bearskin was little more than a charred rag now. Prince George kept the shield ready for the blast.

Up they climbed to the foothills under the cone of the burning mountain. Unicorn's hoofprints swerved around a fiery flow of molten rock onto a ridge to the south of the crater. The rise of the mountain held back the wind here, so swirling eddies of ash and smoke overwhelmed the power of the Nail to cleanse the air about them. The heat was terrific.

Breath came hard to both of them. Prince George wound Lizetta's red scarf around his mouth. He coughed deeply despite regular jolts from the healing horn. Blackie snorted grit from his nose. His throat felt scoured by cinders. His whole body was as dry as his hooves.

Worst of all was the overwhelming sense of futility. There seemed no way Papa could survive this horror. Surely, by now, Unicorn was crushed by this mountain huffing and puffing around them, rolling and rumbling with pent-up power before the final eruption that would bury them all—unicorns and human, horns and bow, shield and spear.

It was too late to escape. Even if they turned to flee, the flood of boiling rock from that great crater would run them down before they reached the plain.

Prince George swung back and forth on Blackie's back, stretching down the Nail to numb Blackie's hooves as he ran. By now, the Prince was shrieking hysterically.

"On, Blackie, on! Though fire and stone and the powers of darkness, we run, we run, we run!"

Blackie would not call it running at this point. He dragged along with heaving chest and aching muscles. His body weighed a ton. He had to focus all his strength to lift hoof after hoof and keep climbing without tumbling back down the rise.

"Poor, poor Prince," came a furtive thought, "if we're buried by the mountain, no one'll hear about this. His greatest adventure left out of his Song."

Prince George swept the air before them with the spear while pounding Blackie's shoulder with the shield.

"Onward, Blackie, onward! We're almost there! I can sense it!"

"On where?" gasped Blackie. "I'm run down . . . run down. I can't climb this . . . this—"

"There!"

Prince George pointed with his spear. Blackie forced up his head, blinking burning eyes to stare through the murk. He saw the nub of a tower sticking up from the ashes, squat, brown, half-buried on the upper side by smoking cinders tumbling down from the crater above.

A wave of revulsion threw Blackie back, but Prince George yanked at his mane.

"Hold on, boy, hold on! I smell it too, the stink, the dragon smell."

That was it, of course. Exhausted as he was, Blackie gagged in the stench of the dragon pouring from the brown tower, the horrible stink of burned bones and rotting flesh. He wobbled on his hooves, struggling to stay erect despite the horror.

Shuddering at the stink, Prince George waved the spear to peer ahead through the fumes.

"Horrible place, hateful, but the hoofprints stop there. Your father, Blackie, the Unicorn, he must have . . . jumped down there!"

"Papa!"

As though responding to the word, the mountain pitched violently with a roar that shot flames high into the air. Blackie's legs gave way. He stumbled back and fell onto Prince George, crushing the man's leg into the burning surface. Dropped by the Prince, the shield spun off to the side while the spear rolled down the hill, the light flashing with each bounce.

Blackie rolled off Prince George and fought to stand again as the Prince howled in agony.

"Gotta get up!" gasped Blackie. "Gotta keep going!"

His flank was scraped and scorched by the clinkers, but the pain recovered his concentration. He pushed to his front hooves, paused for a breath, and kicked to pull up his rear. For once, the mountain helped by lurching upward with a blast that threw him back onto his hooves.

Blackie stood a moment, dizzy with pain under the shower of fiery rock, then turned his horn to the Prince.

"I'm sorry, so sorry."

"Don't talk!" screamed Prince George, clutching for the horn. "Heal me, heal me!"

Blackie closed his eyes, gritted his teeth, and launched a mighty dose of healing power through the Prince. Prince George gasped in relief, but clung to the horn.

"Pull me up! Pull me up! I've fallen into fire!"

Blackie pulled back a couple steps, dragging the Prince to his feet. Kicking out his smoking boots, Prince George threw an arm over Blackie to hold steady while brushing sparks from his clothes.

"Now, I'll help you, Blackie!" he cried. "Where's my spear?"

The spear had slid into a pile of clinkers held by a boulder. The Nail shone clearly at the top end of the shaft while flames licked up from the butt, set afire by the cinders.

Prince George grabbed up the hot shield, then threw an arm over Blackie as they crunched down the shifting mound. The Prince wrapped his fingers in the last rags of his bearskin to seize the spear. After running the hide up and down the shaft to choke the flames, he worked around Blackie to stroke the Nail over his burns.

Blackie closed his eyes with relief from the pain. The Nail seemed to remove his fatigue for the moment. He stood quietly while Prince George pulled the bow and arrow from his back to inspect them. They were coated with ash, but untouched by the sparks.

"We're in miserable shape," groaned the Prince, heaving himself up on Blackie, "but we can fight. Help us, Saint Michael, help us!"

"Amen," whispered Blackie, taking on the Prince's weight with a sigh. He turned back to the squat turret outlined by flames from the cone high above.

Prince George held out the Nail on the smoking spear shaft as Blackie struggled up the shaking height. The mountain roared again. One final time, the Prince caught flying debris on the shield, shook it off, and brushed Blackie's rear with the blackened remnants of the bearskin.

"Around the tower, Blackie!" cried the Prince. "To the top! All this filth piled against it—we can follow the Unicorn!"

Blackie tried to struggle around the tower, but the loose piles of cinders threw him back. He slid to his knees in smoking slag while sparks and ash set Prince George to choking and crying.

The Prince rolled off Blackie to make climbing easier for the beast, but neither could scramble up the shifting grit. They stood together, sobbing and gasping, as the mountain heaved and puffed as though laughing at them.

Frustrated, furious, Prince George swung the spear against the tower.

SPLOTCH!

Instead of striking solid stone, the Nail cut into the tower like a sharp knife through cheese.

"Look!" cried the Prince. "The tower, it's . . . it's—"

He tapped the brown stone with the end of the shaft. The stone felt solid against the wood of the forest, but the iron Nail, saved from the Crucifixion of Christ by the mercy of Gypsies, sliced a door through the tower with ease.

CRASH, CRASH!

Blackie heard loosened stones smashing within.

Now, it was the outraged mountain that gasped as it pulled back for a final explosion. Prince George whirled, his eyes bright again.

"This is it, Blackie, old friend! Unicorn's down there, and we're going after him!"

Wearily, Blackie placed his horn on the Prince's shoulder. He drew in his breath and used his last energy to force a healing charge that straightened the Prince and strengthened his voice.

"God bless us all—the Unicorn, the Princess, even Lazlo the Gypsy! His Nail . . . his Nail—"

Prince George gave Blackie one last hug. He gripped the spear with both hands. He stepped into the hole in the side of tower and disappeared.

Blackie reared on hind hooves to shake fiery cinders from his back. He closed his eyes and leaped after the Prince. The mountain roared in fury as Blackie tumbled into darkness.

CHAPTER THIRTY-NINE

Dragon's Nest

WHAM!

Blackie's head smashed down an instant after his body struck, cracking his bones on the rocky floor of the pit. A cloud of dust puffed up at his fall.

"Aaaah!"

Curled in pain, Blackie didn't notice that his tail had flopped onto the spear fallen from Prince George's hand. Quickly, the Nail worked its spell. It numbed Blackie's body so long as he lay still, though moving was a different story. It hurt to draw breath. Lifting a hoof was agony. Even winking his eyes sent arrows through Blackie's head.

The light of the Nail was smothered behind him, but Blackie could see the dark form of Prince George stretched in the dust a few feet away. Blackie shut his eyes, struck by waves of guilt and misery.

"Where . . . where have I brought us this time? Georgie, here because of me, and Papa! Papa, where are you?"

A rumble shook the den. Blackie half-opened his eyes to look beyond the Prince. All he saw were rocky walls curving around. Blackie knew that he had to move. He couldn't give up. He'd die here, another heap of bones on the floor of the pit.

Sucking in shallow breaths, Blackie lifted his horn slightly. Painfully, he inched toward Prince George till he was halted by a tower stone, holding him back three feet from the human.

"This is dumb," thought Blackie. "Surely, I'm not so . . . so—"

Flattened in the dust, he was too weak to roll over the stone. He had to scoot around it. He couldn't move his legs, could barely lift his tail, but he could shrug his shoulders with his breath. Breath by breath, Blackie hunched his body around the stone. He quivered as spasms of pain ran through him, but he scraped around the sharp corner, bending his neck lower and lower until the tip of his horn almost touched the man's knee.

"One more push. One more push."

He rested a moment, dragging in shuddering breaths. With a supreme effort, he shoved his shoulders forward another inch. Now, his horn pressed against the knee. He lay still, panting, to gain strength. With a sob, he forced a healing jolt into the Prince who stiffened and groaned.

"Wake . . . up!" gasped Blackie. "We can't . . . lie here . . . forever."

"Let me go," moaned the Prince, drawing an arm over his face. "I don't want to—"

Blackie gritted his teeth, trembling at the strain, and shot another dose into the human. Prince George let out a heartrending sigh. Moaning, he pushed up on an elbow.

"Oh, Blackie, why'd you bring me back? I was rising into the light! I was bathed in joy! I wanted to—"

The Prince looked around, gasping. "This horrible place—The stink, the bones, where are we?"

"The . . . pit," groaned Blackie. "Under the tower."

Prince George's elbow slipped. He fell flat, then sat up to gaze in amazement at Blackie.

"Blackie, you can speak!"

"I could always . . . speak," panted Blackie. "You couldn't . . . understand."

Groaning, the Prince crawled over to Blackie. He gently rubbed Blackie's head.

"This is . . . excellent, old fellow," he rasped. "You can talk to me now. You can tell me things! Oh, I have so much to ask you!"

He wiped his brow and took a deep breath.

"What . . . what are we doing here? The Unicorn, where is he? How do you feel, Blackie? You look terrible!"

Blackie sagged to the floor. He closed his eyes. Into his mind came the picture of Papa jumping down here before them. How could Papa keep going after that fall?

A greater mystery was simply how Papa got to this tower in the first place. Blackie wondered if anyone would ever explain how Unicorn gathered the resolve to invade Vile after his lazy, happy life. The only thing Blackie knew for certain was that they were stuck in this pit with the mountain exploding around them when he longed to be a world away, enjoying the spring with his Mama and the Princess and the deer.

"Talk to me, Blackie," pleaded the Prince, shaking his ear. "Where do we go from here?"

"I'm done for," groaned Blackie. "No strength."

"Well, here, I'll use my Nail."

The Prince pushed to his knees and reached for the charred staff of the spear. He swung up the Nail, flashing light around the den, and swept it over Blackie. Again, the Nail eased Blackie's aches, removing the pain from cracked ribs, but it didn't give him strength to rise.

"No good," gasped Blackie, opening his eyes. "No good. I'm broken . . . done for, Georgie. I can't move."

The Prince stood up, shining the spear around the cave.

"I don't have medicines," he muttered. "I wonder if there's anything down that passage over there."

Blackie drew a breath.

"It's hopeless, Georgie. Leave me. Save . . . save yourself. Go . . . go look for Papa."

"Nonsense." Prince George knelt to pat Blackie's neck. "I'm not leaving you, Blackie. You're my friend, my comrade. We're a team, you and me. The Princess put us together like those Greeks, Damon and what's-his-name, Pieface. Let me search out this place. Surely, I can find something to give you strength."

"It's not . . . strength I need, Georgie," gasped Blackie. "It's the fall. It . . . It broke me. You'll have to go on . . . on without me."

Blackie felt anguish as Prince George jumped to his feet. Already, Blackie felt abandoned, left alone to dry up in misery. He knew it had to be, as damaged as he was, but it was hard, hard.

"Go on," he moaned, tears running down his nose. "Leave me. Leave me."

Prince George leaned against the side of the cave as the mountain roared again, dust and bits of rubble shaking down on them. He pulled the spear to his chest, thinking aloud.

"Well, let me see what we've got. There's nothing here, just these bones and that tunnel. It goes off that way. Let me take a peek down there."

Prince George left, his footsteps departing. Darkness fell about Blackie except for the ring of flame at the opening above.

Prince George's voice echoed back to him.

"Oh, yes, it continues this way. Looks like the tunnel goes on and on. There's nothing here to help us, though. Just more bones and—Yuck, the stink gets worse and worse down here!"

Now, the footsteps were gone. Blackie pulled back his neck with an effort, closing his eyes.

"This is it," he thought. "All those deer I chased to the hunters—now I know how they felt."

The moments stretched forever before Blackie heard the Prince returning, the spear thumping against the floor. The light flashed on Blackie's eyelids.

"That's the way we have to go, all right. First thing, we have to get you on your feet. Okay, Blackie, no more lumping around like this! You're as lazy as a lady's maid."

"I don't want to lie here," protested Blackie, following the Prince with an eye. "I can't move."

"Well, I've figured out what to do."

Giving Blackie a gentle pat, the Prince reached for the bow on the floor. He plucked off the arrow, wiped it on his sleeve, and held it up in the air.

"Listen, Arrow, you've never failed me yet. We've shot rabbits in the field and geese in the sky. You brought me a blessed oar from the lake, and I'm sure, if I asked you, you'd bring me a bag of gold. This time, I'm shooting you after a greater treasure than that. I need powerful medicine, a magic to heal the unicorn here. As master of the bow, I'm counting on you. Understand?"

The arrow shook in its eagerness, so Prince George swung up the bow, aimed at the flaring circle in the tower above, and loosed the arrow. It zoomed up and out of sight.

Blackie lowered his ears in disappointment.

"That's it?" he gasped. "An arrow? Oh, I'm . . . I'm doomed if that's all . . . all you can come up with! What do you . . . expect . . . the arrow to bring back? Only a fully grown unicorn's horn—"

"Easy, easy," whispered Prince George, sitting by Blackie and stroking his neck. "Lie quietly, Blackie. Rest while you can. You can trust the arrow. In its way, its magic is as strong as your horn's."

Blackie groaned and closed his eyes. Prince George sat down beside Blackie. He pulled his dagger and began scraping at the charred wood of the spear shaft.

"I'm thirsty, Blackie, dry as an oven. When the arrow returns with your medicine, I'll send it after a waterbag. I'll tell it to bring us the freshest water from the coolest spring in the land. Doesn't that sound good?"

Helpless in the dust, Blackie relaxed with the image in his head of the sparkling stream back home where he'd hurt his baby horn on the stone wall. Thinking of the pain of that blow, his mind slid to the terrors plaguing him now. He fell into a nightmare of the slave pens of Vile.

In his dream, he was squeezed into a chasm gouged from burning rock with thousands of humans weeping about him. As the mountain spewed its sparks, the humans surged against him, each one shrieking, "Save me, unicorn! Save me!"

The stinking, sweating horde piled onto him, pulling at him, clutching, scratching, screaming, "Me, me, me, unicorn! Save me!"

Blind and breathless, Blackie was squashed down into the rock under the wriggling mass. Then a deep voice rolled out over the crowd.

"MOTHER."

There was a pause, the whole mob silent as statues until women began clawing their way out of the pile to raise their arms in the air.

"I'm a mother! Do you come for me?"

"Help me, help me! I have six children!"

"I'm pregnant, now! I'll be a mother in two weeks!"

"Why only mothers?" cried a man next to Blackie. "What about fathers, too?"

The mass broke apart as the humans scrambled off Blackie to jump up, waving and hollering. Moaning, Blackie struggled to lift his head. When his eyes came into focus, he saw a tall, bearded man framed in shining light on the rock above. The man spread his arms to the crowd.

"I COME FOR MY MOTHER."

"My child, my lost child!" cried a woman. "You've found me at last."

"Shut up, you!" shrieked a thin woman, waving a fist at the other woman. "It's Simon, my eldest, come for his mama!"

"MOTHER, CLING TO THIS NET. IT WILL LIFT YOU UP."

The man unwound a long fishing net from his shoulder. He cast down the end. The thin woman seized it.

"I've got it, Simon! Pull me up! Pull me up!"

The man set his strong arms to pull. Simon's mother lifted above the crowd, crowing in glee, "I can smell them! I smell them! The fragrant gardens of Heaven!"

"Take me too!" cried the first woman, jumping to grab for the net. She missed the net, but clutched Simon's mother around her waist.

Simon's mother wriggled and kicked.

"Let go, you! Let go! My son came to save me, not some filthy Samaritan from Gerazim!"

"Don't leave me behind!" shouted a man, throwing his arms around both women. Others grabbed his legs, and still more clung to them. Simon pulled them up like fish on a cord, but his mother was in a fury at these interlopers. She jerked the net, swinging back and forth, kicking and screaming in fury.

"Let go! Let go! This is my net! Get your own sons to save you! I'm not sharing my son with anyone!"

"MOTHER, MOTHER," pleaded Simon with his great voice," HOLD STILL! I CAN PULL YOU ALL. THERE'S ROOM FOR EVERYONE."

"I'm not having it, I'm not having it!" she shrieked. "Shake them off! Shake them off!"

In her fury, she let loose of the net and fell, beating at the woman embracing her waist.

"It's my son, my net! Mine, I tell you, mine!"

They collapsed back on to Blackie, knocking him out of his dream. He awoke with a gasp to find Prince George kneeling over him.

"I told you the arrow could do it!" cried the Prince, gently lifting Blackie's head to dribble water from a gourd down his throat. "I thought the arrow would hunt down the Wise Woman to get her salve, the bone and muscle tonic, remember? No, no, it did better than that, much better! It flew all the way to the Fountain of the Shrine! This'll fix you up in no time."

Blackie felt better with the first drops of Fountain water. He was able to lift his head so Prince George could pour a real drink down his throat. The healing power of the Fountain flowed through his body to the cracked bones and knotted muscles. Filled with joy, Blackie shut his eyes as the burns eased, the bruises healed, the bones grew together.

"Bless the Lord! Bless the Lord," panted the Prince. He lifted the gourd and sucked down his own drink. He sprang up with a cheer, grabbed the arrow hovering above them, and kissed it.

"Thank you, Arrow! Swift Arrow, clever Arrow!"

He dipped the arrowhead into the gourd and the arrow twisted happily. It stiffened when the Prince set it back on the bow.

"Wonderful!" cried Blackie, jumping up beside the Prince. "Drink and medicine with one shot! I think, now, you should shoot the arrow to the Wise Woman for a basket of her cookies."

"Ho, ho, Blackie!" shouted Prince George, pounding Blackie's back. "Thinking of cookies are you? You're coming to yourself again!"

"A jest, a jest," said Blackie, shaking out his muscles. "Hold onto that gourd, Georgie. We'll give Papa a drink when we find him."

"Oh, yes, our quest," said Prince George, corking the hole in the gourd. He bent for the spear. "For a moment, I almost forgot why we're here."

They were reminded at once by the mountain shaking with a dreadful roar. Burning cinders filtered down the hole above to sting them back to their mission.

"I'm afraid for Papa," muttered Blackie, looking to the shadows beyond the light of the Nail. "I can't see how he could survive that fall."

"We'll find out soon." The Prince carefully stowed the gourd in a scorched bag at his waist. He swung the bow to his back and took up his shield. "You sure the Unicorn went this way?"

Blackie nodded. "Oh, yes, I smell Papa down there."

"Let's go then."

Blackie pushed ahead, sniffing Unicorn's trail as Prince George stretched out the Nail, scattering the shadows.

"I'll go first," Blackie insisted.

"But I've got the light," protested the Prince. He shook the spear.

"Hold it high, then," said Blackie, grimly, stepping into the dark passage. "I'll lead the way. This is my job after all. Really, Georgie, I didn't plan to bring you along, but I bless the Lord that you stuck with me. I'd never have gotten this far by myself."

Blackie proceeded carefully through the stinking tunnel, setting down his hooves in the shadows thrown by the light above his tail. Back in the forest, he could see fairly well in the dimmest night, but here, the darkness was absolute. At least, the noise of the eruptions grew muffled as the trail angled downward into the mountain, though the rock shuddered constantly under the scorching anger around them.

"Watch out, Georgie!" Blackie jumped a crack where hissing steam sprayed up. "That steam'll broil anyone who stumbles."

"I hate this place," grunted Prince George, vaulting through the steam on the spear shaft.

"We won't stay long, you can be sure of that," said Blackie. He swung around his horn to give the Prince another healing charge to strengthen him.

Prince George took a deep breath. "Do you still smell your Papa?"

"Oh, yes." Blackie stepped along nervously. "He's coming on strong, but so's the dragon. Keep your spear ready."

"How much further, can you tell?"

"It could be right around this turn."

Blackie's ears were up, his horn low. He stepped along at full alert, ready for anything.

They rounded the curve in the tunnel. Prince George kicked bones aside, shuddering at the stench.

"Horrible, horrible!"

"It's worse than the hospital," said Blackie, grimly, "but I think, we've come to the end of our trail."

"So we're here, are we?" muttered the Prince. He stepped up beside Blackie, gripping the spear with both hands, the Nail burning before them. "Let's go."

Side by side, they stepped around the final turn in the tunnel. Ahead, they saw a fiery glow rise and fall, rise and fall. Blackie's heart quickened, his muscles tightened. Fixing his eyes on the frightful sight, he cried out while Prince George stood frozen in shock.

The tunnel ended at the dragon's nest. Hair and cloth, shoes and bones were scratched into a scraggly pile. There she lay, the great worm, huge and bloody, sprawled wide with broken wings. Her jaws opened, shut, opened, shut, gasping out spurts of smoke. Below her lay Unicorn, his horn buried to his forehead in the dragon's bowels. His white coat was burnt black, a bloody haunch torn from his body.

"Papa!"

Heedless of the dragon, Blackie jumped across the serpent's tail to lick Unicorn's face. Papa didn't move. Blackie turned to Prince George, approaching cautiously, his spear at the ready.

"The water, Georgie, the Fountain water!"

"Try your horn," croaked Prince George. "See if you can bring him around."

"My horn!" Blackie gasped. "Of course, of course!"

Kicking aside the bones under his hooves, Blackie pressed his horn against Unicorn's shoulder. Concentrating all his strength, he shot out a powerful charge that made Unicorn's ears fly up.

Papa stayed dead.

Unfortunately, the healing jolt passed through Unicorn's body and up his horn into the dragon. She came back to life with a shriek. Rolling off Unicorn, she swung her great head around to snatch down at Blackie with her jaws. Prince George lunged up with the Nail. He thrust his spear into the monster's yellow eye.

The dragon screamed. She threw back her head, dragging the Prince off his feet. He lost his grip on the spear and fell into the beating wings. The dragon wrenched her head back and forth, trying to shake the spear loose. She blasted flames around the pit that flared on the cobwebs and threads of hair stuck to the stony walls.

Knocked away by the screaming dragon, Blackie scrambled to his hooves. He charged under the flames, stabbing his horn again and again into the dragon's neck at the point where it joined the body. The monster writhed, scratching at him with her fore claws as Blackie drove into her, the poisonous blood spraying about him.

Prince George jumped away from the smashing tail. He dropped his shield and whipped around the magic bow as the dragon threw back her head for another strike.

TWANG!

543

The arrow caught her high in the throat and tore through the spine. She shrieked. Her body leaped against the roof of the cavern. It smashed down, the head crashing on the floor beside her nest. The leathery wings flapped a time or two. They folded about her, the claws clutching together.

Blackie charged and stabbed, charged and stabbed, until Prince George caught him about the neck and dragged him to a stop.

"She's dead, Blackie! She's dead! We've done it! We've killed the dragon!"

Blackie fell over, sobbing in his breath. Prince George tried to pull him from the filthy nest, but let go when the dragon's blood smoked on Blackie's hide, breaking out in swelling blisters.

"I must clean . . . clean you off!" panted the Prince. "Rub you down! Fountain water. Where's that gourd?"

Prince George had to tug the spear from the huge dragon head to peer about the den. The light of the Nail showed the gourd crushed under the thick tail. Drops sparkled in the fragments when Prince George swung the spear close to the gourd so he unwound Jessica's scarf from his neck to wipe the cloth over the precious drops of Fountain water. Jumping to Blackie's side, Prince George scrubbed at him with the damp scarf.

"It's not really . . . a skin lotion, but it's the only medicine we have."

The holy water cleared up Blackie's hide as it touched him. Grunting, Prince George crawled around Blackie, rubbing him from tail to ears, finishing with the horn that glowed white as he cleaned. Sobbing, Blackie pushed to his feet with one thought on his mind.

"Papa."

Prince George threw the filthy scarf aside. He stood panting. Since the dragon was still, the arrow glided to him, poking him on the shoulder until he caught it. He kissed it and clapped it back on the bow.

By now, Prince George became aware of the violent shaking of the cave as the mountain blew off its rage. He turned to Blackie, flinching as a section of cave roof slammed down somewhere in the tunnel, blasting a cloud of grit and dust over them. He pulled Blackie's ear to awaken him to the danger.

"Come, Blackie. Over here."

The Prince ran to the side of the cave where the curve of the wall offered protection from roof falls, but Blackie stumbled to his father to rub Unicorn with his horn.

"Papa, Papa," he wept. "It's all my fault! I was a terrible son last summer, running away without a word! If only I could tell you how I love you! How sorry . . . sorry—!"

"Come on, Blackie!" urged the Prince, running out to pull Blackie's mane. "Come over to the side. It's safer. The ceiling's falling in!"

"Foul thing, evil thing!"

Blackie kicked the dragon. "You worm, monster! I'd bring you to life if I could! I'd kill you again and again, a hundred times, a thousand times to make up for my Papa!"

"Blackie, Blackie, what are you doing!"

Ducking a stone crashing down beside him, Prince George followed Blackie who climbed over the dragon's neck to the smoking rear of the nest.

"What is it, old boy?" asked the Prince in alarm.

Blackie looked at him with eyes red from weeping. "The eggs, the eggs! We must smash the dragon's eggs—end this curse forever."

"Yes, yes, the eggs," muttered Prince George, looking around, anxiously. "Mustn't forget the eggs."

He stumbled after Blackie, flashing the spear over the nest as the mountain shuddered around them.

"How big would they be?"

Shivering in disgust as his hooves slipped on human bones, Blackie pushed back one of the dragon's wings with his horn. The wing was surprisingly light.

"Big as . . . as these skulls, I guess."

The Prince stepped over the dragon's tail to stand by Blackie.

"If there are eggs, they must be under the monster. I bet she squashed them herself, rolling around like that."

"We have to make sure they're smashed!" cried Blackie, tossing his horn. "No more dragons! No more dragons to serve Vile!"

"Well, then." The Prince leaned the spear on the dragon's neck. "Let's roll her over, see if she's lying on the eggs."

Blackie pushed up the wing to set his horn against the dragon's side.

"One, two, three," called the Prince. They shoved together. The dragon rocked a little, but wouldn't roll all the way over. Blackie kicked her in exasperation.

"Oh, if I were only an elephant!"

"She's not that heavy," said Prince George, rubbing his chin. "It's just that her wing and shoulder hold her back. If I had Godfrey's axe—"

Shaking his head, Blackie stumbled back to Papa.

"Oh, Papa, I've failed you, failed you again. I can't even smash the eggs."

Sighing, Prince George stood beside Blackie. They looked down at the blackened unicorn. Blackie sucked in a long, choking breath.

"Oh, Georgie, Papa was beautiful, so beautiful. How proud he was of his perfect coat!"

The Prince threw his arm over Blackie. "I remember the first time I saw Unicorn. It was dawn. He was eating watercress in a stream. He shone like a star."

"Look . . . look at him now," sobbed Blackie. "Burnt black, blacker than me. What will Mama say?"

"She'll say he died a hero!" cried the Prince, flashing the spear. "No one's ever heard of a unicorn tracking the dragon to her pit, stabbing her on her own nest! Your father proved himself a true unicorn after all! He'll live in all the songs!"

"But Papa hated heroes," sniffed Blackie. "All he wanted was to be left alone. He loved his quiet life with his berries and mushrooms."

Prince George snapped up the shining spear in salute.

"Valiant Unicorn, you have found your destiny! After your lifelong struggle to hide from your fate, the fighting spirit in your blood came through. You proved a warrior at last, the noblest of your kind!"

Blackie pressed his cheek against Unicorn. "He came here for me! It was all for me!"

"You know, what we have to do next," said the Prince, glancing back up the tunnel where another section had crashed down. "You have to be strong now."

Blinded by tears, Blackie turned away. "You have to do it, Georgie. You do it! I can't . . . I can't even watch."

Prince George shook his head. "No, Blackie, no. You must do it, yourself. I'll set it up for you."

Prince George leaned the spear against the wall. He searched over the floor for a large, round stone to roll above Unicorn's head. Lifting the horn with both hands, he kicked the stone underneath till the tip of the horn rested on the stone.

"It's ready, Blackie. I think you should do it."

"No, no!" cried Blackie, swinging his head away. "I can't! I can't! It's too much! Papa's perfect horn! He was so proud it was perfect, no scars, no scratches!"

"Just face it, Blackie," said the Prince in a soothing voice. "You're his son. You'll be glad, later on, that you did it."

Blackie shook his head wildly. "I can't do it! I can't! I can't! Not to Papa! You'll have to do it!"

"Are you sure?"

"Please, please."

Sobbing, Blackie turned away as Prince George took a deep breath. He stood beside Unicorn, head bowed, hands folded.

"Beloved Unicorn," he said, "we have no oil to annoint you for the final blessing. We can only pray that the mercy of God will include his holy beast in his loving salvation. *Kyrie, Kyrie eleison.*"

He bent his knees. Blackie shivered, his ears high, as the Prince crossed himself. He jumped with all his weight on the base of Unicorn's horn.

CRACK!

Blackie yelped when the horn snapped off. Prince George stumbled back. He caught himself and bent to pick up the horn. He shouldered it with a sigh. He picked up his shield and spear. He stepped to Blackie.

"It is finished. Let's go, Blackie. If we can find our way out of this pit, we'll carry this horn to rest with your ancestors in the Fountain."

Prince George limped into the turn of the tunnel. Blackie stepped after him, turning his head back to look at Unicorn darkening as the spear light moved away.

"Oh, Papa!"

CHAPTER FORTY

Escaping Vile

Blackie stumbled against the wall as he lost sight of Unicorn in the darkening tunnel. Prince George turned to him with a cry.

"Oh, Blackie, I'm sorry, so sorry! I know what you've lost. My father—I never knew him. I always, always—"

"I have to go back, see Papa again!" screeched Blackie. "What if we're wrong? What if he's still alive? What if we've—"

The Prince dropped the spear. He turned to hug Blackie.

"He's gone, Blackie! He's gone! You know that your horn would have brought him around if . . . if—We have to go on now. Think of our duty to the Princess and . . . and your Mama. We can't stay in this tunnel. The mountain will bury us. We've got to get out of Vile."

Blackie sobbed blindly as Prince George caught up his spear and hurried on. Blackie staggered after the light, barely noticing the noise and dust raised by sections dropping from the ceiling as the mountain quaked again. He couldn't keep his eyes off the broken horn on George's shoulder. The hollow inside winked white against the shadows as the spear swung back and forth with the rocky footing of the tunnel.

It was the gravel rolling under his hooves that drew Blackie's attention to the cracks in the ceiling. They showed the danger of imminent falls. For the moment at least, the mountain seemed to have roared itself out, but Blackie heard stone crash down in the tunnel behind them.

Prince George stepped over chunks knocked from a knee-high slab filling most of the passage. "I don't know how we'll get out of this pit. It was dumb not to plan our escape before we jumped down here."

Blackie clambered automatically through the stones. His tired mind was worrying over what he'd say to Mama if they ever made it out of Vile.

Should he tell her what the Prince had said, that Papa died a hero? That wouldn't cheer her through lonely winter nights without her mate. Who'd keep her warm in the nest? Who'd she talk to? Who'd she care for? Of course, if she were a grandmother—

"No, no!"

He shivered at that idea. What was he thinking? Surely, there had to be female unicorns somewhere. Someday, he supposed, he'd run across a pretty young beast with a pink horn and hooves, but he wasn't ready for that. Not for a long time, a long, long time.

He didn't need that sort of thing now that Prince George could talk to him. He had a friend to talk with, to run with, to explore with. Why, he'd never seen the City! He'd never smelled the sea! And his Princess, how little time he had actually spent with her! Really, he'd only been with her a day or two, now and then.

When he thought about it, all he'd done this past year was trot back and forth across the Empire with Prince George. It had been exciting at first, and his adventures had forced him to grow up early, to mature. His horn was longer than Papa's, but—

That thought yanked him back to the tunnel, back to the pitiful horn on George's shoulder. He saw the Prince place the horn down on the shield set on a block from the tower. The Nail faded slightly as the Prince looked up the rubble to the light from the tunnel opening above.

"Hey, Blackie, looks like the mountain shook down enough stones for us to climb out with no problem. This'd be a great place for an ambush, though. If I know Prince Vile, he'll jump us at some point. Bring your nose over here. Take a whiff. Do you smell any Hellions or Hounds up there?"

Wearily, Blackie stepped forward. He lifted his front hooves onto a block and stretched up his nose to sniff. The stench of dragon blood was too strong in the pit. It covered other smells.

Blackie shook his head. "Sorry, Georgie, I can't tell. My nose doesn't work here."

"That's all right," shrugged the Prince. "I'll use the arrow."

He placed the spear over the horn on his shield. When he took up the bow, the arrow dropped in his hand.

"This time, Arrow, I want you to scout around out there. Run off any villains you find. If you happen to come across a raven called Crepitar, pin his wings back and drag him down to me, okay?"

The arrow shook its agreement. Prince George snapped the shot through the hole in the ceiling. He sat down on another block to await its return.

"You know, Blackie, I think our luck has changed at last. This erupting mountain has shaken Vile's kingdom to its base. He won't be able to organize his armies to chase us. He probably doesn't even know that we've killed his dragon. And the Hounds, I'm sure they've fled to the farthest hills. This is our chance to escape."

Blackie closed his eyes. His horn drooped as waves of fatigue swept over him. He sighed and relaxed, then it seemed the Prince was shaking him again.

"Wake up, Blackie, the arrow's back."

"I had a dream," whispered Blackie, remembering a deep voice from his slumbers. "This was the second time I dreamed it. It was Saint Peter trying to save his mother from Hell. Let me tell you my dream before I forget it."

"Tell me once we're out of here," said the Prince, shooting the arrow back out the hole to guard their escape. "We can't dally here. I've had too much of this pit already."

Blackie was so tired that Prince George had to help him scramble up the stones. The Prince left the horn and the weapons on the shield while he directed Blackie's footing upward and tried to hold him when he slipped.

"By my boots," he gasped, shouldering Blackie's weight when a gob of mortar broke away under a hoof, "you're heavy, Blackie."

Blackie rested on the Prince a moment, then caught his footing again. Straining his front shoulders, he lurched ahead, pushing against a block with a rear hoof, taking a quick step with the other to support himself. The distance wasn't far, but Blackie was reminded again that his long body was not made to scale stairs or rock heaps.

"Hold on," whispered Prince George just below the surface. "Let me look around before we get out."

Blackie slumped against the blocks while the Prince climbed into the light. A moment later, he crawled back to urge Blackie upward.

"Just a few more feet, Blackie. The arrow's keeping watch. Be careful, though. We've got loose stuff up there, still hot."

Prince George tried to pick secure footholds for the rest of Blackie's climb, pushing shifting stones out of the way and placing Blackie's rear hooves with his hands.

"Up now," he gasped, shoving Blackie's rear when a loose chunk rolled under him. "Reach out, don't kick! Ow, ow!"

"Sorry," grunted Blackie, flailing with a hoof until it caught hold. He tried to be careful with Prince George pushing from behind, but felt a naughty pleasure when his hoof landed on a boot. He knew it wasn't fair, but somehow he blamed Prince George for this awkward climb.

Another heave and his horn popped out into sunlight. The mountain was quiet. Only a wisp of vapor floated from the cone though a layer of fumes hung over the ash and rock covering the land. Blackie crawled out through the ruins of the tower, a few blocks still in place running halfway around the pit. He stood panting until the Prince scrambled up, his arms full of weapons and Papa's horn.

Prince George pointed the spear around the smoking countryside. "See, still dreadful."

The smoke caught him. He doubled up coughing until Blackie touched him with his horn. "Sorry."

Prince George wiped his eyes and pointed again. "This whole area's covered with pumice. And look there—you can see that the mountain was really after us. If she hadn't blown herself out when she did, that lava would have covered the tower ten feet deep."

Blackie looked in alarm at the hissing flow of gloppy gunk hardening into ropy gray shapes a hundred yards above them. A wave of fumes blew down, covering the view, setting the Prince to choking again.

"We gotta get out of this!" gasped Blackie. "Mount up, Georgie! Mount up!"

Prince George scooped up his shield and the horn. He stepped onto a blistering boulder to jump onto Blackie. "Hot, hot!" he screeched. "Oh, my burning boots and ankles, I can't stand these fireballs!"

The scorching ashes woke Blackie to their danger. He took off the instant Prince George was settled on his back, trotting south through fiery cinders and smoking boulders. His hooves felt aflame in a few steps. Prince George swung down the Nail to numb them as Blackie jogged heavily along.

They soon left the worst of the debris though smoke and ash followed across the plain. It settled into their hair and hide until Blackie felt that he carried a layer of Vile on him as he ran. He was especially conscious of Papa's long horn rocking back and forth across his shoulders with each step.

A dozen times, Prince George reached down to grasp Blackie's horn for healing jolts before his lungs felt clear to breathe freely. In an hour, they had run far enough that the cinders had cooled on the matted surface. Blackie's fatigue had worn him down. He demanded a break.

"I don't care if . . . every Hound . . . from Vile's kennel is . . . is after us, Georgie, I've got to rest."

"Of course, old boy," said the Prince, dropping down to rub Blackie's head. "We're out of the worst of it. Take a nap while I run the spear over your legs. Think we have time for me to send the arrow after more Fountain water?"

"I don't care what you doooo," yawned Blackie. "Wake me in a week."

Blackie locked his knees and closed his eyes. He dropped into a mindless daze as Prince George shot the arrow after more water.

"Don't go all the way to the Fountain," he told the arrow. "Just bring a cool drink as quickly as possible."

While he waited, Prince George wiped ashes off Blackie with his filthy shirt, the last fabric he possessed. The Prince pulled his gritty shirt back on and sat down on the rigid metal of the shield, the horn and spear in his lap. He was the one who dropped into a miserable sleep, shivering in the chill until the returning arrow slapped a wet waterbag against his face.

Prince George's idea of a rest was unsatisfactory to Blackie. It seemed as though he'd only relaxed a second before the Prince was shaking him.

"Wake up, Blackie. Here's water. We have to keep moving. This place is too exposed."

Blackie raised his head, blinking. His neck hurt. He swung his head from side to side to shake out the kinks while Prince George sawed a wide slit in the top of the bag with his dagger. He held it open for Blackie to drink.

"Hurry, Blackie. Drink up. Drink up."

"What's the hurry?" groaned Blackie, looking around. The mountain smoked lightly under the sun. Nothing moved on the plain as far as he could see.

Prince George followed his gaze, shivering.

"I'm not easy here. I don't like this plain. Dry as it was in the western desert, there were dips and riverbeds to hide in. Here, there's no place of concealment."

"For Heaven's sake," muttered Blackie, stretching his shoulders, "who do we have to hide from? We've just killed a dragon!"

"Don't argue, Blackie," urged the Prince. "Take your drink."

Shrugging, Blackie lowered his nose into the waterbag and drank deeply. The water tasted of leather, but it eased his thirst a bit. To really satisfy him, it'd take a dozen bags.

Lifting his dripping nose, he said, "Georgie, I want to tell you about my dream."

"Tell me later."

Prince George swung the bow over one shoulder and the strap of the waterbag over the other. He slung the shield on top of the bag and balanced the horn on Blackie's shoulders while he mounted and took up the spear.

"I'm overloaded with this stuff," he complained. "If you had a saddle, Blackie, I could tie it on."

"No saddle," said Blackie, quivering at the touch of the horn against his hide. He stood quietly until the Prince was settled, then trotted off toward the mountains to the south.

Blackie kept up a steady pace as the afternoon passed. In an hour or so, he was out of the cinders from the mountain. He trotted, half-asleep, among the rocks, wiry plants, and scattered potholes of the broad flatlands.

Prince George snored heavily on his neck until Blackie leaped aside at a bird flitting up under his hooves. Grabbing for the mane, the Prince rolled off into a low-spreading thorn bush. He pulled free with a cry.

"Hey, Blackie, watch it! Don't drop me like that!"

"I didn't mean to," croaked Blackie. "Something flew up at me."

Prince George brushed blood from the scratches on his arms. "No damage done, old pal. You can heal me again. How you doing?"

Blackie healed the scratches, then the Prince picked up the horn and spear. He looked back at the mountain to judge how far they'd traveled.

"Surely, we've gone further than this. How long did I sleep?"

"It was hard going back there," protested Blackie, kicking a tiny white flower. "And there's nothing to eat here. I'm tired. I'm hungry. I haven't had a meal since Darr."

"Well, I haven't eaten either," muttered the Prince, "but I don't crab about it."

"No, you sleep like a slug. You snore in my ear while I have to keep running."

Prince George set the horn back on Blackie. "Oh, Blackie, let's not quarrel. This place is bad enough without snapping at each other."

Blackie quieted while Prince George climbed on. Blackie felt like throwing him off again, but that wouldn't make anything better.

"Once again," he grumbled, "once again, it's me has to be the good guy. Carry this, carry that, carry everything for everyone."

Sure enough, Prince George dropped to sleep as soon as Blackie trotted on. At least, the earth smoothed out here, so moving was easier. Blackie fell into a steady shuffle while he dozed. A word slipped into his mind as he trotted, a name, echoing the rhythm of his hooves. He didn't recognize it for a time. When he did, he blinked awake in the declining sun.

"Lizetta, Lizetta, Lizetta."

That brought him to a shivering, sweating stop. Prince George sat up, clutching his spear. He looked in alarm to both sides.

"What is it, the Hounds? Where are we?"

"I just remembered," said Blackie, kicking cinders from his rear hooves. "Lizetta! What about the Gypsy? Aren't we supposed to rescue her while we're here?"

"Is that what you woke me for?" demanded Prince George. "Lizetta?"

"Of course," Blackie nodded. "Didn't we promise Lazlo that we'd rescue her?"

Prince George yawned and shifted his weight.

"Oh, Blackie, we didn't actually promise to rescue Lizetta. I told Lazlo that we'd try to bring the Gypsy back if we happened to run across her. But we didn't see her, did we? We couldn't rescue her."

"Oh, well," Blackie said, not totally convinced. "Somehow, I thought—"

Prince George snorted. "You thought that we'd hang around for Lizetta? Maybe attack Vile's castle and stir up the mountain again, not to mention the Hellions and all those guards? That'd be madness! Didn't you get your fill of adventure from the dragon?"

"I guess so," said Blackie, trotting on with a sigh. "I hate to think of Gypsies in chains, the freest people of the Empire trapped in Vile's slave pens. It seems wrong!"

Prince George slapped Blackie lightly on the neck. "Sure, it's sad for Gypsies to be caged up, but think how quiet the Empire would be without them. Hens would sleep in peace on their roosts, horses in the fields. I told you of the time Lazlo hid those spotted ponies from me. That got me in all kinds of trouble. And you know the Gypsies' song."

> Every man's horses
> as good as our own.

"I don't care," mumbled Blackie. "It's sad to me, humans caged up like that. Even goats hate to be cooped up, and pigs. I don't like to see pig pens."

"Well, I don't want to see swine running loose in the streets!" exclaimed Prince George. "What a mess that'd make! After the tussles I've had with wild hogs, I'd pen them all. A boar threw me into a thorn bush as big as a haystack!"

Prince George grew silent. He fell asleep again as Blackie stumbled along at a steady pace, barely conscious of the chilling wind. Far to the west, the sun was sinking in a greenish glow from the haze that stung Blackie's tired eyes.

Prince George didn't agree to a rest until Blackie grew so weary that he had dropped the man twice. The sun was low and the Nail starting to shine. Prince George had to cover it with the empty waterbag.

"I'm thirsty," croaked Blackie, "and hungry. Why don't you shoot the arrow after more supplies?"

"I would," said the Prince, looking nervously across the dusky plain, "but I want to keep the arrow close at hand. Even if Prince Vile doesn't know about the dragon, the Hounds could be out, or the border patrols. I don't want to face spearmen without the arrow."

Blackie scoffed, "Who's afraid of spearmen? We've killed a dragon!"

Prince George curled up on the ground for a sleep while Blackie stretched his muscles and tried to relax. His empty stomach cried for attention. He could smell tasty stems when he lowered his nose to earth, but the mat was too short to graze on. Listening to Prince George cough in his sleep, Blackie bit off a few strands.

The sun disappeared in a florid burst of crimson and gray that faded into a steely glow in the chill northern air. Hearing a strangled cry behind him, Blackie lifted his head. His tired eyes twitched at the darkness beyond his vision. He perked up his ears to listen, but heard only the sigh of the wind brushing the stubby stems of the field.

He took a step closer to Prince George, reached his nose down to smell the horn in the Prince's arms, and shivered at a thought. Someday, his own horn would be snapped off like Papa's. Would he have a friend to carry it to the Fountain? Would his horn lie broken in a glen somewhere, lost and forgotten?

"Does it matter?" he wondered. "If I've fought my foes and served my Princess, I can sleep peacefully when my time comes. Poor Papa would rest as well with his horn in the pit as he will with it in the Fountain. I suppose we carry it to the Shrine as our offering to the Lord."

Prince George snored through the pale northern night, but Blackie couldn't quiet his mind to sleep. His empty belly wakened worries and regrets to keep him starting at every bird cry and whimper from the Prince. He was awake when Prince George sat up just before dawn.

The Prince reached up for Blackie. "What's the matter, boy? Didn't you sleep?"

"How could I sleep?" snapped Blackie. "Someone had to stand guard with those Hellhounds around. You flattened out like you were knocked in the head."

"I'd have wakened if anything stirred," said the Prince, running fingers through his hair. "I sleep light as a feather. No one could have crept up on me."

He jumped up and stretched. "Oh, I'm staaarved," he yawned. "Who's cooking breakfast today? I'll take eggs and sausages, plus strawberries and a honeybun or three."

"Very funny," snorted Blackie. He shook his head in disgust. He didn't want to hear jokes about food. He didn't feel like carrying anyone either, but he stood for Prince George to climb on.

"Why don't you shoot your stupid arrow for rations?" he muttered.

"I don't think that's necessary," said the Prince, lightheartedly. "Something tells me we're going to be lucky today. With the saints watching over and the Nail on my spear, we're sure to be blessed. And look, you can still talk. I was afraid you'd lose your speech when we climbed out of that pit."

Blackie didn't bother to reply. If the Prince wanted to think it was Blackie who'd changed, he'd leave him to his folly. Blackie bumped along wearily, rocking the Prince George back and forth as the sun burst forth in the east when they neared the border mountains.

At least, the wind was cleaner here with the smoke dispersed and the gritty ash behind them. Blackie had grown so used to the stink that the odor of a flower startled him into stopping.

"Maybe I will send out the arrow after all," said the Prince, waking from his sleep.

"About time," grumbled Blackie.

Prince George jumped to the ground and swung up the bow. He set the arrow to the string.

"This time, Arrow, fly through the passes to Darr and catch up a big bucket of fresh milk. Bring it back without spilling a drop."

He snapped off the shot, watching carefully as the arrow swerved slightly and zoomed out of sight.

"Did you see that?" he pointed. "We've been drifting off our path. We have to angle to the right."

"Good idea about the milk," said Blackie, nodding approval. "That'll refresh us like nothing else."

Prince George leaned on the spear, digging a finger into a hole in his shirt.

"You know, Blackie, the Princess has no idea of the powers of this arrow. She uses it as a see-and-shoot weapon. It's much more useful than that. It's a seeker, a hunter. If I told the arrow to fly back to Prince Vile, I bet it'd hunt him down and stab him in the butt."

Trying to follow that idea, Blackie lifted his weary head. "Do you think that if you'd told the arrow to kill the dragon, it could have saved us all this trouble?"

Prince George stretched his arms, yawning again. "Well, the dragon, I don't know. That's a big job for an arrow. I can see it pestering the monster, stabbing her here and there, but she'd probably burn it up with her breath. The Princess would never forgive me for that."

"Now, that the dragon's gone," suggested Blackie, "we could send the arrow to break all the dragon eggs. It could finish the serpents forever."

Prince George scratched his head.

"Oh, I don't know if we should go that far. Wiping out dragons completely—that's extreme. I'd have to talk to the Bishop about it or the Wizard or someone. Evil as they are, the Lord must have made dragons for some purpose. I don't know if we should try to change that."

"Squash 'em in the shell!" gritted Blackie. "Then we wouldn't have to, you know—"

He pointed a hoof at Unicorn's horn, lying on Prince George's shield.

"I know," said Prince George, patting Blackie's head, "I know. Look, here comes the milk—from the same direction, too."

The arrow eased to a stop before Prince George, the bucket swinging to a halt on the shaft. The Prince carefully lifted the bucket from the arrow and took a long drink. Smacking his lips, he set down the bucket before Blackie.

"Goat's milk, excellent! Good work, Arrow. Are you ready to go after a loaf of bread?"

The arrow bobbed excitedly in the air. Prince George waved it off, and it sailed away.

"Look, I don't even have to shoot it from the bow," he said. "I'll bet I can leave it free like a falcon. It'll fly around to guard us and provide for us. I wonder if it's strong enough to carry a man. I could hang a basket on it, or a washtub, and have it fly me through the air like Pegasus."

Blackie lifted his muzzle from the bucket. "Well, don't spoil the thing for the Princess. What if it gets to like flying free? It might go wild and sail away. Who knows? It might join up with Prince Vile or the bandits."

"Oh, Blackie," said the Prince, confidently, "this arrow's not going to do anything like that. It has to obey its master, I'm sure."

"That may be so," said Blackie, wearily, "but who is its master? We know that the Princess found the bow at Castle Thorn, but who made the thing? Who left it there? Is there a magician out there who can whistle the arrow down and turn it against us? We don't know anything about it."

"You worry too much," said the Prince, turning over the bucket for a step-up to mount Blackie. "Let's go."

"What about the arrow?"

"It'll find us as we ride."

Blackie's pace was smoother after drinking his milk. His body was tired, his eyes scratchy and sore, but his legs fell into his usual easy gait. Soon, as Prince George had promised, the arrow flew back to them stuck through a large loaf of crunchy brown bread.

"See," laughed the Prince, reaching down to stuff a chunk of bread into the side of Blackie's mouth, "I told you we could trust the arrow."

Blackie chewed the bread without breaking stride.

"Maybe you can trust the arrow," he thought, "but where does this bread come from? What if the arrow's swooping down and stealing bread from a poor family. We don't even know who we're robbing. That's no better than Lizetta looting hen houses. Of course, Papa—"

His mind flashed again back to Unicorn, blackened and bloody beside the dragon. His body shook with a cry.

"Oh, Papa!"

Prince George leaned down to hug his neck. "It's all right, Blackie. We'll get the Bishop to offer Masses for Unicorn. The monks at the Shrine will send up prayers forever."

"If only I could have spoken to him," groaned Blackie. "I had so much to tell him."

"Don't worry about Unicorn," said the Prince, patting Blackie's shoulder. "He knows, I'm sure he knows. Think of him feasting at the Lord's table, sending blessings down to us like a saint."

"The Lord's table," sniffed Blackie. "He'd eat the fruit of Paradise, better even than the pineapple at the Shrine. That'd suit Papa all right."

He sighed and peered at the land he was crossing. It was getting rough as they neared the border. Through the morning light, he saw the land slanting up with bright peaks ahead and shadows between them.

Prince George squinted his eyes to scan from left to right.

"We've got to be careful to find the proper trail. If we don't watch out, we could get lost in these ravines. I'll call the arrow back to guide us."

"I could sniff out a trail," offered Blackie, "if that's what we want."

"The arrow will be more direct. It'll save us time."

The Prince waved the spear through the air. In moments, the arrow sped down to float backward over Blackie's horn.

"Take us to the nearest pass across the border," commanded the Prince.

"No, no," Blackie corrected, "the safest pass. We want the safest pass."

"Right, the nearest and safest pass."

Prince George waved the arrow away. It shot out of sight over the ridges, returning with swoops and darts a few minutes later to steer them up a stony way between craggy knolls. Blackie walked slowly, setting his hooves carefully in the rocks, conserving his breath for the climb. Shortly, they turned downward, twisting along a dry stream bed. Blackie smelled snakes there, though he didn't see any.

The arrow was always in motion, speeding out of sight around turns, zooming back to float beside the Prince where he could praise it and stroke its feathers with a finger before it took off again. Lumbering along, Blackie grew annoyed at the thing, so proud of its flight and freedom.

"After all," he thought, "it's only an old stick."

Deep in the hills, the arrow guided them to a trail filled with the smells of travelers. Even Prince George sensed the smoothness of the footing.

"Now, we're getting somewhere!" he cried. "This'll take us back over the border. We'll join the road back to Darr in no time."

Tired as he was, Blackie didn't say anything, but his ears were up and his tail swished back and forth. He felt nervous, trotting between mounting rock walls. Anyone could ambush them here. Vile's guards, hiding in the hills, could roll rocks down to crush them like turtles. It didn't help that Prince George roared a manic laugh.

"Push on, Blackie, push on! If we hurry, we'll reach Castle March by evening. I want a good supper and a bed. And a bath! I swear, I'll scrub myself clean with a horse brush the first chance I get. The stink of Vile, it soaks into you, doesn't it? Leaves you tasting filth with each breath. I haven't smelled anything sweet since Dorinda's perfume back at Croy, that Purple Honesty. I want to smell that again."

Blackie scarcely heard the Prince babbling upon him. Blackie's head was high, his ears stiff. Down the trail ahead of them, he heard shouts and—What was that? Weeping? Singing? Whatever it was, Blackie was sure that it meant trouble.

CHAPTER FORTY-ONE

Storming the Border

"What's that noise?" whispered Prince George as the clamor ahead grew louder.

Blackie dumbly shook his head. Whatever it was, he was too tired to care. He'd stumbled along this last hour like an old mare in a mill, his hooves aching, muscles twitching with fatigue. It was a wonder he could move at all.

"Well, we don't have to worry," rasped the Prince. "The arrow won't lead us into danger."

"That arrow—" thought Blackie, sourly. "Sure, sure, trust our lives to that twig."

He dropped his head, breathing heavily while Prince George cupped a hand to his ear to listen. The Prince slid to ground.

"We don't want to run into another ambush, Blackie. Let me slip ahead to check it out. You wait here, old fellow."

Blackie braced his legs to hold himself up. He closed his eyes, swaying slightly as a meadow floated into his mind, a field of dewy green grass and purple-headed clover humming with bumblebees.

"Ow!"

Something stung Blackie—a bumblebee? He opened his eyes. No, it wasn't a bee. That arrow was poking him in the rump. It backed away a couple inches and poked him again.

"Stop that!" snapped Blackie.

The arrow zoomed around him, bouncing in the air. Blackie stared dully as it jerked forward, the shaft bending to look back at him with its arrowhead.

"Stupid thing wants me to follow," he mumbled. He closed his eyes again.

Next thing he knew, he was backing away from a horde of grinning skeletons, thin, glassy-eyed humans with sharp fingers that poked his hide, plucked his mane, pulled his horn. They flooded around, sweaty and urgent, forcing him forward.

"Hurry on, Unicorn! Hurry, hurry! Bless your heart, we been waitin' and waitin' for you. We need you. That Prince feller says for you to hurry on."

Blackie was carried down the trail by the pressure, the humans reaching to touch him while yelping at him from all sides. He caught scattered words.

"Beatin' . . . starvin' . . . crawlin' . . . waitin' . . . blessed Unicorn!"

Blackie bleated at them to stand back, to let him breathe, but they didn't understand. They squeezed him along like a sausage in its casing, his hooves barely touching the path until he was thrown into a wide gorge packed up both rocky sides with humans talking and weeping and moaning, deafening Blackie by their din. The only thing he could think of was his dream of Saint Peter.

They pulled back when Prince George shoved through to grab Blackie by his horn and hold him a moment until he could support himself.

"Back off!" cried the Prince. "Leave him alone! Let him catch his breath!"

"We love the unicorn!" cried the humans. "He'll save us!"

Ears down, tail limp, Blackie wobbled on his hooves, overwhelmed by the noise and the urgency of the crowd. Prince George knelt before him, gazing into his face.

"Blackie, you've got to pull yourself together! We're stuck here at the border. Vile's guards hold us up on this side of the line, the Darrmen stop us on the other. One bunch won't let us out, the other won't let us in. We've got to break through before the Hellions catch up."

"Who—" gasped Blackie, catching a breath, "who are these wretches?"

"We're fugitives," said a familiar voice, "prisoners of Vile. We escaped when the mountain erupted."

Blackie lifted his head with an effort. He gasped.

A girl stood there clutching Prince George's spear. She wasn't shriveled and scrawny like the other humans. Oh, no, Lizetta bloomed like a blossom. Her arms were round, her cheeks rosy, her eyes bright. She wore bright scarves and a golden gown. Her ears, neck, and arms sparkled with jewels. The only dilapidated thing about her was her sandals. They looked as worn and battered as Prince George's boots.

"Don't worry, sweet unicorn," she cooed. "If you're weary, Lizetta can revive you."

She leaned to scratch Blackie's nose with ringed fingers. Her perfume came to him over the stink of the humans, heavy and hypnotic.

"I have just the medicines for you."

Blackie looked at Prince George with alarm. "What does she mean, medicines? What's she doing here, anyway?"

Prince George shrugged. "Somehow Lizetta organized the slaves to break out during the eruption. She claims that she has drugs to help us break through."

Lizetta's gleaming eyes went back and forth from Blackie to the Prince as Blackie looked suspiciously at the bracelets on her arms.

"She's been in a slave pen? She doesn't look like a prisoner to me."

"What's he saying, Princey?" demanded Lizetta.

Prince George gave her a tired smile. "He doesn't believe you've been in a slave pen, you know, your jewels and all."

"No, no, not me," she said airily, waving crimson-tipped fingers, "never in a pen. The Prince does have his favorites, you know. I was a slave, all right, but I lived in the palace. That's where I stole the poison to remove the warders and get the keys to open the gates for these people."

Blackie was skeptical of that story. "And we're supposed to believe that Prince Vile let her get away with that?"

Lizetta spread her hands with a sigh.

"Is not the truth the truth? When the mountain erupted, Prince Vile ran up to the tower to ring the bell for the dragon. A flying rock knocked him out. His guards were frozen until he recovered, terrified they'd do something wrong. No one moves in Vile, you know, without permission. By now, though, I'm sure that he's recovered, recovered enough to send hundreds of Hellions after us riding great, hungry Hellhounds."

"So you see, Blackie!" broke in the Prince. "With the Hellhounds on our tracks, we have only a few minutes to break through the border to save ourselves."

"How do you . . . know all this?" panted Blackie, closing his eyes. "Perhaps Vile was . . . killed by the rock. Maybe nobody's after us."

"Why, Crepitar," said Lizetta, "the raven told me."

Blackie's eyes popped open again. "Crepitar? Not that devil bird?"

"Oh," said Lizetta, smiling at the Prince, "I've reformed Crepitar. When the mountain erupted, he flew to me with smoking feathers. Now, he spies for me. All he needed was someone that understood him."

Peering behind Lizetta, Blackie saw a sturdy slave holding a black bird on his shoulder. Crepitar flirted his feathers and croaked, "Sweet bird, sweet bird! Crepitar loves Lizetta!"

"We don't have time to talk, Blackie!" cried the Prince, "we've got to charge through these guards and bring these people to safety."

Blackie closed his eyes in fatigue. "Not me, I couldn't . . . couldn't charge through . . . through a spider web."

Lizetta nodded when Prince George explained Blackie's condition.

"Of course, he's tired, poor beast," she smiled. "Don't worry, sweet Prince. Didn't I bring Prince Vile's drug chest with me? That's what Vile's mainly after, I suspect. He won't be able to keep going without his precious medicines to pick him up in the morning and put him down at night. And his poisons—I have them all, the sudden toxins, the sickening venoms. I have a whole range of pepping potions for this unicorn too. I'll select the perfect dose to stimulate him without wearing him down."

She gave the Prince's spear to the man holding Crepitar and took a leather case from another slave.

"Not me!" Blackie protested, a bit of life returning to him at the sight of Lizetta leaning over the box of drugs, humming as she pulled out bottles and boxes. "I'm not taking anything from that Gypsy! And you, Georgie, don't you take anything, either. She'll turn you into a love slave and ride you like a donkey."

"Don't worry!" cried Prince George, taking Blackie's head in his hands. "We can trust Lizetta. She's changed! Look how she helped these people escape. Why, she's a hero herself, leading them across this wide tableland. She wouldn't poison you now, so close to freedom."

"No, no."

Blackie clamped his lips when Lizetta leaned close with a silver spoon.

"Well," she said, lowering the spoon and stroking his forehead with her free hand, "if he doesn't want it— But the poor unicorn is dry, that's his problem. I can feel it on his skin. How can we expect him to help us when he's so thirsty? We must give him water, smuggled across the border. A drink will refresh him."

Blackie watched suspiciously as Lizetta made a great show of pouring the drug back in the little bottle and corking it up. When the water was carried to her, she knelt to hold the bucket in her own hands while Blackie plunged in his muzzle to suck down long, refreshing drafts of cool water.

The effect of the drink was startling. Blackie felt the hair stiffen on his back. Nervous energy coursed through his body. His eyesight sharpened, the pain in his hooves was gone. Far from feeling tired, he felt jittery and excited. Rest was the last thing he needed.

He pranced back and forth, flicking his tail, swinging his head around as though trying to shake off flies. When Prince George spoke to him, the sound was hollow, as though echoing through the bucket.

"Do you feel better, Blackie? Do you feel like helping these people cross the border?"

"After that drink, he'll do whatever I tell him to," said the Gypsy, dropping a kiss on Blackie's horn. "Come along now, sweet unicorn. Obey your mistress. We're going to cross the border."

Crossing the border—that was exactly what Blackie wanted to do. This place, so dry and rocky, he didn't like this place. It was boring. There was nothing to eat here, no grass, no clover, no nothing. He wasn't going to stay here, but where was he going? He tried to remember. Oh, yes, Lizetta reminded him. Darr! She spoke of the green hills of Darr, the grass and leaves, the bushes and flowers of Darr.

Of course, he was going to Darr. That's where Lizetta was going, so he'd go there too. And these humans, they were going with him. He'd save them from slavery if he took them to Darr.

He looked around with affection. The humans crowded about him, admiring him, cheering him. They loved him. And Lizetta was petting him, calling him "sweet unicorn."

This Gypsy, she wasn't so bad. All she wanted was a little freedom. Suddenly, it was important that Lizetta should get what she wanted.

"Save Lizetta!"

The notion echoed in his ears. He had to save Lizetta, sweet, generous Lizetta. Hadn't she given him the water that pepped him up like this?

He couldn't stand here doing nothing. He had to move. He had to act. Who were these border guards to hold him back? How dare they stop him from getting to Darr? He had friends in Darr—Godfrey, Dorinda. Godfrey would throw him a party, serve him apples and oats, carrots and cakes.

"I'm the unicorn," he said, shaking his body, "the black unicorn, and I'm going to Darr!"

"He'll do it!" cried Prince George, watching Blackie closely. "He'll break through to Darr!"

"Of course, he will," laughed Lizetta. "He's revived, sharpened up. He'll do whatever Lizetta tells him to do."

Blackie straightened. He threw up his head while Prince George climbed on his back.

"Give me my spear!" cried the Prince.

Lizetta hesitated, but handed the spear to the Prince. He shook it fiercely. He called to the arrow circling slowly above, "Scout ahead for us, Arrow! Fly back to warn me when we near the border."

The arrow nodded happily and sailed out of sight through the twisting rock walls. Blackie trotted through the humans. They waved and croaked blessings to him as he passed.

"Slow down, sweet Prince!" called Lizetta. "I'm calling up my bruisers to help, the slaves from the mills and mines. They've brought their sledges and crowbars, good as any weapons. We'll break out of here with ease."

Blackie didn't want to slow down. He cantered along, singing a little song to himself.

Trotting to Darr,
Trotting to Darr,
Trotting to Darr with Lizetta.

Lizetta called for him again to slow down. She was riding a little white donkey that clattered over the rocks while a stream of husky brutes marched behind her. Scarred and toughened from toiling in the slave pens, they looked like they'd welcome a chance to hammer on Hellions.

By now, Blackie had passed through the slaves. The gorge ahead widened into a valley with a sandy stream bed. Patches of green grew up the lower walls. His mind on the apples of Darr, Blackie trotted under a moon that rose in the smokeless sky, barely aware of the men following with their tools. They sang as they marched.

> Workin' for the man in the mornin',
> workin' for the man at night.
> You take a breath for a moment—
> you feel the horsewhip bite.

> Workin' for the man when you're weary,
> workin' for the man when you're worn.
> You hate the job you're workin'—
> you curse the day you're born.

> Workin' for the man when it's sunny,
> workin' for the man when it's cold.
> You toil away your childhood—
> you drop before you're old.

The arrow swished back, shivering with excitement, bouncing up and down when Prince George questioned it.

"Just ahead, are they? Lots of 'em? Any bowmen hiding in the rocks to ambush us?"

Blackie stepped around, swinging his tail. He was frantic to charge ahead and smash anyone that tried to stop him, but Prince George held him back.

"Hold still, Blackie! There's time enough to crush our enemies. We have to set the battle order to break through. Arrow, come here."

He gripped the arrow by the stem and spoke to its head.

"Now, listen, Arrow. Your job is to rip into those archers in the hills. Stick 'em and stab 'em, toss 'em down onto the spearmen below. That'll soften 'em up before we charge, got it?"

The arrow arched around his wrist in its eagerness to be off. Prince George threw it up with a cry, "To work now! Jab and stab for Saint Michael!"

The arrow shot away, and Prince George swung Blackie around, calling to Lizetta. "Bring up your bullyboys, your hewers and haulers! Here's their chance to pay the slavers back for all the whips and chains!"

Growling, the bruisers scrambled before him with their tools. They looked as hungry as wolves sniffing a flock of sheep.

"Men," cried the Prince, waving the spear in the air, "men, we have work to do! We're on the verge of freedom. You can smell clean air a mile away. Only one barrier remains, the border! These fools think they can hold us back! Will that stop us?"

"Never, never!" cried the slaves, clashing their tools together.

Blackie rose in the air, trumpeting. Prince George clung to his neck, shouting, "Follow, men, follow! Capture those who submit! Knock down anyone that fights!"

"We'll handle 'em!" cried the slaves. They clashed their tools together.

"We'll bing 'em and bang 'em!"

"Hack 'em and hammer 'em!"

"Pitch 'em and pound 'em!"

"Let's go, Blackie!" cried Prince George, pointing with the spear.

Blackie whirled so quickly he almost threw off the Prince.

"Hold up!" yelled Prince George. "Let me set my shield!"

"What's come over me?" thought Blackie, as he followed the stream bed around the curve at a quickening trot. For a moment, he wondered at this feverish eagerness for action, then he lost himself in his charge.

He barely made out details as he galloped toward the barricade ahead. It bristled with spears, though wounded crossbowmen tumbling down from the mountains were seriously disturbing their concentration. Blackie vaguely heard humans shouting behind as he scrambled over the barrier to stomp and stab while Prince George thrust wildly with his spear.

A huge Hellion appeared before Blackie. Blackie ran him down without thought and charged after another, who threw his club away and fled. Behind him, the slaves were pouring over the barricade to hammer down the Hellions who tried to fight. The human guards were fleeing toward the border where they overwhelmed the Darrmen trying to hold them back.

Most of Vile's men scattered into the mountains beyond and were never seen again. A few set up as bandits to give sport to the Heir when he felt like riding out for a little action on a pleasant autumn morning.

The battle at the border was short. Eighty or ninety prisoners were captured to hand over to the Heir who put them to work building more towers to make Castle March even more formidable. The dead Hellions were shoved into a mountain cavern, formerly the home of bears, then blocked up with boulders after a short funeral service by Father Timothy.

All this had to be explained later to Blackie. As soon as the energy of his charge drained away, Blackie passed out in a snorting, dream-haunted slumber. Unable to wake him, Prince George had Blackie squeezed onto a supply wagon from Sir Burly's castle. Sixty of Lizetta's bruisers hauled him over the mountains. Godfrey set him down in the soft greenness of a little park outside the Chapel at Castle Darr.

Blackie woke two days later with a terrific headache, feeling as dry as an old tree stump. The boys watching over him ran into the castle with the news. Prince George and the Heir hurried down to make over him with love, bringing him buckets of fresh water and wiping his face with cloths.

"It's the medicine," explained Prince George. "Lizetta told us that the drug she slipped in the bucket would leave you dog-tired after your burst of energy."

"Ooooh," moaned Blackie, closing his eyes. "I knew better! I knew better! I'd never have touched anything she gave me if I weren't so tired. Please, Georgie, don't let that Gypsy near me again!"

"What's he saying, my lord?" asked Godfrey.

"Don't worry, Blackie!" cried the Prince, stuffing a nutcake into Blackie's mouth. "That serpent's gone for good! We brought her across the border while you slept, and Lady Dorinda greeted her like a sister. How did she repay us? She dosed the wine at our thanksgiving Mass, knocked out the whole congregation. While we snored on the chapel floor, she stole Godfrey's horses and ran off with a score of bruisers she'd convinced to turn Gypsy."

"Tell him about the spear," urged the Heir.

"Oh, Blackie, my spear, the Nail!" wailed the Prince. "It's gone! Lizetta took that, too! Godfrey sent riders after her, but the only mounts left in the stables were donkeys. They couldn't catch up with her. She's vanished into the Forest of Creeb. I'd shoot the arrow after her, but I'm afraid that she'd witch it over as well!"

"Don't worry, Prince," the Heir tried to reassure him. "You don't need that old spear. You'll do twice the damage with the battle-axe I gave you."

"But I'm used to that spear," insisted Prince George, crushing a nutcake in his hand. "It's part of my legend now, a famous relic, the Nail of the Cross! I killed the dragon with it!"

All this news made Blackie's head hurt worse than ever, but Prince George tugged at his mane.

"Uh, Blackie, if you're awake now, we have a barnful of wounded from the battle. We want to get these boys healed up so they can head home. Godfrey's taking on a few dozen to build up Darr, but the rest of them—"

"All those slaves," Godfrey broke in, "most of 'em sick and weak, hungry as rats after starving at Vile. They're eating up my duchy, that's what! It's impossible to come up with enough rations to feed them this early in the spring. I've got a squad of men hunting mountain goats with the Prince's arrow. You can lend them a hand once you've healed the sick and injured."

Blackie stiffened. "I don't hunt!"

This time, he intended to stick to that vow. It was proper for humans to hunt. Meat was their natural food after all, but a holy beast should never chase his fellow creatures of the field.

He refused to heal humans, too, until he rested. The way he felt, his head would split if he laid his horn to a pimple. He drank a lot of water, ate a few nutcakes, and closed his eyes to sleep again.

"I warned you that he wasn't ready to help," said Prince George, walking away with the Heir.

"I thought you told me he was a fighter," said Godfrey, his voice getting fainter with distance. "He doesn't act like a dragon-killer to me."

"If you knew what he's been through," said the Prince. "If you only knew—"

The sick and injured were still waiting when Blackie finally roused. His headache was gone, but Blackie felt feeble. His muscles trembled.

His eyes watered. He hobbled around on sore hooves. He did have an appetite, though, eating a good meal of sweet grass, oats, and nutcakes, then agreed to tackle the most serious cases.

"Just the worst of them," he croaked to the Prince. "Maybe I'll feel more like healing when I feel better."

"Ask him if he'll treat Lord Brucie, too," suggested the Heir, leading the way through an arch in the castle grounds. "The child hasn't eaten right since Lazlo brought him back to us. My lady thinks the Gypsy put the Evil Eye on him."

"Oh, sure, Godfrey," said Prince George, heartily. "Blackie won't mind healing the boy. It won't take anything out of him."

"That's what you think," muttered Blackie. "Healing always drains me down."

Lady Dorinda greeted them at the barn door in an old dress strained with mucus and blood. After wiping her hands on a rag, she hugged Blackie.

"Oh, dear unicorn, thank Saint Margaret you're finally awake. We pray for the poor souls to hang on, but they're dying by the hour."

"Don't worry, my lady," said Prince George, smiling at Lady Dorinda. "Blackie'll get right to work. And he'll heal Lord Bruce as soon as we see the boy."

"Bless you, my lord," she said, bowing to the Prince. "I'll send for the child immediately, but the unicorn needs to start on these folks. A few of them were wounded in the fight, but most are starved and beaten. I'm glad they're free from Prince Vile. Anyone who treats his slaves like this doesn't deserve them."

Blackie's heart sank when he saw the invalids staring up with dead eyes. These were serious cases requiring powerful healing. They had cracked skin, swollen bellies, protruding bones. Some tried to sit up when they saw Blackie. Others raised feeble arms that flopped down again.

"Most of them were carried by the other prisoners," explained Godfrey. "It's a wonder any of them survived their flight, but Lizetta organized teams to bear them along. She dosed them with medicines to keep them alive."

He spat on the ground. "Lizetta seemed so loving to the slaves that I really believed she'd reformed."

"Not me," said Dorinda, frowning at her husband. "As soon as I saw those beady eyes, I warned my lord about her. He should know you can't trust that sort of woman. He welcomed her like a Christian, even freed Lazlo from the dungeon when she begged him to, then she took my own chestnut mare and ran away to steal more babies!"

Blackie sighed deeply. Nothing seemed to have changed, except that Papa was gone. Here he was again, dealing with sick humans. He limped to the first patient, a young woman with stringy hair hanging about her face, dried up like an old apple.

"This one can't take food," Dorinda explained, kneeling by the bed to hold the woman's hand. "She refused Prince Vile's demands, so he stuck her in a cage to starve."

Shuddering at the sight, Blackie touched the woman with his horn. She didn't stir. He had to tighten his muscles and pour in all his healing power before she came around. With a moan, the woman lifted a hand to touch her withered face.

"It's working!" cried Godfrey. "Blast her again, Blackie! She'll be able to eat."

Blackie took a breath and squeezed out another healing burst. This time, the woman opened her eyes, her mouth twitching. Her skin smoothed and softened as they watched.

"It's a miracle," whispered Dorinda. She squeezed the woman's hand. "The unicorn has saved you, dear. You'll be pretty again. We have soup. You must eat to get well."

"Now, this next one," said Godfrey, leading Blackie along the row of patients, "this one was smashed by a rock from the mountain."

Prince George and Godfrey worked with Blackie, cheering the sick and wounded as he came to them. As they encouraged Blackie to keep healing, Godfrey told him what they'd learned from the slaves.

"Apparently, there'd been rumors for weeks that you were coming. Vile panicked when he heard that you'd broken through the border. He was convinced you were coming after him. Lizetta said he was so terrified that he pulled all his Hellions back to the castle to defend himself. Of course, the mountain cut loose at that time, erupting all over the place and spewing lava so no one could move."

"Oh, yes," said the Prince, grimly, "we know about the lava."

"Well, Lizetta had been waiting for a chance to escape. She'd made herself quite a favorite of the Prince, fawning over him, flattering him, calling him 'noble lord' and 'sweet prince.' You remember, my lord, the way she oiled you up in the old days."

"Oh, yes," said Dorinda, frowning at the Prince. "My lord has told me how you toyed with the Gypsy."

Prince George blushed. He gulped for air, but didn't say anything.

"Anyway," Godfrey went on, "with Vile and the Hellions closed in his castle and the mountain throwing rocks in all directions, Lizetta drugged the guards with medicines. She opened the locks to the slave pens and talked the slaves into escaping. She made the strong ones carry the sick, and they dragged themselves to the border where you met them."

Following Blackie to the next patient, Prince George chuckled dryly. "Yep, Lizetta fooled the black Prince, all right. I admit that she put it over on me, too, once or twice. You add woman's wiles to Gypsy cunning—a man doesn't have a chance around her."

"Woman's wiles, indeed!" snapped Dorinda. "I swear, that witch is worse than Prince Vile. When I first saw her, she was all prayers and penitence, begging us to forgive Lazlo for stealing my child. Then she drugged us at Mass and ran off with my best gowns."

"If I were you," warned the Prince, "I'd check that you've got the right baby. That Gypsy would leave you a beggar's brat if you don't watch out."

"Oh, here he comes now!" cried Lady Dorinda, running to a nurse entering the barn with the child wrapped in a soft blanket. Dorinda took the boy, who whimpered in her arms.

"Now, look at him, Prince. Who could mistake this beautiful lord for any other? I'd know him among a million babies, but those Gypsies have laid a curse on him, I'm sure of it."

Prince George smiled down at the boy, who reached for him with both hands. "Don't worry, my lady. Bring him along to the unicorn. He'll have him hearty as a hawk in no time. Blackie, you've got another patient here. Give him a shot of your strongest healing if you will."

Blackie looked up, blearily. He rolled his eyes at the boy. How many did he have to heal today? This one didn't look sick. They'd told him it was just the saddest cases, but now, they were bringing babies. Oh, well, for Godfrey, the Prince's friend—Blackie knew how fathers worry over their sons.

He pulled himself together, touched his horn to the boy's forehead, and forced out a spark. The little lord roared with laughter and wriggled like a monkey. He grabbed Blackie's horn.

"Oh, thank Heavens!" breathed Lady Dorinda, struggling to hold him. "Now, he's back to himself!"

"That's my son!" beamed the Heir, watching Dorinda carry Brucie out of the barn. "With lungs like that, he'll cry down the wind. You'll have to return in a few years, Blackie. Take the boy out on campaign. By then, the Prince'll be a battered old boot sleeping by the fireside. You'll need a fresh young warrior to run with."

"You should send Lord Bruce to Court as a page," suggested Prince George. "I'll teach him to use his sword and spear. Left to you, he'll grow up thinking that a warrior lives by an axe like a woodchopper."

"Get him a magic bow like you carry, my lord," said Godfrey, "and he can skip all other weapons. That arrow's brought down fifty goats already. We've got enough stew cooking to feed all the slaves."

"Let the arrow doing the hunting," mumbled Blackie. "Not me, I'm not dealing with goats."

Blackie wobbled on his feet, leaning over the next patient. He strained to force out more healing, but it was no use. He was exhausted, totally drained of power. He almost toppled over where he stood, but Godfrey grabbed his shoulder.

"Blackie's done for, Prince. Give us a hand here. The beast needs rest before he can finish the job. Thank the Lord, he healed my son before wearing down completely."

Supported by Prince George and Godfrey, Blackie tottered out of the barn to the park where the men gently settled him down. He stretched out on his side, smelling the grass and fresh air. He slept.

CHAPTER FORTY-TWO

A Day at Darr

It was two weeks later that the Steward, James, spoke over the squeals of playing children. "Lady Dorinda has instructed me, my lord, to inform you that the arrow has returned with a package."

Blackie looked up from the long grass edging the flower beds in the park behind Castle Darr. Prince George was stretched out on a hammock in the shade beside him. The Prince squinted his eyes at the servant.

"Hmmm, hmmm? Oh, thank you, my man. Please inform Lady Dorinda that we'll be up presently to receive the package."

The Prince closed his eyes again. Blackie nipped off a mouthful of buds from a yellow rose bush. He poked the Prince with his horn. "Shouldn't we go see what the arrow's brought?"

"I guess so," sighed the Prince.

The afternoon sun shone warm as spring advanced in the northlands. Bumblebees buzzed around the pink and white blossoms gleaming on the south wall. The grass was fresh and green, and Blackie kept the tender bushes nibbled short.

By now, Blackie was used to Prince George sleeping late. Each morning, they had breakfast together. The Prince would practice a couple hours with the battle-axe before taking his first nap of the afternoon. He came to life in the evenings when Godfrey held court with Lady Dorinda and the old Duke, who'd also slept all day. They feasted long into the night by torchlight. Prince George joked with the Heir, danced with Dorinda's pretty maids, and sang with the minstrels.

The popular ballad of the season was called, "The Dragon's Doom," a song in which Prince George had a leading role. It wasn't what Blackie would call accurate, but the Prince loved to roar out the refrain.

The unicorns did wound the worm,
the royal Prince did kill it.

Today, the children in the park noticed that Blackie had stopped eating. They scampered toward him, begging for rides. Blackie turned to the hammock again.

"Come on, Georgie! Don't sleep away the afternoon. That package could be full of cookies."

"I guess we'd better check it out," yawned the Prince.

He rolled out of the hammock, straightened his tunic, and strolled to the castle gate with Blackie. The children skipped around them, squealing, then ran back to the park as the great door closed with a thump.

Inside the hall, Prince George and Blackie found the Duke snoring in his chair, a half-dozen old dogs curled around his feet. The arrow was poised in the air near Godfrey's table piled with invoices, bills, account books, and legal documents, precisely where Prince George had shot it off to the Princess three days before. The arrow held a long narrow package bound by pretty red ribbons.

Grateful for the interruption, Godfrey looked up from his accounts. He tossed his pen down and wiped ink from his fingers.

"Arrow's back, my lord."

He jumped up to give Blackie a pat. Lady Dorinda looked up, smiling, from her embroidery, and the Duke coughed himself awake.

"What's up? What's up?"

He blinked around, sneezed, and went back to snoring. Two of the dogs stood, yawned, and limped over to sniff Blackie's hooves.

"Oh, heavy package," said the Prince, as the arrow settled its load into his hands.

"Bring it over to the table, my lord," suggested Godfrey, pulling his dagger to cut open the binding. "Let's see what Her Majesty's sent you."

"Don't damage the ribbons!" cried Dorinda, jumping up. "Here, let me untie them."

Prince George set the package down on the table. Dorinda leaned over to pull at the knots, one after the other. Rolling the ribbons around her wrist, she released the arrow which whisked back to the bow leaning against the Prince's throne. The Prince shook open a parchment scroll wrapped around the package. He held it up to the light from the window and glanced down it.

"It's a letter from the Princess."

"Here, my lord," said Godfrey, pulling the covering from the package, "this feels like—"

"It's a sword!" exclaimed Prince George, glimpsing the beechwood scabbard within the wrapping. He sucked in his breath.

"It's my sword, my father's sword!"

Blackie squeezed between them to sniff the sword.

"Your father's sword," he repeated. "Where'd they find it, Georgie? You dropped it in the moat back at that castle."

"Castle Shrems!" said the Prince with emotion. "I dropped it the night we ran from the dragon, remember, Blackie? I thought it was gone for good."

Prince George pulled the sword from the scabbard and slashed it through the air. He swung it up in salute.

"Now, this is a weapon! My father, the King, he carried this sword against Huns and Bulgars and Turks. He killed lions with it. You remember my old lionskin, don't you, Godfrey?"

"Tatty old thing," said Dorinda with a sniff. "You shed hairs wherever you walked."

The Prince kissed the crosspiece at the hilt and held out the sword for Godfrey to inspect. "Now, Godfrey, I can give you back your axe."

Blackie turned away, shrugging. It was nice that the Prince had his sword again, but he was more interested in cookies.

The Prince slipped the sword back in the scabbard and belted it about his waist. "Good, good, I'm armed again. With this sword and the magic bow, I could fight a dozen dragons."

Dorinda crossed herself. "Saint Michael defend you from that, my lord."

"I wish you'd keep the axe," grumbled Godfrey. "I'm not sure that a broadsword can replace that spear of yours."

Blackie sniffed about the snack table by the Duke's chair while Godfrey took up the parchment, smoothed out the letter, and handed it to Prince George.

"You'd better read the message, my lord. Let's see what the Princess has to say."

"I hope she explains how she got the sword," said the Prince, scanning the opening. "At least, this letter's not in Latin."

"She's an accomplished lady," commented Lady Dorinda.

The Prince grunted.

"Well, she likes to appear that way. Hmm, '*To Prince George at Castle Darr*,' and so forth. Why, the first part's written by the Empress, her pretty script. My lady says, oh, my—"

He blushed and rushed over the words.

> "We're all thrilled at your exploits, dear Prince, invading Vile, killing the dragon, rescuing unhappy prisoners from a life of slavery. The Bishop held a special service of thanksgiving for your success with prayers for your future adventures. Please give our love to the unicorn."

The Prince looked at Blackie with tears in his eyes.

"See, Blackie, she remembers you. Her Majesty, she was always . . . always thoughtful like that. The closest thing I ever had to a mother."

Perking up his ears, Blackie stepped around the table. "I can't wait to see her," he said. "If she's like her sister, Countess Amalia, she must be wonderful."

"Oh, yes," nodded Godfrey, when Prince George explained Blackie's comment. "Everyone loves the Empress. It was loyalty to Her Majesty that held the lords to the Crown during the war, those that stayed faithful."

"What else does she say?" asked Blackie.

"Hmm, hmm, just a couple sentences."

> "Tell Blackie that his mother stayed with us a few weeks, then returned to the forest. He must come to us after the pilgrimage. I long to see him."

He paused, looked down the parchment. "The rest of the message—it's written by the Princess."

"Princess Julianna must be pleased with you, too," smiled Dorinda, looking down to her stitching. Her ladies giggled. The Prince took a deep breath and lifted the letter to the sunlight. In an instant, he was red with anger.

"Look how she writes to me—"

> *"What do you mean, Prince, letting my arrow fly around on its own? It could be lost or captured by a sorcerer. I'll send it back with your sword this time, but keep it within eyesight from now on. I'm holding you responsible for its welfare."*

"'Its welfare'!" He crushed the parchment in his hand. "The arrow's welfare! She's more concerned about this arrow than she is with me! She doesn't recognize how clever I am to use the arrow as a messenger. All she cares about is controlling things—keeping the arrow close at hand, holding me responsible. I've killed a dragon, yet she treats me like a child!"

"Does she write anything about the sword, my lord?" asked Godfrey.

"Oh, well, let's see what else she says."

The Prince spread out the sheet of parchment on the table.

"Here she wants five hundred of Vile's slaves sent to the City to replace workmen killed in the War. That's good—jobs for them and they're off your hands, Godfrey. Oh, yes, here it is.

> *"This sword was found during repairs at Castle Shrems. I recognize your father's lion on the hilt. You'll need this sword when you return my bow to me."*

"Well, it's excellent timing for you," said Godfrey, cheerfully. "She sends you the sword just when you lose your spear."

"Oh, I'll get the spear back," growled the Prince, tossing the letter on the table. "That Gypsy can't hide from me."

"Was that all the Princess said?" asked Dorinda.

"Oh, she says something about meeting her down the road. She's assembling the lords for a grand pilgrimage to the Shrine to give thanks for peace. She says we'll deliver the horn to the Fountain then."

A pain pierced Blackie's heart as Dorinda jumped up, clapping her hands with delight.

"Oh, my lord, we must go! This pilgrimage will be historic. We'll be able to bathe little Brucie in the Fountain waters to shield him from the evil eye. When does she travel, Prince? Do I have time to order new shoes?"

Blackie thought of Papa's horn, now resting on the altar of the castle chapel. Godfrey shook his head.

"Ride to the Shrine this spring? Impossible, absolutely impossible! I'm far too busy with the planting. Why, the border's not secure yet. There's bandits on every road."

"Oh, Papa," thought Blackie for the thousandth time, "why, why did I run off, last summer? Now, I'm losing all that remains of you!"

Prince George saw Blackie's misery and comforted him with a friendly hug as Dorinda rushed in with her protest.

"But our father, he's perfectly capable of seeing to the crops. As to the border, the dragon's dead! Prince Vile's defeated! We've never been more secure."

"I'm not sure about that—" began Godfrey, but his lady overwhelmed him with her arguments.

"And look at the Princess! Just weeks after a bitter siege, she feels safe enough to travel from the City. The Empress would never let her go if it was dangerous. And our duchy is surely stronger than the City with its broken walls and towers. Isn't it our duty, my lord, to join this pilgrimage with our liege Lady? What loyalty do we show hiding here in the mountains when the faithful lords join the Princess to celebrate the end of this horrible war?"

"No, no, no," insisted Godfrey, striking the table with his fist, "we're staying home this year! All the Empire knows that I was loyal when it counted. How many lords rode out with five hundred warriors to relieve the Siege?"

"I know, I know, my lord," cried Lady Dorinda, with a deep curtsey to her husband. "You rode out like a hero! I was so proud of you. But think of me! I've been cooped up at Darr since the Contest years ago! I have a dozen new gowns I haven't worn. We never go anywhere for me to wear them!"

581

"Let's go, Blackie," whispered Prince George, nudging Blackie toward the door. "Let's see what's warm at the bakery. They'll be at this for hours."

"Why do they quarrel?" asked Blackie, stepping carefully down the stairs. "Surely, Godfrey knows he must obey if he's called to the pilgrimage. We all obey the Princess."

The Prince grasped his sword hilt to make sure it was still there.

"I guess, he feels insecure with Dorinda. Poor Godfrey's still a mere headsman at heart. He knows that a lord should rule over his lady, so he'll squirm around and argue with her. Just watch, though. He'll give way in the end. With a dozen new gowns to wear, Dorinda's not going to miss this pilgrimage."

They clattered through a passage to the bakery, sniffing the pastry and bread.

"I don't understand females," commented Blackie. "Look at Lizetta, stealing your spear like that. You'd think she'd be grateful to you for saving her from Vile."

"Well, Lizetta," said the Prince, holding the bakery door open for Blackie, "she's one of a kind. The people have a saying, 'She'll dance with the Devil and run off with his broom.' That's Lizetta."

The bakery was a cheery place with its ovens and mixing bowls and racks of baking trays. The Baker greeted the Prince at the door while the Baker's boys bowed to the Prince and petted Blackie with floury hands that left white fingerprints on his coat.

"Anything you want, me lords!" they cried. "Bread in the oven, cookies on the rack!"

"Try my apple tarts," offered a boy, bringing forward a sheet pan piled with steaming triangles.

Blackie nosed out a bowl half-filled with brown circles oozing with honey.

"That?" laughed a boy. "That's fried dough left from breakfast. You won't want that. It's stale."

But Blackie did want the dough rings, as well as the cookies and apple tarts. Stuffed to his ears, Prince George gave up long before Blackie stopped gobbling.

One of the boys ran to the dairy for fresh milk. Prince George took a mug of milk and settled on a stool beside Blackie, who was licking honey from the dough bowl. The Prince put down his mug and dusted off his hands.

"I've got to give up cookies. It's all right for you, Blackie. You're a beast, but I'm a famous warrior. How would it sound in my songs to have me always guzzling cookies like a weaver's apprentice?"

"Give them up if you want," said Blackie with a belch, "not me. I'm going to guzzle every cookie I can get, but I will take it easy with this fried dough. It sits heavy on my belly."

Prince George shifted on his stool. "If you ate like this every day, you'd be fat as a pig."

"Not much chance of that, not the way we live," said Blackie. He licked his lips with his tongue. "I've got to fill up for that ride to the Shrine."

"Oh, but this will be a noble procession," said the Prince, leaning back. He laced his fingers around a knee. "Nothing like our quest, last fall. This time, we'll travel in state with the Princess. We'll take our time, cover a few miles every day. We'll stay in the richest castles. There's nothing like roaming the country in summertime, feasting on the fat of the land. Wherever we stop, there'll be wine and food, songs, sports, stories. You'll see maidens dance around the roasting pig and bonfires every night."

"And nutmeats," added Blackie, remembering last fall.

"Well, nutmeats are scarce in summertime, but you'll have veggies and berries, plums and peaches. Remember how you loved spinach?"

"Oh, the greens," said Blackie, nodding. "Papa loved the greens."

"Yep," the Prince went on, "of course, we may not get away until autumn. That's the best time to travel. In autumn, you have the harvest festivals with grapes and apples and pears—and nuts, all the nutmeats you can eat. Everyone celebrates in October with the sunny, fragrant afternoons and crisp, cool evenings. How the stars crackle in the night sky! And we'd have plenty of time to return to the City by Christmas. We could keep Yule at the castle with the Knights and the royal family, twelve days of constant parties."

"Unless—" Blackie said. He hesitated, and Prince George finished the statement, gesturing with a nutcake.

"I know, Blackie. Unless the Princess runs us out on another quest. She's driven us hard since I met you. This time, though, I think, she's ready to settle down. I know she wants to show you off. She told me she wants to ride you in a parade. Well, the biggest parade of the year is Saint Swithin's Day. That's Carnival before Lent, which would give us all winter to relax in the City."

Blackie took another drink from the milk bucket while one of the baker's boys shyly asked Prince George, "Me lord, can you really understand the unicorn's noises?"

Prince George swallowed his bite of nutcake.

"Sure, lad, that skill came to me in Vile. The unicorn always understood me, you see. He understands you, as far as that goes, but somehow, deep in the dragon's den, I learned his speech and that of horses to an extent."

"So you can ask him things, me lord?"

"Anyone can ask him things," chuckled the Prince. "It's just that I know what he answers. What do you want to ask him?"

"Oh, nothin', nothin', me lord."

The boy backed away, looking at the floor. A bigger boy pushed him forward, hissing, "Go ahead! Ask 'im!"

"Sure, ask away," said Prince George, yawning. "What do you want to know?"

"He wants you to ask the unicorn," said the bigger boy, poking the other, "just how big was the dragon."

The smaller boy nodded with an eager grin.

"Why ask him?" frowned Prince George. "You can ask me. I was there. It was me that killed the worm with my bow."

"Well, don't take all the credit," demanded Blackie, thumping a hoof on the floor. "He'll think you killed it by yourself. It took both of us to kill it—and Papa. Papa was the one that brought it down in the first place."

"Sure, you unicorns wounded it," insisted the Prince, "but I was the one that gave it the *coup*."

"So, me lord," asked the boy, repeating his question, "how big was the monster, if you don't mind us askin'?"

The Prince smiled at him, kindly. "I don't mind at all. You see, the length of the dragon is mostly neck and tail, but if you stretch it out—"

There was a clatter at the door. The boys jumped away to the dirty trays stacked in the sink as Godfrey strode in with one of his warriors.

"Oh, here you are, I thought so."

He spread his hands in resignation. "Well, it's settled, my lord. We're off to the Shrine. It seems we have to attend the Princess whether I want to go or not."

"I thought so," laughed the Prince. "I knew you couldn't stand out against that storm of arguments."

"Well," Godfrey scratched his head, "I told her that the roads weren't safe to travel with the state the Empire's in, but she pointed out that we'll have you and the unicorn to guard us. What could I say after that?"

Prince George exchanged a look with Blackie.

"Don't blame us you can't rule your household," said the Prince with a grin. "Seems to me it's those new gowns that won that discussion."

"Wait until you're married, my lord," said Godfrey with a sigh. "You'll find that things aren't as easy as they should be."

"Well, when do we leave, Godfrey?"

"It depends on the Princess's schedule, of course. I figure we could be ready to leave in a few weeks if we throw ourselves into the preparations—you know, collecting provisions, getting new boots made, cloaks, all the things that ladies need. The biggest problem is horses. I can levy a horse or two from each of my vassals, but we won't have many in reserve."

"Speaking of cloaks—" said the Prince."

Godfrey cut him off. "Don't worry, my lord. Lady Dorinda has noticed how tattered your clothes are. She's ordering new boots and suits for you, and another cloak."

Prince George blushed. "I'll be sure to thank her for that."

This time, it was Godfrey's turn to laugh.

"I fear that she wants you to appear in style. She sees you as a member of her party now, so she doesn't want you to shame her. You've seen how she dresses me."

"Oh, yes," said the Prince with a grin, "I have noticed a—what d'you call it?—a frilly look about you. That pink tunic you wore yesterday, for example. You better tell your lady that I won't wear pink."

"That tunic wasn't pink," Godfrey explained. "My lady said it was 'coral,' the color of seashells or something."

Prince George stood up, straightening his sword belt. "I fear you're too fashionable for me, Godfrey. Pretty soon you'll be as stylish as the Majordomo. Remember me telling you about him?"

Godfrey sighed as they left the Bakery. Blackie followed them around the keep to the courtyard.

"Sometimes," Godfrey said, "sometimes I wish I were back on Martha, that donkey, in my secondhand boots. Things were a lot easier in those days."

Prince George laughed. "I remember when you were eager to become a lord, to hold court and guard your borders.

"Oh, that part's easy enough," said Godfrey. A frustrated note came into his voice. He began to wave his hands.

"It's the finances, the accounts, finding money to pay for everything. Taxes are late if paid at all. Bills pile up! Income never matches expenditures! It's impossible, impossible!"

Blackie threw up his head as they passed the well in the middle of the courtyard.

"Tell Godfrey to leave all that behind. He should ride out with us. We'll hunt down the Gypsies and get your spear back and his horses."

Prince George was astonished. "You want to ride out already, Blackie?"

He explained to Godfrey.

"Blackie suggests you give it up, Godfrey, go questing after the Gypsies."

Godfrey clapped Blackie on the shoulder with a sigh.

"Oh, I wish I could, Blackie, but Lady Dorinda would have a cat-fit if I suggested it. I have to keep to my desk, pouring over those expenses. The old Duke, he can't make head or tail of the accounts. It's all on my shoulders. Things are different now, Prince. Things are different."

When Blackie stopped at the well for another drink, Godfrey and the Prince walked on without him.

"Well, my lord," Godfrey was saying, "let's stop by the blacksmith. I want to get my axe blade sharpened. How's your sword?"

"Dull as a doorknob," said the Prince. "It needs whetting, and I want to talk to you about a saddle for the unicorn."

"A saddle," thought Blackie, lifting his dripping muzzle. "Here we go again. He still complains about riding bareback."

On impulse, Blackie turned away from the castle keep and trotted across the courtyard to the gate. He passed through the northorn barrier where green leaves had spread over the sharp spines. Out in the street, he looked this way and that. He wandered into Market Square before the church, drawn by the crowds flowing among the carts and booths of the traders.

A shout went up at his appearance. He was surrounded at once by children and beggars. Trim maids came running with their baskets, using him as an excuse to stretch out their errands a few more minutes. As always, a crowd of cripples followed him down the street, pleading for healing, but the hearty shoppers pushed them away.

Blackie had just broken free when a crutch hooked onto his horn. He pulled around to see a grinning human in a green hat.

"Hold up, unicorn, old pal! How 'bout another dose of healing?"

"Back off, Lame Alan!" the people cried, pushing the man away. "Leave the unicorn alone!"

"But he knows me!" squealed the man, toppling into a potter's cart.

"Mind the crockery!" cried the potter, reaching to steady a wobbly stack of bowls.

"He remembers me from a year ago!" bawled Lame Alan, struggling back up on his crutch. "Last winter, he and I fought Hellions down at Croy. Oh, the tales I could tell about this unicorn and the Prince he travels with and the beautiful Gypsy witch, that Lizetta! I was watching here at the gate three weeks ago when she rode out with all those horses. I'd have raised the guard, but she bound me to silence with a magic spell."

"With a cup o' beer, you mean!" shouted a woman. All the people laughed.

"Oh, you can mock at me," said Lame Alan, sinking onto a bench outside the tavern, "you can shake your heads, but I knew this unicorn when he was half this size."

Blackie snorted. This was the man that started his troubles by breaking off his bent horn. Lame Alan held up his arm. He spoke in an impressive voice.

"The unicorn's horn was no longer than my forearm back then. It was damaged, twisted like a corkscrew, so I removed it for him."

By now, the people were drawn to Lame Alan's tale. Children squatted around his foot. Someone handed him a half-empty mug of beer. Blackie started to push away, but paused, curious to hear what lies the man would come up with this time.

"Look at the beast," said Lame Alan, gesturing with the mug. "See? He remembers me. And how I remember him! The first evening I met him, I saw the dragon burst out of Castle Shrems at midnight. It chased him through the roads in a firestorm that torched half the haystacks in the country. They burnt all night, every field lit up like a starry sky."

The people gasped and shuddered at that picture. Living so close to Vile, the dragon preyed heavily on their minds.

"My removing the unicorn horn, that's the story needs to be told." Lame Alan took a sip of beer and stretched out his good leg. "It happened in church down at Shrems, last summer. Anyone could see that the unicorn was in pain. You see, his baby horn, the twisted one, was hanging on where the mature horn—that mighty weapon you see there—was pushing to come in. It's like a child losing his baby teeth. He gets the toothache if the old tooth holds back when the new one's on its way."

"True enough, true enough!" cried an old woman, nodding her head. "My baby Ronnie suffered through every one o' his baby teeth."

"Me, though, you have to understand that I hate to see anyone suffer." Lame Alan slapped his chest. "I'm like the Good Sumarian. If I see misery, I want to help out. So I sprung up in Shrems Church and gave that horn a yank. The unicorn fell one way, and I fell the other, but I pulled off the baby horn as slick as a whistle. You wouldn't believe how grateful he was. He offered to let me ride on his back, promised to carry me anywhere I wanted to go, but I refused.

"'No, thank you,' I told him, 'that honor should go to a mighty Prince.'

"And that's how the two of them got together. They went riding up to the castle where they stirred up the dragon and started this war that's just finished. It all began with me pulling off that horn."

Blackie snorted and turned away as a man said skeptically, "So, Lame Alan, if you pulled off the unicorn's horn, let's see it."

Lame Alan looked up innocently. "See what?"

"The horn, the baby unicorn horn. If you pulled it off, you must have it, so just show us the horn to prove your story, Lame Alan."

"Oh," smiled Lame Alan, "the horn. You're asking me how that unicorn horn got took to the Cathedral down in the City where it's set in gold and jewels and carried about on holiday processions. Now, that's another story. A new tale deserves a new beer.

"I get dried out from talking, ye see. Turns out, that's due to my allergy. I met this priest over to Thorn, a few weeks ago, and he told me that his voice drops away while he's preaching, due to his allergy. Seems that a rich liquid brings his voice back. So I need a rich liquid to keep me talking, that's just the way it is."

Blackie yawned. He was tired of being squeezed by the crowd, but he did want to hear what happened to that horn. Mama would be interested. She'd loved his twisted little horn.

"Oh, give him a beer," cried a woman in a brown shawl. "Let's hear another whopper from Lame Alan."

Someone handed the man a foaming mug of beer. Lame Alan held up the mug in salute as a peddler down the market began singing out.

> Lamps and oil,
> lamps and oil—
> light for prayin',
> light for toil.

Lame Alan took a deep drink from his mug. He lowered it and wiped his lip on his sleeve.

"Now, that's more like it," he sighed. "Beer, good warm beer, it stretches the mind and stirs up the stories. That horn now, what a squabble was started over that little horn!"

A rustle ran through the crowd. People leaned against carts or squatted down to listen. Someone whispered, "Lane Alan's at it now."

"That horn I pulled off," mused Lame Alan, looking down into his beer mug, "that was a twisty little poker, a pink little thing. You wouldn't think it amounted to anything, but the priest back there, Father Paul, he crabbed onto that horn like a terrier catching a rat. He declared it was a holy relic and kept it in a big basket in his church. On Saint Luke's Day, he'd bring it out to heal folks of their ailments, other holidays too. Folks lined up to kiss the horn, and the coppers poured in for his church."

"Did it work?" demanded the woman in the shawl.

"Of course, it worked," declared Lame Alan. "It would heal anyone but a sinner. Father Paul preached that sinners have such hard hearts that the healing can't sink in. They had lots of sinners down there in Shrems."

"This unicorn heals everyone," said a man with a little boy on his shoulder, "saved or sinner, he don't care. I saw him heal a lawyer up to the castle, a man so dried out by his Latin and his sins that he looked like a raisin."

"So did the lawyer repent?" asked another man. "Did he stop writin' papers to put folks off their lands?"

"Well, he didn't stop doin' that," admitted the father, "but he fattened up. He looked like a real human after a month or two."

"But that's no good!" exclaimed the woman. "How'd you know to stay away from a lawyer if he looks like anyone else?"

"Oh, he still had that squint in his eye," said the father. "You'd know him if you saw him in the street, peerin' around to see who he could skin next."

People shuddered at that description. Lame Alan spoke loudly to get their attention back to his story.

"That priest I was telling about, now he was the one that got fat at Shrems. He bought a gold-plated rosary to wear around his neck and wore robes trimmed in velvet. He had a colored window put in his church with a picture of the unicorn on it. The picture didn't look much like a unicorn. Folks said it looked more like a one-horned goat, but the beast was black, so you knew who it was.

"By then, people from villages twenty miles away was making pilgrimages to the church, so Father Paul had to give five masses every weekday. Well, he got tired of that quick, so he hired himself a deacon to do the preaching. He'd sit on a cushion in his big chair with the horn in his lap, smiling on the folks like a saint on earth while his deacon did the marrying and the burying."

Lame Alan paused so the picture of the happy priest could sink into the imaginations of his hearers. Bored by the story, Blackie pushed through the crowd to investigate the food booths before the church. Lame Alan's voice followed as Blackie passed a glover's cart, turning his head away from the stink of tanned leather.

"And that's when the Archdeacon showed up to get hold of the horn for the Bishop."

Blackie remembered his baby horn with nostalgia. "How miserable I was when Lame Alan pulled off my horn! I had to run around with that iron spike on my head. That thing caught on every tree branch in the forest."

By now, he was among the chickens hanging by their feet, the ducks and geese and guinea-fowl, all squawking and quacking and honking to startle a deaf-mute. Blackie ran past the smells of roasting turkeys and sausages and pork pies until he reached the vegetable stands.

Blackie was sniffing the asparagus, radishes, and spinach when two dairy women behind him got into a scuffle after one warned a shopper against the moldy curds sold by the other.

"Furry as a stagnant pond, they is!"

"I'll stagnant you!" cried the second woman, and they went at it, pulling hair and wrestling while the humans around whistled and shouted encouragement.

Shaking his head at the brawl, Blackie trotted down the slanting street to the city wall, a handful of children skipping behind. They climbed up a stone staircase to gaze out over the mountains. Blackie watched hawks coast on the breeze over the darkening procession of peaks to the horizon.

"These mountains, I'll remember these mountains when I'm home in the forest with Mama."

"Come on, unicorn," begged the children. "Let's go do something."

CHAPTER FORTY-THREE

Awards Night

Summertime rolled around Darr, sticky and busy. The humans got caught up in the planting and growing and harvesting of crops. Red strawberries were picked, Green apples eaten. It was winemaking season before Blackie carried Prince George across the drawbridge at Castle Minch where they were to meet the Princess for the long-awaited pilgrimage. Dorinda's party had made good time riding down from Darr, except that Godfrey had insisted on a detour to Ord, a barony at the southwest corner of Darr that had refused to send fighters when the Heir called out his liegemen for the war.

They found Ord Village wracked and ruined. Frightened peasants told Godfrey that Baron Ord had ridden off to support Prince Vile's siege of the City. The Baron's fate was a matter of rumor, but the castle was currently held by the Baron's steward, a villain called Old Crow, who showed no sign of welcoming them until Prince George shot the magic arrow through a window of the castle.

Minutes later, the defenders came spilling out the front gate. When Godfrey rode on, Old Crow rested in the dungeon, his stab wounds healed by Blackie, while the banner of Darr flapped over the tower.

Clearing up that little problem cheered Godfrey so much that he grew happy about the pilgrimage. He beamed at Lady Dorinda in her bright blue traveling cloak being welcomed into Castle Minch by Count Basham. The Count escorted them into the hall to meet his Baroness, a tall lady with a toothy smile.

Prince George, entering after Blackie, seemed the only anxious soul in the hall. Blackie went for the snack table in the corner, but the Prince scurried around asking everyone for news of the Princess, who was overdue at the Crossroads. The Prince was relieved to hear that she hadn't chosen the dangerous route of shipping her Court to Herne in boats. Even in summer, when sea travel was at its height, sailing had its perils.

"She only considered sailing to copy my famous voyage with the desert boy, Aleet," Prince George grumbled to Lord Basham. "If she'd asked me, I'd have warned against it. Veteran sea dogs approach any voyage with prayers."

"No worry, no worry, my lord," the Count assured him. "A messenger rode up Tuesday to inform us that Her Majesty is riding straight up the highway. She's a day late and moving briskly to make up the time. We expect her tomorrow morning."

"I must dash off to escort her!" cried Prince George. "Come on, Blackie! We can catch her on the road!"

As Blackie turned from the snack table with cookies in his mouth, Godfrey seized his axe. "I'll ride with you, Prince!"

"No, no, my lord!" protested Lady Dorinda, grabbing his arm. "Didn't you warn me of the dangers of travel in these uncertain times? You must stay to protect your family."

"She's right, Godfrey," said Prince George, collecting a few honeycakes for the road. "Your duty's here with your son. Don't worry about us. Blackie and I are used to traveling alone."

"But . . . but I want to ride with you, Prince!" insisted Godfrey. "A short gallop for old times' sake."

"Of course, you should go," smiled Lord Basham. "You can leave your lady with me, my lord. Everything's peaceful in these parts since I raided the Boyles. We shoved them back into their hills with one sharp strike. The unicorn's friend Mardoc led the assault. He's working out splendidly, by the way, dances every night with the quarrymen."

"*Sposo mio*," Lady Basham hissed to her lord, "Lady Dorinda wants the Heir to stay with her tonight. Lovebirds should stick together, you know, and this is their first vacation since their marriage. I've given them the rose room in the west tower with the view of the lake."

"Thank you, my lady," said Dorinda, blushing. "Of course, we'll let the baby sleep late in the morning. He must be lively when the Princess sees him. She is his godmother, after all."

"You see, Godfrey," said Prince George, patting the Heir on the shoulder, "the ladies have everything arranged for you. We'll put off our ride together. Next summer, perhaps, you can visit the City, and we'll sail down to Sicily to raid the Northmen. You've always wanted to test yourself against their axes."

Godfrey seemed inclined to argue. "But my service to the Princess—"

Lady Dorinda brushed his objections aside with an impatient air. "No, no, my lord, you'll wait with me to greet Her Majesty as a family. There's been talk enough that I was forced to marry a lowly headsman. The Empire must learn that you're a dutiful husband as well as a fierce warrior."

Godfrey gave up with a sigh. He bowed to Dorinda, rolling his eyes at the Prince. "As you desire, my lady. Anything else?"

"Only your clothes." She shook her head at his worn riding cloak. "I've brought fresh garments for you, the violet suit that you wore at the Christening. My lady must see that we're not totally ignorant of fashion, even up in the mountains."

So Prince George and Blackie trotted alone to greet the Princess on this warm, sunny afternoon. Passing under shading trees, Blackie barely noticed the squirrels chattering from the branches. He tingled at the thought that he'd be seeing his Princess in a few hours.

The only thing dampening his joy was the memory of the horn he'd left behind at Castle Minch. It pained him to leave Papa's horn, even to meet the Princess. In just a few days, he'd have to deposit it in the Fountain. He'd be left with only memories of Papa.

Prince George was as excited to meet the Princess as Blackie, but he'd taken the time to prepare himself before leaving Castle Minch. Blackie had watched him dress carefully in the new clothes Lady Dorinda had given him. The Prince sat stiffly, staring in a mirror, while Dorinda's hairdresser trimmed his hair and shaped the little beard that was finally appearing on his chin.

Blackie's thoughts were broken off when they met the first group of outriders sooner than expected, two knights and a dozen spearmen of the Guard who whooped at Prince George in greeting. Passing by, the

Prince grew restless as Blackie galloped with delight, remembering the voice of his Princess, her touch, her smell! And she was only minutes away.

They heard a bugle. Prince George stiffened. His breath caught in his throat. Blackie lifted his head high, ears up, eyes bright, swishing his tail as he pranced along.

"Ho, my lord!"

It was the vanguard of the Princess's party. Sir Vernon, an old comrade, waved to them. In a moment, the horsemen squeezed around Blackie, rubbing his head and shoulders.

"You did it, Prince George!" cried the Knight, shaking the Prince's hand. "You really did it, my lord! You killed the dragon!"

"How did the Princess take the news?" asked Prince George, nervously patting Blackie.

"She was thrilled, Prince, absolutely thrilled. We all were. The Empress declared a holiday in your honor and ordered a statue to be set in the square before the Cathedral."

"A statue of me?" cried the Prince, thumping Blackie's sides with his boots. "Really?"

"You and the unicorn bigger than life, carved in marble! You're spearing the dragon at your feet."

Eager to see the Princess, Blackie accepted a handful of carrots from one of the spearmen before pushing through the horses.

Prince George yelled back, "You'll have to tell me more about that statue!"

Sir Vernon called after them, "I'll see you tonight, my lord, at the castle."

"Just think of that!" said Prince George, hoarsely, rubbing Blackie's ears. "A statue of us—in marble, Blackie! They only make marble statues of kings and saints, you know. Now, the Princess will have to show me some respect."

Chewing the carrots in his jaw, Blackie lowered his head and galloped down the road. They passed another band of knights who cheered the Prince and pounded him on the back, then they had to pull off into the underbrush for banner-bearers and the musicians, toodling merrily away.

Blackie saw her first, his Princess, riding Midnight. She glowed in her green hat and cloak, waving a hand in the air as she chatted with

Lady Jessica, riding beside her. Jessica leaned forward on Butterball, pointing them out. The Princess threw herself into the air, waving her hat.

"Hooray, hooray for the heroes!"

Beaming, she spurred her horse up to them, arms reached forward. Prince George broke into a fit of nervous coughing as Blackie pressed close to sweaty Midnight, stretching up his head to sniff his Princess with delight. Midnight turned her head with a snort as the Princess leaned over to hug Blackie.

The Princess straightened. "Down, Prince, down! After all these months, I want to ride my unicorn!"

Still coughing, red with embarrassment, Prince George slid off into the trampled bushes beside the road.

"Welcome, my lord. It's good to see you," smiled Jessica as the Princess swung over onto Blackie.

Blackie shivered with joy, feeling his lady's weight on his back and her hands in his mane. He swung his head around to watch her from the corner of his eye. She threw her arms around his neck and hugged him again.

"How I love you!" she cried. "My unicorn, my sweet, sweet unicorn, I'm keeping you near me from now on! How are you, dear thing? Did you get terribly burnt by the dragon? The stories we've heard from Vile—They made me sorry I let you go there in the first place! Mother had Masses said for you in every abbey in the land."

Jessica offered Prince George a drink of wine from the Princess's silver cup. He watched resentfully as the Princess scratched Blackie around his horn, murmuring loving words. She leaned forward to kiss him on his ears, then settled back and turned to face the Prince. She threw a green-gloved hand to him.

"And to you, my Prince, bravo, bravo! You've shown the valor I expect from my knights! Did you bring me a dragon claw as a token of your adventure?"

Dropping her hand, Prince George jumped back in exasperation.

"A dragon claw! What do you expect from us, Princess? Haven't you heard that we killed the dragon in a collapsing tunnel? We had a volcano exploding over our heads! Only the grace of God saved our lives as we crawled out through fire and fumes with burning boulders raining down on our heads. We lost everything we had, but our lives and your magic bow!"

"My bow," nodded the Princess, "at least, you preserved my bow. You'd better pass it over now. I'll take charge of it before you lose my arrow, too."

"My lady, that arrow—" began the Prince, holding up the bow.

"I know," interrupted the Princess, snatching the bow out of his hands. "You've been shooting it off indiscriminately, letting it fly about on its own."

She gave the arrow a quick inspection, pulling off a glove to test the sharpness of the point on her finger.

"It's a wonder my arrow didn't get lost somewhere. I'll have the fletcher inspect it to make sure it's not damaged. I'll keep it under proper control from here on."

"Yes, my lady," sighed the Prince.

The Princess looked up the road.

"Well, we can't hang around gossiping, Georgie. I'm pushing everyone to catch up to our schedule. We stop this evening at Minch, some rebel barony up north. I brought your old horse, so you'd have a mount when I get my unicorn back. You can have a young charger if you wish, but that Steed is smart enough to keep you out of trouble for the rest of this journey."

Blackie watched the Prince walk off by himself, his shoulders slumped. The Princess kicked him sharply.

"Wake up, Blackie, move on. Castle Minch is still a few miles away. We've made excellent time so far today, but I want to see my godson. They say that Lady Dorinda hasn't recovered from the shock of that Gypsy stealing the little lord. I'm talking to the Bishop about settling those Gypsies once and for all. I want that Nail for the Castle chapel."

They rode around a curve in the road through a bright grove of trees. Jessica pushed Butterball up beside Blackie.

"My lady," she said. "Don't you think you were a little hard on Prince George, just now?"

The Princess looked at her with surprise. "Hard on him, Jessie? I made him give back my bow, that's all."

"But my lady," said Lady Jessica in her soft voice, "we must remember that the Prince is a hero. He survived terrible dangers with great courage, only to have you jerk away the bow and scold him like a bootboy. You'll break his spirit if you aren't careful."

"Break his spirit?" hooted the Princess. "Georgie? Impossible! You know the boy as well as I do, Jessie. He's like a walnut tree—the more you beat them, the better they bear. He gets uppity if I treat him too well. You've seen how he talks back when I don't smack him down."

She reached for the arrow as a squirrel dashed across the road with a whisk of its tail, but Jessica kept after her.

"You've just met the Prince after his adventures, my lady. He's done great things, but you greet him as though he's returned from some trivial errand. I think you were a little ungracious to the Prince."

"Ungracious, me?" The Princess twisted on Blackie to glare at Jessica. "I'll have you know that I'm never ungracious to anyone! Perhaps I don't fawn over Georgie like everyone else. I'm a warrior Princess. I fought the dragon myself back in the tower. But I'm not ungrateful for his services. Apparently, he did finish off the monster, though I suspect that my unicorn did most of the fighting. At least, the Prince accompanied him throughout the adventure."

"Accompanied me?" thought Blackie, sweeping off a horsefly with his tail, "I'd have been killed without Prince George. I'd tell her that if she could understand me like the Prince."

Though Blackie couldn't defend the Prince, Jessica spoke up for him. "The ballad says that the Prince was terribly burnt while killing the dragon. Don't you think such courage deserves recognition?"

"Oh, Jessie," cried the Princess, pulling Blackie back to Butterball's pace. "Those old ballads! You know better than to believe such ditties! That ballad also says that the magic of the mountain taught Georgie how to speak with the unicorn. Ridiculous! Events are always exaggerated in song and story—that's why lore is filled with such lies. I'm sure the volcano was dangerous. Prince George probably got singed a little, but the minstrels lay it on for effect."

Jessica shook her head, but the Princess swept on. "Why, you've heard the songs about me. From the ballads, you'd think that I saved the City by myself, but remember all the help I had. You, yourself, stayed with me to spot targets. You carried arrows to Aleet when the dragon swooped down on us, but you're not even mentioned in the songs."

"I just think—" gasped Jessica, pressing Butterball to keep up. "I just think you should treat the Prince with kindness!"

"Kindness!" screeched the Princess, shaking her head. "Kindness has no place in a Queen's character! She should be brave and noble and charitable—charitable, certainly, to pardon weakness and folly, but not mewling over people's hurt pride and bruised feelings. The Prince is a knight! He serves for duty and honor, not for compliments like some upstairs maid."

Blackie didn't see Prince George again until the Princess left him off at the stable behind Castle Minch, ordering the Head Groom to rub him well and to polish his horn and hooves for the feast that night. Blackie was feeding on a late cutting of hay when Prince George rode Steed up to the manger. The horse began gobbling hay while the Prince complained.

"You heard her, Blackie, insulting as usual. She could have at least thanked me for spearing the dragon. I'd say that's a bit more dangerous than knocking off a polecat in a hen house."

Steed lifted his head from the manger. "What's the boy blatherin' about now?"

"Oh, he thinks the Princess abuses him," said Blackie. "She doesn't thank him for his exploits."

"If the boy's waitin' for thanks from a human," drawled Steed, blinking his eyes, "he might as well hold his breath. They'll give you an apple one moment and slap your nose the next."

"That's true of the Princess," nodded Prince George.

"You talkin' to that horse, me lord?" asked the Head Groom, taking the shield from the Prince.

"Might as well talk to a horse," said the Prince, dropping into the muck of the yard. "No one else wants to talk to me."

The Head Groom passed the shield to one of the lads. "I'd talk to that horse, if I could. An old veteran like him, he's seen plenty of action if what they say is true."

"Tell me, young unicorn," asked Steed, "how in the world did you teach that boy to speak like a proper e-quine? Last I heard him, he was gibberin' like the rest of the two-legs. Now, he's got some sense in him, talks like he wants to be understood."

"Oh, I don't know," mumbled Blackie, looking around at the Prince. "It just happened up at Vile."

"Don't want to talk about it, eh?" Steed swallowed a mouthful of hay. "Well, I've got stories to tell if nobody else is yammerin' away. I ever tell you 'bout the time I was chasin' pirates with Sir Otley? That was down at the seashore where them hairy Northmen was rowin' up streams to rob churches and carry off horses. Well, we was leadin' this ragtag patrol of guards when we heard the church bell ringin' for help from a village. Sir Otley starts squawkin' to step up the pace, and I—"

"Now, it's horses boring me with their yarns," thought Prince George, trudging around the castle to the entrance. Heartsore over the reception he'd received from the Princess, he barely acknowledged the salute of the guard. Things looked dark without Blackie or the magic bow. The Princess hadn't even thanked him for his service.

"She goes out of her way to slap me down," he groaned. "It's like I was a boy again."

Prince George was even more depressed when he was caught at the gate by the Princess's chaplain. The Prince didn't recognize him at first, but the chubby little priest grabbed him by the sleeve and sputtered out his story.

"Oh, my lord, I don't blame you for not knowing me. I'm Father Paul from Shrems! I've changed so much since you met me—new robes, boots, rosary. This is real gold, the chain as well as the Cross, and I've put on twenty pounds since you knew me as a poor village vicar. It's all due to that unicorn horn you gave me. Now, I'm Provost of the Cathedral—would you believe? I help the Archdeacon with his duties, and the Empress listens to my sermons. Holy Saturday last April, Her Majesty congratulated me on my homily. She said that my notion of the eighth deadly sin made her think."

The Provost offered to repeat his sermon for Prince George, then and there.

"I'm . . . I'm eager to hear it," said the Prince, backing away, "but later, Father Paul, much later. I must clean up for the feast to welcome the Princess."

"Anytime, my lord," promised the Provost, following him, "but the eighth deadly sin, can you guess what it is?"

"Surprise me with it—later!"

Prince George hurried off to the guardroom beside the gate that the knights had taken over for their arms and tackle. He didn't see the

Provost again until the feast that evening when Father Paul showed his thanks for his elevation with extra-long prayers before the meal.

The company celebrated into the night with feasting and singing. Blackie had a wonderful time. Eager to make amends for Lord Minch's crimes, the peasants of the land had come around with their freshest produce. Though Blackie had made a good start on the hay at the stables, he stuffed himself into near collapse in the hall, eating the last veggies of summer, along with pears and grapes, cookies and cakes.

Prince George sulked at the Knights' table in the corner. He rested his chin in his hands until Count Basham struck the floor with his staff and called for silence.

"My royal lady, Princess Julianna—" He bowed. "Lords and Ladies, honored guests, and local dignitaries. As you see, Castle Minch is missing the baron who should have hosted you at this celebration of greeting and sharing. In his absence, it's my honor as feudal overlord to welcome our dear Princess to Castle Minch. I'm sure that all nobles and gentles, as well as our other royal guest, Prince George of Dacia, join me in begging Her Majesty for a few words to complete our joy at this occasion."

Wiping her lips on a napkin, the Princess bounced up from her throne.

"Here comes the Latin," groaned Prince George, but a smile touched his lips as she prettily held up her hands to still the clamor from the Knights' table that greeted her.

"Thank you, my lord Count," she cried with a curtsy to the lord, who returned a deep bow. "Thank you, everyone."

She paused, casting a searching eye around the room to note the few gentles remaining to Barony Minch.

"We have done our best to celebrate tonight," she declared in her clear voice, "though our assembly lacks many of the loyal hearts and smiling faces that should greet a royal visitor. Where are the landholders, the retainers we would expect to greet us at the foot of their baron to welcome their guests? Dead, most of them, I fear, or lost to Vile when the unhappy rebels fled after our righteous victory. We must pray that the very forests of this land are not blasted by their guilt, that the fields are not blighted."

Blackie heard a groan through the hall as a shudder ran over the guests. No one looked at his neighbor. Baby Brucie let out a wail.

601

"But all is not dark!" The Princess threw out her arms. "Light can dawn over the land despite the doom and dishonor of the past! We must look to those heroes that served with faith and courage in the time of troubles. Greatest of all, perhaps, are the unicorns!"

She pointed to Blackie, who lifted his startled head from the basket of cookies. She bowed before Unicorn's broken horn, elevated in a purple-draped cradle as the centerpiece on the table.

"We know, there can be only victory when such heroic beasts rise up to aid us against the forces of evil. This shattered antler—"

"'Antler?'" the Prince questioned that term in a whisper to Sir Vernon. "She's in rare form tonight. I hope this doesn't last long."

"—this unicorn horn reminds us that our pilgrimage to the Shrine joins the cavalcade of sinners from the past who climbed the holy mountain to pray to the martyrs of the ages. May the unicorn horns in the Fountain inspire us all to keep faithful in our weakness despite temptations to the contrary."

Blackie belched. Halfheartedly, he took another mouthful of cookies.

"And my knights!" cried the Princess, turning to the table in the corner where the knights nudged each other and lifted their heads to meet her gaze.

"How many scars, how many wounds, have these warriors suffered in their loyal service during the late rebellion! And," her voice lowered, "how many of their brother knights were lost in the struggle. Oh, the names I could mention—Sir Otley, Sir Robert, Dennis of the Lake, Richard of Gaul—heroes all, who died sword in hand, fighting for the rights of their ruler."

"When will this be over?" thought Blackie, looking back at the Prince. "I love my Princess, but she does talk, and all so sad and gloomy tonight! I want to see her laugh. I want to see her dance."

But now, the Princess was speaking in a happier tone. "Looking about the hall this evening, I see some of the brave hearts that won the war for us. Over here to my left, I must point out the noble Heir of Darr, Lord Godfrey, who fathered the beautiful child we've all been admiring."

Godfrey sat rigid, moving only to grasp his axe, while Lady Dorinda held up the sleeping boy with a radiant smile. The Princess bowed to them both.

"As everyone knows, this hero was once a minor gentleman, a headsman in the service of the Crown. Then I recognized his potential and married him to his beloved Dorinda, the most beautiful lady in the land, creating one of the most loyal Peers of the Empire."

Prince George choked, spitting a mouthful of wine across the table. What a lie! The Princess had not recognized anybody's potential. No, no, it was he, Prince George of Dacia, who had discovered Godfrey as a ragged beggar in the forest.

"I dressed him and mounted him and brought him along on my adventures," fumed the Prince, as the Princess went on complimenting Godfrey. "The world knows that I gave Lady Dorinda to Godfrey after winning her in the Contest. Children memorize my famous speech in which I insisted that Godfrey would make a noble Heir for Darr!"

After condescending to him and belittling him, the Princess was now stealing his fame. What more could she do to him?

"I don't care," he said to himself, gritting his teeth. "What she says doesn't matter. My reputation's secure. Everyone's heard the songs. Besides, as the Provost said in his sermon, all this is but dross. I must keep my mind on higher things than worldly fame. By the Cross on my shield, I serve the highest Lord of all, so let her tell all the lies she wants. I laugh at her. Her insults are but pinpricks to me. She won't break my spirit!"

The Princess had placed a hand on Godfrey's shoulder. She was praising him as though he'd won the war by himself.

"Not only did this great warrior hold his border fastness against the hordes of Vile, but he led an army of hardy mountaineers to break the siege of the City. This is the loyalty we celebrate tonight, a model of valorous service to all gentlemen in the Empire. In this very castle that stands as an emblem of treason and rebellion, I honor Lord Godfrey of the Axe by declaring him to be installed into the order of *Chevaliers d'Honneur*. Moreover, County Bynam to the west of Darr, abandoned by its faithless lord, shall be asseized by Lord Godfrey as his personal domain and attached to the Dukedom of Darr forever."

Prince George gasped, then leaped to his feet with a shout of acclaim. What an honor for Godfrey! Not only was Godfrey entered in the highest circle of knights in the Empire, but to be given County Bynam, expanding the Ducal territory by at least a third—This was a princely gift indeed!

"The saints know that Godfrey deserves the best," he thought, sinking back, "but me . . . me . . ."

Godfrey was purple-faced, wiping his eyes with a sleeve. Lady Dorinda had tossed Baby Brucie to one of her ladies so she could cling to Godfrey with a fierce smile of triumph. Godfrey looked over her shoulder to the Knights' table and waved to the Prince with a wide grin. Prince George forced a smile and waved back while the cheers went on and on.

The Princess was hugging Lady Dorinda now and speaking a mile a minute to Godfrey, who nodding his head up and down like a pigeon. Finally, the applause dropped away, the Darrmen on their bench to the rear keeping it going minutes longer than everyone else. Prince George slumped back to his seat, dropping his head into his arms.

He felt a sudden headache behind his eyes. He must have drunk more wine than he thought. As soon as this nonsense was over, he'd get Blackie to heal his head, then slink off to his narrow cot in the gatehouse. The other knights could stay up drinking if they wanted to, but he was tired tonight. He probably had a cold coming on. An autumn cold, they're the worst! Well, Blackie could heal that too, but the Prince felt worn out tonight. A good sleep would restore him for tomorrow's ride.

The Princess was speaking again.

"I'm sure that we all congratulate Lord Godfrey for his honors, but there is one more hero who requires special attention this evening. While it's always exciting to see a great leader emerge from obscurity, there's a special thrill in watching an old friend fulfill the promise that you saw in him from the beginning. And when that friend exceeds your expectations by joining the great heroes of history, you feel as joyous for him as though you'd done it yourself."

Prince George pushed up his head at this. He peered around the room with slitted eyes. Who was she talking about now? One of the young barons, probably, who'd distinguished himself in the Siege.

During the meal, the minstrel had sung about Lord Piers, who sat with the honored guests at the head table. Supposedly, Piers had killed three Hellions with his dagger after losing his sword in combat—an exaggerated tale, if the Prince had ever heard one, but the sort that might appeal to the Princess, especially since Lord Piers was a good dancer. Sort of a pretty boy, you might say.

"Since my childhood," the Princess was saying, "I've known this warrior. We studied our languages together until he became a fair Latinist, *experto credite*. I've watched him practice his horsemanship, his swordsmanship, and his archery. He almost matches me on the basic bow. I admit that he stumbled a bit in his first quests, but then began a string of victories not known since the ancients, another Aeneas or Hercules."

"Oh, ho, is she puffing this one up," thought Prince George, sourly. "Must be one of the boys from the Castle School with us. Lord Brierwood, I suppose. He held the East Wall during the siege."

"By now," cried the Princess, stepping away from the head table, "everyone knows whom I'm describing—that great hero who captured the unicorn, defeated the Northmen, and killed the dragon!"

Prince George jumped as though stabbed. He looked around stupidly. "Me? She's talking about me?"

The Princess ran across the hall and took him by the hand. She pulled him to his feet and led him, stumbling, to her throne.

"My old playmate, friend, and noblest knight," she declared, "tonight, you sit in glory while the rest of us kneel before you."

She pushed the Prince into her seat while he protested, his face as red as a cherry. "My lady, I can't sit—! This is wrong! You mustn't—!"

The entire company was on its feet, clapping, cheering, whistling, but silenced with a gasp as the Princess actually dropped to her knees before Prince George, forcing all the guests to lower themselves to the floorboards. Blackie ran to Prince George and placed his horn on the Prince's shoulder, shooting in a tremendous charge that made the man shine like Unicorn himself while grinning down on Godfrey and Dorinda and Jessica and Lord Piers and all the knights, who kept shouting. Tears ran down his cheeks as the Princess beamed up at him. The cheers went on and on till Prince George wanted to shrink away and hide. This was too much, too much.

The Princess rose and held up her hands. The applause died away as she turned back to the crowd and took up her speech again.

"I need not list for you the exploits of this noble Prince. His fame has spread from one end of the world to the other. The burning mountain of Vile trembles at his name!"

To the Prince's embarrassment, the shouts began again. "Enough, enough," he muttered, as the Princess quieted them with a gesture.

"As I said, we all know the heroic deeds of my lord Prince. What remains, tonight, is to reward him."

"Give him another Dorinda!" yelled Godfrey, grinning with pride at the Prince.

"Hush, hush, my lord!" whispered Lady Dorinda, jerking Godfrey's sleeve, her face almost as red as the Prince's.

"I'm afraid that's impossible, my lord Godfrey," answered the Princess, smiling at them. "Where could I find another Lady Dorinda to bestow on the Prince? No, no, the prizes we can bestow fall short of the treasure you received."

She spun around to Prince George.

"First, from my mother, the Empress—she sends her love to you. She longs to receive you herself. When we return to the City, she promises a parade through the streets and a thanksgiving service in the Cathedral that will be remembered for generations. For now, she sends you this necklace with the famous Ruby of Wellandor, an heirloom fit for any royal Prince."

Blushing, Prince George lowered his head while the Princess looped the shining necklace over his head.

"It's not the real ruby, Georgie," she whispered in his ear. "Mother fears the thieving Gypsies, so she's keeping the true necklace in the strongroom for your return."

"Oh," said the Prince, feeling oddly resentful at this precaution.

"And then," exclaimed the Princess, again taking Prince George by the hand, as she turned back to the crowd, "to show further the Empress's faith in this great Prince and because like any any lord, he needs lands to support his magnificence—"

She paused for a breath.

"—I have been authorized to announce that this knight, Prince George of Dacia, is to be given seigniorial hold over the Barony of Mandor as personal fief with the customary rights of possession in exchange for service, aid, and counsel, all to be awarded at a Commendation Ceremony back in the City."

Prince George reeled backward, totally caught off guard by this announcement. The Princess was giving him land, which meant rule, security, a home base. He was no longer a poor wandering knight—and he didn't have to marry anyone to gain it!

"Of course," explained the Princess, "my lord Prince knows how this particular barony is suited to him. Seated at the western crossroads of the great highways of the Empire, Mandor controls the traffic of the Empire in four directions. This late rebellion demonstrates why a strong and faithful vassal is needed there to stop treasonous passage and confederations.

"Also, my lord," she added with a nod of her head, "once the Barony is properly organized with the tolls collected from peaceful traffic, Mandor has the potential to become one of the richest holdings in the Empire. You can build that cursed castle into a real home."

Blackie backed away as the throng gathered about the Prince, patting his back and congratulating him.

"Joy, joy!" cried Godfrey. "Now that you have lands, we can visit back and forth, season by season!"

"I'll help decorate your household," promised Lady Dorinda, squeezing his hand, "and I'll find you a wife, a sweet, quiet girl with nice eyes. She'll bear you playmates for our Brucie."

Sir Vernon shook his hand strongly as a brother knight.

"You'll need proper troops to collect those tolls, my lord," he suggested. "Paid troops with a Captain you can trust. I wouldn't mind leaving the City if the post was offered to me."

The Prince's mind was awhirl. He'd dreamed all his life of having wealth and lands, but it hadn't struck him till now how many decisions it involved. With all these people pushing in on him, he couldn't think.

At the end of all the well-wishers came Lady Jessica.

"Congratulations, my lord," she said quietly, bowing before him. "Don't let anyone hurry you into rash decisions. Take your time and arrange things as you wish them to be."

"Thanks, Jessica, thanks," he said fervently, looking into her blue eyes. "You're right, absolutely right. There's no rush, no hurry. I'll get advice, take my time, feel my way into doing things properly."

She gave him a smile and returned to her place by the Princess, who was clapping her hands to restore order.

"We have much to celebrate tonight! Music, please, music for dancing. Step out with me, Prince. We must lead the dance tonight."

At the doorway, Blackie looked back to watch the Princess dance with Prince George under the candles of the hall. Blackie was stuffed and sleepy. He wanted to have a word with old Steed down in the stables. Steed would be interested in the Prince's good fortune. A rich barony meant hayfields and pastures, gardens and groves. It meant plums and peaches and pears, and all the cookies you could eat.

CHAPTER FORTY-FOUR

Stories and Schemes

To Prince George's delight, his lady treated him as a friend and companion on the way to the Shrine. Not only did she lend him Blackie to scout ahead in hazardous country, but she followed his advice when he reported back. In secure areas, she rode quietly with Jessica while he and Godfrey told stories of traveling this road during the Contest.

At first, Prince George was uneasy at such courtesy from his lady. He blustered a bit, exaggerating the dangers he'd faced, but a friendly comment or question calmed him. He relaxed enough to confess the little blunders and accidents that made his adventures interesting to his listeners.

Since this was the first pilgrimage for the ladies, they were especially keen when Prince George could point out the locations of his stories. They rode slowly around the ashes of the Haunted Inn, the horses shying at the dark spirits of the place.

Blackie had been there before, but he listened again when Prince George described the satanic fiddler dancing the pilgrims to sleep with his music. Jessica shrieked as Godfrey recounted how the Prince woke at the last minute to save their lives. The Princess clenched her fist when Prince George described the villains crumbling away into ashes at a blow.

"I'd love to have seen that!"

Blackie stamped his feet in the blasted weeds around the lot. "If I'd have been there, I'd have kicked them all into dust!"

No sooner had they taken to the road again, than Crepitar, the raven, came sailing down with a message. Godfrey caught the bird on his glove and held him out for the Princess. Crepitar was grumpy as usual, squawking that she worked him too hard.

"No rest, no rest, no rest for birdie."

"If you want rest," said the Princess, adjusting her hat, "I'll hood you like a sparrowhawk. Sulky birds molt away in darkness. What does Lady Amalia have to say to me?"

"Lady Ahmm, Lady Ahmm say she go . . . go . . . go to Shrine with you. Meet . . . meet at Monsty."

"Monsty?" asked the Princess.

"The Monastery," explained Prince George, "St. Catherine's. It's an easy ride down from Furland. Lady Amalia is a great patron of the monks."

"An easy ride if you don't have three feet of snow!" laughed Godfrey. "We rode through a blizzard when we traveled this road during the Contest, remember, my lord?"

"Well, Crepitar," said the Princess, "you can fly off, now. Tell the cooks to give you a meal and let you sleep in a warm wagon. I'll have more messages when you're rested."

"Aawk!" cried Crepitar in disgust. He twisted his head to sneer at Prince George before flapping back down the road over the column of travelers. The Prince watched him fly away.

"I wouldn't trust that bird, my lady. Not with any message of importance."

"Oh, he'll be faithful enough," said the Princess, walking Blackie back to the road. "He's learned his lesson. When the Gypsies fled from Darr on Lord Godfrey's horses, the bird showed up in the City begging for mercy. He claims that he hates the deep forest. Too many snakes and hawks for him."

"Most people regard the raven as a demon," added Jessica. "My lady's the only one that would protect him."

"If you ask me," drawled Steed, stepping into his trot. "It's good to see that bird put to work. He's a nasty critter."

"Prince George is right," warned Godfrey. "Crepitar deserted Vile for Lizetta, and now, he's left Lizetta for you. If he ever hears anything of importance, he'll fly back to report it to Vile"

"I think it's safer to send your messages by the arrow," suggested Prince George.

"Perhaps so, my lord," said the Princess, refusing to argue.

The pilgrims had an easy ride that day, stopping for a three-hour lunch break to rest the ladies and the horses. Sitting on her field throne in the warm sunshine, the Princess demanded more stories about the characters Prince George had run across in his travels. Particularly, she questioned him about Lizetta.

"I think it's strange, Prince George," she pointed out, "that you run into that Gypsy wherever you go."

"Oh, she's a pretty one," said Godfrey with a grin. "You should see her when she gets tarted up in her jewels and scarves."

He poked Prince George with an elbow. "Right, my lord?"

"A low type," snapped Lady Dorinda. "I don't see how anyone would call her pretty!"

"I've heard that she's beautiful," said Jessica, lifting an eyebrow at Dorinda. "People say she's a wonderful dancer. Is that true, my lord?"

Everyone looked at Prince George while he examined his wine cup. "Well, uh," he said at last, "she does dance with a certain . . . flair."

"Flair!" cried the Princess. "I've heard that she dances like the Bacchantes. She intoxicates men, drives them mad with desire."

Godfrey grinned again. "Oh, she does have a touch of that, eh, my lord? To see her spinning around like Salome from the Testament, whirling and swirling, throwing out her arms with her eyes aflame! She touches your heart, all right."

"That's before you get to know her!" cried the Prince, kicking out a boot. "I hate her! She's lied to me a thousand times, chained me like a galley slave, stolen my spear. I hope I never see that Gypsy again!"

"I'm sure you'll never have to," said Jessica, hastily, looking at the Princess. "Right, my lady?"

"You never know," said the Princess, smiling to herself. "How far from here to the Monastery, my lord?"

There was a great feast at the Monastery that night. Having known Prince George and Godfrey from years past, the monks welcomed them with joy. The monks told the story of Blackie's ferocious battle to drive off the raiders attacking the compound.

To add to the celebration, the Princess's aunt, Countess Amalia of Furland, was waiting for them. She'd arrived a day earlier with supplies for the monks, food for the feast, and cartloads of gifts. Everyone loved Lady Amalia, especially Prince George, who thought her as kind and generous as the Empress herself.

There was a flurry of hugs and greetings at the monastery gate. After weeping over the Princess, whom she hadn't seen for years, Lady Amalia wanted to meet everyone, especially Dorinda and the baby. Prince George had visited Lady Amalia during the Contest, so she knew Godfrey well.

"Your son, Lord Godfrey," she cried, sweeping up the laughing child in her arms, "what a charmer! I was so pleased when I heard the outcome of the Contest! I knew that you'd make a wonderful husband and father. Lady Dorinda is more beautiful than the songs describe. And my lord Prince—"

She smiled at Prince George over Brucie's head.

"What a hero you've become—winning the Contest, riding the unicorn, killing the dragon! I knew you were destined for great deeds. My people still talk of that giant bear you killed with your dagger. We've mounted the head in my castle. It's as big as a washtub."

She turned to the Princess. "You can see it yourself, Julianna, if you stop with me on the way home. And Prince, dear, I bring you a new fur cloak. Do you still have that bearskin I sent you?"

"That bearskin was burnt up in Vile, Lady Amalia," said Prince George, sadly. "It protected us from flying fireballs."

"Oh," she shuddered, "that's where you killed the dragon, isn't it? To think that you chased her right into the burning mountain. You must still have nightmares over that. And this is your famous unicorn, the healer."

She carried Baby Brucie over to Blackie. The little lord reached for Blackie's horn, crying, "Horsie, horsie, horsie!" Blackie sniffed a trace of the Princess's sweet scent on Lady Amalia.

"He's actually my unicorn, Aunt Amalia," said the Princess, running her hands down Blackie's mane.

"Of course, he is, Julianna," smiled the lady. She scratched Blackie between the ears. "I knew your father, bless his soul. He stayed with me several times during his roaming days. He was a strong, beautiful creature. I will pray over his horn."

"This unicorn's named Blackie," said Prince George, putting a hand on the unicorn's back. "Somehow in Vile, I learned to speak with him. I actually understand what he says."

"So something good came out of Vile!" cried the Duchess. "Something besides horror and death."

There was a stir in the crowd, and the Prior bustled up, followed by monks and novices. The Prior bowed deeply to the Princess.

"Bless you, bless you, my lady. Forgive me for not meeting you. I just learned that you had arrived. I beg you to come into the guest room. We're reserving that room for the ladies, but all are welcome in the refectory. Your horses can go to the stables out back."

"Yes, yes, Julianna," urged Lady Amalia, "come with me to the guest room. It's the only heated room in the monastery, except for the kitchen, so we can clean up there. When it cools in the evening, we'll gather in the courtyard for the bonfire. They put up a canvas windbreak, so it's most pleasant."

Walking behind the Prior with the ladies, Blackie perked his ears as the Princess said, "I bring you a letter from Mother, Aunt Amalia. She's gained her weight back after the Siege, but she's still working too hard helping the people."

"I'm sure of it," said Lady Amalia. "We've heard about the famine all the way out here. I'm having my people dry goat meat and venison to send back with you."

Blackie was turned away at the door, so he ran to Prince George in the courtyard where clusters of Guards and Darrmen stood around the fire with Lady Amalia's foresters. Sandor, the Hunt Master of the Furlanders, who'd ridden with the army, greeted him with a shout.

"There you are, young unicorn!" He stepped forward, grinning. "Stand away, men, make room for the holy beast, just returned from killing the dragon!"

The men watched with awe as Blackie shook himself before the fire and sniffed the bread and beer at a nearby table. Pulling off his gloves, Prince George tossed him a crusty loaf of monastery bread.

Godfrey asked, "Ho, Master, how's the beer? Good as ever?"

"We got a keg over here, Headsman," said Sandor, running to fill him a wooden mug. "Straight from Furland, the best in the country."

Prince George smiled at the men creeping toward Blackie. "Go ahead, fellows. You can pat him, you know. He doesn't mind. He's still the same as ever, fierce to his enemies, but warm to his friends."

The Furlanders crowded around Blackie, quietly chewing his bread.

"Remember me, unicorn?" asked one. "I'm Ritchie. You healed me broken arm back with the troops."

Meanwhile, the Darrmen lined up at the keg to fill their beer mugs while the Knights sent for a cask of the monastery's good wine. Novices were fetching more tables and benches from the building.

A minstrel began tuning his lute and warming up his voice, "La, la, la, laaa."

> A lady and her lover,
> a-walking by a lake . . .

"So it true, me lord, what we've been told," asked the Hunt Master, patting Blackie's back, "you and the unicorn really killed the dragon?"

Prince George nodded. "That worm will never burn another village."

The men sighed in wonder.

"And," added Sandor, "does the unicorn still heal broken bones and catarrh?"

"He's ever the healer," said Prince George, throwing an arm over Blackie. "Wounds close up at the touch of his horn. We'll hold a sick call once he's been fed."

"A true beast and a Christian," said the Master with satisfaction. "Look at him up close, lads. You can tell your grandkids that you seen the unicorn that killed the dragon."

"I got a toothache," said a man, touching his jaw. "Can he can heal that, me lord?"

"Bring all your aches and pains," said Prince George, watching the novices push up a sloshing wine cask in a wheelbarrow. "Blackie can heal anything this side of the grave."

The party went on late into the night. When the night got cool, the novices threw more wood on the fire. Lady Amalia had brought turkeys, hams, and venison while the monks provided their own chickens and ducks, cheese, and bread, so a massive spread was prepared for all.

To honor the Princess, the Prior again relieved the monks from their strict rule for the evening so they could have a bit of the feast in a secluded corner of the courtyard. Some of the older monks were shocked at this license. They stayed on their knees in the chapel, praying for the others, especially when a few of the novices went so far as to sing four-part golliard songs to the ladies late at night.

The bands of warriors—the Princess's Guards, the Darrmen, and the Furlanders—competed at dancing and wrestling. With so many men admiring them and striving to entertain them, the ladies had a wonderful time. Prince George heard several new songs about his exploits.

The Princess was ready to ride at dawn, next morning. While the men packed up and saddled the horses, she waited impatiently as Blackie healed all the broken bones and headaches from last night's feast. The eastern sun had risen far over their heads before the pilgrims trotted off, Prince George riding Steed beside the Princess.

Jessica, just behind, lifted her light, clear voice in one of the songs that made the Prince shiver with embarrassment.

> The handsome Prince was fresh and young.
> The Gypsy Queen said, bold.
> "I'll have this youth, by the light of the moon,
> and warm his blood so cold!"

Prince George swung around in Steed's saddle. "Not that song, please, Jessica. There's not one word of truth in it—lies, all lies, like most of those ballads."

"Most of the ballads, my lord?" asked the Princess, laughing. "You mean the songs about you fighting the dragon?"

And then, they were squabbling again, the ladies ganging up to tease Prince George until he stirred Steed into a trot. Poking along with the Princess, Blackie looked out through the rustling trees of the forest dropping yellow and brown leaves to flutter against his legs. A few green pines towered here and there though the company hadn't yet come to the evergreen forests of the mountains.

Blackie yawned and thought of the Nest. After leaving Papa's horn at the Shrine, he was to carry the Princess to the City to view all the wonders he'd heard about, the Imperial castle, the Cathedral, the statues, the sea. And there was the promised festival for the Prince. He didn't want to miss that. Once Easter was over, Blackie planned to head home to spend the spring with Mama, cheering her and seeing his forest friends. The fawns would now have fawns of their own, he supposed. He muttered to himself, "I hope they didn't hear about my hunting."

The ride to the Shrine went easily. Passing the north lane to Furland, Lady Amalia sent the carts home to be refilled for the return ride. Then she caught up with the Princess, who requested childhood stories of the Empress. The Princess particularly wanted to hear again how the Emperor had won her mother's hand.

"As a girl, my sister shed tears over a dashing count," said Lady Amalia with a smile, "but he broke his neck showing off for her in a horse race. Then the Emperor made his offer. Sister Julia knew he was a steady, comfortable man. She felt that she could do good for the Empire if she accepted him. I'd say, she's been happy with your father despite these troubled times, and she's had the joy of watching you grow up to marriageable age."

Blackie rolled an eye to see the Princess redden.

"You know, my lady," she confided to her aunt, "I may not marry at all. All my life, I've dreamed of being a warrior queen and conquering lands for the Empire. Babies like Brucie are sweet, but I want to do great deeds instead of nursing infants. And choosing a husband, even that could cause trouble. We've already fought a war because Prince Vile demanded my hand."

"But Julianna, don't you think there'll be more trouble if you don't deliver an heir for the crown?"

"Why, Aunt, you don't have children. Who's to inherit Furland when you die?"

Lady Amalia laughed. "Oh, I've taken care of that. I've brought my young cousin Godring into my castle, and I'm training him to rule. Louis, his older brother, is in line to inherit the County, but your mother has promised to set aside his claim at the proper moment."

"But won't that cause trouble?"

"Why, Louis will dream of rebelling when the time comes—he's a nasty, jealous sort. But he'll get a fair payment in silver. To tell you the truth, Julianna, he'd probably prefer the coin. He's always been sort of a miser."

"See, Aunt Amalia," the Princess laughed, "you're just like Mama. The two of you make better rulers than any man. I want to be like you."

The Duchess had to drop back at this point where a fallen tree closed half the road. When she caught up, she looked at her niece and sighed.

"Well, Julianna, I have to warn you—it's hard reigning alone. Tradition's against us. Men resent being ruled by a woman. To be effective, you have to be strong and firm to assert yourselves without turning harsh and cruel. Some queens become monsters despite themselves."

"I think," said the Princess, "that historians are unfair to queens because men write the books. Look at Queen Cleopatra. The men around her were much worse than she was, but she's the one that gets criticized."

"Well, dear, perhaps you should become a scholar. You could correct the histories."

The Princess reached down to pat Blackie. "I'd rather ride with my armies, but you've given me an idea, Aunt. I'll gather learned ladies about me and set them to writing an accurate chronicle of my rule. Yoo hoo, Jessica!"

Jessica was riding behind, talking with Lady Dorinda about the servant problem. Hearing her lady's call, she kicked Butterball to squeeze in next to Blackie.

"Yes, my lady?"

"How would you like to write a book?"

Jessica blinked. "A book, my lady?"

"Yes, I've decided to set up a college of learned ladies to write a true history of my reign. I'll make you the Prioress, if you like."

Jessica rode silently, thinking this over.

"Cat got your tongue, Jessica?" asked the Princess, shortly. "Why so quiet? I'm offering to make you a Prioress."

"I think," said Jessica slowly, "that I'd rather marry and have a family, my lady."

"A family, Jessica?" asked the Princess with surprise. "But as Prioress, you wouldn't have to stay in your convent. You'd travel with me as my chronicler. You'll get to share my adventures and see new countries. Wouldn't you enjoy that?"

Jessica looked away before answering, "I would enjoy serving you, my lady."

"Why look at this, Aunt Amalia," said the Princess, annoyed. "I offer a important post to my old companion. She could travel with me and have a fascinating life, but she says that she'd rather have a family like any stick-in-the-mud tradesman's wife."

"I suspect that she would," said Lady Amalia, kindly. "Most ladies want to marry. Do you have a gentleman in mind as a husband, Lady Jessica?"

Jessica blushed. "I think, I do."

"Oh, you do!" exclaimed the Princess, turning to Jessica with surprise. "Who've you been talking to, one of the young barons?"

Jessica answered in a faint voice. "Not a baron, my lady."

"Oh, ho, Lady Jessica," laughed the Princess, winking an eye, "you have ambitions above yourself. I suspect I know who you dream of! I see you whispering to Georgie, listening to his blown-up tales. Don't set your hopes on that boy. He may like you, but he'll never marry anyone. He's not steady enough to make a husband."

Jessica turned bright red, but her voice was even.

"You always underestimate the Prince, my lady. You didn't think he'd ride into Vile, let alone kill the dragon."

"That did astonish me," admitted the Princess.

"Well, Lady Jessica," asked Countess Amalia, "do you have some reason to think Prince George would marry you?"

Jessica swallowed. She opened her mouth to answer, but was saved from answering by the Page Cedric, riding back to salute the Princess.

"If it please you, my lady, rest stop in ten minutes before we head into the mountains."

"Oh, good," thought Blackie, tossing his head, "this is ridiculous—the idea of Prince George getting married."

The moment Cedric rode away, the Princess turned back to Jessica. "So, Jessica, why in the world would Georgie ever marry you?"

Jessica took a deep breath. "It's . . . it's sort of a secret, my lady."

Blackie felt the Princess rock back. "A secret! You're keeping secrets from me! Out with it, immediately! What are you up to?"

"I . . . I," Jessica stammered. Then she burst out with it. "Oh, I have a bottle of love potion in my purse."

Blackie was as astonished at this as the Princess.

"Love potion?" she cried. "What love potion?"

Jessica sighed. "Oh, my lady, it's a long story. You remember when the refugees began streaming into the City before the Siege. Well, a group came from Shrems, you know, the priest, the tailor, the baker."

The Princess shook her head. "No, Jessica, of course, I don't remember that. I was preparing for a war, remember? I had to attend to important things. I could barely keep track of the lords who showed up, let alone the flood of commoners."

"Of course not, my lady," nodded Jessica, "but you see, leading the villagers was that Wise Woman from the grove. The Woman knows the secrets of the earth, all the herbs and roots and toadstools."

"Yes, yes," said the Princess, patting Blackie's neck, "the Wise Woman I remember, especially her skin creams and lotions."

"Well, when Her Majesty ordered that the lower end of the Cathedral be closed off as a hospital for the wounded, the Wise Woman turned to nursing."

"Of course," yawned the Princess. "Bishop hated it, but we needed the space for the injured. Mother visited the hospital every day."

"So she did," said Jessica. "I helped out a little there, myself, when I wasn't assisting you, and I met this Wise Woman there. She could work wonders among the injured with her salves and potions. Not miracle cures like the unicorn's horn, but natural healing with simples and herbs. We got to talking about marriage one day—you remember the scandal when Lord Pimple tried to put away his wife, Lady Bonnie?"

"No, I don't remember that either!" snapped the Princess. "What has all this gossip got to do with Prince George?"

Jessica looked about to see who was listening. In a half-whisper, she went on.

"The Wise Woman told me a secret as we washed down the wounded. It turns out that Lady Bonnie was keeping her husband faithful by giving him love potion every week, a potion concocted by the Woman."

"Love potion!" snorted the Princess. "Every quack in the Empire claims to have a love potion. They don't really work."

"But this one does," insisted Jessica. "Unfortunately, though, when Lord Pimple rode off with the troops from his home county, the potion wore off and Lord Pimple got a good look at his wife. He demanded an annulment at once. Luckily, the Provost of the Cathedral insisted they have a counseling session to work out their problems. That gave Lady Bonnie a chance to slip another dose in his wine there. Now, they're happy again."

"A pretty story," said the Princess, reining in Blackie as they came to the tents raised for the ladies at the rest stop. Ignoring the lords waiting to attend her, she turned Blackie alongside Butterball for another question.

"So what has all this to do with Prince George?"

"The Wise Woman gave me this vial of love potion," admitted Jessica. "It works on man or beast, so I'm sure it will capture the Prince's heart."

"But Jessica," protested Lady Amalia, pulling her horse to Butterball's other side, "you don't want to win a husband that way. Look at Lady Bonnie. The moment her husband got away from the potion, he tried to escape his marriage."

"And I don't want George to become like Godfrey!" exclaimed the Princess. "I haven't trained the Prince to be a great warrior for him to suck potions and nurse babies. I need him free to lead my armies. He's got to conquer countries for me. I think that you'd better turn over that potion to me, Jessica. I'll make better use of it than you would."

Jessica turned white at this. She began to tremble. Lady Amalia took her hand.

"Lady Jessica, do you really care for this man?"

Pale as a ghost, Jessica nodded. She swallowed and whispered.

"I've known Prince George all my life, you see. We've always . . . always . . . gotten along. He seems to enjoy my company, and he confides his secrets to me. I know, my lady, that he's in the highest rank and I'm nobody. But he's lonely, and, I think . . . I think I'd make him happy."

The Princess looked kindly at Jessica. She patted her on the shoulder. "It's a nice idea, Jessie, but it's not possible. Of course, I know that Georgie likes you, but he's a prince, after all. If he does marry, I'll arrange a political marriage for him. You know, join him to the daughter of some king we need as ally. But don't worry about yourself. I'll find you a handsome young squire for a husband. You'll do better than Lord Pimple."

"But, my lady," protested Jessica, "the Prince wore my token when he rode against the dragon!"

"What do you mean?" asked Lady Amalia.

"My red scarf! He wore my scarf through all his adventure. It was a token of me as his lady love."

"That wasn't a damsel's silken kerchief," insisted the Princess. "It's not like a ballad. That was just the wrap for some bread and cheese."

"Nevertheless—" muttered Jessica, looking stubborn. She burst out, "I love Prince George! I've always loved him, and you don't care about him at all!"

Watching tears run down Jessica's cheeks, Lady Amalia had a suggestion. "You know, Julianna, you've told me over and over how valuable Lord Godfrey was during the War, holding the border against Vile so the northern flank of the Empire was secure. What if Prince George became another such bastion? You're thinking of giving him Mandor to hold for you, but look at the other rebellious baronies in the region. Give him Gerlock and Dorland, too, combine them all into a powerful dutchy. Then you'd have the western half of the Empire held by a faithful prince whose wife is your best friend."

"But who'd I get to lead my armies!" wailed the Princess, sliding off Blackie to the ground."

A knight helped Jessica down. She ran around the horse to the Princess.

"Oh, I'd let Prince George serve whenever you need him," she said eagerly, "like Lady Dorinda sending the Heir off to the siege. Only I'd insist on riding along with him to make sure he gets his potion regularly. I'd have adventures that way. I could even keep a journal about your exploits."

"Well, I have to think about this," said the Princess, pulling off her gloves. "I'll ask Mama what she thinks. It's true that we would be secure if the West were held by a loyal vassal. Conspiracies would be impossible. Rebels would have to stick to the country lanes to combine against us, and we could stop them before they got started."

"And I'm sure," smiled Lady Amalia, "that Prince George would be happy. Lady Jessica would make him a splendid wife. In no time, he'd grow to love her for herself."

"At least," said the Princess, walking into her tent to wash her face, "Jessica would keep him away from Gypsy queens."

Blackie followed the horses around to the watering trough.

"Wow," he said to himself, "what a story to tell Prince George! Imagine the ladies conspiring against him like that! He'll get so nervous when he hears about the love potion that he won't drink anything. I hope he doesn't die of thirst."

Blackie plunged his nose into the trough for a long drink of cold water. "Although," he thought, lifting his dripping nose for a breath, "Georgie might be happy with Jessica. He has known her all his life, and she does listen to his stories. He's always telling me how lonely he is. He might even like staying home for a while. After invading Vile and killing the dragon, he claims that he's ready for a quiet life. Look how Papa loved it."

Full of water, Blackie headed around the tents to find Prince George.

"I think, I'll keep my mouth shut and see what happens," he decided. "I'll let the Princess deal with this. We may have a wedding before I go home in the spring. I've never seen a wedding feast. Georgie's told me of the wonderful banquets they serve with many-level cakes and mountains of cookies!"

CHAPTER FORTY-FIVE

The Shrine

Princess Juliana threw back the fur cloak her aunt had given her. Dropping her hands to her hips, she gazed down the road at Pilgrim's Rest.

"Look at those stragglers! Stretched out for a mile. What kind of entrance will this make for my pilgrimage? I wanted to march into the Shrine with band and banners like a disciplined company."

"That's not going to happen," said Prince George, standing beside her. "Not on this narrow path. And the real climb starts here, Princess. Better drink more Pool water while you wait for a litter. It's not safe to ride here, even on Blackie."

"Pooh!" cried the Princess. "If I can't ride, I'll climb. No one's hauling me up like a sack of barley!"

Working their way up Shrine Mount, they'd camped for two days at Saint Gabriel's Pool before attempting the final climb. This morning, they'd left Steed and the horses at the camp with the grooms and half the Guards before setting out to push to the top in one mighty effort.

Now, the pilgrims were spread widely along the trail. The Princess had ridden ahead on Blackie, who bore also the broken horn strapped to his side. Prince George and Jessica followed on mules. Then came the weaker ladies on litters, carried by teams of troopers. The Knights came last as a rearguard, moving slowly up the narrow path.

Godfrey came out the hermitage door. "Old Hermit's not here, my lord. Looks like he hasn't been around for months."

Blackie nodded. The dog scent was faint.

"It's cute, the way things are arranged in there," said Lady Dorinda, following her lord. "Everything's stored on shelves or hanging from pegs."

"We'd better prepare for the final climb," said the Princess. "I'll change to my sturdy shoes, Jessica. These purple boots aren't made to climb mountains."

She pulled in her cloak. "If it weren't so cold, I'd crawl up on my knees. Humility always looks good in a warrior queen."

Prince George snorted. "Don't worry, Princess. You'll get humble enough when the spirit strikes you up there. Pride melts in the shadow of the Hand."

"I've heard," said Jessica, pulling the shoes from the boot bag, "that queens have cast off their crowns after tasting the Fountain waters. Remember Queen Clotilda? She retired to a convent."

"I'm not Queen Clotilda!" snapped the Princess. "She had that squabbling family. No wonder she wanted to hide away."

"Now, my lord," asked Godfrey, striding to the staircase winding out of sight up the mountain, "how far up from here?"

Prince George walked over to him. "Less than a mile, Godfrey, but it's stair-steps all the way. A thousand steps, they say."

"Only a thousand steps," thought Blackie, looking up beside the Prince. Chopped from the stone with that mile-deep drop-off to the side, the stairway looked as formidable as it had last year.

"One more climb, then I say goodbye to Papa. How I'll miss his beautiful horn! Why didn't I listen to his stories back home? All the forest lore he tried to teach me—I can't even tell good mushrooms from bad. Papa said you can poison yourself if you go by scent alone."

"Wait there, Blackie!" called the Princess, leaning on Lady Amalia while Jessica knelt to tie the shoes on her foot. "I want a couple strong men to hold you as you climb."

"Men hold Blackie?" snorted the Prince. "More likely he'd hold them. He's a unicorn, remember?"

The Princess stamped her feet into the shoes. "I don't trust the wind up there. At this height, he could get dizzy."

"Me, dizzy? Not likely."

Blackie lifted his front legs up three steps and began to climb. Voices called from behind, but he set his hooves firmly. He climbed step after step while the wind whistled down the stairway, catching the horn swinging against his side. Alone with the horn on the mountain, Blackie was swept by memories of Unicorn.

"Papa, Papa, when I saw you last, your silvery coat was black and bloody! You'd already killed the dragon. If we hadn't showed up, she'd have died anyway a few minutes later. All our fame, those songs, those stories, they come from finishing off a dying dragon! Oh, Papa!"

Tears stung his eyes. He had to slow down to set his hooves carefully for the next step.

"Watch out, fellows!" cried a voice from above. "Someone's coming! I hear someone below!"

Blackie stopped as a group of pilgrims groped their way down the stairs, supporting themselves on staffs.

"My stars, it's a unicorn, a black unicorn!"

A short man jumped ahead of the others. He pulled off his gloves to reach for Blackie's horn.

"Another miracle!" he breathed, holding the horn in both hands and bending to kiss it. Blackie stood still, afraid to move, as the man cried out.

"Drinking from that Fountain was a wonder, and now, now, I've kissed a unicorn's horn! Well, if I can't fly after this—"

"Stop, Aaron!" yelled the men behind him, but the short man turned to the drop-off, spread his arms, and leaped. He fell out of sight with a scream.

Blackie gasped. The humans stood paralyzed, clutching each other in shock. One of them dropped to his knees to look down over the edge.

"I . . . I can't see him."

"He didn't fly," said the other man, astonished.

The kneeling man stood up. "Of course, he didn't fly! That was crazy! He was out of his head. We must pray for his soul."

Both men looked sadly at Blackie.

"Don't blame yourself, Unicorn," said the man who'd looked down. "It wasn't your fault. We could tell you stories about Aaron. He was deeply disturbed. We brought him up here to the Shrine to find peace."

Blackie caught his breath as the humans tried to decide what to do. Should they return to the Shrine to pray for Aaron or continue down?

They squeezed against the rock as Blackie edged by. He shook himself, and continued climbing, setting his hooves more firmly as their voices grew thin.

"What do we tell his mother?"

"We'll tell her the truth—that Aaron missed a step when he saw the unicorn."

"Yeah, that's a good story."

Tears came to Blackie's eyes. He drew a ragged breath.

"Now, I've killed Aaron—like Papa! I just stood there when Aaron touched me. I could have healed him. It would have been easy, but it happened so quickly I didn't think of it. I just let him jump. Another soul to pray for. Oh, how I need a blessing! I need the Fountain!"

With the man's cry ringing in his head, Blackie climbed strongly, up, up, up. A thousand steps to go! How far had he climbed? He looked down at the lower peaks stacked behind each other with the shadows falling into smoky gray valleys.

"Aaron fell down there. Why, oh, why, didn't the Fountain heal him? Are there troubles the Shrine can't heal? No, no, that's not possible! Aaron must have not swallowed the holy waters, but still, just smelling the flowers of the Shrine—"

Troubled in his mind, Blackie kept climbing. The wind, by now, was calming and warming as he passed the messages carved into the mountain. The steps were changing from hard stone to yielding gold, much easier on his hooves. His thoughts drifted to the Princess.

How far behind was she? She wanted to parade into the Shrine with flags flying, but he couldn't wait for her. Not on these little treads with his front hooves stretched above his rear. No, he'd have to climb to the Shrine and wait for her there.

At last, the sweetness in the air was cheering him. He bounded past the carving of the Man with the Cross. He heard singing growing louder.

> I lift up my eyes to the mountain.
> That's where I find my help.

Rounding the turn, he saw the Hand reaching for him, its fingers bright with the western light reflecting off the Fountain. Blackie leaped forward through happy humans who drew back for him. He plunged his muzzle into the cool water and drank away the guilt and pain and sorrow of a damaged world.

"Ahh!"

Blackie stepped back, lifting his head. Now, the humans pressed around, hugging and kissing him, but Blackie didn't notice. His horn was high, eyes closed, sending healing from his heart to all the friends he could think of—the Princess and George, of course, but also Lady Amalia and Jessica and Lady Katherine and Lame Alan and Godfrey and Dorinda and Brucie and Papa and Mama and the fawns in the forest, all the deer he'd driven to the bowmen, and the humans surrounding him, even the little boy pulling his tail.

"Bless you, unicorn!" called the humans.

"Look, Ma, I'm touching his horn!"

"Remember me, unicorn? I brought you bread, last autumn. Stay here. I'll fetch another basket."

Blackie prayed for Aaron too, that unhappy soul.

"Look, Blackie!" shouted a voice. "I beat them all!"

The Princess clattered up the last steps leaning on a knobby staff. She'd thrown off her fur in the warmth of the Shrine. She waved to him, her dark hair wild and windblown, her eyes bright, smile dazzling.

"All the way up, Blackie! I made it all the way up in a single day!"

The humans drew back as she limped toward him, waving them out of her way with her stick. She dropped the stick and threw her arms around Blackie's neck.

"What a climb! Georgie's coming behind with Jessica, but I made it by myself! So that's the great Hand, and this, this is the Fountain!"

Her voice stilled as she gazed at the Fountain before her. Blackie walked with her into the Hand. The Princess threw herself to her knees. She leaned forward on her arms to touch her lips to the waters. She drank and drank, strands of hair falling to the surface to plaster about her face when she lifted her smile.

Blackie stepped back to make room as Prince George walked forward, an arm around Jessica. The Prince pointed down.

"Oh, Blackie, Lady Jessica sprained her ankle on a step!"

"I'll heal it!"

Blackie jumped forward to touch his horn to Jessica's ankle. Jessica gasped and straightened, lowering her weight onto the ankle. She leaned away from the Prince.

"Oh, thank you, Blackie. And you, my lord, so gracious of you to help me along." She smiled up at the Prince. "You are very good."

"It's nothing." He turned to the Hand. "Look, the Fountain, you must drink."

"The Fountain," she breathed and walked into the Hand. Prince George turned from her to help the Princess to her feet, then knelt beside Jessica to drink.

The Princess ran lightly to Blackie and kissed his nose.

"All my life, Blackie, I've heard how wonderful the Fountain is, but I didn't suspect it could be so . . . so, satisfying! It fills your imagination, answers all your questions. No one told me that."

She looked back at the stairway. "Here come Godfrey and Dorinda. I must warn her to dip Brucie all the way into the Fountain. She mustn't hold him by the heel like Achilles."

She ran over to Dorinda's litter as Prince George stood smiling at Blackie. Fountain waters dripped from his beard. He ran fingers through Blackie's mane.

"The blessed water still has that kick, doesn't it, Blackie? A drink washes away the suffering—the dragon, the war. Exciting times ahead, old beast. The celebration in the City and then, my own lands! You know what Jessica suggested on the climb up? She thinks that I should tear Castle Mandor down. Raze it to the ground and build a new castle. Build it the way I want it, free of the past. I'd call it Dacia after my kingdom and build it around a holy well."

He laughed happily.

"I know that no well could be like this Fountain, but if you'll give the waters a dose now and then with your horn—"

Blackie tossed his horn. "I'd be happy to, Georgie! No more sick calls! People can heal themselves with a drink from your well. Also, you'll want orchards and gardens and shaded woods with streams."

Jessica joined them, smiling, as the Prince agreed. "Yes, yes, and there'll always be room for you, Blackie. Your own suite of rooms or stables, whatever you want."

"Are you telling him about your castle?" asked Jessica.

"He wants orchards and gardens," said the Prince.

"And of course, my lord," Jessica added, "you'll have chambers for your lady and a nursery for your children."

"Oh, chi . . . children," sputtered the Prince, glancing at the Princess. "I don't know if it'll come to that. Not for a long time, anyway."

"Of course," said Jessica, demurely, "that's for your future, isn't it?"

By now, the officers of the Shrine were advancing to the Prince. The Commander of St. Michael's Knights marched up with Sir Sebastian and the Abbot of the Monks. Prince George accepted their welcome, then introduced them to the Princess. She greeted them with a speech.

"Father Abbot, the Empress sends her love and prayers. And Master Commander, we've not exhausted our thanks for your services during the war. Meeting at this holy place, my heart is full. What a privilege for a mortal to taste a hint of the bliss awaiting the saints. My draught of the holy waters reminds me of the challenges to a righteous ruler who wants to bring happiness to her people. Beyond defending her borders, I see the duty of a queen to rule her people with love, caring for widows and orphans, tending the sick, feeding the poor."

Prince George lifted his eyebrows to Jessica. This was a new Princess! He'd never heard her lecture on love and charity. It was though she'd been infected with her mother's spirit.

"When I govern the people," concluded the Princess, "my service to the Empire can be summed up in one sentence: *"Quod bonum, felix faustumque sit."*

Jessica laughed, while the Prince thought warmly, "Showing off her Latin again! This is the Princess I know. But this love for the people, this concern for their welfare. Has she really changed? She doesn't speak like a warrior queen!"

"Bless you, my lady!" cried the Abbot. "You'll have our prayers for your virtuous rule. Now, the table is prepared for your party. Will it please you to come to the feast of the Lord?"

"Most happily, Father Abbot. First, though—" She lowered her voice to a somber tone and gestured to the horn at Blackie's side. "We have a presentation for the Fountain."

"Absolutely, my lady," said the Commander, coming to attention. "You bring a blessed horn to the Fountain. We have all heard how the heroic beast broke into the dark kingdom to smite the dragon. I'll call up the troops, if I may. We'll do this with style."

629

"If you don't mind, Commander," said the Princess, quietly, "I think, the son would rather have a private dedication, right, Blackie?"

"Please," said Blackie, switching his tail. "Papa wasn't one for pomp and ceremony."

Prince George was surprised again. The Princess passing up a chance for display? He smiled at her and nodded. "Blackie thanks you for your thoughtfulness."

"In that case—" The Commander and his Knights stepped back and came to attention, along with the Princess's Knights and Guards.

Blackie led the way to the Fountain where Jessica and the Princess unstrapped Unicorn's broken horn from Blackie's harness. Prince George held the horn while Blackie sniffed it one last time and kissed it, tears running down his nose.

Blackie's voice choked in his throat. "Do . . . do it now, Georgie," he rasped.

At a nod from the Princess, Prince George held the horn over the Fountain. He spoke quietly, but his words were clear above the ripple of the waters.

"I think I knew Unicorn as well as anyone but Blackie. After all, the first challenge in the Contest for Lady Dorinda was to capture Unicorn. Here, in this holy place, I confess the truth I've kept hidden. No one knows that I caught the unicorn with a trick. You know what they say, 'All's fair in love.' I'm sure that Princess Julianna has a Latin expression for that."

Jessica and the Princess exchanged looks. The Princess nodded and whispered thoughtfully, *"Omnia justa—Omnia justa sunt amore."*

"The truth is," continued the Prince, "I caught Unicorn with a love potion. Mighty as he was, I'd never have caught him any other way. But riding him up to Castle Darr to deliver him to the ladies, I learned to know him as a peace-loving creature who relished the quiet joys of good food and pleasant surroundings. Of course, we all recognize the strength and swiftness of the beast, as well as his downright stubbornness, if I may call it that. He was a creature who insisted on his chosen way of life despite all that was expected of him, even despite the warrior blood that flowed through his veins. But—"

The Prince's voice got stronger.

"—hidden within him was his deep and abiding love for his son. It was that love that shook him out of his life of lethargy. Nothing could hold Unicorn back when he thought that Blackie was in danger. No border could hold him. No monster could stop him. Not even his love for strawberries and mushrooms and the tasty greens of springtime could contain his determination to rescue his son. We can only guess what it cost him to fight his way through the dark kingdom, but we're all better off for his sacrifice. Thanks to him, the dragon is dead. Good has defeated evil one more time, and we have a chance to start our lives afresh."

Prince George lowered the horn and looked soberly at Blackie.

"For all that," he concluded, "we must thank Unicorn. We remember the power of a love strong enough to carry the holy beast from his beloved forest to save his son, surely a reflection of the love of the Almighty who gave his Son to save his creation. Bless the Lord. Bless Unicorn. Bless us all."

Prince George paused and took a deep breath, tears streaming down his cheeks.

"I'll think of him whenever we pass around the cookie platter."

Blackie was sobbing so heavily that he barely saw the Prince lean down, slip the tip of the horn into the Fountain, and let it slide into the pool. The broken tip bobbed high for a moment, then Unicorn's horn sank in a spray of bubbles and rolled to its resting place atop the horns of the ancestors.

After the Abbot said a quiet prayer for the peace of the Empire, Blackie stepped back to the lookout above the stairway. His friends followed to gaze at the red and purple glow over the darkening Empire beyond the radiance of the Fountain.

Thoughts flooded Blackie's mind, but one recognition shook him from horn to tail.

"Papa's gone! From now on, I'm It! I'm the Unicorn! All those horns, the lives of my grandsires, each of them leads straight to me. However I live, whatever I do, I'm doing it for Papa and Grandpa and all the 'Great-Greats' back to the first unicorn in Adam's Garden. How can I bear all this weight, all this responsibility? It's too much!"

Everyone stood quietly, arms around each other, the Princess with Blackie, Jessica with Prince George, Dorinda with Godfrey. Blackie shook with sorrow until a perverse thought wriggled into his mind to raise a small smile.

"The mushrooms, at least, are safe from Papa. I can hear all those little mushlets rolling about on the hills next spring, singing in their damp beds."

He's gone! He's gone! He's gone!
Old Unicorn's gone for good!
Spring can dance in
with blossoms and buds.
No nibbling and noshing,
guzzling and gobbling—
Unicorn's gone for good!

"Georgie," said the Princess after a silence, "ask Blackie about that cry we heard. Someone fell past us while we climbed the mountain."

"Oh, him?" said Blackie with a sigh. "That was Aaron. He was disturbed. He visited the Fountain and he touched my horn. He thought that would give him the power to fly. It didn't."

Prince George patted Blackie and stood silently.

"Well, Georgie," insisted the Princess, "what did Blackie say?"

Prince George looked at her. "Sure you want to know?"

"Of course, I do. If one of my subjects falls from a mountain, I should be concerned."

"Well," said the Prince, thoughtfully, "Blackie told me that he met a sphinx on the stairway. She refused to let Blackie pass until he answered a question. When he answered correctly, she jumped off the mountain."

"She jumped off the mountain?" repeated the Princess. She thought a moment. "So, what was the question?"

"She asked, 'What has two legs in the morning, four legs in the afternoon, and three legs in the evening.'"

"Oh," nodded the Princess, "that's easy. Let's go to the feast, Blackie. We'll celebrate your father together."

They turned and trailed after the Abbot toward the crowded tables. The Guards shouldered their spears and followed.

"Do you really know the answer, my lady?" asked Jessica, curiously.

"Of course."

The Princess stood at the table loaded with bowls of bread, platters of fruit, and pitchers of wine. Jessica, Dorinda, and the other ladies stood beside her while Prince George, Godfrey, and the Knights stood across from them. Between them, Blackie sniffed the bread at the end of the table.

Prince George rubbed Blackie's ears. "So, my lady, what do you think Blackie told the sphinx."

The Princess lowered her head as the Abbot pronounced the benediction. After the "Amens," she sat down on the bench. The others followed.

"I suppose," she said, splitting a piece of bread, "he mentioned those ladders you told me about, the ladders in the plum orchard at Cranch. When folded, they had two legs, and they had four when standing."

"And the three legs?"

"When left leaning against tree trunks at evening, the trees would be the third leg."

"That's not the right answer," objected the Prince.

The Princess reached down the table to pull a bowl of pineapple in front of Blackie. "It's the answer I'd give."

She straightened with a smile.

"My lord Prince, in honor of your heroism, I'm giving you a special treat today. A valiant knight should be served by a beautiful lady. To go along with the wine at this feast, Lady Jessica will bring you water straight from the Fountain in my silver cup."

Prince George was touched by the offer. "Why, thank you, my lady, and thank you, too, Jessica."

"Are you sure, my lady?" whispered Jessica.

The Princess smiled slyly. "As Prince George says, '*Omnia justa—*'"

Blackie rolled his eyes to watch Jessica's hand stray to her purse as she curtseyed to the Prince.

"It is indeed an honor, my lord."

"So all ends well," thought Blackie, slurping up juicy pineapple as Jessica skipped off with the silver cup. "The dragon's dead. Prince Vile's stuck across the border. Princess Julianna will be a righteous queen, and Georgie will be happy with Jessica. As for me, I'll dose their water and eat cookies and and carry their children around the gardens and groves of their castle."

CPSIA information can be obtained at www.ICGtesting.com
Printed in the USA
BVOW041349281212

309298BV00003B/10/P